TOO FAR FROM HOME

The Selected Writings of Paul Bowles

BOOKS BY PAUL BOWLES

NOVELS

The Sheltering Sky

Let It Come Down

The Spider's House

Up Above the World

NOVELLA

Too Far from Home

SHORT STORIES

The Delicate Prey

*A Hundred Camels in
the Courtyard*

The Time of Friendship

*Pages from Cold Point
and Other Stories*

*Things Gone and Things
Still Here*

A Distant Episode

Midnight Mass and Other Stories

*Call at Corazón and
Other Stories*

Collected Stories, 1939–1976

Unwelcome Words

A Thousand Days for Mokhtar

The Stories of Paul Bowles

AUTOBIOGRAPHY

Without Stopping

Days: A Tangier Diary

LETTERS

In Touch: The Letters of Paul Bowles
 (edited by Jeffrey Miller)

POETRY

Two Poems

Scenes

The Thicket of Spring

*Next to Nothing: Collected Poems,
1926–1977*

**NONFICTION, TRAVEL,
ESSAYS, MISCELLANEOUS**

Yallah! (written by Paul Bowles,
 photographs by Peter W.
 Haeberlin)

*Their Heads Are Green and
Their Hands Are Blue*

Points in Time: Tales from Morocco

Paul Bowles: Photographs
 (edited by Simon Bischoff)

TOO FAR FROM HOME

The Selected Writings of
PAUL BOWLES

Introduced by Joyce Carol Oates

Edited and with a Preface by
Daniel Halpern

AN **ecco** BOOK

HARPER PERENNIAL

NEW YORK ● LONDON ● TORONTO ● SYDNEY

ACKNOWLEDGMENTS

Special thanks to Steve Hill, for his careful enlightened reading of the complete works of Paul Bowles. And to Jeffrey Miller, who over the last twenty years has assiduously collected the letters from which this volume's have been selected.

HARPER ● PERENNIAL

The Library of Congress has catalogued the Ecco Press Companions edition as follows:
Bowles, Paul, 1910–.
Too far from home : the selected writings of Paul Bowles / edited and with a preface by Daniel Halpern ; introduction by Joyce Carol Oates.— 1st ed.
p. cm.—(Ecco companions)
Includes biographical references.
I. Halpern, Daniel, 1945–. II. Title. III. Series.
PS3552.O874A6   1992
813'.54   92-27275   CIP

ISBN 0-88001-295-1
ISBN 0-88001-391-5 (pbk.)

ISBN-10: 0-06-113740-5 (pbk.)
ISBN-13: 978-0-06-113740-2 (pbk.)

06   07   08   09   10   RRD   10   9   8   7   6   5   4   3   2   1

Contents

POEMS

TRAVEL ESSAYS

AUTOBIOGRAPHY

JOURNALS

LETTERS

INTERVIEW

BIBLIOGRAPHY

Bowles in Tangier: A Preface

Paul Bowles was at a party, sitting in the far corner of a room crowded with professors from the state university where he was teaching for the semester. He was looking slightly bored, even a little edgy, as though on the lookout for an opportunity to leave the room.

California State University at Northridge is located in a sleepy quarter of the San Fernando Valley in Los Angeles, but this was the late sixties and political activism was in full swing, having arrived at this campus a bit late and then with a vengeance. The university must have seemed a strange place in 1968, filled with militant students, most of whom had never been farther afield than Palm Springs, Las Vegas, or Tijuana. It was in this atmosphere that Paul suddenly found himself, somehow against his will, as he would later explain it—which turned out to be the case for much that happened to him.

Being the only student at the party, I was feeling out of place, too. Paul and I were introduced, and he seemed pleased to meet me when he learned I wrote poetry. He also sensed my discomfort. After a polite moment, he asked if I "drove an automobile"—as if *anyone* who grew up in L.A. didn't—and if I might possibly drive him to the Shangri-La, his hotel on the beach in Santa Monica.

It was on that hour's drive that I received the inimitable Bowles "introduction to Morocco": the *myth of place*, or place *as* myth, as related by Paul Bowles. I had just read *The Sheltering Sky*, a book I still believe changed the course of my life. I was twenty-three at the time and Paul's indelible desert novel about three Americans traveling deep into the Sahara, farther and farther away from what they had known as reality, was at that moment very much part of my consciousness. It was the psychology, or perhaps philosophy, of these characters that revealed a way of thinking about the world that had never occurred to me. We called it "existential" in those days, and perhaps Paul is an existentialist, a character out of Camus, a writer much admired by him.

I think I must have expected a particular *type* of man—secretive, powerful yet distracted, obsessed with thoughts of the time he'd endured in the North African desert. In fact, the person I met was an elegant, gentle-looking man: white hair, trim to wiry in build, wearing a camel-hair sweater and pale leather shoes. His expression, though, was ironic, with the suggestion of considerable darkness just below the surface.

By 1968 Paul had already lived out an extensive expatriate life in France, Germany, Ceylon, Thailand, South America, and most importantly, Tangier, where he settled in 1947 and has lived ever since. Part of Paul's appeal, I believe, is that despite his seeming urbanity, he has chosen to lead a romantic, even exotic life. What drew writers like William Burroughs and Allen Ginsberg to him is the basic enigma of his personality. Beyond the work itself, and what he tells you in conversation about the history and traditions of his adopted country, there is little to hold onto. The rest is saved for his inner life, which I doubt anyone has peered very far into— perhaps he himself least of all.

Driving him in my '56 Nash Rambler along the Pacific Coast Highway, a new album by Jackie McLean on the local jazz station, I began to consider the possibilities of following this elusive expatriate back to Tangier. As we made our way from the Valley to the ocean, I heard about the trance dancing performed by the various Berber religious brotherhoods; the Berber music, which Paul had taped for the Library of Congress some years before; the street life of Tangier and the Café Central, where foreigners sat day and night drinking mint tea and discussing the nature of the world; the month of Ramadan in the Islamic world, when all believers observe the long days of abstinence with a North African stoicism and await the first bowl of Ramadan soup called *harira,* served from large boiling pots at sundown after the cannon is fired. I heard about Aicha Kandisha, a malevolent *djinniya* who makes those who gaze upon her go crazy—she has the body of a beautiful woman and the feet of a goat. And I heard about the little restaurant down the Atlantic coast in Asila, where you can sit in the sun and for a few dollars eat your fill of wonderfully prepared fish pulled from the water an hour earlier. Of course, Paul also profiled some of the more colorful "Tangierines," those English second sons and other non-Moslems who inhabited the Old Mountain outside the center of Tangier. There was, for example, a peculiar Englishman who had a refrigerator in his living room that contained small vials of blood he had relieved from various young Moroccan boys, each labeled with the name of the boy—Mohammed, Ahmed, Larbi. These were offered to his guests. I was pleased to learn Paul was no drinker.

* * *

Three months after that pivotal night on the rim of the Pacific, I found myself stepping off the Algeciras-Tangier ferry. I labored with my rucksack up to the Zoco Chico ("small market") that housed the notorious Café Central, and just off the square I located the small hotel Paul had told me about, the Hotel Carlton. I dumped my things, changed dollars into dirhams, and set off in search of Immeuble Itesa, Paul's apartment house in one of the outlying districts of the city.

When I had spoken with Paul in L.A. about journeying to Morocco, he maintained that it was quite doubtful I'd actually come—typically, he found it impossible to think positively about anything that had to do with the future. As a result, I imagined Paul's reception would be slightly more demonstrative than it turned out to be. He opened the door, saw me, and with a degree of subdued formality and not a trace of surprise, asked me in. We sat down on the *mtarba*, the banquette that is there today, in the small, fading living room where Paul had propped odd primitive paintings by intense local artists against the pale walls. Off this room is a terrace, thick with plants and cages containing a variety of small multicolored singing birds. Paul disappeared onto this terrace from time to time to feed the birds and water the plants and, from what I could tell, look out over the Aïn Hayani, the residential district just below his apartment. It was from the Derb Badr that numerous small fires sent up thick plumes of smoke, hazing the light of late afternoon and placing on the air the scent of woodsmoke.

When he left the room to get my Lapsang tea that first day, Paul said, "Will you excuse me?" And to this day, after the nearly twenty-five years I've known him, he always offers me my Lapsang in exactly this way—with a studied politeness, a considered distance. The longer I was in Morocco the better I understood how this distance allowed Paul to live in comfort among the Moroccans and within himself.

That afternoon of my first visit, Paul took me up the Old Mountain to see the cottages where Tennessee Williams had stayed earlier in the decade. Truman Capote had also visited Bowles during the sixties, as had Gore Vidal, and later the Rolling Stones, and many others. Then we walked to a café overlooking the Strait of Gibraltar, and while the freighters passed in and out of the Mediterranean, he told me tales of his boyhood.

As the sun began to set on my first day in Tangier, we made our way to the large market in the rue de Fez, where Paul was greeted by the owner of each small stall—the tangerine-and-apple man, the man who sold tomatoes and cauliflowers, the spice woman, the baker, the butcher. They greeted him in Moghrebi, the Moroccan dialect, as if they hadn't seen him for months, although this was a daily ritual. He poked through their wares, bought what looked freshest, and placed his purchases in a string shopping bag.

As I boyishly breathed in all that was arrayed before me, he suddenly bade me farewell and headed off at a pace speedier than I imagined he could have moved, weaving through the crowd of earthbrown *djellabas,* the robes of the Moroccan men, working his way back home to greet whoever might be awaiting him. I headed back to Medina and the Zoco Chico, abandoned but buoyant nonetheless at what the future at that moment seemed to hold.

I remember many things about that time in Tangier, but the image that remains strongest is of the heavy green velvet curtain in Paul's apartment. It hangs between the front door and living room, a crucial character in the play of this man's life, acting as a kind of guardian. One is always holding it back for someone else to enter or to leave, and it becomes the medium through which one hears "pilgrims" at the door, asking for a moment with Paul, the local holy man for the Nazarenes, as the non-Moslems in Tangier are called. Like his formality, it is the fabric that separates the man from the visitor. But he refuses no one entry. As the inscription in my first-edition copy of *The Sheltering Sky* reads, "Things don't happen, it depends on who comes along."

* * *

In 1969, Paul offered to put up enough money to launch a magazine, if I were willing to remain in Tangier to edit it. So in the fall of 1969, Paul and I began soliciting material for the first issue of *Antaeus,* a literary quarterly (now semiannual) to which he has remained spiritual advisor ever since. When The Ecco Press came into existence in 1972, our inaugural publishing list included a reissue of Paul's first collection of stories, *The Delicate Prey.* Paul and I have worked together on his books ever since.

In selecting work for *Too Far From Home,* my first goal was to assemble a Bowles reader as representative of the power of his varied oeuvre as possible. I have excerpted two critical passages from *The Sheltering Sky,* and a generous selection of stories from Paul's first collection, *The Delicate Prey* (1950). This novel and these stories are the heart of his early fiction and established his reputation as an important young American writer.

This said, I am pleased to be publishing here for the first time the important new novella that lends this book its title. The story takes for its setting an isolated town in the Niger River valley, the characters a brother and sister, and, as always in the work of Paul Bowles, the hapless characters who find themselves passing through.

From his three other novels—*Up Above the World* (1966), the novel Paul considers his best, *Let it Come Down* (1952), and *The Spider's House* (1955)—I have chosen excerpts that illustrate his range and excellence in this genre. In addition to the early stories taken from *The Delicate Prey*, there is more recent short fiction, such as "Tangier 1975," "In the Red Room," and the haunting "Allal."

Under the category of "Historical Tales" you will find passages from *Points in Time* (1982), a distillation of the very essence of Moroccan culture, condensing experience, emotion, the whole history of a people into a series of short, insightful vignettes—what Tobias Wolff called "a nervy, surprising, completely original performance, so original that it can't be referred to any previous category of fiction or non-fiction."

Their Heads Are Green and Their Hands Are Blue (1963) represents some of the best travel writing on the exotic landscapes of Morocco and Ceylon recorded by a Western sensibility. I have used four essays, including a superb meditation on the Sahara, "Baptism of Solitude," which begins with one of the definitive passages in Bowles:

> Immediately when you arrive in the Sahara, for the first or the tenth time, you notice the stillness. An incredible, absolute silence prevails outside the towns; and within, even in the busy places like the markets, there is a hushed quality in the air, as if the quiet were a conscious force which, resenting the intrusion of sound, minimizes and disperses sound straightway. Then there is the sky, compared to which all other skies seem faint-hearted efforts.

Moving to an autobiographical mode, there are three passages from Paul's elusive but beguiling autobiography *Without Stopping* (1972); the first illuminates his rather rarified childhood; the others, his adventures in Paris and Berlin, where he met the likes of André Gide, Ezra Pound, Jean Cocteau, and Gertrude Stein, who ultimately led Paul to Tangier. I have also excerpted from his journals, *Days* (1991), followed by a selection of letters that address subjects regarding Paul's literary work. Finally, I close with an interview I conducted with Paul at the end of the sixties, where he enlightens us with some vivid insights into his world view, and how it has influenced his writing.

Here then is Paul Bowles, in all his guises save that of composer, his first career. For more than sixty years he has cast a cool and penetrating eye over the landscapes he's lived and imagined, and the people—real and invented—he's placed in them, to see what they will do, the fate they will inherit. It's an eye at once informed, curious, and unforgiving—and finally, indefatigable. As He of the Assembly says, "The eye wants to sleep, but the head is no mattress."

—DANIEL HALPERN
South Harpswell, Maine
August 1992

Introduction

This superb gathering of work by Paul Bowles—prose fiction, essays, poetry, autobiography, and letters—brings together in a single volume the rich and unexpectedly variegated achievement of a major American writer whose "American-ness" is invisible in his work, yet a constant point of reference. Like Ernest Hemingway, whose imagination was aggressively stimulated by the self-defined role, and the romantic adventure of the role, of the expatriate, the voyager into human soul by way of "foreign" peoples and landscapes, Paul Bowles realized his genius by "getting as far away as possible" from home as a young man, as he says in *Without Stopping*, his autobiography; like Hemingway, he fashioned a writerly voice, early on in his career, perfectly suited to the subject matter he would claim as his own. Both writers began their careers with first novels that achieved immediate celebrity, or notoriety, and commercial success: Hemingway's *The Sun Also Rises* (1926) was published when the author was twenty-seven years old; Bowles' *The Sheltering Sky* (1949) was published when the author was thirty-eight years old—but had already had a brilliant career as a composer, music critic, and poet. *The Sun Also Rises* became the very voice of the "Lost Generation" of American expatriates living in Paris in the 1920s, and *The Sheltering Sky* became a cult novel, a stark, ironic, uninflected drama of existential absurdity and fate.

A writer's language is more than merely a vehicle of communication, of course. It is predominantly music created by the rhythm and texture and cadence of words. In his earliest stories, Paul Bowles wrote with the chill omniscient ease of fable—"A Distant Episode," for instance, first published in *Partisan Review* in 1946, unfolds with the horrific calm of a legend, or dream, in which a fate both impersonal and ordained becomes the lot of an American professor of linguistics in Morocco. (The ironic significance of the professor's specialty is an integral part of the story, appropriate to a pitiless world in which, at least in metaphor, the punishment fits the crime.) Bowles' voyager is unnamed, only the Professor; he is both an allegorical figure and a succinctly characterized individual, very likely an alter ego of the author's, like the doomed principals of *The Sheltering Sky* and the isolated Pastor Dowe at Tacaté. The Professor's fate is *not* death—his fate is, horribly, to exist, in a sense, beyond death; to survive as consciousness, bereft of the human. A captive of an outlaw tribe of the Sahara, the Professor perversely lives on, and on, and in the story's mordant climax:

> The tiny inkmarks of which a symphony consists may have been made long ago, but when they are fulfilled in sound they become imminent and mighty. So a kind of music of feeling began to play in the Professor's head, increasing in volume as he looked at the mud wall, and he had the feeling that he was performing what had been written for him long ago.

The Professor has become, unknown to him, a "holy maniac." He runs out into the desert to become "a part of the great silence out there beyond the gate."

"A Distant Episode" is one of those stories, like Poe's "The Tell-Tale Heart" or Kafka's "In the Penal Colony," that, once read, can never be forgotten—even if one should wish to forget it.

Bowles's first gathering of stories, *The Delicate Prey* (1950), a number of which are included in this volume, became too, notably for young writers, a cult book. Published at a time when "the short story" was a fastidiously crafted mannerist genre in which the mores of middle-class Caucasian Americans were subjected to microscopic examination—"A tempest," as Hortense Calisher wittily observed, "in a very small teacup"—*The Delicate Prey* offended, astounded, impressed readers in both the United States and England, and became something of a succès de scandale. Significantly, its dedication page read: "For my mother, who first read me the stories of Poe."

Virtually all of Bowles's fictional work might be so dedicated. Though differing in obvious ways from Poe's insular, claustrophobic, and wildly surrealist tales, as much in their coolness of language as in their keenly recorded camera's-eye observations of Morocco, Mexico, South and Central America, Bowles's fictional works share with Poe's the imagination of nightmare; a simplicity of vision that would seem to predate history; a sense that a man's or a woman's character is fate, and that both are impersonally prescribed. The demonic self-destructive urges to which Poe gave the memorable name "the imp of the perverse" are ubiquitous in Bowles's worlds. From the earliest stories and novels through *Too Far From Home*, the new novella set in the Niger River valley, we encounter men and women, travellers from America, at the mercy of buried wishes experienced as external fate. Indeed, in his 1980 preface to *Let It Come Down,* originally published in 1952, Bowles speaks bluntly of his hero Dyar as a "nonentity, a victim" with a personality "defined solely in terms of situation."

Readers coming to Paul Bowles for the first time are invariably startled by the *uncanniness* his fiction exudes. We are habituated to writers who identify with their characters and whose aim is to maneuver us into an identification with them too. We are habituated to writers whose preoccupations are with human affairs—family crises, politics, marriages, comedies or tragedies of manners. We may be disoriented by a writer whose focus of attention is not upon human beings but upon primitive forces—land- or cityscapes—that express themselves through human beings. The humanist tradition which most educated readers share does not accommodate itself readily to ironic perspectives; we wish to believe, even in the face of Darwinian logic, that the individual matters, and matters greatly. In Bowles's imagination, no such tradition is honored, nor even evoked except ironically. Tennessee Williams, himself the object of passionate attack for his work, warned Bowles, after having read "The Delicate Prey," that he would be considered a monster if he published it. Yet in such monstrousness, such an anti-heroic downscaling of man's spiritual possibilities, is there not, oddly, a kind of modesty?—a most reasonable modesty?

The hapless Pastor Dowe, for instance, deluded in his worthy Protestant mission to bring the "truth" of Jesus Christ to unregenerate South American Indians, realizes one day that the place his church has sent him is "outside God's jurisdiction." The seemingly civilized American husband of "Call at Corazón" detaches himself from hideousness by fixing his attention "upon the given object or situation so that the various elements, all familiar, will regroup themselves. Frightfulness is never more than an unfamiliar pattern": this recipe, as he calls it, allows him to abandon his alcoholic wife to an unspeakable fate in the South American jungle. In "At Paso Rojo" a young Mexican woman surrenders to the atmosphere of brutality that surrounds her and discovers a kinship with spiders living in the crevices of her bedroom walls; in "Allal," a kif-besotted boy is transmogrified into a snake that experiences "the joy of pushing his fangs" into two men before he is killed. In "The Circular Valley," perspective is outside the human altogether: we experience the valley, and human visitors to the valley, through the restive consciousness of the "Atlájala," a demonic spirit capable of passing into sensate creatures:

It would become one of the swallows that made their nests in the rocks beside the top of the waterfall. In the burning sunlight it would plunge again and again into the curtain of mist that rose from far below. . . . It would spend a day as a plant louse, crawling slowly along the underside of the leaves, living quietly in the huge green world down there which is forever hidden from the sky. Or at night, in the velvet body of a panther, it would know the pleasure of the kill. Once . . . it lived in an eel at the bottom of the pool . . .; that was a restful period, but afterward the desire to know again the mysterious life of man had returned—an obsession of which it was useless to try to rid itself.

Even in first-person narratives like "Pages from Cold Point," the reader feels distanced from the speaker, to whom and around whom things happen with an eerie, dreamlike inevitability. In *Too Far From Home*, the narrator is an unstable woman in retreat from a disastrous marriage, who, without knowing what she does, evokes a curse on two young fellow Americans visiting the Niger River valley; in turn, she is herself under the spell of a black servant—in this place where "blacks were the real people and . . . she was the shadow, and . . . even if she went on living here for the rest of her life she would never understand how their minds worked."

Bowles's epigraph to Book 1 of *The Spider's House* (1955) might be an epigraph to all his fiction:

I have understood that the world is a vast emptiness built upon emptiness . . . And so they call me the master of wisdom. Alas! Does anyone know what wisdom is?

> —Song of the Owl,
> *The Thousand and One Nights*

* * *

And then there are Paul Bowles's numerous non-fiction works in which his voice, his first-person persona, is so strikingly different from the voice, or voices, of the fiction.

In the scrupulously observed travel essays collected under the exotic title (from, in fact, Edward Lear) *Their Heads Are Green and Their Hands Are Blue: Scenes from the Non-Christian World* (1963), in the elegantly composed "lyrical history of Morocco" *Points in Time* (1984), in the resolutely unsensational *Without Stopping* (1972) and *Days: Tangier Journal 1987–1989,* and in letters and interviews, Paul Bowles emerges as a dispassionate analyst of culture and of his own life. Temperamentally antithetical to, for instance, Ernest Hemingway and countless fellow writers whose supreme fiction is their self-created image, Bowles declares himself *not* a mythmaker; his efforts are to clarify, not obfuscate. His intelligence is a beacon that illuminates but does not blind, as in the sharply observed anthropological passages in the travel essays; in the autobiographical *Without Stopping,* his tone is one of earnest bemusement with the circumstances of his life and of life generally.

So uninflected in tone and so noncommittal in revealing "secrets" is *Without Stopping,* that Bowles's longtime friend William Burroughs remarked that it might more accurately be titled *Without Telling.* Yet Bowles's account of his long, crowded life is generous with information; he is unsparing in the melancholy details, for instance, of his life as a child. (He was born on December 30, 1911, the only son of a Long Island dentist and his wife: his relations with his abusive father, a thwarted violinist, were always strained. The father had allegedly tried to kill him as an infant and never ceased monitoring and restricting his behavior, with the result that at the age of eleven Bowles "vowed to devote my life to his destruction, even though it meant my own—an infantile conceit, but one which continued to preoccupy me for many years.")

Great memoirs are carefully orchestrated works of art, like Thoreau's *Walden;* they are no more "authentic" than works that announce themselves as fictional texts, though they may contain (or appear to contain) historical veracity. Bowles's memoirs are bluntly direct and honest, for the writer perceives that what he recalls is not an actual event, but merely a memory of the last time the event was recalled; for Bowles, this sort of writing is a kind of journalism, devoid of the strategies of art. His role is to undercut speculation, as he does, for instance, when covering his lengthy expatriated life in Tangier, by saying that he did not choose to live there permanently—"It happened." Similarly, in his autobiography, as in his life, there is little drama because there was no struggle: "I hung on and waited. It seems to me that this must be what most people do."

Bowles's egoless detachment from his own life has allowed him, through the decades of his career, to cast a cold eye upon the world and his own position within it. How significant then that he did find a permanent home in a part of the world that to the American sensibility would indeed seem like a region outside God's jurisdiction—a region where nothing, save the Infinite, is real.

—JOYCE CAROL OATES
June 1992

NOVELS

The Sheltering Sky

He walked through the streets, unthinkingly seeking the darker ones, glad to be alone and to feel the night air against his face. The streets were crowded. People pushed against him as they passed, stared from doorways and windows, made comments openly to each other about him—whether with sympathy or not he was unable to tell from their faces—and they sometimes ceased to walk merely in order to watch him.

"How friendly are they? Their faces are masks. They all look a thousand years old. What little energy they have is only the blind, mass desire to live, since no one of them eats enough to give him his own personal force. But what do they think of me? Probably nothing. Would one of them help me if I were to have an accident? Or would I lie here in the street until the police found me? What motive could any one of them *have* for helping me? They have no religion left. Are they Moslems or Christians? They don't know. They know money, and when they get it, all they want is to eat. But what's wrong with that? Why do I feel this way about them? Guilt at being well fed and healthy among them? But suffering is equally divided among all men; each has the same amount to undergo. . . ." Emotionally he felt that this last idea was untrue, but at the moment it was a necessary belief: it is not always easy to support the stares of hungry people. Thinking that way he could walk on through the streets. It was as if either he or they did not exist. Both suppositions were possible. The Spanish maid at the hotel had said to him that noon: *"La vida es pena."* "Of course," he had replied, feeling false even as he spoke, asking himself if any American can truthfully accept a definition of life which makes it synonymous with suffering. But at the moment he had approved her sentiment because she was old, withered, so clearly of the people. For years it had been one of his superstitions that reality and true perception were to be found in the conversation of the laboring classes. Even though now he saw clearly that their formulas of thought and speech are as strict and as patterned, and thus as far removed from any profound expression of truth as those of any other class, often he found himself still in the act of waiting, with the unreasoning belief that gems of wisdom might yet issue from their mouths. As he walked along, his nervousness was made manifest to him by the sudden consciousness that he was repeatedly tracing rapid figure-eights with his right index finger. He sighed and made himself stop doing it.

His spirits rose a bit as he came out onto a square that was relatively brightly lighted. The cafés on all four sides of the little plaza had put tables and chairs not only across the sidewalks, but in the street as well, so that it would have been impossible for a vehicle to pass through without upsetting them. In the center of the square was a tiny park adorned by four plane trees that had been trimmed to look like open parasols. Underneath the trees there were at least a dozen dogs of various sizes, milling about in a close huddle, and all barking frantically. He made his way slowly across the square, trying to avoid the dogs. As he moved along cautiously under the trees he became aware that at each step he was crushing something beneath his feet. The ground was covered with large insects; their hard shells broke with little explosions that were quite audible to him even amidst the noise the dogs were making. He was aware that ordinarily he would have experienced a thrill of disgust on contact with such a phenomenon, but unreasonably tonight he felt instead a childish triumph. "I'm in a bad way and so what?" The few scattered people sitting at the tables were for the most part silent, but when they spoke, he heard all three of the town's tongues: Arabic, Spanish and French.

Slowly the street began to descend; this surprised him because he imagined that the entire town was built on the slope facing the harbor, and he had consciously chosen to walk inland rather than toward the waterfront. The odors in the air grew ever stronger. They were varied, but they all represented filth of one sort or another. This proximity with, as it were, a forbidden element, served to elate him. He abandoned himself to the perverse pleasure he found in continuing mechanically to put one foot in front of the other, even though he was quite clearly aware of his fatigue. "Suddenly I'll find myself turning around and going back," he thought. But not until then, because he would not make the decision to do it. The impulse to retrace his steps delayed itself from moment to moment. Finally he ceased being surprised: a faint vision began to haunt his mind. It was Kit, seated by the open window, filing her nails and looking out over the town. And as he found his fancy returning more often, as the minutes went by, to that scene, unconsciously he felt himself the protagonist, Kit the spectator. The validity of his existence at that moment was predicated on the assumption that she had not moved, but was still sitting there. It was as if she could still see him from the window, tiny and far away as he was, walking rhythmically uphill and down, through light and shadow; it was as if only she knew when he would turn around and walk the other way.

The street lights were very far apart now, and the streets had left off being paved. Still there were children in the gutters, playing with the garbage and screeching. A small stone suddenly hit him in the back. He wheeled about, but it was too dark to see where it had come from. A few seconds later another stone, coming from in front of him, landed against his knee. In the dim light, he saw a group of small children scattering before him. More stones came from the other direction, this time without hitting him. When he got beyond, to a point where there was a light, he stopped and tried to watch the two groups in battle, but they all ran off into the dark, and so he started up again, his gait as mechanical and rhythmical as before. A wind that was dry and warm, coming up the street out of the blackness before him, met him head on. He sniffed at the fragments of mystery in it, and again he felt an unaccustomed exaltation.

Even though the street became constantly less urban, it seemed reluctant to give up; huts continued to line it on both sides. Beyond a certain point there were no more lights, and the dwellings themselves lay in darkness. The wind, straight from the south, blew across the barren mountains that were invisible ahead of him, over the vast flat sebkha to the edges of the town, raising curtains of dust that climbed to the crest of the hill and lost themselves in the air above the harbor. He stood still. The last possible suburb had been strung on the street's thread. Beyond the final hut the garbage and rubble floor of the road sloped abruptly downward in three directions. In the dimness below were shallow, crooked canyon-like formations. Port raised his eyes to the sky: the powdery course of the Milky Way was like a giant rift across the heavens that let the faint white light through. In the distance he heard a motorcycle. When its sound was finally gone, there was nothing to hear but an occasional cockcrow, like the highest part of a repeated melody whose other notes were inaudible.

He started down the bank to the right, sliding among the fish skeletons and dust. Once below, he felt out a rock that seemed clean and sat down on it. The stench was overpowering. He lit a match, saw the ground thick with chicken feathers and decayed melon rinds. As he rose to his feet he heard steps above him at the end of the street. A figure stood at the top of the embankment. It did not speak, yet Port was certain that it had seen him, had followed him, and knew he was sitting down there. It lit a cigarette, and for a moment he saw an Arab wearing a chechia on his head. The match, thrown into the air, made a fading parabola, the face disappeared, and only the red point of the cigarette remained. The cock crowed several times. Finally the man cried out.

"Qu'est-ce ti cherches là?"

"Here's where the trouble begins," thought Port. He did not move.

The Arab waited a bit. He walked to the very edge of the slope. A dislodged tin can rolled noisily down toward the rock where Port sat.

"Hé! M'sieu! Qu'est-ce ti vo?"

He decided to answer. His French was good.

"Who? Me? Nothing."

The Arab bounded down the bank and stood in front of him. With the characteristic impatient, almost indignant gestures he pursued his inquisition. What are you doing here all alone? Where do you come from? What do you want here? Are you looking for something? To which Port answered wearily: Nothing. That way. Nothing. No.

For a moment the Arab was silent, trying to decide what direction to give the dialogue. He drew violently on his cigarette several times until it glowed very bright, then he flicked it away and exhaled the smoke.

"Do you want to take a walk?" he said.

"What? A walk? Where?"

"Out there." His arm waved toward the mountains.

"What's out there?"

"Nothing."

There was another silence between them.

"I'll pay you a drink," said the Arab. And immediately on that: "What's your name?"

"Jean," said Port.

The Arab repeated the name twice, as if considering its merits. "Me," tapping his chest, "Smaïl. So, do we go and drink?"

"No."

"Why not?"

"I don't feel like it."

"You don't feel like it. What do you feel like doing?"

"Nothing."

All at once the conversation began again from the beginning. Only the now truly outraged inflection of the Arab's voice marked any difference: *"Qu'est-ce ti fi là? Qu'est-ce ti cherches?"* Port rose and started to climb up the slope, but it was difficult going. He kept sliding back down. At once the Arab was beside him, tugging at his arm. "Where are you going, Jean?" Without answering Port made a great effort and gained the top. *"Au revoir,"* he called, walking quickly up the middle of the street. He heard a desperate scrambling behind him; a moment later the man was at his side.

"You didn't wait for me," he said in an aggrieved tone.

"No. I said good-bye."

"I'll go with you."

Port did not answer. They walked a good distance in silence. When they came to the first street light, the Arab reached into his pocket and pulled out a worn wallet. Port glanced at it and continued to walk.

"Look!" cried the Arab, waving it in his face. Port did not look.

"What is it?" he said flatly.

"I was in the Fifth Battalion of Sharpshooters. Look at the paper! Look! You'll see!"

Port walked faster. Soon there began to be people in the street. No one stared at them. One would have said that the presence of the Arab beside him made him invisible. But now he was no longer sure of the way. It would never do to let this be seen. He continued to walk straight ahead as if there were no doubt in his mind. "Over the crest of the hill and down," he said to himself, "and I can't miss it."

Everything looked unfamiliar: the houses, the streets, the cafés, even the formation of the town with regard to the hill. Instead of finding a summit from which to begin the downward walk, he discovered that here the streets all led perceptibly upward, no matter which way he turned; to descend he would have had to go back. The Arab walked solemnly along with him, now beside him, now slipping behind when there was not enough room to walk two abreast. He no longer made attempts at conversation; Port noticed with relish that he was a little out of breath.

"I can keep this up all night if I have to," he thought, "but how the hell will I get to the hotel?"

All at once they were in a street which was no more than a passageway. Above their heads the opposite walls jutted out to within a few inches of each other. For an instant Port hesitated: this was not the kind of street he wanted to walk in, and besides, it so obviously did not lead to the hotel.

In that short moment the Arab took charge. He said: "You don't know this street? It's called Rue de la Mer Rouge. You know it? Come on. There are *cafés arabes* up this way. Just a little way. Come on."

Port considered. He wanted at all costs to keep up the pretense of being familiar with the town.

"Je ne sais pas si je veux y aller ce soir," he reflected, aloud.

The Arab began to pull Port's sleeve in his excitement. *"Si, si!"* he cried. *"Viens!* I'll pay you a drink."

"I don't drink. It's very late."

Two cats nearby screamed at each other. The Arab made a hissing noise and stamped his feet; they ran off in opposite directions.

"We'll have tea, then," he pursued.

Port sighed. *"Bien,"* he said.

The café had a complicated entrance. They went through a low arched door, down a dim hall into a small garden. The air reeked of lilies, and it was also tinged with the sour smell of drains. In the dark they crossed the garden and climbed a long flight of stone steps. The staccato sound of a hand drum came from above, tapping indolent patterns above a sea of voices.

"Do we sit outside or in?" the Arab asked.

"Outside," said Port. He sniffed the invigorating smell of hashish smoke, and unconsciously smoothed his hair as they arrived at the top of the stairs. The Arab noticed even that small gesture. "No ladies here, you know."

"Oh, I know."

Through a doorway he caught a glimpse of the long succession of tiny, brightly-lit rooms, and the men seated everywhere on the reed matting that covered the floors. They all wore either white turbans or red chechias on their heads, a detail which lent the scene such a strong aspect of homogeneity that Port exclaimed: "Ah!" as they passed by the door. When they were on the terrace in the starlight, with an oud being plucked idly in the dark nearby, he said to his companion: "But I didn't know there was anything like this left in this city." The Arab did not understand. "Like this?" he echoed. "How?"

"With nothing but Arabs. Like the inside here. I thought all the cafés were like the ones in the street, all mixed up; Jews, French, Spanish, Arabs together. I thought the war had changed everything."

The Arab laughed. "The war was bad. A lot of people died. There was nothing to eat. That's all. How would that change the cafés? Oh no, my friend. It's the same as always." A moment later he said: "So you haven't been here since the war! But you were here before the war?"

"Yes," said Port. This was true; he had once spent an afternoon in the town when his boat had made a brief call there.

The tea arrived; they chatted and drank it. Slowly the image of Kit sitting in the window began to take shape again in Port's mind. At first, when he became conscious of it, he felt a pang of guilt. Then his fantasy took a hand, and he saw her face, tight-lipped with fury as she undressed and flung her flimsy pieces of clothing across the furniture. By now she had surely given up waiting and gone to bed. He shrugged his shoulders and grew pensive, rinsing what was left of his tea around and around in the bottom of the glass, and following with his eyes the circular motion he was making.

"You're sad," said Smaïl.

"No, no." He looked up and smiled wistfully, then resumed watching the glass.

"You live only a short time. *Il faut rigoler.*"

Port was impatient; he was not in the mood for café philosophizing.

"Yes, I know," he said shortly, and he sighed. Smaïl pinched his arm. His eyes were shining.

"When we leave here, I'll take you to see a friend of mine."

"I don't want to meet him," said Port, adding: "Thank you anyway."

"Ah, you're really sad," laughed Smaïl. "It's a girl. Beautiful as the moon."

Port's heart missed a beat. "A girl," he repeated automatically, without taking his eyes from the glass. He was perturbed to witness his own interior excitement. He looked at Smaïl.

"A girl?" he said. "You mean a whore."

Smaïl was mildly indignant. "A whore? Ah, my friend, you don't know me. I wouldn't introduce you to that. *C'est de la saloperie, ça!* This is a friend of mine, very elegant, very nice. When you meet her, you'll see."

The musician stopped playing the oud. Inside the café they were calling out numbers for the lotto game: *"Ouahad aou tletine! Arbaine!"*

Port said: "How old is she?"

Smaïl hesitated. "About sixteen. Sixteen or seventeen."

"Or twenty or twenty-five," suggested Port, with a leer.

Again Smaïl was indignant. "What do you mean, twenty-five? I tell you she's sixteen or seventeen. You don't believe me? Listen. You meet her. If you don't like her, you just pay for the tea and we'll go out again. Is that all right?"

"And if I do like her?"

"Well, you'll do whatever you want."

"But I'll pay her?"

"But of course you'll pay her."

Port laughed. "And you say she's not a whore."

Smaïl leaned over the table towards him and said with a great show of patience: "Listen, Jean. She's a dancer. She only arrived from her bled in the desert a few weeks ago. How can she be a whore if she's not registered and doesn't live in the quartier? Eh? Tell me! You pay her because you take up her time. She dances in the quartier, but she has no room, no bed there. She's not a whore. So now, shall we go?"

Port thought a long time, looked up at the sky, down into the garden, and all around the terrace before answering: "Yes. Let's go. Now."

* * *

When they left the café it seemed to him that they were going more or less in the same direction from which they had just come. There were fewer people in the streets and the air was cooler. They walked for a good distance through the Casbah, making a sudden exit through a tall gateway onto a high, open space outside the walls. Here it was silent, and the stars were very much in evidence. The pleasure he felt at the unexpected freshness of the air and the relief at being in the open once more, out from under the overhanging houses, served to delay Port in asking the question that was in his mind: "Where are we going?" But as they continued along what seemed a parapet at the edge of a deep, dry moat, he finally gave voice to it. Smaïl replied vaguely that the girl lived with some friends at the edge of town.

"But we're already in the country," objected Port.

"Yes, it's the country," said Smaïl.

It was perfectly clear that he was being evasive now; his character seemed to have changed again. The beginning of intimacy was gone. To Port he was once more the anonymous dark figure that had stood above him in the garbage at the end of the street, smoking a bright cigarette. *You can still break it up. Stop walking. Now.* But the combined even rhythm of their feet on the stones was too powerful. The parapet made a wide curve and the ground below dropped steeply away into a deeper darkness. The moat had ended some hundred feet back. They were now high above the upper end of an open valley.

"The Turkish fortress," remarked Smaïl, pounding on the stones with his heel.

"Listen to me," began Port angrily; "where are we going?" He looked at the rim of uneven black mountains ahead of them on the horizon.

"Down there." Smaïl pointed to the valley. A moment later he stopped walking. "Here are the stairs." They leaned over the edge. A narrow iron staircase was fastened to the side of the wall. It had no railing and led straight downward at a steep angle.

"It's a long way," said Port.

"Ah, yes, it's the Turkish fortress. You see that light down there?" He indicated a faint red glimmer that came and went, almost directly beneath them. "That's the tent where she lives."

"The tent!"

"There are no houses down here. Only tents. There are a lot of them. *On descend?*"

Smaïl went first, keeping close to the wall. "Touch the stones," he said.

As they approached the bottom, he saw that the feeble glow of light was a dying bonfire built in an open space between two large nomad tents. Smaïl suddenly stopped to listen. There was an indistinguishable murmur of male voices. *"Allons-y,"* he muttered; his voice sounded satisfied.

They reached the end of the staircase. There was hard ground beneath their feet. To his left Port saw the black silhouette of a huge agave plant in flower.

"Wait here," whispered Smaïl. Port was about to light a cigarette; Smaïl hit his arm angrily. "No!" he whispered. "But what is it?" began Port, highly annoyed at the show of secrecy. Smaïl disappeared.

Leaning against the cold rock wall, Port waited to hear a break in the monotonous, low-pitched conversation, an exchange of greetings, but nothing happened. The voices went on exactly as before, an uninterrupted flow of expressionless sounds. "He must have gone into the other tent," he thought. One side of the farther tent flickered pink in the light of the bonfire; beyond was darkness. He edged a few steps along the wall, trying to see the entrance of the tent, but it faced in the other direction. Then he listened for the sound of voices there, but none came. For no reason at all he suddenly heard Kit's parting remark as he had left her room: "After all, it's much more your business than it is mine." Even now the words meant nothing in particular to him, but he remembered the tone in which she had said it: she had sounded hurt and rebellious. And it was all about Tunner. He stood up straight. "He's been after her," he whispered aloud. Abruptly he turned and went to the staircase, started up it. After six steps he stopped and looked around. "What can I do tonight?" he thought. "I'm using this as an excuse to get out of here, because I'm afraid. What the hell, he'll never get her."

A figure darted out from between the two tents and ran lightly to the foot of the stairs. "Jean!" it whispered. Port stood still.

"*Ah! Ti es là!* What are you doing up there? Come on!"

Port walked slowly back down. Smaïl stepped out of his way, took his arm.

"Why can't we talk?" whispered Port. Smaïl squeezed his arm. "Shh!" he said into his ear. They skirted the nearer tent, brushing past a clump of high thistles, and made their way over the stones to the entrance of the other.

"Take off your shoes," commanded Smaïl, slipping off his sandals.

"Not a good idea," thought Port. "No," he said aloud.

"Shh!" Smaïl pushed him inside, shoes still on.

The central part of the tent was high enough to stand up in. A short candle stuck on top of a chest near the entrance provided the light, so that the nether parts of the tent were in almost complete darkness. Lengths of straw matting had been spread on the ground at senseless angles; objects were scattered everywhere in utter disorder. There was no one in the tent waiting for them.

"Sit down," said Smaïl, acting the host. He cleared the largest piece of matting of an alarm clock, a sardine can, and an ancient, incredibly greasy pair of overalls. Port sat down and put his elbows on his knees. On the mat next to him lay a chipped enamel bedpan, half filled with a darkish liquid. There were bits of stale bread everywhere. He lit a cigarette without offering one to Smaïl, who returned to stand near the entrance, looking out.

And suddenly she stepped inside—a slim, wild-looking girl with great dark eyes. She was dressed in spotless white, with a white turbanlike headdress that pulled her hair tightly backward, accentuating the indigo designs tattooed on her forehead. Once inside the tent, she stood quite still, looking at Port with something of the expression, he thought, the young bull often wears as he takes the first few steps into the glare of the arena. There was bewilderment, fear, and a passive expectancy in her face as she stared quietly at him.

"Ah, here she is!" said Smaïl, still in a hushed voice. "Her name is Marhnia." He waited a bit. Port rose and stepped forward to take her hand. "She doesn't speak French," Smaïl explained. Without smiling, she touched Port's hand lightly with her own and raised her fingers to her lips. Bowing, she said, in what amounted almost to a whisper: "*Ya sidi, la bess âlik? Eglès, baraka 'laou'fik.*" With gracious dignity and a peculiar modesty of movement, she unstuck the lighted candle from the chest, and walked across to the back of the tent, where a blanket stretched from the ceiling formed a partial alcove. Before disappearing behind the blanket, she turned her head to them, and said, gesturing: "*Agi! Agi menah!*" The two men followed her into the alcove, where an old mattress had been laid on some low boxes in an attempt to make a salon. There was a tiny tea table beside the improvised divan, and a pile of small, lumpy cushions lay on the mat by the table. The girl set the candle down on the bare earth and began to arrange the cushions along the mattress.

"*Essmah!*" she said to Port, and to Smaïl: "*Tsekellem bellatsi.*" Then she went out. He laughed and called after her in a low voice: "*Fhemtek!*" Port was intrigued by the girl, but the language barrier annoyed him, and he was even more irritated by the fact that Smaïl and she could converse together in his presence. "She's gone to get fire," said Smaïl. "Yes, yes," said Port, "but why do we have to whisper?" Smaïl rolled his eyes toward the tent's entrance. "The men in the other tent," he said.

Presently she returned, carrying an earthen pot of bright coals. While she was boiling the water and preparing the tea, Smaïl chatted with her. Her replies were always grave, her voice hushed but pleasantly modulated. It seemed to Port that she was much more like a young nun than a café dancer. At the same time he did not in the least trust her, being content to sit and marvel at the delicate movements of her nimble, henna-stained fingers as she tore the stalks of mint apart and stuffed them into the little teapot.

When she had sampled the tea several times and eventually had found it to her liking, she handed them each a glass, and with a solemn air sat back on her haunches and began to drink hers. "Sit here," said Port, patting the couch beside him. She indicated that she was quite happy where she was, and thanked him politely. Turning her attention to Smaïl, she proceeded to engage him in a lengthy conversation during which Port sipped his tea and tried to relax. He had an oppressive sensation that daybreak was near at hand—surely not more than an hour or so away, and he felt that all this time was being wasted. He looked anxiously at his watch; it had stopped at five minutes of two. But it was still going. Surely it must be later than that. Marhnia addressed a question to Smaïl which seemed to include Port. "She wants to know if you have heard the story about Outka, Mimouna and Aïcha," said Smaïl. "No," said Port. *"Goul lou, goul lou,"* said Marhnia to Smaïl, urging him.

"There are three girls from the mountains, from a place near Marhnia's bled, and they are called Outka, Mimouna and Aïcha." Marhnia was nodding her head slowly in affirmation, her large soft eyes fixed on Port. "They go to seek their fortune in the M'Zab. Most girls from the mountains go to Alger, Tunis, here, to earn money, but these girls want one thing more than everything else. They want to drink tea in the Sahara." Marhnia continued to nod her head; she was keeping up with the story solely by means of the place-names as Smaïl pronounced them.

"I see," said Port, who had no idea whether the story was a humorous one or a tragic one; he was determined to be careful, so that he could pretend to savor it as much as she clearly hoped he would. He only wished it might be short.

"In the M'Zab the men are all ugly. The girls dance in the cafés of Ghardaia, but they are always sad; they still want to have tea in the Sahara." Port glanced again at Marhnia. Her expression was completely serious. He nodded his head again. "So, many months pass, and they are still in the M'Zab, and they are very, very sad, because the men are all so ugly. They are very ugly there, like pigs. And they don't pay enough money to the poor girls so they can go and have tea in the Sahara." Each time he said "Sahara," which he pronounced in the Arabic fashion, with a vehement accent on the first syllable, he stopped for a moment. "One day a Targui comes, he is tall and handsome, on a beautiful mehari; he talks to Outka, Mimouna and Aïcha, he tells them about the desert, down there where he lives, his bled, and they listen, and their eyes are big. Then he says: 'Dance for me,' and they dance. Then he makes love with all three, he gives a silver piece to Outka, a silver piece to Mimouna, and a silver piece to Aïcha. At daybreak he gets on his mehari and goes away to the south. After that they are very sad, and the M'Zabi look uglier than ever to them, and they only are thinking of the tall Targui who lives in the Sahara." Port lit a cigarette;

then he noticed Marhnia looking expectantly at him, and he passed her the pack. She took one, and with a crude pair of tongs elegantly lifted a live coal to the end of it. It ignited immediately, whereupon she passed it to Port, taking his in exchange. He smiled at her. She bowed almost imperceptibly.

"Many months go by, and still they can't earn enough money to go to the Sahara. They have kept the silver pieces, because all three are in love with the Targui. And they are always sad. One day they say: 'We are going to finish like this—always sad, without ever having tea in the Sahara—so now we must go anyway, even without money.' And they put all their money together, even the three silver pieces, and they buy a teapot and a tray and three glasses, and they buy bus tickets to El Goléa. And there they have only a little money left, and they give it all to a bachhamar who is taking his caravan south to the Sahara. So he lets them ride with his caravan. And one night, when the sun is going to go down, they come to the great dunes of sand, and they think: 'Ah, now we are in the Sahara; we are going to make tea.' The moon comes up, all the men are asleep except the guard. He is sitting with the camels playing his flute." Smaïl wriggled his fingers in front of his mouth. "Outka, Mimouna and Aïcha go away from the caravan quietly with their tray and their teapot and their glasses. They are going to look for the highest dune so they can see all the Sahara. Then they are going to make tea. They walk a long time. Outka says: 'I see a high dune,' and they go to it and climb up to the top. Then Mimouna says: 'I see a dune over there. It's much higher and we can see all the way to In Salah from it.' So they go to it, and it is much higher. But when they get to the top, Aïcha says: 'Look! There's the highest dune of all. We can see to Tamanrasset. That's where the Targui lives.' The sun came up and they kept walking. At noon they were very hot. But they came to the dune and they climbed and climbed. When they got to the top they were very tired and they said: 'We'll rest a little and then make tea.' But first they set out the tray and the teapot and the glasses. Then they lay down and slept. And then"—Smaïl paused and looked at Port—"Many days later another caravan was passing and a man saw something on top of the highest dune there. And when they went up to see, they found Outka, Mimouna and Aïcha; they were still there, lying the same way as when they had gone to sleep. And all three of the glasses," he held up his own little tea glass, "were full of sand. That was how they had their tea in the Sahara."

There was a long silence. It was obviously the end of the story. Port looked at Marhnia; she was still nodding her head, her eyes fixed on him. He decided to hazard a remark. "It's very sad," he said. She immediately inquired of Smaïl what he had said. *"Gallik merhmoum b*χ*ef,"* translated Smaïl. She shut her eyes slowly and continued to nod her head. *"Ei oua!"* she said, opening them again. Port turned quickly to Smaïl. "Listen, it's very late. I want to arrange a price with her. How much should I give her?"

Smaïl looked scandalized. "You can't do that as if you were dealing with a whore! *Ci pas une putain, je t'ai dit!"*

"But I'll pay her if I stay with her?"

"Of course."

"Then I want to arrange it now."

"I can't do that for you, my friend."

Port shrugged his shoulders and stood up. "I've got to go. It's late."

Marhnia looked quickly from one man to the other. Then she said a word or two in a very soft voice to Smaïl, who frowned but stalked out of the tent yawning.

They lay on the couch together. She was very beautiful, very docile, very understanding, and still he did not trust her. She declined to disrobe completely, but in her delicate gestures of refusal he discerned an ultimate yielding, to bring about which it would require only time. With time he could have had her confidence; tonight he could only have that which had been taken for granted from the beginning. He reflected on this as he lay, looking into her untroubled face, remembered that he was leaving for the south in a day or two, inwardly swore at his luck, and said to himself: "Better half a loaf." Marhnia leaned over and snuffed the candle between her fingers. For a second there was utter silence, utter blackness. Then he felt her soft arms slowly encircle his neck, and her lips on his forehead.

Almost immediately a dog began to howl in the distance. For a while he did not hear it; when he did, it troubled him. It was the wrong music for the moment. Soon he found himself imagining that Kit was a silent on-looker. The fantasy stimulated him—the lugubrious howling no longer bothered him.

Not more than a quarter of an hour later, he got up and peered around the blanket, to the flap of the tent: it was still dark. He was seized with an abrupt desire to be out of the place. He sat down on the couch and began to arrange his clothing. The two arms stole up again, locked themselves about his neck. Firmly he pulled them away, gave them a few playful pats. Only one came up this time; the other slipped inside his jacket and he felt his chest being caressed. Some indefinable false movement there made him reach inside to put his hand on hers. His wallet was already between her fingers. He yanked it away from her and pushed her back down on the mattress. "Ah!" she cried, very loud. He rose and stumbled noisily through the welter of objects that lay between him and the exit. This time she screamed, briefly. The voices in the other tent became audible. With his wallet still in his hand he rushed out, turned sharply to the left and began to run toward the wall. He fell twice, once against a rock and once because the ground sloped unexpectedly down. As he rose the second time, he saw a man coming from one side to cut him off from the staircase. He was limping, but he was nearly there. He did get there. All the way up the stairs it seemed to him that someone immediately behind him would have hold of one of his legs during the next second. His lungs were an enormous pod of pain, would burst instantly. His mouth was open, drawn down at the sides, his teeth clenched, and the air whistled between them as he drew breath. At the top he turned, and seizing a boulder he could not lift, he did lift it, and hurled it down the staircase. Then he breathed deeply and began to run along the parapet. The sky was palpably lighter, an immaculate gray clarity spreading upward from behind the low hills in the east. He could not run very far. His heart was beating in his head and neck. He knew he never could reach the town. On the side of the road away from the valley there was a wall, too high to be climbed. But a few hundred feet farther on, it had been broken down for a short distance, and a talus of stones and dirt made a perfect stile. He cut back inside the wall in the direction from which he had just come, and hurried panting up a gradual side hill studded with the flat stone beds which are Moslem tombstones. Finally he sat down for a minute, his head in his hands, and was conscious of several things at once: the pain of his head and chest, the fact that he no longer held his wallet, and the loud sound of his own heart, which, however, did not keep him from thinking he heard the excited voices of his pursuers below in the road a moment later. He rose and staggered on upward over the graves. Eventually the hill sloped downward in the other direction. He felt a little safer. But each minute the light of day was nearer; it would be easy to spot his solitary figure from a distance, wandering over the hill. He began to run again, downhill, always in the same direction, staggering now and then, never looking up for fear he should fall; this went on for a long time; the graveyard was left behind. Finally he reached a high spot covered with bushes and cactus, but from which he could dominate the entire immediate countryside. He sat down among the bushes. It was perfectly quiet. The sky was white. Occasionally he stood up carefully and peered out. And so it was that when the sun came up he looked between two oleanders and saw it reflected red across the miles of glittering salt sebkha that lay between him and the mountains.

* * *

It was a long night. They came to a bordj built into the side of a cliff. The overhead light was turned on. The young Arab just in front of Kit, turning around and smiling at her as he lowered the hood of his burnous, pointed at the earth several times and said: *"Hassi Inifel!"*

"Merci," she said, and smiled back. She felt like getting out, and turned to Port. He was doubled up under his coat; his face looked flushed.

"Port," she began, and was surprised to hear him answer immediately. "Yes?" His voice sounded wide awake.

"Let's get out and have something hot. You've slept for hours."

Slowly he sat up. "I haven't slept at all, if you want to know."

She did not believe him. "I see," she said. "Well, do you want to go inside? I'm going."

"If I can. I feel terrible. I think I have grippe or something."

"Oh, nonsense! How could you? You probably have indigestion from eating dinner so fast."

"You go on in. I'll feel better not moving."

She climbed out and stood a moment on the rocks in the wind, taking deep breaths. Dawn was nowhere in sight.

In one of the rooms near the entrance of the bordj there were men singing together and clapping their hands quickly in complex rhythm. She found coffee in a smaller room nearby, and sat down on the floor, warming her hands over the clay vessel of coals. "He *can't* get sick here," she thought. "Neither of us can." There was nothing to do but refuse to be sick, once one was this far away from the world. She went back out and looked through the windows of the bus. Most of the passengers had remained asleep, wrapped in their burnouses. She found Port, and tapped on the glass. "Port!" she called. "Hot coffee!" He did not stir.

"Damn him!" she thought. "He's trying to get attention. He *wants* to be sick!" She climbed aboard and worked her way back to his seat, where he lay inert.

"Port! Please come and have some coffee. As a favor to me." She cocked her head and looked at his face. Smoothing his hair she asked: "Do you feel sick?"

He spoke into his coat. "I don't want anything. Please. I don't want to move."

She disliked to humor him; perhaps by waiting on him she would be playing right into his hands. But in the event he had been chilled he should drink something hot. She determined to get the coffee into him somehow. So she said: "Will you drink it if I bring it to you?"

His reply was a long time in coming, but he finally said: "Yes."

The driver, an Arab who wore a visored cap instead of a turban, was already on his way out of the bordj as she rushed in. "Wait!" she said to him. He stood still and turned around, looking her up and down speculatively. He had no one to whom he could make any remarks about her, since there were no Europeans present, and the other Arabs were not from the city, and would have failed completely to understand his obscene comments.

Port sat up and drank the coffee, sighing between swallows.

"Finished? I've got to give the glass back."

"Yes." The glass was relayed through the bus to the front, where a child waited for it, peering anxiously back lest the bus start up before he had it in his hands.

They moved off slowly across the plateau. Now that the doors had been open, it was colder inside.

"I think that helped," Port said. "Thanks an awful lot. Only I *have* got something wrong with me. God knows I never felt quite like this before. If I could only be in bed and lie out flat, I'd be all right, I think."

"But what do you think it *is?*" she said, suddenly feeling them all there in full force, the fears she had been holding at bay for so many days.

"You tell *me*. We don't get in till noon, do we? What a mess, what a mess!"

"Try and sleep, darling." She had not called him that in at least a year. "Lean over, way over, this way, put your head here. Are you warm enough?" For a few minutes she tried to break the jolts of the bus for him by posting with her body against the back of the seat, but her muscles soon tired; she leaned back and relaxed, letting his head bounce up and down on her breast. His hand in her lap sought hers, found it, held it tightly at first, then loosely. She decided he was asleep, and shut her eyes, thinking: "Of course, there's no escape now. I'm here."

At dawn they reached another bordj standing on a perfectly flat expanse of land. The bus drove through the entrance into a court, where several tents stood. A camel peered haughtily through the window beside Kit's face. This time everyone got out. She woke Port. "Want some breakfast?" she said.

"Believe it or not, I'm a little hungry."

"Why shouldn't you be?" she said brightly. "It's nearly six o'clock."

They had more of the sweet black coffee, and some hardboiled eggs, and dates. The young Arab who had told her the name of the other bordj walked by as they sat on the floor eating. Kit could not help noticing how unusually tall he was, what an admirable figure he cut when he stood erect in his flowing white garment. To efface her feeling of guilt at having thought anything at all about him, she felt impelled to bring him to Port's attention.

"Isn't that one striking!" she heard herself saying, as the Arab moved from the room. The phrase was not at all hers, and it sounded completely ridiculous coming out of her mouth; she waited uneasily for Port's reaction. But Port was holding his hand over his abdomen; his face was white.

"What is it?" she cried.

"Don't let the bus go," he said. He rose unsteadily to his feet and left the room precipitately. Accompanied by a boy he stumbled across the wide court, past the tents where fires burned and babies cried. He walked doubled over, holding his head with one hand and his belly with the other.

In the far corner was a little stone enclosure like a gun-turret, and the boy pointed to it. *"Daoua,"* he said. Port went up the steps and in, slamming the wooden door after him. It stank inside, and it was dark. He leaned back against the cold stone wall and heard the spiderwebs snap as his head touched them. The pain was ambiguous: it was a violent cramp and a mounting nausea, both at once. He stood still for some time, swallowing hard and breathing heavily. What faint light there was in the chamber came up through the square hole in the floor. Something ran swiftly across the back of his neck. He moved away from the wall and leaned over the hole, pushing with his hands against the other wall in front of him. Below were the fouled earth and spattered stones, moving with flies. He shut his eyes and remained in that expectant position for some minutes, groaning from time to time. The bus driver began to blow his horn; for some reason the sound increased his anguish. "Oh, God, shut up!" he cried aloud, groaning immediately afterward. But the horn continued, mixing short blasts with long ones. Finally came the moment when the pain suddenly seemed to have lessened. He opened his eyes, and made an involuntary movement upward with his head, because for an instant he thought he saw flames. It was the red rising sun shining on the rocks and filth beneath. When he opened the door Kit and the young Arab stood outside; between them they helped him out to the waiting bus.

As the morning passed, the landscape took on a gaiety and softness that were not quite like anything Kit had ever seen. Suddenly she realized that it was because in good part sand had replaced rock. And lacy trees grew here and there, especially in the spots where there were agglomerations of huts, and these spots became more frequent. Several times they came upon groups of dark men mounted on mehara. These held the reins proudly, their kohl-farded eyes were fierce above the draped indigo veils that hid their faces.

For the first time she felt a faint thrill of excitement. "It *is* rather wonderful," she thought, "to be riding past such people in the Atomic Age."

Port reclined in his seat, his eyes shut. "Just forget I'm here," he had said when they left the bordj, "and I'll be better able to do the same thing. It's only a few hours more—then bed, thank God."

The young Arab spoke just enough French to be undaunted by the patent impossibility of his engaging in an actual conversation with Kit. It appeared that in his eyes a noun alone or a verb uttered with feeling was sufficient, and she seemed to be of the same mind. He told her, with the usual Arab talent for making a legend out of a mere recounting of facts, about El Ga'a and its high walls with their gates that shut at sunset, its quiet dark streets and its great market where men sold many things that came from the Soudan and from even farther away: salt bars, ostrich plumes, gold dust, leopard skins—he enumerated them in a long list, unconcernedly using the Arabic term for a thing when he did not know the French. She listened with complete attention, hypnotized by the extraordinary charm of his face and his voice, and fascinated as well by the strangeness of what he was talking about, the odd way he was saying it.

The terrain now was a sandy wasteland, strewn with occasional tortured bushlike trees that crouched low in the virulent sunlight. Ahead, the blue of the firmament was turning white with a more fierce glare than she had thought possible: it was the air over the city. Before she knew it, they were riding along beside the gray mud walls. The children cried out as the bus went past, their voices like bright needles. Port's eyes were still shut; she decided not to disturb him until they had arrived. They turned sharply to the left, making a cloud of dust, and went through a big gate into an enormous open square—a sort of antechamber to the city, at the end of which was another gate, even larger. Beyond that the people and animals disappeared into darkness. The bus stopped with a jolt and the driver got out abruptly and walked away with the air of wishing to have nothing further to do with it. Passengers still slept, or yawned and began looking about for their belongings, most of which were no longer in the places where they had put them the night before.

Kit indicated by word and gesture that she and Port would stay where they were until everyone else had left the vehicle. The young Arab said that in that event he would, too, because she would need him to help take Port to the hotel. As they sat there waiting for the leisurely travelers to get down, he explained that the hotel was across the town on the side by the fort, since it was operated exclusively for the few officers who did not have homes, it being very rare that anyone arriving by bus had need of a hotel.

"You are very kind," she said, sitting back in her seat.

"Yes, madame." His face expressed nothing but friendly solicitousness, and she trusted him implicitly.

When at last the bus was empty save for the debris of pomegranate peel and date pits on the floor and seats, he got out and called a group of men to carry the bags.

"We're here," said Kit in a loud voice. Port stirred, opened his eyes, and said: "I finally slept. What a hellish trip. Where's the hotel?"

"It's somewhere around," she said vaguely; she did not like to tell him that it was on the other side of the city.

He sat up slowly. "God, I hope it's near. I don't think I can make it if it isn't. I feel like hell. I really feel like hell."

"There's an Arab here who's helping us. He's taking us there. It seems it isn't right here by the terminal." She felt better letting him discover the truth about the hotel from the Arab; that way she would remain uninvolved in the matter, and whatever resentment Port might feel would not be directed against her.

Outside in the dust was the disorder of Africa, but for the first time without any visible sign of European influence, so that the scene had a purity which had been lacking in the other towns, an unexpected quality of being complete which dissipated the feeling of chaos. Even Port, as they helped him out, noticed the unified aspect of the place. "It's wonderful here," he said, "what I can see of it, anyway."

"What you can see of it!" echoed Kit. "Is something wrong with your eyes?"

"I'm dizzy. It's a fever, I know that much."

She felt his forehead, and said nothing but: "Well, let's get out of this sun."

The young Arab walked on his left and Kit on his right; each had a supporting arm about him. The porters had gone on ahead.

"The first decent place," said Port bitterly, "and I have to feel like this."

"You're going to stay in bed until you're absolutely well. We'll have plenty of time to explore later."

He did not answer. They went through the inner gate and straightway plunged into a long, crooked tunnel. Passersby brushed against them in the dark. People were sitting along the walls at the sides, from where muffled voices rose, chanting long repetitious phrases. Soon they were in the sunlight once more, then there was another stretch of darkness where the street burrowed through the thick-walled houses.

"Didn't he tell you where it was? I can't take much more of this," Port said. He had not once addressed the Arab directly.

"Ten, fifteen minutes," said the young Arab.

He still disregarded him. "It's out of the question," he told Kit, gasping a little.

"My dear boy, you've *got* to go. You can't just sit down in the street here."

"What is it?" said the Arab, who was watching their faces. And on being told, he hailed a passing stranger and spoke with him briefly. "There is a fondouk that way." He pointed. "He can—" He made a gesture of sleeping, his hand against his cheek. "Then we go hotel and get men and *rfed, très bien!*" He made as if to sweep Port off his feet and carry him in his arms.

"No, no!" cried Kit, thinking he really was about to pick him up.

He laughed and said to Port: "You want to go there?"

"Yes."

They turned around and made their way back through a part of the interior labyrinth. Again the young Arab spoke with someone in the street. He turned back to them smiling. "The end. The next dark place."

The fondouk was a small, crowded and dirty version of any one of the bordjes they had passed through during the recent weeks, save that the center was covered with a latticework of reeds as a protection from the sun. It was filled with country folk and camels, all of them reclining together on the ground. They went in and the Arab spoke with one of the guardians, who cleared the occupants from a stall at one side and piled fresh straw in its corner for Port to lie down on. The porters sat on the luggage in the courtyard.

"I can't leave here," said Kit, looking about the filthy cubicle. "Move your hand!" It lay on some camel dung, but he left it there. "Go on, please. *Now,*" he said. "I'll be all right until you get back. But Hurry. Hurry!"

She cast a last anguished glance at him and went out into the court, followed by the Arab. It was a relief to her to be able to walk quickly in the street.

"*Vite! Vite!*" she kept repeating to him, like a machine. They panted as they went along, threading their way through the slow-moving crowd, down into the heart of the city and out on the other side, until they saw the hill ahead with the fort on it. This side of the town was more open than the other, consisting in part of gardens separated from the streets by high walls, above which rose an occasional tall black cypress. At the end of a long alley there was an almost unnoticeable wooden plaque painted with the words: *Hôtel du Ksar,* and an arrow pointing left. "Ah!" cried Kit. Even here at the edge of town it was still a maze; the streets were constructed in such a way that each stretch seemed to be an impasse with walls at the end. Three times they had to turn back and retrace their steps. There were no doorways, no stalls, not even any passersby—only the impassive pink walls baking in the breathless sunlight.

At last they came upon a tiny, but well-bolted door in the middle of a great expanse of wall. *Entrée de l'Hôtel,* said the sign above it. The Arab knocked loudly.

A long time passed and there was no answer. Kit's throat was painfully dry; her heart was still beating very fast. She shut her eyes and listened. She heard nothing.

"Knock again," she said, reaching up to do it herself. But his hand was still on the knocker, and he pounded with greater energy than before. This time a dog began to bark somewhere back in the garden, and as the sound gradually came closer it was mingled with cries of reproof. "*Askout!*" cried the woman indignantly, but the animal continued to bark. Then there was a period during which an occasional stone bumped on the ground, and the dog was quiet. In her impatience Kit pushed the Arab's hand away from the knocker and started an incessant hammering, which she did not stop until the woman's voice was on the other side of the door, screaming: *"Echkoun? Echkoun?"*

The young Arab and the woman engaged in a long argument, he making extravagant gestures while he demanded she open the door, and she refusing to touch it. Finally she went away. They heard her slippered feet shuffling along the path, then they heard the dog bark again, the woman's reprimands, followed by yelps as she struck it, after which they heard nothing.

"What is it?" cried Kit desperately. *"Pourquoi on ne nous laisse pas entrer?"*

He smiled and shrugged his shoulders. "Madame is coming," he said.

"Oh, good God!" she said in English. She seized the knocker and hammered violently with it, at the same time kicking the base of the door with all her strength. It did not budge. Still smiling, the Arab shook his head slowly from side to side. *"Peut pas,"* he told her. But she continued to pound. Even though she knew she had no reason to be, she was furious with him for not having been able to make the woman open the door. After a moment she stopped, with the sensation that she was about to faint. She was shaking with fatigue, and her mouth and throat felt as though they were made of tin. The sun poured down on the bare earth; there was not a square inch of shadow, save at their feet. Her mind went back to the many times when, as a child, she had held a reading glass over some hapless insect, following it along the ground in its frenzied attempts to escape the increasingly accurate focusing of the lens, until finally she touched it with the blinding pinpoint of light, when as if by magic it ceased running, and she watched it slowly wither and begin to smoke. She felt that if she looked up she would find the sun grown to monstrous proportions. She leaned against the wall and waited.

Eventually there were steps in the garden. She listened to their sound grow in clarity and volume, until they came right up to the door. Without even turning her head she waited for it to be opened; but that did not happen.

"Qui est là?" said a woman's voice.

Out of fear that the young Arab would speak and perhaps be refused entrance for being a native, Kit summoned all her strength and cried: *"Vous êtes la propriétaire?"*

There was a short silence. Then the woman, speaking with a Corsican or Italian accent, began a voluble entreaty: *"Ah, madame, allez vous en, je vous en supplie!* . . . *Vous ne pouvez pas entrer ici!* I regret! It is useless to insist. I cannot let you in! No one has been in or out of the hotel for more than a week! It is unfortunate, but you cannot enter!"

"But, madame," Kit cried, almost sobbing, "my husband is very ill!"

"*Aie!*" The woman's voice rose in pitch and Kit had the impression that she had retreated several steps into the garden; her voice, a little farther away, now confirmed it. "*Ah, mon dieu!* Go away! There is nothing I can do!"

"But where?" screamed Kit. "Where can I go?"

The woman already had started back through the garden. She stopped to cry: "Away from El Ga'a! Leave the city! You cannot expect me to let you in. So far we are free of the epidemic, here in the hotel."

The young Arab was trying to pull Kit away. He had understood nothing except that they were not to be let in. "Come. We find fondouk," he was saying. She shook him off, cupped her hands, and called: "Madame, what epidemic?"

The voice came from still farther away. "But, meningitis. You did not know? *Mais oui, madame! Partez! Partez!*" The sound of her hurried footsteps became fainter, was lost. Around the corner of the passageway a blind man had appeared, and was advancing toward them slowly, touching the wall as he moved. Kit looked at the young Arab; her eyes had opened very wide. She was saying to herself: "This is a crisis. There are only a certain number of them in life. I must be calm, and think." He, seeing her staring eyes, and still understanding nothing, put his hand comfortingly on her shoulder and said: "Come." She did not hear him, but she let him pull her away from the wall just before the blind man reached them. And he led her along the street back into the town, as she kept thinking: "This is a crisis." The sudden darkness of a tunnel broke into her self-imposed hypnosis. "Where are we going?" she said to him. The question pleased him greatly; into it he read a recognition of her reliance upon him. "Fondouk," he replied, but some trace of his triumph must have been implicit in the utterance of his word, for she stopped walking and stepped away from him. "*Balak!*" cried a voice beside her, and she was jolted by a man carrying a bundle. The young Arab reached out and gently pulled her toward him. "The fondouk," she repeated vaguely. "Ah, yes." They resumed walking.

In his noisy stable Port seemed to be asleep. His hand still rested on the patch of camel dung—he had not moved at all. Nevertheless he heard them enter and stirred a little to show them he was conscious of their presence. Kit crouched in the straw beside him and smoothed his hair. She had no idea what she was going to say to him, nor, of course, what they were going to do, but it comforted her to be this near to him. For a long time she squatted there, until the position became too painful. Then she stood up. The young Arab was sitting on the ground outside the door. "Port has not said a word," she thought, "but he is expecting the men from the hotel to come and carry him there." At this moment the most difficult part of her task was having to tell him that there was nowhere for him to stay in El Ga'a; she determined not to tell him. At the same time her course of action was decided for her. She knew just what she would do.

And it was all done quickly. She sent the young Arab to the market. Any car, any truck, any bus would do, she had said to him, and price meant nothing. This last enjoinder was wasted on him, of course—he spent nearly an hour haggling over the price three people would pay to be taken in the back of a produce truck that was going to a place called Sbâ that afternoon. But when he came back it was arranged. Once the truck was loaded, the driver would call with it at the New Gate, which was the gate nearest to the fondouk, and would send his mechanic-*copain* to let them know he was waiting for them, and to recruit the men necessary for carrying Port through the town to the vehicle. "It is good luck," said the young Arab. "Two times one month they go to Sbâ." Kit thanked him. During all the time of his absence Port had not stirred, and she had not dared attempt to rouse him. Now she knelt down with her mouth close to his ear and began to repeat his name softly from time to time. "Yes, Kit," he finally said, his voice very faint. "How are you?" she whispered.

He waited a good while before answering. "Sleepy," he said.

She patted his head. "Sleep a while longer. The men will be here in a little while."

But they did not come until nearly sunset. Meanwhile the young Arab had gone to fetch a bowl of food for Kit. Even with her ravenous appetite, she could hardly manage to swallow what he brought her: the meat consisted of various unidentifiable inner organs fried in deep fat, and there were some rather hard quinces cut in halves, cooked in olive oil. There was also bread, and it was of this that she ate most copiously. When the light already was fading, and the people outside in the courtyard were beginning to prepare their evening meal, the mechanic arrived with three fierce-looking Negroes. None of them spoke any French. The young Arab pointed Port out to them, and they unceremoniously lifted him up from his bed of straw and carried him out into the street, Kit following as near to his head as possible, to see that they did not let it fall too low. They walked quickly along the darkening passageways, through the camel and goat market, where there was no sound now but the soft bells worn by some of the animals. And soon they were outside the walls of the city, and the desert was dark beyond the headlights of the waiting truck.

"Back. He goes in back," said the young Arab to her by way of explanation, as the three let their burden fall limply on the sacks of potatoes. She handed him some money and asked him to settle with the Soudanese and the porters. It was not enough; she had to give him more. Then they went away. The chauffeur was racing the motor, the mechanic hopped into the front seat beside him and shut the door. The young Arab helped her up into the back, and she stood there leaning over a stack of wine cases looking down at him. He made as if to jump in with her, but at that instant the truck started to move. The young Arab ran after it, surely expecting Kit to call out to the driver to stop, since he had every intention of accompanying her. Once she had caught her balance, however, she deliberately crouched low and lay down on the floor among the sacks and bundles, near Port. She did not look out until they were miles into the desert. Then she looked with fear, lifting her head and peering quickly as if she expected to see him out there in the cold wasteland, running along the trail behind the truck after her.

The truck rode more easily than she had expected, perhaps because the trail was smooth and there were few curves; the way seemed to lie through a straight, endless valley on each side of which in the distance were high dunes. She looked up at the moon, still tiny, but visibly thicker than last night. And she shivered a little, laying her handbag on her bosom. It gave her momentary pleasure to think of that dark little world, the handbag smelling of leather and cosmetics, that lay between the hostile air and her body. Nothing was changed in there; the same objects fell against each other in the same limited chaos, and the names were still there, still represented the same things. Mark Cross, Caron, Helena Rubinstein. "Helena Rubinstein," she said aloud, and it made her laugh. "I'm going to be hysterical in one minute," she said to herself. She clutched one of Port's inert hands and squeezed the fingers as hard as she could. Then she sat up and devoted all her attention to kneading and massaging the hand, in the hope of feeling it grow warmer under her pressure. A sudden terror swept over her. She put her hand on his chest. Of course, his heart was beating. But he seemed cold. Using all her energy, she pushed his body over onto its side, and stretched herself out behind him, touching him at as many points as possible, hoping in this way to keep him warm. As she relaxed, it struck her that she herself had been cold and that she felt more comfortable now. She wondered if subconsciously part of her desire in lying beside Port had been to warm herself. "Probably, or I never should have thought of it." She slept a little.

And awoke with a start. It was natural, now her mind was clear, that there should be a horror. She tried to keep from thinking what it was. Not Port. That had been going on for a long time now. A new horror, connected with sunlight, dust. . . . She looked away with all her power as she felt her mind being swept into contact with the idea. In a split second it would no longer be possible not to know what it was. . . . There! Meningitis!

The epidemic was in El Ga'a and she had been exposed to it. In the hot tunnels of the streets she had breathed in the poisoned air, she had nestled in the contaminated straw at the fondouk. Surely by now the virus had lodged within her and was multiplying. At the thought of it she felt her back grow stiff. But Port could not be suffering from meningitis: he had been cold since Aïn Krorfa, and he had probably had a fever since the first days in Bou Noura, if they only had had the intelligence between them to find out. She tried to recall what she knew about symptoms, not only of meningitis, but of the other principal contagious diseases. Diphtheria began with a sore throat, cholera with diarrhea, but typhus, typhoid, the plague, malaria, yellow fever, kala azar—as far as she knew they all began with fever and malaise of one sort or another. It was a toss-up. "Perhaps it's amoebic dysentery combined with a return of malaria," she reasoned. "But whatever it is, it's already there in him, and nothing I do or don't do can change the outcome of it." She did not want to feel in any way responsible; that would have been too much to bear at this point. As it was, she felt that she was holding up rather well. She remembered stories of horror from the war, stories whose moral always turned out to be: "One never knows what a person is made of until the moment of stress; then often the most timorous person turns out to be the bravest." She wondered if she were being brave, or just resigned. Or cowardly, she added to herself. That, too, was possible, and there was no way of knowing. Port could never tell her because he knew even less about it. If she nursed him and got him through whatever he had, he doubtless would tell her she had been brave, a martyr, and many other things, but that would be out of gratitude. And then she wondered why she wanted to know—it seemed rather a frivolous consideration at the moment.

The truck roared on and on. Fortunately the back was completely open, or the exhaust fumes would have been troublesome. As it was, she caught a sharp odor now and then, but in the following instant it was dissipated in the cold night air. The moon set, the stars were there, she had no idea how late it was. The noise of the motor drowned out the sound of whatever conversation there may have been in front between the driver and the mechanic, and made it impossible for her to communicate with them. She put her arms about Port's waist, and hugged him closer for warmth. "Whatever he has, he's breathing it away from me," she thought. In her moments of sleep she burrowed with her legs beneath the sacks to keep warm; their weight sometimes woke her, but she preferred the pressure to the cold. She had put some empty sacks over Port's legs. It was a long night.

* * *

As he lay in the back of the truck, protected somewhat from the cold by Kit, now and then he was aware of the straight road beneath him. The twisting roads of the past weeks became alien, faded from his memory; it had been one strict, undeviating course inland to the desert, and now he was very nearly at the center.

How many times his friends, envying him his life, had said to him: "Your life is so simple." "Your life seems always to go in a straight line." Whenever they had said the words he heard in them an implicit reproach: it is not difficult to build a straight road on a treeless plain. He felt that what they really meant to say was: "You have chosen the easiest terrain." But if they elected to place obstacles in their own way—and they so clearly did, encumbering themselves with every sort of unnecessary allegiance—that was no reason why they should object to his having simplified his life. So it was with a certain annoyance that he would say: "Everyone makes the life he wants. Right?" as though there were nothing further to be said.

The immigration authorities at his disembarkation had not been satisfied to leave a blank after the word *Profession* on their papers as he had done in his passport. (That passport, official proof of his existence, racing after him, somewhere behind in the desert!) They had said: "Surely monsieur must do something." And Kit, seeing that he was about to contest the point, had interposed quickly: "Ah, yes. Monsieur is a writer, but he is modest!" They had laughed, filled in the space with the word *écrivain,* and made the remark that they hoped he would find inspiration in the Sahara. For a while he had been infuriated by their stubbornness in insisting upon his having a label, an *état-civil.* Then for a few hours the idea of his actually writing a book had amused him. A journal, filled in each evening with the day's thoughts, carefully seasoned with local color, in which the absolute truth of the theorem he would set forth in the beginning—namely, that the difference between something and nothing is nothing—should be clearly and calmly demonstrated. He had not even mentioned the idea to Kit; she surely would have killed it with her enthusiasm. Since the death of his father he no longer worked at anything, because it was not necessary, but Kit constantly held the hope that he would begin again to write—to write no matter what, so long as he worked at it. "He's a *little* less insupportable when he's working," she explained to others, and by no means totally in jest. And when he saw his mother, which was seldom, she too would say: "Been working?" and look at him with her large sad eyes. He would reply: "Nope," and look back at her insolently. Even as they were driving to the hotel in the taxi, with Tunner saying: "What a hellhole" as he saw the miserable streets, he had been thinking that Kit would be too delighted at the prospect; it would have to be done in secret—it was the only way he would be able to carry it off. But then when he had got settled in the hotel, and they had started their little pattern of café life at the Eckmühl-Noiseux, there had been nothing to write about—he could not establish a connection in his mind between the absurd trivialities which filled the day and the serious business of putting words on paper. He thought it was probably Tunner who prevented him from being completely at ease. Tunner's presence created a situation, however slight, which kept him from entering into the reflective state he considered essential. As long as he was living his life, he could not write about it. Where one left off, the other began, and the existence of circumstances which demanded even the vaguest participation on his part was sufficient to place writing outside the realm of possibility. But that was all right. He would not have written well, and so he would have got no pleasure from it. And even if what he might have written had been good, how many people would have known it? It was all right to speed ahead into the desert leaving no trace.

Suddenly he remembered that they were on their way to the hotel in El

Ga'a. It was another night and they had not yet arrived; there was a contradiction somewhere, he knew, but he did not have the energy to look for it. Occasionally he felt the fever rage within him, a separate entity; it gave him the image of a baseball player winding up, getting ready to pitch. And he was the ball. Around and around he went, then he was flung into space for a while, dissolving in flight.

They stood over him. There had been a long struggle, and he was very tired. Kit was one; the other was a soldier. They were talking, but what they said meant nothing. He left them there standing over him, and went back where he had come from.

"He will be as well off here as anywhere else this side of Sidi-bel-Abbès," said the soldier. "With typhoid all you can do, even in a hospital, is to keep the fever as low as possible, and wait. We have little here in Sbâ in the way of medicine, but these"—he pointed to a tube of pills that lay on an overturned box by the cot—"will bring the fever down, and that is already a great deal."

Kit did not look at him. "And peritonitis?" she said in a low voice.

Captain Broussard frowned. "Do not look for complications, madame," he said severely. "It is always bad enough without that. Yes, of course, peritonitis, pneumonia, heart stoppage, who knows? And you, too, maybe you have the famous El Ga'a meningitis that Madame Luccioni was kind enough to warn you about. *Bien sûr!* And maybe there are fifty cases of cholera here in Sbâ at this moment. I would not tell you even if there were."

"Why not?" she said, finally looking up.

"It would be absolutely useless; and besides, it would lower your morale. No, no. I would isolate the sick, and take measures to prevent the spread of the disease, nothing more. What we have in our hands is always enough. We have a man here with typhoid. We must bring down the fever. That is all. And these stories of peritonitis for him, meningitis for you, do not interest me in the least. You must be realistic, madame. If you stray outside that, you do harm to everyone. You have only to give him his pills every two hours, and try to make him take as much soup as possible. The cook's name is Zina. It would be prudent to be in the kitchen with her now and then to be sure there is always a fire and a big pot of soup constantly hot and ready. Zina is magnificent; she has cooked for us twelve years. But all natives need to be watched, always. They forget. And now, madame, if you will pardon me, I shall get back to my work. One of the men will bring you the mattress I promised you from my house, this afternoon. It will not be very comfortable, doubtless, but what can you expect—you are in Sbâ, not in Paris." He turned in the doorway. *"Enfin, madame, soyez courageuse!"* he said, frowning again, and went out.

Kit stood unmoving, and slowly looked about the bare little room with the door on one side, and a window on the other. Port lay on the rickety cot, facing the wall, breathing regularly with the sheet pulled up around his head. This room was the hospital of Sbâ; it had the one available bed in the town, with real sheets and blankets, and Port was in it only because no member of the military force happened to be ill at the moment. A mud wall came halfway up the window outside, but above that the sky's agonizing light poured in. She took the extra sheet the captain had given her for herself, folded it into a small square the size of the window, got a box of thumbtacks out of Port's luggage, and covered the open space. Even as she stood in the window she was struck with the silence of the place. She could have thought there was not a living being within a thousand miles. The famous silence of the Sahara. She wondered if as the days went by each breath she took would sound as loud to her as it did now, if she would get used to the ridiculous noise her saliva made as she swallowed, and if she would have to swallow as often as she seemed to be doing at the moment, now that she was so conscious of it.

"Port," she said, very softly. He did not stir. She walked out of the room into the blinding light of the courtyard with its floor of sand. There was no one in sight. There was nothing but the blazing white walls, the unmoving sand at her feet and the blue depths of the sky above. She took a few steps, and feeling a little ill, turned and went back into the room. There was not a chair to sit on—only the cot and the little box beside it. She sat down on one of the valises. A tag hung from the handle by her hand. *Wanted on Voyage*, it said. The room had the utterly non-committal look of a storeroom. With the luggage in the middle of the floor there was not even space for the mattress they were going to bring; the bags would have to be piled in one huge heap in a corner. She looked at her hands, she looked at her feet in their lizard-skin pumps. There was no mirror in the room; she reached across to another valise and seized her handbag, pulling out her compact and lipstick. When she opened the compact she discovered there was not enough light to see her face in its little mirror. Standing in the doorway, she made up slowly and carefully.

"Port," she said again, as softly as before. He went on breathing. She locked her handbag into a valise, looked at her wristwatch, and stepped forth once more into the bright courtyard, this time wearing dark glasses.

Dominating the town, the fort sat astride a high hill of sand, a succession of scattered buildings protected by a wandering outer rampart. It was a separate town, alien to the surrounding landscape and candidly military in aspect. The native guards at the gate looked at her with interest as she went through. The town, sand-color, was spread out below with its single-storied, flat-roofed houses. She turned in the other direction and skirted the wall, climbing for a brief distance until she was at the top of the hill. The heat and the light made her slightly dizzy, and the sand kept filling her shoes. From this point she could hear the clear, high-pitched sounds of the town below; children's voices and dogs barking. In all directions, where the earth and sky met, there was a faint, rapidly pulsating haze.

"Sbâ," she said aloud. The word meant nothing to her; it did not even represent the haphazard collection of formless huts below. When she returned to the room someone had left a mammoth white china chamber-pot in the middle of the floor. Port was lying on his back, looking up at the ceiling, and he had pushed the covers off.

She hurried to the cot and pulled them up over him. There was no way of tucking him in. She took his temperature: it had fallen somewhat.

"This bed hurts my back," he said unexpectedly, gasping a little. She stepped back and surveyed the cot: it sagged heavily between the head and the foot.

"We'll fix that in a little while," she said. "Now, be good and keep covered up."

He looked at her reproachfully. "You don't have to talk to me as if I were a child," he said. "I'm still the same person."

"It's just automatic, I suppose, when people are sick," she said, laughing uncomfortably. "I'm sorry."

He still looked at her. "I don't have to be humored in any way," he said slowly. Then he shut his eyes and sighed deeply.

When the mattress arrived, she had the Arab who had brought it go and get another man. Together they lifted Port off the cot and laid him onto the mattress which was spread on the floor. Then she had them pile some of the valises on the cot. The Arabs went out.

"Where are you going to sleep?" asked Port.

"On the floor here beside you," she said.

He did not ask her any more. She gave him his pills and said: "Now sleep." Then she went out to the gate and tried to speak with the guards;

they did not understand any French, and kept saying: *"Non, m'si."* As she was gesticulating with them, Captain Broussard appeared in a nearby doorway and looked at her with a certain suspicion in his eyes. "Do you want something, madame?" he said.

"I want someone to go with me to the market and help me buy some blankets," said Kit.

"Ah, je regrette, madame," he said. "There is no one in the post here who could render you that service, and I do not advise you to go alone. But if you like I can send you blankets from my quarters."

Kit was effusive in her thanks. She went back into the inner courtyard and stood a moment looking at the door of the room, loath to enter. "It's a prison," she thought. "I'm a prisoner here, and for how long? God knows." She went in, sat down on a valise just inside the door, and stared at the floor. Then she rose, opened a bag, pulled out a fat French novel she had bought before leaving for Boussif, and tried to read. When she had got to the fifth page, she heard someone coming through the courtyard. It was a young French soldier carrying three camel blankets. She got up and stepped aside for him to enter, saying: *"Ah, merci. Comme vous êtes aimable!"* But he stood still just outside the door, holding his arm out toward her for her to take the blankets. She lifted them off and laid them on the floor at her feet. When she looked up he already had started away. She stared after him an instant, vaguely perplexed, and then set about collecting various odd pieces of clothing from among her effects, which could serve as a foundation to place underneath the blankets. She finally arranged her bed, lay down on it, and was pleasantly surprised to find it comfortable. All at once she felt an overwhelming desire to sleep. It would be another hour and a half before she must give Port his medicine. She closed her eyes and for a moment was in the back of the truck on her way from El Ga'a to Sbâ. The sensation of motion lulled her, and she immediately fell asleep.

She was awakened by feeling something brush past her face. She started up, saw that it was dark and that someone was moving about in the room. "Port!" she cried. A woman's voice said: *"Voici mangi, madame."* She was standing directly above her. Someone came through the courtyard silently bearing a carbide lamp. It was a small boy, who walked to the door, reached in, and set the light down on the floor. She looked up and saw a large-boned old woman with eyes that were still beautiful. "This is Zina," she thought, and she called her by name. The woman smiled, and stooped down, putting the tray on the floor by Kit's bed. Then she went out.

It was difficult to feed Port; much of the soup ran over his face and down his neck. "Maybe tomorrow you'll feel like sitting up to eat," she said as she wiped his mouth with a handkerchief. "Maybe," he said feebly.

"Oh, my God!" she cried. She had overslept; the pills were long overdue. She gave them to him and had him wash them down with a swallow of tepid water. He made a face. "The water," he said. She sniffed the carafe. It reeked of chlorine. She had put the Halazone tablets in twice by mistake. "It won't hurt you," she said.

She ate her food with relish; Zina was quite a good cook. While she was still eating, she looked over at Port and saw that he was already asleep. The pills seemed each time to have that effect. She thought of taking a short walk after the meal, but she was afraid that Captain Broussard might have given orders to the guards not to let her pass. She went out into the courtyard and walked around it several times, looking up at the stars. An accordion was being played somewhere at the other end of the fort; its sound was very faint. She went into the room, shut the door, locked it, undressed, and lay on her blankets beside Port's mattress, pulling the lamp over near her head so she could read. But the light was not strong enough, and it moved too much, so that her eyes began to hurt, and the smell of it disgusted her. Reluctantly she blew out the flame, and the room fell back into the profoundest darkness. She had scarcely lain down before she sprang up again, and began to scrabble about the floor with her hand, searching for matches. She lit the lamp, which seemed to be smelling stronger than ever since she had blown it out, and said to herself, but moving her lips: "Every two hours. Every two hours."

In the night she awoke sneezing. At first she thought it was the odor of the lamp, but then she put her hand to her face, and felt the grit on her skin. She moved her fingers along the pillow: it was covered with a coating of dust. Then she became conscious of the noise of the wind outside. It was like the roar of the sea. Fearful of waking Port, she tried to stifle the sneeze that was on its way; her effort was unsuccessful. She got up. It seemed cold in the room. She spread Port's bathrobe over him. Then she got two large handkerchiefs out of a suitcase and tied one over the lower part of her face, bandit-fashion. The other one she intended to arrange for Port when she woke him up to give him his pills. It would be only another twenty minutes. She lay down, sneezing again as a result of the dust raised by moving the blankets. She lay perfectly still listening to the fury of the wind as it swept by outside the door.

"Here I am, in the middle of horror," she thought, attempting to exaggerate the situation, in the hope of convincing herself that the worst had happened, was actually there with her. But it would not work. The sudden arrival of the wind was a new omen, connected only with the time to come. It began to make a singular, animal-like sound beneath the door. If she could only give up, relax, and live in the perfect knowledge that there was no hope. But there was never any knowing or any certitude; the time to come always had more than one possible direction. One could not even give up hope. The wind would blow, the sand would settle, and in some as yet unforeseen manner time would bring about a change which could only be terrifying, since it would not be a continuation of the present.

She remained awake the rest of the night, giving Port his pills regularly, and trying to relax in the periods between. Each time she woke him he moved obediently and swallowed the water and the tablet proffered him without speaking or even opening his eyes. In the pale, infected light of daybreak she heard him begin to sob. Electrified, she sat up and stared at the corner where his head lay. Her heart was beating very fast, activated by a strange emotion she could not identify. She listened a while, decided it was compassion she felt, and leaned nearer to him. The sobs came up mechanically, like hiccups or belches. Little by little the sensation of excitement died away, but she remained sitting up, listening intently to the two sounds together: the sobs inside the room and the wind without. Two impersonal, natural sounds. After a sudden, short silence she heard him say, quite distinctly: "Kit. Kit." As her eyes grew wide she said: "Yes?" But he did not answer. After a long time, clandestinely, she slid back down under the blanket and fell asleep for a while. When she awoke the morning had really begun. The inflamed shafts of distant sunlight sifted down from the sky along with the air's fine grit; the insistent wind seemed about to blow away what feeble strands of light there were.

She arose and moved about the room stiffly in the cold, trying to raise as little dust as possible while she made her toilet. But the dust lay thick on everything. She was conscious of a defect in her functioning—it was as if an entire section of her mind were numb. She felt the lack there: an enormous blind spot inside her—but she could not locate it. And as if from a distance she watched the fumbling gestures her hands made as they came in contact with the objects and the garments. "This has got to stop," she said to herself. "This has got to stop." But she did not know quite what she meant. Nothing could stop; everything always went on.

Zina arrived, completely shrouded in a great white blanket, and slamming the door behind her against the blast, drew forth from beneath the folds of her clothing a small tray which bore a teapot and a glass. *"Bonjour, madame. R'mleh bẓef,"* she said, with a gesture toward the sky, and set the tray on the floor beside the mattress.

The hot tea gave her a little strength; she drank it all and sat a while listening to the wind. Suddenly she realized that there was nothing for Port. Tea would not be enough for him. She decided to go in search of Zina to see if there was any way of getting him some milk. She went out and stood in the courtyard, calling: "Zina! Zina!" in a voice rendered feeble by the wind's fury, grinding the sand between her teeth as she caught her breath.

No one appeared. After stumbling into and out of several empty niche-like rooms, she discovered a passageway that led to the kitchen. Zina was there squatting on the floor, but Kit could not make her understand what she wanted. With motions the old woman indicated that she would presently fetch Captain Broussard and send him to the room. Back in the semi-darkness she lay down on her pallet, coughing and rubbing away from her eyes the sand that had gathered on her face. Port was still sleeping.

She herself was almost asleep when the captain came in. He removed the hood of his camel's-hair burnous from around his face, and shook it, then he shut the door behind him and squinted about in the obscurity. Kit stood up. The expected queries and responses regarding the state of the patient were made. But when she asked him about the milk he merely looked at her pityingly. All canned milk was rationed, and that only to women with infants. "And the sheep's milk is always sour and undrinkable in any case," he added. It seemed to Kit that each time he looked at her it was as if he suspected her of harboring secret and reprehensible motives. The resentment she felt at his accusatory gaze helped her to regain a little of her lost sense of reality. "I'm sure he doesn't look at everybody that way," she thought. "Then why me? Damn his soul!" But she felt too utterly dependent upon the man to allow herself the satisfaction of letting him perceive anything of her reactions. She stood, trying to look forlorn, with her right hand outstretched above Port's head in a compassionate gesture, hoping the captain's heart might be moved; she was convinced that he could get her all the canned milk she wanted, if he chose.

"Milk is completely unnecessary for your husband in any case, madame," he said dryly. "The soup I have ordered is quite sufficient, and more digestible. I shall have Zina bring a bowl immediately." He went out; the sand-laden wind still roared.

Kit spent the day reading and seeing to it that Port was dosed and fed regularly. He was utterly disinclined to speak; perhaps he did not have the strength. While she was reading, sometimes she forgot the room, the situation, for minutes at a time, and on each occasion when she raised her head and remembered again, it was like being struck in the face. Once she almost laughed, it seemed so ridiculously unlikely. "Sbâ," she said, prolonging the vowel so that it sounded like the bleat of a sheep.

Toward late afternoon she tired of her book and stretched out on her bed, carefully, so as not to disturb Port. As she turned toward him, she realized with a disagreeable shock that his eyes were open, looking at her across the few inches of bedding. The sensation was so violently unpleasant that she sprang up, and staring back at him, said in a tone of forced solicitude: "How do you feel?" He frowned a little, but did not reply. Falteringly she pursued. "Do you think the pills help? At least they seem to bring the fever down a bit." And now, surprisingly enough, he answered, in a soft but clear voice. "I'm very sick," he said slowly. "I don't know whether I'll come back."

"Back?" she said stupidly. Then she patted his hot forehead, feeling disgusted with herself even as she uttered the words: "You'll be all right."

All at once she decided she must get out of the room for a while before dark—even if just for a few minutes. A change of air. She waited until he had closed his eyes. Then without looking at him again for fear she would see them open once more, she got up quickly and stepped out into the wind. It seemed to have shifted a little, and there was less sand in the air. Even so, she felt the sting of the grains on her cheeks. Briskly she walked out beneath the high mud portal, not looking at the guards, not stopping when she reached the road, but continuing downward until she came to the street that led to the market place. Down there the wind was less noticeable. Apart from an inert figure lying here and there entirely swathed in its burnous, the way was empty. As she moved along through the soft sand of the street, the remote sun fell rapidly behind the flat hammada ahead, and the walls and arches took on their twilight rose hue. She was a little ashamed of herself for having given in to her nervous impatience to be out of the room, but she banished the sentiment by arguing with herself that nurses, like everyone else, must rest occasionally.

She came to the market, a vast, square, open space enclosed on all four sides by whitewashed arcades whose innumerable arches made a monotonous pattern whichever way she turned her head. A few camels lay grumbling in the center, a few palm-branch fires flared, but the merchants and their wares were gone. Then she heard the muezzins calling in three distinct parts of the town, and saw those men who were left begin their evening prayer. Crossing the market, she wandered into a side street with its earthen buildings all orange in the momentary glow. The little shop doors were closed—all but one, in front of which she paused an instant, peering in vaguely. A man wearing a beret crouched inside over a small fire built in the middle of the floor, holding his hands fanwise almost in the flames. He glanced up and saw her, then rising, he came to the door. "*Entrez, madame,*" he said, making a wide gesture. For lack of anything else to do, she obeyed. It was a tiny shop; in the dimness she could see a few bolts of white cloth lying on the shelves. He fitted a carbide lamp together, touched a match to the spout, and watched the sharp flame spring up. "Daoud Zozeph," he said, holding forth his hand. She was faintly surprised: for some reason she had thought he was French. Certainly he was not a native of Sbâ. She sat on the stool he offered her, and they talked a few minutes. His French was quite good, and he spoke it gently in a tone of obscure reproof. Suddenly she realized he was a Jew. She asked him; he seemed astonished and amused at her question. "Of course," he said. "I stay open during the hour of prayer. Afterward there are always a few customers." They spoke of the difficulties of being a Jew here in Sbâ, and then she found herself telling him of her predicament, of Port who lay alone up in the Poste Militaire. He leaned against the counter above her, and it seemed to her that his dark eyes glowed with sympathy. Even this faint impression, unconfirmed as it was, made her aware for the first time of how cruelly lacking in that sentiment was the human landscape here, and of how acutely she had been missing it without realizing she was missing it. And so she talked on and on, even going into her feeling about omens. She stopped abruptly, looked at him a little fearfully, and laughed. But he was very serious; he seemed to understand her very well. "Yes, yes," he said, stroking his beardless chin meditatively. "You are right about all that."

Logically she should not have found such a statement reassuring, but the fact that he agreed with her she found deliciously comforting. However, he continued: "The mistake you make is in being afraid. That is the great mistake. The signs are given us for our good, not for our harm. But when you are afraid you read them wrong and make bad things where good ones were meant to be."

"But I *am* afraid," protested Kit. "How can I change that? It's impossible."

He looked at her and shook his head. "That is not the way to live," he said.

"I know," she said sadly.

An Arab entered the shop, bade her good evening, and purchased a pack of cigarettes. As he went out the door, he turned and spat just inside it on the floor. Then he gave a disdainful toss of his burnous over his shoulder and strode away. Kit looked at Daoud Zozeph.

"Did he spit on purpose?" she asked him.

He laughed. "Yes. No. Who knows? I have been spat upon so many thousand times that I do not see it when it happens. You see! You should be a Jew in Sbâ, and you would learn not to be afraid! At least you would learn not to be afraid of God. You would see that even when God is most terrible, he is never cruel, the way men are."

Suddenly what he was saying sounded ridiculous. She rose, smoothed her skirt, and said she must be going.

"One moment," he said, going behind a curtain into a room beyond. He returned presently with a small parcel. Behind the counter he resumed the anonymous air of a shopkeeper. He handed the parcel across to her, saying quietly: "You said you wanted to give your husband milk. Here are two cans. They were the ration for our baby." He raised his hand as she tried to interrupt. "But it was born dead, last week, too soon. Next year if we have another we can get more."

Seeing Kit's look of anguish, he laughed: "I promise you," he said, "as soon as my wife knows, I will apply for the coupons. There will be no trouble. *Allons!* What are you afraid of now?" And as she still stood looking at him, he raised the parcel in the air and presented it again with such an air of finality that automatically she took hold of it. "This is one of those occasions where one doesn't try to put into words what one feels," she said to herself. She thanked him saying that her husband would be very happy, and that she hoped they would meet again in a few days. Then she went out. With the coming of night, the wind had risen somewhat. She shivered climbing the hill on the way to the fort.

The first thing she did on arriving back in the room was to light the lamp. Then she took Port's temperature: she was horrified to find it higher.

The pills were no longer working. He looked at her with an unaccustomed expression in his shining eyes.

"Today's my birthday," he murmured.

"No, it isn't," she said sharply; then she reflected an instant, and asked with feigned interest: "Is it, really?"

"Yes. This was the one I've been waiting for."

She did not ask him what he meant. He went on: "Is it beautiful out?"

"No."

"I wish you could have said yes."

"Why?"

"I'd have liked it to be beautiful out."

"I suppose you could call it beautiful, but it's just a little unpleasant to walk in."

"Ah, well, we're not out in it," he said.

The quietness of this dialogue made more monstrous the groans of pain which an instant later issued from within him. "What is it?" she cried in a frenzy. But he could not hear her. She knelt on her mattress and looked at him, unable to decide what to do. Little by little he grew silent, but he did not open his eyes. For a while she studied the inert body as it lay there beneath the covers, which rose and fell slightly with the rapid respiration. "He's stopped being human," she said to herself. Illness reduces man to his basic state: a cloaca in which the chemical processes continue. The meaningless hegemony of the involuntary. It was the ultimate taboo stretched out there beside her, helpless and terrifying beyond all reason. She choked back a wave of nausea that threatened her for an instant.

There was a knocking at the door: it was Zina with Port's soup, and a plate of couscous for her. Kit indicated that she wanted her to feed the invalid; the old woman seemed delighted, and began to try to coax him into sitting up. There was no response save a slight acceleration in his breathing. She was patient and persevering, but to no avail. Kit had her take the soup away, deciding that if he wanted nourishment later she would open one of the tins of milk and mix it with hot water for him.

The wind was blowing again, but without fury, and from the other direction. It moaned spasmodically through the cracks around the window, and the folded sheet moved a bit now and then. Kit stared at the spurting white flame of the lamp, trying to conquer her powerful desire to run out of the room. It was no longer the familiar fear that she felt—it was a steadily mounting sentiment of revulsion.

But she lay perfectly still, blaming herself and thinking: "If I feel no sense of duty toward him, at least I can act as if I did." At the same time there was an element of self-chastisement in her immobility. "You're not even to move your foot if it falls asleep. And I hope it hurts." Time passed, expressed in the low cry of the wind as it sought to enter the room, the cry rising and falling in pitch but never quite ceasing. Unexpectedly Port breathed a profound sigh and shifted his position on the mattress. And incredibly, he began to speak.

"Kit." His voice was faint but in no way distorted. She held her breath, as if her least movement might snap the thread that held him to rationality.

"Kit."

"Yes."

"I've been trying to get back. Here." He kept his eyes closed.

"Yes—"

"And now I am."

"Yes!"

"I wanted to talk to you. There's nobody here?"

"No, no!"

"Is the door locked?"

"I don't know," she said. She bounded up and locked it, returning to her pallet, all in the same movement. "Yes, it's locked."

"I wanted to talk to you."

She did not know what to say. She said: "I'm glad."

"There are so many things I want to say. I don't know what they are. I've forgotten them all."

She patted his hand lightly. "It's always that way."

He lay silent a moment.

"Wouldn't you like some warm milk?" she said cheerfully.

He seemed distraught. "I don't think there's time. I don't know."

"I'll fix it for you," she announced, and she sat up, glad to be free.

"Please stay here."

She lay down again, murmuring: "I'm so glad you feel better. You don't know how different it makes *me* feel to hear you talk. I've been going crazy here. There's not a soul around—" She stopped, feeling the momentum of hysteria begin to gather in the background. But Port seemed not to have heard her.

"Please stay here," he repeated, moving his hand uncertainly along the sheet. She knew it was searching for hers, but she could not make herself reach out and let it take hold. At the same moment she became aware of her refusal, and the tears came into her eyes—tears of pity for Port. Still she did not move.

Again he sighed. "I feel very sick. I feel awful. There's no reason to be afraid, but I am. Sometimes I'm not here, and I don't like that. Because then I'm far away and all alone. No one could ever get there. It's too far. And there I'm alone."

She wanted to stop him, but behind the stream of quiet words she heard the entreaty of a moment back: "Please stay here." And she did not have the strength to stop him unless she got up and moved about. But his words made her miserable; it was like hearing him recount one of his dreams—worse, even.

"So alone I can't even remember the idea of not being alone," he was saying. His fever would go up. "I can't even think what it would be like for there to be someone else in the world. When I'm there I can't remember being here; I'm just afraid. But here I can remember being there. I wish I could stop remembering it. It's awful to be two things at once. You know that, don't you?" His hand sought hers desperately. "You do know that? You understand how awful it is? You've got to." She let him take her hand, pull it towards his mouth. He rubbed his rough lips along it with a terrible avidity that shocked her; at the same time she felt the hair at the back of her head rise and stiffen. She watched his lips opening and shutting against her knuckles, and felt the hot breath on her fingers.

"Kit, Kit. I'm afraid, but it's not only that. Kit! All these years I've been living for you. I didn't know it, and now I do. I do know it! But now you're going away." He tried to roll over and lie on top of her arm; he clutched her hand always tighter.

"I'm not!" she cried.

His legs moved spasmodically.

"I'm right here!" she shouted, even louder, trying to imagine how her voice sounded to him, whirling down his own dark halls toward chaos. And as he lay still for a while, breathing violently, she began to think: "He says it's more than just being afraid. But it isn't. He's never lived for me. Never. Never." She held to the thought with an intensity that drove it from her mind, so that presently she found herself lying taut in every muscle without an idea in her head, listening to the wind's senseless monologue. For a time this went on; she did not relax. Then little by little she tried to draw her hand away from Port's desperate grasp. There was a sudden violent activity beside her, and she turned to see him partially sitting up.

"Port!" she cried, pushing herself up and putting her hands on his shoulders. "You've got to lie down!" She used all her strength; he did not budge. His eyes were open and he was looking at her. "Port!" she cried again in a different voice. He raised one hand and took hold of her arm.

"But Kit," he said softly. They looked at each other. She made a slight motion with her head, letting it fall onto his chest. Even as he glanced down at her, her first sob came up, and the first cleared the passage for the others. He closed his eyes again, and for a moment had the illusion of holding the world in his arms—a warm world all tropics, lashed by storm. "No, no, no, no, no, no, no," he said. It was all he had the strength to say. But even if he had been able to say more, still he would have said only: "No, no, no, no."

It was not a whole life whose loss she was mourning there in his arms, but it was a great part of one; above all it was a part whose limits she knew precisely, and her knowledge augmented the bitterness. And presently within her, deeper than the weeping for the wasted years, she found a ghastly dread all formed and growing. She raised her head and looked up at him with tenderness and terror. His head had dropped to one side; his eyes were closed. She put her arms around his neck and kissed his forehead many times. Then, half-pulling and half-coaxing, she got him back down into bed and covered him. She gave him his pill, undressed silently and lay down facing him, leaving the lamp burning so she could see him as she fell asleep. The wind at the window celebrated her dark sensation of having attained a new depth of solitude.

* * *

First of all there was the room. Nothing could change the hard little shell of its existence, its white plaster walls and its faintly arched ceiling, its concrete floor and its windows across which a sheet had been tacked, folded over many times to keep out the light. Nothing could change it because that was all there was of it, that and the mattress on which he lay. When from time to time a gust of clarity swept down upon him, and he opened his eyes and saw what was really there, and knew where he really was, he fixed the walls, the ceiling and the floor in his memory, so that he could find his way back next time. For there were so many other parts of the world, so many other moments in time to be visited; he never was certain that the way back would really be there. Counting was impossible. How many hours he had been like this, lying on the burning mattress, how many times he had seen Kit stretched out on the floor nearby, had made a sound and seen her turn over, get up and then come toward him to give him water—things like that he could not have told, even if he had thought to ask them of himself. His mind was occupied with very different problems. Sometimes he spoke aloud, but it was not satisfying; it seemed rather to hold back the natural development of the ideas. They flowed out through his mouth, and he was never sure whether they had been resolved in the right words. Words were much more alive and more difficult to handle, now; so much so that Kit did not seem to understand them when he used them. They slipped into his head like the wind blowing into a room, and extinguished the frail flame of an idea forming there in the dark. Less and less he used them in his thinking. The process became more mobile; he followed the course of thoughts because he was tied on behind. Often the way was vertiginous, but he could not let go. There was no repetition in the landscape; it was always new territory and the peril increased constantly. Slowly, pitilessly, the number of dimensions was lessening. There were fewer directions in which to move. It was not a clear process, there was nothing definite about it so that he could say: "Now up is gone." Yet he had witnessed occasions when two different dimensions had deliberately, spitefully, merged their identities, as if to say to him: "Try and tell which is which." His reaction was always the same: a sensation in which the outer parts of his being rushed inward for protection, the same movement one sometimes sees in a kaleidoscope on turning it very slowly, when the parts of the design fall headlong into the center. But the center! Sometimes it was gigantic, painful, raw and false, it extended from one side of creation to the other, there was no telling where it was; it was everywhere. And sometimes it would disappear, and the other center, the true one, the tiny burning black point, would be there in its place, unmoving and impossibly sharp, hard and distant. And each center he called "That." He knew one from the other, and which was the true, because when for a few minutes sometimes he actually came back to the room and saw it, and saw Kit, and said to himself: "I am in Sbâ," he could remember the two centers and distinguish between them, even though he hated them both, and he knew that the one which was only *there* was the true one, while the other was wrong, wrong, wrong.

It was an existence of exile from the world. He never saw a human face or figure, nor even an animal; there were no familiar objects along the way, there was no ground below, nor sky above, yet the space was full of things.

Sometimes he saw them, knowing at the same time that really they could only be heard. Sometimes they were absolutely still, like the printed page, and he was conscious of their terrible invisible motion underneath, and of its portent to him because he was alone. Sometimes he could touch them with his fingers, and at the same time they poured in through his mouth. It was all utterly familiar and wholly horrible—existence unmodifiable, not to be questioned, that must be borne. It would never occur to him to cry out.

The next morning the lamp had still been burning and the wind had gone. She had been unable to rouse him to give him his medicine, but she had taken his temperature through his half-open mouth: it had gone much higher. Then she had rushed out to find Captain Broussard, had brought him to the bedside where he had been noncommittal, trying to reassure her without giving her any reason for hope. She had passed the day sitting on the edge of her pallet in an attitude of despair, looking at Port from time to time, hearing his labored breathing and seeing him twist in the throes of an inner torment. Nor could Zina tempt her with food.

When night came and Zina reported that the American lady still would not eat, Captain Broussard decided upon a simple course of action. He went to the room and knocked on the door. After a short interval he heard Kit say: *"Qui est là?"* Then she opened the door. She had not lighted the lamp; the room was black behind her.

"Is it you, madame?" He tried to make his voice pleasant.

"Yes."

"Could you come with me a moment? I should like to speak with you."

She followed him through several courtyards into a brightly lighted room with a blazing fireplace at one end. There was a profusion of native rugs which covered the walls, the divans and the floor. At the far end was a small bar attended by a tall black Soudanese in a very white turban and jacket. The captain gestured nonchalantly toward her.

"Will you take something?"

"Oh, no. Thank you."

"A little apéritif."

Kit was still blinking at the light. "I couldn't," she said.

"You'll have a Cinzano with me." He signaled to his barman. *"Deux Cinzanos.* Come, come, sit down, I beg you. I shall not detain you long."

Kit obeyed, took the glass from the proffered tray. The taste of the wine pleased her, but she did not want to be pleased, she did not want to be ripped from her apathy. Besides, she was still conscious of the peculiar light of suspicion in the captain's eyes when he looked at her. He sat studying her face as he sipped his drink: he had about come to the decision that she was not exactly what he had taken her for at first, that perhaps she really was the sick man's wife after all.

"As Chef de Poste," he said, "I am more or less obliged to verify the identity of the persons who pass through Sbâ. Of course the arrivals are very infrequent. I regret having to trouble you at such a time, naturally. It is merely a question of seeing your identity papers. Ali!" The barman stepped silently to their chairs and refilled the glasses. Kit did not reply for a moment. The apéritif had made her violently hungry.

"I have my passport."

"Excellent. Tomorrow I shall send for both passports and return them to you within the hour."

"My husband has lost his passport. I can only give you mine."

"*Ah, ça!*" cried the captain. It was as he had expected, then. He was furious; at the same time he felt a certain satisfaction in the reflection that his first impression had been correct. And how right he had been to forbid his inferior officers to have anything to do with her. He had expected just something of this sort, save that in such cases it was usually the woman's papers which were difficult to get hold of, rather than the man's.

"Madame," he said, leaning forward in his seat, "please understand that I am in no way interested in probing matters which I consider strictly personal. It is merely a formality, but one which must be carried out. I must see both passports. The names are a matter of complete indifference to me. But two people, two passports, no? Unless you have one together."

Kit thought he had not heard her correctly. "My husband's passport was stolen in Aïn Krorfa."

The captain hesitated. "I shall have to report this, of course. To the commander of the territory." He rose to his feet. "You yourselves should have reported it as soon as it happened." He had had the servant lay a place at table for Kit, but now he did not want to eat with her.

"Oh, but we did. Lieutenant d'Armagnac at Bou Noura knows all about it," said Kit, finishing her glass. "May I have a cigarette, please?" He gave her a Chesterfield, lighted it for her, and watched her inhale. "My cigarettes are all gone." She smiled, her eyes on the pack he held in his hand. She felt better, but the hunger inside her was planting its claws deeper each minute. The captain said nothing. She went on. "Lieutenant d'Armagnac did everything he could for my husband to try and get it back from Messad."

The captain did not believe a word she was saying; he considered it all an admirable piece of lying. He was convinced now that she was not only an adventuress, but a truly suspicious character. "I see," he said, studying the rug at his feet. "Very well, madame. I shall not detain you now."

She rose.

"Tomorrow you will give me your passport, I shall prepare my report and we shall see what the outcome will be." He escorted her back to the room and returned to eat alone, highly annoyed with her for having insisted upon trying to deceive him. Kit stood in the dark room a second, reopened the door slightly and watched the glow cast on the sand by his flashlight disappear. Then she went in search of Zina, who fed her in the kitchen.

When she had finished eating she went to the room and lighted the lamp. Port's body squirmed and his face protested against the sudden light. She put the lamp in a corner behind some valises and stood a while in the middle of the room thinking of nothing. A few minutes later she took up her coat and went out into the courtyard.

The roof of the fort was a great, flat, irregularly shaped mud terrace whose varying heights were a projection, as it were, of the uneven ground below. The ramps and staircases between the different wings were hard to see in the dark. And although there was a low wall around the outer edge, the innumerable courtyards were merely open wells to be skirted with caution. The stars gave enough light to protect her against mishaps. She breathed deeply, feeling rather as if she were on shipboard. The town below was invisible—not a light showed—but to the north glimmered the white ereg, the vast ocean of sand with its frozen swirling crests, its unmoving silence. She turned slowly about, scanning the horizon. The air, doubly still now after the departure of the wind, was like something paralyzed. Whichever way she looked, the night's landscape suggested only one thing to her: negation of movement, suspension of continuity. But as she stood there, momentarily a part of the void she had created, little by little a doubt slipped into her mind, the sensation came to her, first faint, then sure, that some part of this landscape was moving even as she looked at it. She glanced up and grimaced. The whole, monstrous star-filled sky was turning sideways before her eyes. It looked still as death, yet it moved. Every second an invisible star edged above the earth's line on that side, and another fell below on the opposite side. She coughed self-consciously, and started to walk again, trying to remember how much she disliked Captain Broussard. He had not even offered her a pack of cigarettes, in spite of her overt remark. "Oh, God," she said aloud, wishing she had not finished her last Players in Bou Noura.

He opened his eyes. The room was malignant. It was empty. "Now, at last, I must fight against this room." But later he had a moment of vertiginous clarity. He was at the edge of a realm where each thought, each image, had an arbitrary existence, where the connection between each thing and the next had been cut. As he labored to seize the essence of that kind of consciousness, he began to slip back into its precinct without suspecting that he was no longer wholly outside in the open, no longer able to consider the idea at a distance. It seemed to him that here was an untried variety of thinking, in which there was no necessity for a relationship with life. "The thought in itself," he said—a gratuitous fact, like a painting of pure design. They were coming again, they began to flash by. He tried to hold one, believed he had it. "But a thought of what? What is it?" Even then it was pushed out of the way by the others crowding behind it. While he succumbed, struggling, he opened his eyes for help. "The room! The room! Still here!" It was in the silence of the room that he now located all those hostile forces; the very fact that the room's inert watchfulness was on all sides made him distrust it. Outside himself, it was all there was. He looked at the line made by the joining of the wall and the floor, endeavored to fix it in his mind, that he might have something to hang on to when his eyes should shut. There was a terrible disparity between the speed at which he was moving and the quiet immobility of that line, but he insisted. So as not to go. To stay behind. To overflow, take root in what would stay here. A centipede can, cut into pieces. Each part can walk by itself. Still more, each leg flexes, lying alone on the floor.

There was a screaming sound in each ear, and the difference between the two pitches was so narrow that the vibration was like running his fingernail along the edge of a new dime. In front of his eyes clusters of round spots were being born; they were the little spots that result when a photographic cut in a newspaper is enlarged many times. Lighter agglomerations, darker masses, small regions of uninhabited space here and there. Each spot slowly took on a third dimension. He tried to recoil from the expanding globules of matter. Did he cry out? Could he move?

The thin distance between the two high screams became narrower, they were almost one; now the difference was the edge of a razor blade, poised against the tips of each finger. The fingers were to be sliced longitudinally.

A servant traced the cries to the room where the American lay. Captain Broussard was summoned. He walked quickly to the door, pounded on it, and hearing nothing but the continued yelling within, stepped into the room. With the aid of the servant, he succeeded in holding Port still enough to give him an injection of morphine. When he had finished, he glared about the room in an access of rage. "And that woman!" he shouted. "Where in the name of God is she?"

"I don't know, my Captain," said the servant, who thought the question had been addressed to him.

"Stay here. Stand by the door," growled the captain. He was determined to find Kit, and when he found her he was going to tell her what he thought of her. If necessary, he would place a guard outside the door, and force her to stay inside to watch the patient. He went first to the main gate, which was locked at night so that no guard was necessary. It stood open. *"Ah, ça, par exemple!"* he cried, beside himself. He stepped outside, and saw nothing but the night. Going within, he slammed the high portal shut and bolted it savagely. Then he went back to the room and waited while the servant fetched a blanket, and instructed him to stay there until morning. He returned to his quarters and had a glass of cognac to calm his fury before trying to sleep.

As she paced back and forth on the roof, two things happened at once. On one side the large moon swiftly rose above the edge of the plateau, and on the other, in the distant air, an almost imperceptible humming sound became audible, was lost, became audible again. She listened: now it was gone, now it was a little stronger. And so it continued for a long time, disappearing, and coming back always a bit nearer. Now, even though it was still far away, the sound was quite recognizable as that of a motor. She could hear the shifts of speed as it climbed a slope and reached level ground again. Twenty kilometers down the trail, they had told her, you can hear a truck coming. She waited. Finally, when it seemed that the vehicle must already be in the town, she saw a tiny portion of rock far out on the hammada being swept by the headlights as the truck made a curve in its descent toward the oasis. A moment later she saw the two points of light. Then they were lost for a while behind the rocks, but the motor grew ever louder. With the moon casting more light each minute, and the truck bringing people to town, even if the people were anonymous figures in white robes, the world moved back into the realm of the possible. Suddenly she wanted to be present at the arrival down in the market. She hurried below, tiptoed through the courtyards, managed to open the heavy gate, and began to run down the side of the hill toward the town. The truck was making a great racket as it went along between the high walls in the oasis;

as she came opposite the mosque it nosed above the last rise on its way up into the town. There were a few ragged men standing at the entrance of the market place. When the big vehicle roared in and stopped, the silence that followed lasted only a second before the excited voices began, all at once.

She stood back and watched the laborious getting-down of the natives and the leisurely unloading of their possessions: camel saddles that shone in the moonlight, great formless bundles done up in striped blankets, coffers and sacks, and two gigantic women so fat they could barely walk, their bosoms, arms and legs weighted down with pounds of massive silver ornaments. And all these possessions, with their owners, presently disappeared behind the dark arcades and went out of hearing. She moved around so she could see the front end of the truck, where the chauffeur and mechanic and a few other men stood in the glare of the headlights talking. She heard French being spoken—bad French—as well as Arabic. The chauffeur reached in and switched off the lights; the men began to walk slowly up into the market place. No one seemed to have noticed her. She stood still a moment, listening.

She cried: "Tunner!"

One of the figures in a burnous stopped, came running back. On its way, it called: "Kit!" She ran a few steps, saw the other man turning to look, and was being smothered in Tunner's burnous as he hugged her. She thought he would never let go, but he did, and said: "So you're really here!" Two of the men had come over. "Is this the lady you were looking for?" said one. "*Oui, oui!*" Tunner cried, and they said good night.

They stood alone in the market place. "But this is wonderful, Kit!" he said. She wanted to speak, but she felt that if she tried, her words would turn to sobs, so she nodded her head and automatically began to pull him along toward the little public garden by the mosque. She felt weak; she wanted to sit down.

"My stuff is locked in the truck for the night. I didn't know where I'd be sleeping. God, what a trip from Bou Noura! Three blowouts on the way, and these monkeys think changing a tire should always take a couple of hours at least." He went into details. They had reached the entrance to the garden. The moon shone like a cold white sun; the spearlike shadows of the palm branches were black on the sand, a sharp unvaried pattern along the garden walk.

"But let's see you!" he cried, spinning her around so the moon's light

struck her face. "Ah, poor Kit! It must have been hell!" he murmured, as
she squinted up into the brightness, her features distorted by the imminent
outbreaking of tears.

They sat on a concrete bench and she wept for a long time, her face
buried in his lap, rubbing the rough wool of the burnous. From time to time
he uttered consoling words, and as he found her shivering, he enveloped
her in one great wing of the robe. She hated the salt sting of the tears, and
even more she hated the ignominy of her being there, demanding comfort
of Tunner. But she could not, could not stop; the longer she continued to
sob, the more clearly she sensed that this was a situation beyond her control.
She was unable to sit up, dry her tears, and make an attempt to extricate
herself from the net of involvement she felt being drawn around her. She
did not want to be involved again: the taste of guilt was still strong in her
memory. Yet she saw nothing ahead of her but Tunner's will awaiting her
signal to take command. And she would give the signal. Even as she knew
this she was aware of a pervading sense of relief, to struggle against which
would have been unthinkable. What delight, not to be responsible—not to
have to decide anything of what was to happen! To know, even if there was
no hope, that no action one might take or fail to take could change the
outcome in the slightest degree—that it was impossible to be at fault in any
way, and thus impossible to feel regret, or, above all, guilt. She realized the
absurdity of still hoping to attain such a state permanently, but the hope
would not leave her.

The street led up a steep hill where the hot sun was shining, the sidewalks
were crowded with pedestrians looking in the shop windows. He had the
feeling there was traffic in the side streets, but the shadows there were dark.
An attitude of expectancy was growing in the crowd; they were waiting for
something. For what, he did not know. The entire afternoon was tense,
poised, ready to fall. At the top of the street a huge automobile suddenly
appeared, glistening in the sunlight. It came careening over the crest and
down the hill, swerving savagely from one curb to the other. A great yell
rose up from the crowd. He turned and frantically sought a doorway. At
the corner there was a pastry shop, its windows full of cakes and meringues.
He fumbled along the wall. If he could reach the door. . . . He wheeled,
stood transfixed. In the tremendous flash of sunlight reflected from the glass
as it splintered he saw the metal pinning him to the stone. He heard his own

ridiculous cry, and felt his bowels pierced through. As he tried to topple over, to lose consciousness, he found his face a few inches from a row of pastries, still intact on their paper-covered shelf.

They were a row of mud wells in the desert. But how near were they? He could not tell: the debris had pinned him to the earth. The pain was all of existence at that moment. All the energy he could exert would not budge him from the spot where he lay impaled, his bleeding entrails open to the sky. He imagined an enemy arriving to step into his open belly. He imagined himself rising, running through the twisting alleys between the walls. For hours in all directions in the alleys, with never a door, never the final opening. It would get dark, they would be coming nearer, his breath would be failing. And when he willed it hard enough, the gate would appear, but even as he rushed panting through it, he would realize his terrible mistake.

Too late! There was only the endless black wall rising ahead of him, the rickety iron staircase he was obliged to take, knowing that above, at the top, they were waiting with the boulder poised, ready to hurl it when he came near enough. And as he got close to the top it would come hurtling down at him, striking him with the weight of the entire world. He cried out again as it hit, holding his hands over his abdomen to protect the gaping hole there. He ceased imagining and lay still beneath the rubble. The pain could not go on. He opened his eyes, shut his eyes, saw only the thin sky stretched across to protect him. Slowly the split would occur, the sky draw back, and he would see what he never had doubted lay behind advance upon him with the speed of a million winds. His cry was a separate thing beside him in the desert. It went on and on.

The moon had reached the center of the sky when they arrived at the fort and found the gate locked. Holding Tunner's hand, Kit looked up at him. "What'll we do?"

He hesitated, and pointed to the mountain of sand above the fort. They climbed slowly upward along the dunes. The cold sand filled their shoes: they took them off and continued. Up here the brightness was intense; each grain of sand sent out a fragment of the polar light shed from above. They could not walk side by side—the ridge of the highest dune was too steep. Tunner draped his burnous around Kit's shoulders and went ahead. The crest was infinitely higher and further away than they had imagined. When finally they climbed atop it, the ereg with its sea of motionless waves lay all about them. They did not stop to look: absolute silence is too powerful once one has trusted oneself to it for an instant, its spell too difficult to break.

"Down here!" said Tunner.

They let themselves slide forward into a great moonlit cup. Kit rolled over and the burnous slipped off; he had to dig into the sand and climb back after it. He tried to fold it and throw it down at her playfully, but it fell halfway. She let herself roll to the bottom and lay there waiting. When he came down he spread the wide white garment out on the sand. They stretched out on it side by side and pulled the edges up around them. What conversation had eventually taken place down in the garden had centered about Port. Now Tunner looked at the moon. He took her hand.

"Do you remember our night on the train?" he said. As she did not reply, he feared he had made a tactical error, and went on quickly: "I don't think a drop of rain has fallen since that night, anywhere on the whole damned continent."

Still Kit made no answer. His mention of the night ride to Boussif had evoked the wrong memories. She saw the dim lamps swinging, smelled the coal gas, and heard the rain on the windows. She remembered the confused horror of the freight car full of natives; her mind refused to continue further.

"Kit. What's the matter?"

"Nothing. You know how I am. Really, nothing's wrong." She pressed his hand.

His voice became faintly paternal. "He's going to be all right, Kit. Only some of it's up to you, you know. You've got to keep in good shape to take care of him. Can't you see that? And how can you take care of him if you get sick?"

"I know, I know," she said.

"Then I'd have two patients on my hands—"

She sat up. "What hypocrites we are, both of us!" she cried. "You know damned well I haven't been near him for hours. How do we know he's not already dead? He could die there all alone! We'd never know. Who could stop him?"

He caught her arm, held it firmly. "Now, wait a minute, will you? Just for the record, I want to ask you: who could stop him even if we were both there beside him? Who?" He paused. "If you're going to take the worst possible view of everything, you might as well follow it through with a little logic at least, girl. But he's not going to die. You shouldn't even think of it. It's crazy." He shook her arm slowly, as one does to awaken a person from a deep sleep. "Just be sensible. You can't get in to him until morning. So relax. Try and get a little rest. Come on."

As he coaxed, she suddenly burst into tears once again, throwing both arms around him desperately. "Oh, Tunner! I love him so much!" she sobbed, clinging ever more tightly. "I love him! I love him!"

In the moonlight he smiled.

His cry went on through the final image: the spots of raw bright blood on the earth. Blood on excrement. The supreme moment, high above the desert, when the two elements, blood and excrement, long kept apart, merge. A black star appears, a point of darkness in the night sky's clarity. Point of darkness and gateway to repose. Reach out, pierce the fine fabric of the sheltering sky, take repose.

* * *

She opened the door. Port lay in a strange position, his legs wound tightly in the bedcovers. That corner of the room was like a still photograph suddenly flashed on the screen in the middle of the stream of moving images. She shut the door softly, locked it, turned again toward the corner, and walked slowly over to the mattress. She held her breath, bent over, and looked into the meaningless eyes. But already she knew, even to the convulsive lowering of her hand to the bare chest, even without the violent push she gave the inert torso immediately afterward. As her hands went to her own face, she cried: "No!" once—no more. She stood perfectly still for a long, long time, her head raised, facing the wall. Nothing moved inside her; she was conscious of nothing outside or in. If Zina had come to the door it is doubtful whether she would have heard the knock. But no one came. Below in the town a caravan setting out for Atar left the market place, swayed through the oasis, the camels grumbling, the bearded black men silent as they walked along thinking of the twenty days and nights that lay ahead, before the walls of Atar would rise above the rocks. A few hundred feet away in his bedroom Captain Broussard read an entire short story in a magazine that had arrived that morning in his mail, brought by last night's truck. In the room, however, nothing happened.

Much later in the morning, probably out of sheer fatigue, she began to walk in a small orbit in the middle of the room, a few steps one way and a few the other. A loud knock on the door interrupted this. She stood still, staring toward the door. The knock was repeated. Tunner's voice, carefully lowered, said: "Kit?" Again her hands rose to cover her face, and she remained standing that way during the rest of the time he stayed outside the door, now rapping softly, now faster and nervously, now pounding violently. When there was no more sound, she sat down on her pallet for a while, presently lying out flat with her head on the pillow as if to sleep. But her eyes remained open, staring upward almost as fixedly as those beside her. These were the first moments of a new existence, a strange one in which she already glimpsed the element of timelessness that would surround her. The person who frantically has been counting the seconds on his way to catch a train, and arrives panting just as it disappears, knowing the next one is not due for many hours, feels something of the same sudden surfeit of time, the momentary sensation of drowning in an element become too rich and too plentiful to be consumed, and thereby made meaningless, nonexistent. As the minutes went by, she felt no impulse to move; no thought wandered near her. Now she did not remember their many conversations built around the idea of death, perhaps because no idea about death has anything in common with the presence of death. She did not recall how they had agreed that one can *be* anything but *dead,* that the two words together created an antinomy. Nor did it occur to her how she once had thought that if Port should die before she did, she would not really believe he was dead, but rather that he had in some way gone back inside himself to stay there, and that he never would be conscious of her again; so that in reality it would be she who would have ceased to exist, at least to a great degree. She would be the one who had entered partially into the realm of death, while he would go on, an anguish inside her, a door left unopened, a chance irretrievably lost. She had quite forgotten the August afternoon only a little more than a year ago, when they had sat alone out on the grass beneath the maples, watching the thunderstorm sweep up the river valley toward them, and death had become the topic. And Port had said: "Death is always on the way, but the fact that you don't know when it will arrive seems to take away from the finiteness of life. It's that terrible precision that we hate so much. But because we don't know, we get to think of life as an inexhaustible well. Yet everything happens only a certain number of times, and a very small number, really. How many more times will you remember a certain afternoon of your childhood, some afternoon that's so deeply a part of your being that you can't even conceive of your life without it? Perhaps four or five times more. Perhaps not even that. How many more times will you watch the full moon rise? Perhaps twenty. And yet it all seems limitless." She had not listened at the time because the idea had depressed her; now if she had called it to mind it would have seemed beside the point. She was incapable now of thinking about death, and since death was there beside her, she thought of nothing at all.

And yet, deeper than the empty region which was her consciousness, in an obscure and innermost part of her mind, an idea must already have been in gestation, since when in the late afternoon Tunner came again and hammered on the door, she got up, and standing with her hand on the knob, spoke: "Is that you, Tunner?"

"For God's sake, where were you this morning?" he cried.

"I'll see you tonight about eight in the garden," she said, speaking as low as possible.

"Is he all right?"

"Yes. He's the same."

"Good. See you at eight." He went away.

She glanced at her watch: it was quarter of five. Going to her overnight bag, she set to work removing all the fittings; one by one, brushes, bottles and manicuring implements were laid on the floor. With an air of extreme preoccupation she emptied her other valises, choosing here and there a garment or object which she carefully packed into the small bag. Occasionally she stopped moving and listened: the only sound she could hear was her own measured breathing. Each time she listened she seemed reassured, straightway resuming her deliberate movements. In the flaps at the sides of the bag she put her passport, her express checks and what money she had. Soon she went to Port's luggage and searched awhile among the clothing there, returning to her little case with a good many more thousand-franc notes which she stuffed in wherever she could.

The packing of the bag took nearly an hour. When she had finished, she closed it, spun the combination lock, and went to the door. She hesitated a second before turning the key. The door open, the key in her hand, she stepped out into the courtyard with the bag and locked the door after her. She went to the kitchen, where she found the boy who tended the lamps sitting in a corner smoking.

"Can you do an errand for me?" she said.

He jumped to his feet smiling. She handed him the bag and told him to take it to Daoud Zozeph's shop and leave it, saying it was from the American lady.

Back in the room she again locked the door behind her and went over to the little window. With a single motion she ripped away the sheet that covered it. The wall outside was turning pink as the sun dropped lower in the sky; the pinkness filled the room. During all the time she had been moving about packing she had not once glanced downward at the corner. Now she knelt and looked closely at Port's face as if she had never seen it before. Scarcely touching the skin, she moved her hand along the forehead with infinite delicacy. She bent over further and placed her lips on the smooth brow. For a while she remained thus. The room grew red. Softly she laid her cheek on the pillow and stroked his hair. No tears flowed; it was a silent leave-taking. A strangely intense buzzing in front of her made her open her eyes. She watched fascinated while two flies made their brief, frantic love on his lower lip.

Then she rose, put on her coat, took the burnous which Tunner had left with her, and without looking back went out the door. She locked it behind her and put the key into her handbag. At the big gate the guard made as if to stop her. She said good evening to him and pushed by. Immediately afterward she heard him call to another in an inner room nearby. She breathed deeply and walked ahead, down toward the town. The sun had set; the earth was like a single ember alone on the hearth, rapidly cooling and growing black. A drum beat in the oasis. There would probably be dancing in the gardens later. The season of feasts had begun. Quickly she descended the hill and went straight to Daoud Zozeph's shop without once looking around.

She went in. Daoud Zozeph stood behind the counter in the fading light. He reached across and shook her hand.

"Good evening, madame."

"Good evening."

"Your valise is here. Shall I call a boy to carry it for you?"

"No, no," she said. "At least, not now. I came to talk to you." She glanced around at the doorway behind her; he did not notice.

"I am delighted," he said. "One moment. I shall get you a chair, madame." He brought a small folding chair around from behind the counter and placed it beside her.

"Thank you," she said, but she remained standing. "I wanted to ask you about trucks leaving Sbâ."

"Ah, for El Ga'a. We have no regular service. One came last night and left again this afternoon. We never know when the next will come. But Captain Broussard is always notified at least a day in advance. He could tell you better than anyone else."

"Captain Broussard. Ah, I see."

"And your husband. Is he better? Did he enjoy the milk?"

"The milk. Yes, he enjoyed it," she said slowly, wondering a little that the words could sound so natural.

"I hope he will soon be well."

"He is already well."

"Ah, *hamdoul'lah!*"

"Yes." And starting afresh, she said: "Monsieur Daoud Zozeph, I have a favor to ask of you."

"Your favor is granted, madame," he said gallantly. She felt that he had bowed in the darkness.

"A great favor," she warned.

Daoud Zozeph, thinking that perhaps she wanted to borrow money, began to rattle objects on the counter, saying: "But we are talking in the dark. Wait. I shall light a lamp."

"No! Please!" exclaimed Kit.

"But we don't see each other!" he protested.

She put her hand on his arm. "I know, but don't light the lamp, please. I want to ask you this favor immediately. May I spend the night with you and your wife?"

Daoud Zozeph was completely taken aback—both astonished and relieved. "Tonight?" he said.

"Yes."

There was a short silence.

"You understand, madame, we should be honored to have you in our house. But you would not be comfortable. You know, a house of poor people is not like a hotel or a poste militaire. . . ."

"But since I ask you," she said reproachfully, "that means I don't care. You think that matters to me? I have been sleeping on the floor here in Sbâ."

"Ah, that you would not have to do in my house," said Daoud Zozeph energetically.

"But I should be delighted to sleep on the floor. Anywhere. It doesn't matter."

"Ah, no! No, madame! Not on the floor! *Quand-même!*" he objected. And as he struck a match to light the lamp, she touched his arm again.

"*Ecoutez, monsieur,*" she said, her voice sinking to a conspiratorial whisper, "my husband is looking for me, and I don't want him to find me. We have had a misunderstanding. I don't want to see him tonight. It's very simple. I think your wife would understand."

Daoud Zozeph laughed. "Of course! Of course!" Still laughing, he closed the door into the street, bolted it, and struck a match, holding it high in the air. Lighting matches all the way, he led her through a dark inner room and across a small court. The stars were above. He paused in front of a door. "You can sleep here." He opened the door and stepped inside. Again a match flared: she saw a tiny room in disorder, its sagging iron bed covered with a mattress that vomited excelsior.

"This is not your room, I hope?" she ventured, as the match went out.

"Ah, no! We have another bed in our room, my wife and I," he answered, a note of pride in his voice. "This is where my brother sleeps when he comes from Colomb-Béchar. Once a year he visits me for a month, sometimes longer. Wait. I shall bring a lamp." He went off, and she heard him talking in another room. Presently he returned with an oil lamp and a small tin pail of water.

With the arrival of the light, the room took on an even more piteous aspect. She had the feeling that the floor had never yet been swept since the day the mason had finished piling the mud on the walls, the ubiquitous mud that dried, crumbled, and fell in a fine powder day and night. . . . She glanced up at him and smiled.

"My wife wants to know if you like noodles," said Daoud Zozeph.

"Yes, of course," she answered, trying to look into the peeling mirror over the washstand. She could see nothing at all.

"*Bien.* You know, my wife speaks no French."

"Really. You will have to be my interpreter."

There was a dull knocking, out in the shop. Daoud Zozeph excused himself and crossed the court. She shut the door, found there was no key, stood there waiting. It would have been so easy for one of the guards at the fort to follow her. But she doubted that they had thought of it in time. She sat down on the outrageous bed and stared at the wall opposite. The lamp sent up a column of acrid smoke.

The evening meal at Daoud Zozeph's was unbelievably bad. She forced down the amorphous lumps of dough fried in deep fat and served cold, the pieces of cartilaginous meat, and the soggy bread, murmuring vague compliments which were warmly received, but which led her hosts to press more of the food upon her. Several times during the meal she glanced at her watch. Tunner would be waiting in the public garden now, and when he left there he would go up to the fort. At that moment the trouble would begin; Daoud Zozeph could not help hearing of it tomorrow from his customers.

Madame Daoud Zozeph gestured vigorously for Kit to continue eating; her bright eyes were fixed on her guest's plate. Kit looked across at her and smiled.

"Tell madame that because I am a little upset now I am not very hungry," she said to Daoud Zozeph, "but that I should like to have something in my room to eat later. Some bread would be perfect."

"But of course. Of course," he said.

When she had gone to her room, Madame Daoud Zozeph brought her a plate piled high with pieces of bread. She thanked her and said good night, but her hostess was not inclined to leave, making it clear that she was interested in seeing the interior of the traveling case. Kit was determined not to open it in front of her; the thousand-franc notes would quickly become a legend in Sbâ. She pretended not to understand, patted the case, nodded and laughed. Then she turned again toward the plate of bread and repeated her thanks. But Madame Daoud Zozeph's eyes did not leave the valise. There was a screeching and fluttering of wings outside in the court. Daoud Zozeph appeared carrying a fat hen, which he set down in the middle of the floor.

"Against the vermin," he explained, pointing at the hen.

"Vermin?" echoed Kit.

"If a scorpion shows its head anywhere along the floor—tac! She eats it!"

"Ah!" She fabricated a yawn.

"I know madame is nervous. With our friend here she will feel better."

"This evening," she said, "I am so sleepy that nothing could make me nervous."

They shook hands solemnly. Daoud Zozeph pushed his wife out of the room and shut the door. The hen scratched a minute in the dust, then scrambled up onto the rung of the washstand and remained motionless. Kit sat on the bed looking into the uneven flame of the lamp; the room was full of its smoke. She felt no anxiety—only an overwhelming impatience to put all this ludicrous décor behind her, out of her consciousness. Rising, she stood with her ear against the door. She heard the sound of voices, now and then a distant thud. She put on her coat, filled the pockets with pieces of bread, and sat down again to wait.

From time to time she sighed deeply. Once she got up to turn down the wick of the lamp. When her watch said ten o'clock, she went again to the door and listened. She opened it: the court glowed with reflected moonlight. Stepping back inside, she picked up Tunner's burnous and flung it under the bed. The resultant swirl of dust almost made her sneeze. She took her handbag and the valise and went out, taking care to shut the door after her. On her way through the inner room of the shop she stumbled over something and nearly lost her balance. Going more slowly, she moved ahead into the shop, around the end of the counter, feeling lightly along its top with the fingers of her left hand as she went. The door had a simple bolt which she drew back with difficulty; eventually it made a heavy metallic noise. Quickly she swung the door open and went out.

The light of the moon was violent—walking along the white street in it was like being in the sunlight. "Anyone could see me." But there was no one. She walked straight to the edge of town, where the oasis straggled over into the courtyards of the houses. Below, in the wide black mass formed by the tops of the palms, the drums were still going. The sound came from the direction of the ksar, the Negro village in the middle of the oasis.

She turned into a long, straight alley bordered by high walls. On the other side of them the palms rustled and the running water gurgled. Occasionally there was a white pile of dried palm branches stacked against the wall; each time she thought it was a man sitting in the moonlight. The alley swerved toward the sound of the drums, and she came out upon a square, full of little channels and aqueducts running paradoxically in all directions; it looked like a very complex toy railway. Several walks led off into the oasis from here. She chose the narrowest, which she thought might skirt the ksar rather than lead to it, and went on ahead between the walls. The path turned this way and that.

The sound of the drums was louder: now she could hear voices repeating a rhythmical refrain, always the same. They were men's voices, and there seemed to be a great many of them. Sometimes, when she reached the heavy shadows, she stopped and listened, an inscrutable smile on her lips.

The little bag was growing heavy. More and more frequently she shifted it from one hand to the other. But she did not want to stop and rest. At each instant she was ready to turn around and go back to look for another alley, in case she should come out all at once from between the walls into the middle of the ksar. The music seemed quite nearby at times, but it was hard to tell with all the twisting walls and trees in between. Occasionally it sounded almost at hand, as if only a wall and a few hundred feet of garden separated her from it, and then it retreated into the distance and was nearly covered by the dry sound of the wind blowing through the palm leaves.

And the liquid sound of the rivulets on all sides had their effect without her knowing it: she suddenly felt dry. The cool moonlight and the softly moving shadows through which she passed did much to dispel the sensation, but it seemed to her that she would be completely content only if she could have water all around her. All at once she was looking through a wide break in the wall into a garden; the graceful palm trunks rose high into the air from the sides of a wide pool. She stood staring at the calm dark surface of water; straightway she found it impossible to know whether she had thought of bathing just before or just after seeing the pool. Whichever it was, there was the pool. She reached through the aperture in the crumbling wall and set down her bag before climbing across the pile of dirt that lay in her way. Once in the garden she found herself pulling off her clothes. She felt a vague surprise that her actions should go on so far ahead of her consciousness of them. Every movement she made seemed the perfect expression of lightness and grace. "Look out," said a part of her. "Go carefully." But it was the same part of her that sent out the warning when she was drinking too much. At this point it was meaningless. "Habit," she thought. "Whenever I'm about to be happy I hang on instead of letting go." She kicked off her sandals and stood naked in the shadows. She felt a strange intensity being born within her. As she looked about the quiet garden she had the impression that for the first time since her childhood she was seeing objects clearly. Life was suddenly there, she was in it, not looking through the window at it. The dignity that came from feeling a part of its power and grandeur, that was a familiar sensation, but it was years ago that she had last known it. She stepped out into the moonlight and waded slowly toward the center of the pool. Its floor was slippery with clay; in the middle the water came to her waist. As she immersed herself completely, the thought came to her: "I shall never be hysterical again." That kind of tension, that degree of caring about herself, she felt she would never attain them any more in her life.

She bathed lengthily; the cool water on her skin awakened an impulse to sing. Each time she bent to get water between her cupped palms she uttered a burst of wordless song. Suddenly she stopped and listened. She no longer heard the drums—only the drops of water falling from her body into the pool. She finished her bath in silence, her access of high spirits gone; but life did not recede from her. "It's here to stay," she murmured aloud, as she walked toward the bank. She used her coat as a towel, hopping up and down with cold as she dried herself. While she dressed she whistled under her breath. Every so often she stopped and listened for a second, to see if she could hear the sound of voices, or the drums starting up again. The wind came by, up there above her head, in the tops of the trees, and there was the faint trickle of water somewhere nearby. Nothing more. All at once she was seized with the suspicion that something had happened behind her back, that time had played a trick on her: she had spent hours in the pool instead of minutes, and never realized it. The festivities in the ksar had come to an end, the people had dispersed, and she had not even been conscious of the cessation of the drums. Absurd things like that did happen, sometimes. She bent to take her wrist watch from the stone where she had laid it. It was not there; she could not verify the hour. She searched a bit, already convinced that she would never find it: its disappearance was a part of the trick. She walked lightly over to the wall and picked up her valise, flung her coat over her arm, and said aloud to the garden: "You think it matters to me?" And she laughed before climbing back across the broken wall.

Swiftly she walked along, focusing her mind on that feeling of solid delight she had recaptured. She had always known it was there, just behind things, but long ago she had accepted not having it as a natural condition of life. Because she had found it again, the joy of being, she said to herself that she would hang on to it no matter what the effort entailed. She pulled a piece of bread from the pocket of her coat and ate it voraciously.

The alley grew wide, its wall receding to follow the line of vegetation. She had reached the oued, at this point a flat open valley dotted with small dunes. Here and there a weeping tamarisk tree lay like a mass of gray smoke along the sand. Without hesitating she made for the nearest tree and set her bag down. The feathery branches swept the sand on all sides of the trunk—it was like a tent. She put on her coat, crawled in, and pulled the valise in after her. In no time at all she was asleep.

Up Above the World

Dr. Slade had finished his breakfast. The table was set under a khaki-colored parasol in the small patio off the bedroom. He turned his chair around so he could look across the garden. "They've done everything they could for us," he said.

"They've been marvelous, of course. I often wonder what we must have looked like, staggering out of that customs office." Being with Taylor had brought her all the way back into the world; she sat and enjoyed the powerful early morning sunlight and the country smells. "No! I only meant—you don't want to stay here *very* long, do you? They couldn't be sweeter and more generous." She hesitated and took a sip of coffee. "But what have we got in common?"

This of course was the position he had originally taken with regard to his hosts, but at the moment he was in an expansive mood. He stretched back in his chair and yawned. "You're talking too soon, Day. You can't tell. You may love it here."

"You keep inferring there's something here I don't like. I'm divinely happy. I wouldn't want to be anywhere else. But from something you said, I got the impression you felt like staying for quite a while, and I'm just trying to find out how long."

"Since we're here, why don't we just enjoy ourselves? Whenever you want, we can leave."

She sighed. He was not in the habit of being relaxed and casual when it was a question of travel plans. It could be a sign of fatigue. At his age, she reflected, and considering the virulence of the disease, he was fortunate to have rallied this quickly.

"I suppose you're right," she said, feeling a sudden surge of protectiveness toward him. It seemed likely that he needed a thorough rest, and this was the opportunity. She stretched out her feet in front of her and looked at her sandals. "We'll save money, too," she added archly.

He grunted. "It's usually about the same as a hotel by the time you get out, as far as that goes." Her abrupt gesture of agreement had not escaped him; however, he was wary of its motive, and waited.

Late in the afternoon, when the shadows were oblique, they set forth on a walking tour of inspection under the guidance of Señor Soto. Luchita was sullen and silent, and made a point of looking at the sky or the ground beneath her feet each time they stopped to admire a view or examine a plant. She wore a torn shirt, a pair of exaggeratedly dirty Levis, and from what Day could see, nothing else. At one point they came out onto a point of tableland overlooking the river valley and the forest below. "It's dry jungle," said their host. "You can see it's really only a strip that follows the river. We've got about ten thousand acres of good grazing land on the other side over there. Down below here there's a little coffee. Not much, yet. It costs more than it brings in at this point."

Day glanced around for Luchita, and saw her some distance away, seated on a rock, smoking a cigarette. She inhaled with great deliberateness, each time holding the smoke carefully in her lungs for a moment before expelling it. She can't even smoke like other people, she thought. Then she saw that Grove had noticed her, too, and watched his expression cloud over with annoyance. "Come on!" he called. "The *fábrica,* before it gets dark." He led them downward, along a narrow path between boulders and large ceiba trees with fat gray roots.

The *fábrica* was a vast wooden construction, built into the side hill on several levels, partly covered and partly roofless, a chaos of chutes and bins. In Indian file, with Grove leading, they picked their way among the mounds of coffee beans and got to a small office on the dim far side of the shed. A wizened, swarthy young man sat at a desk. "This is my foreman, Enrique Quiroga," said Grove, and they shook hands. Several workmen had taken up unmoving positions from which they could watch through the open door into the office. Grove seized one of several large sombreros that hung from a row of nails on the wall and threw it on his head at an angle. "I feel as though we were on our way to the captain's dinner," Day said to him.

"Not quite. Watch."

A few thin beams of late sunlight pierced the makeshift wall and slanted across the dark interior far above their heads. "Piranese," said Grove, walking ahead.

No one answered. "Come over here and look at this," he said.

Luchita was talking with the foreman. *"Hombre!"* she shouted.

In the corner, up and down, were dozens of webs, like hammocks carelessly slung between the two walls. An enormous black-and-yellow spider lay in each one.

"My God, their bodies are as big as plums!" cried Dr. Slade.

Crushing the crown of the sombrero in one hand, Grove made a long downward scooping gesture with it; the sticky membranes snapped. Then he held the hat up so they could see inside. Dr. Slade adjusted his glasses and stared.

"How many'd I get?"

"Seven or eight."

As Luchita came over to them, Grove bunched the crown together again. "Hold the shadow-maker a minute, will you?"

Dutifully she took it and carried it a few paces. One of the insects, climbing up to escape, touched her hand. She glanced down, screamed, and flung the hat away.

"Oh, I'll kill you, you lousy son of a bitch!" she cried, rushing at Grove to pound him with her fists.

"She hates them," he explained over her shoulder to Day, keeping her hands away from his face.

Behind the *fábrica* were several rows of thatched-roof huts where women chattered and children shrieked. They stood outside of one and looked in at the mud walls and dirt floor; an old woman lay on a pile of burlap sacks in one corner.

"Pretty primitive," said Dr. Slade. Day caught the inflection of criticism in his voice. Perhaps Grove noticed it also. "They're primitive people," he said. "Give them a bed and they put it out for the chickens to roost on. Give them money and they're drunk for two days."

"Still, they must have money sometimes," objected Dr. Slade.

"They don't see it from one year to the next. They get paid in scrip and buy their food at the company store on credit."

"I've read about the system," said Dr. Slade drily.

"They seem happy enough," Day began in an uncertain tone. She was ready to say anything which might forestall discussion of the subject: she knew Taylor.

At one side of the *fábrica*, under a large tree, there was a truck. "Enrique's giving us a lift back to the house," said Grove.

The bumpy trail led through scrub most of the way; it was almost dark when they arrived back at the house. Luchita had made a point of involving herself in a conversation with the foreman as soon as they had got into the truck. When it stopped she jumped down and disappeared.

The main courtyard of the monastery, terraced and open at one end, had not been changed. By daylight there was a view down through the cloistered garden and across the headlands to the curving river with its band of forest. In a corner on the highest terrace, glass walls had been built, and behind these they had dinner. The candles flickered in the breeze. Luchita was sleek and glowing in a close-fitting black gown. As she ate, she stared moodily out toward the invisible river, and when she spoke, her voice was sharp with emotion, alternately indignant and insolent.

"The poor child's still shaken," said Day to Grove. "Those spiders! Why did you do it?"

"Do what?" he cried disgustedly. "It's that very childishness she should be fighting against."

In principle Day agreed with him, but she raised her eyebrows to show disapproval. Looking at him, ruddy and beaming in the candlelight, she thought with faint repulsion: Men are all brutal with young girls. And even Taylor. He too had been sadistic to a small girl, but where had it been? And had he, really, or was it a false memory left over from her sickness?

All day long, here and there, at odd moments, something had been bothering her, and she had put off taking the time to see what it was. And now, as she suddenly came face to face with it, even as Luchita was refusing salad from the bowl the servant held in front of her, she knew in a flash that there was still an empty spot in the past.

She watched the man coming toward her with the salad bowl. Nothing of what was happening was understandable; it could as easily have been something completely different. Until she knew what had gone on before she could not fully accept what was going on now.

For one thing, it struck her as extremely strange that she should feel she knew Grove so well. His voice particularly—it was like a sound she had known all her life. There was something abnormal in the terrible familiarity she felt with its cadence and inflections. And then, What has he got against me? she wondered. Why is he practically vibrating with hostility? Several times during the day she had been nettled by his air of insolent triumph as he looked at her.

All at once she realized that Grove and Taylor were engaged in the argument she had been afraid they would have when they had stood among the workers' huts outside the *fábrica*.

"Yes, but what does the term 'human rights' mean? The American idea is based completely on the fact that Americans have always had more than their share." Grove fixed Dr. Slade with his forefinger. "Put them in the same position as the rest of the people in the world, and they'll understand soon enough that what they've had so far have been only privileges, not rights."

"But for your own protection, in a country like this," pursued Dr. Slade blandly, "it seems you'd do better to cut down the area of possible discontent, don't you think?"

Grove laughed. "Shall we go inside for coffee?" They rose from the table, leaving the candles to gutter in the rising breeze.

In the *sala* Grove stood facing Dr. Slade. "I know, I know," he said with impatience. "A liberal can't say no because he's got nothing to say yes to. But, Doctor, in political theory you keep up with research too."

Dr. Slade bridled. "I'm afraid I don't see the parallel."

They walked over and sat down by the coffee table. Luchita, seeing Grove come into the room, had stopped talking and had assumed a chastened attitude.

"Taylor! Listen to what Pepito said. Tell him, Luchita. It's marvelous!"

Luchita glanced apprehensively at Grove, who seemed amused by her sudden shyness.

"I don't know what's come over her. Ordinarily she doesn't mention the product of her childhood indiscretions," he said.

"Who's Pepito?" demanded Dr. Slade, still ruffled by what he considered Grove's unwarranted attack. But Luchita had risen silently, her face transformed by rage, and was already on her way out of the room. The sound of her heels tapping on the flagstones in the patio died away, and there was silence for an instant.

Finally Day said, "Well!" Grove went on to tell about Indian customs; there was no further reference to the angry exit. A half hour later he too got up, saying he had some work to do, and bade them good night.

They sat on in the *sala* for another few minutes, leafing through magazines in silence. Then, more with mutterings than with words, they agreed to get up and go to their room. Day took with her a copy of *Country Life* and one of *Réalités*. There was a barefoot Indian girl in their bedroom turning down the coverlets and laying out their bathrobes and slippers. She smiled at them and went out.

Dr. Slade stood by the window staring into the faintly lighted patio. Day had gone into the bathroom and was drawing water in the washbasin. He tried without success to remember the last occasion when he and Day had been together in bed. It was unimportant, and yet not knowing when or where it had been disturbed him.

At last she came into the room, radiant in a white peignoir. She walked over to him and put her arm through his. "Darling," he said, turning toward her to embrace her. The smell of her hair always reminded him of sunlight and wind. She did not raise her face to his.

He put his hand under her chin. "What's the matter?"

"Nothing very much," she said smiling; she pulled gently away from him and went to sit at the dressing table.

When he came out of the bathroom in his pajamas, she was sitting up with her sheet over her, looking at *Réalités*. She had tossed the copy of *Country Life* onto his bed. He lay down and stared for a minute at photographs of yew trees and English sitting rooms; then he turned off the lamp on his night table and let the magazine slide to the floor. A moment later Day clicked off her light; the room was in darkness. He heard her yawn faintly. After that there was silence, and then she spoke, tentatively: "Taylor."

"Yes," he murmured, forcing himself back into wakefulness. "What?"

"I wanted to ask you. Have you had any trouble trying to remember things? Since you were sick? Have you noticed anything?"

"A little." He was already wide-awake.

"I've got a big blank in my head. The whole trip is completely gone. It's awful."

"He mentioned the possibility of it. He said it would all come back."

"It's as though a whole section had been simply rubbed out."

"I know. I went through it yesterday," he said hesitantly. "This is one time when you've just got to be patient."

"You have no blank spots?" she insisted.

"I think they've all gone now." He fabricated a yawn; he hoped she would take the hint, and go to sleep. About his own situation he was not so happy as he had tried to appear. Very definitely there was a blind spot in his memory; he could recall nothing that had happened beyond the first two or three days on the ship out of San Francisco. But he had no intention of admitting it to Day; it would deprive her of the very support she most needed at the moment. Besides, he was convinced that between them they would be able to put together the jumbled pieces. Each day one or the other would supply more details, until the picture was complete for both of them.

He listened. She was still; he assumed she was asleep.

Words were deceptive, the very short ones most of all; she thought of the crucial importance of the two small words Taylor had just used: *he said.* He said the forgetfulness would quickly be dissipated. He said it was a result of something called Newbold's Disease. He said the best doctor in the capital had attended them. But would the faculty return intact? Taylor had never heard of Newbold's Disease. It was conceivable that a different doctor could have prescribed a treatment which would have obviated the aftereffects she was suffering. It was demoralizing to know that everything depended on the word of this particular young man. More than ever she distrusted him, and was annoyed only because she could find no more specific material to help her account for her feeling. It seemed to her that the mere fact of his having taken them in and having bothered to bring them all the way here to the ranch could be viewed in a suspicious light. There was a fundamental contradiction in his behavior: he had gone far out of his way to be hospitable and helpful, yet when she was with him she could not perceive even a glimmer of friendliness. He served his charm and courtesy mechanically; it was as if she and Taylor were paying guests and he a professional host. She was convinced that when he had left them an hour ago he had heaved a sigh of relief finally to be rid of them, free to get back to his own life. What his private world was like she could only surmise, but she was certain there was no corner in it for either her or Taylor; in that realm they counted as objects, not as people.

At some point in the night she had a dream. Or it was possible that she was partially awake, and was only remembering a dream? She was alone among the rocks on a dark coast beside the sea. The water surged upward and fell back languidly, and in the distance she heard surf breaking slowly on a sandy shore. It was comforting to be this close to the surface of the ocean and gaze at the intimate nocturnal details of its swelling and ebbing. And as she listened to the faraway breakers rolling up onto the beach, she became aware of another sound entwined with the intermittent crash of waves: a vast horizontal whisper across the bosom of the sea, carrying an ever-repeated phrase, regular as a lighthouse flashing: *Dawn will be breaking soon.* She listened a long time: again and again the scarcely audible words were whispered across the moving water. A great weight was being lifted slowly from her; little by little her happiness became more complete, and she awoke. Then she lay for a few minutes marveling at the dream, and once again fell asleep.

* * *

The next morning, some time after they had finished breakfast, Grove knocked on their door. Day, who had been sunbathing, pulled her bathrobe around her.

"I hate to invade your privacy like this," he said, striding into the patio where they sat. "Everything all right? Anything you need?" As they protested that all the details combined to make perfection, he settled back on a chaise longue and lit a cigarette. In a few minutes the purpose of his visit became clear: he had come to ask Dr. Slade to go with him to visit a nearby silver mine.

"A silver mine! Is that right?" said Dr. Slade with inflections of interest. "Why, I think I might enjoy it."

"Are you going *into* the mine?" Day inquired, looking intently at Grove.

He smiled. "It would be hard to see it from the outside."

"I hate places inside the earth!" she said with feeling, not removing her eyes from his.

"It's a common enough complaint," he told her, his smile even more bland. Suddenly she felt that he was encouraging her to make herself absurd beyond a point of dignified retreat, and so for a while she let the talk go on to other things. Then without warning she asked him, "Is this a modern mine?"

"It's safe, if that's what you mean. It's at least two centuries old. Very solid."

When Dr. Slade got up to leave and was about to follow Grove through the doorway, she said to him in a low voice, but loud enough so that he heard, "I wish you wouldn't go, Taylor."

He stopped and turned. "This is a fine time to tell me! I'll take it easy on the climbs and see you about twelve."

"Yes," she said tonelessly, waving her hand in his direction. He took it as a gesture of dismissal and went on.

When they were in the cloister of the main courtyard, Grove looked at him. "Day's full of anxieties, isn't she?"

"Not at all. She's unusually well balanced," said Dr. Slade. "Her nerves have been a little raw since she was sick, that's all."

Grove smiled tolerantly, shook his head. "Well, Doctor, she's *your* wife. You ought to know. On the other hand, that very intimacy you have might make it impossible for you to see what somebody else meeting her for the first time would see right off. You can't tell."

"I doubt that very much," Dr. Slade said with some force. Grove understood that he was not going to be receptive.

"Why should she be nervous?" he demanded. "She's completely recovered. You can see that."

Dr. Slade stopped walking. "But is she? She's got the same business I have." He tapped his forehead. "There are a whole lot of things she can't remember."

Grove snorted. "More likely it's imaginary. She knows she was out cold for a few days, so she feels the thread's been broken. I think you'll find she can remember, if you ask her the right questions."

They resumed walking, slowly. "I don't know," said Dr. Slade dubiously. "Certainly in my case it's real enough. There's a whole period that's just gone."

"Still missing!" Grove exclaimed.

Since he felt himself being encouraged to talk about it, during the drive he went into describing for Grove the extent of the lapse, using certain landmark dates and counting the days before and after them on his fingers. Between them they calculated that the lost time embraced a period of between thirteen and fifteen days.

"It's my main interest in life at the moment, getting back those days," said Dr. Slade, trying to smile. The hot wind cut violently across his face, making it hard to breathe.

"They'll come home, dragging their tails behind them." Grove was driving much too fast along the rough trail; he never moved his eyes from the track ahead.

Day, continuing her sunbath alone in the increasingly hot patio, went on striving to reconstruct key scenes whose details might call into being a fragment of the missing material. But it was like looking on the shore for yesterday's footprints. She held it against Taylor that he had gone out in spite of her having asked him not to: his absence left her alone with her preoccupation. She was certain that together they had a better chance of solving their difficulties than they ever could have separately.

When the maids came to make up the room she slipped on a shirt and some slacks, and wandered through the house to the front entrance. Outside in the road it seemed a little cooler. There were several dusty trails leading in various directions; the one she chose went along for a way beside the walls of the house and gardens. Soon it dipped and turned to the left. In spite of the heat she continued slowly, scuffing the dust with her sandals as she went along. Then she turned and went back toward the ranch more quickly than she had come. Once in the courtyard, she heard voices coming from the *sala*, and looked in.

"You should have seen it," Taylor told her. "There were brooks of cyanide everywhere."

She laughed shortly and took the cocktail Grove was holding out to her. "That's what I need, some good cyanide."

The dining room was a small museum of pre-Columbian art; its walls were peppered with niches that held masks and sculptures. Grove had wanted to eat here, insisting that it was too hot to be outside. There was a discussion then with Luchita, who protested that the air conditioning made it too cold to be in the dining room. As they sat down to lunch she brought it up again.

"And besides that, you give us vichyssoise with ice in it," she complained.

"Ah, the old teahead freeze. It's hot in here." Grove looked to Day for support.

"It feels just right to me," she said lightly, at the same time twining her legs together, for it seemed uncomfortably chilly.

"Delightful," said Dr. Slade.

"You've got a jacket on," Day told him, and stopped. "What god is that?" she inquired presently, pointing to the huge stone figure that towered at the far end of the room.

Grove glanced at the statue with respect. "That's Xiuloc, god of the life force. They called him the Father of Boils. He weighs fourteen tons."

"I'd have thought a good deal more," said Dr. Slade morosely; he considered it an absurdity to surround a dining table with grimacing faces and snarling muzzles.

"That's the point," Grove told him. "The stone is porous. They broke their boils on it and the stone sucked out the pus."

"Oh," said Day, looking down at her vichyssoise.

"God of the life force," repeated Dr. Slade, as if considering the idea.

"How'd you ever corral all these things?" she asked Grove.

"Everything was dug up on our own land somewhere. The government got the big ones. But there's one mammoth in the studio you've got to see."

"You won't sleep for two weeks if you look at that. I'm telling you the truth," Luchita warned her, speaking with great seriousness.

"I can't wait," she said to Grove. "What is it?"

"Just a divinity. But it's got snakes and spiders in it, and that bothers her."

What am I doing here? she asked herself. It was absurd to be sitting in this glacial room with these two disconnected young people; to prolong the visit would be senseless. She suspected that it was going to be hard to spur Taylor to action. Perhaps a scene would not be necessary, but she was prepared to produce one if he demurred. At least there was satisfaction in knowing that she was no longer of two minds about it.

Immediately after lunch, while Luchita and Dr. Slade were having coffee in the cloister, Grove took her into the room where the big statue was. The light behind it came down from windows high above; she had a strong impression that the object was alive and conscious. A gigantic piece of stone, waiting. Whether it was decorated with snakes and spiders, or hearts and skulls, was beside the point. It was the stone itself that was alive.

From somewhere above their heads came the desperate buzzing of a solitary fly as it banged against a pane of glass. The air in the room was hot and still. The longer they sat without speaking, the more importance the statue would assume.

"I think Luchita and I see it the same way," she finally said. "These Indian things down here give me the shudders."

"Don't you think it's a beauty?" Grove demanded.

"It's magnificent. But I wouldn't want to live anywhere near it. I don't even like to touch these things." Her tone had become one of apology; then it resumed its natural sound. "I think these were pretty terrible civilizations, don't you?"

"Terrible compared to what? Sit down here on the couch where you can look up at it. It has a sense of balance all its own."

She laughed and obligingly seated herself. "It's much worse from here, of course. But you said, Compared to what? Well, to our own Christian civilization, for instance."

Abruptly he sat down beside her. "The one thing Christianity has given the world is a lesson in empathy. Jesus's words are a manual on the technique of putting yourself in the other's place."

"Is that what they are?" If he was hoping to make her angry, she would disappoint him.

"Your husband worries too much about you," he went on, as though continuing the conversation.

"Worries about me?" she exclaimed, astonished.

"I suppose he's concerned about your aftereffects, your hangover of amnesia."

"That's ridiculous," she said, annoyed to hear that they had discussed her. "It's not permanent, is it?"

"No, no." He said only that, and then there was the sound of the fly's agonized attempt to escape. They sat there.

Finally he spoke. "You have to work at it, you know. For instance, when we were out on the terrace, up in the capital, you spoke about coming out of the customhouse at Puerto Farol, and from the way you described it, it seemed like a very sharp and detailed memory."

"Yes," she said uncertainly. The picture as she saw it now was not sharp and detailed at all; it was like remembering a photograph she had once looked at rather than an experience she had lived through.

"You know the part I mean." His voice had overtones of impatience. "When the side of the building and the signboard seemed to buckle as you were falling, and the water in the harbor was flowing like a river? And the uprooted palm trees lying along the waterfront?"

She shut her eyes for a few seconds. When she opened them again her heart was beating violently. Without saying anything she shook her head slowly back and forth.

"Anyway," he went on, "it's not what you saw or thought you saw at that moment, but the fact that those clear memories came right in the middle of your blocked-out period."

She was silent for a moment. Her heart still pounding, she got up quietly and said, "Couldn't we go back?" Without looking again at the statue, she walked toward the door leading out to the cloister.

In the *sala* there was no sign of Luchita or Dr. Slade, and the coffee tray had been cleared away. "Taylor must have gone for his siesta," she said. "I'm going in too, if you don't mind."

"It's hot today," he told her. "The end of the dry season it gets like this."

Taylor had told her about the end of the dry season in that part of the world, how all of nature seemed to be straining to pull a little moisture out of the sky, until one could feel the tension in everything, and the scorpions came out and the lightning flashed more each night, and human nerves grew taut. As she lay back on her pillow, with Taylor snoring gently on the other bed, she tried to find the reason why it had been such an unpleasant experience to have Grove remind her of the arrival in Puerto Farol. It had been like hearing her own dream being told by someone who could tell it far better than she ever could. A few days ago the mention of it on the terrace in the city had been bad, but today's reminder had been infinitely worse, because his unexpected inclusion of the forgotten details of the water in the harbor pouring out to sea and the broken palm trees had given her a terrifying sensation of being dependent upon him, as if she would remember whatever he chose to have her remember. This was manifestly nonsense. She determined not to speak of it to Taylor, who already was treating her with a little of the condescension one shows to invalids.

She listened: the dry wind bore the sound of singing insects as it blew through the patio, and the long, hard leaves of the pandanus bumped one against the next. It would have made her happy to lean across the space between the two beds and take Taylor by the arm. When he was awake she would say, I want to go tomorrow morning.

She sat up. There was no question of relaxing enough to be able to doze off, and if she could not sleep she did not want to be lying there. A walk, even in the burning mid-afternoon sun, would be preferable. She could try a different road—one that might take her to a vantage point where she could see the entire ranch from above.

A few minutes later she stepped out into the wind. There was not a person in sight on any of the roads. The monastery was prolonged by walls for a great distance at each end; she turned to the right and followed the wall. Soon she came to an open door. She peered through and saw some avocado trees. There was a primitive hut back in the deep shade. Turkeys pecked at the dust. One of the maids came out of the hut, caught sight of her, and waved.

She walked on. In the air was the simple odor of the dusty plains, tinged occasionally with a whiff of plant life from the jungle below. The road led upward, over the crest of a small hill. On each side was a living fence of high cactus, and each plant was entirely wrapped in a thick coating of spiderwebs that quivered in the wind. The dust in the road was thick and satiny; no tracks were visible on its recently deposited surface. And in the maze of webs there was nothing but an occasional dry twig or scrap of insect. Yet she repeatedly found herself staring carefully into the tattered gossamer world, as if somewhere inside might be lurking something which would translate itself into the answer to an as yet unformulated question.

The bare hillside had a few rocks and prickly shrubs scattered over it. There was nothing to look at. But the mere act of walking made it easier to accept the fact that she was only waiting for Taylor to finish his nap.

Up here the whole landscape looked scraggy and desolate; its leafless trees and slag-colored expanses made her want to shut her eyes. Whichever way she looked, it was the same: gray and burned out—a landscape imitating death. But when she got to the crest of the hill she found that on the other side it overlooked a bend in the river valley. The tufted tops of the big trees lay steeply below, and in the middle distance she could see stretches of the river as it wandered through the jungle, back and forth across the valley. From where she stood there was no sign of human presence—only the wasteland around her, the valley below, and beyond that more wasteland, rising on and on, to shadows of high mountains on the farthest horizon. After she had stood a while she went back, feeling frustrated.

In the bedroom he was still asleep. She continued into the bathroom and, leaving the door partly open, took a noisy shower. When she came out, he was stirring.

"You're so lucky to be able to sleep that way. Do you want me to ring for tea?"

"I suppose. I've been sweating. It's hot in here."

Ten minutes later, while he was eating an éclair, she began. "You know what I'd like?" she said. "I'd like to pack my things tonight and leave tomorrow morning."

He stared at her. "That seems like rather short notice, doesn't it? They'll think something's wrong."

It annoyed her to hear him include Luchita along with Grove, as if she carried some weight in his household. "Plenty's wrong, and it's all with him. I could fly out of my skin."

"Day, you can't just walk out on people. How do you know what they've got planned for us?"

"Planned!" she cried piteously.

"We can't do it. We've got to give them a little notice."

"I really hate it here," she said in a small, pathetic voice. "I'd like to be in a hotel."

"I got to know him a little this morning," Dr. Slade said meditatively. "You can't help liking the boy. He's had a pretty tough time."

She was contemptuous. "Oh, stop it! He was brought up in the lap of luxury."

"What's that got to do with it? There are other things besides comfort and financial security."

"You'd never guess it."

He shrugged. "You want to be harsh on him, that's all." Then he turned and saw the anxiety in her face. "Why don't we compromise and tell them at dinner we've got to leave day after tomorrow?"

"But definitely? No matter what?"

"Well, of course definitely."

She was silent a moment. "That makes another forty or more hours to get through. God!"

"I wish you'd just relax," he told her.

By dinnertime it had cooled off enough so that they were able to eat in the courtyard under the stars. About halfway through the meal Dr. Slade cleared his throat, and she knew he was going to begin. "Grove, Day and I have been talking it over, and we feel we've got to be getting on." There was a long period of protestation and mutual flattery; she was aware of what Taylor was going through, and she felt sorry for him.

Luchita, looking very pale and sophisticated, had finished her steak and lighted one of her aromatic cigarettes. Her humor was better tonight; from time to time she looked derisively at Grove as he attempted to persuade Dr. Slade to put off his departure. What a rude little bitch she is, Day thought. She might as well have been saying aloud, This isn't what he tells *me*.

It was understood that Grove would drive them to the station at San Felipe and put them on the train for the capital. As they went across the cloister into the *sala*, Grove added, "Luchita's going up anyway on Friday."

Quick as a lizard Luchita turned in the doorway. "Oh, I am?" she cried hoarsely. "You think I am? On the train?"

Day sat down in the place indicated for her, while Grove piled cushions behind her back. She watched the girl closely. Grove turned to her and said in an offhand manner, "Luchita, do you remember a restaurant near the Place de l'Alma called A la Grenouille de Cantal?" Looking earnestly at her, he waited for the reply. And Day was first astonished and then incensed, with the result that she felt impelled to side with the girl. It was a shamefully unequal struggle; Luchita wilted, melted, as if an invisible blow had been struck her. After a moment she said in an almost inaudible voice, "Yes, Vero."

A little while later, when she had the opportunity, Day said in an aside to Grove, "You seem to have *all* the answers."

"Not all," he said, looking carefully at her.

She had hoped to keep the hard edge of her voice covered, but she knew it had cut through; his look at her had been swift and keen. And his astuteness in discerning the hostility she had meant to keep hidden surprised her; it ran counter to certain key prejudices she had regarding him.

When they got to the bedroom and the door was shut behind them, Day stood motionless. "You see what I mean about him?" she demanded.

"He and the girl were on the outs, that's all."

It seemed useless to discuss it. From her bed, propped up against the pillows, she watched Dr. Slade as he shuffled about the room in his bathrobe. Soon he got into the other bed, took off his wristwatch, and reached out to lay it on the night table.

"Has it ever occurred to you," she said, looking at him steadily, "to ask yourself *why* he brought us here?"

He looked incredulous. *"Why?* My God, girl, he's just being hospitable! How can you ask *why?"*

"I can ask anything," she said.

It was twenty-five minutes past eight. From her bed Day heard the rustling of small birds in the patio's shrubs. Because the air was so still she could hear even the distant sounds from the kitchen: a pail being set down, the chatter of women, a door slamming. Taylor lay on his side, asleep. Tomorrow at this time I'll be on the train, she thought, wondering how she would get through the enormous day of waiting that lay ahead of her.

In the dim bathroom as she washed, she was telling herself that each hour equaled about four per cent of the time left, which meant that every fifteen minutes one per cent would tick by. At first her reckoning made the time seem finite and bearable, but after several carefully spaced glances at her watch, she understood that fifteen minutes was a long period of time.

During the course of the morning she gave several small things to the chambermaid to wash out for her, explaining that she must have them all back by evening. Between bouts of packing she sunbathed in the patio with Taylor. Just before they went in to lunch, the girl brought all the clothing back, washed, dried and ironed. "Of course. Everything dries in two minutes in this climate," said Taylor.

At one o'clock they assembled in the *sala* for cocktails. Now there was no sign of friction between Grove and Luchita. "One last round before we go into that icebox," Grove advised, pouring out the drinks for everyone but Luchita, who was still sipping her first.

"Wise girl," commented Dr. Slade. "You don't ever drink much, do you?"

"It makes me feel sick," she told him.

Sitting at the table directly across from Luchita, Day had the opportunity of examining her at close range. What she saw struck her as extraordinarily unpleasant: for the first time in her life she felt she was looking at a zombie. The girl's eyes were almost closed, and a gigantic, meaningless smile lay over her face. When she was spoken to, she appeared to have difficulty finding her voice in order to reply. At least, thought Day, this beatific state augured a quiet meal.

"Well, so this is our last lunch together," said Dr. Slade, spooning up his gazpacho. "It's been so pleasant I hate to get out of the rut. This is certainly one part of the trip I'll never forget."

Day tittered and turned red. Dr. Slade did not seem to have heard. Luchita stared at her, suddenly wide-eyed; then she put her head back and looked down from her own remote heights upon the antics of the alcohol drinker.

"You've missed a great chance, you know, Day." Grove pointed a cigarette at her. "I'd have taken you into San Felipe. A local fiesta."

Day had brought her cocktail in with her; now she sipped it. "Don't tell me," she pleaded. "I don't want to know what I'm missing."

While the others talked, she was busy calculating that already about twenty-two per cent of her time had gone past.

"How about it, Day? You put off your trip and take in the fiesta?"

"You're not serious?"

"Yes."

"Of course we're not going to put off anything. We're leaving tomorrow morning." She laughed in order to seem less ungracious and looked toward Taylor, fearful that he might yet allow the departure to be placed in question. She would not have been astonished at that moment if Grove had spoken out suddenly, declaring that it would be impossible for them to leave. Then she understood that the danger was past and that he would say no more about it.

As they got up from the table, Dr. Slade put his hand on Grove's arm. "Now if you'll forgive me this once, I'll cut the coffee and make straight for my bed."

"Yes," Day said. "I'm sleepy too."

Trying to keep out of the stinging sunlight, they walked slowly along the cloister toward their room. Grove called after them, "Tea in your room at five?"

"Lovely!" said Day. Then she muttered, "Breakfast and tea are the best meals in *this* house. I thought the lunch would never end."

"He makes his drinks too damned strong," Dr. Slade declared.

The curtains were drawn against the glare of the patio. "Will it bother you if I go on packing?" she asked him. He was wrapping his beach bathrobe around him. "Go right ahead," he said. Then, "Whew!" he exclaimed fervently as he fell onto the bed.

For a while she moved aimlessly around the darkened room, carrying objects from one place to another. Finally it became clear to her that everything was packed except the things that had to be left out until the last moment. Common sense told her to stay in the room, where there was no risk of running into Grove and having to engage in conversation with him, but the prospect of lying quietly in the gloom for two or three hours was more than she could face. She was too nervous to read. There was nothing to do but go outside.

It was unlikely that Grove would be wandering around the servants' garden at this hour. There was always life in the neighborhood of the kitchen, and it was soothing to watch people in the act of performing simple tasks. She went out through the big door and followed the road that went along beside the wall. When she came to the garden door, she pushed it open and stepped inside.

At once she had the impression that the place was deserted. The turkeys were there, furrowing the dust with their stiff tailfeathers, and somewhere behind one of the huts farther back in the shade a dog yapped; but she did not hear a human sound.

Leading back to the kitchen door was a long pergola with a trelliswork top where flowering vines drooped. She walked along slowly, marveling at the silence of the afternoon. As she came out into sunlight, she saw on a flagstone at her feet the remains of a small bonfire. Several sheets of typewritten paper had been partially burned; the black-edged, irregular yellow scraps lay beside her foot. She craned her neck a bit and, with her head on one side, looked at what was written there. The word "scaffolding" caught her eye. Then she straightened and walked on to the kitchen door.

There was no sound inside but the steady cheerful dripping of a tap into a sink full of water. The room was very bright; there were glass bricks in the ceiling. She walked in front of the enormous fireplace. It was, of course, the hour of the siesta, when everyone managed to crawl away and lose consciousness for an hour or two, but she would expect to find at least one maid somewhere about. As she continued into the pantry, her movements became stealthy; she felt she had had no right to go through the kitchen.

Surely Grove would consider it a kind of trespassing. In the dining room's cold vault the silence was at its most strident. She went quickly through without glancing at the grinning faces. There was no one in the courtyard. A hammock had been slung across between two pillars, and a book lay open in it, face down. The wind hissed among the thousands of twigs in the lemon tree and pushed the tendrils of overhanging vines out to touch her.

When she came to the turning that led to their room, she hesitated an instant, and then continued straight ahead to the front door. This time she took the road that led downward toward the river. On the promontory that was visible from where they had sat at lunch there were a few low shaggy trees where buzzards perched, and a small partially ruined chapel. This was where the workmen were installing the swimming pool; half of it would be shaded by the apse and the rest would be in the sunlight. She could see the mounds of earth and the wheelbarrows in front of the baroque façade, but no workmen.

It gave her pleasure to scuff her feet through the thick dust, raising a long cloud that moved off behind her across the empty land. The dust was everywhere on her; she thought voluptuously of the shower she would take on returning. It would be more fun to have something visible to wash off.

When the road began to descend too steeply she climbed up over the rocks at the side to get a view across the highest branches of the trees that loomed ahead, and if possible to get a glimpse of the river. Then she stood there staring out at the savage landscape. Directly below her, half covered by trees, was the red roof of the coffee *fábrica*. The ribbon of jungle wound deliberately through the barren country, covering great distances back and forth across the valley; of the river itself there was no sign. Only one more meal to sit through, she reflected with satisfaction.

It was not quite ten to five when she got back to the room, but Taylor had already drunk his tea and gone back to sleep. The tray was there, the teapot empty. He would always drink it while it was hot, without waiting for her, no matter when they brought it. But she was annoyed with Grove. He had said five; here she was, just in time, and there was no tea for her.

Taylor was asleep on his back. It looked like an uncomfortable position, but there was no question of waking him to make him change it. After she had taken her shower she lay out flat on her bed, hoping to relax for a few minutes. Occasionally she rose and walked slowly around the room. When it was twilight she went through the curtained door and into the rosy gray light of the patio. She stood, feeling the slight wind go past.

When the stars are really out I'll wake him up, she thought. With the trip in view it was good that he was sleeping so long. If she changed for dinner now, he could have the bathroom to himself when he got up.

A half hour later, when she was dressed to go in for cocktails, she wandered once more out into the patio and stared up at the sky. The wind had dropped; there were a few stars, but most of them were hidden by great masses of distant cumulus, still white with daylight from behind the horizon. As she watched, tongues of lightning moved between the clouds, and they glowed and flickered with yellow light from deep inside.

She went back in and, opening one of Taylor's valises, took out a pack of playing cards. She sat sideways on her bed and unthinkingly began to play a kind of solitaire she had not thought of since her childhood. Suddenly she made her decision. "Taylor!" she said. She looked over at him and thought she saw him breathe more deeply. "Come on. It's seven-thirty."

His eyes were still shut, and his hands were folded comfortably on his chest.

"Taylor!" she cried. She leaned across and seized his arm, shook it roughly. Already she was certain that nothing was going to rouse him. She jumped up. Standing directly over him, looking down upon his head, feeling his forehead, she thought: He's going to die. This time he's going to die.

It was not much later when she pushed the wall button to call the maid. Then she felt his pulse, and sat intent on the insistent throbs beneath the ball of her finger. There was no knock at the door; she rang again. In the bathroom she dampened a towel and brought it to put around his head. As she pushed the folds of wet linen against his hair she saw that she should have wrung out the towel much more firmly. The water trickled onto the pillow. If by now no one had come in answer to her call, no one was going to come, because the house was empty.

She went in the direction of the corridor. The lights were burning there. When she got to the far side of the courtyard she saw Grove standing inside the doorway of the *sala*.

Together they stood in the room looking at Taylor, Grove nodding his head slowly as he studied the inert form that lay there.

"Can't we call a doctor?" she said finally.

"I'm afraid he wouldn't thank us for calling in Dr. Solera." He smiled wryly at her. "It's nothing, nothing," he added almost impatiently. "If he doesn't come around by midnight I'll give him a shot."

He led her into the *sala*, where he handed her a double vodka martini.

"I'm really master of the house tonight," he said with relish. "I let the whole staff go to the fiesta. Everybody."

"I noticed the quiet. You mean there are really just the four of us in the house tonight?"

"Three," he said, rising to take his cigarette case from the mantel. "Luchita went up this afternoon." He smiled ingenuously. "You were wrong. You see what happened. She took the station wagon."

She felt her eyes growing wide with dismay. To offset the impression that might make, she slowly let her face expand into a delighted grin.

"No trains for Luchita!" she said, trying to laugh, shaking her head. Suddenly she knew he was at her again, studying each muscle of her face as it moved from one expression to another. I can't let him see I'm afraid, she kept thinking. It was as though he were waiting for her to betray herself.

"Who's getting dinner?" she said.

"I am. We are. If you don't mind helping me."

"No," she said, trying to sound pleasant.

"I'll show you the kitchen."

In her mind's eye she saw the whitewashed walls, the black beams overhead, and the huge fireplace. "Have you installed gadgets?" she asked him. "Or do you use the old kitchen, the way it was?"

"It's not old. It's just smoky." He was eying her in a curious manner, perhaps a little in the way a painter would look at a model he was about to begin sketching. "It looks old, I admit. It's an addition from the turn of the century."

Feeling the wind sweep all at once into the room and inundate her with its sweet forest smell, she looked around toward the door. "What's happening out there?"

"It's capricious this time of year," he said. "Off and on, up and down."

The wind had brought the wilderness into the room; her ear now focused on the sounds it was making in the vegetation outside.

"You never talk about yourself," she told him, as he handed her a second double martini.

"I'm always talking about myself."

"I mean your life. When you were a boy, for instance."

He laughed scornfully, but although she waited, he still said nothing.

She rose. "I've got to get something to put around my shoulders. The wind's blowing right on me."

He did not offer to go with her. As she hurried along toward the bedroom, she found herself marveling that she should be able to go on talking while Taylor lay unconscious. It seemed to help prove the truth of a suspicion she had long entertained: people could not really get very close to one another; they merely imagined they were close. (It was not a relapse, merely a part of the tapering off, Grove had said. There was no danger.)

She hunted out the stole she wanted and put it around her shoulders. "Don't disturb him. The thing is to leave him alone." She went over to Taylor's bed and took away the wet towel from around his head. With a fresh towel she dried the strands of damp hair as well as she could. His breathing was regular, slow and profound, and his face looked neither flushed nor pale. It seemed cruel to leave him alone in order to go and sit in the *sala* making meaningless conversation.

As she turned the corner of the cloister, she glanced down the long corridor that lost itself in a dim confusion of plants and furniture. A man in a white shirt had stood for a second at the far end before stepping ahead into the darkness of the courtyard; he did not reappear.

Grove had turned on some jazz and was stretched out full-length on the floor. She went in, and since he did not get up, she stood a moment and then sat down in a chair by the door, where the sound of the music was not so deafening. When the final cymbal crash had announced the end of the piece, he rose and turned off the machine.

"Sometimes I like it so loud it hurts," he told her.

"You said there was no one in the house," she began. "But there's somebody out there. I just saw him."

"Where?" he demanded, staring at her. The idea hovered in her mind that he might be afraid.

"Way down at the end of the colonnade. He went out into the bushes."

"There's a night guard on, down at the generator. He must have come up for something."

"I was surprised," she said, laying her hand over her heart. "I'm on edge, naturally."

"Yes." It was clear that he was thinking about something different. "Of course." Then he turned to her abruptly. "If you're worrying about the doctor, don't."

She looked at him almost tearfully for an instant. "Of course I'm worried!" she cried.

"But you're a fool—" he raised his hand—"if you let him take that trip tomorrow, no matter how he feels."

"I'm for calling your doctor right now." She felt certain of being able to manage the doctor; he would give his permission, and Taylor could go. "Is he so bad?"

"He's not so good; I can tell you that."

"At least he's a doctor," she said reproachfully.

"You don't want another drink, do you? Let's go out and get dinner. We can talk while we work."

As he piloted her through the dim dining room she was telling herself that from the instant they went through the doorway into the pantry she must behave as though she were seeing everything for the first time. Halfway through the pantry she said, "This is an older wing, isn't it?"

He was not listening. "There are some mangoes and papayas in the icebox that have got to be cut up." They were in the kitchen; she looked up at the vaulted beams.

Grove filled a large pot, and another small one, with water, set them on the stove, and lighted the gas burners. "Now we've got direct contact," he said under his breath. While the water heated, she helped him cut up the fruit on the big center table. Then she stood back against the sink and watched while he opened tins and packets and began silently to stir up a sauce over the flame.

"Do you think Luchita's gone for good?" she asked him.

He looked up in surprise. "Why would I think that? She didn't run away."

"Why don't you marry her, Grove?" she said softly.

"You're serious?" He stopped stirring for an instant and saw that she was. "You've seen her," he said, emptying a box of spaghetti into the cauldron of boiling water.

"Oh, marry her, for God's sake! What's the matter with you?"

Turning to the smaller vessel he held up his arm and let some of the sauce drip from the spoon back into the pot, watching it carefully as it fell. "In this country," he told her, speaking slowly, "they say you might as well make a political speech as give unwanted advice. Nobody's going to listen in either case."

She dropped her cigarette into the sink behind her. "Well, I can tell you, you'll never be happy until you do what you know's the right thing. That's what life's about, after all."

"What life's about!" he cried incredulously. "What *is* life about? Yes. What's the subject matter?" He stirred the sauce. "It's about who's going to clean up the shit."

"I don't know what you mean," she said, her voice hostile.

"The work's got to be done. If *you* don't want to do it, you've got to be able to make somebody else do it. That's what life's about. Or isn't that the way you like to hear it?"

She hesitated. "I don't understand. You seem like a mature man. Why you haven't outgrown all this, I mean. If you were ten years younger it wouldn't be so surprising." She would have enjoyed being able to say "so repulsive," because that was the way she felt, but to risk a break would be a kind of abdication; she must stay with him and prove, at least to herself, that she was not afraid of him. Turning her head so he would not see the expression of distaste she knew was on her face, she finally said, "But, isn't it boring eventually? All this animosity, year after year, hating, hating? How do you keep up interest?"

"Life makes it easy. You don't have to worry about that."

She shrugged. "It's not my problem."

"Only a drooling idiot would tell his troubles to a woman," he said suddenly, with some bitterness.

"Troubles?" She eyed him as she lighted another cigarette. "You have troubles?"

His face darkened; he studied the sauce more closely. "Yes. I have troubles." He had said the word without choosing it, but now he seemed to be considering its meaning.

She looked at him and believed him. "I'm sorry," she said. "But whatever they are, I have a feeling you'll get them behind you. It's a question of making up your mind."

He seemed to stiffen. "In what way?"

"I mean setting your mind to putting them behind you."

He wheeled to face her, and she saw with a cold dread that he had had his eyes shut for the past few seconds; they were still shut as he turned. When he opened them, he opened his mouth as well, and laughed once. It sounded like a young dog trying to bark.

"*Abajo* San Felipe!" he cried. "I'm no cook." She had the impression now that he had clambered back inside himself and shut the door.

"I didn't have to let them all go," he went on. "It seemed like a cheap way of reinforcing goodwill between master and servant. You have to keep shoring it up, you know. It wears away like a sea wall. Why don't we sit down right here? Or would you rather put everything on trays and take it into the dining room?"

She went on looking at him, aware suddenly that there was a shadowy bond between them. It was at that instant she first felt the cold impact of physical fear. And for some hidden reason she hoped never to discover, he was afraid of her.

They sat down at a long marble-topped table near the fireplace. The smell of garlic and spices was in the steam that rose from the sauce, but she had no appetite for it when he passed it to her. It had been a fraction of a second that she had looked into his eyes as they opened after having been focused on an inner world of torment, but she had been caught up and drawn into orbit along with him. By the time she had thought: I am I, it was finished, yet for that flash the difference between them had been next to nothing. It was a fact as much as the water dripping from the tap (now into a shallow dish) or the electric clock whirring on top of the refrigerator, or the smoky façade of the chimney above the fireplace.

After the first few mouthfuls she found it easier to eat. He told her several unlikely stories about the abbot of the monastery; she listened and watched him, remembering that at least time was going past. The trouble with Grove was, she thought, trying to be objective about him for a minute, that it was impossible to be relaxed in his presence: he was too desperate and final in his manner.

"There's always a pan of ice cream in the fridge for me," he said when they had finished. "I hope to hell it's there tonight. They get excited by fiestas. Anything can happen."

He got up and peered into the freezing compartment. "It's here," he announced. "Would you like some?"

She let him heap it into a bowl for her. "We'll eat it by the fire," he told her.

Reclining on piles of cushions in the familiar *sala*, she felt a little better, although she longed to get to her own room. He turned on the tape recorder; this time the jazz was a scarcely audible background.

They talked sporadically. Betweentimes the music went on playing. Finally the soft curtain of jazz had become empty silence; the machine continued to run. She could hear the long trills of the night insects in the higher branches of the lemon tree outside. Now and then a languorous stirring of the wind reached her where she sat.

Grove was up, had stopped the tape recorder, was spinning the tape ahead. "I have a wonderful jungle sequence somewhere on here. Just sounds at night." He started the tape, turned up the volume, and the dry, metallic song of the forest night filled the room.

"Beautiful," she said. After a suitable period of listening, she stood up.

"He's all right. Believe me," he told her, rising. "The thing is to let him wake up by himself. If he's hungry, or you want anything, my room's the last one on the right going down, at the end."

"Thank you." She was too tired to think of anything else to say.

Everything was the same in the room: the lighted floor lamp, the curtains across the doorway into the little garden, the nightgown draped over the cowhide back of the chair. Dr. Slade, however, was not in the bed. She saw the depression in the mattress, and the flattened part of the pillow where his head had been lying. It was too much what she had hoped for; it could not be true. "Taylor," she called softly, standing beside the bathroom door.

No sound. She opened the door a crack; it was dark inside. She pushed open the door and stared into the empty bathroom. She pulled aside the curtains and went out into the patio. It was fairly dark out there, but she could see the whitewashed walls all around, and the sharp black forms of the plants against them. There was no one there.

Back in the room standing near the foot of her bed, she turned slowly, looking at each wall in succession. There was no point in going to the door and shouting his name up and down the cloister; nevertheless she stepped outside for an instant and cried "Taylor!" once, into the darkened court-yard. A moment later she began to walk swiftly along under the arches toward the far open end of the cloister. The last door had a sliver of light under it. She knocked four times, quickly.

It seemed a long time before Grove, wearing a white bathrobe, stepped outside and shut the door behind him.

They stood in the dark. He waited, and so she spoke. "He's gotten up and gone out of the room. I don't know where to look for him."

He knotted the belt of the bathrobe tighter about his waist. "He's somewhere around. He won't have gone far."

"Somewhere around," she repeated without conviction. "In the dark?" She gestured with an arm, indicating the vast unlighted expanse of the courtyard. "He shouldn't be wandering around. Suppose he's delirious or walking in his sleep?"

He patted her on the shoulder. "Why don't you just go to bed? He'll be back. He probably wanted a little air."

This was more than she could take. "Are you out of your mind?" she cried. "I've got to find him."

"Feel free to go anywhere. There's generally a light switch on the right inside each door. I don't think you'll find him. As you say, he's not likely to be standing around in a dark house." He stepped toward the doorway.

There was a long silence. "I see," she said. "I thought you might be willing to help."

He did not reply, merely stood there with his hand on the doorknob.

At last he's showing his true colors, she thought. She listened to the wind in the vines. A rooster crowed nearby.

"If he's not in the house, he's gone out," he said. "If he's gone out he'll be back. He's not a child."

"The fact that he's been sick, the fact that only an hour ago he was still unconscious, none of that means anything to you?"

He opened his door a crack and started in. "It doesn't because it's irrelevant. I'd advise you to go back and get into bed."

"You're incredible!" she told him, but her voice was so tight with rage that she doubted he heard her. In her anger she spun around and began to walk very fast. The sound of her heeltaps on the stones struck her as ridiculous even as she heard his door shut. Her fancy was beset with images of pummeling him, clawing his face, kicking him; the black hatred he had aroused spread to the house itself and the countryside around it, and she found herself at the main entrance door, which she opened. She stood there, looking out at the road and the trees swimming in the moonlight. Suddenly she felt certain that Taylor was out here—not in the house.

First she went to the gate that led into the garden. It was unlocked. Inside, the huts were all dark, and the thatch of their roofs was mottled with tiny patches of moonlight that sifted down through the high trees. She stepped uncertainly ahead into the gloom, and then she stopped moving and listened. What she heard in the distance sounded like a drum beating a fast, irregular rhythm. The generator, she thought, and there was a man on duty there. She walked on into the tunnel of shadow. When the avenue of trees and huts had finished, she came out into an open space, and there was a flight of steps leading down. The sound was very loud here; she could see a little building in the bushes below, but no light. The moonlight was bright on the steps. Until she got around to the other side of the cabin and walked under the banana plants that grew in front of it she did not hear the radio. Then she saw a man squatting just outside the open door, his transistor on the ground in front of him. He grunted, jumped up and snapped on a light in the doorway; a tawny Indian youth in a visored cap stared at her with suspicion. She smiled, but could think of no explanation to give for her sudden intrusion. The boy did not return the smile. Instead, he called out, "Señor Torny!"

There was the sound of heavy boots coming nearer on the other side of the plants. A tall young man in cowboy uniform moved into view, and remained looking impassively in her direction for what seemed a long time. Like the nasty one in a Western, she thought. The Indian boy did not move again. Suddenly the cowboy spoke in a low thin voice, and she jerked her head up in surprise. His English was perfect.

"Looking for something in particular or just taking a walk?"

"Oh, I heard the sound and I came down," she said, knowing that what she was saying was absurd, unconvincing. He still waited, and an idea came to her. "I think you were right in the beginning. I did want something."

She waited again. "Yes," he finally said.

"What I really needed but didn't dare hope for was a ride into San Felipe."

"You mean tonight, now?"

"That's what I meant."

He stepped toward her. "I'd do it, baby, but the truck isn't mine."

She hesitated. "I just wanted to get to a doctor."

Again he merely looked at her.

She was not certain how he was going to react, but she went ahead anyway. "It would be worth a hundred dollars to me to get there."

"I see." Now he stared at the ground.

Eventually he looked up at her. "The problem's still the same, but I'll risk it. When do you want to go?"

"Right now."

"I'll have to get the keys. Wait there." He turned away. The sound of his boots on the gravel became fainter. She moved aimlessly around in the open space in front of the banana plants while the Indian boy stared at her. Now and then she felt a compulsion to go back to the bedroom: Taylor could be there waiting. But she did not believe it, and she would not go into the house again until she had Dr. Solera with her. She heard the cowboy's feet pounding the earth as he approached.

"Ready," he said from behind the wall of banana leaves. They walked, partly through garden and partly through wasteland, to the garage where a truck stood in the moonlight. He got in, leaned across and opened the door for her. The hard seat was very high off the floor, and the motor made a fantastic amount of noise when he started it. Then they swung around and began to move along the driveway. As a precaution he had opened the gate when he went to get the keys. They slid through and the ranch was behind them.

He turned to her. "Have you got enough clothes on, baby? It's a lot cooler up there, you know."

Even had she known that the streets of San Felipe were going to be deep with snow, she would not have considered going back to get a coat. She looked through the windshield at the sky full of stars. "Why do you say baby?" she asked him.

He was startled. "Why do I say baby? It's the way I talk, that's all. Why, don't you like it?"

"I don't mind it," she said thoughtfully.

He did not reply. The truck roared along the highway, in and out of arroyos, through desert and brushland. At a gap between two hills he stopped and jumped out, slamming the door. After she had managed to get her door open, she too got down. He was standing in the cold at the back of the truck, looking down into the valley they had just left behind. Seeing her, he turned and began to kick the tires. "I'm paranoid about flats," he said. Far down the valley she saw the lights of a car moving along toward them.

"O.K.?" They got in, slammed the doors, and moved off. As they approached the first cantinas on the outskirts of the town, he looked briefly over at her. "You want a doctor? That means Solera."

"Yes," she said impatiently.

"But with this fiesta, I don't know. We'll have to walk." He had slowed down. Through the window, above the sound of the truck's motor, came the ceaseless rattle of firecrackers, and she could hear two or three bands playing at once.

He stopped under some tamarind trees near the empty marketplace. Men were lying at the base of the trees and in front of the dark stalls. They got out, and he locked the doors. "Come on," he said.

"Do you know where he lives?"

"Sure I know. That doesn't mean much tonight, though."

The din of marimbas, cornets, fireworks and screams came closer as they walked through the market; the crowd was at the end of the street, ahead of them. Now and then a skyrocket rushed almost horizontally to explode just above their heads.

Day was not used to seeing several thousand masked men and women shouting into one another's faces. It was clear that the fireworks were dangerous: several rockets had gone directly into the mass of people. She tried to slow their pace a bit, but he kept going until they were in the crowded plaza, under the lights and streamers, engulfed by the mob. They began to fight their way through in order to cross the square.

"Do we have to get into the middle of it?" she shouted. He seemed not to hear her, and only shoved her ahead. She felt the bodies pushing and twisting against her on all sides, saw the shiny painted masks: skulls, monkeys, demons—and the purpose of the fiesta came to her. It was not meant to celebrate the glory of God, or the saint in whose honor it was named. Instead, it was a night of collective fear, when everyone agreed to be frightened. Each person was out to scare the next; their voices were sharp with apprehensiveness. And no one knew where the skyrockets and Roman candles were going to belch their fire.

The crush had started out by being overwhelming; then it had become painful and a little unpleasant. She was sure that beneath the masks the faces were unfriendly.

In the center of the plaza was a kiosk plastered over with posters. REVINDICACIÓN, REDENCIÓN, REVOLUCIÓN, they proclaimed. She let herself be forced back into the pocket against the wall of the kiosk, where there was partial shelter from the moving throng.

"I sort of hoped we might find him here," he told her. "The important citizens are usually up there sitting with the band."

"Is he really a very bad doctor?"

"Couldn't tell you."

They stood a while watching; the uproar did not encourage conversation. But once she looked and he was not there, and her heart missed a beat. Then she began desperately to examine all the taller men nearby, thinking, He can't just have walked off without his hundred dollars. When she was satisfied that he was not there, she lowered her head. Suddenly she understood that he had betrayed her to Grove. She started ahead fiercely into the crowd. I'll get to Dr. Solera by myself. She clamped her jaws together and put all her force into pushing her body forward.

Eventually she was ejected from the central core of pressure, spinning and staggering, to land against a concrete bench. A group of youths stood on top of it, peering over the heads of the multitude. As she bumped against their legs, they stared at her in surprise. One of them jumped down and stood on the ground beside her. Quickly she began in careful Spanish, *"Buenas noches.* I should like a hotel."

They started to walk. She was being buffeted so often by people rushing past that he took her arm to steady her. A skyrocket emptied its fire into a group just ahead of them, and a girl was led away sobbing, her hands over her face.

They finally left the plaza behind and walked in the small dark streets. From time to time, when the breeze shifted and blew up from across the swampland below, an evil odor filled the air—a wide, greasy stench that expanded slowly through the streets until a new wind dispersed it. The Indians sat quietly in the dust, burning candles and carbide lamps, arranging their herbs and copal in small designs on the ground in front of them, their empty eyes fixed upon a point beyond the town.

There was another plaza, smaller and deserted save for a few drunken mestizos lying on the benches and against the tree trunks. On the far side at the end of a row of humble houses was a door with a small plaque above it: PENSIÓN FÉNIX. CAMAS.

She stood quietly, listening to the distant excitement while he knocked. There might be no one to open the door. But then an old woman stood there, her black rebozo pulled tightly about her head, blinking and frowning at them. When the youth had spoken with her for a moment, she opened the door wider. *"A sus órdenes,"* he murmured, turning and running down the street. Day stepped inside.

There was a small patio full of furniture and plants. From there the old woman led her into a room that had nothing in it but a brass bed and a round table that held a bowl of dusty wax flowers. "Dr. Solera," she began. "Where is his house? I want to see him."

The old woman spoke for a while; Day interpreted her words as meaning that the thing would not be possible before morning. Still she insisted. She could be shown his house at least. But the old woman pulled the rebozo more firmly around her wrinkled forehead and began to mutter and sigh to herself. *"No se puede,"* she said, going out into the patio. Day followed her.

In the center was a tall cage covered with chicken wire where birds fluttered and hopped among the branches of a dead tree. The old woman stood by the cage watching the birds move in the dark, and her face assumed an expression which could have denoted satisfaction.

Day hovered in the background, waiting for a propitious moment, when the old woman might become receptive again. On a small wicker table covered with lace doilies was a frayed photograph album. She held it under the light bulb and fingered the pages. The pictures were old postcards, all of them views of a local volcano. She put the album back and took up a magazine. There were photographs of huge groups of nuns standing in rows, and a full-page portrait of the Pope. When she heard the four quick knocks on the entrance door she was absolutely certain it was Grove; it was almost as if his voice had spoken. She dropped the magazine to her side and, standing very still, looked up at the stars.

Let It Come Down

The Beidaouis' Sunday evenings were unique in that any member of one of the various European colonies could attend without thereby losing face, probably because the fact that the hosts were Moslems automatically created among the guests a feeling of solidarity which they welcomed without being conscious of its origin. The wife of the French minister could chat with the lowest American lady tourist and no one would see anything extraordinary about it. This certainly did not mean that if the tourist caught sight of Mme. D'Arcourt the next day and had the effrontery to recognize her, she in turn would be recognized. Still, it was pleasant and democratic while it lasted, which was generally until about nine. Very few Moslems were invited, but there were always three or four men of importance in the Moslem world: perhaps the leader of the Nationalist Party in the Spanish Zone, or the editor of the Arabic daily in Casablanca, or a wealthy manufacturer from Tunis, or the advisor to the Jalifa of Tetuan. In reality the gatherings were held in order to entertain these few Moslem guests, to whom the unaccountable behavior of Europeans never ceased to be a fascinating spectacle. Most of the Europeans, of course, thought the Moslem gentlemen were invited to add local color, and praised the Beidaoui brothers for their cleverness in knowing so well just what sort of Moroccan could mix properly with foreigners. These same people, who prided themselves upon the degree of intimacy to which they had managed to attain in their relationships with the Beidaoui, were nevertheless quite unaware that the two brothers were married, and led intense family lives with their women and children in a part of the house where no European had ever entered. The Beidaouis would certainly not have hidden the fact had they been asked, but no one had ever thought to question them about such things. It was taken for granted that they were two debonair bachelors who loved to surround themselves with Europeans.

That morning, on one of his frequent walks along the waterfront, where he was wont to go when he had a hangover or his home life had grown too oppressive for his taste, Thami had met with an extraordinary piece of good luck. He had wandered out onto the breakwater of the inner port, where the fishermen came to unload, and was watching them shake out the black nets, stiff with salt. A small, old-fashioned motor-boat drew alongside the dock. The man in it, whom Thami recognized vaguely, threw a rope to a boy standing nearby. As the boatman, who wore a turban marking him as a member of the Jilala cult, climbed up the steps to the pier, he greeted Thami briefly. Thami replied, asking if he had been fishing. The man looked at him a little more closely, as if to see exactly who it was he had spoken to so carelessly. Then he smiled sadly, and said that he never had used his little boat for fishing, and that he hoped the poor old craft would be spared such a fate until the day it fell to pieces. Thami laughed; he understood perfectly that the man meant it was a fast enough boat to be used for smuggling. He moved along the dock and looked down into the motor-boat. It must have been forty years old; the seats ran lengthwise and were covered with decaying canvas cushions. There was an ancient two-cylinder Fay and Bowen engine in the center. The man noticed his scrutiny, and inquired if he were interested in buying the boat. "No," said Thami contemptuously, but he continued to look. The other remarked that he hated to sell it but had to, because his father in Azemmour was ill, and he was going back there to live. Thami listened with an outward show of patience, waiting for a figure to be mentioned. He had no intention of betraying his interest by suggesting one himself. Eventually, as he tossed his cigarette into the water and made as if to go, he heard the figure: ten thousand pesetas. "I don't think you'll get more than five," he replied, turning to move off. "Five!" cried the man indignantly. "Look at it," said Thami, pointing down at it. "Who's going to give more?" He started to walk slowly away, kicking pieces of broken concrete into the water as he went. The man called after him. "Eight thousand!" He turned around, smiling, and explained that he was not interested himself, but that if the Jilali really wanted to sell the boat, he should put a sensible price on it, one that Thami could quote to his friends in case one of them might know a possible buyer. They argued a while, and Thami finally went away with six thousand as an asking price. He felt rather pleased with himself, because although it was by no means the beautiful speed boat he coveted, it was at least a tangible and immediate possibility whose realization would not involve either an import license or any very serious tampering with his heritage. He had thought of asking the American, whom he liked, and who he felt had a certain sympathy for him, to purchase the boat in his name. It would have been a way around the license. But he thought he did not know him well enough, and beyond a doubt it would have been a foolish move: he would have had to rely solely on the American's honesty for proof of ownership. As to the price, it was negligible, even at six thousand, and he was positive he could get it down to five. There was even a faint possibility, although he doubted it, really, that he could get Abdelmalek to lend him the sum. In any case, among his bits of property there was a two-room house without lights or water at the bottom of a ravine behind the Marshan, which ought to bring just about five thousand pesetas in a quick sale.

The end of the afternoon was splendid: the clouds had been blown away by a sudden wind from the Atlantic. The air smelled clean, the sky had become intense and luminous. As Dyar waited in front of the door of his hotel, a long procession of Berbers on donkeys passed along the avenue on their way from the mountains to the market. The men's faces were brown and weather-burned, the women were surprisingly light of skin, with salient, round red cheeks. Dispassionately he watched them jog past, not realizing how slowly they moved until he became aware of the large American convertible at the end of the line, whose horn was being blown frantically by the impatient driver. "What's the hurry?" he thought. The little waves on the beach were coming in quietly, the hills were changing color slowly with the dying of the light behind the city, a few Moroccans strolled deliberately along the walk under the wind-stirred branches of the palms. It was a pleasant hour whose natural rhythm was that of leisure; the insistent blowing of the trumpet-like horn made no sense in that ensemble. Nor did the Berbers on their donkeys give any sign of hearing it. They passed peacefully along, the little beasts taking their measured steps and nodding their heads. When the last one had come opposite Dyar, the car swung toward the curb and stopped. It was the Marquesa de Valverde. "Mr. Dyar!" she called. As he shook her hand she said: "I'd have been here earlier, darling, but I've been bringing up the rear of this parade for the past ten minutes. Don't ever buy a car here. It's the most nerve-racking spot in this world to drive in. God!"

"I'll bet," he said; he went around to the other side and got in beside her.

They drove up through the modern town at a great rate, past new apartment houses of glaring white concrete, past empty lots crammed to bursting with huts built of decayed signboards, packing cases, reed latticework and old blankets, past new cinema palaces and night clubs whose sickly fluorescent signs already glowed with light that was at once too bright and too dim. They skirted the new market, which smelled tonight of fresh meat and roses. To the south stretched the sandy wasteland and the green scrub of the foothills. The cypresses along the road were bent by years of wind. "This Sunday traffic is dreadful. Ghastly," said Daisy, looking straight ahead. Dyar laughed shortly; he was thinking of the miles of strangled parkways outside New York. "You don't know what traffic is," he said. But his mind was not on what was being said, nor yet on the gardens and walls of the villas going past. Although he was not given to analyzing his states of mind, since he never had been conscious of possessing any sort of apparatus with which to do so, recently he had felt, like a faint tickling in an inaccessible region of his being, an undefined need to let his mind dwell on himself. There were no formulated thoughts, he did not even daydream, nor did he push matters so far as to ask himself questions like: "What am I doing here?" or "What do I want?" At the same time he was vaguely aware of having arrived at the edge of a new period in his existence, an unexplored territory of himself through which he was going to have to pass. But his perception of the thing was limited to knowing that lately he had been wont to sit quietly alone in his room saying to himself that he was here. The fact kept repeating itself to him: "Here I am." There was nothing to be deduced from it; the saying of it seemed to be connected with a feeling almost of anaesthesia somewhere within him. He was not moved by the phenomenon; even to himself he felt supremely anonymous, and it is difficult to care very much what is happening inside a person one does not know. At the same time, that which went on outside was remote and had no relationship to him; it might almost as well not have been going on at all. Yet he was not indifferent—indifference is a matter of the emotions, whereas this numbness affected a deeper part of him.

They turned into a somewhat narrower, curving street. On the left was a windowless white wall at least twenty feet high which went on ahead, flush with the street, as far as the eye could follow. "That's it," said Daisy, indicating the wall. "The palace?" said Dyar, a little disappointed. "The Beidaoui Palace," she answered, aware of the crestfallen note in his voice. "It's a strange old place," she added, deciding to let him have the further surprise of discovering the decayed sumptuousness of the interior for himself. "It sure looks it," he said with feeling. "How do you get in?"

"The gate's a bit farther up," replied Daisy, and without transition she looked directly at him as she said: "You've missed out on a good many things, haven't you?" His first thought was that she was pitying him for his lack of social advantages; his pride was hurt. "I don't think so," he said quickly. Then with a certain heat he demanded: "What sort of things? What do you mean?"

She brought the car to a stop at the curb behind a string of others already parked there. As she took out the keys and put them into her purse she said: "Things like friendship and love. I've lived in America a good deal. My mother was from Boston, you know, so I'm part American. I know what it's like, Oh, God, only too well!"

They got out. "I guess there's as much friendship there as anywhere else," he said. He was annoyed, and he hoped his voice did not show it. "*Or* love."

"Love!" she cried derisively.

An elderly Sudanese swung the grilled gate. They went into a dark room where several other bearded men were stretched out on mats in a niche that ran the length of the wall. These greeted Daisy solemnly, without moving. The old servant opened a door, and they stepped out into a vast dim garden in which the only things Dyar could identify with certainty were the very dark, tall cypresses, their points sharp against the evening sky, and the very white marble fountains in which water splashed with an uneven sound. They went along the gravel walk in silence between the sweet and acid floral smells. There were thin strains of music ahead. "I expect they're dancing to the gramophone," said Daisy. "This way." She led him up a walk toward the right, to a wide flight of marble stairs. "Evenings they entertain in the European wing. And in European style. Except that they themselves don't touch liquor, of course." Above the music of the tango came the chatter of voices. As they arrived at the top of the stairway a grave-faced man in a white silk gown stepped forward to welcome them.

"Dear Abdelmalek!" Daisy cried delightedly, seizing his two hands. "*What* a lovely party! This is Mr. Dyar of New York." He shook Dyar's hand warmly. "It is very kind of Madame la Marquise to bring you to my home," he said. Daisy was already greeting other friends; M. Beidaoui, still grasping Dyar's hand, led him to a nearby corner where he presented him to his brother Hassan, a tall chocolate-colored gentleman also clothed in white robes. They spoke a minute about America, and Dyar was handed a whiskey-soda by a servant. As his hosts turned away to give their attention to a new arrival, he began to look about him. The room was large, comfortable and dark, being lighted only by candles that rested in massive candelabra placed here and there on the floor. It was irregularly shaped, and the music and dancing were going on in a part hidden from his vision. Along the walls nearby were wide, low divans occupied exclusively by women, all of whom looked over forty, he noted, and certain of whom were surely at least seventy. Apart from the Beidaoui brothers there were only two other Moslems in view. One was talking to Daisy by an open window and the other was joking with a fat Frenchman in a corner. In spite of the Beidaouis, whom he rather liked, he felt smothered and out of place, and he wished he had not come.

As Dyar was about to move off and see who was taking part in the dancing, Hassan tapped him on the arm. "This is Madame Werth," he said. "You speak French?" The dark-eyed woman in black to whom he was being presented smiled. "No," said Dyar, confused. "It does not matter," she said. "I speak a little English." "You speak very well," said Dyar, offering her a cigarette. He had the feeling that someone had spoken to him about her, but he could not remember who, or what it was that had been said. They conversed a while, standing there with their drinks, in the same spot where they had been introduced, and the idea persisted that he knew something about her which he was unable to call to mind. He had no desire to be stuck with her all evening, but for the moment he saw no way out. And she had just told him that she was in mourning for her husband; she looked rather forlorn, and he felt sorry for her. Suddenly he saw Eunice Goode's flushed face appear in the doorway. "How do you do?" she said to Hassan Beidaoui. Behind her was Hadija, looking very smart indeed. "How do you do?" said Hadija, with the identical inflection of Eunice Goode. A third woman entered with them, small and grim-faced, who scarcely acknowledged the greeting extended to her, but immediately began to inspect the guests with care, one by one, as if taking a rapid inventory of the qualities and importance of each. There was not enough light for the color of her hair to be noticeable, so, since no one seemed to know her, no one paid her any attention for the moment. Dyar was too much astonished at seeing Hadija to continue his conversation; he stood staring at her. Eunice Goode held her by the hand and was talking very fast to Hassan.

"You'll be interested to know that one of my dearest friends was Crown

Prince Rupprecht. We were often at Karlsbad together. I believe he knew your father." As the rush of words went on, Hassan's face showed increasing lack of comprehension; he moved backward a step after each few sentences, saying: "Yes, yes," but she followed along, pulling Hadija with her, until she had backed him against the wall and Dyar could no longer hear what she was saying. Somewhat embarrassed, he again became conscious of Madame Werth's presence beside him.

"—and I hope you will come to make a visit to me when I am returning from Marrakech," she was saying.

"Thank you, I'd like very much to." It was then that he recalled where he had heard her name. The canceled reservation at the hotel there which he had been going to give to Daisy had originally been Madame Werth's.

"Do you know Marrakech?" she asked him. He said he did not. "Ah, you must go. In the winter it is beautiful. You must have a room at the Mamounia, but the room must have a view on the mountains, the snow, you know, and a terrace above the garden. I would love to go tomorrow, but the Mamounia is always full now and my reservation is not before the twenty of the month."

Dyar looked at her very hard. She noticed the difference in his expression, and was slightly startled.

"You're going to the Hotel Mamounia in Marrakech on the twentieth?" he said. Then, seeing the suggestion of bewilderment on her face he looked down at her drink. "Yours is nearly finished," he remarked. "Let me get you another." She was pleased; he excused himself and went across the room with a glass in each hand.

It all made perfectly good sense. Now at last he understood Daisy's request of him and the secrecy with which she had surrounded it. Madame Werth would simply have been told that there had been a most regrettable misunderstanding, and Wilcox's office would have been blamed, but the Marquise de Valverde would already have been installed in the room and there would have been no dislodging her. As he realized how close he had come to doing her the favor he felt a rush of fury against her. "The bitch!" he said between his teeth. The little revelation was unpleasant, and it somehow extended itself to the whole room and everyone in it.

He saw Daisy out of the corner of his eye as he passed the divan where she sat; she was talking to a pale young man with spectacles and a girl with a wild head of red hair. As he was on his way back she caught sight of him and called out: "Mr. Dyar! When you've made your delivery I want you to come over here." He held the glasses up higher and grinned. "Just a second," he said. He was wondering if Madame Werth would be capable of the same sort of throatslitting behavior as Daisy, and decided against the likelihood of it. She looked too helpless, which was doubtless precisely why Daisy had singled her out as a likely prospective victim.

Back, standing again beside Madame Werth, he said as she sipped her new drink: "Do you know the Marquesa de Valverde?"

Madame Werth seemed enthusiastic. "Ah, what a delightful woman! Such vivacity! And very kind. I have seen her pick out from the street young dogs, poor thin ones with bones, and take them to her home and care for them. The entire world is her charity."

Dyar laughed abruptly; it must have sounded derisive, for Madame Werth said accusingly: "You think kindness does not matter?"

"Sure it matters. It's very important." At the moment he felt expansive and a little reckless; it would be pleasurable to sit beside Daisy and worry her. She could not see whom he was talking to from where she sat, and he wanted to watch her reaction when he told her. Presently a Swiss gentleman joined them and began speaking with Madame Werth in French. Dyar slipped away, finishing his drink quickly and getting another before he went over to the divan where Daisy was.

"Two compatriots of yours," she said, moving over so he could squeeze in beside her. "Mr. Dyar. Mrs. Holland, Mr. Richard Holland." The two acknowledged the introduction briefly, with what seemed more diffidence than coldness.

"We were talking about New York," said Daisy. "Mr. and Mrs. Holland are from New York, and they say they feel quite as much at home here as they do there. I told them that was scarcely surprising, since Tangier is more New York than New York. Don't you agree?"

Dyar looked at her closely; then he looked at Mrs. Holland, who met his gaze for a startled instant and began to inspect her shoes. Mr. Holland was staring at him with great seriousness, like a doctor about to arrive at a diagnosis, he thought. "I don't think I see what you mean," said Dyar. "Tangier like New York? How come?"

"In spirit," said Mr. Holland with impatience. "Not in appearance, naturally. Are you from New York? I thought Madame de Valverde said you were." Dyar nodded. "Then you must see how alike the two places are. The life revolves wholly about the making of money. Practically everyone is dishonest. In New York you have Wall Street, here you have the Bourse.

Not like the bourses in other places, but the soul of the city, its *raison d'être*. In New York you have the slick financiers, here the money-changers. In New York you have your racketeers. Here you have your smugglers. And you have every nationality and no civic pride. And each man's waiting to suck the blood of the next. It's not really such a far-fetched comparison, is it?"

"I don't know," said Dyar. At first he had thought he agreed, but then the substance of Holland's argument had seemed to slip away from him. He took a long swallow of whiskey. The phonograph was playing *"Mamá Inez."* "I guess there are plenty of untrustworthy people here, all right," he said.

"Untrustworthy!" cried Mr. Holland. "The place is a model of corruption!"

"But darling," Daisy interrupted. "Tangier's a one-horse town that happens to have its own government. And you know damned well that all government lives on corruption. I don't care what sort—socialist, totalitarian, democratic—it's all the same. Naturally in a little place like this you come in contact with the government constantly. God knows, it's inevitable. And so you're always conscious of the corruption. It's that simple."

Dyar turned to her. "I was just talking with Madame Werth over there." Daisy looked at him calmly for a moment. It was impossible to tell what she was thinking. Then she laughed. "I being the sort of person I am, and you being the sort of person you are, I think we can skip over *that*. Tell me, Mrs. Holland, have you read *The Thousand and One Nights?*"

"The Mardrus translation," said Mrs. Holland without looking up.

"All of it?"

"Well, not quite. But most."

"And do you adore it?"

"Well, I admire it terribly. But Dick's the one who loves it. It's a little direct for me, but then I suppose the culture had no nuances either."

Dyar had finished his drink and was again thinking of getting in to where the dancing was going on. He sat still, hoping the conversation might somehow present him with a possibility of withdrawing gracefully. Daisy was addressing Mr. Holland. "Have you ever noticed how completely illogical the end of each one of those thousand and one nights actually is? I'm curious to know."

"Illogical?" said Mr. Holland. "I don't think so."

"Oh, my dear! Really! Doesn't it say, at the end of each night: 'And Scheherazade, perceiving the dawn, discreetly became silent'?"

"Yes."

"And then doesn't it say: 'And the King and Scheherazade went to bed and remained locked in one another's arms until morning'?"

"Yes."

"Isn't that rather a short time? Especially for Arabs?"

Mrs. Holland directed an oblique upward glance at Daisy, and returned to the contemplation of her feet.

"I think you misunderstand the time-sequence," said Mr. Holland, sitting up straight with a sudden spasmodic movement, as if he were getting prepared for a discussion. Dyar got quickly to his feet. He had decided he did not like Mr. Holland, who he imagined found people agreeable to the extent that they were interested in hearing him expound his theories. Also he was a little disappointed to find that Daisy had met his challenge with such bland complacency. "She didn't bat an eyelash," he thought. It had been no fun at all to confront her with the accusation. Or perhaps she had not even recognized his remark as such. The idea occurred to him as he reached the part of the room where the phonograph was, but he rejected it. Her reply could have meant only that she admitted she had been found out, and did not care. She was even more brazen than he had imagined. For no particular reason, knowing this depressed him, put him back into the gray mood of despair he had felt the night of his arrival on the boat, enveloped him in the old uneasiness.

A few couples were moving discreetly about the small floor-space, doing more talking than dancing. As Dyar stood watching the fat Frenchman swaying back and forth on his feet, trying to lead an elderly English woman in a turban who had taken a little too much to drink, Abdelmalek Beidaoui came up to him bringing with him a tall Portuguese girl, cadaver-thin and with a cast in one eye. It was obvious that she wanted to dance, and she accepted with eagerness. Although she kept her hips against his as they danced, she leant sharply backward from the waist and peered at him fixedly while she told him bits of gossip about the people in the other part of the room. In speaking she kept her lips drawn back so that her gums were fully visible. "Jesus, I've got to get out of here," Dyar thought. But they went on, record after record. At the close of a samba, he said to her, panting somewhat exaggeratedly: "Tired?" "No, no!" she cried. "You are marvelous dancer."

Here and there candles had begun to go out; the room was chilly, and a damp wind came through the open door from the garden. It was that moment of the evening when everyone had arrived and no one had yet thought of going home; one could have said that the party was in full swing, save that there was a peculiar deadness about the gathering which made it difficult to believe that a party was actually in progress. Later, in retrospect, one might be able to say that it had taken place, but now, while it still had not finished, it was somehow not true.

The Portuguese girl was telling him about Estoril, and how Monte Carlo even at its zenith never had been so glamorous. If at that moment someone had not taken hold of his arm and yanked on it violently he would probably have said something rather rude. As it was, he let go of the girl abruptly and turned to face Eunice Goode, who was by then well primed with martinis. She was looking at the frowning Portuguese girl with a polite leer. "I'm afraid you've lost your dancing partner," she said, steadying herself by putting one hand against the wall. "He's coming with me into the other room."

Under ordinary circumstances Dyar would have told her she was mistaken, but right now the idea of sitting down with a drink, even with Eunice Goode along, seemed the preferable, the less strenuous of two equally uninteresting prospects. He excused himself lamely, letting her lead him away across the room into a small, dim library whose walls were lined to the ceiling with graying encyclopaedias, reference books and English novels. Drawn up around a fireplace with no fire in it were three straight-backed chairs, in one of which sat Mme. Jouvenon, staring ahead of her into the cold ashes. She did not turn around when she heard them come into the room.

"Here we are," said Eunice brightly, and she introduced the two, sitting down so that Dyar occupied the chair between them.

For a few minutes Eunice valiantly made conversation; she asked questions of them both and answered for both. The replies were doubtless not the ones that either Mme. Jouvenon or Dyar would have given, but in their respective states of confusion and apathy they said: "Ah, yes" and "That's right" when she took it upon herself to explain to each how the other felt. Dyar was bored, somewhat drunk, and faintly alarmed by Mme. Jouvenon's expression of fierce preoccupation, while she, desperately desirous of gaining his interest, was casting about frantically in her mind for a proper approach. With each minute that passed, the absurd situation in the cold little library became more untenable. Dyar shifted about on his chair and tried to see behind him through the doorway into the other room; he hoped to catch sight of Hadija. Someone put on a doleful Egyptian record. The groaning baritone voice filled the air.

"You have been to Cairo?" said Mme. Jouvenon suddenly.

"No." It did not seem enough to answer, but he had no further inspiration.

"You are inter-r-rested in the Middle East, also?"

"Madame Jouvenon has spent most of her life in Constantinople and Baghdad and Damascus, and other fascinating places," said Eunice.

"Not Baghdad," corrected Mme. Jouvenon sternly. "Bokhara."

"That must be interesting," said Dyar.

The Egyptian record was interrupted in mid-lament, and a French music-hall song replaced it. Then there was the sound of one of the heavy candelabra being overturned, accompanied by little cries of consternation. Taking advantage of the moment, which he felt might not present itself again even if he waited all night, Dyar sprang to his feet and rushed to the door. Directly behind him came Mme. Jouvenon, picking at his sleeve. She had decided to be bold. If, as Eunice Goode claimed, the young man was short of funds, it was likely he would accept an invitation to a meal, and so she promptly extended one for the following day, making it clear that he was to be her guest. "That's a splendid idea," said Eunice hurriedly. "I'm sure you two will have a great deal to give each other. Mr. Dyar has been in the consular service for years, and you probably have dozens of mutual friends." He did not even bother to correct her: she was too far gone, he thought. He had just had a glimpse of Hadija dancing with one of the Beidaoui brothers, and he turned to Mme. Jouvenon to decline her kind invitation. But he was not quick enough.

"At two tomorrow. At the Empire. You know where this is. The food is r-rather good. I will have the table at end, by where the bar is. This will give me gr-reat pleasure. We cannot speak here." And so it was settled, and he escaped to the table of drinks and got another.

"You rather bungled that," Eunice Goode murmured.

Mme. Jouvenon looked at her. "You mean he will not come?"

"*I* shouldn't if I were he. Your behavior. . . ." She stopped on catching sight of Hadija engaged in a rumba with Hassan Beidaoui; they smiled fatuously as they wriggled about. "The little idiot," she thought. The sight was all too reminiscent of the Bar Lucifer. "She's surely speaking Arabic with him." Uneasily she walked toward the dance floor, and presently was gratified to hear Hadija cry: "Oh, yes!" to something Hassan had said.

Without being invited this time, Dyar went and sat down beside Daisy. The room seemed immense, and much darker. He was feeling quite drunk; he slid down into a recumbent position and stretched his legs out straight in front of him, his head thrown back so that he was staring up at the dim white ceiling far above. Richard Holland sat in a chair facing Daisy, holding forth, with his wife nestling on the floor at his feet, her head on his knee. The old English lady with the turban was at the other end of the divan, smoking a cigarette in a very long, thin holder. Eunice Goode wandered over to the group, followed by Mme. Jouvenon, and stood behind Holland's chair drinking a glass of straight gin. She looked down at the back of his head, and said in a soft but unmistakably belligerent voice: "I don't know who you are, but I think that's all sheer balls."

He squirmed around and looked up at her; deciding she was drunk he ignored her, and went on talking. Presently Mme. Jouvenon whispered to Eunice that she must go, and the two went toward the door where Abdelmalek stood, his robes blowing in the breeze.

"Who is that extraordinary woman with Miss Goode?" asked the English lady. "I don't recall ever having seen her before." No one answered. "Don't any of you know?" she pursued fretfully.

"Yes," said Daisy at length. She hesitated a moment, and then, her voice taking on a vaguely mysterious tone: "I know who she is."

But Mme. Jouvenon had left quickly, and Eunice was already back, dragging a chair with her, which she installed as close as possible to Richard Holland's, and in which she proceeded to sit suddenly and heavily.

From time to time Dyar closed his eyes, only to open them again quickly when he felt the room sliding forward from under him. Looking at the multitude of shadows on the ceiling he did not think he felt the alcohol too much. But it became a chore to keep his eyes open for very long at a stretch. He heard the voices arguing around him; they seemed excited, and yet they were talking about nothing. They were loud, and yet they seemed far away. As he fixed one particular part of a monumental shadow stretching away into the darker regions of the ceiling, he had the feeling suddenly that he was seated there surrounded by dead people—or perhaps figures in a film that had been made a long time before. They were speaking, and he heard their voices, but the actual uttering of the words had been done many years ago. He must not let himself be fooled into believing that he could commu-

nicate with them. No one would hear him if he should try to speak. He felt
the cold rim of his glass on his leg where he held it; it had wet through his
trousers. With a spasmodic movement he sat up and took a long drink. If
only there had been someone to whom he could have said: "Let's get out
of here." But they all sat there in another world, talking feverishly about
nothing, approving and protesting, each one delighted with the sound his
own ideas made when they were turned into words. The alcohol was like
an ever-thickening curtain being drawn down across his mind, isolating it
from everything else in the room. It blocked out even his own body, which,
like the faces around him, the candle flames and the dance music, became
also increasingly remote and disconnected. "God damn it!" he cried sud-
denly. Daisy, intent on what Richard Holland was saying, distractedly
reached out and took his hand, holding it tightly so he could not withdraw
it without an effort. He let it lie in hers; the contact helped him a little to
focus his attention upon the conversation.

"Oh no!" said Holland, "The species is not at all intent on destroying
itself. That's nonsense. It's intent on being something which happens
inevitably to entail its destruction, that's all."

A man came through the door from the garden and walked quickly
across the room to where Abdelmalek stood talking with several of his
guests. Dyar was not alert enough to see his face as he moved through the
patches of light in the center of the room, but he thought the figure looked
familiar.

"Give me a sip," said Holland, reaching down and taking his wife's glass
out of her hand. "There's nothing wrong in the world except that man has
persuaded himself he's a rational being, when really he's a moral one. And
morality must have a religious basis, not a rational one. Otherwise it's just
play-acting."

The old English lady lit another cigarette, throwing the match on the
floor to join the wide pile of ashes she had scattered there. "That's all very
well," she said with a touch of petulance in her cracked voice, "but
nowadays religion and rationality are not mutually exclusive. We're not
living in the Dark Ages."

Holland laughed insolently; his eyes were malignant. "Do you want to
see it get dark?" he shouted. "Stick around a few years." And he laughed
again. No one said anything. He handed the glass back to Mrs. Holland. "I
don't think anyone will disagree if I say that religion all over the world is
just about dead."

"*I* certainly shall," said the English lady with asperity. "But no matter."

"I'm sorry, but in most parts of the world today, professing a religion is purely a matter of politics, and has practically nothing to do with faith. The Hindus are busy letting themselves be seen riding in Cadillacs instead of smearing themselves with sandalwood paste and bowing in front of Ganpati. The Moslems would rather miss evening prayer than the new Disney movie. The Buddhists think it's more important to take over in the name of Marx and Progress than to meditate on the four basic sorrows. And we don't even have to mention Christianity or Judaism. At least, I hope not. But there's absolutely nothing that can be done about it. You can't *decide* to be irrational. Man is rational now, and rational man is lost."

"I suppose," said the English lady acidly, "that you're going to tell us we can no longer choose between good and evil? It seems to me that would come next on your agenda."

"God, the man's pretentious," Daisy was thinking. As she grew increasingly bored and restive, she toyed with Dyar's fingers. And to himself Dyar said: "I don't want to listen to all this crap." He never had been one to believe that discussion of abstractions could lead to anything but more discussion. Yet he did listen, perhaps because in his profound egotism he felt that in some fashion Holland was talking about him.

"Oh, that!" said Holland, pretending to sound infinitely patient. "Good and evil are like white and black on a piece of paper. To distinguish them you need at least a glimmer of light, otherwise you can't even see the paper. And that's the way it is now. It's gotten too dark to tell." He snickered. "Don't talk to *me* about the Dark Ages. Right now no one could presume to know where the white ends and the black begins. We know they're both there, that's all."

"Well, I must say I'm glad to hear we know that much, at least," said the English lady testily. "I was on the point of concluding that there was absolutely no hope." She laughed mockingly.

Holland yawned. "Oh, it'll work itself out, all right. Until then, it would be better not to be here. But if anyone's left afterward, they'll fix it all up irrationally and the world will be happy again."

Daisy was examining Dyar's palm, but the light was too dim. She dropped the hand and began to arrange her hair, preparatory to getting up. "*Enfin*, none of it sounds very hopeful," she remarked, smiling.

"It *isn't* very hopeful," Holland said pityingly; he enjoyed his role as diagnostician of civilization's maladies, and he always arrived at a negative prognosis. He would happily have continued all night with an appreciative audience.

"Excuse me. I've got to have another drink," said Dyar, lunging up onto his feet. He took a few steps forward, turned partially around and smiled at Daisy, so as not to seem rude, and saw Mrs. Holland rise from her uncomfortable position on the floor to occupy the place on the divan which he had just vacated. Then he went on, found himself through the door, standing on the balcony in the damp night wind. There seemed to be no reason for not going down the wide stairs, and so he went softly down and walked along the path in the dark until he came to a wall. There was a bench; he sat down in the quiet and stared ahead of him at the nearby silhouettes of moving branches and vines. No music, no voices, not even the fountains could be heard here. But there were other closer sounds: the leaves of plants rubbed together, stalks and pods hardened by the winter rattled and shook, and high in a palmyra tree not far away the dry slapping of an enormous fan-shaped branch (it covered and uncovered a certain group of stars as it waved back and forth) was like the distant slamming of an old screen door. It was difficult to believe a tree in the wind could make that hard, vaguely mechanical noise.

For a while he sat quite still in the dark, with nothing in his mind save an awareness of the natural sounds around him; he did not even realize that he was welcoming these sounds as they washed through him, that he was allowing them to cleanse him of the sense of bitter futility which had filled him for the past two hours. The cold wind eddied around the shrubbery at the base of the wall; he hugged himself but did not move. Shortly he would have to rise and go back into the light, up the steps into the room whose chaos was only the more clearly perceived for the polite gestures of the people who filled it. For the moment he stayed sitting in the cold. "Here I am," he told himself once again, but this time the melody, so familiar that its meaning was gone, was faintly transformed by the ghost of a new harmony beneath it, scarcely perceptible and at the same time, merely because it was there at all, suggestive of a direction to be taken which made those three unspoken words more than a senseless reiteration. He might have been saying to himself: "Here I am and something is going to happen." The infinitesimal promise of a possible change stirred him to physical movement: he unwrapped his arms from around himself and lit a cigarette.

Back in the room Eunice Goode, on her way to being a little more drunk than usual (the presence of many people around her often led her to such excesses), was in a state of nerves. A recently arrived guest, a young man whom she did not know, and who in spite of his European attire was obviously a Moslem, had come up to Hadija as she and Eunice stood together by the phonograph, and greeted her familiarly in Arabic. Fortunately Hadija had had the presence of mind to answer: "What you sigh?" before turning her back on him, but that had not ended the incident. A moment later, while Eunice was across the room having her glass replenished, the two had somehow begun to dance. When she returned and saw them she had wanted terribly to step in and separate them, but of course there was no way she could do such a thing without having an excuse of some sort. "I shall make a fearful scene if I start," she said to herself, and so she hovered about the edge of the dance floor, now and then catching hold of a piece of furniture for support. At least, as long as she remained close to Hadija the girl would not be so likely to speak Arabic. That was the principal danger.

Hadija was in misery. She had not wanted to dance (indeed, she considered that her days of enforced civility to strange men, and above all Moslem men, had come to a triumphant close), but he had literally grabbed her. The young man, who was squeezing her against him with such force that she had difficulty in breathing, refused to speak anything but Arabic with her, even though she kept her face set in an intransigent mask of hauteur and incomprehension. "Everyone knows you're a Tanjaouia," he was saying. But she fought down the fear that his words engendered. Only her two protectors, Eunice and the American gentleman, knew. Several times she tried to push him away and stop dancing, but he only held her with increased firmness, and she realized unhappily that any more vehement efforts on her part would attract the attention of the other dancers, of whom there were now only two couples. Occasionally she said in a loud voice: "O.K." or "Oh, yes!" so as to reassure Eunice, whom she saw watching her desperately.

"*Ch' aândek?* What's the matter with you? What are you trying to do?" the young man was saying indignantly. "Are you ashamed of being a Moslem? It's very bad, what you are doing. You think I don't remember you from the Bar Lucifer? Ha! *Hamqat, entina! Hamqat!*" His breath smelled strongly of the brandy he had been drinking all day.

Hadija was violently indignant. "*Ana hamqat?*" she began, and realized too late that she had given herself away. The young man laughed delightedly, and tried to get her to go on, but she froze into absolute silence.

Finally she cried out in Arabic: "You're hurting me!" and breaking from his embrace hurried to Eunice's side, where she stood rubbing her shoulder. "Wan fackin bastard," she said under her breath to Eunice, who had witnessed her linguistic indiscretion and realized that as far as the young man was concerned the game was up.

"Shut up!" She seized Hadija's arm and pulled her off into an empty corner.

"I want wan Coca-Cola," objected Hadija. "Very hot. That lousy guy dance no good."

"Who is he, anyway?"

"Wan Moorish man live in Tangier."

"I know, but who? What's he doing in the Beidaoui Palace?"

"He plenty drunk."

Eunice mused a moment, letting go of Hadija's arm. With as much dignity as she could summon, she strode across the room toward Hassan Beidaoui, who, seeing her coming, turned around and managed to be talking animatedly with Mme. Werth by the time she reached him. The maneuver proved quite worthless, of course, since Eunice's piercing "I say" began while she was still ten feet away. She tapped Hassan's arm and he faced her patiently, prepared to listen to another series of incomprehensible reminiscences about Crown Prince Rupprecht.

"I say!" She indicated Hadija's recent dancing partner. "I say, isn't that the eldest son of the Pacha of Fez? I'm positive I remember him from Paris."

"No," said Hassan quietly. "That is my brother Thami. Would you like to meet him?" (This suggestion was prompted less by a feeling of amiability toward Eunice Good than by one of spite toward Thami, whose unexpected appearance both Hassan and Abdelmalek considered an outrage. They had suggested he leave, but being a little drunk he had only laughed. If anyone present could precipitate his departure, thought Hassan, it was this outlandish American woman.) "Will you come?" He held out his arm. Eunice reflected quickly, and said she would be delighted.

She was not surprised to find Thami exactly the sort of Moroccan she most disliked and habitually inveighed against: outwardly Europeanized but inwardly conscious that the desired metamorphosis would remain forever unaccomplished, and therefore defiant, on the offensive to conceal his defeat, irresponsible and insolent. For his part, Thami behaved in a particularly obnoxious fashion. He was in a foul humor, having met with no success either in attempting to get the money for the boat from his brothers, or in persuading them to agree to the sale of his house in the Marshan. And again, this hideous woman was his idea of the typical tourist who admired his race only insofar as its members were picturesque.

"You want us all to be snake-charmers and scorpion-eaters," he raged, at one point in their conversation, which he had inevitably maneuvered in such a direction as to permit him to make his favorite accusations.

"Naturally," Eunice replied in her most provoking manner. "It would be far preferable to being a nation of tenth-rate pseudo-civilized rug-sellers." She smiled poisonously, and then belched in his face.

At that moment Dyar came in. The candlelight seemed bright to him and he blinked his eyes. Seeing Thami in the center of the room, he looked surprised for an instant, and then went up to him and greeted him warmly. Without seeming to see Eunice, he took him by the arm and led him aside. "I want to settle my little debt with you, from the other night."

"Oh, that's all right," said Thami, looking at him expectantly. And as the money changed hands, Thami said: "She's here. You have seen her?"

"Yeah, sure."

"You brought her?"

"No. Miss Goode over there." Dyar jerked his chin in her direction, and Thami fell to thinking.

From where she stood Eunice watched them, saw Dyar slip some notes into Thami's hand, and guessed correctly that Thami had been the friend who had lent him the money to pay Hadija at the Bar Lucifer. It was the realization of her worst fears, and in her present unbalanced state she built it up into a towering nightmare. The two men held her entire future happiness in their hands. If anyone had observed her face closely at that moment, he would unhesitatingly have declared her mad, and he would probably have moved quickly away from her. It had suddenly flashed upon her, the realization of how supremely happy she had been at the Beidaouis' this evening—at least, it seemed so to her now. Hadija belonged completely to her, she had been accepted, was even having a small success at the moment as Miss Kumari, chatting in monosyllables with Dr. Waterman in a corner. But Miss Kumari's feet were planted at the edge of a precipice, and it required the merest push from either of the two men there (she clenched her fists) to topple her over the brink. The American was the more dangerous, however, and she already had set in motion the apparatus that was destined to get rid of him. "It can't fail," she thought desperately. But of course it could fail. There was no particular reason to believe that he would keep the appointment so clumsily arranged by Mme. Jouvenon for tomorrow, nor were there any grounds for confidence in her ability to make matters go as they were supposed to go. She opened her mouth wide and after some difficulty belched again. The room was going away from her; she felt it draining off into darkness. Making a tremendous effort, she prevented herself from tipping sideways toward the floor, and took a few steps forward, perhaps with the intention of speaking to Dyar. But the effort was too much. Her final remaining energy was used in reaching a nearby empty chair; she slid into it and lost consciousness.

Daisy had joined Dyar, without, however, paying any notice to Thami, who unobtrusively walked away. "Good God!" she cried, seeing Eunice's collapse. "That's a lovely sight. I don't intend to be delegated to carry it home, though, which is exactly what will happen unless I leave." She paused, and seemed to be changing her mind. "No! Her little Greek friend can just call a taxi and the servants can dump her in. I'm damned if I'll play chauffeur to Uncle Goode, and I'm damned if I'll go home to keep from doing it, either. Hassan—aren't they both sweet? don't you love them?—" Dyar assented. "—He's offered to show us the great room, and that doesn't happen every day. I've seen it only once, and I'm longing to see it again. So there's going to be no victim here, making a Red Cross ambulance out of the car, and going up that fiendish narrow street to the Metropole. God!" She paused, then went on. "They're not ready to take us yet. They want to wait till a few more people have left. But I must talk to you before you disappear again. I saw you run out, darling. You've got to stop acting like a pariah. Come over here and sit down. I've got two things to say to you, and both are important, and not very pleasant."

"What do you mean?"

"Just let me do the talking, and listen." They sat down on the same divan where they had been sitting a half hour ago. The fresh air had made him feel better, and he had decided not to take any more whiskey. She laid her hand on his arm; the diamonds of her bracelets shone in the candlelight. "I'm practically certain Jack Wilcox is about to get himself into trouble. It seems *most* suspicious, the fact that he's keeping you out of his office. The moment you told me that, I knew something peculiar was going on. He's always been an ass in his business dealings, and he's no less of one now.

By ass I mean stupidly careless. God, the idiots and scoundrels he's taken
into his confidence! You know, everyone here's got some little peccadillo
he's hoping to hide. You know, *ça va sans dire.* Everyone has to make a
living, and here no one asks questions. But Jack practically *advertises* his
business indiscretions. He can't make a move now without the entire scum
of the Zone knowing about it. Which would be all right if there were any
protection, which obviously there can't be in such cases. You just have to
take your chances."

Dyar was listening, but at the same time he was uneasily watching the
other end of the room where he had observed Hadija and Thami engaged
in what appeared to be an intense and very private conversation. *"What* are
you talking about?" he demanded rudely, turning suddenly to stare at her.

Daisy misinterpreted his question. "My dear, certainly no one but an
imbecile would think of trying to enlist the help of the Police in such
matters. I love Jack; I think he's a dear. But I certainly think you should
be warned. *Don't* get involved in any of his easy-money schemes. They
crack up. There are plenty of ways of making a living here, and quite as
easy, without risking getting stabbed or shot."

Now Dyar looked at her squarely and laughed.

"I know I'm drunk," she said. "But I also know what I'm saying. I can
see you're going to laugh even more at the other thing I've got to tell you."
Dyar cast a troubled glance behind him at Hadija and Thami.

Daisy's voice was suddenly slightly harsh. "Oh, stop breaking your
neck. He's not going to run off with your girlfriend."

Dyar turned his head back swiftly and faced her, his mouth open a little
with astonishment. "What?"

She laughed. "Why are you so surprised? I told you everyone knows
everything here. What do you think I have a good pair of Zeiss field-glasses
in my bedroom for, darling? You didn't know I had such a thing? Well,
I have, and they were in use today. There's a short stretch of shore-line
visible from one corner of the room. But that's not what I was going to tell
you," she went on, as Dyar, trying to picture to himself just what incidents
of his outing she might have seen, felt his face growing hot. "I'd like to sock
her in that smug face," he thought, but she caught the unspoken phrase.
"You're angry with me, darling, aren't you?" He said nothing. "I don't
blame you. It was a low thing to do, but I'm making amends for it now
by giving you some *very* valuable advice." She began to speak more slowly
and impressively. "Madame Jouvenon, that frightful little woman you went

off into the other room with, is a Russian agent. A spy, if you like the word better." She sat back and squinted at him, as if to measure the effect of that piece of news.

It seemed to have brought him around to a better humor, for he chuckled, took her hand and smoothed the fingers slowly; she made no effort to withdraw it. "At least," she continued, "I've heard it from two distinct sources, neither of which I have any reason to doubt. Of course, it's a perfectly honorable way of making a living, and we all have our agents around, and I daresay she's not even a particularly efficient one, but there you are. So those are my two little warnings for tonight, my dear young man, and you can take them or leave them, whichever you like." She pulled her hand away to smooth her hair. "I shouldn't have told you, really. God knows how much of a chatterbox you are. But if you quote me I shall deny ever having said a word."

"I'll *bet* you would. And the same goes for the room in Marrakech. Right?"

She took the tip of one of his fingers between her thumb and forefinger, squeezed it hard, and looked at him seriously a moment before she said: "I suppose you think that was immoral."

The company was thinning; people were leaving now in groups. Abdelmalek and Hassan Beidaoui stood one on each side of the door, bowing and smiling. There were not more than ten guests left, including the Hollands, who had found an old swing record in the pile, and were now doing some very serious jitterbugging, alone on the floor. One of the two Moroccan gentlemen stood watching them, an expression of satisfaction on his face, as though at last he were seeing what he had come here to see.

Thami and Hadija still conversed, but the important points in their talk had all been touched upon, with the result that Thami now suspected that the money for his boat might conceivably be donated by Eunice Goode. Many members of the lower stratum of society in Tangier naturally knew perfectly well who Hadija was, but there was next to no contact between that world of cast-off clothing, five-peseta cognac and cafés whose patrons sat on mats smoking kif and playing ronda, and this other more innocent world up here in which it was only one step from wanting a thing to having it. Nevertheless, he knew both worlds; he was the point of contact. It was a privileged position and he felt it could be put to serious use. Nothing of all this had been said to Hadija; encouraged by him she had told all the important facts. No Moroccan is foolish enough to let another Moroccan know that both are stalking the same prey—after all, there is only a limited amount of flesh on any given carcass. And while the tentative maximum set by Thami was only whatever the price of the boat should finally turn out to be, still, he knew that Hadija would consider as her rightful property every peseta that went to him. Like most girls with her training, basically Hadija thought only in terms of goods delivered and payment received; it did not occur to her that often the largest sums go to those who agree to do nothing more than stay out of the way. This is not to say that she was unaware of the position of power enjoyed by Thami in the present situation. "You won't say a word?" she whispered anxiously.

"We're friends. More than friends," he assured her, looking steadily into her eyes. "Like brother and sister. And Muslimin, both of us. How could I betray my sister?"

She was satisfied. But he continued. "And tonight, what are you doing?" She knew what that meant. If it had to be, there was nothing to do about it, and tonight was the most likely time, with Eunice in her present state. Hadija glanced across at the massive body sprawled on the chair.

"Call a taxi," went on Thami. "Get the servants to put her in. Take her home and see that she's in bed. Meet me outside the Wedad pastry shop in the dark part there at the foot of the steps to the garden. I'll be there before you, so you won't have to wait."

"Ouakha," she agreed. She was going to get nothing for it, yet it had to be done. To remain Miss Kumari she must go back and be the Hadija of the pink room behind the Bar Lucifer. She looked at him with undissimulated hatred. He saw it and laughed; it made her more desirable.

"Little sister," he murmured, his lips so close to the lobe of her ear that they brushed it softly in forming the word.

She got up. Save for Eunice they were alone in the room. The remaining guests had gone out, were being taken through the blue court, the jasmine court, the marble pavilion, to the vast, partially ruined ballroom where several sultans had dined. But Hadija was too much perturbed to notice that she had not been invited to make the tour along with the others.

"You call a taxi. The telephone is in there." He indicated the little library. "I'll take care of her." He went out to the entrance lodge and got two of the guards to come in and carry Eunice to the gate, where they laid her on a mat along one of the niches until the cab arrived. He sat in front with the driver and went along as far as Bou Araqía, where he got out and after saying a word through the open window to Hadija, walked off into the dark in the direction of the Zoco de Fuera.

The European guests were not taken back into the European wing; Abdelmalek and Hassan led them directly to the gate on the street, bade them a gracious good-bye, and stepped behind the high portals which were closed and noisily bolted. It was a little like the expulsion from Eden, thought Daisy, and she turned and grinned at the Hollands.

"May I drive you to your hotel?" she offered.

They protested that it was nearby, but Daisy snorted with impatience. She knew she was going to take them home, and she wanted to start. "Get in," she said gruffly. "It's a mile at least to the Pension Acacias."

The final good nights were called as the other guests drove off.

"But it's out of your way," objected Richard Holland.

"Stuff and nonsense! Get in! How do you know where I'm going? I've got to meet Luis more or less in that neighborhood."

"Sh! What's that?" Mrs. Holland held up a silencing finger. From somewhere in the dark on the other side of the street came a faint chorus of high, piercing mews.

"Oh, God! It's a family of abandoned kittens," moaned Daisy. "The Moors are always doing it. When they're born they simply throw them out in a parcel into the street like garbage."

"The poor things!" cried Mrs. Holland, starting across the pavement toward the sound.

"Come back here!" shouted her husband. "Where do you think you're going?"

She hesitated. Daisy had got into the car, and sat at the wheel.

"I'm afraid it's hopeless, darling," she said to Mrs. Holland.

"Come *on!*" Holland called. Reluctantly she returned and got in. When she was beside him in the back seat he said: "What did you think you were going to do?"

She sounded vague. "I don't know. I thought we might take them somewhere and give them some milk." The car started up, skirting the wall for a moment and then turning through a park of high eucalyptus trees.

Dyar, sitting in front with Daisy, and infinitely thankful to be out of the Beidaoui residence, felt pleasantly relaxed. He had been listening to the little scene with detached interest, rather as if it were part of a radio program, and he expected now to hear an objection from Holland based on grounds of practicality. Instead he heard him say: "Why in hell try to keep them alive? They're going to die anyway, sooner or later."

Dyar turned his head sideways and shouted against the trees going by: "So are you, Holland. But in the meantime you eat, don't you?"

There was no reply. In the back, unprotected from the wet sea wind, the Hollands were shivering.

The Spider's House

There were four cafés on the square, and each one had a large space in front of it which was ordinarily full of tables and chairs. Today, these had prudently not been set out, so that the sides of the square presented a deserted aspect which was emphasized by the fact that the center also was empty, for no one was walking in it. True, it was hot, and there would have been few strollers at this hour in any case, but the absence of people was so complete that the scene—even if the line of police could have been disregarded—had no element of the casualness which ordinarily gave the place its character.

"*Very* strange," Stenham muttered.

"Am I wrong," she said, "or does this look sort of sinister?"

"Come on." He took her arm and they hurried across to the café nearest the waiting buses. One of the *mokhaznia* standing by the footbridge across the stream looked at them dubiously, but did not stop them from passing. In the café, a group of thirty or forty men sat and stood quietly near the windows, peering out through the hanging fronds of the pepper trees at the emptiness of the sunny square. More than by the unusual tenseness of these faces, Stenham was at once struck by the silence of the place, by the realization that no one was talking, or, if someone did speak, it was in a low voice scarcely pitched above a whisper. Of course, without the radio there was no need to shout as they ordinarily had to do, but he felt that even had the radio been playing, together with all its extra amplifiers for the smaller rooms, they still would only have murmured. And he did not like the expressions on their faces when they looked up and saw him. It was the first time in many years that he had read enmity in Moroccan faces. Once more than twenty years ago he had ventured alone inside the *horm* of Moulay Idriss—not the sanctuary itself, but the streets surrounding it—and then he had seen hatred on a few faces; he had never forgotten the feeling it had given him. It was a physical thing that those fierce faces had confronted him with, and his reaction to it had likewise been purely physical; he had felt his spine stiffen and the hair at the back of his neck bristle.

He began to speak with Lee in a loud voice, not paying much attention to what he was saying, but using what he thought would be an unmistakably American intonation. He saw her glance at him once with surprise.

"There are a lot of little rooms out in the back," he went on. "Let's get one that's not so crowded." She was annoyed; he could see that. He could also see that the only result his bit of play-acting had brought him was that a good many more of the bearded, turbaned and *tarbouched* individuals had looked away from the window and were staring at them with equally hostile countenances.

"Let's just sit anywhere and stop being so conspicuous," she said nervously; at the same time she took several steps toward an unoccupied table by the wall opposite the entrance. But Stenham wanted, if it were possible, to get out of the range of these unfriendly faces. In the next room they found a party of elderly men from the country sprawled out, smoking kif and eating. A boy stood in the doorway to a further room. Behind him the room appeared to be empty. Stenham stepped across and peered in; the boy did not move. There was no one in there at all. Through a back window he caught sight of a sheet of water shining in the sun.

"Lee!" he called. She slipped through the doorway and they sat down.

"Are you yelling so they'll think you're an American? Is that it?" she demanded.

"It's very important they shouldn't think we're French, at least."

"But you sounded so funny!" She began to laugh. "It would have been so much more effective if you'd just roared: 'O.K., give money, twenty dollar, very good, yes, no, get outa here, god damned son of a bitch!' Perhaps they'd have gotten the point then. The way you did it, I don't think you got it across to them for a minute."

"Well, I did my best." Now that he was in the inner room out of sight of the inimical faces, he felt better.

Presently the waiter came in with a glass of tea for the boy at the other table. Stenham ordered tea and pastries.

"Damnation!" he said. "I forgot to leave a note for Moss."

"It's my fault," she declared.

"Very sweet of you, but completely untrue."

"You could phone him."

"No. There's no phone here. I don't know. Sometimes I wonder what's wrong with me. I know just how to behave, but only before or after the fact. When the moment's there in front of me, I don't seem to function."

"You're no different from anybody else," she said.

He suspected that she was waiting for an adverse reaction to this statement, so he said nothing. They were both silent for a minute. The Arab boy was sipping his tea with the customary Moslem noisiness. Stenham, in good spirits, did not mind his presence; he was a bit of native decoration. He would not have objected even if the boy had begun to make the loud belches that polite Moroccans make when they wish to show their appreciation of what they have eaten or drunk. The boy however did not belch; instead he rose from his table and taking up a good-sized stone from the floor, started to pound on the bolt of the door that led to the little garden outside. Stenham leaned across the table and took Lee's hand. He had never noticed the wedding ring until this minute—a simple gold band. "It's good to see you," he told her, and then immediately wished he had sat still and said nothing, for at the contact of his hand her face had clouded. "It's always good to see you," he added with less buoyancy, watching her closely. For a time she seemed to be trying to decide whether or not to speak. Then she said: "Why do you do that?"

"Why shouldn't I?" He spoke quietly because he wanted to avoid stirring up another argument.

Her expression was one of utter candor. "Because it puts me in a false position," she told him. "It makes me so uncomfortable. I can't help feeling that something's expected of me. I feel I should either go coquettish or prudish on you, and I don't want to be either one."

"Why don't you just be natural?" he suggested gently.

"I'm *trying* to be natural now," she said with impatience, "but you don't seem to understand. You put me in a position where it's next to impossible to be natural."

"Is it that bad?" he said, smiling sadly.

"They say you can't tell any man that you don't find him sexually attractive, that a woman's whole success in life is based on the principle of making every man feel that given the right circumstances she'd rush to bed with him. But I think there must be a few men bright enough to hear the news without going into a fit of depression. Don't you think so?" She smiled provocatively.

He said slowly: "I think you know that isn't true. What's being bright got to do with it? You might as well say an intelligent man won't mind being hungry as much as a slow-witted one will."

"Well, maybe that's true," she said gaily. "Who knows?"

He was hurt; to keep her from knowing it he held her hand tighter. "I'm not that easy to discourage," he assured her lightly. She shrugged and looked down at the table. "I was just being friendly," she pouted. "Because I really like you. I like just being with you. If that isn't enough—" she shrugged again— "well, then, the hell with it."

"Fine, fine. Maybe you'll change."

"Maybe I will. I like to think I have an open mind."

He did not answer, but sat back and looked out the window. The boy had taken off his shoes and was wading in the pool, a sight which, because of his state of mind, did not at once strike him as peculiar. When he saw him bend over and fish a large, bedraggled insect out of the water, he became interested. Now the boy held his hand very close to his face, studying his prey, smiling at it; he even moved his lips a few times, as though he were talking to it.

"What is it? What are you staring at?" she asked.

"Trying to make out what that kid's doing out there, standing in the middle of the water."

Suddenly the insect had flown away. The boy stood looking after it, his face expressing satisfaction rather than the disappointment Stenham had expected to see. He climbed out of the pool and sat down at its edge where he had been before.

Stenham shook his head. "Now, that was a strange bit of behavior. The boy made a special trip into the water just to pull out some kind of insect."

"Well, he's kind-hearted."

"I know, but they're not. That's the whole point. In all my time here I've never seen anyone do a thing like that."

He looked at the boy's round face, heavy, regular features, and curly black hair.

"He could be a Sicilian, or a Greek," he said as if to himself. "If he's not a Moroccan, there's nothing surprising about his deed. But if he is, then I give up. Moroccans just don't do things like that."

Lee stood up briefly and looked out the window; then she sat down again. "He looks like the model for all the worst paintings foreigners did in Italy a hundred years ago. *Boy at Fountain, Gipsy Carrying Water Jar;* you know?"

"You want another tea?"

"No!" she said. "One's plenty. It's so sweet. But anyway, I don't believe you can make such hard and fast general rules about people."

"You can in this case. I've watched them for years. I know what they're like."

"That doesn't mean you know what each one is like individually, after all."

"But the whole point is, they're not individuals in the sense you mean," he said.

"You're on dangerous ground," she warned him.

For fear that she might take exception to his words, he was quiet, did not attempt to explain to her how living among a less evolved people enabled him to see his own culture from the outside, and thus to understand it better. It was her express desire that all races and all individuals be "equal," and she would accept no demonstration which did not make use of that axiom. In truth, he decided, it was impossible to discuss anything at all with her, because instead of seeing each part of total reality as a complement to the other parts, with dogged insistence she forged ahead seeing only those things which she could twist into the semblance of an illustration for her beliefs.

From somewhere outside there came a faint sound which, if he had not known it was being made by human voices, he might have imagined sounded like the wind soughing through pine branches. The boy, who sat by the pool as though he were the express reason for the sun's existence at that moment, seemed to hear the sound, too. Stenham glanced at Lee: apparently she heard nothing. There were only two bits of stage business, he reflected, of which she was capable. One was to pull out her compact and occupy herself by looking into its mirror, and the other was to light a cigarette. On this occasion she used the compact.

He watched her. For her the Moroccans were backward onlookers standing on the sidelines of the parade of progress; they must be exhorted to join, if necessary pulled by force into the march. Hers was the attitude of the missionary, but whereas the missionary offered a complete if unusable code of thought and behavior, the modernizer offered nothing at all, save a place in the ranks. And the Moslems, who with their blind intuitive wisdom had triumphantly withstood the missionaries' cajoleries, now were going to be duped into joining the senseless march of universal brotherhood; for the privilege each man would have to give up only a small part of himself—just enough to make him incomplete, so that instead of looking into his own heart, to Allah, for reassurance, he would have to look to the others. The new world would be a triumph of frustration, where all humanity would be lifting itself by its own bootstraps—the equality of the damned. No wonder the religious leaders of Islam identified Western culture with the works of Satan: they had seen the truth and were expressing it in the simplest terms.

The sound of shouting suddenly increased in volume; it was obviously coming from a moving column of men. How many thousand throats did it take, he wondered, to make a sound like that?

"Listen," said Lee.

The progress through the streets was slow, and the acoustics, changing from moment to moment, brought the sound nearer, then removed it to a more distant plane. But it was clear that the crowd was on its way up toward Bou Jeloud.

"Here comes your trouble," he said to her.

She bit her upper lip for a second, and looked at him distraughtly. "What do you think we ought to do? Get out?"

"Sure, if you like."

The boy came through the door, glanced shyly at them, and turned to sit down at his table. Stenham called out to him: *"Qu'est-ce qui se passe dehors?"* The boy stared at him, uncomprehending. So he was a Moroccan, after all. *"Smahli,"* Stenham said. *"Chnou hadek el haraj?"*

The other looked at him with wide eyes, clearly wondering how anyone could be so stupid. "That's people yelling," he said.

"Are they happy or angry?" Stenham wanted to know.

The boy struggled to keep his sudden suspiciousness from becoming visible in his face. He smiled, and said: "Maybe some are happy, some are angry. Each man knows what is in his own heart."

"A philosopher," Stenham laughed in an aside to Lee.

"What does he say? What is it?" she asked impatiently.

"He's being cagey. *Egless.*" He indicated the third chair at their table, and the boy sat down carefully, never taking his eyes from Stenham's face. "I'd better offer him a cigarette," Stenham said, and did so. The boy refused, smiling. "Tea?" asked Stenham. "I've drunk it. Thank you," said the boy.

"Ask him what he thinks about staying here," Lee said nervously.

"You can't hurry these people," he told her. "You get nothing out of them if you do."

"I know, but if we're going to go we should go, don't you think?"

"Well, yes, if we are. But I'm not sure it's such a good idea to go out there running around looking for a cab now, do you think?"

"You're the expert. How should I know? But for God's sake try and make sense at this point. I don't feel like being massacred."

He laughed, then turned his head to face her completely. "Lee, if I thought there were any serious danger you don't think I'd have suggested coming here, do you?"

"How do I know what you'd have suggested? I'm just telling you that if there's any question of a mob smashing into this café I want to get out now, and not wait until it's too late."

"What's this sudden hysteria?" he demanded. "I don't understand."

"Hysteria!" She laughed scornfully. "I don't think you've ever seen a hysterical woman in your life."

"Listen. If you want to go, we'll go now."

"That's just what I *didn't* say. I merely asked you to be serious and realize that you've got the responsibility for us both, and act accordingly. That's all."

What a schoolmarm, he thought angrily. "All right," he said. "Let's sit right here. This is an Arab café. There are about fifty police outside and there's a *poste de garde* right across the square. I don't know where we could be safer, except in the Ville Nouvelle. Certainly not in the hotel."

She did not answer. The noise of the crowd had become much louder; it sounded now like prolonged cheering. He turned to the boy again.

"The people are coming this way."

"Yes," said the boy; it was evident that he did not want to discuss the subject. Another tack, a different approach, thought Stenham, but not a personal one, either. "Do you like this café?" he said after a moment, remembering too late that statements were better than questions in the task of trying to establish contact with the Moroccans.

The boy hesitated. "I like it," he said grudgingly, "but it's not a good café."

"I thought it was a good café. I like it. It has water on both sides."

"Yes," the boy admitted. "I like to come and sit. But it's not a good café." He lowered his voice. "The owner has buried something outside the door. That's not good."

Stenham, bewildered, said: "I see."

The noise now could not be disregarded; its rhythmical chanting had grown into a gigantic roar, unmistakably of anger, and it was at last possible to hear details in its pattern. It had ceased being a unified wall of sound, and become instead a great, turbulent mass of innumerable separate human cries.

"*Smahli,*" said the boy. "I'm going to look." Quickly he rose and went out of the room.

"Are you nervous?" Stenham asked her.

"Well, I'm not exactly relaxed. Give me a cigarette. I've run out."

While he was lighting her cigarette there came the sound of one lone shot—a small dull pop which nevertheless carried above the roar of voices. They both froze; the roar subsided for a second or two, then rose to a chaos of frenzy. Their wide eyes met, but only by accident. Then from what they would have said was the front of the café there was a phrase of machine-gun fire, a short sequence of rapidly repeated, shattering explosions.

They both jumped up and ran to the door. The other room was empty now, Stenham noticed as they went through it, save for one old man sitting on the floor in the corner, holding a kif pipe in his hand. They went only as far as the doorway of the large front room. There men were still falling over each other in their haste to get to the windows. Two waiters were sliding enormous bolts across the closed entrance door. When they had finished doing that they hurriedly pushed a large chest in front of the door, and wedged tables between it and a pillar near by. They did the work automatically, as though it were the only reaction conceivable in such a situation. Then they went behind a wall of bottle cases and peered worriedly out a small window there. From where they stood in the inner doorway Lee and Stenham could see, through the florid designs of the grillwork in the windows, only a series of senseless vignettes which had as their background the hard earth of the square. Occasionally part of a running figure passed through one of the frames. The noise at the moment was largely one of screaming; there was also the tinkle of shattering glass at intervals. Suddenly, like so many huge motors starting up, machine-guns fired from all around the square. When they had finished, there was relative silence, broken by a few single revolver shots from further away. A police whistle sounded, and it was even possible to hear individual voices shouting commands in French. A man standing in one of the windows in front of them began to beat on the grillwork like a caged animal, shrieking imprecations; hands reached out from beside him and pulled him back, and a brief struggle ensued as he was forced to the floor by his companions. Stenham seized Lee by the wrist and wheeled her around, saying: "Come on." They returned to their little room.

"Sit down," said Stenham. Then he stepped out into the sunlight, looked up at the walls around the patio, sighed, and went back in. "No way out there," he said. "We'll just have to sit here."

Lee did not reply; she sat looking down at the table, her chin cupped in her hands. He observed her: he could not be certain, but it seemed to him that she was shivering. He put his hand on her shoulder, felt it tremble.

"Wouldn't you like some hot tea, without the sugar?" he asked her.

"It's all right," she said after a pause, without glancing up. "I'm all right."

He stood there helplessly, looking down at her. "Maybe——"

"Please sit down."

Automatically he obeyed. Then he lighted a cigarette. Presently she raised her head. "Give me one," she said. Her teeth were chattering. "I might as well smoke. I can't do anything else."

Someone was standing in the doorway. Swiftly Stenham turned his head. It was the boy, staring at them. Stenham rose and went over, pulling him with him out into the next room. The old man still sprawled in the corner in a cloud of kif smoke.

"Try and get a glass of tea for the *mra*," he told the boy, who did not appear to understand. "The lady wants some tea." He's looking at me as though I were a talking tree, thought Stenham. He took the boy's arm and squeezed it, but there was no reaction. The eyes were wide, and there was nothing in them. He looked back into the room and saw Lee hunched over the table, sobbing. Pulling the boy by the arm, he led him to the chair beside her and made him sit down. Then he went out to the main room to the alcove where the fire was, and ordered three teas from the *qaouaji;* he too seemed to be in a state bordering on catalepsy. "Three teas, three teas," Stenham repeated. "One with only a little sugar." It'll give him something to do, he thought.

The feeble chaos outside was now almost covered by the voices of the onlookers within the café. They were not talking loud, but they spoke with frantic intensity, and all together, so that no one was listening to anyone else. Happily, this occupied them; they paid him no attention. He felt that if he left the *qaouaji* to prepare the tea and bring it by himself, he would be likely to fall back into his lethargy; he determined to remain with him until it was ready. From where he stood, through the small window in front of him, he could see only a part of the center of the square. Usually it was empty, but when a figure appeared, moving across the space made by the window's frame, it was always a policeman or a *mokhazni*. What had happened was fairly clear: the crowd had attempted to pass out of the Medina through Bab Bou Jeloud, and had been stopped at the gate itself. Now there were small skirmishes taking place well within the gate as the marchers retreated. When he heard a cavalcade of trucks begin to arrive, he knew it would be safe to go and look out the window, and so he squeezed himself into the narrow corridor between the piles of cases of empty bottles and the wall, and went to peer out. There were four big army trucks and they had drawn up in a line behind the two abandoned buses. Berber soldiers in uniform, their rifles in their hands, were still leaping out of the backs of the trucks, running toward the gate. There must be about two hundred of them, he calculated.

Now a slow massacre would begin, inside the walls, in the streets and alleys, until every city-dweller who was able had reached some sort of shelter and no one was left outside but the soldiers. Even as he was thinking this, the pattern of the shooting changed from single, desultory shots to whole volleys of them, like strings of fire-crackers exploding. He stood there watching tensely, although there was nothing to see; it was like seeing a newsreel of the event, where what is presented is the cast of characters and the situation before and afterward, but never the action itself. Even the gunfire might as well have been a sound-track; it was hard to believe that the rifles he had seen two minutes before were at this moment being used to kill people; were firing the shots that he was hearing. If you had had no previous contact with this sort of violence, he reflected, even when it was happening where you were, it remained unreal.

He went back to the alcove where the fire was, and was pleasantly surprised to see that the *qaouaji* had nearly finished making the tea. When it was done, he followed the man as unobtrusively as he could to the back room. When he looked at the table he did not know whether he was annoyed or delighted to find Lee and the boy engaged in a mysterious bilingual dialogue.

"Have some hot tea," he told her.

She looked up; there was no sign on her face that she had been crying. "Oh, that's sweet of you," she said, lifting the glass, finding it too hot, and putting it down again. "These people are really amazing. It took this child about two minutes to get me over feeling sorry for myself. The first thing I knew he was tugging at my sleeve and turning on the most irresistible smile and saying things in his funny language, but with such gentleness and sweetness that there I was, feeling better, that's all."

"That *is* strange," Stenham said, thinking of the state the boy himself had been in when he had left him. He turned to him and said: "*O deba labès enta?* You feel better? You were a little sick."

"No, I wasn't sick," the boy said firmly, but his face showed three consecutive expressions: shame, resentment, and finally a certain trusting humility, as if by the last he meant that he threw himself upon Stenham's mercy not to tell Lee of his weakness.

"When can we get out of here? We want to go home," Stenham said to him.

The boy shook his head. "This isn't the time to go into the street."

"But the lady wants to go to the hotel."

"Of course." The boy laughed, as though Lee's desires were those of an unreasoning animal, and were to be taken no more seriously. "This café is a very good place for her. The soldiers won't know she's in here."

"The soldiers won't know?" echoed Stenham sharply, his intuition warning him that there was more import to the words than his mind had yet grasped. "What do you mean? *Chnou bghitsi ts'qoulli?*"

"Didn't you see the soldiers? I heard them come when you were getting the tea. If they know she's in here they'll break the door and come in."

"But why?" demanded Stenham idiotically.

The boy replied succinctly and in unequivocal terms.

"No, no." Stenham was incredulous. "They couldn't. The French."

"What French?" said the boy bitterly. "The French aren't with them. They send them out alone, so they can break the houses and kill the men and take the girls and steal what they want. The Berbers don't fight for the French just for those few francs a day they give them. You didn't know that? This way the French don't have to spend any money, and the city people are kept poor, and the Berbers are happy in their heads, and the people hate the Berbers more than they hate the French. Because if everybody hated the French they couldn't stay here. They'd have to go back to France."

"I see. And how do you know all that?" Stenham asked, impressed by the clarity of the boy's simple analysis.

"I know it because everybody knows it. Even the donkeys and mules know that. And the birds," he added with complete seriousness.

"If you know all that, maybe you know what's going to happen next," Stenham suggested, half in earnest.

"There will be more and more poison in the hearts of the Moslems, and more and more and more"—his face screwed itself up into a painful grimace—"until they all burst, just from hating. They'll set everything on fire and kill each other."

"I mean today. What's going to happen now? Because we want to go home."

"You must look out the window and wait until the only men there are French and *mokhaznia*—no partisans at all. Then you make the man open the door and let you out, and go to a policeman, and he'll take you home."

"But we don't like the French," objected Stenham, thinking this was as good a moment as any to reassure the boy as to where their sympathies lay; he did not want him to regret his candor when the excitement of the instant had passed.

A cynical smile appeared on the young face. *"Binatzkoum.* That's between you and them," he said impassively. "How did you get to Fez?"

"On the train."

"And where do you live?"

"At the Mérinides Palace."

"Binatzkoum, binatzkoum. You came with the French and you live with the French. What difference does it make whether you like them or not? If they weren't here you couldn't be here. Go to a French policeman. But don't tell him you don't like him."

"Look!" said Lee suddenly. "I don't feel like sitting here while you take an Arab lesson. I want to get out of here. Has he given you any information at all?"

"If you'll just have a little patience," said Stenham, nettled, "I'll get all the details. You can't hurry these people; I've told you that."

"I'm sorry. But it *is* going to be dark soon and we *have* got to get all the way back to the hotel. What I meant was, I hope you're not just having an ordinary conversation."

"We're not," Stenham assured her. He looked at his watch. "It's only four-twenty," he said. "It won't be dark for a long time. The boy doesn't think we ought to go outside quite yet. I'm inclined to think he's right."

"He probably doesn't know as much about it as you do, if you come down to that," she said. "But go ahead and talk."

The sounds of shooting had retreated into the distance. "Why don't you go and look out the window?" Stenham suggested to the boy, "and see what's happening."

Obediently the boy rose and went out.

"He's a good kid," said Stenham. "Bright as they come."

"Oh, he's a darling. I think we should each give him something when we go."

It was a long while before he returned, and when he came in they saw immediately that he was in a completely different state of mind. He walked slowly to his chair and sat down, looking ready to burst into tears.

"*Chnou?* What is it?" Stenham demanded impatiently.

The boy looked straight ahead of him, a picture of despair.

"Now *you* be patient," Lee said.

"You can go," the boy said finally in a toneless voice. "The man will open the door for you. There's nothing to be afraid of."

Stenham waited a moment for the boy to say more, but he merely sat there, his hands in his lap, his head bent forward, looking at the air. "What is it?" he finally asked him, conscious that both his experience and his Arabic were inadequate for dealing with a situation which demanded tact and delicacy. The boy shook his head very slowly without moving his eyes. "Did you see something bad?"

The boy heaved a deep sigh. "The city is closed," he said. "All the gates are closed. No one can go in. No one can come out."

Stenham relayed the information to Lee, adding: "I suppose that means going through hell to get into the hotel. Officially it's inside the walls."

She clicked her tongue with annoyance. "We'll get in. But what about him? Where does he live?"

Stenham talked with the boy for a bit, drawing only the briefest answers from him. At the end of a minute or so, he said to Lee: "He doesn't know where he's going to eat or sleep. That's the trouble. His family lives way down in the Medina. It's a mess, isn't it? And of course he has no money. They never have any. I think I'll give him a thousand. That ought to help some."

Lee shook her head. "Money's not what the poor kid needs. What good's money going to be to him?"

"What good is it!" exclaimed Stenham. "What else can you give him?"

Lee reached over and tapped the boy's shoulder. "Look!" she said, pointing at him. "You. Come." She waggled her fingers like two legs. "Him." She indicated Stenham. "Me." She pointed her thumb at herself. "Hotel." She described a wide arc with her hand. "Yes? *Oui?*"

"You're crazy," Stenham told her. A flicker of hope had appeared in the boy's eyes. Warming to her game, Lee bent forward and went on with her dumb-show. Stenham rose, saying: "Why get him all worked up? It's cruel." She paid him no attention.

"I'm going to take a look into the other room," he said, and he left them there, leaning toward each other intently, Lee gesticulating and uttering single words with exaggeratedly clear enunciation—like a schoolteacher, he thought again.

"What does she want? Gratitude?" He knew how it would end: the boy would disappear, and afterward it would be discovered that something was missing—a camera, a watch, a fountain pen. She would be indignant, and he would patiently explain that it had been inevitable from the start, that such behavior was merely an integral part of "their" ethical code.

The other room was quiet. Only a few men stood in the windows looking out. Of the rest, some talked and the others merely sat. He went to the little window where he had gone before, and peered out. In the square there was activity: the soldiers were piling sandbags in a curved line across the lower end, just outside the gate. A large calendar hung on the wall beside the window; its text written in Arabic characters, it showed an unmistakably American girl lifting a bottle of Coca-Cola to her lips. As he went back across the room two or three men turned angry faces toward him, and he heard the word *mericani,* as well as a few unflattering epithets. He was relieved: at least they all knew he was not French. It was unlikely that there would be any trouble.

In the middle room the old man had slumped to one side and closed his eyes: so many pipes of kif in one afternoon had proven more than he could manage. When Stenham stepped through the further doorway Lee stood up, smoothed her skirt, and said: "Well, it's all settled. Amar's coming with us. They can find somewhere for him to sleep, and if they won't, I'll simply take a room for him tonight."

Stenham smiled pityingly. "Well, your intentions are good, anyway. Is that his name? Amar?"

"Ask him. That's what he told me. He can say my name, but he pronounces it Bali. It's rather nice—certainly prettier than Polly."

"I see," said Stenham. "It means old, applied to objects. If you want to lug him along it's all right with me."

The boy was still seated, looking up at them anxiously, from her face to his and back again.

"Suppose he hadn't happened to meet us," Stenham suggested. "What would he have done then?"

"He'd probably have gone back into the town before the trouble started and gotten home somehow. Don't forget it was you who spoke to him and asked him to sit down with us."

"You're sure you wouldn't just like to give him some money and let it go at that?"

"Yes, I'm sure," she said flatly.

"All right. Then I guess we'd better go."

He handed the boy five hundred francs. "*Chouf.* Pay for the tea and *cabrhozels,* and ask the *qaouaji* to open the door for us." Amar went out. It was perfectly possible, thought Stenham, that the proprietor of the café would refuse to run the risk of opening the door; they had no one's word but the boy's to the contrary. He stepped to the back door and looked out once again at the pool. The sun had gone behind the walls; in the afternoon shade the patio had taken on an austere charm. The surface of the water was smooth, but the plants along the edges, trembling regularly, betrayed the current beneath. A swallow came careening down from the ramparts toward the pool, obviously with the intention of touching the water. Seeing Stenham, it changed its direction violently, and went off in blind haste toward the sky. He listened: the shooting was not audible at the moment, there were no street-vendors' shouts, no watersellers' bells jangling, and the high murmur of human voices that formed the city's usual backdrop of sound was missing. What he heard was the sharp confusion of bird-cries. It was the hour of the swallows. Each evening at this time they set to wheeling and darting by the tens of thousands, in swift, wide circles above the walls and gardens and alleys and bridges, their shrill screams presaging the advent of twilight.

So, he thought, it's happened. They've done it. Whatever came to pass now, the city would never be the same again. That much he knew. He heard Lee's voice behind him.

"Amar says they've unlocked the door for us. Shall we go?"

NOVELLA

Too Far From Home

By day her empty room had four walls, and the walls enclosed a definite space. At night the room continued forever into the darkness.

"If there are no mosquitos why do we have mosquito nets?"

"The beds are low and we have to tuck ourselves in with the nets, so that our hands can't fall out and touch the floor," Tom said. "You don't know what might be crawling there."

The day she arrived, the first thing he did after showing her the room where she would sleep, was to take her on a tour of the house. It was dim and clean. Most of the rooms were empty. It seemed to her that the help occupied the greater part of the building. In one room five women sat in a row along the wall. She was presented to all of them. Tom explained that only two of them were employed in the house; the others were visitors. There was the sound of men's voices in another room, a sound which turned swiftly to silence at Tom's knock on the door. A tall, very black man in a white turban appeared. She had the instant impression that he resented her presence, but he bowed gravely. "This is Sekou," Tom told her. "He runs things around here. You might not guess it, but he's extremely bright." She glanced at her brother nervously; he seemed to know why. "Don't worry," he added. "Nobody knows a word of English here."

She could not go on talking about this man while she stood facing him. But when they were on the roof later, under the improvised awning, she continued the conversation. "What made you assume that I thought your man was stupid? I know you didn't say that; but you as much as said it. I'm not a racist, you know. Do *you* think he looks slow-witted?"

"I was just trying to help you see the difference between him and the others, that's all."

"Oh," she said. "There's an obvious difference, of course. He's taller, blacker, and with finer features than the others."

"But there's a basic difference, too," Tom told her. "You see, he's not a servant like them. Sekou is not his name. It's his title. He's a kind of chief."

"But I saw him sweeping the courtyard," she objected.

"Yes, but that's just because he wants to. He likes to be in this house. I don't mind having him here. He keeps the other men in order."

They wandered to the edge of the roof. The sun was blinding.

"I can't believe that," she laughed. "He has the face of a tyrant."

"I doubt if anyone suffers under him. You know," he went on, suddenly raising his voice, "you *are* a racist. If Sekou were white, the idea would never have occurred to you."

She faced him, there in the burning sunlight. "If he were white, he'd have a different face. After all, it's the features that give a face expression. And I'm willing to bet anything that if he keeps the men in order he does it through fear."

"I don't think it's likely," he said. "But even so, why not?"

She went inside and stood in the doorway to her room. The maid had changed the position of her rug and mattress, so that they both lay at a ninety-degree angle to the way they had been arranged before. This disturbed her, although she did not know why.

II

My Dear Dorothy:

I was shocked to read the letter you wrote after your accident. Lucky you weren't going fast. By the time you get this your leg will probably be in good condition. I hope so. I'm always surprised that any mail at all can get here, as it's really the end of the world. When I think that the nearest town to the town where we are is Timbuctoo, I get a sort of sinking feeling. It's only momentary, however. What I have to remember is that I'm here because at the time it seemed an ideal solution, and all things considered, really the only thing to do. What else would have got me out of that depression that came over me after the divorce, except a long stay in a sanatorium. And who knows? Even that might not have done the trick. And financially it would have been ausgeschlossen, in any case. With Tom coming on his Guggenheim this seemed perfect. The idea was to get away from everything that could remind me in any way of what I'd been going through. This is certainly the antithesis of New York and of any place you can think of in the U.S.A. I was worried about food, but so far neither of us has been sick. Probably the important thing is that the cook is civilized enough to believe in the existence of bacteria, and is very careful to sterilize whatever needs sterilizing. The Niger River Valley is no place to come down with any disease. Fortunately we can get French mineral water for drinking. If its delivery should be cut off, or if it should not arrive in time, we'd have to drink what there is here, boiled and with Halazone. All this may sound silly, but living here makes one into a hypochondriac. You may wonder why I don't describe the place, tell you what it looks like. I can't. I don't believe I could be objective about it, which would mean that when I finished you'd have less of an idea what it's like than before I started. You'll have to wait until you see what Tom does with it, although he hasn't yet painted any landscapes at all—only what he sees in the kitchen: vegetables, fruit, fish, and a few sketches of natives bathing in the river. You'll see it all when we get back.

Elaine Duncan is such a nut. Imagine her asking me if I don't miss Peter. How does a mind like that work? At first I thought she was pulling my leg, but then I realized she was perfectly serious. I suppose it's just her kind of sentimentality. She knows what I was going through and what it cost me to make the final decision. She also knows me well enough to realize that once I'd decided to get out of it, it was because I understood I couldn't stay any longer with Peter, and most assuredly wasn't of two minds about it. It's clear she's hoping I regret having got out of the marriage. I'm afraid she's in for a big disappointment. At last I feel free. I can have my own thoughts, without anybody offering me a penny for them. Tom works all day in silence, and doesn't notice whether I talk or not. It's so refreshing to be with somebody who pays no attention to you, doesn't notice whether you're there or not. All feelings of guilt evaporate. This is all very personal, of course. But in a place like this you become autoanalytical.

I do hope you're completely recovered from the effects of the accident, and that you'll keep warm. Here it's generally just a little over a hundred degrees Fahrenheit. You can imagine how much energy I have!

Devotedly,
Anita

III

Nights were slow in passing. Sometimes as she lay in the silent blackness it seemed to her that the night had come down and seized the earth so tightly that daylight would be unable to show through. It could already be noon of the next day and no one would know it. People would go on sleeping as long as it remained dark, Tom in the next room, and Johara and the watchman whose name she never could remember, in one of the empty rooms across the courtyard. They were very quiet, those two. They retired early and they rose early, and the only sound she ever heard from their side of the house was an occasional dry cough from Johara. It bothered her that there was no door to her room. They had hung a dark curtain over the doorway between Tom's room and hers, so that the light of his roaring Coleman lamp would not bother her. He liked to sit up reading until ten o'clock, but immediately after the evening meal she was always somnolent, and had to go to bed, where she would sleep heavily for two or three hours before she awoke to lie in the dark, hoping that it was nearly morning. The crowing of cocks near and far was meaningless. They crowed at any time during the night.

In the beginning it had seemed quite natural that Johara and her husband should be black. In New York there had always been two or three black servants around the house. There she thought of them as shadows of people, not really at home in a country of whites, not sharing the same history or culture and thus, in spite of themselves, outsiders. Slowly, however, she had begun to see that these people here were masters of their surroundings, completely at home with the culture of the place. It was to be expected, of course, but it was something of a shock to realize that the blacks were the real people and that she was the shadow, and that even if she went on living here for the rest of her life she would never understand how their minds worked.

IV

Dear Elaine:

I should have written you ages ago when I first got here, but I've been under the weather for the past few weeks—not physically, really, except

that the spirit and the flesh aren't separated. When I'm depressed, every-
thing in my body seems to go to pieces. I suppose that's normal, perhaps
it isn't. God knows.

It's true, when I first looked out at the flat land that went on and on to
the horizon, I felt my depression dissolving in all that brightness. It didn't
seem possible that there could be so much light. And the stillness that
surrounded each little sound! You feel that the town is built on a cushion
of silence. That was something new—an amazing sensation, and I was very
conscious of it. I felt that all this was exactly what I needed, to get my mind
off the divorce and the rest of the trouble. There was nothing that had to
be done, no one I had to see. I was my own master, and didn't even have
to bother with the servants if I didn't want to. It was like camping out in
a big empty house. Of course in the end I did have to bother with the
servants, because they did everything wrong. Tom would tell me: Leave
them alone. They know what they're doing. I suppose they do know what
they mean to do, but they don't seem to be able to do it. If I find fault with
the food, the cook looks bewildered and aggrieved. This is because she
knows she's famous in the Gao region as the woman whose cuisine pleases
the Europeans. She listens and agrees, but in the manner of one soothing
a deranged invalid. I suspect she thinks of me in just such terms.

By being completely aware of, and focusing his attention on the smallest
details of the life going on around him, Tom manages to objectify the
details, and so he remains outside, and far from them. He paints whatever
is in front of his eyes at any moment, in the kitchen, or the market, or the
edge of the river: vegetables and fruit being sliced, often with the knife still
embedded in the flesh, bathers and fish from the Niger. My trouble is that
this life sweeps me along with it in spite of me. I mean that I am being
forced to participate in some sort of communal consciousness that I really
hate. I don't know anything about these people. They're all black, but
nothing like "our" blacks in the States. They're simpler, more friendly and
straightforward, and at the same time very remote.

Something is wrong with night here. Logic would have it that night is
only the time when the sky's door is open and one can look out on infinity,
and thus that the spot from which one looks out is of no importance. Night
is night, no matter from where perceived. Night here is no different from
night somewhere else. It's only logic that says this. Day is huge and bright
and it's impossible to see farther than the sun. I realize that by "here" I
don't mean "here in the middle of the Sahara on the banks of the River

Niger" but "here in this house where I'm living." Here in this house with the floors of smooth earth where the servants go barefoot and you never hear anyone coming until he's already in the room.

I've been trying to get used to this crazy life here, but it takes some getting used to, I can tell you. There are many rooms in the house. In fact, it's enormous, and the rooms are big. And they look even larger, without furniture, of course. There is no furniture at all except for the mats on the floors of the rooms where we sleep and our suitcases and the wardrobes where we hang the few clothes we have with us. It was because of these wardrobes that the house was available, because they made it count as a "furnished house," and that made the rent so high that no one wanted to take it. By our standards, of course, it's very cheap, and God knows it should be, with no electricity and no water, without even a chair to sit in or a table to eat at, or, for that matter, a bed to sleep in.

Naturally I knew it was going to be hot, but I hadn't imagined this sort of heat—solid, no change from day to day, no breeze. And remember, no water, so to take even a sponge bath is an entire production number. Tom is angelic about the water. He lets me have about all we can get hold of. He says females need more than men do. I don't know whether that's an insult or not, and I don't care as long as I can get the water. He also says it's not hot. But it is. I don't know how to convert Centigrade into Fahrenheit, but if you do, change 46° C into F., and you'll see that I'm right. 46° was what my thermometer registered this morning.

I don't know which is worse, day or night. In the daytime, of course, it's a little hotter, although not much. They don't believe in windows here, so the house is dark inside, and that gives you a shut-in feeling. Tom does a lot of his work on the roof in the sun. He claims he doesn't mind it, but I can't believe it's not bad for him. I know it would be the end of me if I sat up there the way he does, hours at a time and with no break.

I had to laugh when I read your question about how I felt after the divorce, whether I "still cared" a little for Peter. What a crazy question! How could I still care for him? The way I feel now, if I never see another man it will be too soon. I'm really fed up with their hypocrisy, and I'd willingly send them all to Hell. Not Tom, of course, because he's my brother, even though trying to live with him under these conditions isn't easy. But trying to live at all in this place is hard. You can't imagine how remote from everything it makes you feel.

The mail service here is not perfect. How could it be? But it's not impossible. I do get letters, so be sure and write me. After all, the post office is this end of the umbilical cord that keeps me attached to the world. (I almost added: *and to sanity*.)

I hope all is well with you, and that New York hasn't grown any worse than it was last year; although I'm sure it has.

Much love, and write.

Anita

V

At first there would be memories—small, precise images complete with the sounds and odors of a certain incident in a certain summer. They had not meant anything to her at the time of experiencing them, but now she strove desperately to stay with them, to relive them and not let them fade into the enveloping darkness where a memory lost its contours and was replaced by something else. The formless entities which followed on the memories were menacing because indecipherable, and her heartbeat and breathing accelerated at this point. "As though I'd had coffee," she thought, although she never drank it. Whereas a few moments earlier she had been living in the past, she was now fully surrounded by the present instant, face to face with a senseless fear. Her eyes would fly open, to fix on what was not there in the blackness.

She was not fond of the food, claiming that it was much too hot with red pepper and at the same time without flavor.

"And you realize," he said, "that we've got the most famous cook in these parts."

She remarked that it was hard to believe.

They were eating lunch on the roof, not in the sun, but in the vicious glare of a white sheet stretched above them. There was an expression of distaste on her face.

"I feel sorry for the girl who marries you," she said presently.

"It's an abstraction," he told her. "Don't even think about it. Let her pity herself once she's married to me."

"Oh, she will, all right. I can promise you that."

After a fairly long silence he looked at her.

"What's making you so belligerent all of a sudden?"

"Belligerent? I was just thinking how hard it is for you to show sympathy. You know I haven't been feeling too well lately. But have I ever noticed a shred of sympathy?" (She wondered, too late, if she ought to have made this admission.)

"You're perfectly well," he said, adopting his gruff manner.

VI

Dear Peg:

It's evident that Tom is doing everything in his power to keep any day from being exactly like the preceding one. He arranges a walk down to the river or a jaunt into "town," as he calls the nondescript collection of shacks around the market. No matter where we go, I'm expected to snap pictures. Some of it can be fun. The rest is tiring. It's quite clear that he does all this to keep me from boredom, which means it's a kind of therapy, which in turn means that he believes I might become a mental case and is afraid. This I find very troubling. It means that there is something between us that can't be mentioned. It's embarrassing and makes for tension. I'd like to be able to turn to him and say: "Relax. I'm not about to crack up." But I can pretty well imagine the disastrous effect such a straightforward statement would have. For him it would only be proof that I was not certain of my mental stability, and of course, all he needs to ruin his year is a jittery sister. Why should there be any question of my being in anything but the best of health? I suppose it's simply because I'm terrified that he'll suspect I'm not. I can't bear the idea of being a spoilsport, or of his thinking that I am.

We were walking, Tom and I, along the edge of the river yesterday. A wide beach of hard dirt. He tries to get me to walk nearer the water where the ground is softer, saying it's easier on the bare feet. God knows what parasites live in this water. It seems dangerous enough to me to go barefoot anywhere around here, without going into the water. Tom has very little patience with me when I take care of myself. He claims it's just part of my generally negative approach to life. Being used to his critical remarks, I let them slide off my duck's back. He did say one thing which stuck in my mind, which was that extreme self-centeredness invariably caused dissatis-faction and poor health. It's clear he considers me a paragon of egocentricity. So today when I went up onto the roof I faced him with it. The dialogue went something like this:

"You seem to be under the impression that I'm incapable of being interested in anything besides myself."

"Yes. That's the impression I'm under."

"Well, you don't have to be so cavalier about it."

"As long as we've started this conversation we might as well push ahead with it. Tell me then; what are you interested in?"

"When you're asked point-blank like that, it's hard to pluck something out of the air, you know."

"But don't you see that that means you can't think of anything? And that's because you have no interests. Apparently you don't realize feigning interest, kindles interest. Like the old French saying about love being born through making the gestures of love."

"So you think salvation lies in pretending?"

"Yes, and I'm serious. You've never yet looked at my work, much less thought about it."

"I've looked at everything you've done here."

"Looked at. But seen?"

"How do you expect me to appreciate your paintings? I have a poor visual sense. You know that."

"I don't care whether you appreciate them, or even like them. We're not talking about my paintings. We're talking about you. That's just a small example. You could take an interest in the servants and their families. Or how the architecture in the town fits the exigencies of the climate. I realize that's a pretty ridiculous suggestion, but there are a thousand things to care about."

"Yes, if you care in the first place. Hard to do if you don't."

I knew (or felt pretty certain) when I agreed to come here that I was letting myself in for something unpleasant. I realize that I'm writing now as though there had been some dreadful occurrence, when as a matter of fact nothing whatever has happened. And let's hope it doesn't.

Lots of love.
Anita

VII

Hi, Ross! The enclosed shows the view looking south from the roof. It certainly is a lot of nothing. Yet it's strange how one lone man in such a vast landscape takes on importance. It's not a place I'd recommend to anybody. I didn't recommend it even to Anita; she just came. I think she's happy here—that is, as much as she's ever happy. Some days she's crankier than usual, but I disregard that. I don't think she enjoys celibate life. Too bad she didn't think of that before she came. Myself, I do very little besides work. I can feel it's going well. It would take a major act of God to stop me at this point.

Tom

VIII

One morning when she had finished her breakfast and set her tray on the floor beside her bed, she ran up onto the roof for a little sunlight and fresh air. Normally she was careful not to climb up because Tom sat there most of the day, generally not working, merely sitting. When she once had been thoughtless enough to inquire what he was doing, instead of answering "Communing with nature" or "meditating" as more pretentious painters might have replied, he said: "Getting ideas." This directness was tantamount to expressing a desire for privacy; so she respected that privacy and seldom went up onto the roof. This morning he gave no sign of minding. "I heard the call to prayer this morning for the first time," she told him. "It was still dark."

"Yes, you can sometimes hear that one," he said, "when there's no other sound to cover it."

"It was sort of comforting. Made me feel that things were under control."

He did not seem to be paying attention. "Listen, Nita, you could do me a great favor, if you will. Yes?"

"Well, sure," she said, with no idea of what was coming next. It was something she was not expecting, given his unusual manner of prefacing it.

"Could you go into town and get some films? I want to take a lot more pictures. You know Mother's been asking for shots of you and me together. I've got plenty of photos, but not of us. I'd go myself, but I can't spare the time. It's not nine yet. The shop that sells films is on the other side of the market. They don't shut until ten."

"But Tom, you seem to forget that I don't know my way anywhere."

"Well, Sekou'll go with you. You won't get lost. Tell them you want black and white."

"I know Mother'd rather have them in color."

"You're right. Old people and kids like color better. Get two rolls of color and two black and white. Sekou's waiting for you by the front door."

She was sorry she needed a guide to show her the shop, and even more sorry that the guide had to be the black man she had already decided was hostile toward her. But it was still early and the air in the street would feel relatively fresh.

"Don't wear those sandals," Tom told her, continuing to work, not looking up. "Wear thick socks and regular shoes. God knows what germs are in the dust."

So she stood at the door in the prescribed footgear, and Sekou came across the courtyard and greeted her in French. His wide smile made her think that perhaps she had been mistaken, that he did not resent her presence in the house after all. And suppose he does? she thought defiantly. There was a limit to the depth at which one could decently bury one's ego. Beyond that depth the whole game of selflessness became abject. She knew it was in her nature to refuse to admit being a "person." It was so much simpler to hide in the shadow of neutrality, even when there was no possibility of a confrontation. One could scarcely care about the reactions of an African servant. For in spite of what Tom had told her, she still thought of Sekou as a kind of servant—a factotum, perhaps with the stature of a jester.

It was an insane thing to be doing, walking along the main street of the town, side by side with this tall black man. An unlikely couple, God knows. The idea of being photographed at the moment made her smile. If she were to send a copy of such a picture to her mother she knew more or less what the reply would be. "The ultimate in exoticism." She certainly did not feel that this street was exotic or picturesque: it was dirty and squalid.

"He may try to make conversation," she thought, and determined to pretend not to understand. Then she would have only to smile and shake her head. Presently he did say something which, since she had already decided that there were to be no words between them, she failed to understand. An instant later she heard his phrase with its interrogatory inflection, and realized that he had said: *"Tu n'as pas chaud?"* He had slowed his gait; he was waiting for her reply.

"The hell with it," she thought, and so she answered his question, but indirectly. Rather than saying: "Yes, I am hot," she said: "It's hot."

Now he stopped walking altogether, and indicated, on their left, an improvised nook between piles of crates, where a table and two chairs had been placed. A large sign was laid across the entire space, creating an inviting area of shade, which quickly grew to be irresistible once one had even entertained the possibility of stepping in and sitting down.

Obsessively, her thoughts turned to her mother. What would be her reaction if she could see her only daughter sitting beside a black man in this dark little refuge? "If he takes advantage of you, remember that you asked for it. It's just tempting Providence. You can't treat people like that as equals. They don't understand it."

The drink was Pepsi Cola, surprisingly cold, but unusually sweet. "Ah," she said, appreciative.

Sekou's fluent French put her to shame. "How can this be?" she thought, with a certain indignation. Being conscious of her own halting French made it more difficult to engage in conversation. These empty moments when neither of them had anything to say made the silence more apparent, and for her more embarrassing. The sounds of the street—footsteps on the sand, children running and now and then a dog's bark, were curiously muted by the piles of crates and the covering overhead. It was an astonishingly quiet town, she reflected. Since they had left the house she had not heard the sound of one automobile, even in the distance. But now, as she became aware of listening, she could discern the far-off alternative whining and braying of a motorcycle, sounds she particularly disliked.

Sekou rose and went to pay the owner. She had meant to do that, but now it seemed quite impossible. She thanked him. Then they were back in the street, and the air was hotter than ever. This was the moment to ask herself why she had allowed Tom to send her off on this absurd errand. It would have been better, she thought, if she had gone to the kitchen and asked the cook not to serve fried potatoes. The woman seemed to consider potatoes, no matter how prepared, a succulent dish, but those available here did not lend themselves to any mode of cooking save perhaps mashing. She had mentioned this to Tom on various occasions, but his opinion was that mashing would be more work for Johara, and that most likely she would not know how to perform the operation properly, so that the result would be less tasty than what she served now.

The insane noise of the motorcycle in imitation of a siren came from a good deal nearer at present. "It's coming this way," she thought. If only we could get to the market before it arrives. She had been once with Tom to buy food, and she remembered the colonnades and pillars. No motorcycle could roar through there. "Where *is* the market?" she demanded suddenly. Sekou gestured. "Ahead."

Now the dragonlike machine was visible, far up the long street, bouncing and raising a cloud of dust which seemed partly to precede it. Even that far away she could see pedestrians bolting and scurrying to keep out of its way.

The noise was growing unbelievably loud. She had an impulse to cover her ears, like a child. The thing was coming. It was coming straight at them. She jumped to the side of the road just as the motorcyclist braked to avoid hitting Sekou straight on. He had refused to duck and escape its impact. The flamboyant vehicle lay in the dust, partially covering the bare legs and arms of the riders. Two nearly naked youths pulled themselves up, holding their red and yellow helmets in their hands. They glared and shouted at Sekou. She was not surprised to hear American speech.

"You blind?"

"You're one lucky son of a bitch. We could have killed you."

As Sekou paid no attention to them, but continued to walk, they became abusive.

"A real downhome uppity nigger."

Sekou ignored the two with supreme aplomb.

From her side of the road Anita stepped forth to face them. "If we're going to talk about who might be killed by your impossible apparatus, I'm first on the list. You came straight at me. Isn't that what's known as sowing panic? Does it make you feel better to frighten people?"

"Sorry we scared you, ma'am. That wasn't what we had in mind."

"I'll bet it wasn't." Now being startled had turned to being indignant. "I'll bet what you had in mind was one big zero." She had not heard the apology. "You've gone too far from home, my friends, and you're going to have trouble."

A leer. "Oh yeah?"

She could feel her anger pushing up inside her. "Yeah!" she cried. "Trouble! And I hope I'll have a chance to see it." A moment later she spat: "Monsters."

Sekou, who had not even glanced at them once, now stopped and turned to see if she were coming. As she caught up with him, he remarked without looking at her that tourists were always ignorant.

When they got to the shop that sold films, she was surprised to find it being run by a middle-aged French woman. If Anita had not been breathless with rage and excitement, she would have liked to engage the woman in conversation: to ask how long she had been living here and what her life was like. The moment was not propitious for such a move.

As they walked back toward the house in the increasing heat, there was no sign or sound of the hellish machine. She noticed that Sekou was limping a bit, and looked carefully at him. There was blood on the lower part of his white robe, and she realized that the motorcycle had collided with his leg. Her appraisal seemed to annoy him; she could not bring herself to ask to see the injury, or even to speak of it.

IX

At lunch she avoided all mention of the motorcycle accident.

"It wasn't too far, was it?"

"It was hot," she replied.

"I've been thinking," Tom said at length. "This house would be so cheap to buy. It would be worthwhile. I wouldn't mind coming here regularly."

"I think you'd be out of your mind!" she cried. "You could never really live here. It's an uncomfortable temporary campsite, nothing more. Anyway, whatever property you buy in a third-world country is lost before you even pay for it. You know that. Renting makes sense. Then when things go crazy, you're free."

Johara stood beside her, offering her more creamed onions. She served herself.

"Things don't always go crazy," Tom said.

"Oh, yes they do!" she cried. "In these countries? It's inescapable."

After a bit, she went on. "Well, of course. You'll do as you please. I don't suppose you'd lose much."

While they were having fruit, Anita volunteered: "I dreamed of Mother last night."

"You did?" said Tom without interest. "What was she doing?"

"Oh, I can't even remember. But when I woke up I began thinking about her. You know she had absolutely no sense of humor, and yet she could be very funny. I remember she was giving a rather fancy dinner one night, and suddenly she turned to you and said: 'How old are you, Tom?' And you said: 'Twenty-six.' She waited a little, and then said: 'When William the Silent was your age he had conquered half of Europe.' And she sounded so disgusted that everyone at the table burst out laughing. Do you remember? I still think that's funny, although I'm sure she didn't mean it to be."

"I wouldn't be too sure. I think she was playing to the gallery. She couldn't laugh herself, naturally. Too dignified. But she wasn't above making others laugh."

X

Another day they sat on the floor having breakfast in Tom's room. The cook had just brought them more toast.

"I'd like to drive a few miles down the river and have a look at the next village," said Tom, signalling to the cook to wait. "How about it? I can rent Bessier's old truck. How does that strike you?"

"I'm game," she said. "The road's straight and flat, isn't it?"

"We won't get lost. Or stuck in the sand."

"Is there something special you want to see?"

"I just need to see something else. The smallest change gives me all sorts of new ideas."

They agreed to go the following day. When he asked Johara to prepare them a *casse-croûte*, she became excited upon hearing that they planned to go to Gargouna. Her sister lived there, she said, and she gave Tom instructions as to how to find her house, along with messages she hoped he would deliver.

The little truck had no cabin. They were cooled by the breeze they created. It was stimulating to be driving along the edge of the river in the early morning air. The road was completely flat, with no potholes or obstacles.

"It's fine now," said Tom, "but it won't be so good coming back, with nothing between us and the sun."

"We've got our topis," she reminded him, glancing at the two helmets on the seat between them. She had with her a pair of powerful field glasses, bought in Kobe the previous year, and in spite of the movement she kept them trained on the river where men fished and women bathed.

"It's nice, isn't it?" said Tom.

"It's certainly a lot prettier with the black bodies than it would be if they were all whites."

This was only moderate enthusiasm, but it seemed to please him. He was very eager for her to appreciate the Niger Valley. But at the moment he was intent on not passing the road on the left that led to Gargouna. "Fifty kilometres, more or less," he murmured. Soon he said: "Here it is, but I'm not going to risk that sand." He stopped the truck and shut off the motor. The silence was overpowering. They sat without moving. Occasionally there was a cry from the river, but the open and wide landscape made the voices sound like birdcries.

"One of us has to stay with the car, and that's you."

Tom jumped down. "I'm going to do it on foot, find the village and Johara's sister. It ought to take ten minutes, not much more. You'll be all right here, won't you?" They had not seen another vehicle since setting out. "We're right in the middle of the road," she told him.

"I know, but if I move off to the right, I'll be in the sand. That's the one thing I don't want. If it makes you nervous, get out and walk around. It's not hot yet."

She was not afraid to have been left alone, but she was nervous. This was one occasion when Tom could have brought along one of the several men who spent their days sitting in the kitchen. It suddenly occurred to her that she had not seen Sekou since the day of the motorcycle incident, and this made her wonder how badly his leg or foot had been hurt. Thinking of him, she got down and began to walk along the same path Tom had taken. She could not see him ahead, because the region was one of low dunes with occasional thorn bushes. She wondered why it was impossible for the sky here to be really blue, why instead it always had a grey tinge.

Thinking that she might get a glimpse of Gargouna, she climbed one of the small hills of sand, but had a view only of rather larger thorn bushes ahead. She was particularly eager to see the village; she could imagine it: a group of circular huts lying fairly far apart, each with a cleared space around it, where poultry pecked in the sand. She turned to the right, where the dunes appeared to be somewhat higher, and followed a kind of path which led over and around them. There were little valleys between the dunes, some of them quite deep. The crests of the dunes all seemed to run parallel to each other, so that it was difficult to get from one dune to the next without going down and then climbing immediately. There was one dune not far ahead which dominated the others, and from which she felt certain she could see the truck waiting in the road. She reached it and stood atop it, a bit breathless. With the aid of the field glasses she saw that the truck was there, and to the left in the distance there were a few leafless trees. The village was in that direction, she supposed. Then, looking across into the depression between two dunes, she saw something that accelerated the beating of her heart, a senseless sculpture in vermillion enamel and chromium. There were large boulders down there; the cycle had skidded, hurling the suntanned torsos against the rocks. The machine was twisted grotesquely and the two bodies were jumbled together and uniformly spattered with blood. They were not in a condition to call for help; they lay motionless there in the declivity, invisible to all save to one who might stand exactly where she was standing. She turned and ran quickly down the side of the dune. "Monsters," she muttered, but without indignation.

She was sitting in the truck when Tom returned. "Did you find her, Johara's sister?"

"Oh, yes. It's a tiny village. Everybody knows everybody, of course. Let's eat. Here or down the shore?"

Her heart was still beating rapidly and with force. She said: "Let's go down to the river. There might be a little breeze down there." She was surprised now to recall that her first feeling upon seeing the wreck of the motorcycle had been one of elation. She could still induce the little chill of pleasure that had run through her at that instant. As they walked along the shore, she was thankful once again that she had never mentioned to Tom the confrontation with the two Americans.

XI

"Are you sleeping better now?" Tom asked her.

She hesitated. "Not really."

"What do you mean, not really?"

"I have a problem," she sighed.

"A problem?"

"Oh, I might as well tell you."

"Of course."

"Tom, I think Sekou comes to my room at night."

"What?" he cried. "You're crazy. What do you mean, he comes to your room?"

"Just that."

"What does he do? Does he say anything?"

"No, no. He just stands beside my bed in the dark."

"That's insane."

"I know."

"You've never seen him?"

"How could I? It's pitch dark."

"You've got a flashlight."

"Oh, that terrifies me more than anything. To turn it on and actually see him. Who knows what he'd do then, once he knew I'd seen him."

"He's not a criminal. God, why are you so damned nervous? You're safer here than you would be anywhere back in New York."

"I believe you," she said. "But that's not the point."

"What *is* the point? You think he comes and stands by your bed. Why do you think he does that?"

"That's the worst part of all. I can't tell you. It's too frightening."

"Why? Do you think he's planning to rape you?"

"Oh, no! It's nothing like that. What I feel is that he's *willing* me to dream. He's willing me to dream a dream I can't bear."

"A dream about him?"

"No. He's not even in the dream."

Tom was exasperated. "But what is this? What are we talking about, finally? You say Sekou wants you to have a certain dream, and you have it. So then he comes the next night, and you're afraid you'll have it again. According to you, why does he do this? I mean, what interest would he have in doing it?"

"I don't know. That makes it more horrible. I know you think it's ridiculous. Or you think I'm imagining it all."

"No, I don't say that. But since you've never seen anything, how can you be sure it's Sekou and not somebody else?"

Later in the day he said to her, "Anita, are you taking vitamins?"

She laughed. "Lord, yes. Dr. Kirk gave me all kinds. Vitamins and minerals. He said the soil here probably was deficient in mineral salts. Oh, I'm sure you think I have some sort of chemical imbalance that causes the dreaming. That could be. But it isn't the dream itself that scares me. Although God knows it's too repulsive to talk about."

He interrupted. "Is it sexual?"

"If it were," she said, "it would be a lot easier to describe. The thing is, I *can't* describe it." She shuddered. "It's too confusing. And it makes me feel sick to think of it."

"Maybe you should let me be your analyst. What happens during the dream?"

"Nothing happens. I only know something terrible is on its way. But as I say, it's not the dream that bothers me. It's knowing I'm being obliged to have it, knowing that black man is standing there inventing it and forcing me into it. That's too much."

XII

A wooden sign, nailed above a wooden door, with the words *Yindall & Fambers, Apothecaries* painted on it. Inside, a counter, an athletic young man standing behind it. At first glance he looks naked, but he is wearing red and blue shorts. Instead of saying: "Hi, I'm Bud," he says: "I'm Mr. Yindall. May I help you?" The voice is dry and grey.

"I want a small bottle of Sweet Spirits of Nitre and a box of Slippery Elm lozenges."

"Right away." But something is wrong with his face. He turns to go into the back room, hesitates. "You haven't come to see Mr. Yindall, have you?"

"But you said you were Mr. Yindall."

"He gets mixed up sometimes. As a rule he doesn't admit people."

"I didn't say I wanted to see him."

"But you do." He reaches across the counter, and a hand of steel takes hold. "He's waiting in the basement. Fambers speaking."

"I don't want to see Mr. Yindall, thank you."

"It's too late to say that."

A portion of the counter is on hinges. He lifts it up to allow passage, still pressing with a hand of steel.

Protestations all the way to the cellar. A chromium throne against one wall shining in the glare of spotlights trained upon it. Two muscular thighs growing from a man's shoulders, the legs bent at the knees. Between the thighs a thick neck from which the head has been severed. The arms, attached to the hips, hang loosely, the fingers twitching.

"This is Mr. Fambers. He can't see you, of course. His head had to be removed. It got in the way. But his neck is filled with highly sensitive protoplasm. If you bite it or even nibble it, you establish instant communication. Just lean over and push your mouth into his neck."

The hand of steel guides. The substance inside the neck feels like water-soaked bread, its slightly sulfurous odor is like that of turnips.

"Push with your tongue. Don't gag."

At the first pressure of the tongue, the substance in the neck pulses, bubbles, splashes warm liquid upward.

"It's only blood. I think you'd better stay here a while."

"No, no, no, no!" Rolling in her vomit on the floor.

"No, no, no!" Trying to rub the blood from her lips and face.

Down, down, blood and all, vomit and all, into the feather-bedded floor. Only the turnip stench to breathe in an airless pocket. Then, choking, having been smothered, she rose from below and breathed deeply of the open black air around her, sickened by the nature of the dream, certain that it would be repeated, terrified above all by the thought that the orders governing this phenomenon should be coming from without, from another mind. This was unacceptable.

XIII

Tom found her reasoning faulty. "You had a nightmare, and of course that's not something to worry about. But to be obsessed by the idea that Sekou or anyone else is in charge of your dreams is pure paranoia. It's based on nothing at all. Can't you see that?"

"I can see how *you* think that, yes."

"I'm convinced that once you told it, all of it, it would stop worrying you."

"It makes me feel like throwing up just to think of it."

The steady burning of the pressure lamp between them on the floor inspired Anita to exclaim: "It's too bright, too noisy, and too hot."

"Don't pay it any attention. Forget about it."

"It's rather hard to do that."

"You know if I turn it down we won't be able to see anything."

After a moment she said: "These vegetables here are really abject. I don't understand you. You paint practically nothing but food, yet you don't care what you eat."

"What d'you mean, I don't care? I care very much. I don't complain, if that's what you're expecting. The vegetables here are what there is, unless you want French canned food, which, knowing you, I don't believe you do. I think it's a miracle they can get even this much out of the sand."

Suddenly Johara was in the room; she announced the next course.

"I didn't hear her come upstairs, did you?"

She snorted. "With this lamp going you wouldn't hear an elephant."

"No, but even without the lamp, have you noticed that you never hear any footsteps in this house?"

She laughed. "I'm only too aware of it. That's part of what bothers me at night. I've never heard a sound in my room when it's night. Any number of people could be there and I wouldn't know it."

Tom said nothing; his mind obviously was on something else. For a few minutes they sat in silence. When she began to speak again, her voice made it clear that she had been ruminating.

"Tom, did you ever hear of slippery elm?"

He sat up straight. "Of course. Granny used to swear by it for sore throat. They put it out in tablets, like cough-drops. I remember how upset she was when they stopped manufacturing them. I doubt that slippery elm exists today in any form."

He stole a glance at her, suspecting that this was her devious way of dealing with the material of the dream. He waited.

Her next question struck him as comic. "Isn't saltpeter what they put into prisoners' food?"

"They used to, I don't know whether they do nowadays. What are you doing, preparing a compendium of useless knowledge?"

"No, I just wondered."

He arranged the cushions behind him and stretched out.

"You want to know who I think Sekou is?" he asked her.

"How do you mean, who he is?"

"Who he is for you, I mean. I think he's Mother."

"What?!" she cried, very loud.

"I'm serious. I remember how Mother used to come and stand beside my bed in the dark, and just stand there. And I was always terrified she'd know I was awake. So I had to breathe calmly and not move a muscle. And she used to do the same thing by your bed. I'd hear her go into your room. Didn't you ever find her there, right beside your bed, standing perfectly still?"

"I don't remember. It's a pretty crazy idea, to have a black African play the role of your mother."

"You're just looking at it from the outside. But I'm willing to bet it's a guilt dream, and who's the one who always makes you feel guilty? Mother, every time."

"I'm not a Freudian," she told him. "But even if you admit—which I don't for a minute—that the dream comes from feeling guilt, and that I'm remembering Mother from when I was little, it gets nowhere in explaining why I'm so sure Mother's being played by Sekou. Haven't you got a theory for that?"

"A very good one. There's just no connection between what's in the dream and why you think you dream it. Try putting Sekou into the dream when you go over it in your mind, and see how he reacts."

"I never go over it in my mind. It's bad enough to have to experience it without playing around with it when I'm awake."

"Well, all I can say, Nita, is that it'll go on bothering you until you pull it to pieces and examine it carefully."

"The day I decide what I'm guilty of, I'll tell you."

XIV

Everyone in the town knew of Mme. Massot. She and her husband had lived there when the French ruled the region. Then, just after Independence, when Mme. Massot was not yet twenty years old, her husband had died, leaving her with a photographer's studio and very little else. She had a darkroom and she had learned how to develop and print photographs. Having a monopoly on this service was not as remunerative as it might have been elsewhere, for there was very little call for it. Of late the number of young people with cameras had increased, so that she not only developed and printed, but sold film as well. A few young natives who had lived in Europe repeatedly tried to persuade her to stock video tapes, but she explained that she did not have the capital to invest.

After the death of Monsieur Massot she had briefly entertained the idea of returning to France, but she soon decided that she did not really want to do that. Life in Montpellier would be a good deal more expensive, and there was no guarantee that she would find a suitable place to live, with an extra room to be used as a darkroom.

Only a handful of white people found it strange that she was willing to stay on alone in a city of blacks. As for her, from the day of her arrival directly after her marriage, she had found the black people sympathetic, kind, generous and well-disposed. She could find no fault in them save a tendency to be careless about time. Often they seemed not to know either the hour or the day. The younger citizens were aware that Europeans considered this a defect in their countrymen, and did their utmost to be punctual when they were dealing with foreigners. Although Mme. Massot was cordial with the other French inhabitants, she had established her particular friendships with the families of the native bourgeoisie. She had never learned to speak any of the local tongues, but these people spoke a passable French, and their sons were surprisingly proficient in the language.

Seldom did she find herself wishing to be in France, and then only fleetingly. The climate here was pleasant if one did not mind the heat, which she did not, and with her asthmatic condition it was ideal. People in Europe continually surprised her by assuming that the city must be dirty and unhealthy, and very likely she surprised them by maintaining that the streets were cleaner and more free of objectionable odors than those of any European city. She knew how to live in the desert, and she managed to remain in excellent health all during the year. The difficult months were May and June, when the heat became trying and the wind covered one with sand if one went outside, and July and August, when rain fell and the air was damp, and reminded her that she had suffered from asthma in her early days.

Before Anita's arrival Mme. Massot and Tom had become friends, principally, he supposed, because she had worked for a year at a small art gallery in the rue Vignon, and being unusually aware had absorbed a good deal of painter lore during that time, all of which had remained with her since then. She was still able to discuss the private lives of several painters of the era and the prices fetched by their canvases, and Tom found this appealing. Her year in Paris had made a kind of gossip between them possible. He thought now of inviting her once again for a meal. This was always a risky undertaking because she was an expert cook, particularly of local dishes using native ingredients. Unlike many autodidacts she was not averse to sharing her discoveries with anyone who had the same interest in cooking as she. With her encouragement Tom had learned to prepare two or three dishes successfully.

"I'll have her for lunch on Monday," he told Anita. "And you can do me a great favor once again if you go to her shop and invite her. You can get some films at the same time. You know the way now, so you won't need anybody to go with you. Do you mind? I'd lose a morning's work if I went."

"I don't mind. But I should think a little exercise would be good for you."

"I get my exercise running on the shore before breakfast. You know that. I don't need more. So you tell Mme. Massot we'll expect her for lunch Monday, will you? She speaks English."

"You forget I majored in French."

She had no desire to walk through the town, but she rose, saying, "Well, I'm off while the air is only at blood temperature."

When she came to the stand where she and Sekou had sat and had cold drinks, she found it shut. She had not been eager to come on this errand for Tom because she had a superstitious conviction that the encounter with the two American barbarians might repeat itself. She even found herself listening for the detestable sound of their motorcycle in the distance. Before she got to the market she decided that the two had left the town and gone to another place where they could terrify a new lot of natives, the people here undoubtedly having grown used to their presence.

Mme. Massot seemed to be delighted with the invitation. "How's Tom?" she said. "You came to the shop not long ago, but I haven't seen Tom in a very long time."

Back in the house she climbed to the roof where Tom was working, and told him: "She'll come Monday. Is she a dyke, d'you think?"

Tom cried: "Good Lord! How would I know? I never asked her. Where'd you get such an idea?"

"I don't know. It just occurred to me as we were talking. She's so serious."

"I'd be very surprised if she were."

Recently the air had been charged with dust, and each day there seemed to be more of it. Apparently it was politer to call it sand, or so Tom said, but he agreed that if it was sand, it was pulverized sand, which is another term for dust. There was no avoiding it. Certain downstairs rooms let less of it in, but the doors could not really be shut, and the powder was being propelled by a constant wind which carried it into the narrowest spaces.

XV

When Monday came, the dust had reached such a state of opacity that from the roof it was impossible to distinguish forms in the street below. Tom decided that they would have to eat in one of the downstairs rooms with the door shut. "It'll be claustrophobic," he said, "but what else can we do?"

"I know one thing we can do," Anita told him. "Not today, but fast, just the same. And that's to get out of this town. Think of our lungs. We might as well be living in a coal mine. And it's going to start raining soon. Then what do we have? Mud City. You've always said the place was uninhabitable half the year."

Mme. Massot was shown upstairs by a kitchen maid, lighting the way in the gloom with a guttering candle. She held in front of her what looked like a shoe box, which she immediately presented to Tom.

"The herbs I promised you," she said. "Only it's a little late to be giving them to you now."

He opened the box. Inside, it was divided into three small compartments, all filled with black earth, out of which grew small fringes and feathers of green. "Oregano, marjoram and tarragon," she said, pointing. "But you have to keep the box covered at this season. The sand will choke the plants."

"I love it," Anita volunteered, examining the box. "It's like a little portable garden."

"I keep all my herbs inside the house and covered up."

"We should have made this appointment two weeks ago," Tom said. "I hate to think of you walking all the way through this hellish weather. And how do you manage to arrive here looking so unruffled, so svelte and chic?"

Anita had been thinking exactly that. Mme. Massot was impeccably clothed in a khaki ensemble, clearly something designed for use in the desert, but which would have been equally elegant on the rue de Faubourg St. Honoré. "Ah," she said, unwinding the turban from her head and shaking it. "The secret is that Monsieur Bessier passed me in the market and drove me straight here in his truck. So it was a question of two minutes rather than forty."

"What a fantastic garment!" Anita cried with enthusiasm, stretching forth her hand to touch the lower part. "Do you mind?"

Mme. Massot raised her arms behind her head to facilitate the examination. "It's really an adaptation of Saharan serrouelles combined with the local boubou," she explained. "It's my own invention."

"It's absolutely perfect," Anita told her. "But you didn't get the material here."

"No, no. I got it in Paris, and had it made up there. I'm not very good with a needle and thread. But the design is so simple that I'm convinced a local tailor could make a copy easily. The trick is in the cutting on the bias, so that the top seems to be a part of the trousers, and the whole thing, from the shoulders to the ankles, is one line, seamless."

"It's certainly the right color for today," Tom told her.

"I don't mind the weather," she said. "This is the price we have to pay for what we get the rest of the year. It's a nuisance, but I find it a challenge. That doesn't mean that I don't often rush off to France at this time of the year, because I do. My brother has a farm not far from Narbonne. Summer in Provence is lovely. But you know, I'm here today primarily to see your pictures."

"Yes." Tom looked unhappy. "Too bad you can't see them by daylight, but it'll have to be downstairs, and by pressure lamp. I can't unpack them up here with this dust and sand."

Lunch was announced by Johara, and the same kitchen maid guided them down the dark stairway, holding her candle aloft. "It's really a shame," Anita remarked, "having to eat down here. It's so much pleasanter on the terrace under the awning. But there's certainly no help for it."

As she ate, Mme. Massot demanded suddenly: "Who is responsible for this delicious food, monsieur? You?"

"I'm afraid not. It was Johara."

"How lucky you are to have that woman. As soon as you're gone, I'm going to try to get her."

"But you don't need her. You can prepare any dish you want by yourself."

"Yes, if I don't mind spending the entire day in the kitchen. Besides, it's less of a pleasure to eat the food one has cooked oneself."

"I imagine she'll be delighted to go from one job directly to another," said Tom.

"Oh, you never know with these people. They're not greedy. They're not ambitious. What seems to be most important for them is their relationship with their employer. He may be impossibly severe or completely casual. If they like him, they like him. This dish is superb," she went on. "I know how it's made, but I haven't had much luck with it so far."

"How *is* it made?" asked Tom.

"The base is tiny millet cakes. The caramel sauce is no problem, but the cream over it is a bit difficult. It's the white meat of the coconut, macerated in a little of the coconut milk. It's hard to get the right consistency. But your cook has done it to perfection."

Tom was busy removing his paintings from the metal case in which he kept them. "I'll just bring out the most recent things. I think they're the best, anyway."

"Oh, no!" objected Mme. Massot. "I want to see everything. Whatever you've done here, in any case."

"That would take all night. You don't realize how prolific I am."

"Just show me what you want to show me, and I'll be happy." He passed her a sheaf of gouaches done on paper.

She studied each piece intently and at length. Suddenly she cried out in delight. "But these paintings are phenomenal! Of a subtlety! And of a beauty! Let me see more! They're like nothing I've ever seen, I assure you."

As she continued to look, from time to time she murmured: "*Invraisemblable.*"

Anita, until now a spectator, spoke. "Show her *La Boucle du Niger*," she urged Tom. "Can you get at it? I think it's one of the most successful of all."

He seemed annoyed by her declaration. "In what way successful?"

"I love the landscape on the far side of the river," she explained.

"I'll come to it," he said gruffly. "I've got them arranged the way I want them."

Mme. Massot continued to study the pictures. "I begin to understand your method," she murmured. "It's very clever. Often a question of letting pure chance in one detail decide the treatment of the entire painting. You remain flexible up to the final moment. Isn't that true?"

"Sometimes," he agreed, noncommittally. A moment later he said: "I think that's enough to give you an idea of what I've been doing here."

Mme. Massot's eyes shone. "You're a genius! You'll surely have an enormous success with these. They're irresistible."

When Johara had cleared away the coffee cups, Mme. Massot rose. "I still intend to try to get that woman when you've gone," she told them. "You're going this week?"

"As soon as we can get out," Anita said.

"Let's go upstairs and see how the weather is behaving," Tom suggested. "You haven't got Monsieur Bessier to drive you home."

He and Mme. Massot walked to the door. "You coming?" he asked Anita. She shook her head, and he shut the door from the outside.

They were gone longer than was necessary for determining whether or not the wind had diminished. She sat in the shut-in room, feeling that the lunch had been a waste of time. When they came down, Mme. Massot was insisting that it was unnecessary for Tom to accompany her home. Anita saw, however, that he was determined to go with her. "But everyone knows me here," she was objecting, "and it's not yet dark. No one would think of bothering me. Anyway, the wind has died down and there's practically no dust in the air. Do stay here."

"I wouldn't dream of it."

XVI

When Mme. Massot had made a somewhat formal adieu to Anita, they went out, and Anita hurried upstairs onto the roof, to breathe some fresh air. The wind was no longer raging, and the town's soft landscape of mud was once more visible. It was very quiet; only an occasional dog barked to pierce the silence. The knowledge that very soon she would be leaving buoyed up her spirits, so that she was able to feel a certain sense of responsibility vis-à-vis the house. It seemed to her that it would be a good idea to go down and thank Johara for having taken such pains to prepare an excellent dinner for their guest. Johara, standing in the kitchen lighted by two candles, received the praise with her usual imperturbable dignity. Communication with her was difficult, so Anita smiled and went out into the courtyard, turning her flashlight in all directions. Then she went back to the room where they had eaten, and where the pressure lamp was roaring. She had left the door open when she had gone up onto the roof, and the room was now aired. She sat down on the cushions and began to read.

Sooner than she expected, he was back, his T-shirt completely wet.

"Why all the sweat?" she said. "It's not that hot."

"I practically jogged all the way back."

"You didn't have to do that. There's no hurry."

She read a few more lines, and put the book on the couch beside her. "Anyway, now we know she's not a dyke," she said.

"Are you out of your mind?" he cried. "Still thinking about that? Besides, why do we know now and didn't before? Because she didn't make a pass at you?"

She glanced at him an instant. "Ah, shut your beak! It was pretty clear to me that she's interested in you."

"What made it so clear?"

"Oh, the way she purred over your pictures, for one thing."

"Just French manners."

"Yes. I know. But no etiquette demands such fulsome praise as she was dishing out."

"Fulsome? It was perfectly sincere. As a matter of fact, a lot of what she said was very much to the point."

"I can see you respond to flattery."

"You can't believe that anyone could get excited about my painting, I know."

"Oh, Tom, you're impossible. I didn't say that, but my personal opinion is that it wasn't your pictures that excited her today."

"You mean she has a sexual interest?"

"What do you think I mean?"

"Well, suppose she did, and suppose I reciprocated it, would that be important?"

"Obviously not. But I think it's interesting."

"You were just trying to keep me on the straight and narrow as far as my work is involved. You're right, of course, and I ought to appreciate it. But I don't. It's too much fun to be told how good you are. You want to stay up there for a while, savoring all the nice things you've just been told."

"I'm sorry," she said. "I certainly didn't mean to belittle your work, or depress you."

"Probably you didn't, but talking about it now depresses me."

"Sorry," she said, not sounding sorry. "On the way to her house did Mme. Massot go on about your painting?"

He was angry. "She did not." A moment later he continued. "She had a long complicated story to tell, about two students from Yale who were found dead last week out near Gargouna. We never hear anything here. Old Monsieur Bessier was called in. The police had heard that his truck had been seen out there a couple of days before they found them. Of course it had, because we were in it. The kids had a motorcycle, and they were trying to run it in the sand."

"They had an accident?" She managed to keep her voice normal. "There's no need," she thought. "No one knows anything."

"They went into some big rocks, and were pretty much cut up. But apparently it wasn't their injuries that killed them."

"What was it?" Her voice was much too feeble, but he did not notice. "I've got to continue this dialogue as though it meant absolutely nothing," she told herself.

"It was insolation. The damn fools were wearing no clothes. Only shorts. Nobody's sure when the accident happened, but they must have lain there naked for two or three days, getting more burned and scorched by the hour. It's a mystery why nobody from the village saw them before that. But people don't wander around in the dunes much, of course. And by the time somebody did see them, the sun had finished them off."

"What a shame." She saw the two again, the bright red and blue shorts, the blood on the bronzed bodies and the bent chromium cage above them. "The poor boys. How awful."

Tom went on talking, but she did not hear him. A little later she murmured: "How terrible."

XVII

Now, when they were within a few days of leaving to go to Paris, Anita began to feel an acute need to clear her mind of the fog of doubts and fears that had been plaguing her since the day at Gargouna. The dream was of course at the core; she had not experienced it for several nights. There was also the question of Sekou. If she left here without a satisfactory explanation of his connection with the dream, she would consider it a major failure on her part. The monsters were dead. Sekou was alive; he might be of help.

"Is Sekou around?" she inquired of Tom. He looked surprised. "Why? You want to see him?"

"I'd like to take a walk along the river, and I thought he might go with me."

Tom hesitated. "I don't know whether he's up to it. He's been having trouble with an infected leg. I'll see if he's in the house somewhere and let you know."

He found him sitting in a room near the kitchen, and suggested that he let him sterilize the wound again. Sekou became hesitant when he saw Anita standing outside the door.

"You can come in and watch, if you want," Tom told her. He had no patience with the excessive prudery of the local males. "It's a mean gash, all the way from the ankle up to the knee. I don't wonder it got infected. But it's a lot better." He tore away the strips that held the bandage in place. "It's all dry," he announced. There's no use asking him if it hurts, because he'll say no, even if the pain is killing him. *"Tout va bien maintenant?"* Sekou smiled and said: *"Merci beaucoup. La plaie s'est fermee."*

"He'll be able to walk with you," Tom said.

Sekou seemed relieved when Tom pulled his gandoura down and covered the leg.

As they went along the edge of the river, Anita inquired what had happened to cause such a deep cut. "You saw," he said, surprised at the question. "You were there. You saw how the tourists ran their machine into me."

"I thought so," she said. "Oh, those two monsters." It helped to speak of them thus, even knowing that she was partially responsible for their deaths.

The wind was beginning again to blow, and the air was being filled with dust. There were not many fishermen in the river today. It was twilight at mid-morning.

"You say they were devils," proceeded Sekou. "But they weren't devils. They were ignorant young men. I know you were very angry with them, and you put a curse on them."

Anita was astonished. "What?" she cried.

"You said they were going to be in trouble and you would be happy to see them suffering. I think they have gone away."

Her impulse was to say: "They're dead," but she held her tongue, thinking it strange that he had not heard the news.

"I had already forgiven them, but I know you had not. When my leg hurt very much, Monsieur Tom gave me an injection. I told myself maybe the pain would stop if you forgave them, too. One night I dreamed I went and spoke to you. I wanted to hear you say it. But you said: 'No. They are devils. They nearly killed me. Why should I forgive them?' Then I knew that you would never forgive them."

"Monsters," Anita murmured, "not devils." He seemed not to have heard her.

"Then thanks to God, Monsieur Tom made my leg well again."

"Shall we go back? The air is full of dust." They turned and began to walk in the other direction. For some minutes they were silent. Eventually Anita said: "In your dream, did you want me to go and see them, tell them I forgave them?"

"It would have made me very happy, yes. But I did not dare ask you to do that. I thought it would be enough to hear you say 'I forgive them.' "

"It doesn't do any good for me to say now 'I forgive them,' does it? But I do forgive them." Her voice was a bit tearful. He noticed it, and stood still.

"Of course it does! It does good for you. If you have anger inside yourself it's poison for you. Everyone should always forgive everyone."

During the rest of the walk she was silent, thinking of her own dream in which forgiveness played no part, for Yindall and Fambers could only be what she had decided they were beforehand. They were monsters, thus her unconscious had to supply a world for them where everything was monstrous.

She thought of Sekou's interpretation of her furious words to the cyclists. In a sense it was quite accurate. Her behavior was exactly what constituted putting a curse on someone, although she would not have described the thing in those terms. Without understanding the words, he had seized their import. Basic emotions have their own language.

She had been right. Sekou's intense desire had, through his dream, put him in contact with the dark side of her mind and forced her to seek out Yindall and Fambers. (She had no other names to give them.)

XVIII

The following morning Tom, who had gone out early not to run beside the river, but to walk to the market, returned in a state of excitement. "A real stroke of luck!" he cried. "I ran into Bessier. His nephew's here and he's leaving tomorrow, and he says there's room for us in his Land Rover. That way we're sure of getting to Mopti before the rain starts."

Anita, delighted by the prospect of going, nevertheless asked: "Why Mopti before the rain?"

"Because the road between here and there is impassable once the rain begins. From Mopti on it's relatively smooth sailing. The ride'll save us a lot of worry. And I won't have to pay out a fortune to rent a vehicle that would get us through. So, can you get packed?"

She laughed. "I've got practically nothing with me, you know. I can get it all together in a half hour."

The idea of leaving, of seeing a landscape different from the endless lightstruck emptiness here stimulated her. She felt, however, a certain ambivalence. She had begun to care for the flat sand-colored town, knowing that she would never see another place quite like it. Nor, it occurred to her, would she ever find another person with the same uncomplicated purity of Sekou. (She knew that she would continue to think of him in the days to come.)

The morning of departure Tom was busy handing out money to those who had performed services of one sort or another in the house. Anita went with him to the kitchen and shook Johara's hand. She was hoping to see Sekou and bid him good-bye, but it was too early for him to have come around.

"I'm really disappointed," she said, as they stood outside the house waiting for Bessier's nephew.

"You finally decided to like Sekou," Tom remarked. "You see, he didn't want to rape you."

She could not help saying: "But he dreamed of me."

"He did?" Tom seemed amused. "How do you know that?"

"He told me. He dreamed he came and stood by my bed." She decided to stop there and say no more. Tom's expression was despairing. He shook his head. "Well, it's all too much for me."

She was glad to see the Land Rover approaching.

When they were far out in the desert she was still reviewing the no longer painful story. Sekou knew much of it, but she knew it all, and she promised herself that never would anyone else hear of it.

STORIES

The Delicate Prey

There were three Filala who sold leather in Tabelbala—two brothers and the young son of their sister. The two older merchants were serious, bearded men who liked to engage in complicated theological discussions during the slow passage of the hot hours in their *hanoute* near the market-place; the youth naturally occupied himself almost exclusively with the black-skinned girls in the small *quartier réservé*. There was one who seemed more desirable than the others, so that he was a little sorry when the older men announced that soon they would all leave for Tessalit. But nearly every town has its *quartier*, and Driss was reasonably certain of being able to have any lovely resident of any *quartier*, whatever her present emotional entanglements; thus his chagrin at hearing of the projected departure was short-lived.

The three Filala waited for the cold weather before starting out for Tessalit. Because they wanted to get there quickly they chose the western-most trail, which is also the one leading through the most remote regions, contiguous to the lands of the plundering Reguibat tribes. It was a long time since the uncouth mountain men had swept down from the *hammada* upon a caravan; most people were of the opinion that since the war of the Sarrho they had lost the greater part of their arms and ammunition, and, more important still, their spirit. And a tiny group of three men and their camels could scarcely awaken the envy of the Reguibat, traditionally rich with loot from all Río de Oro and Mauretania.

Their friends in Tabelbala, most of them other Filali leather merchants, walked beside them sadly as far as the edge of the town; then they bade them farewell, and watched them mount their camels to ride off slowly toward the bright horizon.

"If you meet any Reguibat, keep them ahead of you!" they called.

The danger lay principally in the territory they would reach only three or four days' journey from Tabelbala; after a week the edge of the land haunted by the Reguibat would be left entirely behind. The weather was cool save at midday. They took turns sitting guard at night; when Driss stayed awake he brought out a small flute whose piercing notes made the older uncle frown with annoyance, so that he asked him to go and sit at some distance from the sleeping-blankets. All night he sat playing whatever sad songs he could call to mind; the bright ones in his opinion belonged to the *quartier*, where one was never alone.

When the uncles kept watch, they sat quietly, staring ahead of them into the night. There were just the three of them.

And then one day a solitary figure appeared, moving toward them across the lifeless plain from the west. One man on a camel; there was no sign of any others, although they scanned the wasteland in every direction. They stopped for a while; he altered his course slightly. They went ahead; he changed it again. There was no doubt that he wanted to speak with them.

"Let him come," grumbled the older uncle, glaring about the empty horizon once more. "We each have a gun."

Driss laughed. To him it seemed absurd even to admit the possibility of trouble from one lone man.

When finally the figure arrived within calling distance, it hailed them in a voice like a muezzin's: "*S'l'm aleikoum!*" They halted, but did not dismount, and waited for the man to draw nearer. Soon he called again; this time the older uncle replied, but the distance was still too great for his voice to carry, and the man did not hear his greeting. Presently he was close enough for them to see that he did not wear Reguiba attire. They muttered to one another: "He comes from the north, not the west." And they all felt glad. However, even when he came up beside them they remained on the camels, bowing solemnly from where they sat, and always searching in the new face and in the garments below it for some false note which might reveal the possible truth—that the man was a scout for the Reguibat, who would be waiting up on the *hammada* only a few hours distant, or even now moving parallel to the trail, closing in upon them in such a manner that they would not arrive at a point within visibility until after dusk.

Certainly the stranger himself was no Reguiba; he was quick and jolly, with light skin and very little beard. It occurred to Driss that he did not like his small, active eyes which seemed to take in everything and give out nothing, but this passing reaction became only a part of the general initial distrust, all of which was dissipated when they learned that the man was a Moungari. Moungar is a holy place in that part of the world, and its few residents are treated with respect by the pilgrims who go to visit the ruined shrine nearby.

The newcomer took no pains to hide the fear he had felt at being alone in the region, or the pleasure it gave him to be now with three other men. They all dismounted and made tea to seal their friendship, the Moungari furnishing the charcoal.

During the third round of glasses he made the suggestion that since he was going more or less in their direction he accompany them as far as Taoudeni. His bright black eyes darting from one Filali to the other, he explained that he was an excellent shot, that he was certain he could supply them all with some good gazelle meat en route, or at least an *aoudad*. The Filala considered; the oldest finally said: "Agreed." Even if the Moungari turned out to have not quite the hunting prowess he claimed for himself, there would be four of them on the voyage instead of three.

Two mornings later, in the mighty silence of the rising sun, the Moungari pointed at the low hills that lay beside them to the east: *"Timma. I know this land. Wait here. If you hear me shoot, then come, because that will mean there are gazelles."*

The Moungari went off on foot, climbing up between the boulders and disappearing behind the nearest crest. "He trusts us," thought the Filala. "He has left his *mehari*, his blankets, his packs." They said nothing, but each knew that the others were thinking the same as he, and they all felt warmly toward the stranger. They sat waiting in the early-morning chill while the camels grumbled.

It seemed unlikely that there would prove to be any gazelles in the region, but if there should be any, and the Moungari were as good a hunter as he claimed to be, then there was a chance they would have a *mechoui* of gazelle that evening, and that would be very fine.

Slowly the sun mounted in the hard blue sky. One camel lumbered up and went off, hoping to find a dead thistle or a bush between the rocks, something left over from a year when rain might have fallen. When it had disappeared, Driss went in search of it and drove it back to the others, shouting: *"Hut!"*

He sat down. Suddenly there came a shot, a long empty interval, and then another shot. The sounds were fairly distant, but perfectly clear in the absolute silence. The older brother said: "I shall go. Who knows? There may be many gazelles."

He clambered up the rocks, his gun in his hand, and was gone.

Again they waited. When the shots sounded this time, they came from two guns.

"Perhaps they have killed one!" Driss cried.

"*Yemkin*. With Allah's aid," replied his uncle, rising and taking up his gun. "I want to try my hand at this."

Driss was disappointed: he had hoped to go himself. If only he had got up a moment ago, it might have been possible, but even so it was likely that he would have been left behind to watch the *mehara*. In any case, now it was too late; his uncle had spoken.

"Good."

His uncle went off singing a song from Tafilalet: it was about date palms and hidden smiles. For several minutes Driss heard snatches of the song, as the melody reached the high notes. Then the sound was lost in the enveloping silence.

He waited. The sun began to be very hot. He covered his head with his burnoose. The camels looked at each other stupidly, craning their necks, baring their brown and yellow teeth. He thought of playing his flute, but it did not seem the right moment: he was too restless, too eager to be up there with his gun, crouching behind the rocks, stalking the delicate prey. He thought of Tessalit and wondered what it would be like. Full of blacks and Touareg, certainly more lively than Tabelbala, because of the road that passed through it. There was a shot. He waited for others, but no more came this time. Again he imagined himself there among the boulders, taking aim at a fleeing beast. He pulled the trigger, the animal fell. Others appeared, and he got them all. In the dark the travelers sat around the fire gorging themselves with the rich roasted flesh, their faces gleaming with grease. Everyone was happy, and even the Moungari admitted that the young Filali was the best hunter of them all.

In the advancing heat he dozed, his mind playing over a landscape made of soft thighs and small hard breasts rising like sand dunes; wisps of song floated like clouds in the sky, and the air was thick with the taste of fat gazelle meat.

He sat up and looked around quickly. The camels lay with their necks stretched along the ground in front of them. Nothing had changed. He stood up, uneasily scanned the stony landscape. While he had slept, a hostile presence had entered into his consciousness. Translating into thought what he already sensed, he cried out. Since first he had seen those small, active eyes he had felt mistrust of their owner, but the fact that his uncles had accepted him had pushed suspicion away into the dark of his mind. Now, unleashed in his slumber, it had bounded back. He turned toward the hot hillside and looked intently between the boulders, into the black shadows. In memory he heard again the shots up among the rocks, and he knew what they had meant. Catching his breath in a sob, he ran to mount his *mehari*, forced it up, and already had gone several hundred paces before he was aware of what he was doing. He stopped the animal to sit quietly a moment, glancing back at the campsite with fear and indecision. If his uncles were dead, then there was nothing to do but get out into the open desert as quickly as possible, away from the rocks that could hide the Moungari while he took aim.

And so, not knowing the way to Tessalit, and without sufficient food or water, he started ahead, lifting one hand from time to time to wipe away the tears.

For two or three hours he continued that way, scarcely noticing where the *mehari* walked. All at once he sat erect, uttered an oath against himself, and in a fury turned the beast around. At that very moment his uncles might be seated in the camp with the Moungari, preparing a *mechoui* and a fire, sadly asking themselves why their nephew had deserted them. Or perhaps one would already have set out in search of him. There would be no possible excuse for his conduct, which had been the result of an absurd terror. As he thought about it, his anger against himself mounted: he had behaved in an unforgivable manner. Noon had passed; the sun was in the west. It would be late when he got back. At the prospect of the inevitable reproaches and the mocking laughter that would greet him, he felt his face grow hot with shame, and he kicked the *mehari*'s flanks viciously.

A good while before he arrived at the camp he heard singing. This surprised him. He halted and listened: the voice was too far away to be identified, but Driss felt certain it was the Moungari's. He continued around the side of the hill to a spot in full view of the camels. The singing stopped, leaving silence. Some of the packs had been loaded back on to the beasts, preparatory to setting out. The sun had sunk low, and the shadows of the rocks were stretched out along the earth. There was no sign that they had caught any game. He called out, ready to dismount. Almost at the same instant there was a shot from very nearby, and he heard the small rushing sound of a bullet go past his head. He seized his gun. There was another shot, a sharp pain in his arm, and his gun slipped to the ground.

For a moment he sat there holding his arm, dazed. Then swiftly he leapt down and remained crouching among the stones, reaching out with his good arm for the gun. As he touched it, there was a third shot, and the rifle moved along the ground a few inches toward him in a small cloud of dust. He drew back his hand and looked at it: it was dark and blood dripped from it. At that moment the Moungari bounded across the open space between them. Before Driss could rise the man was upon him, had pushed him back down to the ground with the barrel of his rifle. The untroubled sky lay above; the Moungari glanced up at it defiantly. He straddled the supine youth, thrusting the gun into his neck just below the chin, and under his breath he said: "Filali dog!"

Driss stared up at him with a certain curiosity. The Moungari had the upper hand; Driss could only wait. He looked at the face in the sun's light, and discovered a peculiar intensity there. He knew the expression: it comes from hashish. Carried along on its hot fumes, a man can escape very far from the world of meaning. To avoid the malevolent face he rolled his eyes from side to side. There was only the fading sky. The gun was choking him a little. He whispered: "Where are my uncles?"

The Moungari pushed harder against his throat with the gun, leaned partially over and with one hand ripped away his *serouelles*, so that he lay naked from the waist down, squirming a little as he felt the cold stones beneath him.

Then the Moungari drew forth rope and bound his feet. Taking two steps to his head, he abruptly faced in the other direction, and thrust the gun into his navel. Still with one hand he slipped the remaining garments off over the youth's head and lashed his wrists together. With an old barber's razor he cut off the superfluous rope. During this time Driss called his uncles by name, loudly, first one and then the other.

The man moved and surveyed the young body lying on the stones. He ran his finger along the razor's blade; a pleasant excitement took possession of him. He stepped over, looked down, and saw the sex that sprouted from the base of the belly. Not entirely conscious of what he was doing, he took it in one hand and brought his other arm down with the motion of a reaper wielding a sickle. It was swiftly severed. A round, dark hole was left, flush with the skin; he stared a moment, blankly. Driss was screaming. The muscles all over his body stood out, moved.

Slowly the Moungari smiled, showing his teeth. He put his hand on the hard belly and smoothed the skin. Then he made a small vertical incision there, and using both hands, studiously stuffed the loose organ in until it disappeared.

As he was cleaning his hands in the sand, one of the camels uttered a sudden growling gurgle. The Moungari leapt up and wheeled about savagely, holding his razor high in the air. Then, ashamed of his nervousness, feeling that Driss was watching and mocking him (although the youth's eyes were unseeing with pain), he kicked him over on to his stomach where he lay making small spasmodic movements. And as the Moungari followed these with his eyes, a new idea came to him. It would be pleasant to inflict an ultimate indignity upon the young Filali. He threw himself down; this time he was vociferous and leisurely in his enjoyment. Eventually he slept.

At dawn he awoke and reached for his razor, lying on the ground nearby. Driss moaned faintly. The Moungari turned him over and pushed the blade back and forth with a sawing motion into his neck until he was certain he had severed the windpipe. Then he rose, walked away, and finished the loading of the camels he had started the day before. When this was done he spent a good while dragging the body over to the base of the hill and concealing it there among the rocks.

In order to transport the Filala's merchandise to Tessalit (for in Taoudeni there would be no buyers) it was necessary to take their *mehara* with him. It was nearly fifty days later when he arrived. Tessalit is a small town. When the Moungari began to show the leather around, an old Filali living there, whom the people called Ech Chibani, got wind of his presence. As a prospective buyer he came to examine the hides, and the Moungari was unwise enough to let him see them. Filali leather is unmistakable, and only the Filala buy and sell it in quantity. Ech Chibani knew the Moungari had come by it illicitly, but he said nothing. When a few days later another caravan arrived from Tabelbala with friends of the three Filala who asked after them and showed great distress on hearing that they never had arrived, the old man went to the Tribunal. After some difficulty he found a Frenchman who was willing to listen to him. The next day the commandant and two subordinates paid the Moungari a visit. They asked him how he happened to have the three extra *mehara*, which still carried some of their Filali trappings; his replies took a devious turn. The Frenchmen listened seriously, thanked him, and left. He did not see the commandant wink at the others as they went out into the street. And so he remained sitting in his courtyard, not knowing that he had been judged and found guilty.

The three Frenchmen went back to the Tribunal, where the newly arrived Filali merchants were sitting with Ech Chibani. The story had an old pattern; there was no doubt at all about the Moungari's guilt. "He is yours," said the commandant. "Do what you like with him."

The Filala thanked him profusely, held a short conference with the aged Chibani, and strode out in a group. When they arrived at the Moungari's dwelling he was making tea. He looked up, and a chill moved along his spine. He began to scream his innocence at them; they said nothing, but at the point of a rifle bound him and tossed him into a corner, where he continued to babble and sob. Quietly they drank the tea he had been brewing, made some more, and went out at twilight. They tied him to one of the *mehara,* and mounting their own, moved in a silent procession (silent save for the Moungari) out through the town gate into the infinite wasteland beyond.

Half the night they continued, until they were in a completely unfrequented region of the desert. While he lay raving, bound to the camel, they dug a well-like pit, and when they had finished they lifted him off, still trussed tightly, and stood him in it. Then they filled all the space around his body with sand and stones, until only his head remained above the earth's surface. In the faint light of the new moon his shaved pate without its turban looked rather like a rock. And still he pleaded with them, calling upon Allah and Sidi Ahmed Ben Moussa to witness his innocence. But he might have been singing a song for all the attention they paid to his words. Presently they set off for Tessalit; in no time they were out of hearing.

When they had gone the Moungari fell silent, to wait through the cold hours for the sun that would bring first warmth, then heat, thirst, fire, visions. The next night he did not know where he was, did not feel the cold. The wind blew dust along the ground into his mouth as he sang.

A Distant Episode

The September sunsets were at their reddest the week the Professor decided to visit Aïn Tadouirt, which is in the warm country. He came down out of the high, flat region in the evening by bus, with two small overnight bags full of maps, sun lotions and medicines. Ten years ago he had been in the village for three days; long enough, however, to establish a fairly firm friendship with a café keeper, who had written him several times during the first year after his visit, if never since. "Hassan Ramani," the Professor said over and over, as the bus bumped downward through ever warmer layers of air. Now facing the flaming sky in the west, and now facing the sharp mountains, the car followed the dusty trail down the canyons into air which began to smell of other things besides the endless ozone of the heights: orange blossoms, pepper, sun-baked excrement, burning olive oil, rotten fruit. He closed his eyes happily and lived for an instant in a purely olfactory world. The distant past returned—what part of it, he could not decide.

The chauffeur, whose seat the Professor shared, spoke to him without taking his eyes from the road. *"Vous êtes géologue?"*

"A geologist? Ah, no! I'm a linguist."

"There are no languages here. Only dialects."

"Exactly. I'm making a survey of variations on Maghrebi."

The chauffeur was scornful. "Keep on going south," he said. "You'll find some languages you never heard of before."

As they drove through the town gate, the usual swarm of urchins rose up out of the dust and ran screaming beside the bus. The Professor folded his dark glasses, put them in his pocket; and as soon as the vehicle had come to a standstill he jumped out, pushing his way through the indignant boys who clutched at his luggage in vain, and walked quickly into the Grand Hotel Saharien. Out of its eight rooms there were two available—one facing the market and the other, a smaller and cheaper one, giving onto a tiny yard full of refuse and barrels, where two gazelles wandered about. He took the smaller room, and pouring the entire pitcher of water into the tin basin, began to wash the grit from his face and ears. The afterglow was nearly gone from the sky, and the pinkness in objects was disappearing, almost as he watched. He lit the carbide lamp and winced at its odor.

After dinner the Professor walked slowly through the streets to Hassan Ramani's café, whose back room hung hazardously out above the river. The entrance was very low, and he had to bend down slightly to get in. A man was tending the fire. There was one guest sipping tea. The *qaouaji* tried to make him take a seat at the other table in the front room, but the Professor walked airily ahead into the back room and sat down. The moon was shining through the reed latticework and there was not a sound outside but the occasional distant bark of a dog. He changed tables so he could see the river. It was dry, but there was a pool here and there that reflected the bright night sky. The *qaouaji* came in and wiped off the table.

"Does this café still belong to Hassan Ramani?" he asked him in the Maghrebi he had taken four years to learn.

The man replied in bad French: "He is deceased."

"Deceased?" repeated the Professor, without noticing the absurdity of the word. "Really? When?"

"I don't know," said the *qaouaji*. "One tea?"

"Yes. But I don't understand . . ."

The man was already out of the room, fanning the fire. The Professor sat still, feeling lonely, and arguing with himself that to do so was ridiculous. Soon the *qaouaji* returned with the tea. He paid him and gave him an enormous tip, for which he received a grave bow.

"Tell me," he said, as the other started away. "Can one still get those little boxes made from camel udders?"

The man looked angry. "Sometimes the Reguibat bring in those things. We do not buy them here." Then insolently, in Arabic: "And why a camel-udder box?"

"Because I like them," retorted the Professor. And then because he was feeling a little exalted, he added, "I like them so much I want to make a collection of them, and I will pay you ten francs for every one you can get me."

"*Khamstache,*" said the *qaouaji,* opening his left hand rapidly three times in succession.

"Never. Ten."

"Not possible. But wait until later and come with me. You can give me what you like. And you will get camel-udder boxes if there are any."

He went out into the front room, leaving the Professor to drink his tea and listen to the growing chorus of dogs that barked and howled as the moon rose higher into the sky. A group of customers came into the front room and sat talking for an hour or so. When they had left, the *qaouaji* put out the fire and stood in the doorway putting on his burnoose. "Come," he said.

Outside in the street there was very little movement. The booths were all closed and the only light came from the moon. An occasional pedestrian passed, and grunted a brief greeting to the *qaouaji*.

"Everyone knows you," said the Professor, to cut the silence between them.

"Yes."

"I wish everyone knew me," said the Professor, before he realized how infantile such a remark must sound.

"*No* one knows you," said his companion gruffly.

They had come to the other side of the town, on the promontory above the desert, and through a great rift in the wall the Professor saw the white endlessness, broken in the foreground by dark spots of oasis. They walked through the opening and followed a winding road between rocks, downward toward the nearest small forest of palms. The Professor thought: "He may cut my throat. But his café—he would surely be found out."

"Is it far?" he asked, casually.

"Are you tired?" countered the *qaouaji*.

"They are expecting me back at the Hotel Saharien," he lied.

"You can't be there and here," said the *qaouaji*.

The Professor laughed. He wondered if it sounded uneasy to the other.

"Have you owned Ramani's café long?"

"I work there for a friend." The reply made the Professor more unhappy than he had imagined it would.

"Oh. Will you work tomorrow?"

"That is impossible to say."

The Professor stumbled on a stone, and fell, scraping his hand. The *qaouaji* said: "Be careful."

The sweet black odor of rotten meat hung in the air suddenly.

"Agh!" said the Professor, choking. "What is it?"

The *qaouaji* had covered his face with his burnoose and did not answer. Soon the stench had been left behind. They were on flat ground. Ahead the path was bordered on each side by a high mud wall. There was no breeze and the palms were quite still, but behind the walls was the sound of running water. Also, the odor of human excrement was almost constant as they walked between the walls.

The Professor waited until he thought it seemed logical for him to ask with a certain degree of annoyance: "But where are we going?"

"Soon," said the guide, pausing to gather some stones in the ditch.

"Pick up some stones," he advised. "Here are bad dogs."

"Where?" asked the Professor, but he stooped and got three large ones with pointed edges.

They continued very quietly. The walls came to an end and the bright desert lay ahead. Nearby was a ruined marabout, with its tiny dome only half standing, and the front wall entirely destroyed. Behind it were clumps of stunted, useless palms. A dog came running crazily toward them on three legs. Not until it got quite close did the Professor hear its steady low growl. The *qaouaji* let fly a large stone at it, striking it square in the muzzle. There was a strange snapping of jaws and the dog ran sideways in another direction, falling blindly against rocks and scrambling haphazardly about like an injured insect.

Turning off the road, they walked across the earth strewn with sharp stones, past the little ruin, through the trees, until they came to a place where the ground dropped abruptly away in front of them.

"It looks like a quarry," said the Professor, resorting to French for the word "quarry," whose Arabic equivalent he could not call to mind at the moment. The *qaouaji* did not answer. Instead he stood still and turned his head, as if listening. And indeed, from somewhere down below, but very far below, came the faint sound of a low flute. The *qaouaji* nodded his head slowly several times. Then he said: "The path begins here. You can see it well all the way. The rock is white and the moon is strong. So you can see well. I am going back now and sleep. It is late. You can give me what you like."

Standing there at the edge of the abyss which at each moment looked deeper, with the dark face of the *qaouaji* framed in its moonlit burnoose close to his own face, the Professor asked himself exactly what he felt. Indignation, curiosity, fear, perhaps, but most of all relief and the hope that this was not a trick, the hope that the *qaouaji* would really leave him alone and turn back without him.

He stepped back a little from the edge, and fumbled in his pocket for a loose note, because he did not want to show his wallet. Fortunately there was a fifty-franc bill there, which he took out and handed to the man. He knew the *qaouaji* was pleased, and so he paid no attention when he heard him saying: "It is not enough. I have to walk a long way home and there are dogs. . . ."

"Thank you and good-night," said the Professor, sitting down with his legs drawn up under him, and lighting a cigarette. He felt almost happy.

"Give me only one cigarette," pleaded the man.

"Of course," he said, a bit curtly, and he held up the pack.

The *qaouaji* squatted close beside him. His face was not pleasant to see. "What is it?" thought the Professor, terrified again, as he held out his lighted cigarette toward him.

The man's eyes were almost closed. It was the most obvious registering of concentrated scheming the Professor had ever seen. When the second cigarette was burning, he ventured to say to the still-squatting Arab: "What are you thinking about?"

The other drew on his cigarette deliberately, and seemed about to speak. Then his expression changed to one of satisfaction, but he did not speak. A cool wind had risen in the air, and the Professor shivered. The sound of the flute came up from the depths below at intervals, sometimes mingled with the scraping of nearby palm fronds one against the other. "These people are not primitives," the Professor found himself saying in his mind.

"Good," said the *qaouaji*, rising slowly. "Keep your money. Fifty francs is enough. It is an honor." Then he went back into French: *"Ti n'as qu'à discendre, to' droit."* He spat, chuckled (or was the Professor hysterical?), and strode away quickly.

The Professor was in a state of nerves. He lit another cigarette, and found his lips moving automatically. They were saying: "Is this a situation or a predicament? This is ridiculous." He sat very still for several minutes, waiting for a sense of reality to come to him. He stretched out on the hard, cold ground and looked up at the moon. It was almost like looking straight at the sun. If he shifted his gaze a little at a time, he could make a string of weaker moons across the sky. "Incredible," he whispered. Then he sat up quickly and looked about. There was no guarantee that the *qaouaji* really had gone back to town. He got to his feet and looked over the edge of the precipice. In the moonlight the bottom seemed miles away. And there was nothing to give it scale; not a tree, not a house, not a person. . . . He listened for the flute, and heard only the wind going by his ears. A sudden violent desire to run back to the road seized him, and he turned and looked in the direction the *qaouaji* had taken. At the same time he felt softly of his wallet in his breast pocket. Then he spat over the edge of the cliff. Then he made water over it, and listened intently, like a child. This gave him the impetus to start down the path into the abyss. Curiously enough, he was not dizzy. But prudently he kept from peering to his right, over the edge. It was a steady and steep downward climb. The monotony of it put him into a frame of mind not unlike that which had been induced by the bus ride. He was murmuring "Hassan Ramani" again, repeatedly and in rhythm. He stopped, furious with himself for the sinister overtones the name now suggested to him. He decided he was exhausted from the trip. "And the walk," he added.

He was now well down the gigantic cliff, but the moon, being directly overhead, gave as much light as ever. Only the wind was left behind, above, to wander among the trees, to blow through the dusty streets of Aïn Tadouirt, into the hall of the Grand Hotel Saharien, and under the door of his little room.

It occurred to him that he ought to ask himself why he was doing this irrational thing, but he was intelligent enough to know that since he was doing it, it was not so important to probe for explanations at that moment.

Suddenly the earth was flat beneath his feet. He had reached the bottom sooner than he had expected. He stepped ahead distrustfully still, as if he expected another treacherous drop. It was so hard to know in this uniform, dim brightness. Before he knew what had happened the dog was upon him, a heavy mass of fur trying to push him backward, a sharp nail rubbing down his chest, a straining of muscles against him to get the teeth into his neck. The Professor thought: "I refuse to die this way." The dog fell back; it looked like an Eskimo dog. As it sprang again, he called out, very loud: "Ay!" It fell against him, there was a confusion of sensations and a pain somewhere. There was also the sound of voices very near to him, and he could not understand what they were saying. Something cold and metallic was pushed brutally against his spine as the dog still hung for a second by his teeth from a mass of clothing and perhaps flesh. The Professor knew it was a gun, and he raised his hands, shouting in Maghrebi: "Take away the dog!" But the gun merely pushed him forward, and since the dog, once it was back on the ground, did not leap again, he took a step ahead. The gun kept pushing; he kept taking steps. Again he heard voices, but the person directly behind him said nothing. People seemed to be running about; it sounded that way, at least. For his eyes, he discovered, were still shut tight against the dog's attack. He opened them. A group of men was advancing toward him. They were dressed in the black clothes of the Reguibat. "The Reguiba is a cloud across the face of the sun." "When the Reguiba appears the righteous man turns away." In how many shops and marketplaces he had heard these maxims uttered banteringly among friends. Never to a Reguiba, to be sure, for these men do not frequent towns. They send a representative in disguise, to arrange with shady elements there for the disposal of captured goods. "An opportunity," he thought quickly, "of testing the accuracy of such statements." He did not doubt for a moment that the adventure would prove to be a kind of warning against such foolishness on his part—a warning which in retrospect would be half sinister, half farcical.

Two snarling dogs came running from behind the oncoming men and threw themselves at his legs. He was scandalized to note that no one paid any attention to this breach of etiquette. The gun pushed him harder as he tried to sidestep the animals' noisy assault. Again he cried: "The dogs! Take them away!" The gun shoved him forward with great force and he fell, almost at the feet of the crowd of men facing him. The dogs were wrenching at his hands and arms. A boot kicked them aside, yelping, and then with increased vigor it kicked the Professor in the hip. Then came a chorus of kicks from different sides, and he was rolled violently about on the earth for a while. During this time he was conscious of hands reaching into his pockets and removing everything from them. He tried to say: "You have all my money; stop kicking me!" But his bruised facial muscles would not work; he felt himself pouting, and that was all. Someone dealt him a terrific blow on the head, and he thought: "Now at least I shall lose consciousness, thank Heaven." Still he went on being aware of the guttural voices he could not understand, and of being bound tightly about the ankles and chest. Then there was black silence that opened like a wound from time to time, to let in the soft, deep notes of the flute playing the same succession of notes again and again. Suddenly he felt excruciating pain everywhere—pain and cold. "So I have been unconscious, after all," he thought. In spite of that, the present seemed only like a direct continuation of what had gone before.

It was growing faintly light. There were camels near where he was lying; he could hear their gurgling and their heavy breathing. He could not bring himself to attempt opening his eyes, just in case it should turn out to be impossible. However, when he heard someone approaching, he found that he had no difficulty in seeing.

The man looked at him dispassionately in the gray morning light. With one hand he pinched together the Professor's nostrils. When the Professor opened his mouth to breathe, the man swiftly seized his tongue and pulled on it with all his might. The Professor was gagging and catching his breath; he did not see what was happening. He could not distinguish the pain of the brutal yanking from that of the sharp knife. Then there was an endless choking and spitting that went on automatically, as though he were scarcely a part of it. The word "operation" kept going through his mind; it calmed his terror somewhat as he sank back into darkness.

The caravan left sometime toward mid-morning. The Professor, not unconscious, but in a state of utter stupor, still gagging and drooling blood, was dumped doubled-up into a sack and tied at one side of a camel. The lower end of the enormous amphitheater contained a natural gate in the rocks. The camels, swift *mehara,* were lightly laden on this trip. They passed through single file, and slowly mounted the gentle slope that led up into the beginning of the desert. That night, at a stop behind some low hills, the men took him out, still in a state which permitted no thought, and over the dusty rags that remained of his clothing they fastened a series of curious belts made of the bottoms of tin cans strung together. One after another of these bright girdles was wired about his torso, his arms and legs, even across his face, until he was entirely within a suit of armor that covered him with its circular metal scales. There was a good deal of merriment during this decking-out of the Professor. One man brought out a flute and a younger one did a not ungraceful caricature of an Ouled Naïl executing a cane dance. The Professor was no longer conscious; to be exact, he existed in the middle of the movements made by these other men. When they had finished dressing him the way they wished him to look, they stuffed some food under the tin bangles hanging over his face. Even though he chewed mechanically, most of it eventually fell out onto the ground. They put him back into the sack and left him there.

Two days later they arrived at one of their own encampments. There were women and children here in the tents, and the men had to drive away the snarling dogs they had left there to guard them. When they emptied the Professor out of his sack, there were screams of fright, and it took several hours to convince the last woman that he was harmless, although there had been no doubt from the start that he was a valuable possession. After a few days they began to move on again, taking everything with them, and traveling only at night as the terrain grew warmer.

Even when all his wounds had healed and he felt no more pain, the Professor did not begin to think again; he ate and defecated, and he danced when he was bidden, a senseless hopping up and down that delighted the children, principally because of the wonderful jangling racket it made. And he generally slept through the heat of the day, in among the camels.

Wending its way southeast, the caravan avoided all stationary civilization. In a few weeks they reached a new plateau, wholly wild and with a sparse vegetation. Here they pitched camp and remained, while the *mehara* were turned loose to graze. Everyone was happy here; the weather was cooler and there was a well only a few hours away on a seldom-frequented trail. It was here they conceived the idea of taking the Professor to Fogara and selling him to the Touareg.

It was a full year before they carried out this project. By this time the Professor was much better trained. He could do a handspring, make a series of fearful growling noises which had, nevertheless, a certain element of humor; and when the Reguibat removed the tin from his face they discovered he could grimace admirably while he danced. They also taught him a few basic obscene gestures which never failed to elicit delighted shrieks from the women. He was now brought forth only after especially abundant meals, when there was music and festivity. He easily fell in with their sense of ritual, and evolved an elementary sort of "program" to present when he was called for: dancing, rolling on the ground, imitating certain animals, and finally rushing toward the group in feigned anger, to see the resultant confusion and hilarity.

When three of the men set out for Fogara with him, they took four *mehara* with them, and he rode astride his quite naturally. No precautions were taken to guard him, save that he was kept among them, one man always staying at the rear of the party. They came within sight of the walls at dawn, and they waited among the rocks all day. At dusk the youngest started out, and in three hours he returned with a friend who carried a stout cane. They tried to put the Professor through his routine then and there, but the man from Fogara was in a hurry to get back to town, so they all set out on the *mehara*.

In the town they went directly to the villager's home, where they had coffee in the courtyard sitting among the camels. Here the Professor went into his act again, and this time there was prolonged merriment and much rubbing together of hands. An agreement was reached, a sum of money paid, and the Reguibat withdrew, leaving the Professor in the house of the man with the cane, who did not delay in locking him into a tiny enclosure off the courtyard.

The next day was an important one in the Professor's life, for it was then that pain began to stir again in his being. A group of men came to the house, among whom was a venerable gentleman, better clothed than those others who spent their time flattering him, setting fervent kisses upon his hands and the edges of his garments. This person made a point of going into classical Arabic from time to time, to impress the others, who had not learned a word of the Koran. Thus his conversation would run more or less as follows: "Perhaps at In Salah. The French there are stupid. Celestial vengeance is approaching. Let us not hasten it. Praise the highest and cast thine anathema against idols. With paint on his face. In case the police wish to look close." The others listened and agreed, nodding their heads slowly and solemnly. And the Professor in his stall beside them listened, too. That is, he was *conscious* of the sound of the old man's Arabic. The words penetrated for the first time in many months. Noises, then: "Celestial vengeance is approaching." Then: "It is an honor. Fifty francs is enough. Keep your money. Good." And the *qaouaji* squatting near him at the edge of the precipice. Then "anathema against idols" and more gibberish. He turned over panting on the sand and forgot about it. But the pain had begun. It operated in a kind of delirium, because he had begun to enter into consciousness again. When the man opened the door and prodded him with his cane, he cried out in a rage, and everyone laughed.

They got him onto his feet, but he would not dance. He stood before them, staring at the ground, stubbornly refusing to move. The owner was furious, and so annoyed by the laughter of the others that he felt obliged to send them away, saying that he would await a more propitious time for exhibiting his property, because he dared not show his anger before the elder. However, when they had left he dealt the Professor a violent blow on the shoulder with his cane, called him various obscene things, and went out into the street, slamming the gate behind him. He walked straight to the street of the Ouled Naïl, because he was sure of finding the Reguibat there among the girls, spending the money. And there in a tent he found one of them still abed, while an Ouled Naïl washed the tea glasses. He walked in and almost decapitated the man before the latter had even attempted to sit up. Then he threw his razor on the bed and ran out.

The Ouled Naïl saw the blood, screamed, ran out of her tent into the next, and soon emerged from that with four girls who rushed together into the coffeehouse and told the *qaouaji* who had killed the Reguiba. It was only a matter of an hour before the French military police had caught him at a friend's house, and dragged him off to the barracks. That night the Professor had nothing to eat, and the next afternoon, in the slow sharpening of his consciousness caused by increasing hunger, he walked aimlessly about the courtyard and the rooms that gave onto it. There was no one. In one room a calendar hung on the wall. The Professor watched nervously, like a dog watching a fly in front of its nose. On the white paper were black objects that made sounds in his head. He heard them: *"Grande Épicerie du Sahel. Juin. Lundi, Mardi, Mercredi. . . ."*

The tiny inkmarks of which a symphony consists may have been made long ago, but when they are fulfilled in sound they become imminent and mighty. So a kind of music of feeling began to play in the Professor's head, increasing in volume as he looked at the mud wall, and he had the feeling that he was performing what had been written for him long ago. He felt like weeping; he felt like roaring through the little house, upsetting and smashing the few breakable objects. His emotion got no further than this one overwhelming desire. So, bellowing as loud as he could, he attacked the house and its belongings. Then he attacked the door into the street, which resisted for a while and finally broke. He climbed through the opening made by the boards he had ripped apart, and still bellowing and shaking his arms in the air to make as loud a jangling as possible, he began to gallop along the quiet street toward the gateway of the town. A few people looked at him with great curiosity. As he passed the garage, the last building before the high mud archway that framed the desert beyond, a French soldier saw him. *"Tiens,"* he said to himself, "a holy maniac."

Again it was sunset time. The Professor ran beneath the arched gate, turned his face toward the red sky, and began to trot along the Piste d'In Salah, straight into the setting sun. Behind him, from the garage, the soldier took a potshot at him for good luck. The bullet whistled dangerously near the Professor's head, and his yelling rose into an indignant lament as he waved his arms more wildly, and hopped high into the air at every few steps, in an access of terror.

The soldier watched a while, smiling, as the cavorting figure grew smaller in the oncoming evening darkness, and the rattling of the tin became a part of the great silence out there beyond the gate. The wall of the garage as he leaned against it still gave forth heat, left there by the sun, but even then the lunar chill was growing in the air.

Call at Corazón

"But why would you want a little horror like that to go along with us? It doesn't make sense. You know what they're like."

"I know what they're like," said her husband. "It's comforting to watch them. Whatever happens, if I had that to look at, I'd be reminded of how stupid I was ever to get upset."

He leaned further over the railing and looked intently down at the dock. There were baskets for sale, crude painted toys of hard natural rubber, reptile-hide wallets and belts, and a few whole snakeskins unrolled. And placed apart from these wares, out of the hot sunlight, in the shadow of a crate, sat a tiny, furry monkey. The hands were folded, and the forehead was wrinkled in sad apprehensiveness.

"Isn't he wonderful?"

"I think you're impossible—and a little insulting," she replied.

He turned to look at her. "Are you serious?" He saw that she was.

She went on, studying her sandaled feet and the narrow deck boards beneath them: "You know I don't really mind all this nonsense, or your craziness. Just let me finish." He nodded his head in agreement, looking back at the hot dock and the wretched tin-roofed village beyond. "It goes without saying I don't mind all that, or we wouldn't be here together. You might be here alone . . ."

"You don't take a honeymoon alone," he interrupted.

"*You* might." She laughed shortly.

He reached along the rail for her hand, but she pulled it away, saying, "I'm still talking to you. I expect you to be crazy, and I expect to give in to you all along. I'm crazy too, I know. But I wish there were some way I could just once feel that my giving in meant anything to you. I wish you knew how to be gracious about it."

"You think you humor me so much? I haven't noticed it." His voice was sullen.

"I don't *humor* you at all. I'm just trying to live with you on an extended trip in a lot of cramped little cabins on an endless series of stinking boats."

"What do you mean?" he cried excitedly. "You've always said you loved the boats. Have you changed your mind, or just lost it completely?"

She turned and walked toward the prow. "Don't talk to me," she said. "Go and buy your monkey."

An expression of solicitousness on his face, he was following her. "You know I won't buy it if it's going to make you miserable."

"I'll be more miserable if you don't, so please go and buy it." She stopped and turned. "I'd love to have it. I really would. I think it's sweet."

"I don't get you at all."

She smiled. "I know. Does it bother you very much?"

After he had bought the monkey and tied it to the metal post of the bunk in the cabin, he took a walk to explore the port. It was a town made of corrugated tin and barbed wire. The sun's heat was painful, even with the sky's low-lying cover of fog. It was the middle of the day and few people were in the streets. He came to the edge of the town almost immediately. Here between him and the forest lay a narrow, slow-moving stream, its water the color of black coffee. A few women were washing clothes; small children splashed. Gigantic gray crabs scuttled between the holes they had made in the mud along the bank. He sat down on some elaborately twisted roots at the foot of a tree and took out the notebook he always carried with him. The day before, in a bar at Pedernales, he had written: "Recipe for dissolving the impression of hideousness made by a thing: Fix the attention upon the given object or situation so that the various elements, all familiar, will regroup themselves. Frightfulness is never more than an unfamiliar pattern."

He lit a cigarette and watched the women's hopeless attempts to launder the ragged garments. Then he threw the burning stub at the nearest crab, and carefully wrote: "More than anything else, woman requires strict ritualistic observance of the traditions of sexual behavior. That is her definition of love." He thought of the derision that would be called forth should he make such a statement to the girl back on the ship. After looking at his watch, he wrote hurriedly: "Modern, that is, intellectual education, having been devised by males for males, inhibits and confuses her. She avenges . . ."

Two naked children, coming up from their play in the river, ran screaming past him, scattering drops of water over the paper. He called out to them, but they continued their chase without noticing him. He put his pencil and notebook into his pocket, smiling, and watched them patter after one another through the dust.

When he arrived back at the ship, the thunder was rolling down from the mountains around the harbor. The storm reached the height of its hysteria just as they got under way.

She was sitting on her bunk, looking through the open porthole. The shrill crashes of thunder echoed from one side of the bay to the other as they steamed toward the open sea. He lay doubled up on his bunk opposite, reading.

"Don't lean your head against that metal wall," he advised. "It's a perfect conductor."

She jumped down to the floor and went to the washstand.

"Where are those two quarts of White Horse we got yesterday?"

He gestured. "In the rack on your side. Are you going to drink?"

"I'm going to *have* a drink, yes."

"In this heat? Why don't you wait until it clears, and have it on deck?"

"I want it now. When it clears I won't need it."

She poured the whiskey and added water from the carafe in the wall bracket over the washbowl.

"You realize what you're doing, of course."

She glared at him. "What am I doing?"

He shrugged his shoulders. "Nothing, except just giving in to a passing emotional state. You could read, or lie down and doze."

Holding her glass in one hand, she pulled open the door into the passageway with the other, and went out. The noise of the slamming door startled the monkey, perched on a suitcase. It hesitated a second, and hurried under its master's bunk. He made a few kissing sounds to entice it out, and returned to his book. Soon he began to imagine her alone and unhappy on the deck, and the thought cut into the pleasure of his reading. He forced himself to lie still a few minutes, the open book face down across his chest. The boat was moving at full speed now, and the sound of the motors was louder than the storm in the sky.

Soon he rose and went on deck. The land behind was already hidden by the falling rain, and the air smelled of deep water. She was standing alone by the rail, looking down at the waves, with the empty glass in her hand. Pity seized him as he watched, but he could not walk across to her and put into consoling words the emotion he felt.

Back in the cabin he found the monkey on his bunk, slowly tearing the pages from the book he had been reading.

The next day was spent in leisurely preparation for disembarking and changing of boats: in Villalta they were to take a smaller vessel to the opposite side of the delta.

When she came in to pack after dinner, she stood a moment studying the cabin. "He's messed it up, all right," said her husband, "but I found your necklace behind my big valise, and we'd read all the magazines anyway."

"I suppose this represents Man's innate urge to destroy," she said, kicking a ball of crumpled paper across the floor. "And the next time he tries to bite you, it'll be Man's basic insecurity."

"You don't know what a bore you are when you try to be caustic. If you want me to get rid of him, I will. It's easy enough."

She bent to touch the animal, but it backed uneasily under the bunk. She stood up. "I don't mind him. What I mind is you. *He* can't help being a little horror, but he keeps reminding me that you could if you wanted."

Her husband's face assumed the impassivity that was characteristic of him when he was determined not to lose his temper. She knew he would wait to be angry until she was unprepared for his attack. He said nothing, tapping an insistent rhythm on the lid of a suitcase with his fingernails.

"Naturally I don't really mean you're a horror," she continued.

"Why not mean it?" he said, smiling pleasantly. "What's wrong with criticism? Probably I am, to you. I like monkeys because I see them as little model men. You think men are something else, something spiritual or God knows what. Whatever it is, I notice you're the one who's always being disillusioned and going around wondering how mankind can be so bestial. I think mankind is fine."

"Please don't go on," she said. "I know your theories. You'll never convince yourself of them."

When they had finished packing, they went to bed. As he snapped off the light behind his pillow, he said, "Tell me honestly. Do you want me to give him to the steward?"

She kicked off her sheet in the dark. Through the porthole, near the horizon, she could see stars, and the calm sea slipped by just below her. Without thinking she said, "Why don't you drop him overboard?"

In the silence that followed she realized she had spoken carelessly, but the tepid breeze moving with languor over her body was making it increasingly difficult for her to think or speak. As she fell asleep it seemed to her she heard her husband saying slowly, "I believe you would. I believe you would."

The next morning she slept late, and when she went up for breakfast her husband had already finished his and was leaning back, smoking.

"How are you?" he asked brightly. "The cabin steward's delighted with the monkey."

She felt a flush of pleasure. "Oh," she said, sitting down, "did you give it to him? You didn't have to do that." She glanced at the menu; it was the same as every other day. "But I suppose really it's better. A monkey doesn't go with a honeymoon."

"I think you're right," he agreed.

Villalta was stifling and dusty. On the other boat they had grown accustomed to having very few passengers around, and it was an unpleasant surprise to find the new one swarming with people. Their new boat was a two-decked ferry painted white, with an enormous paddle wheel at the stern. On the lower deck, which rested not more than two feet above the surface of the water, passengers and freight stood ready to travel, packed together indiscriminately. The upper deck had a salon and a dozen or so narrow staterooms. In the salon the first-class passengers undid their bundles of pillows and opened their paper bags of food. The orange light of the setting sun flooded the room.

They looked into several of the staterooms.

"They all seem to be empty," she said.

"I can see why. Still, the privacy would be a help."

"This one's double. And it has a screen in the window. This is the best one."

"I'll look for a steward or somebody. Go on in and take over." He pushed the bags out of the passageway where the *cargador* had left them, and went off in search of an employee. In every corner of the boat the people seemed to be multiplying. There were twice as many as there had been a few moments before. The salon was completely full, its floor space occupied by groups of travelers with small children and elderly women, who were already stretched out on blankets and newspapers.

"It looks like Salvation Army headquarters the night after a major disaster," he said as he came back into the stateroom. "I can't find anybody. Anyway, we'd better stay in here. The other cubicles are beginning to fill up."

"I'm not so sure I wouldn't rather be on deck," she announced. "There are hundreds of cockroaches."

"And probably worse," he added, looking at the bunks.

"The thing to do is take those filthy sheets off and just lie on the mattresses." She peered out into the corridor. Sweat was trickling down her neck. "Do you think it's safe?"

"What do you mean?"

"All those people. This old tub."

He shrugged his shoulders.

"It's just one night. Tomorrow we'll be at Ciénaga. And it's almost night now."

She shut the door and leaned against it, smiling faintly.

"I think it's going to be fun," she said.

"The boat's moving!" he cried. "Let's go on deck. If we can get out there."

Slowly the old boat pushed across the bay toward the dark east shore. People were singing and playing guitars. On the bottom deck a cow lowed continuously. And louder than all the sounds was the rush of water made by the huge paddles.

They sat on the deck in the middle of a vociferous crowd, leaning against the bars of the railing, and watched the moon rise above the mangrove swamps ahead. As they approached the opposite side of the bay, it looked as if the boat might plow straight into the shore, but a narrow waterway presently appeared, and the boat slipped cautiously in. The people immediately moved back from the railing, crowding against the opposite wall. Branches from the trees on the bank began to rub against the boat, scraping along the side walls of the cabins, and then whipping violently across the deck.

They pushed their way through the throng and walked across the salon to the deck on the other side of the boat; the same thing was happening there.

"It's crazy," she declared. "It's like a nightmare. Whoever heard of going through a channel no wider than the boat! It makes me nervous. I'm going in and read."

Her husband let go of her arm. "You can never enter into the spirit of a thing, can you?"

"You tell me what the spirit is, and I'll see about entering into it," she said, turning away.

He followed her. "Don't you want to go down onto the lower deck? They seem to be going strong down there. Listen." He held up his hand. Repeated screams of laughter came up from below.

"I certainly don't!" she called, without looking around.

He went below. Groups of men were seated on bulging burlap sacks and wooden crates, matching coins. The women stood behind them, puffing on black cigarettes and shrieking with excitement. He watched them closely, reflecting that with fewer teeth missing they would be a handsome people. "Mineral deficiency in the soil," he commented to himself.

Standing on the other side of a circle of gamblers, facing him, was a muscular young native whose visored cap and faint air of aloofness suggested official position of some sort aboard the boat. With difficulty the traveler made his way over to him, and spoke to him in Spanish.

"Are you an employee here?"

"Yes, sir."

"I am in cabin number eight. Can I pay the supplementary fare to you?"

"Yes, sir."

"Good."

He reached into his pocket for his wallet, at the same time remembering with annoyance that he had left it upstairs locked in a suitcase. The man looked expectant. His hand was out.

"My money is in my stateroom." Then he added, "My wife has it. But if you come up in half an hour I can pay you the fare."

"Yes, sir." The man lowered his hand and merely looked at him. Even though he gave an impression of purely animal force, his broad, somewhat simian face was handsome, the husband reflected. It was surprising when, a moment later, that face betrayed a boyish shyness as the man said, "I am going to spray the cabin for your señora."

"Thank you. Are there many mosquitoes?"

The man grunted and shook the fingers of one hand as if he had just burned them.

"Soon you will see how many." He moved away.

At that moment the boat jolted violently, and there was great merriment among the passengers. He pushed his way to the prow and saw that the pilot had run into the bank. The tangle of branches and roots was a few feet from his face, its complex forms vaguely lighted by the boat's lanterns. The boat backed laboriously and the channel's agitated water rose to deck level and lapped the outer edge. Slowly they nosed along the bank until the prow once more pointed to midstream, and they continued. Then almost immediately the passage curved so sharply that the same thing happened again, throwing him sideways against a sack of something unpleasantly soft and wet. A bell clanged below deck in the interior of the boat; the passengers' laughter was louder.

Eventually they pushed ahead, but now the movement became painfully slow as the sharpness of the curves in the passage increased. Under the water the stumps groaned as the boat forced its sides against them. Branches cracked and broke, falling onto the forward and upper decks. The lantern at the prow was swept into the water.

"This isn't the regular channel," muttered a gambler, glancing up.

Several travelers exclaimed, "What?" almost in unison.

"There's a pile of passages through here. We're picking up cargo at Corazón."

The players retreated to a square inner arena which others were forming by shifting some of the crates. The husband followed them. Here they were comparatively safe from the intruding boughs. The deck was better lighted here, and this gave him the idea of making an entry in his notebook. Bending over a carton marked VERMIFUGO SANTA ROSALIA, he wrote: "November 18. We are moving through the bloodstream of a giant. A very dark night." Here a fresh collision with the land knocked him over, knocked over everyone who was not propped between solid objects.

A few babies were crying, but most of them still slept. He slid down to the deck. Finding his position fairly comfortable, he fell into a dozing state which was broken irregularly by the shouting of the people and the jolting of the boat.

When he awoke later, the boat was quite stationary, the games had ceased, and the people were asleep, a few of the men continuing their conversation in small groups. He lay still, listening. The talk was all about places; they were comparing the unpleasant things to be found in various parts of the republic: insects, weather, reptiles, diseases, lack of food, high prices.

He looked at his watch. It was half past one. With difficulty he got to his feet, and found his way to the stairs. Above, in the salon, the kerosene lamps illumined a vast disorder of prostrate figures. He went into the corridor and knocked on the door marked with an eight. Without waiting for her to answer, he opened the door. It was dark inside. He heard a muffled cough nearby, and decided that she was awake.

"How are the mosquitoes? Did my monkey man come and fix you up?" he asked.

She did not answer, so he lit a match. She was not in the bunk on the left. The match burned his thumb. With the second one, he looked at the right-hand bunk. A tin insecticide sprayer lay there on the mattress; its leak had made a large circle of oil on the bare ticking. The cough was repeated. It was someone in the next cabin.

"Now what?" he said aloud, uncomfortable at finding himself upset to this degree. A suspicion seized him. Without lighting the hanging lamp, he rushed to open her valises, and in the dark felt hurriedly through the flimsy pieces of clothing and the toilet articles. The whiskey bottles were not there.

This was not the first time she had gone on a solitary drinking bout, and it would be easy to find her among the passengers. However, being angry, he decided not to look for her. He took off his shirt and trousers and lay down on the left-hand bunk. His hand touched a bottle standing on the floor by the head of the bunk. He raised himself enough to smell it; it was beer and the bottle was half full. It was hot in the cabin, and he drank the remaining warm, bitter liquid with relish and rolled the bottle across the room.

The boat was not moving, but voices shouted out here and there. An occasional bump could be felt as a sack of something heavy was heaved aboard. He looked through the little square window with the screen in it. In the foreground, dimly illumined by the boat's lanterns, a few dark men, naked save for their ragged underdrawers, stood on a landing made in the mud and stared toward the boat. Through the endless intricacies of roots and trunks behind them he saw a bonfire blazing, but it was far back in the swamp. The air smelled of stagnant water and smoke.

Deciding to take advantage of the relative silence, he lay down and tried to sleep; he was not surprised, however, by the difficulty he found in relaxing. It was always hard to sleep when she was not there in the room. The comfort of her presence was lacking, and there was also the fear of being awakened by her return. When he allowed himself to, he would quickly begin to formulate ideas and translate them into sentences whose recording seemed the more urgent because he was lying comfortably in the dark. Sometimes he thought about her, but only as an unclear figure whose character lent flavor to a succession of backdrops. More often he reviewed the day just completed, seeking to convince himself that it had carried him a bit further away from his childhood. Often for months at a time the strangeness of his dreams persuaded him that at last he had turned the corner, that the dark place had finally been left behind, that he was out of hearing. Then, one evening as he fell asleep, before he had time to refuse, he would be staring closely at a long-forgotten object—a plate, a chair, a pincushion—and the accustomed feeling of infinite futility and sadness would recur.

The motor started up, and the great noise of the water in the paddle wheel recommenced. They pushed off from Corazón. He was pleased. "Now I shan't hear her when she comes in and bangs around," he thought, and fell into a light sleep.

He was scratching his arms and legs. The long-continued, vague malaise eventually became full consciousness, and he sat up angrily. Above the sounds made by the boat he could hear another sound, one which came through the window: an incredibly high and tiny tone, tiny but constant in pitch and intensity. He jumped down from the berth and went to the window. The channel was wider here, and the overhanging vegetation no longer touched the sides of the boat. In the air, nearby, far away, everywhere, was the thin wail of mosquito wings. He was aghast, and completely delighted by the novelty of the phenomenon. For a moment he watched the tangled black wilderness slip past. Then with the itching he remembered the mosquitoes inside the cabin. The screen did not reach quite to the top of the window; there was ample space for them to crawl in. Even there in the dark as he moved his fingers along the frame to find the handle he could feel them; there were that many.

Now that he was fully awake, he lighted a match and went to her bunk. Of course she was not there. He lifted the Flit gun and shook it. It was empty, and as the match went out, he saw that the spot on the mattress had spread even further.

"Son of a bitch!" he whispered, and going back to the window he tugged the screen vigorously upward to close the crack. As he let go of it, it fell out into the water, and almost immediately he was conscious of the soft caress of tiny wings all about his head. In his undershirt and trousers he rushed out into the corridor. Nothing had changed in the salon. Almost everyone was asleep. There were screen doors giving onto the deck. He inspected them: they appeared to be more firmly installed. A few mosquitoes brushed against his face, but it was not the horde. He edged in between two women who were sleeping sitting with their backs against the wall, and stayed there in acute discomfort until again he dozed. It was not long before he opened his eyes to find the dim light of dawn in the air. His neck ached. He arose and went out onto the deck, to which most of the people from the salon had already crowded.

The boat was moving through a wide estuary dotted with clumps of plants and trees that rose out of the shallow water. Along the edges of the small islands stood herons, so white in the early gray light that their brightness seemed to come from inside them.

It was half past five. At this moment the boat was due in Ciénaga, where it was met on its weekly trip by the train that went into the interior. Already a thin spit of land ahead was being identified by eager watchers. Day was coming up swiftly; sky and water were the same color. The deck reeked of the greasy smell of mangoes as people began to breakfast.

And now at last he began to feel pangs of anxiety as to where she might be. He determined to make an immediate and thorough search of the boat. She would be instantly recognizable in any group. First, he looked methodically through the salon, then he exhausted the possibilities on the upper decks. Then he went downstairs, where the gambling had already begun again. Toward the stern, roped to two flimsy iron posts, stood the cow, no longer bellowing. Nearby was an improvised lean-to, probably the crew's quarters. As he passed the small door, he peered through the low transom above it, and saw her lying beside a man on the floor. Automatically he walked on; then he turned and went back. The two were asleep, and half-clothed. In the warm air that came through the screened transom there was the smell of whiskey that had been drunk and whiskey that had been spilled.

He went upstairs, his heart beating violently. In the cabin, he closed her two valises, packed his own, set them all together by the door and laid the raincoats on top of them. He put on his shirt, combed his hair carefully, and went on deck. Ciénaga was there ahead, in the mountains' morning shadow: the dock, a line of huts against the jungle behind, and the railway station to the right beyond the village.

As they docked, he signaled the two urchins who were waving for his attention, screaming, *"Equipajes!"* They fought a bit with one another until he made them see his two fingers held aloft. Then to make them certain, he pointed at each of them in turn, and they grinned. Still grinning, they stood beside him with the bags and coats, and he was among the first of the upper-deck passengers to get on land. They went down the street to the station with the parrots screaming at them from each thatched gable along the way.

On the crowded, waiting train, with the luggage finally in the rack, his heart beat harder than ever, and he kept his eyes painfully on the long dusty street that led back to the dock. At the far end, as the whistle blew, he thought he saw a figure in white running among the dogs and children toward the station, but the train started up as he watched, and the street was lost to view. He took out his notebook, and sat with it on his lap, smiling at the shining green landscape that moved with increasing speed past the window.

Pages from Cold Point

Our civilization is doomed to a short life: its component parts are too heterogeneous. I personally am content to see everything in the process of decay. The bigger the bombs, the quicker it will be done. Life is visually too hideous for one to make the attempt to preserve it. Let it go. Perhaps some day another form of life will come along. Either way, it is of no consequence. At the same time, I am still a part of life, and I am bound by this to protect myself to whatever extent I am able. And so I am here. Here in the Islands vegetation still has the upper hand, and man has to fight even to make his presence seen at all. It is beautiful here, the trade winds blow all year, and I suspect that bombs are extremely unlikely to be wasted on this unfrequented side of the island, if indeed on any part of it.

I was loath to give up the house after Hope's death. But it was the obvious move to make. My university career always having been an utter farce (since I believe no reason inducing a man to "teach" can possibly be a valid one), I was elated by the idea of resigning, and as soon as her affairs had been settled and the money properly invested, I lost no time in doing so.

I think that week was the first time since childhood that I had managed to recapture the feeling of there being a content in existence. I went from one pleasant house to the next, making my adieux to the English quacks, the Philosophy fakirs and so on—even to those colleagues with whom I was merely on speaking terms. I watched the envy in their faces when I announced my departure by Pan American on Saturday morning; and the greatest pleasure I felt in all this was in being able to answer, "Nothing," when I was asked, as invariably I was, what I intended to do.

When I was a boy people used to refer to Charles as "Big Brother C.," although he is only a scant year older than I. To me now he is merely "Fat Brother C.," a successful lawyer. His thick, red face and hands, his back-slapping joviality and his fathomless hypocritical prudery—these are the qualities which make him truly repulsive to me. There is also the fact that he once looked not unlike the way Racky does now. And after all, he still is my big brother, and disapproves openly of everything I do. The loathing I feel for him is so strong that for years I have not been able to swallow a morsel of food or a drop of liquid in his presence without making a prodigious effort. No one knows this but me—certainly not Charles, who would be the last one I should tell about it. He came up on the late train two nights before I left. He got quickly to the point—as soon as he was settled with a highball.

"So you're off for the wilds," he said, sitting forward in his chair like a salesman.

"If you can call it the wilds," I replied. "Certainly it's not wild like Mitichi." (He has a lodge in northern Quebec.) "I consider it really civilized."

He drank and smacked his lips together stiffly, bringing the glass down hard on his knee.

"And Racky. You're taking him along?"

"Of course."

"Out of school. Away. So he'll see nobody but you. You think that's good."

I looked at him. "I do," I said.

"By God, if I could stop you legally, I would!" he cried, jumping up and putting his glass on the mantel. I was trembling inwardly with excitement, but I merely sat and watched him. He went on. "You're not fit to have custody of the kid!" he shouted. He shot a stern glance at me over his spectacles.

"You think not?" I said gently.

Again he looked at me sharply. "D'ye think I've forgotten?"

I was understandably eager to get him out of the house as soon as I could. As I piled and sorted letters and magazines on the desk, I said: "Is that all you came to tell me? I have a good deal to do tomorrow and I must get some sleep. I probably shan't see you at breakfast. Agnes'll see that you eat in time to make the early train."

All he said was: "God! Wake up! Get wise to yourself! You're not fooling anybody, you know."

That kind of talk is typical of Charles. His mind is slow and obtuse; he constantly imagines that everyone he meets is playing some private game of deception with him. He is so utterly incapable of following the functioning of even a moderately evolved intellect that he finds the will to secretiveness and duplicity everywhere.

"I haven't time to listen to that sort of nonsense," I said, preparing to leave the room.

But he shouted, "You don't want to listen! No! Of course not! You just want to do what you want to do. You just want to go on off down there and live as you've a mind to, and to hell with the consequences!" At this point I heard Racky coming downstairs. C. obviously heard nothing, and he raved on. "But just remember, I've got your number all right, and if there's any trouble with the boy I'll know who's to blame."

I hurried across the room and opened the door so he could see that Racky was there in the hallway. That stopped his tirade. It was hard to know whether Racky had heard any of it or not. Although he is not a quiet young person, he is the soul of discretion, and it is almost never possible to know any more about what goes on inside his head than he intends one to know.

I was annoyed that C. should have been bellowing at me in my own house. To be sure, he is the only one from whom I would accept such behavior, but then, no father likes to have his son see him take criticism meekly. Racky simply stood there in his bathrobe, his angelic face quite devoid of expression, saying: "Tell Uncle Charley good night for me, will you? I forgot."

I said I would, and quickly shut the door. When I thought Racky was back upstairs in his room, I bade Charles good night. I have never been able to get out of his presence fast enough. The effect he has on me dates from an early period of our lives, from days I dislike to recall.

Racky is a wonderful boy. After we arrived, when we found it impossible to secure a proper house near any town where he might have the company of English boys and girls his own age, he showed no sign of chagrin, although he must have been disappointed. Instead, as we went out of the renting office into the glare of the street, he grinned and said: "Well, I guess we'll have to get bikes, that's all."

The few available houses near what Charles would have called "civiliza-tion" turned out to be so ugly and so impossibly confining in atmosphere that we decided immediately on Cold Point, even though it was across the island and quite isolated on its seaside cliff. It was beyond a doubt one of the most desirable properties on the island, and Racky was as enthusiastic about its splendors as I.

"You'll get tired of being alone out there, just with me," I said to him as we walked back to the hotel.

"Aw, I'll get along all right. When do we look for the bikes?"

At his insistence we bought two the next morning. I was sure I should not make much use of mine, but I reflected that an extra bicycle might be convenient to have around the house. It turned out that the servants all had their own bicycles, without which they would not have been able to get to and from the village of Orange Walk, eight miles down the shore. So for a while I was forced to get astride mine each morning before breakfast and pedal madly along beside Racky for a half hour. We would ride through the cool early air, under the towering silk-cotton trees near the house, and out to the great curve in the shoreline where the waving palms bend landward in the stiff breeze that always blows there. Then we would make a wide turn and race back to the house, loudly discussing the degrees of our desires for the various items of breakfast we knew were awaiting us there on the terrace. Back home we would eat in the wind, looking out over the Caribbean, and talk about the news in yesterday's local paper, brought to us by Isiah each morning from Orange Walk. Then Racky would disappear for the whole morning on his bicycle, riding furiously along the road in one direction or the other until he had discovered an unfamiliar strip of sand along the shore that he could consider a new beach. At lunch he would describe it in detail to me, along with a recounting of all the physical hazards involved in hiding the bicycle in among the trees, so that natives passing along the road on foot would not spot it, or in climbing down unscalable cliffs that turned out to be much higher than they had appeared at first sight, or in measuring the depth of the water preparatory to diving from the rocks, or in judging the efficacy of the reef in barring sharks and barracuda. There is never any element of bragadoccio in Racky's relating of his exploits— only the joyous excitement he derives from telling how he satisfies his inexhaustible curiosity. And his mind shows its alertness in all directions at once. I do not mean to say that I expect him to be an "intellectual." That is no affair of mine, nor do I have any particular interest in whether he turns out to be a thinking man or not. I know he will always have a certain boldness of manner and a great purity of spirit in judging values. The former will prevent his becoming what I call a "victim": he never will be brutalized by realities. And his unerring sense of balance in ethical consider-ations will shield him from the paralyzing effects of present-day materialism.

For a boy of sixteen Racky has an extraordinary innocence of vision. I do not say this as a doting father, although God knows I can never even think of the boy without that familiar overwhelming sensation of delight and gratitude for being vouchsafed the privilege of sharing my life with him. What he takes so completely as a matter of course, our daily life here together, is a source of never-ending wonder to me; and I reflect upon it a good part of each day, just sitting here being conscious of my great good fortune in having him all to myself, beyond the reach of prying eyes and malicious tongues. (I suppose I am really thinking of C. when I write that.) And I believe that a part of the charm of sharing Racky's life with him consists precisely in his taking it all so utterly for granted. I have never asked him whether he likes being here—it is so patent that he does, very much. I think if he were to turn to me one day and tell me how happy he is here, that somehow, perhaps, the spell might be broken. Yet if he were to be thoughtless and inconsiderate, or even unkind to me, I feel that I should be able only to love him the more for it.

I have reread that last sentence. What does it mean? And why should I even imagine it could mean anything more than it says?

Still, much as I may try, I can never believe in the gratuitous, isolated fact. What I must mean is that I feel that Racky already has been in some way inconsiderate. But in what way? Surely I cannot resent his bicycle treks; I cannot expect him to want to stay and sit talking with me all day. And I never worry about his being in danger; I know he is more capable than most adults of taking care of himself, and that he is no more likely than any native to come to harm crawling over the cliffs or swimming in the bays. At the same time there is no doubt in my mind that something about our existence annoys me. I must resent some detail in the pattern, whatever that pattern may be. Perhaps it is just his youth, and I am envious of the lithe body, the smooth skin, the animal energy and grace.

For a long time this morning I sat looking out to sea, trying to solve that small puzzle. Two white herons came and perched on a dead stump east of the garden. They stayed a long time there without stirring. I would turn my head away and accustom my eyes to the bright sea horizon, then I would look suddenly at them to see if they had shifted position, but they would always be in the same attitude. I tried to imagine the black stump without them—a purely vegetable landscape—but it was impossible. All the while I was slowly forcing myself to accept a ridiculous explanation of my annoyance with Racky. It had made itself manifest to me only yesterday, when instead of appearing for lunch, he sent a young colored boy from

Orange Walk to say that he would be lunching in the village. I could not help noticing that the boy was riding Racky's bicycle. I had been waiting lunch a good half hour for him, and I had Gloria serve immediately as the boy rode off, back to the village. I was curious to know in what sort of place and with whom Racky could be eating, since Orange Walk, as far as I know, is inhabited exclusively by Negroes, and I was sure Gloria would be able to shed some light on the matter, but I could scarcely ask her. However, as she brought on the dessert, I said: "Who was that boy that brought the message from Mister Racky?"

She shrugged her shoulders. "A young lad of Orange Walk. He's named Wilmot."

When Racky returned at dusk, flushed from his exertion (for he never rides casually), I watched him closely. His behavior struck my already suspicious eye as being one of false heartiness and a rather forced good humor. He went to his room early and read for quite a while before turning off his light. I took a long walk in the almost day-bright moonlight, listening to the songs of the night insects in the trees. And I sat for a while in the dark on the stone railing of the bridge across Black River. (It is really only a brook that rushes down over the rocks from the mountain a few miles inland, to the beach near the house.) In the night it always sounds louder and more important than it does in the daytime. The music of the water over the stones relaxed my nerves, although why I had need of such a thing I find it difficult to understand, unless I was really upset by Racky's not having come home for lunch. But if that were true it would be absurd, and moreover, dangerous—just the sort of thing the parent of an adolescent has to beware of and fight against, unless he is indifferent to the prospect of losing the trust and affection of his offspring permanently. Racky must stay out whenever he likes, with whom he likes, and for as long as he likes, and I must not think twice about it, much less mention it to him, or in any way give the impression of prying. Lack of confidence on the part of a parent is the one unforgivable sin.

Although we still take our morning dip together on arising, it is three weeks since we have been for the early spin. One morning I found that Racky had jumped onto his bicycle in his wet trunks while I was still swimming, and gone by himself, and since then there has been an unspoken agreement between us that such is to be the procedure; he will go alone. Perhaps I held him back; he likes to ride so fast.

Young Peter, the smiling gardener from Saint Ives Cove, is Racky's special friend. It is amusing to see them together among the bushes, crouched over an anthill or rushing about trying to catch a lizard, almost of an age the two, yet so disparate—Racky with his tan skin looking almost white in contrast to the glistening black of the other. Today I know I shall be alone for lunch, since it is Peter's day off. On such days they usually go together on their bicycles into Saint Ives Cove, where Peter keeps a small rowboat. They fish along the coast there, but they have never returned with anything so far.

Meanwhile I am here alone, sitting on the rocks in the sun, from time to time climbing down to cool myself in the water, always conscious of the house behind me under the high palms, like a large glass boat filled with orchids and lilies. The servants are clean and quiet, and the work seems to be accomplished almost automatically. The good, black servants are another blessing of the islands; the British, born here in this paradise, have no conception of how fortunate they are. In fact, they do nothing but complain. One must have lived in the United States to appreciate the wonder of this place. Still, even here ideas are changing each day. Soon the people will decide that they want their land to be a part of today's monstrous world, and once that happens, it will be all over. As soon as you have that desire, you are infected with the deadly virus, and you begin to show the symptoms of the disease. You live in terms of time and money, and you think in terms of society and progress. Then all that is left for you is to kill the other people who think the same way, along with a good many of those who do not, since that is the final manifestation of the malady. Here for the moment at any rate, one has a feeling of staticity—existence ceases to be like those last few seconds in the hourglass when what is left of the sand suddenly begins to rush through to the bottom all at once. For the moment, it seems suspended. And if it seems, it is. Each wave at my feet, each birdcall in the forest at my back, does *not* carry me one step nearer the final disaster. The disaster is certain, but it will suddenly have happened, that is all. Until then, time stays still.

I am upset by a letter in this morning's mail: the Royal Bank of Canada requests that I call in person at its central office to sign the deposit slips and other papers for a sum that was cabled from the bank in Boston. Since the central office is on the other side of the island, fifty miles away, I shall have to spend the night over there and return the following day. There is no point in taking Racky along. The sight of "civilization" might awaken a longing for it in him; one never knows. I am sure it would have in me when I was his age. And if that should once start, he would merely be unhappy, since there is nothing for him but to stay here with me, at least for the next two years, when I hope to renew the lease, or, if things in New York pick up, buy the place. I am sending word by Isiah when he goes home into Orange Walk this evening, to have the McCoigh car call for me at seven-thirty tomorrow morning. It is an enormous old open Packard, and Isiah can save the ride out to work here by piling his bicycle into the back and riding with McCoigh.

The trip across the island was beautiful, and would have been highly enjoyable if my imagination had not played me a strange trick at the very outset. We stopped in Orange Walk for gasoline, and while that was being seen to, I got out and went to the corner store for some cigarettes. Since it was not yet eight o'clock, the store was still closed, and I hurried up the side street to the other little shop which I thought might be open. It was, and I bought my cigarettes. On the way back to the corner I noticed a large black woman leaning with her arms on the gate in front of her tiny house, staring into the street. As I passed by her, she looked straight into my face and said something with the strange accent of the island. It was said in what seemed an unfriendly tone, and ostensibly was directed at me, but I had no notion what it was. I got back into the car and the driver started it. The sound of the words had stayed in my head, however, as a bright shape outlined by darkness is likely to stay in the mind's eye, in such a way that when one shuts one's eyes one can see the exact contour of the shape. The car was already roaring up the hill toward the overland road when I suddenly reheard the very words. And they were: "Keep your boy at home, mahn." I sat perfectly rigid for a moment as the open countryside rushed past. Why should I think she had said that? Immediately I decided that I was giving an arbitrary sense to a phrase I could not have understood even if I had been paying strict attention. And then I wondered why my subconscious should have chosen that sense, since now that I whispered the words over to myself they failed to connect with any anxiety to which my mind might have been disposed. Actually I have never given a thought to Racky's wanderings about Orange Walk. I can find no such preoccupation no matter how I put the question to myself. Then, could she really have said those words? All the way through the mountains I pondered the question, even though it was obviously a waste of energy. And soon I could no longer hear the sound of her voice in my memory: I had played the record over too many times, and worn it out.

Here in the hotel a gala dance is in progress. The abominable orchestra, comprising two saxophones and one sour violin, is playing directly under my window in the garden, and the serious-looking couples slide about on the waxed concrete floor of the terrace, in the light of strings of paper lanterns. I suppose it is meant to look Japanese.

At this moment I wonder what Racky is doing there in the house with only Peter and Ernest the watchman to keep him company. I wonder if he is asleep. The house, which I am accustomed to think of as smiling and benevolent in its airiness, could just as well be in the most sinister and remote regions of the globe, now that I am here. Sitting here with the absurd orchestra bleating downstairs, I picture it to myself, and it strikes me as terribly vulnerable in its isolation. In my mind's eye I see the moonlit point with its tall palms waving restlessly in the wind, its dark cliffs licked by the waves below. Suddenly, although I struggle against the sensation, I am inexpressibly glad to be away from the house, helpless there, far on its point of land, in the silence of the night. Then I remember that the night is seldom silent. There is the loud sea at the base of the rocks, the droning of the thousands of insects, the occasional cries of the night birds—all the familiar noises that make sleep so sound. And Racky is there surrounded by them as usual, not even hearing them. But I feel profoundly guilty for having left him, unutterably tender and sad at the thought of him, lying there alone in the house with the two Negroes the only human beings within miles. If I keep thinking of Cold Point I shall be more and more nervous.

I am not going to bed yet. They are all screaming with laughter down there, the idiots; I could never sleep anyway. The bar is still open. Fortunately it is on the street side of the hotel. For once I need a few drinks.

Much later, but I feel no better; I may be a little drunk. The dance is over and it is quiet in the garden, but the room is too hot.

As I was falling asleep last night, all dressed, and with the overhead light shining sordidly in my face, I heard the black woman's voice again, more clearly even than I did in the car yesterday. For some reason this morning there is no doubt in my mind that the words I heard are the words she said. I accept that and go on from there. Suppose she did tell me to keep Racky home. It could only mean that she, or someone else in Orange Walk, has had a childish altercation with him; although I must say it is hard to conceive of Racky's entering into any sort of argument or feud with those people. To set my mind at rest (for I do seem to be taking the whole thing with great seriousness), I am going to stop in the village this afternoon before going home, and try to see the woman. I am extremely curious to know what she could have meant.

I had not been conscious until this evening when I came back to Cold Point how powerful they are, all those physical elements that go to make up its atmosphere: the sea and wind sounds that isolate the house from the road, the brilliancy of the water, sky and sun, the bright colors and strong odors of the flowers, the feeling of space both outside and within the house. One naturally accepts these things when one is living here. This afternoon when I returned I was conscious of them all over again, of their existence and their strength. All of them together are like a powerful drug; coming back made me feel as though I had been disintoxicated and were returning to the scene of my former indulgences. Now at eleven it is as if I had never been absent an hour. Everything is the same as always, even to the dry palm branch that scrapes against the window screen by my night table. And indeed, it is only thirty-six hours since I was here; but I always expect my absence from a place to bring about irremediable changes.

Strangely enough, now that I think of it, I feel that something *has* changed since I left yesterday morning, and that is the general attitude of the servants—their collective aura, so to speak. I noticed that difference immediately upon arriving back, but was unable to define it. Now I see it clearly. The network of common understanding which slowly spreads itself through a well-run household has been destroyed. Each person is by himself now. No unfriendliness, however, that I can see. They all behave with the utmost courtesy, excepting possibly Peter, who struck me as looking unaccustomedly glum when I encountered him in the kitchen after dinner. I meant to ask Racky if he had noticed it, but I forgot and he went to bed early.

In Orange Walk I made a brief stop on the pretext to McCoigh that I wanted to see the seamstress in the side street. I walked up and back in front of the house where I had seen the woman, but there was no sign of anyone.

As for my absence, Racky seems to have been perfectly content, having spent most of the day swimming off the rocks below the terrace. The insect sounds are at their height now, the breeze is cooler than usual, and I shall take advantage of these favorable conditions to get a good long night's rest.

Today has been one of the most difficult days of my life. I arose early, we had breakfast at the regular time, and Racky went off in the direction of Saint Ives Cove. I lay in the sun on the terrace for a while, listening to the noises of the household's regime. Peter was all over the property, collecting dead leaves and fallen blossoms in a huge basket and carrying them off to the compost heap. He appeared to be in an even fouler humor than last night. When he came near to me at one point on his way to another part of the garden I called to him. He set the basket down and stood looking at me; then he walked across the grass toward me slowly—reluctantly, it seemed to me.

"Peter, is everything all right with you?"

"Yes, sir."

"No trouble at home?"

"Oh, no, sir."

"Good."

"Yes, sir."

He went back to his work. But his face belied his words. Not only did he seem to be in a decidedly unpleasant temper; out here in the sunlight he looked positively ill. However, it was not my concern, if he refused to admit it.

When the heavy heat of the sun reached the unbearable point for me, I got out of my chair and went down the side of the cliff along the series of steps cut there into the rock. A level platform is below, and a diving board, for the water is deep. At each side, the rocks spread out and the waves break over them, but by the platform the wall of rock is vertical and the water merely hits against it below the springboard. The place is a tiny amphitheatre, quite cut off in sound and sight from the house. There too I like to lie in the sun; when I climb out of the water I often remove my trunks and lie stark naked on the springboard. I regularly make fun of Racky because he is embarrassed to do the same. Occasionally he will do it, but never without being coaxed. I was spread out there without a stitch on, being lulled by the slapping of the water, when an unfamiliar voice very close to me said: "Mister Norton?"

I jumped with nervousness, nearly fell off the springboard, and sat up, reaching at the same time, but in vain, for my trunks, which were lying on the rock practically at the feet of a middle-aged mulatto gentleman. He was in a white duck suit, and wore a high collar with a black tie, and it seemed to me that he was eyeing me with a certain degree of horror.

My next reaction was one of anger at being trespassed upon in this way. I rose and got the trunks, however, donning them calmly and saying nothing more meaningful than: "I didn't hear you come down the steps."

"Shall we go up?" said my caller. As he led the way, I had a definite premonition that he was here on an unpleasant errand. On the terrace we sat down, and he offered me an American cigarette which I did not accept.

"This is a delightful spot," he said, glancing out to sea and then at the end of his cigarette, which was only partially aglow. He puffed at it.

I said, "Yes," waiting for him to go on; presently he did.

"I am from the constabulary of this parish. The police, you see." And seeing my face, "This is a friendly call. But still it must be taken as a warning, Mister Norton. It is very serious. If anyone else comes to you about this it will mean trouble for you, heavy trouble. That's why I want to see you privately this way and warn you personally. You see."

I could not believe I was hearing his words. At length I said faintly: "But what about?"

"This is not an official call. You must not be upset. I have taken it upon myself to speak to you because I want to save you deep trouble."

"But I *am* upset!" I cried, finding my voice at last. "How can I help being upset, when I don't know what you're talking about?"

He moved his chair close to mine, and spoke in a very low voice.

"I have waited until the young man was away from the house so we could talk in private. You see, it is about him."

Somehow that did not surprise me. I nodded.

"I will tell you very briefly. The people here are simple country folk. They make trouble easily. Right now they are all talking about the young man you have living here with you. He is your son, I hear." His inflection here was skeptical.

"Certainly he's my son."

His expression did not change, but his voice grew indignant. "Whoever he is, that is a bad young man."

"What do you mean?" I cried, but he cut in hotly: "He may be your son; he may not be. I don't care who he is. That is not my affair. But he is bad through and through. We don't have such things going on here, sir. The people in Orange Walk and Saint Ives Cove are very cross now. You don't know what these folk do when they are aroused."

I thought it my turn to interrupt. "Please tell me why you say my son is bad. What has he done?" Perhaps the earnestness in my voice reached him, for his face assumed a gentler aspect. He leaned still closer to me and almost whispered.

"He has no shame. He does what he pleases with all the young boys, and the men too, and gives them a shilling so they won't tell about it. But they talk. Of course they talk. Every man for twenty miles up and down the coast knows about it. And the women too, they know about it." There was a silence.

I had felt myself preparing to get to my feet for the last few seconds because I wanted to go into my room and be alone, to get away from that scandalized stage whisper. I think I mumbled "Good morning" or "Thank you," as I turned away and began walking toward the house. But he was still beside me, still whispering like an eager conspirator into my ear: "Keep him home, Mister Norton. Or send him away to school, if he is your son. But make him stay out of these towns. For his own sake."

I shook hands with him and went to lie on my bed. From there I heard his car door slam, heard him drive off. I was painfully trying to formulate an opening sentence to use in speaking to Racky about this, feeling that the opening sentence would define my stand. The attempt was merely a sort of therapeutic action, to avoid thinking about the thing itself. Every attitude seemed impossible. There was no way to broach the subject. I suddenly realized that I should never be able to speak to him directly about it. With the advent of this news he had become another person—an adult, mysterious and formidable. To be sure, it did occur to me that the mulatto's story might not be true, but automatically I rejected the doubt. It was as if I wanted to believe it, almost as if I had already known it, and he had merely confirmed it.

Racky returned at midday, panting and grinning. The inevitable comb appeared and was used on the sweaty, unruly locks. Sitting down to lunch, he exclaimed: "Gosh! Did I find a swell beach this morning! But what a job to get to it!" I tried to look unconcerned as I met his gaze; it was as if our positions had been reversed, and I were hoping to stem his rebuke. He prattled on about thorns and vines and his machete. Throughout the meal I kept telling myself: "Now is the moment. You must say something." But all I said was: "More salad? Or do you want dessert now?" So the lunch passed and nothing happened. After I had finished my coffee I went into my bedroom and looked at myself in the large mirror. I saw my eyes trying to give their reflected brothers a little courage. As I stood there I heard a commotion in the other wing of the house: voices, bumpings, the sound of a scuffle. Above the noise came Gloria's sharp voice, imperious and excited: "No, mahn! Don't strike him!" And louder: "Peter, mahn, no!"

I went quickly toward the kitchen, where the trouble seemed to be, but on the way I was run into by Racky, who staggered into the hallway with his hands in front of his face.

"What is it, Racky?" I cried.

He pushed past me into the living room without moving his hands away from his face; I turned and followed him. From there he went into his own room, leaving the door open behind him. I heard him in his bathroom running the water. I was undecided what to do. Suddenly Peter appeared in the hall doorway, his hat in his hand. When he raised his head, I was surprised to see that his cheek was bleeding. In his eyes was a strange, confused expression of transient fear and deep hostility. He looked down again.

"May I please talk with you, sir?"

"What was all the racket? What's been happening?"

"May I talk with you outside, sir?" He said it doggedly, still not looking up.

In view of the circumstances, I humored him. We walked slowly up the cinder road to the main highway, across the bridge, and through the forest while he told me his story. I said nothing.

At the end he said: "I never wanted to, sir, even the first time, but after the first time I was afraid, and Mister Racky was after me every day."

I stood still, and finally said: "If you had only told me this the first time it happened, it would have been much better for everyone."

He turned his hat in his hands, studying it intently. "Yes, sir. But I didn't know what everyone was saying about him in Orange Walk until today. You know I always go to the beach at Saint Ives Cove with Mister Racky on my free days. If I had known what they were all saying I wouldn't have been afraid, sir. And I wanted to keep on working here. I needed the money." Then he repeated what he had already said three times. "Mister Racky said you'd see about it that I was put in the jail. I'm a year older than Mister Racky, sir."

"I know, I know," I said impatiently; and deciding that severity was what Peter expected of me at this point I added: "You had better get your things together and go home. You can't work here any longer, you know."

The hostility in his face assumed terrifying proportions as he said: "If you killed me I would not work anymore at Cold Point, sir."

I turned and walked briskly back to the house, leaving him standing there in the road. It seems he returned at dusk, a little while ago, and got his belongings.

In his room Racky was reading. He had stuck some adhesive tape on his chin and over his cheekbone.

"I've dismissed Peter," I announced. "He hit you, didn't he?"

He glanced up. His left eye was swollen, but not yet black.

"He sure did. But I landed him one, too. And I guess I deserved it anyway."

I rested against the table. "Why?" I asked nonchalantly.

"Oh, I had something on him from a long time back that he was afraid I'd tell you."

"And just now you threatened to tell me?"

"Oh, no! He said he was going to quit the job here, and I kidded him about being yellow."

"Why did he want to quit? I thought he liked the job."

"Well, he did, I guess, but he didn't like me." Racky's candid gaze betrayed a shade of pique. I still leaned against the table.

I persisted. "But I thought you two got on fine together. You seemed to."

"Nah. He was just scared of losing his job. I had something on him. He was a good guy, though; I liked him all right." He paused. "Has he gone yet?" A strange quaver crept into his voice as he said the last words, and I understood that for the first time Racky's heretofore impeccable histrionics were not quite equal to the occasion. He was very much upset at losing Peter.

"Yes, he's gone," I said shortly. "He's not coming back, either." And as Racky, hearing the unaccustomed inflection in my voice, looked up at me suddenly with faint astonishment in his young eyes, I realized that this was the moment to press on, to say: "What did you have on him?" But as if he had arrived at the same spot in my mind a fraction of a second earlier, he proceeded to snatch away my advantage by jumping up, bursting into loud song, and pulling off all his clothes simultaneously. As he stood before me naked, singing at the top of his lungs, and stepped into his swimming trunks, I was conscious that again I should be incapable of saying to him what I must say.

He was in and out of the house all afternoon: some of the time he read in his room, and most of the time he was down on the diving board. It is strange behavior for him; if I could only know what is in his mind. As evening approached, my problem took on a purely obsessive character. I walked to and fro in my room, always pausing at one end to look out the window over the sea, and at the other end to glance at my face in the mirror. As if that could help me! Then I took a drink. And another. I thought I might be able to do it at dinner, when I felt fortified by the whiskey. But no. Soon he will have gone to bed. It is not that I expect to confront him with any accusations. That I know I never can do. But I must find a way to keep him from his wanderings, and I must offer a reason to give him, so that he will never suspect that I know.

We fear for the future of our offspring. It is ludicrous, but only a little more palpably so than anything else in life. A length of time has passed; days which I am content to have known, even if now they are over. I think that this period was what I had always been waiting for life to offer, the recompense I had unconsciously but firmly expected, in return for having been held so closely in the grip of existence all these years.

That evening seems long ago only because I have recalled its details so many times that they have taken on the color of legend. Actually my problem already had been solved for me then, but I did not know it. Because I could not perceive the pattern, I foolishly imagined that I must cudgel my brains to find the right words with which to approach Racky. But it was he who came to me. That same evening, as I was about to go out for a solitary stroll which I thought might help me hit upon a formula, he appeared at my door.

"Going for a walk?" he asked, seeing the stick in my hand.

The prospect of making an exit immediately after speaking with him made things seem simpler. "Yes," I said, "but I'd like to have a word with you first."

"Sure. What?" I did not look at him because I did not want to see the watchful light I was sure was playing in his eyes at this moment. As I spoke I tapped with my stick along the designs made by the tiles in the floor. "Racky, would you like to go back to school?"

"Are you kidding? You know I hate school."

I glanced up at him. "No, I'm not kidding. Don't look so horrified. You'd probably enjoy being with a bunch of fellows your own age." (That was not one of the arguments I had meant to use.)

"I might like to be with guys my own age, but I don't want to have to be in school to do it. I've had school enough."

I went to the door and said lamely: "I thought I'd get your reactions."

He laughed. "No, thanks."

"That doesn't mean you're not going," I said over my shoulder as I went out.

On my walk I pounded the highway's asphalt with my stick, stood on the bridge having dramatic visions which involved such eventualities as our moving back to the States, Racky's having a bad spill on his bicycle and being paralyzed for some months, and even the possibility of my letting events take their course, which would doubtless mean my having to visit him now and then in the governmental prison with gifts of food, if it meant nothing more tragic and violent. "But none of these things will happen," I said to myself, and I knew I was wasting precious time; he must not return to Orange Walk tomorrow.

I went back toward the point at a snail's pace. There was no moon and very little breeze. As I approached the house, trying to tread lightly on the cinders so as not to awaken the watchful Ernest and have to explain to him that it was only I, I saw that there were no lights in Racky's room. The house was dark save for the dim lamp on my night table. Instead of going in, I skirted the entire building, colliding with bushes and getting my face sticky with spiderwebs, and went to sit awhile on the terrace where there seemed to be a breath of air. The sound of the sea was far out on the reef, where the breakers sighed. Here below, there were only slight watery chugs and gurgles now and then. It was unusually low tide. I smoked three cigarettes mechanically, having ceased even to think, and then, my mouth tasting bitter from the smoke, I went inside.

My room was airless. I flung my clothes onto a chair and looked at the night table to see if the carafe of water was there. Then my mouth opened. The top sheet of my bed had been stripped back to the foot. There on the far side of the bed, dark against the whiteness of the lower sheet, lay Racky asleep on his side, and naked.

I stood looking at him for a long time, probably holding my breath, for I remember feeling a little dizzy at one point. I was whispering to myself, as my eyes followed the curve of his arm, shoulder, back, thigh, leg: "A child. A child." Destiny, when one perceives it clearly from very near, has no qualities at all. The recognition of it and the consciousness of the vision's clarity leave no room on the mind's horizon. Finally I turned off the light and softly lay down. The night was absolutely black.

He lay perfectly quiet until dawn. I shall never know whether or not he was really asleep all that time. Of course he couldn't have been, and yet he lay so still. Warm and firm, but still as death. The darkness and silence were heavy around us. As the birds began to sing, I sank into a soft, enveloping slumber; when I awoke in the sunlight later, he was gone.

I found him down by the water, cavorting alone on the springboard; for the first time he had discarded his trunks without my suggesting it. All day we stayed together around the terrace and on the rocks, talking, swimming, reading, and just lying flat in the hot sun. Nor did he return to his room when night came. Instead, after the servants were asleep, we brought three bottles of champagne in and set the pail on the night table.

Thus it came about that I was able to touch on the delicate subject that still preoccupied me, and profiting by the new understanding between us, I made my request in the easiest, most natural fashion.

"Racky, would you do me a tremendous favor if I asked you?"

He lay on his back, his hands beneath his head. It seemed to me his regard was circumspect, wanting in candor.

"I guess so," he said. "What is it?"

"Will you stay around the house for a few days—a week, say? Just to please me? We can take some rides together, as far as you like. Would you do that for me?"

"Sure thing," he said, smiling.

I was temporizing, but I was desperate.

Perhaps a week later—(it is only when one is not fully happy that one is meticulous about time, so that it may have been more or less)—we were having breakfast. Isiah stood by, in the shade, waiting to pour us more coffee.

"I noticed you had a letter from Uncle Charley the other day," said Racky. "Don't you think we ought to invite him down?"

My heart began to beat with great force.

"Here? He'd hate it here," I said casually. "Besides, there's no room. Where would he sleep?" Even as I heard myself saying the words, I knew that they were the wrong ones, that I was not really participating in the conversation. Again I felt the fascination of complete helplessness that comes when one is suddenly a conscious onlooker at the shaping of one's fate.

"In my room," said Racky. "It's empty."

I could see more of the pattern at that moment than I had ever suspected existed. "Nonsense," I said. "This is not the sort of place for Uncle Charley."

Racky appeared to be hitting on an excellent idea. "Maybe if I wrote and invited him," he suggested, motioning to Isiah for more coffee.

"Nonsense," I said again, watching still more of the pattern reveal itself, like a photographic print becoming constantly clearer in a tray of developing solution.

Isiah filled Racky's cup and returned to the shade. Racky drank slowly, pretending to be savoring the coffee.

"Well, it won't do any harm to try. He'd appreciate the invitation," he said speculatively.

For some reason, at this juncture I knew what to say, and as I said it, I knew what I was going to do.

"I thought we might fly over to Havana for a few days next week."

He looked guardedly interested, and then he broke into a wide grin. "Swell!" he cried. "Why wait till next week?"

The next morning the servants called "Good-bye" to us as we drove up the cinder road in the McCoigh car. We took off from the airport at six that evening. Racky was in high spirits; he kept the stewardess engaged in conversation all the way to Camagüey.

He was delighted also with Havana. Sitting in the bar at the Nacional, we continued to discuss the possibility of having C. pay us a visit at the island. It was not without difficulty that I eventually managed to persuade Racky that writing him would be inadvisable.

We decided to look for an apartment right there in Vedado for Racky. He did not seem to want to come back here to Cold Point. We also decided that living in Havana he would need a larger income than I. I am already having the greater part of Hope's estate transferred to his name in the form of a trust fund which I shall administer until he is of age. It was his mother's money, after all.

We bought a new convertible, and he drove me out to Rancho Boyeros in it when I took my plane. A Cuban named Claudio with very white teeth, whom Racky had met in the pool that morning, sat between us.

We were waiting in front of the landing field. An official finally un-hooked the chain to let the passengers through. "If you get fed up, come to Havana," said Racky, pinching my arm.

The two of them stood together behind the rope, waving to me, their shirts flapping in the wind as the plane started to move.

The wind blows by my head; between each wave there are thousands of tiny licking and chopping sounds as the water hurries out of the crevices and holes; and a part-floating, part-submerged feeling of being in the water haunts my mind even as the hot sun burns my face. I sit here and I read, and I wait for the pleasant feeling of repletion that follows a good meal, to turn slowly, as the hours pass along, into the even more delightful, slightly stirring sensation deep within, which accompanies the awakening of the appetite.

I am perfectly happy here in reality, because I still believe that nothing very drastic is likely to befall this part of the island in the near future.

The Circular Valley

The abandoned monastery stood on a slight eminence of land in the middle of a vast clearing. On all sides the ground sloped gently downward toward the tangled, hairy jungle that filled the circular valley, ringed about by sheer, black cliffs. There were a few trees in some of the courtyards, and the birds used them as meeting places when they flew out of the rooms and corridors where they had their nests. Long ago bandits had taken whatever was removable out of the building. Soldiers had used it once as headquarters, had, like the bandits, built fires in the great windy rooms so that afterward they looked like ancient kitchens. And now that everything was gone from within, it seemed that never again would anyone come near the monastery. The vegetation had thrown up a protecting wall; the first story was soon quite hidden from view by small trees which dripped vines to lasso the cornices of the windows. The meadows roundabout grew dank and lush; there was no path through them.

At the higher end of the circular valley a river fell off the cliffs into a great cauldron of vapor and thunder below; after this it slid along the base of the cliffs until it found a gap at the other end of the valley, where it hurried discreetly through with no rapids, no cascades—a great thick black rope of water moving swiftly downhill between the polished flanks of the canyon. Beyond the gap the land opened out and became smiling; a village nestled on the side hill just outside. In the days of the monastery it was there that the friars had got their provisions, since the Indians would not enter the circular valley. Centuries ago when the building had been constructed the Church had imported the workmen from another part of the country. These were traditional enemies of the tribes thereabouts, and had another language; there was no danger that the inhabitants would communicate with them as they worked at setting up the mighty walls. Indeed, the construction had taken so long that before the east wing was completed the workmen had all died, one by one. Thus it was the friars themselves who had closed off the end of the wing with blank walls, leaving it that way, unfinished and blind-looking, facing the black cliffs.

Generation after generation, the friars came, fresh-cheeked boys who grew thin and gray, and finally died, to be buried in the garden beyond the courtyard with the fountain. One day not long ago they had all left the monastery; no one knew where they had gone, and no one thought to ask. It was shortly after this that the bandits, and then the soldiers had come. And now, since the Indians do not change, still no one from the village went up through the gap to visit the monastery. The Atlájala lived there; the friars had not been able to kill it, had given up at last and gone away. No one was surprised, but the Atlájala gained in prestige by their departure. During the centuries the friars had been there in the monastery, the Indians had wondered why it allowed them to stay. Now, at last, it had driven them out. It always had lived there, they said, and would go on living there because the valley was its home, and it could never leave.

In the early morning the restless Atlájala would move through the halls of the monastery. The dark rooms sped past, one after the other. In a small patio, where eager young trees had pushed up the paving stones to reach the sun, it paused. The air was full of small sounds: the movements of butterflies, the falling to the ground of bits of leaves and flowers, the air following its myriad courses around the edges of things, the ants pursuing their endless labors in the hot dust. In the sun it waited, conscious of each gradation in sound and light and smell, living in the awareness of the slow, constant disintegration that attacked the morning and transformed it into afternoon. When evening came, it often slipped above the monastery roof and surveyed the darkening sky: the waterfall would roar distantly. Night after night, along the procession of years, it had hovered here above the valley, darting down to become a bat, a leopard, a moth for a few minutes or hours, returning to rest immobile in the center of the space enclosed by the cliffs. When the monastery had been built, it had taken to frequenting the rooms, where it had observed for the first time the meaningless gestures of human life.

And then one evening it had aimlessly become one of the young friars. This was a new sensation, strangely rich and complex, and at the same time unbearably stifling, as though every other possibility besides that of being enclosed in a tiny, isolated world of cause and effect had been removed forever. As the friar, it had gone and stood in the window, looking out at the sky, seeing for the first time, not the stars, but the space between and beyond them. Even at that moment it had felt the urge to leave, to step outside the little shell of anguish where it lodged for the moment, but a faint curiosity had impelled it to remain a little longer and partake a little further of the unaccustomed sensation. It held on; the friar raised his arms to the sky in an imploring gesture. For the first time the Atlájala sensed opposition, the thrill of a struggle. It was delicious to feel the young man striving to free himself of its presence, and it was immeasurably sweet to remain there. Then with a cry the friar had rushed to the other side of the room and seized a heavy leather whip hanging on the wall. Tearing off his clothing he had begun to carry out a ferocious self-beating. At the first blow of the lash the Atlájala had been on the point of letting go, but then it realized that the immediacy of that intriguing inner pain was only made more manifest by the impact of the blows from without, and so it stayed and felt the young man grow weak under his own lashing. When he had finished and said a prayer, he crawled to his pallet and fell asleep weeping, while the Atlájala slipped out obliquely and entered into a bird which passed the night sitting in a great tree on the edge of the jungle, listening intently to the night sounds, and uttering a scream from time to time.

Thereafter the Atlájala found it impossible to resist sliding inside the bodies of the friars; it visited one after the other, finding an astonishing variety of sensation in the process. Each was a separate world, a separate experience, because each had different reactions when he became conscious of the other being within him. One would sit and read or pray, one would go for a long troubled walk in the meadows, around and around the building, one would find a comrade and engage in an absurd but bitter quarrel, a few wept, some flagellated themselves or sought a friend to wield the lash for them. Always there was a rich profusion of perceptions for the Atlájala to enjoy, so that it no longer occurred to it to frequent the bodies of insects, birds and furred animals, nor even to leave the monastery and move in the air above. Once it almost got into difficulties when an old friar it was occupying suddenly fell back dead. That was a hazard it ran in the frequenting of men: they seemed not to know when they were doomed, or if they did know, they pretended with such strength not to know, that it amounted to the same thing. The other beings knew beforehand, save when it was a question of being seized unawares and devoured. And that the Atlájala was able to prevent: a bird in which it was staying was always avoided by the hawks and eagles.

When the friars left the monastery, and, following the government's orders, doffed their robes, dispersed and became workmen, the Atlájala was at a loss to know how to pass its days and nights. Now everything was as it had been before their arrival: there was no one but the creatures that always had lived in the circular valley. It tried a giant serpent, a deer, a bee: nothing had the savor it had grown to love. Everything was the same as before, but not for the Atlájala; it had known the existence of man, and now there were no men in the valley—only the abandoned building with its empty rooms to make man's absence more poignant.

Then one year bandits came, several hundred of them in one stormy afternoon. In delight it tried many of them as they sprawled about cleaning their guns and cursing, and it discovered still other facets of sensation: the hatred they felt for the world, the fear they had of the soldiers who were pursuing them, the strange gusts of desire that swept through them as they sprawled together drunk by the fire that smoldered in the center of the floor and the insufferable pain of jealousy which the nightly orgies seem to awaken in some of them. But the bandits did not stay long. When they had left, the soldiers came in their wake. It felt very much the same way to be a soldier as to be a bandit. Missing were the strong fear and the hatred, but the rest was almost identical. Neither the bandits nor the soldiers appeared to be at all conscious of its presence in them; it could slip from one man to another without causing any change in their behavior. This surprised it, since its effect on the friars had been so definite, and it felt a certain disappointment at the impossibility of making its existence known to them.

Nevertheless, the Atlájala enjoyed both bandits and soldiers immensely, and was even more desolate when it was left alone once again. It would become one of the swallows that made their nests in the rocks beside the top of the waterfall. In the burning sunlight it would plunge again and again into the curtain of mist that rose from far below, sometimes uttering exultant cries. It would spend a day as a plant louse, crawling slowly along the underside of the leaves, living quietly in the huge green world down there which is forever hidden from the sky. Or at night, in the velvet body of a panther, it would know the pleasure of the kill. Once for a year it lived in an eel at the bottom of the pool below the waterfall, feeling the mud give slowly before it as it pushed ahead with its flat nose; that was a restful period, but afterward the desire to know again the mysterious life of man had returned—an obsession of which it was useless to try to rid itself. And now it moved restlessly through the ruined rooms, a mute presence, alone, and thirsting to be incarnate once again, but in man's flesh only. And with the building of highways through the country it was inevitable that people should come once again to the circular valley.

A man and a woman drove their automobile as far as a village down in a lower valley; hearing about the ruined monastery and the waterfall that dropped over the cliffs into the great amphitheatre, they determined to see these things. They came on burros as far as the village outside the gap, but there the Indians they had hired to accompany them refused to go any farther, and so they continued alone, upward through the canyon and into the precinct of the Atlájala.

It was noon when they rode into the valley; the black ribs of the cliffs glistened like glass in the sun's blistering downward rays. They stopped the burros by a cluster of boulders at the edge of the sloping meadows. The man got down first, and reached up to help the woman off. She leaned forward, putting her hands on his face, and for a long moment they kissed. Then he lifted her to the ground and they climbed hand in hand up over the rocks. The Atlájala hovered near them, watching the woman closely: she was the first ever to have come into the valley. The two sat beneath a small tree on the grass, looking at one another, smiling. Out of habit, the Atlájala entered into the man. Immediately, instead of existing in the midst of the sunlit air, the bird calls and the plant odors, it was conscious only of the woman's beauty and her terrible imminence. The waterfall, the earth, and the sky itself receded, rushed into nothingness, and there were only the woman's smile and her arms and her odor. It was a world more suffocating and painful than the Atlájala had thought possible. Still, while the man spoke and the woman answered, it remained within.

"Leave him. He doesn't love you."

"He would kill me."

"But I love you. I need you with me."

"I can't. I'm afraid of him."

The man reached out to pull her to him; she drew back slightly, but her eyes grew large.

"We have today," she murmured, turning her face toward the yellow walls of the monastery.

The man embraced her fiercely, crushing her against him as though the act would save his life. "No, no, no. It can't go on like this," he said. "No."

The pain of his suffering was too intense; gently the Atlájala left the man and slipped into the woman. And now it would have believed itself to be housed in nothing, to be in its own spaceless self, so completely was it aware of the wandering wind, the small flutterings of the leaves, and the bright air that surrounded it. Yet there was a difference: each element was magnified in intensity, the whole sphere of being was immense, limitless. Now it understood what the man sought in the woman, and it knew that he suffered because he never would attain that sense of completion he sought. But the Atlájala, being one with the woman, had attained it, and being aware of possessing it, trembled with delight. The woman shuddered as her lips met those of the man. There on the grass in the shade of the tree their joy reached new heights; the Atlájala, knowing them both, formed a single channel between the secret springs of their desires. Throughout, it remained within the woman, and began vaguely to devise ways of keeping her, if not inside the valley, at least nearby, so that she might return.

In the afternoon, with dreamlike motions, they walked to the burros and mounted them, driving them through the deep meadow grass to the monastery. Inside the great courtyard they halted, looking hesitantly at the ancient arches in the sunlight, and at the darkness inside the doorways.

"Shall we go in?" said the woman.

"We must get back."

"I want to go in," she said. (The Atlájala exulted.) A thin gray snake slid along the ground into the bushes. They did not see it.

The man looked at her perplexedly. "It's late," he said.

But she jumped down from her burro by herself and walked beneath the arches into the long corridor within. (Never had the rooms seemed so real as now when the Atlájala was seeing them through her eyes.)

They explored all the rooms. Then the woman wanted to climb up into the tower, but the man took a determined stand.

"We must go back now," he said firmly, putting his hand on her shoulder.

"This is our only day together, and you think of nothing but getting back."

"But the time . . ."

"There is a moon. We won't lose the way."

He would not change his mind. "No."

"As you like," she said. "I'm going up. You can go back alone if you like."

The man laughed uneasily. "You're mad." He tried to kiss her.

She turned away and did not answer for a moment. Then she said: "You want me to leave my husband for you. You ask everything from me, but what do you do for me in return? You refuse even to climb up into a little tower with me to see the view. Go back alone. Go!"

She sobbed and rushed toward the dark stairwell. Calling after her, he followed, but stumbled somewhere behind her. She was as sure of foot as if she had climbed the many stone steps a thousand times before, hurrying up through the darkness, around and around.

In the end she came out at the top and peered through the small apertures in the cracking walls. The beams which had supported the bell had rotted and fallen; the heavy bell lay on its side in the rubble, like a dead animal. The waterfall's sound was louder up here; the valley was nearly full of shadow. Below, the man called her name repeatedly. She did not answer. As she stood watching the shadow of the cliffs slowly overtake the farthest recesses of the valley and begin to climb the naked rocks to the east, an idea formed in her mind. It was not the kind of idea which she would have expected of herself, but it was there, growing and inescapable. When she felt it complete there inside her, she turned and went lightly back down. The man was sitting in the dark near the bottom of the stairs, groaning a little.

"What is it?" she said.

"I hurt my leg. Now are you ready to go or not?"

"Yes," she said simply. "I'm sorry you fell."

Without saying anything he rose and limped after her out into the courtyard where the burros stood. The cold mountain air was beginning to flow down from the tops of the cliffs. As they rode through the meadow she began to think of how she would broach the subject to him. (It must be done before they reached the gap. The Atlájala trembled.)

"Do you forgive me?" she asked him.

"Of course," he laughed.

"Do you love me?"

"More than anything in the world."

"Is that true?"

He glanced at her in the failing light, sitting erect on the jogging animal.

"You know it is," he said softly.

She hesitated.

"There is only one way, then," she said finally.

"But what?"

"I'm afraid of him. I won't go back to him. You go back. I'll stay in the village here." (Being that near, she would come each day to the monastery.) "When it is done, you will come and get me. Then we can go somewhere else. No one will find us."

The man's voice sounded strange. "I don't understand."

"You do understand. And that is the only way. Do it or not, as you like. It is the only way."

They trotted along for a while in silence. The canyon loomed ahead, black against the evening sky.

Then the man said, very clearly: "Never."

A moment later the trail led out into an open space high above the swift water below. The hollow sound of the river reached them faintly. The light in the sky was almost gone; in the dusk the landscape had taken on false contours. Everything was gray—the rocks, the bushes, the trail—and nothing had distance or scale. They slowed their pace.

His word still echoed in her ears.

"I won't go back to him!" she cried with sudden vehemence. "You can go back and play cards with him as usual. Be his good friend the same as always. I won't go. I can't go on with both of you in the town." (The plan was not working; the Atlájala saw it had lost her, yet it still could help her.)

"You're very tired," he said softly.

He was right. Almost as he said the words, that unaccustomed exhilaration and lightness she had felt ever since noon seemed to leave her; she hung her head wearily, and said: "Yes, I am."

At the same moment the man uttered a sharp, terrible cry; she looked up in time to see his burro plunge from the edge of the trail into the grayness below. There was a silence, and then the faraway sound of many stones sliding downward. She could not move or stop the burro; she sat dumbly, letting it carry her along, an inert weight on its back.

For one final instant, as she reached the pass which was the edge of its realm, the Atlájala alighted tremulously within her. She raised her head and a tiny exultant shiver passed through her; then she let it fall forward once again.

Hanging in the dim air above the trail, the Atlájala watched her indistinct figure grow invisible in the gathering night. (If it had not been able to hold her there, still it had been able to help her.)

A moment later it was in the tower, listening to the spiders mend the webs that she had damaged. It would be a long, long time before it would bestir itself to enter into another being's awareness. A long, long time— perhaps forever.

At Paso Rojo

When old Señora Sanchez died, her two daughters Lucha and Chalía decided to visit their brother at his ranch. Out of devotion they had agreed never to marry while their mother lived, and now that she was gone and they were both slightly over forty there seemed just as little likelihood of a wedding in the family as there ever had. They would probably not admit this even to themselves, however. It was with complete understanding of his two sisters that Don Federico suggested they leave the city and go down to Paso Rojo for a few weeks.

Lucha arrived in black crêpe. To her, death was one of the things that happen in life with a certain regularity, and it therefore demanded outward observance. Otherwise her life was in no way changed, save that at the ranch she would have to get used to a whole new staff of servants.

"Indians, poor things, animals with speech," she said to Don Federico the first night as they sat having coffee. A barefooted girl had just carried the dessert dishes out.

Don Federico smiled. "They are good people," he said deliberately. Living at the ranch so long had lowered his standards, it was said, for even though he had always spent a month or so of each year in the capital, he had grown increasingly indifferent to the social life there.

"The ranch is eating his soul little by little," Lucha used to say to Señora Sanchez.

Only once the old lady had replied. "If his soul is to be eaten, then let the ranch do it."

She looked around the primitive dining room with its dry decorations of palm leaves and branches. "He loves it here because everything is his," she thought, "and some of the things could never have been his if he had not purposely changed to fit them." That was not a completely acceptable thought. She knew the ranch had made him happy and tolerant and wise; to her it seemed sad that he could not have been those things without losing his civilized luster. And that he certainly had lost. He had the skin of a peasant—brown and lined everywhere. He had the slowness of speech of men who have lived for long periods of time in the open. And the inflections of his voice suggested the patience that can come from talking to animals rather than to human beings. Lucha was a sensible woman; still, she could not help feeling a certain amount of regret that her little brother, who at an earlier point in his life had been the best dancer among the members of the country club, should have become the thin, sad-faced, quiet man who sat opposite her.

"You've changed a great deal," she suddenly said, shaking her head from side to side slowly.

"Yes. You change here. But it's a good place."

"Good, yes. But so sad," she said.

He laughed. "Not sad at all. You get used to the quiet. And then you find it's not quiet at all. But you never change much, do you? Chalía's the one who's different. Have you noticed?"

"Oh, Chalía's always been crazy. She doesn't change either."

"Yes. She is very much changed." He looked past the smoking oil lamp, out into the dark. "Where is she? Why doesn't she take coffee?"

"She has insomnia. She never takes it."

"Maybe our nights will put her to sleep," said Don Federico.

Chalía sat on the upper veranda in the soft night breeze. The ranch stood in a great clearing that held the jungle at bay all about, but the monkeys were calling from one side to the other, as if neither clearing nor ranch house existed. She had decided to put off going to bed—that way there was less darkness to be borne in case she stayed awake. The lines of a poem she had read on the train two days before were still in her mind: "*Aveces la noche*. . . . Sometimes the night takes you with it, wraps you up and rolls you along, leaving you washed in sleep at the morning's edge." Those lines were comforting. But there was the terrible line yet to come: "And sometimes the night goes on without you." She tried to jump from the image of the fresh sunlit morning to a completely alien idea: the waiter at the beach club in Puntarenas, but she knew the other thought was waiting there for her in the dark.

She had worn riding breeches and a khaki shirt open at the neck, on the trip from the capital, and she had announced to Lucha her intention of going about in those clothes the whole time she was at Paso Rojo. She and Lucha had quarreled at the station.

"Everyone knows Mamá has died," said Lucha, "and the ones who aren't scandalized are making fun of you."

With intense scorn in her voice Chalía had replied, "You have asked them, I suppose."

On the train as it wound through the mountains toward *tierra caliente* she had suddenly said, apropos of nothing: "Black doesn't become me." Really upsetting to Lucha was the fact that in Puntarenas she had gone off and bought some crimson nail polish which she had painstakingly applied herself in the hotel room.

"You can't, Chalía!" cried her sister, wide-eyed. "You've never done it before. Why do you do it now?"

Chalía had laughed immoderately. "Just a whim!" she had said, spreading her decorated hands in front of her.

Loud footsteps came up the stairs and along the veranda, shaking it slightly. Her sister called: "Chalía!"

She hesitated an instant, then said, "Yes."

"You're sitting in the dark! Wait. I'll bring out a lamp from your room. What an idea!"

"We'll be covered with insects," objected Chalía, who, although her mood was not a pleasant one, did not want it disturbed.

"Federico says no!" shouted Lucha from inside. "He says there are no insects! None that bite, anyway!"

Presently she appeared with a small lamp which she set on a table against the wall. She sat down in a nearby hammock and swung herself softly back and forth, humming. Chalía frowned at her, but she seemed not to notice.

"What heat!" exclaimed Lucha finally.

"Don't exert yourself so much," suggested Chalía.

They were quiet. Soon the breeze became a strong wind, coming from the direction of the distant mountains; but it too was hot, like the breath of a great animal. The lamp flickered, threatened to go out. Lucha got up and turned it down. As Chalía moved her head to watch her, her attention was caught by something else, and she quickly shifted her gaze to the wall. Something enormous, black and swift had been there an instant ago; now there was nothing. She watched the spot intently. The wall was faced with small stones which had been plastered over and whitewashed indifferently, so that the surface was very rough and full of large holes. She rose suddenly and approaching the wall, peered at it closely. All the holes, large and small, were lined with whitish funnels. She could see the long, agile legs of the spiders that lived inside, sticking out beyond some of the funnels.

"Lucha, this wall is full of monsters!" she cried. A beetle flew near to the lamp, changed its mind and lighted on the wall. The nearest spider darted forth, seized it and disappeared into the wall with it.

"Don't look at them," advised Lucha, but she glanced about the floor near her feet apprehensively.

Chalía pulled her bed into the middle of the room and moved a small table over to it. She blew out the lamp and lay back on the hard mattress. The sound of the nocturnal insects was unbearably loud—an endless, savage scream above the noise of the wind. All the vegetation out there was dry. It made a million scraping sounds in the air as the wind swept through it. From time to time the monkeys called to each other from different sides. A night bird scolded occasionally, but its voice was swallowed up in the insistent insect song and the rush of wind across the hot countryside. And it was absolutely dark.

Perhaps an hour later she lit the lamp by her bed, rose, and in her nightgown went to sit on the veranda. She put the lamp where it had been before, by the wall, and turned her chair to face it. She sat watching the wall until very late.

At dawn the air was cool, full of the sound of continuous lowing of cattle, nearby and far. Breakfast was served as soon as the sky was completely light. In the kitchen there was a hubbub of women's voices. The dining room smelled of kerosene and oranges. A great platter heaped with thick slices of pale pineapple was in the center of the table. Don Federico sat at the end, his back to the wall. Behind him was a small niche, bright with candles, and the Virgin stood there in a blue and silver gown.

"Did you sleep well?" said Don Federico to Lucha.

"Ah, wonderfully well!"

"And you?" to Chalía.

"I never sleep well," she said.

A hen ran distractedly into the room from the veranda and was chased out by the serving girl. Outside the door a group of Indian children stood guard around a square of clothesline along which was draped a red assortment of meat: strips of flesh and loops of internal organs. When a vulture swooped low, the children jumped up and down, screaming in chorus, and drove it into the air again. Chalía frowned at their noise. Don Federico smiled.

"This is all in your honor," he said. "We killed a cow yesterday. Tomorrow all that will be gone."

"Not the vultures!" exclaimed Lucha.

"Certainly not. All the cowboys and servants take some home to their families. And they manage to get rid of quite a bit of it themselves."

"You're too generous," said Chalía. "It's bad for them. It makes them dissatisfied and unhappy. But I suppose if you didn't give it to them, they'd steal it anyway."

Don Federico pushed back his chair.

"No one here has ever stolen anything from me." He rose and went out.

After breakfast while it was still early, before the sun got too high in the sky, he regularly made a two-hour tour of the ranch. Since he preferred to pay unexpected visits to the vaqueros in charge of the various districts, he did not always cover the same regions. He was explaining this to Lucha as he untethered his horse outside the high barbed-wire fence that enclosed the house. "Not because I hope to find something wrong. But this is the best way always to find everything right."

Like Chalía, Lucha was skeptical of the Indians' ability to do anything properly. "A very good idea," she said. "I'm sure you are much too lenient with those boys. They need a strong hand and no pity."

Above the high trees that grew behind the house the red and blue macaws screamed, endlessly repeating their elliptical path in the sky. Lucha looked up in their direction and saw Chalía on the upper porch, tucking a khaki shirt into her breeches.

"Rico, wait! I want to go with you," she called, and rushed into her room.

Lucha turned back to her brother. "You won't take her? She couldn't! With Mamá . . ."

Don Federico cut her short, so as not to hear what would have been painful to him. "You both need fresh air and exercise. Come, both of you."

Lucha was silent a moment, looking aghast into his face. Finally she said, "I couldn't," and moved away to open the gate. Several cowboys were riding their horses slowly up from the paddock toward the front of the house. Chalía appeared on the lower porch and hurried to the gate, where Lucha stood looking at her.

"So you're going horseback riding," said Lucha. Her voice had no expression.

"Yes. Are you coming? I suppose not. We should be back soon; no, Rico?"

Don Federico disregarded her, saying to Lucha: "It would be good if you came."

When she did not reply, but went through the gate and shut it, he had one of the cowboys dismount and help Chalía onto his horse. She sat astride the animal beaming down at the youth.

"Now, you can't come. You have no horse!" she cried, pulling the reins taut violently so that the horse stood absolutely still.

"Yes, señora. I shall go with the señores." His speech was archaic and respectful, the speech of the rustic Indian. Their soft, polite words always annoyed her, because she believed, quite erroneously, that she could detect mockery underneath. "Like parrots who've been taught two lines of Góngora!" she would laugh, when the subject was being discussed. Now she was further nettled by hearing herself addressed as señora. "The idiot!" she thought. "He should know that I'm not married." But when she looked down at the cowboy again she noticed his white teeth and his very young face. She smiled, saying, "How hot it is already," and undid the top button of her shirt.

The boy ran to the paddock and returned immediately, riding a larger and more nervous horse. This was a joke to the other cowboys, who started ahead, laughing. Don Federico and Chalía rode side by side, and the boy went along behind them, by turns whistling a tune and uttering soothing words to his skittish horse.

The party went across the mile or so of open space that lay between the house and the jungle. Then the high grass swept the riders' legs as the horses went downward to the river, which was dry save for a narrow stream of water in the middle. They followed the bed downstream, the vegetation increasing the height along the banks as they progressed. Chalía had enameled her fingernails afresh before starting out and was in a good humor. She was discussing the administration of the ranch with Don Federico. The expenses and earning capacity interested her particularly, although she had no clear idea of the price of anything. She had worn an enormous soft straw sombrero whose brim dropped to her shoulders as she rode. Every few minutes she turned around and waved to the cowboy who still remained behind, shouting to him: "Muchacho! You're not lost yet?"

Presently the river was divided into two separate beds by a large island which loomed ahead of them, its upper reaches a solid wall of branches and vines. At the foot of the giant trees among some gray boulders was a score or so of cows, looking very small indeed as they lay hunched up in the mud or ambled about seeking the thickest shade. Don Federico galloped ahead suddenly and conferred loudly with the other vaqueros. Almost simultaneously Chalía drew in her reins and brought her horse to a halt. The boy was quickly abreast of her. As he came up she called to him: "It's hot, isn't it?"

The men rode on ahead. He circled around her. "Yes, señora. But that is because we are in the sun. There"——he indicated the island——"it is shady. Now they are almost there."

She said nothing, but took off her hat and fanned herself with the brim. As she moved her hand back and forth she watched her red nails. "What an ugly color," she murmured.

"What, señora?"

"Nothing." She paused. "Ah, what heat!"

"Come, señora. Shall we go on?"

Angrily she crumpled the crown of the sombrero in her fist. "I am not señora," she said distinctly, looking at the men ahead as they rode up to the cows and roused them from their lethargy. The boy smiled. She went on. "I am señorita. That is not the same thing. Or perhaps you think it is?"

The boy was puzzled; he was conscious of her sudden emotion, but he had no idea of its cause. "Yes, señorita," he said politely, without conviction. And he added, with more assurance, "I am Roberto Paz, at your orders."

The sun shone down upon them from above and was reflected by the mica in the stones at their feet. Chalía undid another button of her shirt.

"It's hot. Will they come back soon?"

"No, señorita. They return by the road. Shall we go?" He turned his horse toward the island ahead.

"I don't want to be where the cows are," said Chalía with petulance. "They have *garrapatas*. The *garrapatas* get under your skin."

Roberto laughed indulgently. "The *garrapatas* will not molest you if you stay on your horse, señorita."

"But I want to get down and rest. I'm so tired!" The discomfort of the heat became pure fatigue as she said the words; this made it possible for the annoyance she felt with him to transform itself into a general state of self-pity and depression that came upon her like a sudden pain. Hanging her head she sobbed: *"Ay, madre mía!* My poor mamá!" She stayed that way a moment, and her horse began to walk slowly toward the trees at the side of the riverbed.

Roberto glanced perplexedly in the direction the others had taken. They had all passed out of sight beyond the head of the island; the cows were lying down again. "The señorita should not cry."

She did not reply. Since the reins continued slack, her horse proceeded at a faster pace toward the forest. When it had reached the shade at the edge of the stream, the boy rode quickly to her side. "Señorita!" he cried.

She sighed and looked up at him, her hat still in her hand. "I'm very tired," she repeated. "I want to get down and rest."

There was a path leading into the forest. Roberto went ahead to lead the way, hacking at stray vines and bushes with his machete. Chalía followed, sitting listlessly in the saddle, calmed by the sudden entrance into the green world of silence and comparative coolness.

They rode slowly upward through the forest for a quarter of an hour or so without saying anything to each other. When they came to a gate Roberto opened it without dismounting and waited for Chalía to pass through. As she went by him she smiled and said: "How nice it is here."

He replied, rather curtly, she thought: "Yes, señorita."

Ahead, the vegetation thinned, and beyond lay a vast, open, slightly undulating expanse of land, decorated here and there, as if by intent, with giant white-trunked ceiba trees. The hot wind blew across this upland terrain, and the cry of cicadas was in the air. Chalía halted her horse and jumped down. The tiny thistlelike plants that covered the ground crackled under her boots. She seated herself carefully in the shade at the very edge of the open land.

Roberto tied the two horses to a tree and stood looking at her with the alert, hostile eyes of the Indian who faces what he does not understand.

"Sit down. Here," she said.

Stonily he obeyed, sitting with his legs straight on the earth in front of him, his back very erect. She rested her hand on his shoulder. *"Qué calor,"* she murmured.

She did not expect him to answer, but he did, and his voice sounded remote. "It is not my fault, señorita."

She slipped her arm around his neck and felt the muscles grow tense. She rubbed her face over his chest; he did not move or say anything. With her eyes shut and her head pressing hard against him, she felt as if she were hanging to consciousness only by the ceaseless shrill scream of the cicadas. She remained thus, leaning over more heavily upon him as he braced himself with his hands against the earth behind him. His face had become an impenetrable mask; he seemed not to be thinking of anything, not even to be present.

Breathing heavily, she raised her head to look at him, but found she did not have the courage to reach his eyes with her gaze. Instead she watched his throat and finally whispered, "It doesn't matter what you think of me. It's enough for me to hold you like this."

He turned his head stiffly away from her face, looking across the landscape to the mountains. Gruffly he said, "My brother could come by this place. We must go back to the river."

She tried to bury her face in his chest, to lose herself once more in the delicious sensation. Without warning, he moved quickly and stood up, so that she tumbled forward with her face against the ground.

The surprise of her little fall changed her mood instantly. She sprang up, dashed blindly for the nearer of the two horses, was astride it in an instant, and before he could cry, "It's the bad horse!" had pounded the animal's flanks with her heels. It raised its head wildly; with a violent bound it began to gallop over the countryside. At the first movement she realized dimly that there had been a change, that it was not the same horse, but in her excitement she let her observation stop there. She was delighted to be moving swiftly across the plain against the hot wind. Roberto was left behind.

"Idiota!" she screamed into the air. *"Idiota! Idiota!"* with all her might. Ahead of her a tremendous vulture, panic-stricken at the approaching hoof sounds, flapped clumsily away into the sky.

The saddle, having been strapped on for less vigorous action, began to slip. She gripped the pommel with one hand, and seizing her shirt with the other gave it a convulsive tug that ripped it completely open. A powerful feeling of exultation came to her as she glanced down and saw her own skin white in the sunlight.

In the distance to one side, she dimly saw some palm trees reaching above a small patch of lower vegetation. She shut her eyes: the palms looked like shiny green spiders. She was out of breath from the jolting. The sun was too hot. The saddle kept slipping further; she could not right it. The horse showed no sign of being aware of her existence. She pulled on the reins as hard as she could without falling over backward, but it had no effect on the horse, which continued to run at top speed, following no path and missing some of the trees by what seemed no more than inches.

"Where shall I be in an hour?" she asked herself. "Dead, perhaps?" The idea of death did not frighten her the way it did some people. She was afraid of the night because she could not sleep; she was not afraid of life and death because she did not feel implicated to any extent in either one. Only other people lived and died, had their lives and deaths. She, being inside herself, existed merely as herself and not as a part of anything else. People, animals, flowers and stones were objects, and they all belonged to the world outside. It was their juxtapositions that made hostile or friendly patterns. Sometimes she looked at her own hands and feet for several minutes, trying to fight off an indefinite sensation they gave her of belonging also to the world outside. But this never troubled her deeply. The impressions were received and accepted without question; at most she could combat them when they were too strong for her comfort.

Here in the hot morning sun, being pulled forward through the air, she began to feel that almost all of her had slipped out of the inside world, that only a tiny part of her was still she. The part that was left was full of astonishment and disbelief; the only discomfort now lay in having to accept the fact of the great white tree trunks that continued to rush by her.

She tried several times to make herself be elsewhere: in her rose garden at home, in the hotel dining room at Puntarenas, even as a last resort which might prove feasible since it too had been unpleasant, in her bed back at the ranch, with the dark around her.

With a great bound, the horse cleared a ditch. The saddle slipped completely around and hung underneath. Having no pommel to cling to, she kept on as best she could, clutching the horse's flanks with her legs and always pulling on the reins. Suddenly the animal slowed down and stepped briskly into a thicket. There was a path of sorts; she suspected it was the same one they had used coming from the river. She sat listlessly, waiting to see where the horse would go.

Finally it came out into the riverbed as she had expected, and trotted back to the ranch. The sun was directly overhead when they reached the paddock. The horse stood outside, waiting to be let in, but it seemed that no one was around. Making a great effort, she slid down to the ground and found she had difficulty in standing because her legs were trembling so. She was furious and ashamed. As she hobbled toward the house she was strongly hoping Lucha would not see her. A few Indian girls appeared to be the only people about. She dragged herself upstairs and shut herself in her room. The bed had been pushed back against the wall, but she did not have the force to pull it out into the center where she wanted it.

*   *   *

When Don Federico and the others returned, Lucha, who had been reading downstairs, went to the gate. "Where's Chalía?" she cried.

"She was tired. One of the boys brought her back a while ago," he said. "It's just as well. We went halfway to Las Cañas."

Chalía had her lunch in bed and slept soundly until late in the afternoon. When she emerged from her room onto the veranda, a woman was dusting the rocking chairs and arranging them in a row against the wall.

"Where's my sister?" demanded Chalía.

"Gone to the village in the truck with the señor," the woman replied, going to the head of the stairs and beginning to dust them one by one, as she went down backward.

Chalía seated herself in a chair and put her feet up on the porch railing, reflecting as she did so that if Lucha had been there she would have disapproved of the posture. There was a bend in the river—the only part of it that came within sight of the house—just below her, and a portion of the bank was visible to her through the foliage from where she sat. A large breadfruit tree spread its branches out almost to the opposite side of the stream. There was a pool at the turn, just where the tree's trunk grew out of the muddy bank. An Indian sauntered out of the undergrowth and calmly removed his trousers, then his shirt. He stood there a moment, stark naked, looking at the water, before he walked into it and began to splash and swim. When he had finished bathing he stood again on the bank, smoothing his blue-black hair. Chalía was puzzled, knowing that few Indians would be so immodest as to bathe naked in full view of the upstairs veranda. With a sudden strange sensation as she watched him, she realized it was Roberto and that he was wholly conscious of her presence at that moment.

"He knows Rico is gone and that no one can see him from downstairs," she thought, resolving to tell her brother when he came home. The idea of vengeance upon the boy filled her with a delicious excitement. She watched his deliberate movements as he dressed. He sat down on a rock with only his shirt on and combed his hair. The late-afternoon sun shone through the leaves and gave his brown skin an orange cast. When finally he had gone away without once glancing up at the house, she rose and went into her room. Maneuvering the bed into the middle of the floor once more, she began to walk around it; her mood was growing more and more turbulent as she circled about the room.

She heard the truck door slam, and a moment later, voices downstairs. With her finger to her temple, where she always put it when her heart was beating very fast, she slipped out onto the veranda and downstairs. Don Federico was in the commissary, which he opened for a half hour each morning and evening. Chalía stepped inside the door, her mouth already open, feeling the words about to burst from her lungs. Two children were pushing their copper coins along the counter, pointing at the candy they wanted. By the lamp a woman was looking at a bolt of goods. Don Federico was on a ladder, getting down another bolt. Chalía's mouth closed slowly. She looked down at her brother's desk by the door beside her, where he kept his ledgers and bills. In an open cigar box almost touching her hand was a pile of dirty bank notes. She was back in the room before she knew it. She shut the door and saw that she had four ten-colón notes in her hand. She stuffed them into her breeches pocket.

At dinner they made fun of her for having slept all the afternoon, telling her that now she would lie awake again all night.

She was busy eating. "If I do, so much the worse," she said, without looking up.

"I've arranged a little concert after dinner," said Don Federico. Lucha was ecstatic. He went on: "The cowboys have some friends here, over from Bagaces, and Raul has finished building his marimba."

The men and boys began to assemble soon after dinner. There was laughter, and guitars were strummed in the dark on the terrace. The two sisters went to sit at the end near the dining room, Don Federico was in the middle with the vaqueros, and the servants were ranged at the kitchen end. After several solo songs by various men with guitars, Raul and a friend began to play the marimba. Roberto was seated on the floor among the cowboys who were not performing.

"Suppose we all dance," said Don Federico, jumping up and seizing Lucha. They moved about together at one end of the terrace for a moment, but no one else stirred.

"*A bailar!*" Don Federico shouted, laughing.

Several of the girls started to dance timidly in couples, with loud giggling. None of the men would budge. The marimba players went on pounding out the same piece over and over again. Don Federico danced with Chalía, who was stiff from her morning ride; soon she excused herself and left. Instead of going upstairs to bed she crossed onto the front veranda and sat looking across the vast moonlit clearing. The night was thick with eternity. She could feel it there, just beyond the gate. Only the monotonous, tinkling music kept the house within the confines of time, saved it from being engulfed. As she listened to the merrymaking progress, she had the impression that the men were taking more part in it. "Rico has probably opened them a bottle of rum," she thought with fury.

At last it sounded as though everyone were dancing. Her curiosity having risen to a high pitch, she was about to rise and return to the terrace, when a figure appeared at the other end of the veranda. She needed no one to tell her it was Roberto. He was walking soundlessly toward her; he seemed to hesitate as he came up to her, then he squatted down by her chair and looked up at her. She had been right: he smelled of rum.

"Good evening, señorita."

She felt impelled to remain silent. Nevertheless, she said, "Good evening." She put her hand into her pocket, saying to herself that she must do this correctly and quickly.

As he crouched there with his face shining in the moonlight, she bent forward and passed her hand over his smooth hair. Keeping her fingers on the back of his neck, she leaned still further forward and kissed his lips. The rum was very strong. He did not move. She began to whisper in his ear, very low: "Roberto, I love you. I have a present for you. Forty *colones*. Here."

He turned his head swiftly and said out loud, "Where?"

She put the bills into his hand, still holding his head, and whispered again: "Sh! Not a word to anyone. I must go now. I'll give you more tomorrow night." She let go of him.

He rose and went out the gate. She went straight upstairs to bed, and as she went to sleep the music was still going on.

Much later she awoke and lit her lamp. It was half past four. Day would soon break. Feeling full of an unaccustomed energy, Chalía dressed, extinguished the lamp and went outdoors, shutting the gate quietly behind her. In the paddock the horses stirred. She walked by it and started along the road to the village. It was a very silent hour: the night insects had ceased their noises and the birds had not yet begun their early-morning twitter. The moon was low in the sky, so that it remained behind the trees most of the time. Ahead of her Venus flared like a minor moon. She walked quickly, with only a twinge of pain now and then in her hip.

Something dark lying in the road ahead of her made her stop walking.

It did not move. She watched it closely, stepping cautiously toward it, ready to run the other way. As her eyes grew accustomed to its form, she saw that it was a man lying absolutely still. And as she drew near, she knew it was Roberto. She touched his arm with her foot. He did not respond. She leaned over and put her hand on his chest. He was breathing deeply, and the smell of liquor was almost overpowering. She straightened and kicked him lightly in the head. There was a tiny groan from far within. This also, she said to herself, would have to be done quickly. She felt wonderfully light and powerful as she slowly maneuvered his body with her feet to the right-hand side of the road. There was a small cliff there, about twenty feet high. When she got him to the edge, she waited a while, looking at his features in the moonlight. His mouth was open a little, and the white teeth peeked out from behind the lips. She smoothed his forehead a few times and with a gentle push rolled him over the edge. He fell very heavily, making a strange animal sound as he hit.

She walked back to the ranch at top speed. It was getting light when she arrived. She went into the kitchen and ordered her breakfast, saying: "I'm up early." The entire day she spent around the house, reading and talking to Lucha. She thought Don Federico looked preoccupied when he set out on his morning tour of inspection, after closing the commissary. She thought he still did when he returned; she told him so at lunch.

"It's nothing," he said. "I can't seem to balance my books."

"And you've always been such a good mathematician," said Chalía.

During the afternoon some cowboys brought Roberto in. She heard the commotion in the kitchen and the servants' cries of *"Ay, Dios!"* She went out to watch. He was conscious, lying on the floor with all the other Indians staring at him.

"What's the matter?" she said.

One of the cowboys laughed. "Nothing of importance. He had too much—" the cowboy made a gesture of drinking from a bottle, "and fell off the road. Nothing but bruises, I think."

After dinner Don Federico asked Chalía and Lucha into his little private office. He looked drawn, and he spoke more slowly than usual. As Chalía entered she saw that Roberto was standing inside the door. He did not look at her. Lucha and Chalía sat down; Don Federico and Roberto remained standing.

"This is the first time anyone has done this to me," said Don Federico, looking down at the rug, his hands locked behind him. "Roberto has stolen from me. The money is missing. Some of it is in his pocket still, more than his monthly wages. I know he has stolen it because he had no money yesterday and because"—he turned to Chalía—"because he can account for having it only by lying. He says you gave it to him. Did you give Roberto any money yesterday?"

Chalía looked puzzled. "No," she said. "I thought of giving him a *colón* when he brought me back from the ride yesterday morning. But then I thought it would be better to wait until we were leaving to go back to the city. Was it much? He's just a boy."

Don Federico said: "It was forty *colones*. But that's the same as forty *centavos*. Stealing . . ."

Chalía interrupted him. "Rico!" she exclaimed. "Forty *colones!* That's a great deal! Has he spent much of it? You could take it out of his wages little by little." She knew her brother would say what he did say, a moment later.

"Never! He'll leave tonight. And his brother with him."

In the dim light Chalía could see the large purple bruise on Roberto's forehead. He kept his head lowered and did not look up, even when she and Lucha rose and left the room at a sign from their brother. They went upstairs together and sat down on the veranda.

"What barbarous people they are!" said Lucha indignantly. "Poor Rico may learn someday how to treat them. But I'm afraid one of them will kill him first."

Chalía rocked back and forth, fanning herself lazily. "With a few more lessons like this he may change," she said. "What heat!"

They heard Don Federico's voice below by the gate. Firmly it said, "*Adiós.*" There were muffled replies and the gate was closed. Don Federico joined his sisters on the veranda. He sat down sadly.

"I didn't like to send them away on foot at night," he said, shaking his head. "But that Roberto is a bad one. It was better to have him go once and for all, quickly. Juan is good, but I had to get rid of him too, of course."

"*Claro, claro,*" said Lucha absently. Suddenly she turned to her brother full of concern. "I hope you remembered to take away the money you said he still had in his pocket."

"Yes, yes," he assured her, but from the tone of his voice she knew he had let the boy keep it.

* * *

Don Federico and Lucha said good night and went to bed. Chalía sat up a while, looking vaguely at the wall with the spiders in it. Then she yawned and took the lamp into her room. Again the bed had been pushed back against the wall by the maid. Chalía shrugged her shoulders, got into the bed where it was, blew out the lamp, listened for a few minutes to the night sounds, and went peacefully to sleep, thinking of how surprisingly little time it had taken her to get used to life at Paso Rojo, and even, she had to admit now, to begin to enjoy it.

Pastor Dowe at Tacaté

Pastor Dowe delivered his first sermon in Tacaté on a bright Sunday morning shortly after the beginning of the rainy season. Almost a hundred Indians attended, and some of them had come all the way from Balaché in the valley. They sat quietly on the ground while he spoke to them for an hour or so in their own tongue. Not even the children became restive; there was the most complete silence as long as he kept speaking. But he could see that their attention was born of respect rather than of interest. Being a conscientious man he was troubled to discover this.

When he had finished the sermon, the notes for which were headed "Meaning of Jesus," they slowly got to their feet and began wandering away, quite obviously thinking of other things. Pastor Dowe was puzzled. He had been assured by Dr. Ramos of the University that his mastery of the dialect was sufficient to enable his prospective parishioners to follow his sermons, and he had had no difficulty conversing with the Indians who had accompanied him up from San Gerónimo. He stood sadly on the small thatch-covered platform in the clearing before his house and watched the men and women walking slowly away in different directions. He had the sensation of having communicated absolutely nothing to them.

All at once he felt he must keep the people here a little longer, and he called out to them to stop. Politely they turned their faces toward the pavilion where he stood, and remained looking at him, without moving. Several of the smaller children were already playing a game, and were darting about silently in the background. The pastor glanced at his wrist watch and spoke to Nicolás, who had been pointed out to him as one of the most intelligent and influential men in the village, asking him to come up and stand beside him.

Once Nicolás was next to him, he decided to test him with a few questions. "Nicolás," he said in his dry, small voice, "what did I tell you today?"

Nicolás coughed and looked over the heads of the assembly to where an enormous sow was rooting in the mud under a mango tree. Then he said: "Don Jesucristo."

"Yes," agreed Pastor Dowe encouragingly. *"Bai,* and Don Jesucristo what?"

"A good man," answered Nicolás with indifference.

"Yes, yes, but what more?" Pastor Dowe was impatient; his voice rose in pitch.

Nicolás was silent. Finally he said, "Now I go," and stepped carefully down from the platform. The others again began to gather up their belongings and move off. For a moment Pastor Dowe was furious. Then he took his notebook and his Bible and went into the house.

At lunch Mateo, who waited on table, and whom he had brought with him from Ocosingo, stood leaning against the wall smiling.

"Señor," he said, "Nicolás says they will not come again to hear you without music."

"Music!" cried Pastor Dowe, setting his fork on the table. "Ridiculous! What music? We have no music."

"He says the father at Yalactín used to sing."

"Ridiculous!" said the pastor again. "In the first place I can't sing, and in any case it's unheard of! *Inaudito!"*

"Sí, verdad?" agreed Mateo.

The pastor's tiny bedroom was breathlessly hot, even at night. However, it was the only room in the little house with a window on the outside; he could shut the door onto the noisy patio where by day the servants invariably gathered for their work and their conversations. He lay under the closed canopy of his mosquito net, listening to the barking of the dogs in the village below. He was thinking about Nicolás. Apparently Nicolás had chosen for himself the role of envoy from the village to the mission. The pastor's thin lips moved. "A troublemaker," he whispered to himself. "I'll speak with him tomorrow."

Early the next morning he stood outside Nicolás's hut. Each house in Tacaté had its own small temple: a few tree trunks holding up some thatch to shelter the offerings of fruit and cooked food. The pastor took care not to go near the one that stood nearby; he already felt enough like a pariah, and Dr. Ramos had warned him against meddling of that sort. He called out.

A little girl about seven years old appeared in the doorway of the house. She looked at him wildly a moment with huge round eyes before she squealed and disappeared back into the darkness. The pastor waited and called again. Presently a man came around the hut from the back and told him that Nicolás would return. The pastor sat down on a stump. Soon the little girl stood again in the doorway; this time she smiled coyly. The pastor looked at her severely. It seemed to him she was too old to run about naked. He turned his head away and examined the thick red petals of a banana blossom hanging nearby. When he looked back she had come out and was standing near him, still smiling. He got up and walked toward the road, his head down, as if deep in thought. Nicolás entered through the gate at that moment, and the pastor, colliding with him, apologized.

"Good," grunted Nicolás. "What?"

His visitor was not sure how he ought to begin. He decided to be pleasant.

"I am a good man," he smiled.

"Yes," said Nicolás. "Don Jesucristo is a good man."

"No, no, no!" cried Pastor Dowe.

Nicolás looked politely confused, but said nothing.

Feeling that his command of the dialect was not equal to this sort of situation, the pastor wisely decided to begin again. "Hachakyum made the world. Is that true?"

Nicolás nodded in agreement, and squatted down at the pastor's feet, looking up at him, his eyes narrowed against the sun.

"Hachakyum made the sky," the pastor began to point, "the mountains, the trees, those people there. Is that true?"

Again Nicolás assented.

"Hachakyum is good. Hachakyum made you. True?" Pastor Dowe sat down again on the stump.

Nicolás spoke finally, "All that you say is true."

The pastor permitted himself a pleased smile and went on. "Hachakyum made everything and everyone because He is mighty and good."

Nicolás frowned. "No!" he cried. "That is not true! Hachakyum did not make everyone. He did not make you. He did not make guns or Don Jesucristo. Many things He did not make!"

The pastor shut his eyes a moment, seeking strength. "Good," he said at last in a patient voice. "Who made the other things? Who made me? Please tell me."

Nicolás did not hesitate. "Metzabok."

"But who is Metzabok?" cried the pastor, letting an outraged note show in his voice. The word for God he had always known only as Hachakyum.

"Metzabok makes all the things that do not belong here," said Nicolás.

The pastor rose, took out his handkerchief and wiped his forehead. "You hate me," he said, looking down at the Indian. The word was too strong, but he did not know how to say it any other way.

Nicolás stood up quickly and touched the pastor's arm with his hand.

"No. That is not true. You are a good man. Everyone likes you."

Pastor Dowe backed away in spite of himself. The touch of the brown hand was vaguely distasteful to him. He looked beseechingly into the Indian's face and said, "But Hachakyum did not make me?"

"No."

There was a long pause.

"Will you come next time to my house and hear me speak?"

Nicolás looked uncomfortable.

"Everyone has work to do," he said.

"Mateo says you want music," began the pastor.

Nicolás shrugged. "To me it is not important. But the others will come if you have music. Yes, that is true. They like music."

"But *what* music?" cried the pastor in desperation.

"They say you have a *bitrola*."

The pastor looked away, thinking: "There is no way to keep anything from these people." Along with all his other household goods and the things left behind by his wife when she died, he had brought a little portable phonograph. It was somewhere in the storeroom piled with the empty valises and cold-weather garments.

"Tell them I will play the *bitrola*," he said, going out the gate.

The little girl ran after him and stood watching him as he walked up the road.

On his way through the village the pastor was troubled by the reflection that he was wholly alone in this distant place, alone in his struggle to bring the truth to its people. He consoled himself by recalling that it is only in each man's own consciousness that the isolation exists; objectively man is always a part of something.

When he arrived home he sent Mateo to the storeroom to look for the portable phonograph. After a time the boy brought it out, dusted it and stood by while the pastor opened the case. The crank was inside. He took it out and wound the spring. There were a few records in the compartment at the top. The first he examined were "Let's Do It," "Crazy Rhythm," and "Strike Up the Band," none of which Pastor Dowe considered proper accompaniments to his sermons. He looked further. There was a recording of Al Jolson singing "Sonny Boy" and a cracked copy of "She's Funny

That Way." As he looked at the labels he remembered how the music on each disk had sounded. Unfortunately Mrs. Dowe had disliked hymn music; she had called it "mournful."

"So here we are," he sighed, "without music."

Mateo was astonished. "It does not play?"

"I can't play them this music for dancing, Mateo."

"Cómo nó, señor! They will like it very much!"

"No, Mateo!" said the pastor forcefully, and he put on "Crazy Rhythm" to illustrate his point. As the thin metallic tones issued from the instrument, Mateo's expression changed to one of admiration bordering on beatitude. *"Qué bonito!"* he said reverently. Pastor Dowe lifted the tone arm and the hopping rhythmical pattern ceased.

"It cannot be done," he said with finality, closing the lid.

Nevertheless on Saturday he remembered that he had promised Nicolás there would be music at the service, and he decided to tell Mateo to carry the phonograph out to the pavilion in order to have it there in case the demand for it should prove to be pressing. This was a wise precaution, because the next morning when the villagers arrived they were talking of nothing but the music they were to hear.

His topic was "The Strength of Faith," and he had got about ten minutes into the sermon when Nicolás, who was squatting directly in front of him, quietly stood up and raised his hand. Pastor Dowe frowned and stopped talking.

Nicolás spoke: "Now music, then talk. Then music, then talk. Then music." He turned around and faced the others. "That is a good way." There were murmurs of assent, and everyone leaned a bit further forward on his haunches to catch whatever musical sounds might issue from the pavilion.

The pastor sighed and lifted the machine onto the table, knocking off the Bible that lay at the edge. "Of course," he said to himself with a faint bitterness. The first record he came to was "Crazy Rhythm." As it started to play, an infant nearby, who had been singsonging a series of meaningless sounds, ceased making its parrotlike noises, remaining silent and transfixed as it stared at the platform. Everyone sat absolutely quiet until the piece was over. Then there was a hubbub of approbation. "Now more talk," said Nicolás, looking very pleased.

The pastor continued. He spoke a little haltingly now, because the music had broken his train of thought, and even by looking at his notes he could not be sure just how far he had got before the interruption. As he continued, he looked down at the people sitting nearest him. Beside Nicolás he noticed the little girl who had watched him from the doorway, and he was gratified to see that she was wearing a small garment which managed to cover her. She was staring at him with an expression he interpreted as one of fascinated admiration.

Presently, when he felt that his audience was about to grow restive (even though he had to admit that they never would have shown it outwardly) he put on "Sonny Boy." From the reaction it was not difficult to guess that this selection was finding less favor with its listeners. The general expression of tense anticipation at the beginning of the record soon relaxed into one of routine enjoyment of a less intense degree. When the piece was finished, Nicolás got to his feet again and raised his hand solemnly, saying: "Good. But the other music is more beautiful."

The pastor made a short summation, and, after playing "Crazy Rhythm" again, he announced that the service was over.

In this way "Crazy Rhythm" became an integral part of Pastor Dowe's weekly service. After a few months the old record was so badly worn that he determined to play it only once at each gathering. His flock submitted to this show of economy with bad grace. They complained, using Nicolás as emissary.

"But the music is old. There will be no more if I use it all," the pastor explained.

Nicolás smiled unbelievingly. "You say that. But you do not want us to have it."

The following day, as the pastor sat reading in the patio's shade, Mateo again announced Nicolás, who had entered through the kitchen and, it appeared, had been conversing with the servants there. By now the pastor had learned fairly well how to read the expressions on Nicolás's face; the one he saw there now told him that new exactions were at hand.

Nicolás looked respectful. "Señor," he said, "we like you because you have given us music when we asked you for it. Now we are all good friends. We want you to give us salt."

"Salt?" exclaimed Pastor Dowe, incredulous. "What for?"

Nicolás laughed good-naturedly, making it clear that he thought the pastor was joking with him. Then he made a gesture of licking. "To eat," he said.

"Ah, yes," murmured the pastor, recalling that among the Indians rock salt is a scarce luxury.

"But we have no salt," he said quickly.

"Oh, yes, señor. There." Nicolás indicated the kitchen.

The pastor stood up. He was determined to put an end to this haggling, which he considered a demoralizing element in his official relationship with the village. Signaling for Nicolás to follow, he walked into the kitchen, calling as he entered, "Quintina, show me our salt."

Several of the servants, including Mateo, were standing in the room. It was Mateo who opened a low cupboard and disclosed a great stack of grayish cakes piled on the floor. The pastor was astonished. "So many kilos of salt!" he exclaimed. *"Cómo se hace?"*

Mateo calmly told him it had been brought with them all the way from Ocosingo. "For us," he added, looking about at the others.

Pastor Dowe seized upon this, hoping it was meant as a hint and could be recognized as one. "Of course," he said to Nicolás. "This is for my house."

Nicolás looked unimpressed. "You have enough for everyone in the village," he remarked. "In two Sundays you can get more from Ocosingo. Everyone will be very happy all the time that way. Everyone will come each time you speak. You give them salt and make music."

Pastor Dowe felt himself beginning to tremble a little. He knew he was excited and so he was careful to make his voice sound natural.

"I will decide, Nicolás," he said. "Good-bye."

It was clear that Nicolás in no way regarded these words as a dismissal. He answered, "Good-bye," and leaned back against the wall calling, "Marta!" The little girl, of whose presence in the room the pastor now became conscious, moved out from the shadows of a corner. She held what appeared to him to be a large doll, and was being very solicitous of it. As the pastor stepped out into the bright patio, the picture struck him as false, and he turned around and looked back into the kitchen, frowning. He remained in the doorway in an attitude of suspended action for a moment, staring at little Marta. The doll, held lovingly in the child's arms, and swaddled in a much-used rag, was making spasmodic movements.

The pastor's ill humor was with him; probably he would have shown it no matter what the circumstances. "What is it?" he demanded indignantly. As if in answer the bundle squirmed again, throwing off part of the rag that covered it, and the pastor saw what looked to him like a comic-strip caricature of Red Riding Hood's wolf peering out from under the grandmother's nightcap. Again Pastor Dowe cried, "What is it?"

Nicolás turned from his conversation, amused, and told Marta to hold it up and uncover it so the señor could see it. This she did, pulling away the wrapping and exposing to view a lively young alligator which, since it was being held more or less on its back, was objecting in a routine fashion to the treatment by rhythmically paddling the air with its little black feet. Its rather long face seemed, however, to be smiling.

"Good heavens!" cried the pastor in English. The spectacle struck him as strangely scandalous. There was a hidden obscenity in the sight of the mildly agitated little reptile with its head wrapped in a rag, but Marta was still holding it out toward him for his inspection. He touched the smooth scales of its belly with his fingers, and withdrew his hand, saying, "Its jaws should be bound. It will bite her."

Mateo laughed. "She is too quick," and then said it in dialect to Nicolás, who agreed, and also laughed. The pastor patted Marta on the head as she returned the animal to her bosom and resumed cradling it tenderly.

Nicolás's eyes were on him. "You like Marta?" he asked seriously.

The pastor was thinking about the salt. "Yes, yes," he said with the false enthusiasm of the preoccupied man. He went to his bedroom and shut the door. Lying on the narrow bed in the afternoon was the same as lying on it at night: there was the same sound of dogs barking in the village. Today there was also the sound of wind going past the window. Even the canopy of mosquito netting swayed a little from time to time as the air came into the room. The pastor was trying to decide whether or not to give in to Nicolás. When he got very sleepy, he thought: "After all, what principle am I upholding in keeping it from them? They want music. They want salt. They will learn to want God." This thought proved relaxing to him, and he fell asleep to the sound of the dogs barking and the wind shrilling past the window.

During the night the clouds rolled down off the mountains into the valley, and when dawn came they remained there, impaled on the high trees. The few birds that made themselves heard sounded as though they were singing beneath the ceiling of a great room. The wet air was thick with woodsmoke, but there was no noise from the village; a wall of cloud lay between it and the mission house.

From his bed, instead of the wind passing the window, the pastor heard the slow drops of water falling upon the bushes from the eaves. He lay still awhile, lulled by the subdued chatter of the servants' voices in the kitchen. Then he went to the window and looked out into the grayness. Even the nearest trees were invisible; there was a heavy odor of earth. He dressed, shivering as the damp garments touched his skin. On the table lay a newspaper:

BARCELONA BOMBARDEADO POR
DOSCIENTOS AVIONES

As he shaved, trying to work up a lather with the tepid water Quintina had brought him, full of charcoal ashes, it occurred to him that he would like to escape from the people of Tacaté and the smothering feeling they gave him of being lost in antiquity. It would be good to be free from that infinite sadness even for a few hours.

He ate a larger breakfast than usual and went outside to the sheltered platform, where he sat down in the dampness and began to read the Seventy-eighth Psalm, which he had thought of using as the basis of a sermon. As he read he looked out at the emptiness in front of him. Where he knew the mango tree stood he could see only the white void, as if the land dropped away at the platform's edge for a thousand feet or more.

"He clave the rocks in the wilderness, and gave them drink as out of the great depths." From the house came the sound of Quintina's giggling. "Mateo is probably chasing her around the patio," thought the pastor; wisely he had long since given up expecting any Indian to behave as he considered an adult should. Every few seconds on the other side of the pavilion a turkey made its hysterical gobbling sound. The pastor spread his Bible out on the table, put his hands to his ears, and continued to read: "He caused an east wind to blow in the heaven: and by His power He brought in the south wind."

"Passages like that would sound utterly pagan in the dialect," he caught himself thinking. He unstopped his ears and reflected: "But to their ears *everything* must have a pagan sound. Everything I say is transformed on the way to them into something else." This was a manner of thinking that Pastor Dowe had always taken pains to avoid. He fixed his eyes on the text with determination, and read on. The giggling in the house was louder; he could hear Mateo too now. "He sent divers sorts of flies among them; . . . and frogs, which destroyed them." The door into the patio was opened and the pastor heard Mateo coughing as he stood looking out. "He certainly has tuberculosis," said the pastor to himself, as the Indian spat repeatedly. He shut his Bible and took off his glasses, feeling about on the table for their case. Not encountering it, he rose, and taking a step forward, crushed it under his heel. Compassionately, he stooped down and picked it up. The hinges were snapped and the metal sides under their artificial leather covering were bent out of shape. Mateo could have hammered it back into a semblance of its form, but Pastor Dowe preferred to think: "All things have their death." He had had the case eleven years. Briefly he summed up its life: the sunny afternoon when he had bought it on the little side street in downtown Havana; the busy years in the hills of southern Brazil; the time in Chile when he had dropped the case, with a pair of dark glasses in it, out the bus window, and everyone in the bus had got out and helped him look for it; the depressing year in Chicago when for some reason he had left it in a bureau drawer most of the time and had carried his glasses loose in his coat pocket. He remembered some of the newspaper clippings he had kept in the case, and many of the little slips of paper with ideas jotted down on them. He looked tenderly down at it, thinking: "And so this is the place and time, and these are the circumstances of its death." For some reason he was happy to have witnessed this death; it was comforting to know exactly how the case had finished its existence. He still looked at it with sadness for a moment. Then he flung it out into the white air as if the precipice were really there. With his Bible under his arm he strode to the door and brushed past Mateo without saying a word. But as he walked into his room it seemed to him that Mateo had looked at him in a strange fashion, as if he knew something and were waiting to see when the pastor would find out, too.

Back in his suffocating little room the pastor felt an even more imperious need to be alone for a time. He changed his shoes, took his cane and went out into the fog. In this weather there was only one path practicable, and that led downward through the village. He stepped ahead over the stones with great caution, for although he could discern the ground at his feet and the spot where he put the tip of his cane each time, beyond that on all sides was mere whiteness. Walking along thus, he reflected, was like trying to read a text with only one letter visible at a time. The wood smoke was sharp in the still air.

For perhaps half an hour Pastor Dowe continued this way, carefully putting one foot before the other. The emptiness around him, the lack of all visual detail, rather than activating his thought, served to dull his perceptions. His progress over the stones was laborious but strangely relaxing. One of the few ideas that came into his head as he moved along was that it would be pleasant to pass through the village without anyone's noticing him, and it seemed to him that it might be managed; even at ten feet he would be invisible. He could walk between the huts and hear the babies crying, and when he came out at the other end no one would know he had been there. He was not sure where he would go then.

The way became suddenly rougher as the path went into a zigzagging descent along the steep side of a ravine. He had reached the bottom before he raised his head once. "Ah," he said, standing still. The fog was now above him, a great gray quilt of cloud. He saw the giant trees that stood around him and heard them dripping slowly in a solemn, uneven chorus onto the wild coca leaves beneath.

"There is no such place as this on the way to the village," thought the pastor. He was mildly annoyed, but more astonished, to find himself standing by these trees that looked like elephants and were larger than any other trees he had seen in the region. Automatically he turned around in the path and started back up the slope. Beside the overpowering sadness of the landscape, now that it was visible to him, the fog up there was a comfort and a protection. He paused for a moment to stare back at the fat, spiny tree trunks and the welter of vegetation beyond. A small sound behind him made him turn his head.

Two Indians were trotting down the path toward him. As they came up they stopped and looked at him with such expectancy on their dark little faces that Pastor Dowe thought they were going to speak. Instead the one ahead made a grunting sound and motioned to the other to follow. There was no way of effecting a detour around the pastor, so they brushed violently against him as they went by. Without once looking back they hurried on downward and disappeared among the green coca leaves.

This unlikely behavior on the part of the two natives vaguely intrigued him; on an impulse he determined to find an explanation for it. He started after them.

Soon he had gone beyond the spot where he had turned back a moment ago. He was in the forest; the plant odor was almost unbearable—a smell of living and dead vegetation in a world where slow growth and slow death are simultaneous and inseparable. He stopped once and listened for footsteps. Apparently the Indians had run on ahead of him; nevertheless he continued on his way. Since the path was fairly wide and well broken in, it was only now and then that he came into contact with a hanging tendril or a projecting branch.

The posturing trees and vines gave the impression of having been arrested in furious motion, and presented a monotonous succession of tortured tableaux vivants. It was as if, for the moment while he watched, the desperate battle for air had been suspended and would be resumed only when he turned away his head. As he looked, he decided that it was precisely this unconfirmable quality of surreptitiousness which made the place so disquieting. Now and then, high above his head, a blood-colored butterfly would float silently through the gloom from one tree trunk to another. They were all alike; it seemed to him that it must be always the same insect. Several times he passed the white grillwork of great spiderwebs flung across between the plants like gates painted on the dark wall behind. But all the webs looked uninhabited. The large, leisurely drops of water still continued to fall from above; even if it had been raining hard, the earth could not have been wetter.

The pastor was astigmatic, and since he was beginning to be dizzy from watching so many details, he kept his eyes looking straight ahead as he walked, deviating his gaze only when he had to avoid the plant life that had grown across the path. The floor of the forest continued flat. Suddenly he became aware that the air around him was reverberating with faint sounds. He stood still, and recognized the casual gurgle a deep stream makes from time to time as it moves past its banks. Almost immediately ahead of him was the water, black and wide, and considering its proximity, incredibly quiet in its swift flowing. A few paces before him a great dead tree, covered with orange fungus, lay across the path. The pastor's glance followed the trunk to the left; at the small end, facing him, sat the two Indians. They were looking at him with interest, and he knew they had been waiting for him. He walked over to them, greeted them. They replied solemnly, never taking their shining eyes from his face.

As if they had rehearsed it, they both rose at the same instant and walked to the water's edge, where they stood looking down. Then one of them glanced back at the pastor and said simply, "Come." As he made his way around the log he saw that they were standing by a long bamboo raft which was beached on the muddy bank. They lifted it and dropped one end into the stream.

"Where are you going?" asked the pastor. For reply they lifted their short brown arms in unison and waved them slowly in the direction of downstream. Again the one who had spoken before said, "Come." The pastor, his curiosity aroused, looked suspiciously at the delicate raft, and back at the two men. At the same time he felt that it would be pleasanter to be riding with them than to go back through the forest. Impatiently he again demanded, "Where are you going? Tacaté?"

"Tacaté," echoed the one who up to this point had not spoken.

"Is it strong?" queried the pastor, stooping to push lightly on a piece of bamboo. This was merely a formality; he had perfect faith in the Indians' ability to master the materials of the jungle.

"Strong," said the first. "Come."

The pastor glanced back into the wet forest, climbed onto the raft, and sat doubled up on its bottom in the stern. The two quickly jumped aboard and pushed the frail craft from the bank with a pole.

Then began a journey which almost at once Pastor Dowe regretted having undertaken. Even as the three of them shot swiftly ahead, around the first bend in the stream, he wished he had stayed behind and could be at this moment on his way up the side of the ravine. And as they sped on down the silent waterway he continued to reproach himself for having come along without knowing why. At each successive bend in the tunnellike course, he felt farther from the world. He found himself straining in a ridiculous effort to hold the raft back: it glided far too easily along the top of the black water. Farther from the world, or did he mean farther from God? A region like this seemed outside God's jurisdiction. When he had reached that idea he shut his eyes. It was an absurdity, manifestly impossible—in any case, inadmissible—yet it had occurred to him and was remaining with him in his mind. "God is always with me," he said to himself silently, but the formula had no effect. He opened his eyes quickly and looked at the two men. They were facing him, but he had the impression of being invisible to them; they could see only the quickly dissipated ripples left behind on the surface of the water, and the irregular arched ceiling of vegetation under which they had passed.

The pastor took his cane from where it was lying hidden, and gesticulated with it as he asked, "Where are we going?" Once again they both pointed vaguely into the air, over their shoulders, as if the question were of no interest, and the expression on their faces never changed. Loath to let even another tree go past, the pastor mechanically immersed his cane in the water as though he would stop the constant forward thrusting of the raft; he withdrew it immediately and laid it dripping across the bottom. Even that much contact with the dark stream was unpleasant to him. He tried to tell himself that there was no reason for his sudden spiritual collapse, but at the same time it seemed to him that he could feel the innermost fibers of his consciousness in the process of relaxing. The journey downstream was a monstrous letting go, and he fought against it with all his power. "Forgive me, O God, I am leaving You behind. Forgive me for leaving You behind." His nails pressed into his palms as he prayed.

And so he sat in agonized silence while they slid ahead through the forest and out into a wide lagoon where the gray sky was once more visible. Here the raft went much more slowly, and the Indians propelled it gently with their hands toward the shore where the water was shallow. Then one of them poled it along with the bamboo stick. The pastor did not notice the great beds of water hyacinths they passed through, nor the silken sound made as they rubbed against the raft. Out here under the low-hanging clouds there was occasionally a bird cry or a sudden rustle in the high grass by the water's edge. Still the pastor remained sunk within himself, feeling, rather than thinking: "Now it is done. I have passed over into the other land." And he remained so deeply preoccupied with this emotional certainty that he was not aware of it when they approached a high escarpment rising sheer from the lagoon, nor when they drew up onto the sand of a small cove at one side of the cliff. When he looked up the two Indians were standing on the sand, and one of them was saying, "Come." They did not help him get ashore; he did this with some difficulty, although he was conscious of none.

As soon as he was on land they led him along the foot of the cliff that curved away from the water. Following a tortuous track beaten through the undergrowth they came out all at once at the very foot of the wall of rock. There were two caves—a small one opening to the left, and a wider, higher one to the right. They halted outside the smaller. "Go in," they said to the pastor. It was not very light inside, and he could see very little. The two remained at the entrance. "Your god lives here," said one. "Speak with him."

The pastor was on his knees. "O Father, hear my voice. Let my voice come through to you. I ask it in Jesus' name. . . ." The Indian was calling to him, "Speak in our tongue." The pastor made an effort, and began a halting supplication in the dialect. There were grunts of satisfaction outside. The concentration demanded in order to translate his thoughts into the still unfamiliar language served to clear his mind somewhat. And the comforting parallel between this prayer and those he offered for his congregation helped to restore his calm. As he continued to speak, always with fewer hesitations, he felt a great rush of strength going through him. Confidently he raised his head and went on praying, his eyes on the wall in front of him. At the same moment he heard the cry: "Metzabok hears you now. Say more to him."

The pastor's lips stopped moving, and his eyes saw for the first time the red hand painted on the rock before him, and the charcoal, the ashes, the flower petals and the wooden spoons strewn about. But he had no sensation of horror; that was over. The important thing now was that he felt strong and happy. His spiritual condition was a physical fact. Having prayed to Metzabok was also a fact, of course, but his deploring of it was in purely mental terms. Without formulating the thought, he decided that forgiveness would be forthcoming when he asked God for it.

To satisfy the watchers outside the cave he added a few formal phrases to his prayer, rose, and stepped out into the daylight. For the first time he noticed a certain animation in the features of the two little men. One said, "Metzabok is very happy." The other said, "Wait." Whereupon they both hurried over to the larger of the two apertures and disappeared inside. The pastor sat on a rock, resting his chin on the hand that held the head of his cane. He was still suffused with the strange triumphant sensation of having returned to himself.

He heard them muttering for a quarter of an hour or so inside the cave. Presently they came out, still looking very serious. Moved by curiosity the pastor risked a question. He indicated the larger cave with a finger and said, "Hachakyum lives there?" Together they assented. He wanted to go further and ask if Hachakyum approved of his having spoken with Metzabok, but he felt the question would be imprudent; besides, he was certain the answer would be in the affirmative.

They arrived back in the village at nightfall, after having walked all the way. The Indians' gait had been far too swift for Pastor Dowe, and they had stopped only once to eat some sapotes they had found under the trees. He asked to be taken to the house of Nicolás. It was raining lightly when they reached the hut. The pastor sat down in the doorway beneath the overhanging eaves of cane. He felt utterly exhausted; it had been one of the most tiring days of his life, and he was not home yet.

His two companions ran off when Nicolás appeared. Evidently he already knew of the visit to the cave. It seemed to the pastor that he had never seen his face so full of expression or so pleasant. "*Utz, utz,*" said Nicolás. "Good, good. You must eat and sleep."

After a meal of fruit and maize cakes, the pastor felt better. The hut was filled with wood smoke from the fire in the corner. He lay back in a low hammock which little Marta, casually pulling on a string from time to time, kept in gentle motion. He was overcome with a desire to sleep, but his host seemed to be in a communicative mood, and he wanted to profit by it. As he was about to speak, Nicolás approached, carrying a rusty tin biscuit box. Squatting beside the hammock he said in a low voice: "I will show you my things." The pastor was delighted; this bespoke a high degree of friendliness. Nicolás opened the box and took out some sample-size squares of printed cloth, an old vial of quinine tablets, a torn strip of newspaper, and four copper coins. He gave the pastor time to examine each carefully. At the bottom of the box were a good many orange and blue feathers which Nicolás did not bother to take out. The pastor realized that he was seeing the treasures of the household, that these items were rare objects of art. He looked at each thing with great seriousness, handing it back with a verbal expression of admiration. Finally he said: "Thank you," and fell back into the hammock. Nicolás returned the box to the women sitting in the corner. When he came back over to the pastor he said: "Now we sleep."

"Nicolás," asked the pastor, "is Metzabok bad?"

"*Bai*, señor. Sometimes very bad. Like a small child. When he does not get what he wants right away, he makes fires, fever, wars. He can be very good, too, when he is happy. You should speak with him every day. Then you will know him."

"But you never speak with him."

"*Bai*, we do. Many do, when they are sick or unhappy. They ask him to take away the trouble. I never speak with him"—Nicolás looked pleased—"because Hachakyum is my good friend and I do not need Metzabok. Besides, Metzabok's home is far—three hours' walk. I can speak with Hachakyum here." The pastor knew he meant the little altar outside. He nodded and fell asleep.

The village in the early morning was a chaos of shrill sounds: dogs, parrots and cockatoos, babies, turkeys. The pastor lay still in his hammock awhile listening, before he was officially wakened by Nicolás. "We must go now, señor," he said. "Everyone is waiting for you."

The pastor sat up, a little bit alarmed. "Where?" he cried.

"You speak and make music today."

"Yes, yes." He had quite forgotten it was Sunday.

The pastor was silent, walking beside Nicolás up the road to the mission. The weather had changed, and the early sun was very bright. "I have been fortified by my experience," he was thinking. His head was clear; he felt amazingly healthy. The unaccustomed sensation of vigor gave him a strange nostalgia for the days of his youth. "I must always have felt like this then. I remember it," he thought.

At the mission there was a great crowd—many more people than he had ever seen attend a sermon at Tacaté. They were chatting quietly, but when he and Nicolás appeared there was an immediate hush. Mateo was standing in the pavilion waiting for him, with the phonograph open. With a pang the pastor realized he had not prepared a sermon for his flock. He went into the house for a moment, and returned to seat himself at the table in the pavilion, where he picked up his Bible. He had left his few notes in the book, so that it opened to the Seventy-eighth Psalm. "I shall read them that," he decided. He turned to Mateo. "Play the *disco*," he said. Mateo put on "Crazy Rhythm." The pastor quickly made a few pencil alterations in the text of the psalm, substituting the names of minor local deities, like Usukun and Sibanaa for such names as Jacob and Ephraim, and local place names for Israel and Egypt. And he wrote the word Hachakyum each time the word God or the Lord appeared. He had not finished when the record stopped. "Play it again," he commanded. The audience was delighted, even though the sound was abominably scratchy. When the music was over for the second time, he stood and began to paraphrase the psalm in a clear voice. "The children of Sibanaa, carrying bows to shoot, ran into the forest to hide when the enemy came. They did not keep their promises to Hachakyum, and they would not live as he told them to live." The audience was electrified. As he spoke, he looked down and saw the child Marta staring up at him. She had let go of her baby alligator, and it was crawling with a surprising speed toward the table where he sat. Quintina, Mateo and the two maids were piling up the bars of salt on the ground to one side. They kept returning to the kitchen for more. He realized that what he was saying doubtless made no sense in terms of his listeners' religion, but it was a story of the unleashing of divine displeasure upon an unholy people, and they were enjoying it vastly. The alligator, trailing its rags, had crawled to within a few inches of the pastor's feet, where it remained quiet, content to be out of Marta's arms.

Presently, while he was still speaking, Mateo began to hand out the salt, and soon they all were running their tongues rhythmically over the large rough cakes, but continuing to pay strict attention to his words. When he was about to finish, he motioned to Mateo to be ready to start the record again the minute he finished; on the last word he lowered his arm as a signal, and "Crazy Rhythm" sounded once more. The alligator began to crawl hastily toward the far end of the pavilion. Pastor Dowe bent down and picked it up. As he stepped forward to hand it to Mateo, Nicolás rose from the ground, and taking Marta by the hand, walked over into the pavilion with her.

"Señor," he said, "Marta will live with you. I give her to you."

"What do you mean?" cried the pastor in a voice which cracked a little. The alligator squirmed in his hand.

"She is your wife. She will live here."

Pastor Dowe's eyes grew very wide. He was unable to say anything for a moment. He shook his hands in the air and finally he said "No" several times.

Nicolás's face grew unpleasant. "You do not like Marta?"

"Very much. She is beautiful." The pastor sat down slowly on his chair. "But she is a little child."

Nicolás frowned with impatience. "She is already large."

"No, Nicolás. No. No."

Nicolás pushed his daughter forward and stepped back several paces, leaving her there by the table. "It is done," he said sternly. "She is your wife. I have given her to you."

Pastor Dowe looked out over the assembly and saw the unspoken approval in all the faces. "Crazy Rhythm" ceased to play. There was silence. Under the mango tree he saw a woman toying with a small, shiny object. Suddenly he recognized his glasses case; the woman was stripping the Leatheroid fabric from it. The bare aluminum with its dents flashed in the sun. For some reason even in the middle of this situation he found himself thinking: "So I was wrong. It is not dead. She will keep it, the way Nicolás has kept the quinine tablets."

He looked down at Marta. The child was staring at him quite without expression. Like a cat, he reflected.

Again he began to protest. "Nicolás," he cried, his voice very high, "this is impossible!" He felt a hand grip his arm, and turned to receive a warning glance from Mateo.

Nicolás had already advanced toward the pavilion, his face like a thundercloud. As he seemed about to speak, the pastor interrupted him quickly. He had decided to temporize. "She may stay at the mission today," he said weakly.

"She is your wife," said Nicolás with great feeling. "You cannot send her away. You must keep her."

"Diga que sí," Mateo was whispering. "Say yes, señor."

"Yes," the pastor heard himself saying. "Yes. Good." He got up and walked slowly into the house, holding the alligator with one hand and pushing Marta in front of him with the other. Mateo followed and closed the door after them.

"Take her into the kitchen, Mateo," said the pastor dully, handing the little reptile to Marta. As Mateo went across the patio leading the child by the hand, he called after him. "Leave her with Quintina and come to my room."

He sat down on the edge of his bed, staring ahead of him with unseeing eyes. At each moment his predicament seemed to him more terrible. With relief he heard Mateo knock. The people outdoors were slowly leaving. It cost him an effort to call out, *"Adelante."* When Mateo had come in, the pastor said, "Close the door."

"Mateo, did you know they were going to do this? That they were going to bring that child here?"

"Sí, señor."

"You knew it! But why didn't you say anything? Why didn't you tell me?"

Mateo shrugged his shoulders, looking at the floor. "I didn't know it would matter to you," he said. "Anyway, it would have been useless."

"Useless? Why? You could have stopped Nicolás," said the pastor, although he did not believe it himself.

Mateo laughed shortly. "You think so?"

"Mateo, you must help me. We must oblige Nicolás to take her back."

Mateo shook his head. "It can't be done. These people are very severe. They never change their laws."

"Perhaps a letter to the administrator at Ocosingo . . ."

"No, señor. That would make still more trouble. You are not a Catholic." Mateo shifted on his feet and suddenly smiled thinly. "Why not let her stay? She doesn't eat much. She can work in the kitchen. In two years she will be very pretty."

The pastor jumped, and made such a wide and vehement gesture with his hands that the mosquito netting, looped above his head, fell down about his face. Mateo helped him disentangle himself. The air smelled of dust from the netting.

"You don't understand anything!" shouted Pastor Dowe, beside himself. "I can't talk to you! I don't want to talk to you! Go out and leave me alone." Mateo obediently left the room.

Pounding his left palm with his right fist, over and over again, the pastor stood in his window before the landscape that shone in the strong sun. A few women were still eating under the mango tree; the rest had gone back down the hill.

He lay on his bed throughout the long afternoon. When twilight came he had made his decision. Locking his door, he proceeded to pack what personal effects he could into his smallest suitcase. His Bible and notebooks went on top with his toothbrush and Atabrine tablets. When Quintina came to announce supper he asked to have it brought to his bed, taking care to slip the packed valise into the closet before he unlocked the door for her to enter. He waited until the talking had ceased all over the house, until he knew everyone was asleep. With the small bag not too heavy in one hand he tiptoed into the patio, out through the door into the fragrant night, across the open space in front of the pavilion, under the mango tree and down the path leading to Tacaté. Then he began to walk fast, because he wanted to get through the village before the moon rose.

There was a chorus of dogs barking as he entered the village street. He began to run, straight through to the other end. And he kept running even then, until he had reached the point where the path, wider here, dipped beneath the hill and curved into the forest. His heart was beating rapidly from the exertion. To rest, and to try to be fairly certain he was not being followed, he sat down on his little valise in the center of the path. There he remained a long time, thinking of nothing, while the night went on and the moon came up. He heard only the light wind among the leaves and vines. Overhead a few bats reeled soundlessly back and forth. At last he took a deep breath, got up, and went on.

He of the Assembly

He salutes all parts of the sky and the earth where it is bright. He thinks the color of the amethysts of Aguelmous will be dark if it has rained in the valley of Zerekten. The eye wants to sleep, he says, but the head is no mattress. When it rained for three days and water covered the flatlands outside the ramparts, he slept by the bamboo fence at the Café of the Two Bridges.

It seems there was a man named Ben Tajah who went to Fez to visit his cousin. The day he came back he was walking in the Djemaa el Fna, and he saw a letter lying on the pavement. He picked it up and found that his name was written on the envelope. He went to the Café of the Two Bridges with the letter in his hand, sat down on a mat and opened the envelope. Inside was a paper which read: "The sky trembles and the earth is afraid, and the two eyes are not brothers." Ben Tajah did not understand, and he was very unhappy because his name was on the envelope. It made him think that Satan was nearby. He of the Assembly was sitting in the same part of the café. He was listening to the wind in the telephone wires. The sky was almost empty of daytime light. "The eye wants to sleep," he thought, "but the head is no mattress. I know what that is, but I have forgotten it." Three days is a long time for rain to keep falling on flat bare ground. "If I got up and ran down the street," he thought, "a policeman would follow me and call to me to stop. I would run faster, and he would run after me. When he shot at me, I'd duck around the corners of houses." He felt the rough dried mud of the wall under his fingertips. "And I'd be running through the streets looking for a place to hide, but no door would be open, until finally I came to one door that was open, and I'd go in through the rooms and courtyards until finally I came to the kitchen. The old woman would be there." He stopped and wondered for a moment why an old woman should be there alone in the kitchen at that hour. She was stirring a big kettle of soup on the stove. "And I'd look for a place to hide there in the kitchen, and there'd be no place. And I'd be waiting to hear the policeman's footsteps, because he wouldn't miss the open door. And I'd look in the dark corner of the room where she kept the charcoal, but it wouldn't be dark enough. And the old woman would turn and look at me and say: 'If you're trying to get away, my boy, I can help you. Jump into the soup kettle.' " The wind sighed in the telephone wires. Men came into the Café of the Two Bridges with their garments flapping. Ben Tajah sat on his mat. He had put the letter away, but first he had stared at it a long time. He of the Assembly leaned back and looked at the sky. "The old woman," he said to himself. "What is she trying to do? The soup is hot. It may be a trap. I may find there's no way out, once I get down there." He wanted a pipe of kif, but he was afraid the policeman would run into the kitchen before he was able to smoke it. He said to the old woman: "How can I get in? Tell me." And it seemed to him that he heard footsteps in the street, or perhaps even in one of the rooms of the house. He leaned over the stove and looked down into the kettle. It was dark and very hot down in there. Steam was coming up in clouds, and there was a thick smell in the air that made it hard to breathe. "Quick!" said the old woman, and she unrolled a rope ladder and hung it over the edge of the kettle. He began to climb down, and she leaned over and looked after him. "Until the other world!" he shouted. And he climbed all the way down. There was a rowboat below. When he was in it he tugged on the ladder and the old woman began to pull it up. And at that instant the policeman ran in, and two more were with him, and the old woman had just the time to throw the ladder down into the soup. "Now they are going to take her to the commissariat," he thought, "and the poor woman only did me a favor." He rowed around in the dark for a few minutes, and it was very hot. Soon he took off his clothes. For a while he could see the round top of the kettle up above, like a porthole in the side of a ship, with the heads of the policemen looking down in, but then it grew smaller as he rowed, until it was only a light. Sometimes he could find it and sometimes he lost it, and finally it was gone. He was worried about the old woman, and he thought he must find a way to help her. No policeman can go into the Café of the Two Bridges because it belongs to the sultan's sister. This is why there is so much kif smoke inside that a *berrada* can't fall over even if it is pushed, and why most customers like to sit outside, and even there keep one hand on their money. As long as the thieves stay inside and their friends bring them food and kif, they are all right. One day police headquarters will forget to send a man to watch the café, or one man will leave five minutes before the other gets there to take his place. Outside everyone smokes kif too, but only for an hour or two—not all day and night like the ones inside. He of the Assembly had forgotten to light his *sebsi*. He was in a café where no policeman could come, and he wanted to go away to a kif world where the police were chasing him. "This is the way we are now," he thought. "We work backwards. If we have something good, we look for something bad instead." He lighted the *sebsi* and smoked it. Then he blew the hard ash out of the *chqaf*. It landed in the brook beside the second bridge. "The world is too good. We can only work forward if we make it bad again first." This made him sad, so he stopped thinking, and filled his *sebsi*. While he was smoking it, Ben Tajah looked in his direction, and although they were facing each other, He of the Assembly did not notice Ben Tajah until he got up and paid for his tea. Then he looked at him because he took such a long time getting up off the floor. He saw his face and he thought: "That man has no one in the world." The idea made him feel cold. He filled his *sebsi* again and lighted it. He saw the man as he was going to go out of the café and walk alone down the long road outside the ramparts. In a little while he himself would have to go out to the *souks* to try to borrow money for dinner. When he smoked a lot of kif he did not like his aunt to see him, and he did not want to see her. "Soup and bread. No one can want more than that. Will thirty francs be enough the fourth time? The *qaouaji* wasn't satisfied last night. But he took it. And he went away and let me sleep. A Moslem, even in the city, can't refuse his brother shelter." He was not convinced, because he had been born in the mountains, and so he kept thinking back and forth in this way. He smoked many *chqofa*, and when he got up to go out into the street he found that the world had changed.

Ben Tajah was not a rich man. He lived alone in a room near Bab Doukkala, and he had a stall in the bazaars where he sold coat hangers and chests. Often he did not open the shop because he was in bed with a liver attack. At such times he pounded on the floor from his bed, using a brass pestle, and the postman who lived downstairs brought him up some food. Sometimes he stayed in bed for a week at a time. Each morning and night the postman came in with a tray. The food was not very good because the postman's wife did not understand much about cooking. But he was glad to have it. Twice he had brought the postman a new chest to keep clothes and blankets in. One of the postman's wives a few years before had taken a chest with her when she had left him and gone back to her family in Kasba Tadla. Ben Tajah himself had tried having a wife for a while because he needed someone to get him regular meals and to wash his clothes, but the girl was from the mountains, and was wild. No matter how much he beat her she would not be tamed. Everything in the room got broken, and finally he had to put her out into the street. "No more women will get into my house," he told his friends in the bazaars, and they laughed. He took home many women, and one day he found that he had *en nòua*. He knew that was a bad disease, because it stays in the blood and eats the nose from inside. "A man loses his nose only long after he has already lost his head." He asked a doctor for medicine. The doctor gave him a paper and told him to take it to the Pharmacie de l'Étoile. There he bought six vials of penicillin in a box. He took them home and tied each little bottle with a silk thread, stringing them so that they made a necklace. He wore this always around his neck, taking care that the glass vials touched his skin. He thought it likely that by now he was cured, but his cousin in Fez had just told him that he must go on wearing the medicine for another three months, or at least until the beginning of the moon of Chouwal. He had thought about this now and then on the way home, sitting in the bus for two days, and he had decided that his cousin was too cautious. He stood in the Djemaa el Fna a minute watching the trained monkeys, but the crowd pushed too much, so he walked on. When he got home he shut the door and put his hand in his pocket to pull out the envelope, because he wanted to look at it again inside his own room, and be sure that the name written on it was beyond a doubt his. But the letter was gone. He remembered the jostling in the Djemaa el Fna. Someone had reached into his pocket and imagined his hand was feeling money, and taken it. Yet Ben Tajah did not truly believe this. He was convinced that he would have known such a theft was happening. There had been a letter in his pocket. He was not even sure of that. He sat down on the cushions. "Two days in the bus," he thought. "Probably I'm tired. I found no letter." He searched in his pocket again, and it seemed to him he could still remember how the fold of the envelope had felt. "Why would it have my name on it? I never found any letter at all." Then he wondered if anyone had seen him in the café with the envelope in one hand and the sheet of paper in the other, looking at them both for such a long time. He stood up. He wanted to go back to the Café of the Two Bridges and ask the *qaouaji:* "Did you see me an hour ago? Was I looking at a letter?" If the *qaouaji* said, "Yes," then the letter was real. He repeated the words aloud: "The sky trembles and the earth is afraid, and the two eyes are not brothers." In the silence afterward the memory of the sound of the words frightened him. "If there was no letter, where are these words from?" And he shivered because the answer to that was: "From Satan." He was about to open the door when a new fear stopped him. The *qaouaji* might say, "No," and this would be still worse, because it would mean that the words had been put directly into his head by Satan, that Satan had chosen him to reveal Himself to. In that case He might appear at any moment. *"Ach haddou laillaha ill' Allah . . . ,"* he prayed, holding his two forefingers up, one on each side of him. He sat down again and did not move. In the street the children were crying. He did not want to hear the *qaouaji* say: "No. You had no letter." If he knew that Satan was coming to tempt him, he would have that much less power to keep Him away with his prayers, because he would be more afraid.

He of the Assembly stood. Behind him was a wall. In his hand was the *sebsi*. Over his head was the sky, which he felt was about to burst into light. He was leaning back looking at it. It was dark on the earth, but there was still light up there behind the stars. Ahead of him was the pissoir of the carpenters' souk which the French had put there. People said only Jews used it. It was made of tin, and there was a puddle in front of it that reflected the sky and the top of the pissoir. It looked like a boat in the water. Or like a pier where boats land. Without moving from where he stood, He of the Assembly saw it approaching slowly. He was going toward it. And he remembered he was naked, and put his hand over his sex. In a minute the rowboat would be bumping against the pier. He steadied himself on his legs and waited. But at that moment a large cat ran out of the shadow of the wall and stopped in the middle of the street to turn and look at him with an evil face. He saw its two eyes and for a while could not take his own eyes away. Then the cat ran across the street and was gone. He was not sure what had happened, and he stood very still looking at the ground. He looked back at the pissoir reflected in the puddle and thought: "It was a cat on the shore, nothing else." But the cat's eyes had frightened him. Instead of being like cats' eyes, they had looked like the eyes of a person who was interested in him. He made himself forget he had this thought. He was still waiting for the rowboat to touch the landing pier, but nothing had happened. It was going to stay where it was, that near the shore but not near enough to touch. He stood still a long time, waiting for something to happen. Then he began to walk very fast down the street toward the bazaars. He had just remembered that the old woman was in the police station. He wanted to help her, but first he had to find out where they had taken her. "I'll have to go to every police station in the Medina," he thought, and he was not hungry anymore. It was one thing to promise himself he would help her when he was far from land, and another when he was a few doors from a commissariat. He walked by the entrance. Two policemen stood in the doorway. He kept walking. The street curved and he was alone. "This night is going to be a jewel in my crown," he said, and he turned quickly to the left and went along a dark passageway. At the end he saw flames, and he knew that Mustapha would be there tending the fire of the bakery. He crawled into the mud hut where the oven was. "Ah, the jackal has come back from the forest!" said Mustapha. He of the Assembly shook his head. "This is a bad world," he told Mustapha. "I've got no money," Mustapha said. He of the Assembly did not understand. "Everything goes backwards," he said. "It's bad now, and we have to make it still worse if we want to go forwards." Mustapha saw that He of the Assembly was *mkiyif ma rassou* and was not interested in money. He looked at him in a more friendly way and said: "Secrets are not between friends. Talk." He of the Assembly told him that an old woman had done him a great favor, and because of that three policemen had arrested her and taken her to the police station. "You must go for me to the commissariat and ask them if they have an old woman there." He pulled out his *sebsi* and took a very long time filling it. When he finished it he smoked it himself and did not offer any to Mustapha, because Mustapha never offered him any of his. "You see how full of kif my head is," he said laughing. "I can't go." Mustapha laughed too and said it would not be a good idea, and that he would go for him.

"I was there, and I heard him going away for a long time, so long that he had to be gone, and yet he was still there, and his footsteps were still going away. He went away and there was nobody. There was the fire and I moved away from it. I wanted to hear a sound like a muezzin crying *Allah akbar!* or a French plane from the Pilot Base flying over the Medina, or news on the radio. It wasn't there. And when the wind came in the door it was made of dust high as a man. A night to be chased by dogs in the Mellah. I looked in the fire and I saw an eye in there, like the eye that's left when you burn *chibb* and you know there was a *djinn* in the house. I got up and stood. The fire was making a noise like a voice. I think it was talking. I went out and walked along the street. I walked a long time and I came to Bab el Khemiss. It was dark there and the wind was cold. I went to the wall where the camels were lying and stood there. Sometimes the men have fires and play songs on their *aouadas*. But they were asleep. All snoring. I walked again and went to the gate and looked out. The big trucks went by full of vegetables and I thought I would like to be on a truck and ride all night. Then in another city I would be a soldier and go to Algeria. Everything would be good if we had a war. I thought a long time. Then I was so cold I turned around and walked again. It was as cold as the belly of the oldest goat of Ijoukak. I thought I heard a muezzin and I stopped and listened. The only thing I heard was the water running in the *seguia* that carries the water out to the gardens. It was near the *mçid* of Moulay Boujemaa. I heard the water running by and I felt cold. Then I knew I was cold because I was afraid. In my head I was thinking: 'If something should happen that never happened before, what would I do?' You want to laugh? Hashish in your heart and wind in your head. You think it's like your grandmother's prayer mat. This is the truth. This isn't a dream brought back from another world past the customs like a teapot from Mecca. I heard the water and I was afraid. There were some trees by the path ahead of me. You know at night sometimes it's good to pull out the *sebsi* and smoke. I smoked and I started to walk. And then I heard something. Not a muezzin. Something that sounded like my name. But it came up from below, from the *seguia*, *Allah istir!* And I walked with my head down. I heard it again saying my name, a voice like water, like the wind moving the leaves in the trees, a woman. It was a woman calling me. The wind was in the trees and the water was running, but there was a woman too. You think it's kif. No, she was calling my name. Now and then, not very loud. When I was under the trees it was louder, and I heard that the voice was my mother's. I heard that the way I can hear you. Then I knew the cat was not a cat, and I knew that Aïcha Qandicha wanted me. I thought of other nights when perhaps she had been watching me from the eyes of a cat or a donkey. I knew she was not going to catch me. Nothing in the seven skies could make me turn around. But I was cold and afraid and when I licked my lips my tongue had no spit on it. I was under the *safsaj* trees and I thought: 'She's going to reach down and try to touch me. But she can't touch me from the front and I won't turn around, not even if I hear a pistol.' I remembered how the policeman had fired at me and how I'd found only one door open. I began to yell: 'You threw me the ladder and told me to climb down. You brought me here! The filthiest whore in the Mellah, with the pus coming out of her, is a thousand times cleaner than you, daughter of all the *padronas* and dogs in seven worlds.' I got past the trees and I began to run. I called up to the sky so she could hear my voice behind: 'I hope the police put a hose in your mouth and pump you full of salt water until you crack open!' I thought: 'Tomorrow I'm going to buy *fasoukh* and *tib* and *nidd* and *hasalouba* and *mska* and all the *bakhour* in the Djemaa, and put them in the *mijmah* and burn them, and walk back and forth over the *mijmah* ten times slowly, so the smoke can clean out all my clothes. Then I'll see if there's an eye in the ashes afterwards. If there is, I'll do it all over again right away. And every Thursday I'll buy the *bakhour* and every Friday I'll burn it. That will be strong enough to keep her away.' If I could find a window and look through and see what they're doing to the old woman! If only they could kill her! I kept running. There were a few people in the streets. I didn't look to see where I was going, but I went to the street near Mustapha's oven where the commissariat was. I stopped running before I got to the door. The one standing there saw me before that. He stepped out and raised his arm. He said to me: 'Come here.' "

He of the Assembly ran. He felt as though he were on horseback. He did not feel his legs moving. He saw the road coming toward him and the doors going by. The policeman had not shot at him yet, but it was worse than the other time because he was very close behind and he was blowing his whistle. "The policeman is old. At least thirty-five. I can run faster." But from any street others could come. It was dangerous and he did not want to think about danger. He of the Assembly let songs come into his head. When it rains in the valley of Zerekten the amethysts are darker in Aguelmous. The eye wants to sleep but the head is no mattress. It was a song. Ah, my brother, the ink on the paper is like smoke in the air. What words are there to tell how long a night can be? Drunk with love, I wander in the dark. He was running through the dye souk, and he splashed into a puddle. The whistle blew again behind him, like a crazy bird screaming. The sound made him feel like laughing, but that did not mean he was not afraid. He thought: "If I'm seventeen I can run faster. That has to be true." It was very dark ahead. He had to slow his running. There was no time for his eyes to get used to the dark. He nearly ran into the wall of the shop at the end of the street. He turned to the right and saw the narrow alley ahead of him. The police had tied the old woman naked to a table with her thin legs wide apart and were sliding electrodes up inside her. He ran ahead. He could see the course of the alley now even in the dark. Then he stopped dead, moved to the wall, and stood still. He heard the footsteps slowing down. "He's going to turn to the left." And he whispered aloud: "It ends that way." The footsteps stopped and there was silence. The policeman was looking into the silence and listening into the dark to the left and to the right. He of the Assembly could not see him or hear him, but he knew that was what he was doing. He did not move. When it rains in the valley of Zerekten. A hand seized his shoulder. He opened his mouth and swiftly turned, but the man had moved and was pushing him from the side. He felt the wool of the man's *djellaba* against the back of his hand. He had gone through a door and the man had shut it without making any noise. Now they both stood still in the dark, listening to the policeman walking quickly by outside the door. Then the man struck a match. He was facing the other way, and there was a flight of stairs ahead. The man did not turn around, but he said, "Come up," and they both climbed the stairs. At the top the man took out a key and opened a door. He of the Assembly stood in the doorway while the man lit a candle. He liked the room because it had many mattresses and cushions and a white sheepskin under the tea tray in the corner of the floor. The man turned around and said: "Sit down." His face looked serious and kind and unhappy. He of the Assembly had never seen it before, but he knew it was not the face of a policeman. He of the Assembly pulled out his *sebsi*.

Ben Tajah looked at the boy and asked him: "What did you mean when you said down there: 'It ends that way'? I heard you say it." The boy was embarrassed. He smiled and looked at the floor. Ben Tajah felt happy to have him there. He had been standing outside the door downstairs in the dark for a long time, trying to make himself go to the Café of the Two Bridges and talk to the *qaouaji*. In his mind it was almost as though he had already been there and spoken with him. He had heard the *qaouaji* telling him that he had seen no letter, and he had felt his own dismay. He had not wanted to believe that, but he would be willing to say yes, I made a mistake and there was no letter, if only he could find out where the words had come from. For the words were certainly in his head: ". . . and the two eyes are not brothers." That was like a footprint found in the garden the morning after a bad dream, the proof that there had been a reason for the dream, that something had been there after all. Ben Tajah had not been able to go or to stay. He had started and stopped so many times that now, although he did not know it, he was very tired. When a man is tired he mistakes the hopes of children for the knowledge of men. It seemed to him that He of the Assembly's words had a meaning all for him. Even though the boy might not know it, he could have been sent by Allah to help him at that minute. In a nearby street a police whistle blew. The boy looked at him. Ben Tajah did not care very much what the answer would be, but he said: "Why are they looking for you?" The boy held out his lighted *sebsi* and his *mottoui* fat with kif. He did not want to talk because he was listening. Ben Tajah smoked kif only when a friend offered it to him, but he understood that the police had begun once more to try to enforce their law against kif. Each year they arrested people for a few weeks, and then stopped arresting them. He looked at the boy, and decided that probably he smoked too much. With the *sebsi* in his hand he was sitting very still listening to the voices of some passersby in the street below. "I know who he is," one said. "I've got his name from Mustapha." "The baker?" "That's the one." They walked on. The boy's expression was so intense that Ben Tajah said to him: "It's nobody. Just people." He was feeling happy because he was certain that Satan would not appear before him as long as the boy was with him. He said quietly: "Still you haven't told me why you said: 'It ends that way.' " The boy filled his *sebsi* slowly and smoked all the kif in it. "I meant," he said, "thanks to Allah. Praise the sky and the earth where it is bright. What else can you mean when something ends?" Ben Tajah nodded his head. Pious thoughts can be of as much use for keeping Satan at a distance as camphor or *bakhour* dropped onto hot coals. Each holy word is worth a high column of smoke, and the eyelids do not smart afterward. "He has a good heart," thought Ben Tajah, "even though he is probably a guide for the Nazarenes." And he asked himself why it would not be possible for the boy to have been sent to protect him from Satan. "Probably not. But it could be." The boy offered him the *sebsi*. He took it and smoked it. After that Ben Tajah began to think that he would like to go to the Café of the Two Bridges and speak to the *qaouaji* about the letter. He felt that if the boy went with him the *qaouaji* might say there had been a letter, and that even if the man could not remember, he would not mind so much because he would be less afraid. He waited until he thought the boy was not nervous about going into the street, and then he said: "Let's go out and get some tea." "Good," said the boy. He was not afraid of the police if he was with Ben Tajah. They went through the empty streets, crossed the Djemaa el Fna and the garden beyond. When they were near the café, Ben Tajah said to the boy: "Do you know the Café of the Two Bridges?" The boy said he always sat there, and Ben Tajah was not surprised. It seemed to him that perhaps he had even seen him there. He seized the boy's arm. "Were you there today?" he asked him. The boy said, "Yes," and turned to look at him. He let go of the arm. "Nothing," he said. "Did you ever see me there?" They came to the gate of the café and Ben Tajah stopped walking. "No," the boy said. They went across the first bridge and then the second bridge, and sat down in a corner. Not many people were left outside. Those inside were making a great noise. The *qaouaji* brought the tea and went away again. Ben Tajah did not say anything to him about the letter. He wanted to drink the tea quietly and leave trouble until later.

When the muezzin called from the minaret of the Koutoubia, He of the Assembly thought of being in the Agdal. The great mountains were ahead of him and the olive trees stood in rows on each side of him. Then he heard the trickle of water and he remembered the *seguia* that is there in the Agdal, and he swiftly came back to the Café of the Two Bridges. Aïcha Qandicha can be only where there are trees by running water. "She comes only for single men by trees and fresh moving water. Her arms are gold and she calls in the voice of the most cherished one." Ben Tajah gave him the *sebsi*. He filled it and smoked it. "When a man sees her face he will never see another woman's face. He will make love with her all the night, and every night, and in the sunlight by the walls, before the eyes of children. Soon he will be an empty pod and he will leave this world for his home in Jehennem." The last carriage went by, taking the last tourists down the road beside the ramparts to their rooms in the Mamounia. He of the Assembly thought: "The eye wants to sleep. But this man is alone in the world. He wants to talk all night. He wants to tell me about his wife and how he beat her and how she broke everything. Why do I want to know all those things? He is a good man but he has no head." Ben Tajah was sad. He said: "What have I done? Why does Satan choose me?" Then at last he told the boy about the letter, about how he wondered if it had had his name on the envelope and how he was not even sure there had been a letter. When he finished he looked sadly at the boy. "And you didn't see me." He of the Assembly shut his eyes and kept them shut for a while. When he opened them again he said: "Are you alone in the world?" Ben Tajah stared at him and did not speak. The boy laughed. "I did see you," he said, "but you had no letter. I saw you when you were getting up and I thought you were old. Then I saw you were not old. That's all I saw." "No, it isn't," Ben Tajah said. "You saw I was alone." He of the Assembly shrugged. "Who knows?" He filled the *sebsi* and handed it to Ben Tajah. The kif was in Ben

Tajah's head. His eyes were small. He of the Assembly listened to the wind in the telephone wires, took back the *sebsi* and filled it again. Then he said: "You think Satan is coming to make trouble for you because you're alone in the world. I see that. Get a wife or somebody to be with you always, and you won't think about it anymore. That's true. Because Satan doesn't come to men like you." He of the Assembly did not believe this himself. He knew that Father Satan can come for anyone in the world, but he hoped to live with Ben Tajah, so he would not have to borrow money in the souks to buy food. Ben Tajah drank some tea. He did not want the boy to see that his face was happy. He felt that the boy was right, and that there never had been a letter. "Two days on a bus is a long time. A man can get very tired," he said. Then he called the *qaouaji* and told him to bring two more glasses of tea. He of the Assembly gave him the *sebsi*. He knew that Ben Tajah wanted to stay as long as possible in the Café of the Two Bridges. He put his finger into the *mottoui*. The kif was almost gone. "We can talk," he said. "Not much kif is in the *mottoui*." The *qaouaji* brought the tea. They talked for an hour or more. The *qaouaji* slept and snored. They talked about Satan and the bad thing it is to live alone, to wake up in the dark and know that there is no one else nearby. Many times He of the Assembly told Ben Tajah that he must not worry. The kif was all gone. He held his empty *mottoui* in his hand. He did not understand how he had got back to the town without climbing up out of the soup kettle. Once he said to Ben Tajah: "I never climbed back up." Ben Tajah looked at him and said he did not understand. He of the Assembly told him the story. Ben Tajah laughed. He said: "You smoke too much kif, brother." He of the Assembly put his *sebsi* into his pocket. "And you don't smoke and you're afraid of Satan," he told Ben Tajah. "No!" Ben Tajah shouted. "By Allah! No more! But one thing is in my head, and I can't put it out. The sky trembles and the earth is afraid, and the two eyes are not brothers. Did you ever hear those words? Where did they come from?" Ben Tajah looked hard at the boy. He of the Assembly understood that these had been the words on the paper, and he felt cold in the middle of his back because he had never heard them before and they sounded evil. He knew, too, that he must not let Ben Tajah know this. He began to laugh. Ben Tajah took hold of his knee and shook it. His face was troubled. "Did you ever hear them?" He of the Assembly went on laughing. Ben Tajah shook his leg so hard that he stopped and said: "Yes!" When Ben Tajah waited and he said nothing more, he saw the man's face growing angry, and so he said: "Yes, I've heard them. But will you tell me what happened to me and how I got out of the soup kettle if I tell you about those words?" Ben Tajah understood that the kif was going away from the boy's head. But he saw that it had not all gone, or he would not have been asking that question. And he said: "Wait a while for the answer to that question." He of the Assembly woke the *qaouaji* and Ben Tajah paid him, and they went out of the café. They did not talk while they walked. When they got to the Mouassine mosque, Ben Tajah held out his hand to say good-night, but He of the Assembly said: "I'm looking in my head for the place I heard your words. I'll walk to your door with you. Maybe I'll remember." Ben Tajah said: "May Allah help you find it." And he took his arm and they walked to Ben Tajah's door while He of the Assembly said nothing. They stood outside the door in the dark. "Have you found it?" said Ben Tajah. "Almost," said He of the Assembly. Ben Tajah thought that perhaps when the kif had gone out of the boy's head he might be able to tell him about the words. He wanted to know how the boy's head was, and so he said: "Do you still want to know how you got out of the soup kettle?" He of the Assembly laughed. "You said you would tell me later," he told Ben Tajah. "I will," said Ben Tajah. "Come upstairs. Since we have to wait, we can sit down." Ben Tajah opened the door and they went upstairs. This time He of the Assembly sat down on Ben Tajah's bed. He yawned and stretched. It was a good bed. He was glad it was not the mat by the bamboo fence at the Café of the Two Bridges. "And so, tell me how I got out of the soup kettle," he said laughing. Ben Tajah said: "You're still asking me that? Have you thought of the words?" "I know the words," the boy said. "The sky trembles. . . ." Ben Tajah did not want him to say them again. "Where did you hear them? What are they? That's what I want to know." The boy shook his head. Then he sat up very straight and looked beyond Ben Tajah, beyond the wall of the room, beyond the streets of the Medina, beyond the gardens, toward the mountains where the people speak Tachelhait. He remembered being a little boy. "This night is a jewel in my crown," he thought. "It went this way." And he began to sing, making up a melody for the words Ben Tajah had told him. When he had finished ". . . and the two eyes are not brothers," he added a few more words of his own and stopped singing. "That's all I remember of the song," he said. Ben Tajah clapped his hands together hard. "A song!" he cried. "I must have heard it on the radio." He of the Assembly shrugged. "They play it sometimes," he said. "I've made him happy," he thought. "But I won't ever tell him another lie. That's the only one. What I'm going to do now is not the same as lying." He got up off the bed and went to the window. The muezzins were calling the *fjer*. "It's almost morning," he said to Ben Tajah. "I still have kif in my head." "Sit down," said Ben Tajah. He was sure now there had been no letter. He of the Assembly took off his *djellaba* and got into bed. Ben Tajah looked at him in surprise. Then he undressed and got into bed beside him. He left the candle burning on the floor beside the bed. He meant to stay awake, but he went to sleep because he was not used to smoking kif and the kif was in his head. He of the Assembly did not believe he was asleep. He lay for a long time without moving. He listened to the voices of the muezzins, and he thought that the man beside him would speak or move. When he saw that Ben Tajah was surely asleep, he was angry. "This is how he treats a friend who has made him happy. He forgets his trouble and his friend too." He thought about it more and he was angrier. The muezzins were still calling the *fjer*. "Before they stop, or he will hear." Very slowly he got out of the bed. He put on his *djellaba* and opened the door. Then he went back and took all the money out of Ben Tajah's pockets. In with the bank notes was an envelope that was folded. It had Ben Tajah's name written across it. He pulled out the piece of paper inside and held it near the candle, and then he looked at it as he would have looked at a snake. The words were written there. Ben Tajah's face was turned toward the wall and he was snoring. He of the Assembly held the paper above the flame and burned it, and then he burned the envelope. He blew the black paper ashes across the floor. Without making any noise he ran downstairs and let himself out into the street. He shut the door. The money was in his pocket and he walked fast to his aunt's house. His aunt awoke and was angry for a while. Finally he said: "It was raining. How could I come home? Let me sleep." He had a little kif hidden under his pillow. He smoked a pipe. Then he looked across his sleep to the morning and thought: "A pipe of kif before breakfast gives a man the strength of a hundred camels in the courtyard."

The Time of Friendship

The trouble had been growing bigger each year, ever since the end of the war. From the beginning, although aware of its existence, Fräulein Windling had determined to pay it no attention. At first there were only whispered reports of mass arrests. People said: "Many thousands of Moslems have been sent to prison in France." Soon some of her own friends had begun to disappear, like young Bachir and Omar ben Lakhdar, the postmaster of Timimoun, who suddenly one morning were gone, or so she was told, for when she returned the following winter they were not there, and she never had seen them since. The people simply made their faces blank when she tried to talk about it. After the hostilities had begun in earnest, even though the nationalists had derailed the trains and disrupted the trans-Saharan truck service on several occasions, still it was possible to get beyond the disturbed region to her oasis. There in the south the fighting was far away, and the long hours of empty desert that lay between made it seem much farther, almost as though it had been across the sea. If the men of her oasis should ever be infected by the virus of discontent from the far-off north—and this seemed to her almost inconceivable—then in spite of the fact that she was certain that war could bring them nothing but unhappiness, she would have no recourse but to hope for their victory. It was their own land they would be fighting for, their own lives they would be losing in order to win the fight. In the meantime people did not talk; life was hard but peaceful. Each one was aware of the war that was going on in the north, and each one was glad it was far away.

Summers, Fräulein Windling taught in the Freiluftschule in Bern, where she entertained her pupils with tales of the life led by the people in the great desert in Africa. In the village where she lived, she told them, everything was made by the people themselves out of what the desert had to offer. They lived in a world of objects fashioned out of baked earth, woven grass, palmwood and animal skins. There was no metal. Although she did not admit it to the children, this was no longer wholly true, since recently the women had taken to using empty oil tins for carrying water, instead of the goathide bags of a few years before. She had tried to discourage her friends among the village women from this innovation, telling them that the tins could poison the water; they had agreed, and gone on using them. "They are lazy," she decided. "The oil tins are easier to carry."

When the sun went down and the cool air from the oasis below with its sting of woodsmoke rose to the level of the hotel, she would smell it inside her room and stop whatever she was doing. Then she would put on her burnoose and climb the stairs to the roof. The blanket she lay on while she sunbathed each morning would be there, and she would stretch out on it facing the western sky, and feel the departed sun's heat still strong underneath her body. It was one of the pleasures of the day, to watch the light changing in the oasis below, when dusk and the smoke from the evening fires slowly blotted out the valley. There always came a moment when all that was left was the faint outline, geometric and precise, of the mass of mud prisms that was the village, and a certain clump of high date palms that stood outside its entrance. The houses themselves were no longer there, and eventually the highest palm disappeared; and unless there was a moon all that remained to be seen was the dying sky, the sharp edges of the rocks on the hammada, and a blank expanse of mist that lay over the valley but did not reach as far up the cliffs as the hotel.

Perhaps twice each winter a group of the village women would invite Fräulein Windling to go with them up into the vast land of the dunes to look for firewood. The glare here was cruel. There was not even the trace of a twig or a stem anywhere on the sand, yet as they wandered along the crests barefoot the women could spot the places where roots lay buried beneath the surface, and then they would stoop, uncover them, and dig them up. "The wind leaves a sign," they told her, but she was never certain of being able to identify the sign, nor could she understand how there might be a connection between the invisible roots in the sand and the wind in the air above. "What we have lost, they still possess," she thought.

Her first sight of the desert and its people had been a transfiguring experience; indeed, it seemed to her now that before coming here she had never been in touch with life at all. She believed firmly that each day she spent here increased the aggregate of her resistance. She coveted the rugged health of the natives, when her own was equally strong, but because she was white and educated, she was convinced that her body was intrinsically inferior.

All the work in the hotel was done by one quiet, sad-faced man named

Boufelja. He had been there when she had first arrived many years ago; for Fräulein Windling he had come to be as much a part of the place as the cliffs across the valley. She often sat on at her table by the fireplace after lunch, playing cards by herself, until the logs no longer gave out heat. There were two very young French soldiers from the fort opposite, who ate in the hotel dining room. They drank a great amount of wine, and it annoyed her to see their faces slowly turning red as they sat there. At first the soldiers had tipped their caps to her as they went out, and they had stopped their laughing long enough to say, *"Bonjour, madame,"* to her, but now they no longer did. She was happy when they had left, and savored the moment before the fire burned out, while it still glowed under the gusts of wind that wandered down the wide chimney.

Almost always the wind sprang up early in the afternoon, a steady, powerful blowing that roared through the thousands of palms in the oasis below and howled under each door in the hotel, covering the more distant village sounds. This was the hour when she played solitaire, or merely sat, watching the burnt-out logs as they fell to pieces before her eyes. Later she would go along the terrace, a high, bright place like the deck of a great ship sailing through the desert afternoon, hurrying into her room for an instant to get her sweater and cane, and start out on a walk. Sometimes she went southward following the river valley, along the foot of the silent cliffs and through the crooked gorges, to an abandoned village built in a very hot place at a turn in the canyon. The sheer walls of rock behind it sent back the heat, so that the air burned her throat as she breathed it in. Or she went farther, to where the cliff dwellings were, with their animals and symbols incised in the rock.

Returning along the road that led to the village, deep in the green shade of the thickest part of the palm forest, she was regularly aware of the same group of boys sitting at the turn of the road, at a place just before it led up the hill to the shops and the village. They squatted on the sand behind the feathery branches of a giant tamarisk, quietly talking. When she came up to them she greeted them, and they always replied, remained silent a moment until she had passed by, and then resumed their conversation. As far as she could tell, there was never any reference to her by word, and yet this year it sometimes seemed to her that once she had gone by, their inflection had subtly altered, as though there had been a modulation into another key. Did their attitude border on derision? She did not know, but since this was the first time during all her years in the desert that the idea had ever suggested itself to her, she put it resolutely out of her mind. "A new generation requires a new technique if one is to establish contact," she thought. "It is for me to find it." Nevertheless she was sorry that there was no other way of getting into the village save along this main road where they invariably gathered. Even the slight tension caused by having to go past them marred the pleasure of her walks.

One day she realized with a slight shock of shame that she did not even know what the boys looked like. She had seen them only as a group from a distance; when she drew near enough to say good-day to them, she always had her head down, watching the road. The fact that she had been afraid to look at them was unacceptable; now, as she came up to them, she stared into the eyes of one after the other, carefully. Nodding gravely, she went on. Yes, they were insolent faces, she thought—not at all like the faces of their elders. The respectful attitudes into which they had been startled were the crudest sort of shamming. But the important thing to her was that she had won: she was no longer preoccupied with having to pass by them every day. Slowly she even grew to recognize each boy.

There was one, she noted, younger than the others, who always sat a little apart from them, and it was this shy one who stood talking to Boufelja in the hotel kitchen early one morning when she went in. She pretended not to notice him. "I am going to my room to work on the machine for about an hour," she told Boufelja. "You can come then to make up the room," and she turned to go out. As she went through the doorway she glanced at the boy's face. He was looking at her, and he did not turn away when his eyes met hers. "How are you?" she said. Perhaps half an hour later, when she was typing her second letter, she raised her head. The boy was standing on the terrace looking at her through the open door. He squinted, for the wind was strong; behind his head she saw the tops of the palms bending.

"If he wants to watch, let him watch," she said to herself, deciding to pay him no attention. After a while he went away. While Boufelja served her lunch, she questioned him about the boy. "Like an old man," said Boufelja. "Twelve years old but very serious. Like some old, old man." He smiled, then shrugged. "It's the way God wanted him to be."

"Of course," she said, remembering the boy's alert, unhappy face. "A young dog that everyone has kicked," she thought, "but he hasn't given up."

In the days that followed, he came often to the terrace and stood watching her while she typed. Sometimes she waved to him, or said: "Good morning." Without answering he would take a step backward, so that he was out of her range. Then he would continue to stand where he was. His behavior irked her, and one day when he had done this, she quickly got up and went to the door. "What is it?" she asked him, trying to smile as she spoke.

"I didn't do anything," he said, his eyes reproachful.

"I know," she answered. "Why don't you come in?"

The boy looked swiftly around the terrace as if for help; then he bowed his head and stepped inside the door. Here he stood waiting, his head down, looking miserable. From her luggage she brought out a bag of hard candy, and handed him a piece. Then she put a few simple questions to him, and found that his French was much better than she had expected. "Do the other boys know French as well as you?" she asked him.

"Non, madame," he said, shaking his head slowly. "My father used to be a soldier. Soldiers speak good French."

She tried to keep her face from expressing the disapproval she felt, for she despised everything military. "I see," she said with some asperity, turning back to her table and shuffling the papers. "Now I must work," she told him, immediately adding in a warmer voice, "but you come back tomorrow, if you like." He waited an instant, looking at her with unchanged wistfulness. Then slowly he smiled, and laid the candy wrapper, folded into a tiny square, on the corner of her table. *"Au revoir, madame,"* he said, and went out of the door. In the silence she heard the scarcely audible thud of his bare heels on the earth floor of the terrace. "In this cold," she thought. "Poor child! If I ever buy anything for him it will be a pair of sandals."

Each day thereafter, when the sun was high enough to give substance to the still morning air, the boy would come stealthily along the terrace to her door, stand a few seconds, and then say in a lost voice that was all the smaller and more hushed for the great silence outside: *"Bonjour, madame."* She would tell him to come in, and they would shake hands gravely, he afterward raising the backs of his fingers to his lips, always with the same slow ceremoniousness. She sometimes tried to fathom his countenance as he went through this ritual, to see if by any chance she could detect a shade of mockery there; instead she saw an expression of devotion so convincing that it startled her, and she looked away quickly. She always kept a bit of bread or some biscuits in a drawer of the wardrobe; when she had brought the food out and he was eating it, she would ask him for news about the families in his quarter of the village. For discipline's sake she offered him a piece of candy only every other day. He sat on the floor by the doorway, on a torn old camel blanket, and he watched her constantly, never turning his head away from her.

She wanted to know what he was called, but she was aware of how secretive the inhabitants of the region were about names, seldom giving their true ones to strangers; this was a peculiarity she respected because she knew it had its roots in their own prehistoric religion. So she forbore asking him, sure that the time would come when he trusted her enough to give it of his own volition. And the moment happened one morning unexpectedly, when he had just recounted several legends involving the great Moslem king of long ago, whose name was Solomon. Suddenly he stopped, and forcing himself to gaze steadily at her without blinking, he said: "And my name too is Slimane, the same as the king."

She tried to teach him to read, but he did not seem able to learn. Often just as she felt he was about to connect two loose ends of ideas and perhaps at last make a contact which would enable him to understand the principle, a look of resignation and passivity would appear in his face, and he would willfully cut off the stream of effort from its source, and remain sitting, merely looking at her, shaking his head from side to side to show that it was useless. It was hard not to lose patience with him at such moments.

The following year she decided not to go on with the lessons, and to use Slimane instead as a guide, bearer and companion, a role which she immediately saw was more suited to his nature than that of pupil. He did not mind how far they went or how much equipment he had to carry; on the contrary, to him a long excursion was that much more of an event, and whatever she loaded onto him he bore with the air of one upon whom an honor is conferred. It was probably her happiest season in the desert, that winter of comradeship when together they made the countless pilgrimages down the valley. As the weeks passed the trips grew in scope, and the hour of departure was brought forward until it came directly after she had finished her breakfast. All day long, trudging in the open sun and in the occasional shade of the broken fringe of palms that skirted the riverbed, she conversed passionately with him. Sometimes she could see that he felt like telling her what was in his head, and she let him speak for as long as his enthusiasm lasted, often reviving it at the end with carefully chosen questions. But usually it was she who did the speaking as she walked behind him. Pounding the stony ground with her steel-tipped stick each time her right foot went down, she told him in great detail the story of the life of Hitler, showing why he was hated by the Christians. This she thought necessary since Slimane had been under a different impression, and indeed had imagined that the Europeans thought as highly of the vanished leader as did he and the rest of the people in the village. She talked a good deal about Switzerland, casually stressing the cleanliness, honesty and good health of her countrymen in short parables of daily life. She told him about Jesus, Martin Luther and Garibaldi, taking care to keep Jesus distinct from the Moslem prophet Sidna Aissa, since even for the sake of argument she could not agree for an instant with the Islamic doctrine according to which the Savior was a Moslem. Slimane's attitude of respect bordering on adoration with regard to her never altered unless she inadvertently tangled with the subject of Islam; then, no matter what she said (for at that point it seemed that automatically he was no longer within hearing) he would shake his head interminably and cry: "No, no, no, no! Nazarenes know nothing about Islam. Don't talk, madame, I beg you, because you don't know what you're saying. No, no, no!"

Long ago she had kept the initial promise to herself that she would buy him sandals; this purchase had been followed by others. At fairly regular intervals she had taken him to Benaissa's store to buy a shirt, a pair of baggy black cotton trousers of the kind worn by the Chaamba camel drivers and ultimately a new white burnoose, despite the fact that she knew the entire village would discuss the giving of so valuable an object. She also knew that it was only the frequent bestowing of such gifts that kept Slimane's father from forbidding him to spend his time with her. Even so, according to reports brought by Slimane, he sometimes objected. But Slimane himself, she was sure, wanted nothing, expected nothing.

It was each year when March was drawing to a close that the days began to be painfully hot and even the nights grew breathless; then, although it always required a strenuous effort of the will to make herself take the step which would bring about renewed contact with the outside world, she would devote two or three days to washing her clothing and preparing for the journey. When the week set for her departure had come, she went over to the fort and put in a call to the café at Kerzaz, asking the proprietor to tell the driver of the next northbound truck to take the detour that would enable her to catch him at a point only about three kilometers from the village.

She and Slimane had come back to the hotel on the afternoon of their last excursion down the valley; Fräulein Windling stood on the terrace looking out at the orange mountains of sand behind the fort. Slimane had taken the packs into the room and put them down. She turned and said: "Bring the big tin box." When he had pulled it out from under the bed he carried it to her, dusting it off with the sleeve of his shirt, and she led the way up the stairs to the roof. They sat down on the blanket; the glow of the vanished sun's furnace heated their faces. A few flies still hovered, now and then attacking their necks. Slimane handed her the biscuit tin and she gave him a fistful of chocolate-covered cakes. "So many all at once?"

"Yes," she said. "You know I'm going home in four days."

He looked down at the blanket a moment before replying. "I know," he murmured. He was silent again. Then he cried out aggrievedly: "Boufelja says it's hot here in the summer. It's not hot! In our house it's cool. It's like the oasis where the big pool is. You would never be hot there."

"I have to earn money. You know that. I want to come back next year."

He said sadly: "Next year, madame! Only Moulana knows how next year will be."

Some camels growled as they rolled in the sand at the foot of the fort; the light was receding swiftly. "Eat your biscuits," she told him, and she ate one herself. "Next year we'll go to Abadla with the caid, *incha' Allah.*"

He sighed deeply. "Ah, madame!" he said. She noted, at first with a pang of sympathy and then, reconsidering, with disapproval, the anguish that lent his voice its unaccustomed intensity. It was the quality she least liked in him, this faintly theatrical self-pity. "Next year you'll be a man," she told him firmly. Her voice grew less sure, assumed a hopeful tone. "You'll remember all the things we talked about?"

She sent him a postcard from Marseille, and showed her classes photographs they had taken of one another, and of the caid. The children were impressed by the caid's voluminous turban. "Is he a Bedouin?" asked one.

When she left the embassy office she knew that this was the last year she would be returning to the desert. There was not only the official's clearly expressed unfriendliness and suspicion: for the first time he had made her answer a list of questions which she found alarming. He wanted to know what subjects she taught in the Freiluftschule, whether she had ever been a journalist, and exactly where she proposed to be each day after arriving in the Sahara. She had almost retorted: I go where I feel like going. I don't make plans. But she had merely named the oasis. She knew that Frenchmen had no respect for elderly Swiss ladies who wore woolen stockings; this simply made them more contemptible in her eyes. However, it was they who controlled the Sahara.

The day the ship put into the African port it was raining. She knew the gray terraced ramps of the city were there in the gloom ahead, but they were invisible. The ragged European garments of the dockworkers were soaked with rain. Later, the whole rain-sodden city struck her as grim, and the people passing along the streets looked unhappy. The change, even from the preceding year, was enormous; it made her sad to sit in the big, cold café where she went for coffee after dinner, and so she returned to her hotel and slept. The next day she got on the train for Perrégaux. The rain fell most of the day. In Perrégaux she took a room in a hotel near the station, and stayed in it, listening to the rain rattle down the gutter by her window. "This place would be a convenient model for Hell," she wrote to a friend in Basel before going to sleep that night. "A full-blown example of the social degeneracy achieved by forced cultural hybridism. Populace debased and made hostile by generations of merciless exploitation. I take the south-bound narrow-gauge train tomorrow morning for a happier land, and trust that my friend the sun will appear at some point during the day. *Seien Sie herzlich gegrüsst von Ihrer Maria.*"

As the train crawled southward, up over the high plateau land, the clouds were left behind and the sun took charge of the countryside. Fräulein Windling sat attentively by the smeared window, enveloped in an increasing sadness. As long as it had been raining, she had imagined the rain as the cause of her depression: the gray cloud light gave an unaccustomed meaning to the landscape by altering forms and distances. Now she understood that the more familiar and recognizable the contours of the desert were to become, the more conscious she would be of having no reason to be in it, because it was her last visit.

Two days later, when the truck stopped to let her out, Boufelja stood in the sun beside the boulders waving; one of the men of the village was with him to help carry the luggage. Once the truck had gone and its cloud of yellow dust had fled across the hammada, the silence was there; it seemed that no sound could be louder than the crunch of their shoes on the ground.

"How is Slimane?" she asked. Boufelja was noncommittal. "He's all right," he said. "They say he tried to run away. But he didn't get very far." The report might be true, or it might be false; in any case she determined not to allude to it unless Slimane himself mentioned it first.

She felt an absurd relief when they came to the edge of the cliffs and she saw the village across the valley. Not until she had made the rounds of the houses where her friends lived, discussed their troubles with them and left some pills here and some candy there, was she convinced that no important change had come to the oasis during her absence. She went to the house of Slimane's parents: he was not there. "Tell him to come and see me," she said to his father as she left the house.

On the third morning after her arrival Slimane appeared, and stood there in the doorway smiling. Once she had greeted him and made him sit down and have coffee with her, she plied him with questions about life in the village while she had been in Europe. Some of his friends had gone to become patriots, he said, and they were killing the French like flies. Her heart sank, but she said nothing. As she watched him smiling she was able to exult in the reflection that Slimane had been reachable, after all; she had proved that it was possible to make true friends of the younger people. But even while she was saying, "How happy I am to see you, Slimane," she remembered that their time together was now limited, and an expression of pain passed over her face as she finished the phrase. "I shall not say a word to him about it," she decided. If he, at least, still had the illusion of unbounded time lying ahead, he would somehow retain his aura of purity and innocence, and she would feel less anguish during the time they spent together.

One day they went down the valley to see the caid, and discussed the long-planned trip to Abadla. Another day they started out at dawn to visit the tomb of Moulay Ali ben Said, where there was a spring of hot water. It was a tiny spot of oasis at the edge of a ridge of high dunes; perhaps fifty palms were there around the decayed shrine. In the shade of the rocks below the walls there was a ruined cistern into which the steaming water dribbled. They spread blankets on the sand nearby, at the foot of a small tamarisk, and took out their lunch. Before starting to eat, they drank handfuls of the water, which Slimane said was famed for its holiness. The palms rattled and hissed in the wind overhead.

"Allah has sent us the wind to make us cool while we eat," Slimane said when he had finished his bread and dates.

"The wind has always been here," she answered carelessly, "and it always will be here."

He sat up straight. "No, no!" he cried. "When Sidna Aissa has returned for forty days there will be no more Moslems and the world will end.

Everything, the sky and the sun and the moon. And the wind too. Everything." He looked at her with an expression of such satisfaction that she felt one of her occasional surges of anger against him.

"I see," she said. "Stand over by the spring a minute. I want to take your picture." She had never understood why it was that the Moslems had conceded Jesus even this Pyrrhic victory, the coda to all creation: its inconsistency embarrassed her. Across the decayed tank she watched Slimane assume the traditional stiff attitude of a person about to be photographed, and an idea came into her head. For Christmas Eve, which would come within two weeks, she would make a crèche. She would invite Slimane to eat with her by the fireplace, and when midnight came she would take him in to see it.

She finished photographing Slimane; they gathered up the equipment and set out against the hot afternoon wind for the village. The sand sometimes swept by, stinging their faces with its invisible fringe. Fräulein Windling led the way this time, and they walked fast. The image of the crèche, illumined by candles, occurred to her several times on the way back over the rocky erg; it made her feel inexpressibly sad, for she could not help connecting it with the fact that everything was ending. They came to the point north of the village where the empty erg was cut across by the wandering river valley. As they climbed slowly upward over the fine sand, she found herself whispering: "It's the right thing to do." " 'Right' is not the word," she thought, without being able to find a better one. She was going to make a crèche because she loved Christmas and wanted to share it with Slimane. They reached the hotel shortly after sunset, and she sent Slimane home in order to sit and plan her project on paper.

It was only when she began actually to put the crèche together that she realized how much work it was going to be. Early the next morning she asked Boufelja to find her an old wooden crate. Before she had been busy even a half hour, she heard Slimane talking in the kitchen. Quickly she pushed everything under the bed and went out onto the terrace.

"Slimane," she said. "I'm very busy. Come in the afternoon." And that afternoon she told him that since she was going to be working every morning until after the day of the Christ Child, they would not be making any more long trips during that time. He received the information glumly. "I know," he said. "You are getting ready for the holy day. I understand."

"When the holy day comes, we will have a feast," she assured him.

"If Allah wills."

"I'm sorry," she said, smiling.

He shrugged. "Good-bye," he told her.

Afternoons they still walked in the oasis or had tea on the roof, but her mornings she spent in her room sewing, hammering and sculpting. Once she had the platform constructed, she had to model the figures. She carried up a great mass of wet clay from the river to her room. It was two days before she managed to make a Virgin whose form pleased her. From an old strip of muslin she fashioned a convincing tent to house the Mother and the Child in its nest of tiny white chicken feathers. Shredded tamarisk needles made a fine carpet for the interior of the tent. Outside she poured sand, and then pushed the clay camels' long legs deep into it; one animal walked behind the other over the dune, and a Wise Man sat straight on top of each, his white *djellaba* falling in long pointed folds to either side of the camel's flanks. The Wise Men would come carrying sacks of almonds and very small liqueur chocolates wrapped in colored tinfoil. When she had the crèche finished, she put it on the floor in the middle of the room and piled tangerines and dates in front of it. With a row of candles burning behind it, and one candle on each side in front, it would look like a Moslem religious chromolithograph. She hoped the scene would be recognizable to Slimane; he might then be more easily persuaded of its poetic truth. She wanted only to suggest to him that the god with whom he was on such intimate terms was the god worshiped by the Nazarenes. It was not an idea she would ever try to express in words.

An additional surprise for the evening would be the new flashbulb attachment to her camera, which Slimane had not yet seen. She intended to take a good many pictures of the crèche and of Slimane looking at it; these she would enlarge to show her pupils. She went and bought a new turban for Slimane; he had been wearing none for more than a year now. This was a man's turban, and very fine: ten meters of the softest Egyptian cotton.

The day before Christmas she overslept, duped by the heavy sky. Each winter the oasis had a few dark days; they were rare, but this was one of them. While she still lay there in bed, she heard the roar of the wind, and when she got up to look out the window she found no world outside—only a dim rose-gray fog that hid everything. The swirling sand sprayed ceaselessly against the glass; it had formed in long drifts on the floor of the terrace. When she went for breakfast, she wore her burnoose with the hood up around her face. The blast of the wind as she stepped out onto the terrace struck her with the impact of a solid object, and the sand gritted on the concrete floor under her shoes. In the dining room Boufelja had bolted the shutters; he greeted her enthusiastically from the gloom inside, glad of her presence.

"A very bad day for your festival, alas, mademoiselle!" he observed as he set her coffeepot on the table.

"Tomorrow's the festival," she said. "It begins tonight."

"I know. I know." He was impatient with Nazarene feasts because the hours of their beginnings and ends were observed in so slipshod a manner. Moslem feasts began precisely, either at sundown or an hour before sunup, or when the new moon was first visible in the western sky at twilight. But the Nazarenes began their feasts whenever they felt like it.

She spent the morning in her room writing letters. By noon the air outside was darker with still more sand; the wind shook the hotel atop its rock as if it would hurl it over the tips of the palms below into the riverbed. Several times she rose and went to the window to stare out at the pink emptiness beyond the terrace. Storms made her happy, although she wished this one could have come after Christmas. She had imagined a pure desert night—cold, alive with stars, and the dogs yapping from the oasis. It might yet be that; there was still time, she thought, as she slipped her burnoose over her head to go in to lunch.

With the wind, the fireplace was an unsure blessing: besides the heat it gave, it provided the only light in the dining room, but the smoke that belched from it burned her eyes and throat. The shutters at the windows rattled and pounded, covering the noise of the wind itself.

She got out of the dining room as soon as she had finished eating, and hurried back to her room to sit through the slowly darkening afternoon, as she continued with her letter-writing and waited for the total extinction of daylight. Slimane was coming at eight. There would be enough time to carry everything into the dining room before that, and to set the crèche up in the dark unused wing into which Boufelja was unlikely to go. But when she came to do it, she found that the wind's force was even greater than she had imagined. Again and again she made the trip between her room and the dining room, carrying each object carefully wrapped in her burnoose. Each time she passed in front of the kitchen door she expected Boufelja to open it and discover her. She did not want him there when she showed the crèche to Slimane; he could see it tomorrow at breakfast.

Protected by the noise of the gale she succeeded in transporting all the parts to the far dark corner of the dining room without alerting Boufelja.

Long before dinnertime the crèche was in readiness, awaiting only the lighting of the candles to be brought alive. She left a box of matches on the table beside it, and hurried back to her room to arrange her hair and change her clothing. The sand had sifted through her garments and was now everywhere; it showered from her underwear and stuck like sugar to her skin. Her watch showed a few minutes after eight when she went out.

Only one place had been laid at table. She waited, while the blinds chattered and banged, until Boufelja appeared carrying the soup tureen.

"What a bad night," he said.

"You forgot to prepare for Slimane," she told him. But he was not paying attention. "He's stupid!" he exclaimed, beginning to ladle out the soup.

"Wait!" she cried. "Slimane's coming. I mustn't eat until he comes."

Still Boufelja misunderstood. "He wanted to come into the dining room," he said. "And he knows it's forbidden at dinnertime."

"But I invited him!" She looked at the lone soup plate on the table. "Tell him to come in, and set another place."

Boufelja was silent. He put the ladle back into the tureen. "Where is he?" she demanded, and without waiting for him to reply she went on. "Didn't I tell you he was going to have dinner with me tonight?" For suddenly she suspected that in her desire for secrecy she might indeed have neglected to mention the invitation to Boufelja.

"You didn't say anything," he told her. "I didn't know. I sent him home. But he'll be back after dinner."

"Oh, Boufelja!" she cried. "You know Slimane never lies."

He looked down at her with reproach on his face. "I didn't know anything about mademoiselle's plans," he said aggrievedly. This made her think for a swift instant that he had discovered the crèche, but she decided that if he had he would have spoken of it.

"Yes, yes, I know. I should have told you. It's my fault."

"That's true, mademoiselle," he said. And he served the remaining courses observing a dignified silence which she, still feeling some displeasure with him, did not urge him to break. Only at the end of the meal, when she had pushed back her chair from the table and sat studying the pattern of the flames in the fireplace, did he decide to speak. "Mademoiselle will take coffee?"

"I do want some," she said, trying to bring a note of enthusiasm into her voice. "*Bien,*" murmured Boufelja, and he left her alone in the room.

When he returned carrying the coffee, Slimane was with him, and they were laughing, she noted, quite as though there had been no misunderstanding about dinner. Slimane stood by the door an instant, stamping his feet and shaking the sand from his burnoose. As he came forward to take her hand, she cried: "Oh, Slimane, it's my fault! I forgot to tell Boufelja. It's terrible!"

"There is no fault, madame," he said gravely. "This is a festival."

"Yes, this is a festival," she echoed. "And the wind's still blowing. Listen!"

Slimane would not take coffee, but Boufelja, ceding to her pressure, let her pour him out a cup, which he drank standing by the fireplace. She suspected him of being secretly pleased that Slimane had not managed to eat with her. When he had finished his coffee, he wished them good-night and went off to bed in his little room next to the kitchen.

They sat a while watching the fire, without talking. The wind rushed past in the emptiness outside, the blinds hammered. Fräulein Windling was content. Even if the first part of the celebration had gone wrong, the rest of the evening could still be pleasant.

She waited until she was sure that Boufelja had really gone to bed, and then she reached into her bag and brought out a small plastic sack full of chocolate creams, which she placed on the table.

"Eat," she said carelessly, and she took a piece of candy herself. With some hesitation Slimane put out his hand to take the sack. When he had a chocolate in his mouth, she began to speak. She intended to tell him the story of the Nativity, a subject she already had touched upon many times during their excursions, but only in passing. This time she felt she should tell him the entire tale. She expected him to interrupt when he discovered that it was a religious story, but he merely kept his noncommittal eyes on her and chewed mechanically, showing that he followed her by occasionally nodding his head. She became engrossed in what she was saying, and began to use her arms in wide gestures. Slimane reached for another chocolate and went on listening.

She talked for an hour or more, aware as from a distance of her own eloquence. When she told him about Bethlehem she was really describing Slimane's own village, and the house of Joseph and Mary was the house down in the *ksar* where Slimane had been born. The night sky arched above the Oued Zousfana and its stars glared down upon the cold hammada. Across the erg on their camels came the Wise Men in their burnooses and turbans, pausing at the crest of the last great dune to look ahead at the valley where the dark village lay. When she had finished, she blew her nose.

Slimane appeared to be in a state bordering on trance. She glanced at him, expected him to speak, but as he did not, she looked more closely at him. His eyes had an obsessed, vacant expression, and although they were still fixed on her face, she would have said that he was seeing something much farther away than she. She sighed, not wanting to make the decision to rouse him. The possibility she would have liked to entertain, had she not been so conscious of its unlikelihood, was that the boy somehow had been captivated by the poetic truth of the story, and was reviewing it in his imagination. "Certainly it could not be the case," she decided; it was more likely that he had ceased some time back to listen to her words, and was merely sitting there, only vaguely aware that she had come to the end of her story.

Then he spoke. "You're right. He was the King of Men."

Fräulein Windling caught her breath and leaned forward, but he went on. "And later Satan sent a snake with two heads. And Jesus killed it. Satan was angry with Him. He said: 'Why did you kill my friend? Did it hurt you, perhaps?' And Jesus said: 'I knew where it came from.' And Satan put on a black burnoose. That's true," he added, as he saw the expression of what he took to be simple disbelief on her face.

She sat up very straight and said: "Slimane, what are you talking about? There are no such stories about Jesus. Nor about Sidna Aissa either." She was not sure of the accuracy of this last statement; it was possible, she supposed, that such legends did exist among these people. "You know those are just stories that have nothing to do with the truth."

He did not hear her because he had already begun to talk. "I'm not speaking of Sidna Aissa," he said firmly. "He was a Moslem prophet. I'm talking about Jesus, the prophet of the Nazarenes. Everyone knows that Satan sent Him a snake with two heads."

She listened to the wind for an instant. "Ah," she said, and took another chocolate; she did not intend to carry the argument further. Soon she dug into her bag again and pulled out the turban, wrapped in red and white tissue paper.

"A present for you," she said, holding it out to him. He seized it mechanically, placed it on his lap and remained staring down at it. "Aren't you going to open it?" she demanded.

He nodded his head twice and tore open the paper. When he saw the pile of white cotton he smiled. Seeing his face at last come to life, she jumped up. "Let's put it on you!" she exclaimed. He gave her one end, which she pulled taut by walking all the way to the door. Then with his hand holding the other end to his forehead, he turned slowly round and round, going toward her all the time, arranging the form of the turban as it wound itself about his head. "Magnificent!" she cried. He went over to the row of black windows to look at himself.

"Can you see?" she asked.

"Yes, I can see the sides of it," he told her. "It's very beautiful."

She walked back toward the center of the room. "I'd like to take your picture, Slimane," she said, seeing an immediate look of puzzlement appear in his face. "Would you do me a favor? Go to my room and get the camera."

"At night? You can take a picture at night?"

She nodded, smiling mysteriously. "And bring me the yellow box on the bed."

Keeping the turban on his head, he got into his burnoose, took her flashlight and went out, letting the wind slam the door. She hoped the sound had not wakened Boufelja; for an instant she listened while there was no sound but the roar of air rushing through the corridor outside. Then she ran to the dark wing of the room and struck a match. Quickly she lighted all the candles around the crèche, straightened a camel in the sand, and walked back around the corner to the fireplace. She would not have thought the candles could give so much light. The other end of the room was now brighter than the end where she stood. In a moment the door burst open and Slimane came back in, carrying the camera slung over his shoulder. He put it down carefully on the table. "There was no yellow box on the bed," he told her. Then his glance caught the further walls flickering with the unfamiliar light, and he began to walk toward the center of the room. She saw that this was the moment. "Come," she said, taking his arm and pulling him gently around the corner to where the crèche was finally visible, bright with its multiple shuddering points of light. Slimane said nothing; he stopped walking and stood completely still. After a moment of silence, she plucked tentatively at his arm. "Come and see," she urged him. They continued to walk toward the crèche; as they came up to it she had the impression that if she had not been there he would have reached out his hand and touched it, perhaps would have lifted the tiny gold-clad infant Jesus out of His bed of feathers. But he stood quietly, looking at it. Finally he said: "You brought all that from Switzerland?"

"Of course not!" It was a little disappointing that he should not have recognized the presence of the desert in the picture, should not have sensed that the thing was of his place, and not an importation. "I made it all here," she said. She waited an instant. "Do you like it?"

"Ah, yes," he said with feeling. "It's beautiful. I thought it came from Switzerland."

To be certain that he understood the subject matter, she began to identify the figures one by one, her voice taking on such an unaccustomed inflection of respect that he glanced up at her once in surprise. It was almost as if she too were seeing it for the first time. "And the Wise Men are coming down out of the erg to see the child."

"Why did you put all those almonds there?" asked Slimane, touching some with his forefinger.

"They're gifts for the little Jesus."

"But what are you going to do with them?" he pursued.

"Eat them, probably, later," she said shortly. "Take one if you like. You say there was no yellow box on the bed?" She wanted to take the photographs while the candles were still of equal height.

"There was nothing but a sweater and some papers, madame."

She left him there by the crèche, crossed the room and put on her burnoose. The darkness in the corridor was complete; there was no sign that Boufelja had awakened. She knew her room was in great disorder, and she played the beam of the flashlight around the floor before entering. In the welter of displaced things that strewed the little room there seemed small chance of finding anything. The feeble ray illumined one by one the meaningless forms made by the piling of disparate objects one on the other; the light moved over the floor, along the bed, behind the flimsy curtain of the armoire. Suddenly she stopped and turned the beam under the bed. The box was in front of her face; she had put it with the crèche.

"I mustn't fall," she thought, running along the corridor. She forced herself to slow her pace to a walk, entered the dining room and shut the door after her carefully. Slimane was on his knees in the middle of the room, a small object of some sort in his hand. She noted with relief that he was amusing himself. "I'm sorry it took me so long," she exclaimed. "I'd forgotten where I'd put it." She was pulling her burnoose off over her head; now she hung it on a nail by the fireplace, and taking up the camera and the yellow box, she walked over to join him.

Perhaps a faint glimmer of guilt in his expression as he glanced up made her eyes stray along the floor toward another object lying nearby, similar to the one he held in his hand. It was one of the Wise Men, severed at the hips from his mount. The Wise Man in Slimane's hand was intact, but the camel had lost its head and most of its neck.

"Slimane! What are you doing?" she cried with undisguised anger. "What have you done to the crèche?" She advanced around the corner and looked in its direction. There was not really much more than a row of candles and a pile of sand that had been strewn with tangerine peel and date stones; here and there a carefully folded square of lavender or pink tinfoil had been planted in the sand. All three of the Wise Men had been enlisted in Slimane's battle on the floor, the tent ravaged in the campaign to extricate the almonds piled inside, and the treasure sacks looted of their chocolate liqueurs. There was no sign anywhere of the infant Jesus or his gold-lamé garment. She felt tears come into her eyes. Then she laughed shortly, and said: "Well, it's finished. Yes?"

"Yes, madame," he said calmly. "Are you going to make the photograph now?" He got to his feet and laid the broken camel on the platform in the sand with the other debris.

Fräulein Windling spoke evenly. "I wanted to take a picture of the crèche."

He waited an instant, as if he were listening to a distant sound. Then he said: "Should I put on my burnoose?"

"No." She began to take out the flashbulb attachment. When she had it ready, she took the picture before he had time to strike a pose. She saw his astonishment at the sudden bright light prolong itself into surprise that the thing was already done, and then become resentment at having been caught off his guard; but pretending to have seen nothing, she went on snapping covers shut. He watched her as she gathered up her things. "Is it finished?" he said, disappointed. "Yes," she replied. "It will be a very good picture."

"*Incha' Allah.*"

She did not echo his piety. "I hope you've enjoyed the festival," she told him.

Slimane smiled widely. "Ah, yes, madame. Very much. Thank you."

She let him out into the camel-square and turned the lock in the door. Quickly she went back into her room, wishing it were a clear night like other nights, when she could stand out on the terrace and look at the dunes and stars, or sit on the roof and hear the dogs, for in spite of the hour she was not sleepy. She cleared her bed of all the things that lay on top of it, and got in, certain that she was going to lie awake for a long time. For it had shaken her, the chaos Slimane had made in those few minutes of her absence. Across the seasons of their friendship she had come to think of him as being very nearly like herself, even though she knew he had not been that way when she first had met him. Now she saw the dangerous vanity at the core of that fantasy: she had assumed that somehow his association with her had automatically been for his ultimate good, that inevitably he had been undergoing a process of improvement as a result of knowing her. In her desire to see him change, she had begun to forget what Slimane was really like. "I shall never understand him," she thought helplessly, sure that just because she felt so close to him she would never be able to observe him dispassionately.

"This is the desert," she told herself. Here food is not an adornment; it is meant to be eaten. She had spread out food and he had eaten it. Any argument which attached blame to that could only be false. And so she lay there accusing herself. "It has been too much head and high ideals," she reflected, "and not enough heart." Finally she traveled on the sound of the wind into sleep.

At dawn when she awoke she saw that the day was going to be another dark one. The wind had dropped. She got up and shut the window. The early-morning sky was heavy with clouds. She sank back into bed and fell asleep. It was later than usual when she rose, dressed and went into the dining room. Boufelja's face was strangely expressionless as he wished her good morning. She supposed it was the memory of last night's misunderstanding, still with him—or possibly he was annoyed at having had to clean up the remains of the crèche. Once she had sat down and spread her napkin across her lap, he unbent sufficiently to say to her: "Happy festival."

"Thank you. Tell me, Boufelja," she went on, changing her inflection. "When you brought Slimane back in after dinner last night, do you know where he had been? Did he tell you?"

"He's a stupid boy," said Boufelja. "I told him to go home and eat and come back later. You think he did that? Never. He walked the whole time up and down in the courtyard here, outside the kitchen door, in the dark."

"I understand!" exclaimed Fräulein Windling triumphantly. "So he had no dinner at all."

"I had nothing to give him," he began, on the defensive.

"Of course not," she said sternly. "He should have gone home and eaten."

"Ah, you see?" grinned Boufelja. "That's what I told him to do."

In her mind she watched the whole story being enacted: Slimane aloofly informing his father that he would be eating at the hotel with the Swiss lady, the old man doubtless making some scornful reference to her, and Slimane going out. Unthinkable, once he had been refused admittance to the dining room, for him to go back and face the family's ridicule. "Poor boy," she murmured.

"The commandant wants to see you," said Boufelja, making one of his abrupt conversational changes. She was surprised, since from one year to the next the captain never gave any sign of being aware of her existence; the hotel and the fort were like two separate countries. "Perhaps for the festival," Boufelja suggested, his face a mask.

"Perhaps," she said uneasily.

When she had finished her breakfast, she walked across to the gates of the fort. The sentry seemed to be expecting her. One of the two young French soldiers was in the compound painting a chair. He greeted her, saying that the captain was in his office. She went up the long flight of stairs and paused an instant at the top, looking down at the valley in the unaccustomed gray light, noting how totally different it looked from its usual self, on this dim day.

A voice from inside called out: *"Entrez, s'il vous plaît!"* She opened the door and stepped in. The captain sat behind his desk; she had the unwelcome sensation of having played this same scene on another occasion, in another place. And she was suddenly convinced that she knew what he was going to say. She seized the back of the empty chair facing his desk. "Sit down, Mademoiselle Windling," he said, rising halfway out of his seat, waving his arm, and sitting again quickly.

There were several topographical maps on the wall behind him, marked with lavender and green chalk. The captain looked at his desk and then at her, and said in a clear voice: "It is an unfortunate stroke of chance that I should have to call you here on this holiday." Fräulein Windling sat down in the chair; leaning forward, she seemed about to rest her elbow on his desk, but instead crossed her legs and folded her arms tight.

"Yes?" she said, tense, waiting for the message. It came immediately, for which she was conscious, even then, of being grateful to him. He told her simply that the entire area had been closed to civilians; this order applied to French nationals as well as to foreigners, so she must not feel discriminated against. The last was said with a wry attempt at a smile.

"This means that you will have to take tomorrow morning's truck," he continued. "The driver has already been advised of your journey. Perhaps another year, when the disturbances are over. . . ." ("Why does he say that?" she thought, "when he knows it's the end, and the time of friendship is finished?") He rose and extended his hand.

She could not remember going out of the room and down the long stairway into the compound, but now she was standing outside the sentry gate beside the wall of the fort, with her hand on her forehead. "Already," she thought. "It came so soon." And it occurred to her that she was not going to be given the time to make amends to Slimane, so that it was really true she was never going to understand him. She walked up to the parapet to look down at the edge of the oasis for a moment, and then went back to her room to start packing. All day long she worked in her room, pulling out boxes, forcing herself to be aware only of the decisions she was making as to what was to be taken and what was to be left behind once and for all.

At lunchtime Boufelja hovered near her chair. "Ah, mademoiselle, how many years we have been together, and now it is finished!" "Yes," she thought, but there was nothing to do about it. His lamentations made her nervous and she was short with him.

Then she felt guilt-stricken and said slowly, looking directly at him: "I am very sad, Boufelja."

He sighed. "Ay, mademoiselle, I know!"

By nightfall the pall of clouds had been blown away across the desert, and the western sky was partly clear. Fräulein Windling had finished all her packing. She went out onto the terrace, saw the dunes pink and glowing, and climbed the steps to the roof to look at the sunset. Great skeins of fiery stormcloud streaked the sky. Mechanically she let her gaze follow the meanders of the river valley as it lost itself in the darkening hammada to the south. "It is in the past," she reminded herself; this was already the new era. The desert out there looked the same as it always had looked. But the sky, ragged, red and black, was like a handbill that had just been posted above it, announcing the arrival of war.

It was a betrayal, she was thinking, going back down the steep stairs, running her hand along the familiar rough mud wall to steady herself, and the French of course were the culprits. But beyond that she had the irrational and disagreeable conviction that the countryside itself had connived in the betrayal, that it was waiting to be transformed by the struggle. She went into her room and lit the small oil lamp; sitting down, she held her hands over it to warm them. At some point there had been a change: the people no longer wanted to go on living in the world they knew. The pressure of the past had become too great, and its shell had broken.

In the afternoon she had sent Boufelja to tell Slimane the news, and to ask him to be at the hotel at daybreak. During dinner she discussed only the details of departure and travel; when Boufelja tried to pull the talk in emotional directions, she did not reply. His commiseration was intolerable; she was not used to giving voice to her despair. When she got to her room she went directly to bed. The dogs barked half the night.

It was cold in the morning. Her hands ached as she gathered up the wet objects from around the washbowl on the table, and somehow she drove a sliver deep under the nail of her thumb. She picked some of it out with a needle, but the greater part remained. Before breakfast she stepped outside.

Standing in the wasteland between the hotel and the fort, she looked down at the countryside's innocent face. The padlocked gasoline pump, triumphant in fresh red and orange paint, caught the pure early sunlight. For a moment it seemed the only living thing in the landscape. She turned around. Above the dark irregular mass of palm trees rose the terraced village, calm under its morning veil of woodsmoke. She shut her eyes for an instant, and then went into the hotel.

She could feel herself sitting stiffly in her chair while she drank her coffee, and she knew she was being distant and formal with Boufelja, but it was the only way she could be certain of being able to keep going. Once he came to tell her that Slimane had arrived bringing the donkey and its master for her luggage. She thanked him and set down her coffee cup. "More?" said Boufelja. "No," she answered. "Drink another, mademoiselle," he urged her. "It's good on a cold morning." He poured it out and she drank part of it. There was a knocking at the gate. One of the young soldiers had been sent with a jeep to carry her out to the truck stop on the trail.

"I can't!" she cried, thinking of Slimane and the donkey. The young soldier made it clear that he was not making an offer, but giving an order. Slimane stood beside the donkey outside the gate.

While she began to speak with him the soldier shouted: "Does he want to come, the *gosse?* He can come too, if he likes." Slimane ran to get the luggage and Fräulein Windling rushed inside to settle her bill. "Don't hurry," the soldier called after her. "There's plenty of time."

Boufelja stood in the kitchen doorway. Now for the first time it occurred to her to wonder what was going to become of him. With the hotel shut he would have no work. When she had settled her account and given him a tip which was much larger than she could afford, she took both his hands in hers and said: "*Mon cher* Boufelja, we shall see one another very soon."

"Ah, yes," he cried, trying to smile. "Very soon, mademoiselle."

She gave the donkey driver some money, and got into the jeep beside the soldier. Slimane had finished bringing out the luggage and stood behind the jeep, kicking the tires. "Have you got everything?" she called to him. "Everything?" She would have liked to see for herself, but she was loath to go back into the room. Boufelja had disappeared; now he came hurrying out, breathless, carrying a pile of old magazines. "It's all right," she said. "No, no! I don't want them." The jeep was already moving ahead down the hill. In what seemed to her an unreasonably short time they had reached the boulders. When Fräulein Windling tried to lift out her briefcase the pain of the sliver under her nail made the tears start to her eyes, and she let go with a cry. Slimane glanced at her, surprised. "I hurt my hand," she explained. "It's nothing."

The bags had been piled in the shade. Sitting on a rock near the jeep, the soldier faced Fräulein Windling; from time to time he scanned the horizon behind her for a sign of the truck. Slimane examined the jeep from all sides; eventually he came to sit nearby. They did not say very much to one another. She was not sure whether it was because of the soldier with them, or because her thumb ached so constantly, but she sat quietly waiting, not wanting to talk.

It was a long time before the far-off motor made itself heard. When the truck was still no more than a puff of dust between sky and earth, the soldier was on his feet watching; an instant later Slimane jumped up. "It is coming, madame," he said. Then he bent over, putting his face very close to hers. "I want to go with you to Colomb-Bechar," he whispered. When she did not respond, because she was seeing the whole story of their friendship unrolled before her, from the end back to its beginning, he said louder, with great urgency: "Please, madame."

Fräulein Windling hesitated only an instant. She raised her head and looked carefully at the smooth brown face that was so near. "Of course, Slimane," she said. It was clear that he had not expected to hear this; his delight was infectious, and she smiled as she watched him run to the pile of bags and begin carrying them out into the sunlight to align them in the dust beside the edge of the trail.

Later, when they were rattling along the hammada, she in front beside the driver and Slimane squatting in the back with a dozen men and a sheep, she considered her irresponsible action in allowing him to make this absurd trip with her all the way to Colomb-Bechar. Still, she knew she wanted to give this ending to their story. A few times she turned partially around in her seat to glance at him through the dirty glass. He sat there in the smoke and dust, laughing like the others, with the hood of his burnoose hiding most of his face.

It had been raining in Colomb-Bechar; the streets were great puddles to reflect the clouded sky. At the garage they found a surly Negro boy to help them carry the luggage to the railway station. Her thumb hurt a little less.

"It's a cold town," Slimane said to her as they went down the main street. At the station they checked the bags and then went outside to stand and watch a car being unloaded from an open freight train: the roof of the automobile was still white with snow from the high steppes. The day was dark, and the wind rippled the surface of the water in the flooded empty lots. Fräulein Windling's train would not be leaving until late in the afternoon. They went to a restaurant and ate a long lunch.

"You really will go back home tomorrow?" she asked him anxiously at one point, while they were having fruit. "You know we have done a very wicked thing to your father and mother. They will never forgive me." A curtain seemed to draw across Slimane's face.

"It doesn't matter," he said shortly.

After lunch they walked in the public garden and looked at the eagles in their cages. A fine rain had begun to be carried on the wind. The mud of the paths grew deeper. They went back to the center of the town and sat down on the terrace of a large, shabby modern café. The table at the end was partly sheltered from the wet wind; they faced an empty lot strewn with refuse. Nearby, spread out like the bones of a camel fallen on the trail, were the rusted remains of an ancient bus. A long, newly felled date palm lay diagonally across the greater part of the lot. Fräulein Windling turned to look at the wet orange fiber of the stump, and felt an idle pity for the tree. "I'm going to have a Coca-Cola," she declared. Slimane said he, too, would like one.

They sat there a long time. The fine rain slanted through the air outside the arcades and hit the ground silently. She had expected to be approached by beggars, but none arrived, and now that the time had come to leave the café and go to the station she was thankful to see that the day had passed so easily. She opened her pocketbook, took out three thousand francs, and handed them to Slimane, saying: "This will be enough for everything. But you must buy your ticket back home today. When you leave the railway station. Be very careful of it."

Slimane put the money inside his garments, rearranged his burnoose, and thanked her. "You understand, Slimane," she said, detaining him with her hand, for he seemed about to rise from the table. "I'm not giving you any money now, because I need what I have for my journey. But when I get to Switzerland I shall send you a little, now and then. Not much. A little."

His face was swept by panic; she was perplexed.

"You haven't got my address," he told her.

"No, but I shall send it to Boufelja's house," she said, thinking that would satisfy him. He leaned toward her, his eyes intense.

"No, madame," he said with finality. "No. I have your address, and I shall send you mine. Then you will have it, and you can write to me."

It did not seem worth arguing about. For most of the afternoon her thumb had not hurt too much; now, as the day waned, it had begun to ache again. She wanted to get up, find the waiter and pay him. The fine rain still blew; the station was fairly far. But she saw Slimane had something more to say. He leaned forward in his chair and looked down at the floor. "Madame," he began.

"Yes?" she said.

"When you are in your country and you think of me you will not be happy. It's true, no?"

"I shall be very sad," she answered, rising.

Slimane got slowly to his feet and was quiet for an instant before going on. "Sad because I ate the food out of the picture. That was very bad. Forgive me."

The shrill sound of her own voice exclaiming, "No!" startled her. "No!" she cried. "That was good!" She felt the muscles of her cheeks and lips twisting themselves into grimaces of weeping; fiercely she seized his arm and looked down into his face. "*Oh, mon pauvre petit!*" she sobbed, and then covered her face with both hands. She felt him gently touching her sleeve. A truck went by in the main street, shaking the floor.

With an effort she turned away and scratched in her bag for a handkerchief. "Come," she said, clearing her throat. "Call the waiter."

They arrived at the station cold and wet. The train was being assembled; passengers were not allowed to go out onto the platform and were sitting on the floor inside. While Fräulein Windling bought her ticket Slimane went to get the bags from the checkroom. He was gone for a long time. When he arrived he came with his burnoose thrown back over his shoulders, grinning triumphantly, with three valises piled on his head. A man in ragged European jacket and trousers followed behind carrying the rest. As he came nearer she saw that the man held a slip of paper between his teeth.

The ancient compartment smelled of varnish. Through the window she could see, above some remote western reach of wasteland, a few strips of watery white sky. Slimane wanted to cover the seats with the luggage, so that no one would come into the compartment. "No," she said. "Put them in the racks." There were very few passengers in the coach. When everything was in place, the porter stood outside in the corridor and she noticed that he still held the slip of paper between his teeth. He counted the coins she gave him and pocketed them. Then quickly he handed the paper to Slimane, and was gone.

Fräulein Windling bent down a bit, to try and see her face in the narrow mirror that ran along the back of the seat. There was not enough light; the oil lantern above illumined only the ceiling, its base casting a leaden shadow over everything beneath. Suddenly the train jolted and made a series of crashing sounds. She took Slimane's head between her hands and kissed the middle of his forehead. "Please get down from the train," she told him. "We can talk here." She pointed to the window and began to pull on the torn leather strap that lowered it.

Slimane looked small on the dark platform, staring up at her as she leaned out. Then the train started to move. She thought surely it would go only a few feet and then stop, but it continued ahead, slowly. Slimane walked with it, keeping abreast of her window. In his hand was the paper the porter had given him. He held it up to her, crying: "Here is my address! Send it here!"

She took it, and kept waving as the train went faster, kept calling: "Good-bye!" He continued to walk quickly along beside the window, increasing his gait until he was running, until all at once there was no more platform. She leaned far out, looking backward, waving; straightway he was lost in the darkness and rain. A bonfire blazed orange by the track, and the smoke stung in her nostrils. She pulled up the window, glanced at the slip of paper she had in her hand and sat down. The train jolted her this way and that; she went on staring at the paper, although now it was in shadow; and she remembered the first day, long ago, when the child Slimane had stood outside the door watching her, stepping back out of her range of vision each time she turned to look at him. The words hastily printed for him on the scrap of paper by the porter were indeed an address, but the address was in Colomb-Bechar. "They said he tried to run away. But he didn't get very far." Each detail of his behavior as she went back over it clarified the pattern for her. "He's too young to be a soldier," she told herself. "They won't take him." But she knew they would.

Her thumb was hot and swollen; sometimes it seemed almost that its throbbing accompanied the side-to-side jolting of the coach. She looked out at the few remaining patches of colorless light in the sky. Sooner or later, she argued, he would have done it.

"Another year, perhaps," the captain had said. She saw her own crooked, despairing smile in the dark window glass beside her face. Maybe Slimane would be among the fortunate ones, an early casualty. "If only death were absolutely certain in wartime," she thought wryly, "the waiting would not be so painful." Listing and groaning, the train began its long climb upward over the plateau.

Tangier 1975

I first met her just after she'd bought the big villa overlooking the valley
Saudis have it now they've got most of the good properties I remember she
asked Anton and me to tea we hadn't been married very long then she
seemed very much interested in him she'd seen him dance years ago in Paris
before his accident and they talked about those days it was all very correct
she had delicious petits fours strange how that impressed itself on my mind
of course at that time you must remember we were frightfully poor living
on the cheapest sort of food fortunately Anton was a fantastic cook or we
should have starved he knew how to make a meal out of nothing at all I
assure you well it wasn't a fortnight later that she invited us to lunch
terribly formal a large staff everything perfect and afterward I remember we
were having coffee and liqueurs beside the fireplace and she suddenly
offered us this little house she had on the property there were several extra
cottages hidden around you know guest houses but most of them were up
above nearer the big house this one was way down in the woods far from
everything except a duck pond I was absolutely stunned it was the last thing
I should have expected of her then she took us down to see it very simple
but charming tastefully furnished and a rather primitive kitchen and bath
but there were heaps of flowers growing outside and lovely views from the
windows we were enchanted of course you understand there was nothing
to pay we were simply given the use of the house for as long as we wished
I admit it was a very kind gesture for her to make although at the time I
suspected that she had her eye on Anton I was quite wrong as it happened
in any case having the house made an enormous difference to us it was a
gift from the gods there was a matter of fact one drawback for me Anton
didn't seem to mind them but there were at least twenty peacocks in an
enormous aviary in the woods not far away and some nights they'd scream
you know how hair-raising the sound is especially in the middle of the night
it took me weeks to get used to it lying there in the dark listening to those
insane screams eventually I was able to sleep through it well once we'd
moved in our hostess never came near us which was her privilege naturally

but it did seem a bit peculiar at least she wasn't after Anton the months went by and we never caught sight of her you see we had a key to the gate at the bottom of the estate so we always used the lower road to come and go it was much easier than climbing up past the big house so of course in order for us to see her she'd have had to come down to our part of the property but she never ventured near us time went on then all at once we began to hear from various directions a strange rumor that whenever she spoke of us she referred to us as her squatters I was all for going up and having it out with her on the spot is that why you invited us here so you could ridicule us wherever you go but Anton said I'd got no proof it could simply be the typical sort of malicious gossip that seems to be everywhere in this place he said to wait until I heard it with my own ears well clearly she wasn't likely to say it in front of me then one morning I went to take a little walk in the woods and what should I see but several freshly painted signs that had been put up along the paths all saying DEFENSE DE TOUCHER AUX FLEURS obviously they'd been put there for us there was no one else isn't it extraordinary the way people's minds work we didn't want her beastly flowers we'd never touched them I don't like cut flowers I much prefer to see them growing Anton said best pay no attention if we have words she'll put us out and he was right of course but it was very hard to take at all events you know she had lovers always natives of course what can one expect that's all right I'm not so narrow-minded I'd begrudge her that dubious pleasure but there are ways and ways of doing things you'd expect a woman of her age and breeding to have a certain amount of discretion that is she'd make everything as unnoticeable as possible but no not at all in the first place she allowed them to live with her quite as if they were man and wife and that gave them command over the servants which is unthinkable but worse she positively flourished those wretched lovers of hers in the face of the entire town never went out without the current incumbent if people didn't include him she didn't accept the invitation she was the sort of woman one couldn't imagine ever having felt embarrassment but she could have managed to live here without alienating half the Europeans you know in those days people felt strongly about such things natives couldn't even enter the restaurants it wasn't that she had lovers or even that her lovers were natives but that she appeared with them in public that was a slap in the face for the European colony and they didn't forgive it but she couldn't be bothered to care what anybody felt what I'm leading up to is the party we never caught a glimpse of her from one month to the next you understand and suddenly one day she came to call on us friendly as you please she said she had a favor to ask of us she was giving this enormous party she'd sent out two hundred invitations that had to be surrendered at the gate she said there were always too many gate-crashers at her parties the tourists would pay the guides to get them in and this time nobody was to get in excepting the ones she'd invited what she wanted us to do was to stand in a booth she'd built just outside the gate it had a little window and a counter Anton was to examine the invitations and give a sign to one of the policemen stationed outside to admit the holder I had a big ledger with all the names alphabetically listed and as Anton passed me the invitation I was to make a red check opposite the name she wanted to be sure later who had come and who hadn't I've got ten servants she said and not one of them can read or write it's discouraging then I thought of you and decided to ask this great favor of you is everything all right in your little house do you enjoy living here so of course we said oh yes everything is lovely we'd be glad to help you what fools we were it won't take long she said two hours at most it's a costume party drinks dinner and dancing by moonlight in the lower garden the musicians begin to play at half past seven after she'd gone I said to Anton two hundred invitations indeed she hasn't got twenty friends in this entire city well the night of the party came and we were up there in our little sentry box working like coolies the sweat was pouring down my back sometimes a dozen people came all together half of them already drunk and they didn't at all like having to wait and be admitted one at a time they kept arriving on and on I thought they'd never stop coming at midnight we were still there finally I told Anton this is too much I don't care who comes I'm not going to stand here another minute and Anton said you're right and he spoke to the guard and said that's it no more people are coming don't let anybody else in and good night and so on and we went down to where the party was the costumes were very elaborate we stood for a few minutes at the end of the garden watching them dancing suddenly a tall man in robes with a false beard and a big turban came up to us I had no idea who he was but Anton claimed he recognized him at once anyway it was her lover if you please she'd sent him to tell us that if we were going to come to the party would we please go and put on our costumes as if we had any costumes to put on I was staggered after getting us to stand for almost five hours in a suffocating little box she has the infernal gall to ask us to leave yes and not even the common courtesy to come and speak to us herself no she sends her native lover to do it I was starved there was plenty of food on the buffet but it was a hundred feet away from us at the other end of the garden when we got back down to our house I told Anton I hate that woman I know it's wrong but I really hate her to make things worse the next day she came down to see us again not as you might think to thank us far from that on the contrary she'd come to complain that we'd let in people who had no invitations what do you mean I cried look at the cards and look at the book they tally what are you talking about and she said the Duchesse de Saint Somethingorother was missing her evening bag where she'd put her emerald earrings and I said just what has that got to do with us will you please tell me well she said we'd left our post our post she called it as though we were in the army and after we'd gone some other people had arrived and the police let them in Anton asked if they'd presented their invitations well she said she hadn't been able to get hold of that particular policeman so she didn't know but if we'd been there it wouldn't have happened my dear lady I said do you realize we were in that booth for five hours you told us it wouldn't take more than two I hope you're aware of that well it's most unfortunate she said I've had to call in the police that made me laugh *eh bien madame* I said since according to you it was the police who let the thief in it ought to be very simple I don't see that we have anything to do with it then she raised her voice all I can say is I'm sorry I was foolish enough to count on you I shall know better another time and she went out it was then that I said to Anton look we can't go on living in this woman's house we've got to find somewhere else he was earning a little at that time working in an export-import office practically nothing but enough to pay rent on a small cottage he thought we should hang on there and hope that things would return to normal but I began to go out by myself nearly every day to look for somewhere we could move to this turned out later to have been very useful at least I'd seen a good many houses and knew which ones were possible you see the party was only the prelude to the ghastly thing that happened less than a month afterward one night some teenage hoodlums got into the big house the lover had gone to Marrakech for the weekend so she was alone yes she made the servants sleep in cabins in the upper garden she was alone in the house and you know these people they're always convinced that Europeans must have vast sums of money hidden about the premises so they tortured her all night long trying to make her tell where it was she was beaten and burned and choked and cut and both her arms were broken she must have screamed I should think but maybe they covered her face with pillows at all events no one heard a thing the maids found her in the morning she was alive but she died in hospital that afternoon we knew nothing about it until the police suddenly arrived two days later and said the property was being padlocked and everybody had to leave immediately meaning the servants and gardeners and us so out we went with all our things it was terrible but as Anton said at least we lived for more than a year without paying rent he always insisted on seeing the positive side of things in a way that was helpful later when I heard the details I was frightfully upset because you see the police traced the hooligans through a gold cigarette case and some other things they'd taken the night they tortured her and then it was discovered that they also had the Duchess's evening bag one of the criminals had arrived late the night of the party and slipped in along with a group of Spaniards after Anton and I had left the gate and of course that gave him the opportunity of examining the house and grounds for the break-in later so I felt terribly guilty of course I knew it wasn't my fault but I couldn't keep myself from thinking that if we'd only stayed on a little longer she'd still have been alive I was certain at first that the lover had had some part in it you see he never left her side she wouldn't hear of it and all at once he goes off to Marrakech for a weekend no it seemed too pat it fitted too well but apparently he had nothing to do with it besides he'd had every chance to make off with whatever he wanted and never had touched a thing so he must have been fairly intelligent at least he knew better than to bite the hand that was feeding him except that in the end he got nothing for his good behavior poor wretch I've tried to think back to that night and sometimes it seems to me that in my sleep maybe I did hear screams but I'd heard those blasted peacocks so many times that I paid no attention and now it makes my blood run cold to think that perhaps I actually did hear her calling for help and thought it was the birds except that the big house was so far away she'd have had to be screaming from a window that looked over the valley so I keep telling myself I couldn't possibly have heard her they wouldn't have let her get near a window but it's upsetting all the same

Allal

He was born in the hotel where his mother worked. The hotel had only three dark rooms which gave on a courtyard behind the bar. Beyond was another smaller patio with many doors. This was where the servants lived, and where Allal spent his childhood.

The Greek who owned the hotel had sent Allal's mother away. He was indignant because she, a girl of fourteen, had dared to give birth while she was working for him. She would not say who the father was, and it angered him to reflect that he himself had not taken advantage of the situation while he had had the chance. He gave the girl three months' wages and told her to go home to Marrakech. Since the cook and his wife liked the girl and offered to let her live with them for a while, he agreed that she might stay on until the baby was big enough to travel. She remained in the back patio for a few months with the cook and his wife, and then one day she disappeared, leaving the baby behind. No one heard of her again.

As soon as Allal was old enough to carry things, they set him to work. It was not long before he could fetch a pail of water from the well behind the hotel. The cook and his wife were childless, so that he played alone.

When he was somewhat older he began to wander over the empty tableland outside. There was nothing else up here but the barracks, and they were enclosed by a high blind wall of red adobe. Everything else was below in the valley: the town, the gardens, and the river winding southward among the thousands of palm trees. He could sit on a point of rock far above and look down at the people walking in the alleys of the town. It was only later that he visited the place and saw what the inhabitants were like. Because he had been left behind by his mother they called him a son of sin, and laughed when they looked at him. It seemed to him that in this way they hoped to make him into a shadow, in order not to have to think of him as real and alive. He awaited with dread the time when he would have to go each morning to the town and work. For the moment he helped in the kitchen and served the officers from the barracks, along with the few motorists who passed through the region. He got small tips in the restaurant, and free food and lodging in a cell of the servants' quarters, but the Greek gave him no wages. Eventually he reached an age when this situation seemed shameful, and he went of his own accord to the town below and began to work, along with other boys of his age, helping to make the mud bricks people used for building their houses.

Living in the town was much as he had imagined it would be. For two years he stayed in a room behind a blacksmith's shop, leading a life without quarrels, and saving whatever money he did not have to spend to keep himself alive. Far from making any friends during this time, he formed a thorough hatred for the people of the town, who never allowed him to forget that he was a son of sin, and therefore not like others, but *meskhot*— damned. Then he found a small house, not much more than a hut, in the palm groves outside the town. The rent was low and no one lived nearby. He went to live there, where the only sound was the wind in the trees, and avoided the people of the town when he could.

One hot summer evening shortly after sunset he was walking under the arcades that faced the town's main square. A few paces ahead of him an old man in a white turban was trying to shift a heavy sack from one shoulder to the other. Suddenly it fell to the ground, and Allal stared as two dark forms flowed out of it and disappeared into the shadows. The old man pounced upon the sack and fastened the top of it, at the same time beginning to shout: Look out for the snakes! Help me find my snakes!

Many people turned quickly around and walked back the way they had come. Others stood at some distance, watching. A few called to the old man: Find your snakes fast and get them out of here! Why are they here? We don't want snakes in this town!

Hopping up and down in his anxiety, the old man turned to Allal. Watch this for me a minute, my son. He pointed at the sack lying on the earth at his feet, and snatching up a basket he had been carrying, went swiftly around the corner into an alley. Allal stood where he was. No one passed by.

It was not long before the old man returned, panting with triumph. When the onlookers in the square saw him again, they began to call out, this time to Allal: Show that *berrani* the way out of the town! He has no right to carry those things in here. Out! Out!

Allal picked up the big sack and said to the old man: Come on.

They left the square and went through the alleys until they were at the edge of town. The old man looked up then, saw the palm trees black against the fading sky ahead, and turned to the boy beside him.

Come on, said Allal again, and he went to the left along the rough path that led to his house. The old man stood perplexed.

You can stay with me tonight, Allal told him.

And these? he said, pointing first at the sack and then at the basket. They have to be with me.

Allal grinned. They can come.

When they were sitting in the house Allal looked at the sack and the basket. I'm not like the rest of them here, he said.

It made him feel good to hear the words being spoken. He made a contemptuous gesture. Afraid to walk through the square because of a snake. You saw them.

The old man scratched his chin. Snakes are like people, he said. You have to get to know them. Then you can be their friends.

Allal hesitated before he asked: Do you ever let them out?

Always, the old man said with energy. It's bad for them to be inside like this. They've got to be healthy when they get to Taroudant, or the man there won't buy them.

He began a long story about his life as a hunter of snakes, explaining that each year he made a voyage to Taroudant to see a man who bought them for the Aissaoua snake charmers in Marrakech. Allal made tea while he listened, and brought out a bowl of kif paste to eat with the tea. Later, when they were sitting comfortably in the midst of the pipe smoke, the old man chuckled. Allal turned to look at him.

Shall I let them out?

Fine!

But you must sit and keep quiet. Move the lamp nearer.

He untied the sack, shook it a bit, and returned to where he had been sitting. Then in silence Allal watched the long bodies move cautiously out into the light. Among the cobras were others with markings so delicate and perfect that they seemed to have been designed and painted by an artist. One reddish-gold serpent, which coiled itself lazily in the middle of the floor, he found particularly beautiful. As he stared at it, he felt a great desire to own it and have it always with him.

The old man was talking. I've spent my whole life with snakes, he said. I could tell you some things about them. Did you know that if you give them *majoun* you can make them do what you want, and without saying a word? I swear by Allah!

Allal's face assumed a doubtful air. He did not question the truth of the other's statement, but rather the likelihood of his being able to put the knowledge to use. For it was at that moment that the idea of actually taking the snake first came into his head. He was thinking that whatever he was to do must be done quickly, for the old man would be leaving in the morning. Suddenly he felt a great impatience.

Put them away so I can cook dinner, he whispered. Then he sat admiring the ease with which the old man picked up each one by its head and slipped it into the sack. Once again he dropped two of the snakes into the basket, and one of these, Allal noted, was the red one. He imagined he could see the shining of its scales through the lid of the basket.

As he set to work preparing the meal Allal tried to think of other things. Then, since the snake remained in his mind in spite of everything, he began to devise a way of getting it. While he squatted over the fire in a corner, he mixed some kif paste in a bowl of milk and set it aside.

The old man continued to talk. That was good luck, getting the two snakes back like that, in the middle of the town. You can never be sure what people are going to do when they find out you're carrying snakes. Once in El Kelaa they took all of them and killed them, one after the other, in front of me. A year's work. I had to go back home and start all over again.

Even as they ate, Allal saw that his guest was growing sleepy. How will things happen? he wondered. There was no way of knowing beforehand precisely what he was going to do, and the prospect of having to handle the snake worried him. It could kill me, he thought.

Once they had eaten, drunk tea and smoked a few pipes of kif, the old man lay back on the floor and said he was going to sleep. Allal sprang up. In here! he told him, and led him to his own mat in an alcove. The old man lay down and swiftly fell asleep.

Several times during the next half hour Allal went to the alcove and peered in, but neither the body in its burnoose nor the head in its turban had stirred.

First he got out his blanket, and after tying three of its corners together, spread it on the floor with the fourth corner facing the basket. Then he set the bowl of milk and kif paste on the blanket. As he loosened the strap from the cover of the basket the old man coughed. Allal stood immobile, waiting to hear the cracked voice speak. A small breeze had sprung up, making the palm branches rasp one against the other, but there was no further sound from the alcove. He crept to the far side of the room and squatted by the wall, his gaze fixed on the basket.

Several times he thought he saw the cover move slightly, but each time he decided he had been mistaken. Then he caught his breath. The shadow along the base of the basket was moving. One of the creatures had crept out from the far side. It waited for a while before continuing into the light, but when it did, Allal breathed a prayer of thanks. It was the red and gold one.

When finally it decided to go to the bowl, it made a complete tour around the edge, looking in from all sides, before lowering its head toward the milk. Allal watched, fearful that the foreign flavor of the kif paste might repel it. The snake remained there without moving.

He waited a half hour or more. The snake stayed where it was, its head in the bowl. From time to time Allal glanced at the basket, to be certain that the second snake was still in it. The breeze went on, rubbing the palm branches together. When he decided it was time, he rose slowly, and keeping an eye on the basket where apparently the other snake still slept, he reached over and gathered together the three tied corners of the blanket. Then he lifted the fourth corner, so that both the snake and the bowl slid to the bottom of the improvised sack. The snake moved slightly, but he did not think it was angry. He knew exactly where he would hide it: between some rocks in the dry riverbed.

Holding the blanket in front of him he opened the door and stepped out under the stars. It was not far up the road, to a group of high palms, and then to the left down into the oued. There was a space between the boulders where the bundle would be invisible. He pushed it in with care, and hurried back to the house. The old man was asleep.

There was no way of being sure that the other snake was still in the basket, so Allal picked up his burnoose and went outside. He shut the door and lay down on the ground to sleep.

Before the sun was in the sky the old man was awake, lying in the alcove coughing. Allal jumped up, went inside, and began to make a fire in the *mijmah*. A minute later he heard the other exclaim: They're loose again! Out of the basket! Stay where you are and I'll find them.

It was not long before the old man grunted with satisfaction. I have the black one! he cried. Allal did not look up from the corner where he crouched, and the old man came over, waving a cobra. Now I've got to find the other one.

He put the snake away and continued to search. When the fire was blazing, Allal turned and said: Do you want me to help you look for it?

No, no! Stay where you are.

Allal boiled the water and made the tea, and still the old man was crawling on his knees, lifting boxes and pushing sacks. His turban had slipped off and his face ran with sweat.

Come and have tea, Allal told him.

The old man did not seem to have heard him at first. Then he rose and went into the alcove, where he rewound his turban. When he came out he sat down with Allal, and they had breakfast.

Snakes are very clever, the old man said. They can get into places that don't exist. I've moved everything in this house.

After they had finished eating, they went outside and looked for the snake between the close-growing trunks of the palms near the house. When the old man was convinced that it was gone, he went sadly back in.

That was a good snake, he said at last. And now I'm going to Taroudant.

They said good-bye, and the old man took his sack and basket and started up the road toward the highway.

All day long as he worked, Allal thought of the snake, but it was not until sunset that he was able to go to the rocks in the oued and pull out the blanket. He carried it back to the house in a high state of excitement.

Before he untied the blanket, he filled a wide dish with milk and kif paste, and set it on the floor. He ate three spoonfuls of the paste himself and sat back to watch, drumming on the low wooden tea table with his fingers. Everything happened just as he had hoped. The snake came slowly out of the blanket, and very soon had found the dish and was drinking the milk. As long as it drank he kept drumming; when it had finished and raised its head to look at him, he stopped, and it crawled back inside the blanket.

Later that evening he put down more milk, and drummed again on the table. After a time the snake's head appeared, and finally all of it, and the entire pattern of action was repeated.

That night and every night thereafter, Allal sat with the snake, while with infinite patience he sought to make it his friend. He never attempted to touch it, but soon he was able to summon it, keep it in front of him for as long as he pleased, merely by tapping on the table, and dismiss it at will. For the first week or so he used the kif paste; then he tried the routine without it. In the end the results were the same. After that he fed it only milk and eggs.

Then one evening as his friend lay gracefully coiled in front of him, he began to think of the old man, and formed an idea that put all other things out of his mind. There had not been any kif paste in the house for several weeks, and he decided to make some. He bought the ingredients the following day, and after work he prepared the paste. When it was done, he mixed a large amount of it in a bowl with milk and set it down for the snake. Then he himself ate four spoonfuls, washing them down with tea.

He quickly undressed, and moving the table so that he could reach it, stretched out naked on a mat near the door. This time he continued to tap on the table, even after the snake had finished drinking the milk. It lay still, observing him, as if it were in doubt that the familiar drumming came from the brown body in front of it.

Seeing that even after a long time it remained where it was, staring at him with its stony yellow eyes, Allal began to say to it over and over: Come here. He knew it could not hear his voice, but he believed it could feel his mind as he urged it. You can make them do what you want, without saying a word, the old man had told him.

Although the snake did not move, he went on repeating his command, for by now he knew it was going to come. And after another long wait, all at once it lowered its head and began to move toward him. It reached his hip and slid along his leg. Then it climbed up his leg and lay for a time across his chest. Its body was heavy and tepid, its scales wonderfully smooth. After a time it came to rest, coiled in the space between his head and his shoulder.

By this time the kif paste had completely taken over Allal's mind. He lay in a state of pure delight, feeling the snake's head against his own, without a thought save that he and the snake were together. The patterns forming and melting behind his eyelids seemed to be the same ones that covered the snake's back. Now and then in a huge frenzied movement they all swirled up and shattered into fragments which swiftly became one great yellow eye, split through the middle by the narrow vertical pupil that pulsed with his own heartbeat. Then the eye would recede, through shifting shadow and sunlight, until only the designs of the scales were left, swarming with renewed insistence as they merged and separated. At last the eye returned, so huge this time that it had no edge around it, its pupil dilated to form an aperture almost wide enough for him to enter. As he stared at the blackness within, he understood that he was being slowly propelled toward the opening. He put out his hands to touch the polished surface of the eye on each side, and as he did this he felt the pull from within. He slid through the crack and was swallowed by darkness.

On awakening Allal felt that he had returned from somewhere far away. He opened his eyes and saw, very close to him, what looked like the flank of an enormous beast, covered with coarse stiff hair. There was a repeated vibration in the air, like distant thunder curling around the edges of the sky. He sighed, or imagined that he did, for his breath made no sound. Then he shifted his head a bit, to try and see beyond the mass of hair beside him. Next he saw the ear, and he knew he was looking at his own head from the outside. He had not expected this; he had hoped only that his friend would come in and share his mind with him. But it did not strike him as being at all strange; he merely said to himself that now he was seeing through the eyes of the snake, rather than through his own.

Now he understood why the serpent had been so wary of him: from here the boy was a monstrous creature, with all the bristles on his head and his breathing that vibrated inside him like a far-off storm.

He uncoiled himself and glided across the floor to the alcove. There was a break in the mud wall wide enough to let him out. When he had pushed himself through, he lay full length on the ground in the crystalline moonlight, staring at the strangeness of the landscape, where shadows were not shadows.

He crawled around the side of the house and started up the road toward the town, rejoicing in a sense of freedom different from any he had ever imagined. There was no feeling of having a body, for he was perfectly contained in the skin that covered him. It was beautiful to caress the earth with the length of his belly as he moved along the silent road, smelling the sharp veins of wormwood in the wind. When the voice of the muezzin floated out over the countryside from the mosque, he could not hear it, or know that within the hour the night would end.

On catching sight of a man ahead, he left the road and hid behind a rock until the danger had passed. But then as he approached the town there began to be more people, so that he let himself down into the *seguia*, the deep ditch that went along beside the road. Here the stones and clumps of dead plants impeded his progress. He was still struggling along the floor of the *seguia*, pushing himself around the rocks and through the dry tangles of matted stalks left by the water, when dawn began to break.

The coming of daylight made him anxious and unhappy. He clambered up the bank of the *seguia* and raised his head to examine the road. A man walking past saw him, stood quite still, and then turned and ran back. Allal did not wait; he wanted now to get home as fast as possible.

Once he felt the thud of a stone as it struck the ground somewhere behind him. Quickly he threw himself over the edge of the *seguia* and rolled squirming down the bank. He knew the terrain here: where the road crossed the oued, there were two culverts not far apart. A man stood at some distance ahead of him with a shovel, peering down into the *seguia*. Allal kept moving, aware that he would reach the first culvert before the man could get to him.

The floor of the tunnel under the road was ribbed with hard little waves of sand. The smell of the mountains was in the air that moved through. There were places in here where he could have hidden, but he kept moving, and soon reached the other end. Then he continued to the second culvert and went under the road in the other direction, emerging once again into the *seguia*. Behind him several men had gathered at the entrance to the first culvert. One of them was on his knees, his head and shoulders inside the opening.

He now set out for the house in a straight line across the open ground, keeping his eye on the clump of palms beside it. The sun had just come up, and the stones began to cast long bluish shadows. All at once a small boy appeared from behind some nearby palms, saw him, and opened his eyes and mouth wide with fear. He was so close that Allal went straight to him and bit him in the leg. The boy ran wildly toward the group of men in the *seguia*.

Allal hurried on to the house, looking back only as he reached the hole between the mud bricks. Several men were running among the trees toward him. Swiftly he glided through into the alcove. The brown body still lay near the door. But there was no time, and Allal needed time to get back to it, to lie close to its head and say: Come here.

As he stared out into the room at the body, there was a great pounding on the door. The boy was on his feet at the first blow, as if a spring had been released, and Allal saw with despair the expression of total terror in his face, and the eyes with no mind behind them. The boy stood panting, his fists clenched. The door opened and some of the men peered inside. Then with a roar the boy lowered his head and rushed through the doorway. One of the men reached out to seize him, but lost his balance and fell. An instant later all of them turned and began to run through the palm grove after the naked figure.

Even when, from time to time, they lost sight of him, they could hear the screams, and then they would see him, between the palm trunks, still running. Finally he stumbled and fell face downward. It was then that they caught him, bound him, covered his nakedness, and took him away, to be sent one day soon to the hospital at Berrechid.

That afternoon the same group of men came to the house to carry out the search they had meant to make earlier. Allal lay in the alcove, dozing. When he awoke, they were already inside. He turned and crept to the hole. He saw the man waiting out there, a club in his hand.

The rage always had been in his heart; now it burst forth. As if his body were a whip, he sprang out into the room. The men nearest him were on their hands and knees, and Allal had the joy of pushing his fangs into two of them before a third severed his head with an axe.

In the Red Room

When I had a house in Sri Lanka, my parents came out one winter to see me. Originally I had felt some qualms about encouraging their visit. Any one of several things—the constant heat, the unaccustomed food and drinking water, even the presence of a leprosy clinic a quarter of a mile from the house—might easily have an adverse effect on them in one way or another. But I had underestimated their resilience; they made a greater show of adaptability than I had thought possible, and seemed entirely content with everything. They claimed not to mind the lack of running water in the bathrooms, and regularly praised the curries prepared by Appuhamy, the resident cook. Both of them being in their seventies, they were not tempted by the more distant or inaccessible points of interest. It was enough for them to stay around the house reading, sleeping, taking twilight dips in the ocean, and going on short trips along the coast by hired car. If the driver stopped unexpectedly at a shrine to sacrifice a coconut, they were delighted, and if they came upon a group of elephants lumbering along the road, the car had to be parked some distance up ahead, so that they could watch them approach and file past. They had no interest in taking photographs, and this spared me what is perhaps the most taxing duty of a cicerone: the repeated waits while the ritual between man and machine is observed. They were ideal guests.

Colombo, where all the people I knew lived, was less than a hundred miles away. Several times we went up for weekends, which I arranged with friends by telephone beforehand. There we had tea on the wide verandas of certain houses in Cinnamon Gardens, and sat at dinners with professors from the University, Protestant ministers, and assorted members of the government. (Many of the Sinhalese found it strange that I should call my parents by their first names, Dodd and Hannah; several of them inquired if I were actually their son or had been adopted.) These weekends in the city were hot and exhausting, and they were always happy to get back to the house, where they could change into comfortable clothing.

One Sunday not long before they were due to return to America, we decided to take in the horse races at Gintota, where there are also some botanical gardens that Hannah wanted to see. I engaged rooms at the New Oriental in Galle and we had lunch there before setting out.

As usual, the events were late in starting. It was the spectators, in any case, who were the focus of interest. The phalanx of women in their shot-silk saris moved Hannah to cries of delight. The races themselves were something of a disappointment. As we left the grounds, Dodd said with satisfaction: It'll be good to get back to the hotel and relax.

But we were going to the Botanical Gardens, Hannah reminded him. I'd like to have just a peek at them.

Dodd was not eager. Those places cover a lot of territory, you know, he said.

We'll just look inside and come out again, she promised.

The hired car took us to the entrance. Dodd was tired, and as a result was having a certain amount of difficulty in walking. The last year or so I find my legs aren't always doing exactly what I want 'em to do, he explained.

You two amble along, Hannah told us. I'll run up ahead and find out if there's anything to see.

We stopped to look up at a clove tree; its powerful odor filled the air like a gas. When we turned to continue our walk, Hannah was no longer in sight. We went on under the high vegetation, around a curve in the path, looked ahead, and still there was no sign of her.

What does your mother think she's doing? The first thing we know she'll be lost.

She's up ahead somewhere.

Soon, at the end of a short lane overhung by twisted lianas, we saw her, partially hidden by the gesticulating figure of a Sinhalese standing next to her.

What's going on? Dodd hastened his steps. Run over there, he told me, and I started ahead, walking fast. Then I saw Hannah's animated smile, and slowed my pace. She and the young man stood in front of a huge bank of brown spider orchids.

Ah! I thought we'd lost you, I said.

Look at these orchids. Aren't they incredible?

Dodd came up, nodded at the young man, and examined the display of flowers. They look to me like skunk cabbage, he declared.

The young man broke into wild laughter. Dodd stared at him.

This young man has been telling me the history of the garden, Hannah began hurriedly. About the opposition to it, and how it finally came to be planted. It's interesting.

The Sinhalese beamed triumphantly. He wore white flannels and a crimson blazer, and his sleek black hair gave off a metallic-blue glint in the sunlight.

Ordinarily I steer a determined course away from the anonymous person who tries to engage me in conversation. This time it was too late; encouraged by Hannah, the stranger strolled beside her, back to the main path. Dodd and I exchanged a glance, shrugged, and began to follow along behind.

Somewhere up at the end of the gardens a pavilion had been built under the high rain trees. It had a veranda where a few sarong-draped men reclined in long chairs. The young man stopped walking. Now I invite you to a cold ginger beer.

Oh, Hannah said, at a loss. Well, yes. That would be nice. I'd welcome a chance to sit down.

Dodd peered at his wristwatch. I'll pass up the beer, but I'll sit and watch you.

We sat and looked out at the lush greenness. The young man's conversation leapt from one subject to another; he seemed unable to follow any train of thought farther than its inception. I put this down as a bad sign, and tried to tell from the inflections of Hannah's voice whether she found him as disconcerting as I did.

Dodd was not listening. He found the heat of low-country Ceylon oppressive, and it was easy to see that he was tired. Thinking I might cover up the young man's chatter, I turned to Dodd and began to talk about whatever came into my head: the resurgence of mask making in Ambalangoda, devil dancing, the high incidence of crime among the fishermen converted to Catholicism. Dodd listened, but did no more than move his head now and then in response.

Suddenly I heard the young man saying to Hannah: I have just the house for you. A godsend to fill your requirements. Very quiet and protected.

She laughed. Mercy, no! We're not looking for a house. We're only going to be here a few weeks more.

I looked hard at her, hoping she would take my glance as a warning against going on and mentioning the place where she was staying. The young man was not paying attention, in any case. Quite all right. You are not buying houses. But you should see this house and tell your friends. A superior investment, no doubt about that. Shall I introduce myself, please? Justus Gonzag, called Sonny by friends.

His smile, which was not a smile at all, gave me an unpleasant physical sensation.

Come anyway. A five-minute walk, guaranteed. He looked searchingly at Hannah. I intend to give you a book of poems. My own. Autographed for you with your name. That will make me very happy.

Oh, Hannah said, a note of dismay in her voice. Then she braced herself and smiled. That would be lovely. But you understand, we can't stay more than a minute.

There was a silence. Dodd inquired plaintively: Can't we go in the car, at least?

Impossible, sir. We are having a very narrow road. Car can't get through. I am arranging in a jiffy. He called out. A waiter came up, and he addressed him in Sinhalese at some length. The man nodded and went inside. Your driver is now bringing your car to this gate. Very close by.

This was going a little too far. I asked him how he thought anyone was going to know which car was ours.

No problem. I was present when you were leaving the Pontiac. Your driver is called Wickramasinghe. Up-country resident, most reliable. Down here people are hopeless.

I disliked him more each time he spoke. You're not from around here? I asked him.

No, no! I'm a Colombo chap. These people are impossible scoundrels. Every one of the blighters has a knife in his belt, guaranteed.

When the waiter brought the check, he signed it with a rapid flourish and stood up. Shall we be going on to the house, then?

No one answered, but all three of us rose and reluctantly moved off with him in the direction of the exit gate. The hired car was there; Mr. Wickramasinghe saluted us from behind the wheel.

The afternoon heat had gone, leaving only a pocket here and there beneath the trees where the air was still. Originally the lane where we were walking had been wide enough to admit a bullock cart, but the vegetation encroaching on each side had narrowed it to little more than a footpath.

At the end of the lane were two concrete gateposts with no gate between them. We passed through, and went into a large compound bordered on two sides by ruined stables. With the exception of one small ell, the house was entirely hidden by high bushes and flowering trees. As we came to a doorway the young man stopped and turned to us, holding up one finger. No noises here, isn't it? Only birds.

It was the hour when the birds begin to awaken from their daytime lethargy. An indeterminate twittering came from the trees. He lowered his finger and turned back to the door. Mornings they are singing. Now not.

Oh, it's lovely, Hannah told him.

He led us through a series of dark empty rooms. Here the dhobi was washing the soiled clothing! This is the kitchen, you see? Ceylon style. Only the charcoal. My father was refusing paraffin and gas both. Even in Colombo.

We huddled in a short corridor while he opened a door, reached in, and flooded the space inside with blinding light. It was a small room, made to seem still smaller by having been given glistening crimson walls and ceiling. Almost all the space was filled by a big bed with a satin coverlet of a slightly darker red. A row of straight-backed chairs stood along one wall. Sit down and be comfy, our host advised us.

We sat, staring at the bed and at the three framed pictures on the wall above its brass-spoked headboard: on the left a girl, in the middle our host, and on the right another young man. The portraits had the imprecision of passport photographs that have been enlarged many times their original size.

Hannah coughed. She had nothing to say. The room gave off a cloying scent of ancient incense, as in a disused chapel. The feeling of absurdity I got from seeing us sitting there side by side, wedged in between the bed and the wall, was so powerful that it briefly paralyzed my mental processes. For once the young man was being silent; he sat stiffly, looking straight ahead, like someone at the theater.

Finally I had to say something. I turned to our host and asked him if he slept in this room. The question seemed to shock him. Here? he cried, as if the thing were inconceivable. No, no! This house is unoccupied. No one sleeping on the premises. Only a stout chap to watch out at night. Excuse me one moment.

He jumped up and hurried out of the room. We heard his footsteps echo in the corridor and then grow silent. From somewhere in the house there came the sonorous chiming of a grandfather's clock; its comfortable sound made the shiny blood-colored cubicle even more remote and unlikely.

Dodd stirred uncomfortably in his chair; the bed was too close for him to cross his legs. As soon as he comes back, we go, he muttered.

He's looking for the book, I imagine, said Hannah.

We waited a while. Then I said: Look. If he's not back in two minutes, I move we just get up and leave. We can find our way out all right.

Hannah objected, saying it would be unpardonable.

Again we sat in silence, Dodd now shielding his eyes from the glare. When Sonny Gonzag returned, he was carrying a glass of water which he drank standing in the doorway. His expression had altered: he now looked preoccupied, and he was breathing heavily.

We slowly got to our feet. Hannah still looking expectant.

We are going, then? Come. With the empty glass still in his hand he turned off the lights, shut the door behind us, opened another, and led us quickly through a sumptuous room furnished with large divans, Coromandel screens and bronze Buddhas. We had no time to do more than glance from side to side as we followed him. As we went out through the front door, he called one peremptory word back into the house, presumably to the caretaker.

There was a wide unkempt lawn on this side, where a few clumps of high areca palms were being slowly strangled by the sheaths of philodendron roots and leaves that encased their trunks. Creepers had spread themselves unpleasantly over the tops of shrubs like the meshes of gigantic cobwebs. I knew that Hannah was thinking of snakes. She kept her eyes on the ground, stepping carefully from flagstone to flagstone as we followed the exterior of the house around to the stables, and thence out into the lane.

The swift twilight had come down. No one seemed disposed to speak. When we reached the car Mr. Wickramasinghe stood beside it.

Cheery-bye, then, and tell your friends to look for Sonny Gonzag when they are coming to Gintota. He offered his hand to Dodd first, then me, finally to Hannah, and turned away.

They were both very quiet on the way back to Galle. The road was narrow and the blinding lights of oncoming cars made them nervous. During dinner we made no mention of the afternoon.

At breakfast, on the veranda swept by the morning breeze, we felt sufficiently removed from the experience to discuss it. Hannah said: I kept waking up in the night and seeing that awful bed.

Dodd groaned.

I said it was like watching television without the sound. You saw everything, but you didn't get what was going on.

The kid was completely non compos mentis. You could see that a mile away, Dodd declared.

Hannah was not listening. It must have been a maid's room. But why would he take us there? I don't know; there's something terribly depressing about the whole thing. It makes me feel a little sick just to think about it. And that bed!

Well, stop thinking about it, then! Dodd told her. I for one am going to put it right out of my mind. He waited. I feel better already. Isn't that the way the Buddhists do it?

The sunny holiday continued for a few weeks more, with longer trips now to the east, to Tissamaharama and the wild elephants in the Yala Preserve. We did not go to Colombo again until it was time for me to put them onto the plane.

The black weather of the monsoons was blowing in from the southwest as we drove up the coast. There was a violent downpour when we arrived in mid-afternoon at Mount Lavinia and checked into our rooms. The crashing of the waves outside my room was so loud that Dodd had to shut the windows in order to hear what we were saying.

I had taken advantage of the trip to Colombo to arrange a talk with my lawyer, a Telugu-speaking Indian. We were to meet in the bar at the Galleface, some miles up the coast. I'll be back at six, I told Hannah. The rain had abated somewhat when I started out.

Damp winds moved through the lobby of the Galleface, but the smoky air in the bar was stirred only by fans. As I entered, the first person I noticed was Weston of the Chartered Bank. The lawyer had not yet come in, so I stood at the bar with Weston and ordered a whiskey.

Didn't I see you in Gintota at the races last month? With an elderly couple?

I was there with my parents. I didn't notice you.

I couldn't tell. It was too far away. But I saw the same three people later with a local character. What did you think of Sonny Gonzag?

I laughed. He dragged us off to his house.

You know the story, I take it.

I shook my head.

The story, which he recounted with relish, began on the day after Gonzag's wedding, when he stepped into a servant's room and found his bride in bed with the friend who had been best man. How he happened to have a pistol with him was not explained, but he shot them both in the face, and later chopped their bodies into pieces. As Weston remarked: That sort of thing isn't too uncommon, of course. But it was the trial that caused the scandal. Gonzag spent a few weeks in a mental hospital, and was discharged.

You can imagine, said Weston. Political excitement. The poor go to jail for a handful of rice, but the rich can kill with impunity, and that sort of thing. You still see references to the case in the press now and then.

I was thinking of the crimson blazer and the Botanical Gardens. No. I never heard about it, I said.

He's mad as a hatter, but there he is, free to do whatever he feels like. And all he wants now is to get people into that house and show them the room where the great event took place. The more the merrier as far as he's concerned.

I saw the Indian come into the bar. It's unbelievable, but I believe it, I told Weston.

Then I turned to greet the lawyer, who immediately complained of the stale air in the bar. We sat and talked in the lounge.

I managed to get back to Mount Lavinia in time to bathe before dinner. As I lay in the tepid water, I tried to imagine the reactions of Hannah and Dodd when I told them what I had heard. I myself felt a solid satisfaction at knowing the rest of the story. But being old, they might well brood over it, working it up into an episode so unpleasant in retrospect that it stained the memory of their holiday. I still had not decided whether to tell them or not, when I went to their room to take them down to dinner.

We sat as far away from the music as we could get. Hannah had dressed a little more elaborately than usual, and they both were speaking with more than their accustomed animation. I realized that they were happy to be returning to New York. Halfway through the meal they began to review what they considered the highlights of their visit. They mentioned the Temple of the Tooth, the pair of Bengal tiger cubs in Dehiwala which they had petted but regretfully declined to purchase, the Indonesian dinner on Mr. Bultjen's lawn, where the mynah bird had hopped over to Hannah and said: "Eat it up," the cobra under the couch at Mrs. de Sylva's tea party.

And that peculiar young man in the *strange* house, Hannah added meditatively.

Which one was that? asked Dodd, frowning as he tried to remember. Then it came to him. Oh, God, he muttered. Your special friend. He turned to me. Your mother certainly can pick 'em.

Outside, the ocean roared. Hannah seemed lost in thought. *I* know what it was like! she exclaimed suddenly. It was like being shown around one of the temples by a bhikku. Isn't that what they call them?

Dodd sniffed. Some temple! he chuckled.

No, I'm serious. That room had a particular meaning for him. It was like a sort of shrine.

I looked at her. She had got to the core without needing the details.

I felt that, too, I said. Of course, there's no way of knowing.

She smiled. Well, what you don't know won't hurt you.

I had heard her use the expression a hundred times without ever being able to understand what she meant by it, because it seemed so patently untrue. But for once it was apt. I nodded my head and said: That's right.

HISTORICAL TALES

Points in Time

He dreamed of a hawk that hovered. A warning, the others said. And they went down to Asana, and a blind man at the entrance to the city raised his hand and spoke.

Pay heed to the wind that moves above this place. The drums you hear are not of our people, nor are the hands that hit the skins.

He saw the blind man's face and remembered the hawk. Behind the walls and higher were the hills, white and hard against the noonday sky.

And they did not enter Asana, but turned southward over an empty plain, and came to the bank of a river.

Asana was destroyed. Only dust was there.

The Moorish Sultan (who had suffered at Sierra Morena such a defeat by the Spaniards that for several days the victors used no other fuel than the pikes, lances and arrows of their fallen enemies) answered his captors with great dignity that he had lately read the Book of Paul's Epistles, which he liked so much that were he to choose another faith it should be Christianity.

But for his part (Nazarenes have the minds of small children) he thought every man should die in the religion into which he was born. (And this will probably not get through into those pork-nourished brains.) The only fault I find with Paul is that he deserted Judaism, he told them, smiling.

In the course of his travels in Portugal, Fra Andrea of Spoleto had met a man for whom he felt great sympathy, and the man happened to be a Moslem. Heretofore he had not known anyone professing that faith, none having chanced to visit the Franciscan monastery where he had lived, and he was amazed, after an hour's talk with this Moroccan gentleman, to find him not only wholly conversant with Christian doctrine, but actually in accord with certain of its tenets.

They saw one another often during that year. As a result of their growing friendship, Si Musa conceived the idea of inviting Fra Andrea to Fez, in order to set up a small Franciscan mission there. Initially the concept struck the monk as purely a fantasy, and quite unrealizable. Then Si Musa let fall the information that his wife was the sister of King Mohammed VIII who at that time ruled Morocco from Fez.

As you know, His Majesty has had ample opportunity to study the works of the Christians, Si Musa remarked with a wry smile. Fra Andrea nodded; he understood that his friend was referring to the unfortunate king's long incarceration by the Portuguese.

Solitude and study can make a man tolerant, you know, he went on. It would give him great pleasure to have you and your friends in Fez, so that the public could see for itself that not all infidels are savages.

Here Fra Andrea guffawed. Si Musa smiled politely, not understanding the reason for his mirth. It was this very ingenuousness in the Moroccan which delighted the monk, and which doubtless was instrumental in persuading him to accept his unlikely suggestion.

Three years later Fra Andrea arrived in Fez, along with Fra Antonio and Fra Giacomo, two other Franciscans who had gone because they considered it their duty to be on hand in Fez, where they might be able to intercede on behalf of Christian hostages being held for ransom. Fra Andrea was looking forward particularly to having religious discussions with the several Moslem intellectuals to whom Si Musa had given him letters of introduction.

From the moment of their arrival everything went wrong for the three. When Fra Andrea tried to find the men to whom he had the notes, he discovered that they were all mysteriously absent from Fez. The old palace near the Fondouq Nejjarine which Si Musa had assured him would be put at his disposal proved not to be available. Indeed, the mere mention of Si Musa's name brought forth unfriendly stares.

It did not take him long to learn the reason. While they had been en route to Fez a new monarch had been crowned: King Ahmed III. The friars received this news with inexpressive faces, but among themselves they discussed it dolefully, agreeing that it did not bode well for their project.

They were advised to look for a house in Fez Djedid, where foreigners

were not regarded with quite such antipathy as in the Medina. The house
they found was not far from the entrance to the Mellah. It had only three
small rooms, but there was a patio, which they soon filled with potted
plants.

Fra Antonio and Fra Giacomo quickly accustomed themselves to the
static life of their new dwelling. They seemed to be contented in the dreary
little house. But Fra Andrea was restless; he had been counting on passing
long hours in the company of new friends with whom he could talk.

The few excursions he made into the Medina persuaded him that he
would do better to stay out of it. Thus he took to wandering in the Mellah,
where it is true that he was stared at with much the same hostility as in the
Medina, the difference being that he was not afraid of the Jews. He did not
believe that they would attack him physically, even though they must have
felt considerable rancour towards his Church for the recent deportations of
Jews from Spain. Fra Andrea considered theirs a politically motivated
hostility, whereas the hatred he had encountered in the Medina transcended
such considerations. He felt free to walk in the alleys of the Mellah, and to
listen to the Spanish conversation of the passers-by.

One evening as he stood leaning against a wall, enjoying the scraps of
domestic conversation that reached him from inside the houses, a portly
gentleman came along the alley, saw him standing there, and bade him good
evening. Embarrassed at having been caught eavesdropping, Fra Andrea
replied briefly and started to walk away.

The other spoke again, and pointed at a door. This was his house, he
said, and he invited him to come in. Only when the monk stood inside a
well-lighted room did he see that his host was a rabbi.

In this way Fra Andrea came to know Rabbi Harun ben Hamu and to
pay him regular visits. He had found a Moroccan with whom he might
conceivably have religious and metaphysical discussions. Rabbi Harun ben
Hamu was exceedingly courteous, and showed a willingness to engage in
serious conversation, but Fra Andrea felt the need to study the Talmud
carefully before expressing any opinions touching on Judaic law. He could
read Hebrew haltingly, and this small knowledge gained early in life served
him perfectly in his present project.

For more than a year he spent most of his time in intensive study. He
filled a book with notations and learned the Mishnah by heart. During this
time he paid constant visits to the rabbi's house, where eventually he was
presented to two other men, Rabbi Judah ibn Danan and Rabbi Shimon

Saqali. He saw that these two did not entirely accept the presence of an anonymous Christian friar in their midst, and this gave him a powerful desire to impress them. It was hard for him to sit by and be silent when he was so eager to discuss their religion with them, but he was preparing himself for the day when he would be able to meet them on an equal footing in the arena of religious polemics, so he held his tongue.

When he had decided that he knew the Law as well as they knew it, and perhaps understood its relation to Islam and Christianity rather better than they, he determined to speak on the next occasion when they should find themselves together.

He had not been wrong in expecting them to show incredulity and amazement when he began to address them. They listened, nodding their heads slowly, puzzled by his strange metamorphosis. At one point he remarked that the halakkic material had little to do with God, and that even the haggadic midrashim contained no passages dealing with the nature of God.

Rabbi Shimon Saqali stiffened. Every phrase contains an infinite number of meanings, he said.

And an infinite number of meanings is equivalent to no meaning at all! cried Fra Andrea. Then, seeing the expressions on the faces of the three men, he decided to make a joke of it, and laughed, but this seemed only to mystify them.

As the discussion progressed, he found in himself a strong desire to confound them, to confront them with their own contradictions. He had behind him years of practice in the art of theological argument, and this had given him an extraordinary memory. He could recall the exact words which had come from the lips of each man during the evening, and he quoted them accurately, his eye on the one who had uttered them.

Even Rabbi Harun ben Hamu was astounded, not so much by his friend's sudden burst of erudition as by his masterly use of logic. Rabbi Shimon and Rabbi Judah were appalled by Fra Andrea; after he had left they told their host as much. Never before had they been baited and humiliated in such a manner, they declared.

Rabbi Harun, who felt mildly possessive about his foreign friend, tried to reassure them. The Christian meant no offence, he told them. He's not one of us, after all.

Then, as they made no answer, he added: a brilliant man.

Yes, unnaturally brilliant, said Rabbi Judah.

Fra Andrea walked back to his house that night highly satisfied with the effect he had produced upon his listeners. Strangely enough, Rabbi Harun ben Hamu continued to invite the other two rabbis and the monk together, and they continued to meet around his table. After his first indiscretion Fra Andrea was careful not to express his personal opinions regarding the Talmud. The discussions were limited to Christian theology. With his diabolically clever mind and tongue Fra Andrea invariably silenced the others. Rabbi Harun ben Hamu greatly enjoyed being host to these fiery harangues. And little by little he found himself accepting many of the monk's premises. The other two noticed with misgiving his growing tendency to agree with him in small matters. This troubled them, and in private they discussed it.

One evening as they sat around Rabbi Harun ben Hamu's table, Fra Andrea in passing thoughtlessly qualified the Targumim as inaccurate and inexcusably vulgar exegeses. Rabbi Judah smote the table with his fist, but this warning sign escaped Fra Andrea's notice.

The Targum to the Megilloth, for instance, he continued, is a piece of unparalleled nonsense. How can anyone credit such absurdities?

Then with great gusto he proceeded to demolish the Second Targum of Esther, not heeding the pallid rigidity in the faces of both Rabbi Judah and Rabbi Shimon.

All at once Rabbi Judah laid his hand on Rabbi Shimon's arm. As one man they rose and left the house. Fra Andrea ceased to speak, looking to Rabbi Harun for an explanation. But his host was staring straight ahead, an expression of mingled doubt and terror on his face.

Fra Andrea waited. Slowly Rabbi Harun raised his head and as if in supplication pointed to the door. Please, he said.

He did not rise from the table when his guest went out. He understood that the other two rabbis had come to the conclusion that the monk was in league with Satan. Although Rabbi Harun ben Hamu was a fairly learned man, the possibility of such a thing did not seem to him at all unlikely. He resolved that under no circumstances would he see the Christian again.

It never became necessary for him to implement his decision. Two days later all the notables and elders of the Mellah (save Rabbi Harun ben Hamu, whom his colleagues considered to be already contaminated by the power of evil) went in a procession to the palace. There they protested at the presence in Fez of a foreign sorcerer who had been sent to sow discord among their people. They charged Fra Andrea with "conspiracy and the practice of magic."

The Moslems, only too happy to have a pretext for ridding their city of this undesirable Christian, agreed to arrest him.

Fra Andrea was given no opportunity of defending himself against the charges, but was thrown straightway into a cell where they tortured him for a few hours. Finally someone impaled his body on a lance.

Heavy sea and a gale from the east.

An English privateer sailed into the bay at daybreak. We dispatched four men to bring the ship into harbour. Then we all went quickly to the shore at the foot of the cliffs and waited.

When the prow hit the reef we swam out and climbed aboard. Some of the passengers dived into the water.

The captain and the crew were on deck. This time we had orders to kill as few as possible. We took them all alive save for one English woman who drowned when she jumped overboard.

We had the chains ready, and we drove them ahead of us through Tangier.

That night there was more wind and rain, and our tents were spread on the sand at the edge of the Oued Tahadartz.

Three at a time we brought in the crew, and they sat with their chains in our tent.

Abdeslam ben Larbi spoke with them in their tongue. Embrace the true faith, and you need not be slaves.

A few screamed curses, but the rest agreed.

They were poor youths, not likely to be ransomed.

During the last hour of darkness they were unshackled and silently taken across the river. We did not see them again.

When daybreak came we set out with our captives. To be safe, we took away their heavy footgear. They walked barefoot like us, and protested greatly, claiming that it caused them much pain.

Each day more of the prisoners had bloody and swollen feet. Some could no longer walk, and we left them behind. Had it taken many days more to reach Meknes, we should have lost them all.

The sound of the sea on the wind blowing through the streets of Essaouira today is the same as it was two hundred years ago, when Andrew Layton had a small exporting business there, together with two Frenchmen, Messieurs Secard and Barre. The three men often set out on their horses into the countryside roundabout, Layton's greyhounds accompanying them. There were very few Europeans in the town, so that these excursions had become their favourite pastime.

One day the three, along with a clerk who worked in their office, went out of the town on their horses. To escape the wind they rode inland, rather than skirting the dunes to the south. Their route led them past several small Chleuh villages. The dogs raced here and there across the scrubland. They passed a hamlet where men and women were working in the fields, while cows grazed nearby. The greyhounds rushed onto the scene and made a concerted attack upon the cattle. As a calf fell, a farmer in the field raised his gun and shot one of the dogs. The others scattered.

The Europeans had seen. They rode up and dismounted, but before they had even begun to speak, the field-workers were hurling stones at them. Monsieur Barre received the most serious bruises. A general mêlée ensued, in the course of which Layton and his associates made free use of their riding-whips. Then they turned and galloped back to Essaouira in a state of high indignation. The occurrence was unusual, and by their standards, outrageous. They went immediately to see the Pacha.

To appease the Europeans, with whom he was on friendly terms, the Pacha first advised them henceforth to ride southward along the beach, notwithstanding the wind, rather than going inland past the villages. Then he agreed to call in the offending farmers. The following day a large group of them appeared in the town. They were in a state of great excitement, and straightway began a frenzied clamour for retribution. A village woman was missing two teeth, which she insisted that Layton had broken. Again and again the villagers called, in the name of Allah and the Prophet, for justice.

Perplexed by the turn events had taken, the Pacha decided to refer the matter to the Sultan. In due course a reply came from His Majesty, ordering all the parties concerned to report to the palace at Marrakech.

At the hearing, which finally took place in the presence of the Sultan, Layton was ingenuous enough to give a straightforward account of the incident. Included was his admission that he had struck the woman in the face with the butt of his whip, thus breaking two of her incisors. He offered to make monetary payment, but the villagers were adamant in their refusal.

They had not come to Marrakech expecting money, they declared. What they demanded was precise retaliation: Layton must furnish them with two of his own teeth. Nothing else was acceptable.

Since the peasants were within their rights in asking that the law of the land be applied, the Sultan had no choice but to order the extractions to be performed then and there. The official tooth-puller stepped forward, ready to start. Layton, although considerably disconcerted, had the presence of mind to ask that the teeth to be pulled be two molars which recently had been giving him trouble. The complainants agreed to the suggestion. Back teeth being larger and heavier than front teeth, they felt that they were getting the better of the bargain.

The operation went ahead under the intent scrutiny of the villagers. They were waiting to hear the infidel's cries of pain. Layton, however, preserved a stoical silence throughout the ordeal. The molars were washed and presented to the claimants, who went away entirely satisfied.

The Sultan had watched the proceedings with growing interest, and he arranged to hold a private conversation with Layton on the following day, when he apologized, at the same time expressing his admiration for the Englishman's fortitude. He could scarcely do less, he said, than agree to grant whatever favour his guest might ask of him.

Layton replied that he desired only that the permit to export a cargo of wheat from Essaouira be expedited. His modesty and candour impelled the monarch to take a personal interest in him, and the two became fast friends.

It was the Emperor's hope that Layton might eventually be persuaded to accept the post of British Consul in Marrakech. There at least, he argued, he would not have to contend with the wind. But the prospect did not appeal to Layton, who preferred to continue his life at Essaouira with his horses and dogs. He had got used to the wind, he said.

Whenever his own tribe won a victory in a battle with another tribe, Si Abdallah el Hassoun inwardly rejoiced. At the same time he considered this pleasure a base emotion, one unworthy of him. Thus, to fortify his sanctity he bade farewell to his students and went to live in Slâ, which is by the sea.

It was not long before the divinity students of his school sent several of their number to Si Abdallah, imploring him to return to them. Without replying, the saint led them to the rocks at the edge of the sea.

How turbulent the water is! he exclaimed. The students agreed. Then Si Abdallah filled a jar with the water and set it on a rock. Yet the water in here is still, he said, pointing at the jar. Why?

A student answered: Because it has been taken out of the place where it was.

Now you see why I must stay here, Si Abdallah said.

For thousands of afternoons in the Fondouq Askour, while the whores squabbled and shrieked in the courtyard outside his room, Sidi Moussa ed Douqqali worked at his obsessive task. He hoped to make asphodel stalks edible, but he died without having succeeded.

Sidi bel Abbes es Sebti was only fifteen when, realizing that he was a saint, he went to Marrakech to live a saint's life. For forty years he walked through the streets of the medina, wearing only a pair of serrouelles, while he extolled the virtues of poverty. He was known for the foul language he used in upbraiding those who took issue with him.

Sidi Belyout, tamer of wild beasts, was never to be seen without his entourage of pet lions. And Sidi Abderrahman el Mejdoub, who dealt in epigram and prophecy, was not only a saint. He was also mentally deranged, thus in direct natural contact with the source of all knowledge.

Along the Oued Tensift beyond the walls, there were caves that had been hollowed in the red earth cliffs. The entrance to Sidi Youssef's cave was protected by high thorn bushes and could not be seen from the river. He sought solitude, and although he was known for his great holiness, the people of Marrakech granted him his privacy, for he had leprosy. He claimed that the disease had been conferred upon him by Allah as a reward for his piety. When pieces of his flesh caught on the thorns and remained hanging there, he gave heartfelt thanks for these extra proofs of divine favour.

A century and a half ago, in one of the twisting back streets of the Mellah in Fez, there lived a respectable couple, Haim and Simha Hachuel. There would be no record of them today had their daughter Sol not been favoured with exceptional beauty.

Since Jewish girls were free to walk in the streets unveiled, the beauty of Sol Hachuel soon became legendary throughout the city.

Moslem youths climbed up from the Medina to stroll through the Mellah in the hope of catching sight of Sol on her way to a fountain to fetch water.

Having seen her once, Mohammed Zrhouni came each day and waited until she appeared, merely to gaze upon her. Later he spoke with her, and still later suggested that they marry.

Sol's parents rejected the idea outright: it would entail her abandonment of Judaism.

The Zrhouni family likewise strongly disapproved: they did not want a Jewess in the house, and they believed, like most Moslems, that no Jew's conversion to Islam could be considered authentic.

Mohammed was not disposed in any case to take a Moslem bride, since that would involve accepting the word of his female relatives as to the girl's desirability; by the time he was finally able to see her face, he would already be married to her. Since the considerations of his family would necessarily be based on the bride-price, he strongly doubted that any girl chosen by them could equal the jewel he had discovered in the Mellah.

For her part, Sol was infatuated with her Moslem suitor. Her parents' furious tirades only increased the intensity of her obsession. Like Mohammed, she saw no reason to let herself be swayed by the opinions of her elders.

The inevitable occurred: she went out of the house one day and did not return. Mohammed covered her with a haik and went with her down into the Medina and across the bridge to his parents' house in the Keddane.

Mohammed lived with his mother, aunts and sisters, his father having died the previous year. Out of deference to him the women of the household received his bride with correctness, if not enthusiasm, and the wedding, with its explicit conversion of the bride to Islam, was performed.

His mother remarked in an aside to Mohammed that at least the bride had cost nothing, and he understood that this was the principal reason for her grudging acceptance of Sol as her daughter-in-law.

Almost immediately Sol realized that she had made an error. Although she was conversant with Moslem customs, it had not occurred to her that she would be forbidden ever to go outside the Zrhouni house.

When she remonstrated with Mohammed, saying that she needed to go out for a walk in the fresh air, he answered that it was common knowledge that a woman goes out only three times during her life: once when she is born and leaves her mother's womb, once when she marries and leaves her father's house, and once when she dies and leaves this world. He advised her to walk on the roof like other women.

The aunts and sisters, instead of coming little by little to accept Sol as a member of the family, made her feel increasingly like an interloper. They whispered among themselves and grew silent when they saw her approaching.

The months went by. Sol pleaded to be allowed to visit her mother and father. They could not come to see her, since the house would be profaned by their presence.

It seemed unjust to Sol that women were not allowed to enter the mosque; if only it had been possible to go with Mohammed and pray, her life would have been easier to bear. She missed the regular visits to the synagogue where she sat upstairs with her mother and listened to her father as he chanted below with the other men.

The Zrhouni house had become a prison, and she resolved to escape from it. Accordingly, one day when she had managed to get hold of the key to the outer door, she wrapped herself in her haik and quietly slipped out into the street. Not looking to right or to left, she hurried up the Talâa to the top, and then set out for the Mellah.

The happiness in the Hachuel home lasted one day. Enraged and humiliated by his wife's dereliction, Mohammed had gone directly to the ulema and told them the story. They listened, consulted together, and declared his wife to be guilty of apostasy from Islam.

On the following afternoon a squad of mokhaznia pounded on the door of the house in the Mellah, and amid shrieks and lamentations, seized the girl. They pulled her out of the house and dragged her through the streets of Fez Djedid, with a great crowd following behind.

Outside Bab Segma the crowd spread out and formed a circle. Screaming and struggling against the ropes that bound her, Sol was forced to kneel in the dust.

A tall mokhazni unsheathed his sword, raised it high in the air, and beheaded her.

Days of less substance than the nights that slipped between. And in the streets they whispered: Where is he?

The murmuring filled the souq at sunset as the goods were stacked away. In irons. In Fez.

Abdeljbar.

Raised eyebrows, swift smiles, nods of understanding. For when the Riffians had burned a Nazarene ship, Sultan Abderrahman, hoping to placate the owners, had sent his soldiers to the Rif. They went directly to the caids and cheikhs, offering silver *reales* in exchange for the names of the guilty ones.

In the town where Cheikh Abdeljbar lived there was a youth named El Aroussi, admired by everyone for the strength in his body and the beauty of his features. For some unexplained reason Cheikh Abdeljbar detested the young man, and this was the subject of many discussions in the souq. It was difficult to find the cause of his hostility.

Those who most disliked the cheikh said it was probable that at some time El Aroussi had repulsed the older man's attempts to seduce him. Others believed that, being of a jealous disposition, the cheikh could not forgive the youth for the many qualities Allah had bestowed upon him—particularly those qualities which made the girls and women wait for hours behind their lattices in order to see him walk by. People admired El Aroussi; they did not admire the cheikh.

El Aroussi knew nothing of the burned ship, and the cheikh was quite aware of this. All the same he named the youth as one of the raiders. El Aroussi was manacled and dragged off to a dungeon in Fez.

There in the Rif injustice was the daily bread. Everyone in the town knew what had happened, and everyone whispered. El Aroussi was a hero. The people were certain he would escape.

Time proved them right. Less than a year later the rumour was going around that he was in Tangier. Probably it did not reach the ears of Cheikh Abdeljbar. Perched above the town in his towers, he spoke only with men of importance, like himself.

The cheikh was ambitious. He hoped to marry his daughter Rahmana to the son of the Pacha of Slâ.

Included among his lands there was a castle on an estate in the Gharb, not far from Slâ, where he decided to take his family for a visit.

El Aroussi had indeed escaped from his confinement in Fez. He returned to his native town, where the people in the streets welcomed him, and commiserated with him for the unjust treatment he had received.

He listened impatiently, almost seeming not to hear them. He had grown bitter and silent. He was obliged to avenge himself against the cheikh. No other course of action was open to him. But the cheikh had gone to the Gharb.

As El Aroussi sat brooding one evening in his father's house, he came upon an idea as to how he might proceed. He knew it would be necessary for him to go and stay, perhaps for many months, in the vicinity of the castle near Slâ, but having no access to money, he could see no way of keeping alive during the time of waiting. Now, however, he thought he had the solution.

The following morning he sought out his friends and put the question to them: would they be willing to go with him and live as bandits in the Forest of Mamora while they waited to carry out the attack upon Cheikh Abdeljbar?

In the end he recruited more than two dozen young men, all of them eager to help him clear his honour.

During the months while Cheikh Abdeljbar was making repeated visits to Slâ, as the arrangements for the forthcoming wedding slowly took form, El Aroussi and his friends lost no time in becoming the fiercest band of brigands in the region. The terror they caused throughout the Gharb was understandable, for they thought it safer to kill their victims before robbing them.

For generations the Forest of Mamora had been notorious as a robber-infested region. The outlaws raided the convoys of those unwise enough to pass within easy striking distance of the forest itself. If Cheikh Abdeljbar had spoken with the peasants working on his land, he might have been able to identify the new bandit chief from descriptions of his person in the gossip that was on everyone's lips. But the cheikh was far too busy in Slâ settling the bride-price with the pacha, and the details of the wedding-feast with his future son-in-law, Sidi Ali.

And Rahmana lay among the cushions swallowing pellets of almond paste with sesame and honey, while maidservants massaged her body with creams and oils.

Guests began to arrive at the castle several days before the wedding feast. On the final night the entire party, led by the bride and groom, set out on horseback in a torchlit procession for Slâ, where the festivities would be continued at the palace of the pacha when they arrived on the following day.

Their way led through a countryside of boulders and high cactus. The moon gave great clarity, and a cold sharp wind ran westward. There were songs, accompanied only by the hoofbeats of a hundred horses.

As they passed between the walls of a winding gorge, a great voice suddenly sounded from somewhere among the rocks nearby.

Ha huwa! El Aroussi!

There was a second's silence, and then the noise of thirty rifles firing into the procession from above.

In the stampede over the bodies of horses and men that followed, only the bridegroom was aware of the horseman who appeared from behind a boulder and rode straight at the bridal couple, at the last instant lifting Rahmana from her mount, and disappearing with her at a gallop into the night.

Cheikh Abdeljbar was unhurt. He and his son-in-law continued to Slâ and consulted with the pacha.

A few days later the Sultan sent soldiers to help the wronged father and husband. Cheikh Abdeljbar and Sidi Ali had taken a solemn oath to search for Rahmana until they found her.

On many occasions as they rode with the soldiers they had glimpses of the bandits just before they vanished into the depths of the forest. There were skirmishes in which both sides bore losses, but the leader was never seen among his henchmen.

It took more than a year for the soldiers to encircle the densest region of the forest. Those of El Aroussi's followers who were left had seen the danger in time and fled.

The weeks went by, while the Sultan's soldiers drew an always tightening ring around the part of the forest from which they were sure El Aroussi had not escaped.

It was Sidi Ali's dogs that finally led to his discovery. They found him in a cave by the edge of a stream, his body wasted with hunger, his face haggard and scarred.

They trussed him and took him to one of the tents at the campsite, where they dumped him onto the ground.

Then Sidi Ali squatted down, drew his dagger, and slowly amputated all ten of the captive's toes, tossing them one by one into El Aroussi's face.

When he had finished with this task, he withdrew to another tent to confer with Cheikh Abdeljbar on the form of death to provide for their prisoner the next morning.

They sat up half the night diverting themselves and each other with suggestions which grew increasingly more grotesque.

By the time the cheikh rose to retire to his own tent, he was in favour of cutting a horizontal line around El Aroussi's waist and then flaying him, pulling the skin upwards over his head and eventually twisting it around his neck to strangle him.

This did not seem sufficiently drastic to Sidi Ali, who thought it would be more fitting to cut off his ears and nose and force him to swallow them, then to slash open his stomach, pull them out and make him swallow them again, and so on, for as long as he remained alive.

The older man reflected for a moment. Then, wishing his son-in-law a pleasant night, he said that with Allah's consent they would continue their discussion in the morning.

The dialogue was never resumed. During the black hour before dawn, the cheikh awoke, frozen by the sound of a voice that cried: *Ha huwa!* El Aroussi!

The cheikh sprang up and rushed out. The prisoner's tent was empty. He ran to Sidi Ali's tent. The young man lay dead. A spear was buried in his eye.

As the cheikh stood staring down in disbelief, there was the sound of a horse's hoofbeats outside. They grew fainter and were gone. El Aroussi had mounted the cheikh's own steed and ridden off on it.

The next morning, after washing and burying Sidi Ali (for they could not carry his body as far as Slâ), Cheikh Abdeljbar and the soldiers set out once more in pursuit.

Before noon they met the horse walking slowly in their direction, its saddle and flanks smeared with blood. The cheikh dismounted and ran to get astride it, turning it and making it retrace its steps. The forest was dense and difficult to push through, but the animal seemed to know its way.

They came soon to a small clearing where a rude hut had been built. The door was open.

Cheikh Abdeljbar stood in the doorway, trying to see into the dark interior. El Aroussi lay supine on the floor. It was clear that he was dead.

Then the cheikh saw the girl crouching by the body, while she kissed the stumps of El Aroussi's toes, one by one. He called her name, already fearful that she would not respond.

She did not seem to hear her father's outcry. When he lifted her up to embrace her, she stared at him and drew away. The soldiers were obliged to bind her in order to get her out of the hut and onto the horse with her father.

Cheikh Abdeljbar took Rahmana back to the Castle of Mamora. He hoped that with the passage of time she would cease her constant calling out of El Aroussi's name.

One day when she was in the garden, she found a gate unlocked, and quickly stepped outside. What happened to her after that is a mystery, for she was not seen again. The people of the countryside claimed that she had returned to the forest in search of El Aroussi. They sang a song about her:

> Days of less substance than the nights that slip
> between
> And Rahmana wanders in the forest, and the branches
> catch her hair.

POEMS

Delicate Song

It was a long trip back.
White lilies waved by walls.
The sweat from blue grapes
Shone like glass.
A wind blown straight from the harbor
Brushed the long grass.
I suppose we thought of the harbor
And of how it looked with its blue water
And its sailboats moving.

But even though the wind smelt of the waves
And of the swamp grass nearer
Our thoughts were of the road.

Flutes are scarcer these days
And flutists are unskilled.
The white lilies were by walls.

No Village

I

What tentacles of clematis have been declared? The ashes of dawn are in a million throats, and a thousand motors press upon the heart. Into the lavender crevices of evening the otters have been pushed, and slowly rises the one dark fume of the lake. Kill this unswerving figure. Into what green halls has it been led? Under what long hills has it smothered softly during the night? In the dark the yards at the edge of the jungle are hot. Panthers move dankly on wet leaves and the breath of the trees falls heavily in festoons of fetid mist. On the earth all is laughter. Where have you led me, Astrea? Are the hills always as remote as they are this night? Is every lane as cold as your finger? There will be no more declarations. There can be no hour uncounted. The floor of the garden will heave silently and in the sea nearby there will be a great explosion. Lava from the beaches will congeal to form starfish and all the universe will be submerged in a sea of fire-coral. Seawrack will twist to choke the throats of poets and the moon rising from behind the lagoon of phosphorus will blind the armadillos. Each crystal hill will shiver into a home for octopi. I shall hear no more the drip of whaleblood on the floor of the cabin. The wind in the trees will linger but a while. All the fronds of the climbing vines at the pane will shrivel to shrill music and the ants will perform a subterranean adagio. No hands will celebrate the ritual with mystery.

II

Carrion in the noon field, shame the vultures. They have awakened me from sleep. Flies that hum in sedge beneath the linden, there is no retreat. There is no more conversation. The fruit in the meadow is drying in the drought, and the brook that whispers somewhere under the witchgrass moves but seldom. Mud, rise from your limestone bed in the gulley, come to me, smear me with coolth. Mountains that flock on the far horizon, camels of the eastern plains, chase no more the long cirrus. Over the ashtrees listen no longer to the laughter of starflowers.

III

A flamingo plunges into the pool and the silk curtain ripples into the chamber. Glow-worms light the terrace. The walls die slowly with the moonset. No light shines into the room. The wind sobs in the tangle of weeds beneath the window. Plant stalks creak one against the other and the fountain is nauseated beside the marble basin. There is a constellation above the wilderness. A cry hurtles through the midnight. I disappear, a black meteor over the moor. The remnants of the manor groan far away in the copse. A shore of guitar-rhythms dances ahead. Oil slakes the noonday thirst. A clamor of womanvoices moves the sky and owls creep into hollow trees in the clearings of the forest. Tambourines wreak tears from children and bangles tinkle in the tents. The day has turned inside out. In the valley the firtrees crack and the glaciers sigh. The chateau crumbles into the ravine and the feet of wolves form a rallentando over the snowcrust. The church-steeple sways and fruitrinds roll down the gutter. The public square sinks into a delirium as memories crash against pale ceilings. Astrea! A glass crocodile rips the quivering morning into a bloody face. Serpents proclaim the heat of strawberries and the hospital rises into a falsehood. Olive trees line the hillside and the bakeries smile with odors. Astrea! Have I died in this room this evening? Lice swarm on my hands and the ignus fatuus on the heather runs before me. Disappearance has become a failure. Cattle low by the saltlick at the end of the lane. My teeth grind caraway seeds as I stare at the hawks where the hill begins. Astrea! Long ago the roses climbed to the top of the vine. I shall never forget this dream, broken smoke of my suburbs. Return. One more cry, before my throat splits across and my heart gushes from my forehead. One more cry while I exist a cube in this hollow, while the moon sinks still, behind the end of the garden. While the leaves tremble with tears of my joy. One more cry, Astrea, while still the poolwater circles from the splash and the hyenas plunder the cemetery. Rub out the walls of this chamber and touch my cheek with a fingernail. Scream that the marshes shall not have me.

I V

Now the sun will reach this rock, but the music of the glen will remain a monotone between the cliffs. You have brought me deep into this place and no one remains here but two souls. The sun cooks the hemlock needles above the shale and your hand, your hand lies on the bank, nearing the sunlight. Leeches writhe anchored to the streambed and your arms already shine silver in the sun. And ever more distinctly the one tone of the glen is heard, heard now below the cliffs. Soon the sun will shade patterns on your shoulders, on your back. The sheen of your back will blind the birds above and the sun will race across the sky to the night. Slowly we shall leave behind the sound of continuous water, forgetting that we have existed. The ferns will scatter clouds of spores and a harmony of quiet will burst from our warm lips. Do you doubt? The sun knows your hair, and wild raspberries fall down the bank at my feet. The glen hums and a dragonfly disappears. Where in the forest could I see a yellow bird were it not for your watchful eyes? When could I spot savory mushrooms pushing from old leaves and dry needles had you not a delicate sense? Had I not you, of what avail would be the path to the glen? The sallow late sky shrieks as a locomotive crawls across the canyon. Three lizards hurry to hide beneath flat stones and you move your arm out of the pale sunlight. Jewelweed bursts to remind the landscape of cows plashing in pastures after rain. A toad squats by a stone and milkweed down sails over our heads. You have brought me deep into this place and there is no retreat. Even at night there will be no respite. The monotone of water travelling on circular clouds under pebbles will continue; the water will rush.

V

On the far pampas the hurricane withers the gourdvines. The mockingbird shrivels in the hedge and reeds no longer sprout by morass. At the border of the alkali lake the sassafras droops. Tiny tornados of dust pattern the land and the acid air is a concavity. The locusts have broken their oboes and under the arch where the cataract hurried it is still. Plantain stems are snapped by the wind and the mudflats near the bay crackle. The odor of limetrees becomes an axiom. A red star flames above the mountainridge and the trestle shakes with the weight of its light. A wagon rumbles on the clay road beyond the knoll. In the pumice cave where the fungus forms a carpet the serpent eggs ripen, and the wind dips into the canal. Dynamite blasts the quarry and the foxes listen from the moor. Strike, bell in the tower, and we shall see the rings of petalled light that scatter outward. The centipede runs along the ditch and the eagles wheel above the plum-orchard. The afternoon is wind-driven across the desert. The cathedral drops into the dusk.

Balconies rattle into fandangos. The sun flies screaming through fire-flooded streets. Ulcerlipped women seek refuge in blazing basements. The ape is seared upon the branch and worms draw up into knots. The palms in the plaza smoulder and the beggar is scorched. Smoke girdles the panorama and the wing of the moth is singed. Across the mountain highway bugle notes are cries of pain. The markets are filled with ashes and sparks spatter upon the hillside. Tunnels belch cinders and the crickets utter a finale. Chasms glow red from great distances and the typhoon roars above the gulf.

The hand is placed upon the hand and silence holds stars and wind. Thrush notes fall upon the buds behind the brook.

VI

The tarantula claws the clown in frenzy and the lightning streaks through the sickly sky. Astrea, where the statues laugh in pestilence these fingers fall apart. The Malay plantation rots beneath the crescent moon, and where the melonvines run along the field despairing crows reel in flocks. Close your eyes, my little spider in mourning, and ignore the decaying year that fills all the crevasses with heavy pollen. Close those peering eyes and come away into the enigma where the water flows beneath the ground. Cease weeping in garlands of sound. The lichens flatten themselves to the rocks and the mountainwind sweeps the bare summit clean of dust. The shepherd's cry is a faroff spiral against the granite cliff. The steamboat scarcely moves upon the sea and clouds smother the sight. And where the doldrums reign the seaweed floats in soggy rags and chokes the water-surface. The porpoises avoid the coralreefs and the equator cuts the noon into shreds.

Mica shines in the moonlight on the beach and the frogs drone all night in the jungle. In the valley the twigs clink under the falling snow. The salamanders chant a pebblesong on the hill road and the storm advances between the mountains. Astrea, convince me that resolution means an elegy, and say but one word. The night sky, now white, now black, performs a mute miracle above the lowering sleetstorm. The lighthouse sways at the edge of the farthest cliff and a crab crawls into a yellowed skull at low tide. Give me your hand here on the sanddune, and explain to me the wisdom of winter. The gulls disappear into the northeast and the ocean groans darkly grey in the halflight.

VII

The black butterfly wings without sound through the pine woods and the wasp burrows into the loam. Carols are sung at evening and the sun leaves a wake of trembling colors above the hills. The peasant treads the sandy road. A whippoorwill mourns behind the farmhouse and fieldmice creep carefully beneath the grass. Woodsmoke mingles with mist on the heather and the brook runs unseen beneath the thick reeds. A locomotive cries behind distant hills and leaves the valleys full of long sounds. Murmur, bushes in the pasture, and slink, grey cat in undergrowth. The millwheel turns unceasingly and the owl sits in the oaktree waiting for darkness. In the east the moon shows a white horn and a wind spreads from up the valley. A chill moves restlessly over the country and the bat flies drunken by the pond.

VIII

Astrea, I shall tell you the final place where the eyes will rest. The lemontrees line the harbor and the sharktooth is buried in the foam. The noonday sand glitters and sailors enter the squalid cafés. The whistle of a steamboat beyond the promontory is an ague and the redhaired woman eats a tangerine. The yellow pennant shakes in the seawind and the butcher on the sidestreet eats his lunch. In the park the swans croak and barnacles are scraped from the ship's side. The narrow streets shudder with heat as the cactus on the hillside hides the scorpion. The mechanical piano vomits a sour melody. In the patio the fountain dribbles. Stretch, cape, sixteen miles away, and stop the larger tropic waves. The octopus is languid in the aquarium and the lizards run along the gravel by the roses. On the quay the beggar dozes and horses stamp hungrily in the square. The day lunges into the hot afternoon and the wind shrills angrily across the beach. The lighthouse stands a white obelisk and urchins bathe by the causeway at the edge of the town. The girl sobs in the courtyard. Two raging cats rack the air with cries. The wheels on the cobblestones make a presto and from the hill the mountainrange is topped with snow. And in the lazy valley there is no village.

Next to Nothing

At first there was mud, and the sound of breathing.
and no one was sure of where we were.
When we found out, it was much too late.
Now nothing can happen save as it has to happen.
And then I was alone, and it did not matter.
Only because by that time nothing could matter.

The next year there were knifing matches in the stadium.
I think the people are ready for it, the mayor said.
Total involvement. A new concept in sports.
The loser does not leave the ring alive.

But no one can know where he is until he knows where he has
    been.
I sat quietly, and the air changed then, and I looked up.
And the black branches trailing in the living water
stirred slowly with the change of air.
Piropos, you said. El aire les hace piropos.

> Have you change for this banknote?
> It is closed off for the time being.
> Take me to the other end of the city
> where they slice up the sharks on the sand.

> The double tariff applies after sundown.
> It is forbidden to pass beyond this railing.
> Take me to the other end of the city
> where nobody wants to go.

Yes, I said we would need the machine-guns by next March,
but I also warned against saying life was easy.

I mixed hoops and coffins, cradles and needles
while the lights twinkled on far-off Monte Tomás.
We sat in a park that smelled of pine trees,
and that night there were voices in the corridors
and I remembered the empty face of the blind man as he sang.

> Tu misma tienes la culpa
> de lo que has hecho conmigo.

You will find yourself among people.
There is no help for this
nor should you want it otherwise.
The passages where no one waits are dark
and hard to navigate.
The wet walls touch your shoulders on each side.
When the trees were there I cared that they were there.
And now they are gone, does it matter?
The passages where no one waits go on
and give no promise of an end.
You will find yourself among people,
Faces, clothing, teeth and hair
and words, and many words.
When there was life, I said that life was wrong.
What do I say now? You understand?

> Something is going on these recent days.
> The clouds that lie in trees
> Can skim your head as you run uphill.
> After sunset birds fly down
> push inside the grill and eat the plants.
> Seafog swells across the lowlands
> and the slow ships moan.
>
> Yes, something is going on.
> You said you saw them together
> but they were not together.
>
> Who loves the fog?
> Why do the birds come?
> As to the clouds, you may be innocent.

Living branches trail in black water. Nothing moves.
And how do I know what you are to me?
Our theories are untested. You must not laugh.
We thought there were other ways.
Probably there are, but they are hidden
and we shall never find them.

       What's his name?
       God forbid.
       Where does he live?
       Nobody knows.
       How do we get there?
       Ask the conductor.
       That's his face?
       Nobody knows.
       Now shall I ask him?
       God forbid.

Take me to the other end of the city
where no one knows the difference between you and me.
I went back. I did not find him.
And what do I say now? You understand?

       The woman pointed.
       That's the model we
       should have had with us.
       We thought about it,
       hung back and didn't.

       Wished a thousand times we had.
       But that's the way those things go.

       You never can know
       until afterwards.
       Roads of nothing but
       sharp pebbles and stones.

       And they say there are
       snakes behind the rocks.

You see no snakes but
you know they are there.

And after you've gone
down into seven
empty valleys, one
after the other,

you find that you've been
quietly crying
for the past half hour.
Or at least I did.

Because there was no
connection. No more
connection to any-
thing at all. Nothing.

It might not have been
such an awful trip
if we'd had that one.

The woman pointed.
That's the model we
ought to have chosen.

It will be raining up there by the time you arrive.
Try to get through quickly. The forest's cold green breath
is best left undisturbed, coiled close to the boughs.
In open country again you can breathe.
That is the theory, but our theories are untested.
Things are not the way they were.
How can we be sure? New laws apply,
and who knows the difference between the law and the wind?
And who knows the difference between you and me?
Y tu misma tienes la culpa
de lo que has hecho conmigo.

I should like to see the bottom of the
    fountain.
Do not go too near the edge.
Does this path lead to the artificial lake?
The band concert has been postponed.
Is there a waterfall behind these rocks?
The guardian is not on duty.

I have no idea of what is going to
    happen
or in which parts the pain will be.
We are only in spring, and spring has a
    twisting light.
Spring's images are made of crystal and
    cannot be recalled.
There will be suffering, but you know
    how to coax it.
There will be memories, but they can be
    deflected.
There will be your heart still moving
in the wind that has not stopped flying
    westward,
and you will give a signal. Will someone
    see it?

We thought there were other ways.
The darkness would stay outside.
We are not it, we said. It is not in us.

        Yes, yes, go with her. The old man smiled.
        You will be back. You will not find me.

There was a time when life moved on a straighter line.
We still drank the water from the lake,
and the bucket came up cold
and sweet with the smell of deep water.
The song was everywhere that year, an absurd refrain:
It's only that it seems so long, and isn't.

It's only that it seems so many years,
and perhaps it's one.
When the trees were there I cared that they were there,
and now they are gone.
On our way out we used the path that goes around the swamp.
When we started back the tide had risen.
There was another way, but it was far above and hard to get to.
And so we waited here, and everything is still the same.

There were many things I wanted to say to you
before you left. Now I shall not say them.
Though the light spills onto the balcony
making the same shadows in the same places,
only I can see it, only I can hear the wind
and it is much too loud.

The world seethes with words. Forgive me.
I love you, but I must not think of you.
That is the law. Not everyone obeys it.
Though time moves past and the air is never the same
I shall not change. That is the law, and it is right.

> Yes, yes, I went with her. Yes.
> In the shine of morning and the glow of
>   afternoon.

> Piropos, you said. El tiempo te hace
>   piropos.
> There will never be a way of knowing.
> I did go back. The old man was gone.

> Do no thinking, give no reasons,
> have no sensations, make no apologies.
> The anguish was not real enough,
> the age of terror too short-lived.
> They thought all that was finished, left
>   behind.
> They were sure there must be other
>   ways.

I am the spider in your salad, the bloodsmear on your bread.
I am the rusted scalpel, the thorn beneath your nail.
Some day I shall be of use to you, as you can never be to me.
The goats leap from grave to grave, and nibble at last year's
  thistles.
In the name of something more than nothing, of Sidi Bouayad,
and all who have wisdom and power and art,
I am the wrong direction, the dead nerve-end, the unfinished
  scream.
One day my words may comfort you, as yours can never comfort
  me.

TRAVEL ESSAYS

Africa Minor

It had taken the truck fourteen hours to get from Kerzaz to Adrar and, except for the lunch stop in the oasis of El Aougherout, the old man had sat the whole time on the floor without moving, his legs tucked up beneath him, the hood of his burnoose pulled up over his turban to protect his face from the fine dust that sifted up through the floor. First-class passage on vehicles of the Compagnie Générale Transsaharienne entitled the voyager to travel in the glassed-in compartment with the driver, and that was where I sat, occasionally turning to look through the smeared panes at the solitary figure sitting sedately in the midst of the tornado of dust behind. At lunch, when I had seen his face with its burning brown eyes and magnificent white beard, it had occurred to me that he looked like a handsome and very serious Santa Claus.

The dust grew worse during the afternoon, so that by sunset, when we finally pulled into Adrar, even the driver and I were covered. I got out and shook myself, and the little old man clambered out of the back, cascades of dust spilling from his garments. Then he came around to the front of the truck to speak to the driver, who, being a good Moslem, wanted to get a shower and wash himself. Unfortunately he was a city Moslem as well as being a good one, so that he was impatient with the measured cadence of his countryman's speech and suddenly slammed the door, unaware that the old man's hand was in the way.

Calmly the old man opened the door with his other hand. The tip of his middle finger dangled by a bit of skin. He looked at it an instant, then quietly scooped up a handful of that ubiquitous dust, put the two parts of the finger together and poured the dust over it, saying softly, "Thanks be to Allah." With that, the expression on his face never having changed, he picked up his bundle and staff and walked away. I stood looking after him, full of wonder, and reflecting upon the difference between his behavior and what mine would have been under the same circumstances. To show no outward sign of pain is unusual enough, but to express no resentment against the person who has hurt you seems very strange, and to give thanks to God at such a moment is the strangest touch of all.

Clearly, examples of such stoical behavior are not met every day, or I should not have remembered this one; my experience since then, however, has shown me that it is not untypical, and it has remained with me and become a symbol of that which is admirable in the people of North Africa. "This world we see is unimportant and ephemeral as a dream," they say. "To take it seriously would be an absurdity. Let us think rather of the heavens that surround us." And the landscape is conducive to reflections upon the nature of the infinite. In other parts of Africa you are aware of the earth beneath your feet, of the vegetation and the animals; all power seems concentrated in the earth. In North Africa the earth becomes the less important part of the landscape because you find yourself constantly raising your eyes to look at the sky. In the arid landscape the sky is the final arbiter. When you have understood that, not intellectually but emotionally, you have also understood why it is that the great trinity of monotheistic religions—Judaism, Christianity and Islam—which removed the source of power from the earth itself to the spaces outside the earth—were evolved in desert regions. And of the three, Islam, perhaps because it is the most recently evolved, operates the most directly and with the greatest strength upon the daily actions of those who embrace it.

For a person born into a culture where religion has long ago become a thing quite separate from daily life, it is a startling experience to find himself suddenly in the midst of a culture where there is a minimum of discrepancy between dogma and natural behavior, and this is one of the great fascinations of being in North Africa. I am not speaking of Egypt, where the old harmony is gone, decayed from within. My own impressions of Egypt before Nasser are those of a great panorama of sun-dried disintegration. In any case, she has had a different history from the rest of Mediterranean Africa; she is ethnically and linguistically distinct and is more a part of the Levant than of the region we ordinarily mean when we speak of North Africa. But in Tunisia, Algeria and Morocco there are still people whose lives proceed according to the ancient pattern of concord between God and man, agreement between theory and practice, identity of word and flesh (or however one prefers to conceive and define that pristine state of existence we intuitively feel we once enjoyed and now have lost).

I don't claim that the Moslems of North Africa are a group of mystics, heedless of bodily comfort, interested only in the welfare of the spirit. If you have ever bought so much as an egg from one of them, you have learned that they are quite able to fend for themselves when it comes to money matters. The spoiled strawberries are at the bottom of the basket, the pebbles inextricably mixed with the lentils and the water with the milk, the same as in many other parts of the world, with the difference that if you ask the price of an object in a rural market, they will reply, all in one breath, "Fifty, how much will you give?" I should say that in the realm of *beah o chra* (selling and buying; note that in their minds selling comes first), they are surpassed only by the Hindus, who are less emotional about it and therefore more successful, and by the Chinese, acknowledged masters of the Oriental branch of the science of commerce.

In Morocco you go into a bazaar to buy a wallet and somehow find yourself being propelled toward the back room to look at antique brass and rugs. In an instant you are seated with a glass of mint tea in your hand and a platter of pastries in your lap, while smiling gentlemen modeling ancient caftans and marriage robes parade in front of you, the salesman who greeted you at the door having completely vanished. Later on you may once again ask timidly to see the wallets, which you noticed on display near the entrance. Likely as not, you will be told that the man in charge of wallets is at the moment saying his prayers, but that he will soon be back, and in the meantime would you not be pleased to see some magnificent jewelry from the court of Moulay Ismail? Business is business and prayers are prayers, and both are a part of the day's work.

When I meet fellow Americans traveling about here in North Africa, I ask them, "What did you expect to find here?" Almost without exception, regardless of the way they express it, the answer, reduced to its simplest terms, is: a sense of mystery. They expect mystery, and they find it, since fortunately it is a quality difficult to extinguish all in a moment. They find it in the patterns of sunlight filtering through the latticework that covers the souks, in the unexpected turnings and tunnels of the narrow streets, in the women whose features still go hidden beneath the *litham*, in the secretiveness of the architecture, which is such that even if the front door of a house is open it is impossible to see inside. If they listen as well as look, they find it too in the song the lone camel driver sings by his fire before dawn, in the calling of the muezzins at night, when their voices are like bright beams of sound piercing the silence, and, most often, in the dry beat of the *darbouka*, the hand drum played by the women everywhere, in the great city houses and in the humblest country hut.

It is a strange sensation, when you are walking alone in a still, dark street late at night, to come upon a pile of cardboard boxes soaked with rain, and, as you pass by it, to find yourself staring into the eyes of a man sitting upright behind it. A thief? A beggar? The night watchman of the quarter? A spy for the secret police?

You just keep walking, looking at the ground, hearing your footsteps echo between the walls of the deserted street. Into your head comes the idea that you may suddenly hear the sound of a conspiratorial whistle and that something unpleasant may be about to happen. A little farther along you see, deep in the recess of an arcade of shops, another man reclining in a deck chair, asleep. Then you realize that all along the street there are men both sleeping and sitting quietly awake, and that even in the hours of its most intense silence the place is never empty of people.

It is only since the end of 1955 that Morocco has had its independence, but already there is a nucleus of younger Moslems who fraternize freely with the writers and painters (most of whom are American girls and youths) who have wandered into this part of the world and found it to their liking. Together they give very staid, quiet parties which show a curious blend of Eastern and Western etiquette. Usually no Moslem girls are present. Everyone is either stretched out on mattresses or seated on the floor, and *kif* and hashish are on hand, but half the foreigners content themselves with highballs. A good many paintings are looked at, and there is a lot of uninformed conversation about art and expression and religion. When food is passed around, the Moslems, for all their passionate devotion to European manners, not only adhere to their own custom of using chunks of bread to sop up the oily *mruq* at the bottom of their plates, but manage to impose the system on the others as well, so that everybody is busy rubbing pieces of bread over his plate. Why not? The food is cooked to be eaten in that fashion, and is less tasty if eaten in any other way.

Many of the Moslems paint, too; after so many centuries of religious taboo with regard to the making of representational images, abstraction is their natural mode of expression. You can see in their canvases the elaboration of design worked out by the Berbers in their crafts: patterns that show constant avoidance of representation but manage all the same to suggest recognizable things. Naturally, their paintings are a great success with the visiting artists, who carry their admiration to the point of imitation. The beat-generation North Africans are music-mad, but they get their music via radio, phonograph and tape-recorder. They are enthusiastic about the music of their own country, but unlike their fathers, they don't sing or play it. They are also fond of such exotic items as Congo drumming, the music of

India, and particularly the more recent American jazz (Art Blakey, Horace Silver, Cannonball Adderley).

At the moment, writing about any part of Africa is a little like trying to draw a picture of a roller coaster in motion. You can say: It *was* thus and so, or, it *is becoming* this or that, but you risk making a misstatement if you say categorically that anything *is*, because likely as not you will open tomorrow's newspaper to discover that it has changed. On the whole the new governments of Tunisia and Morocco wish to further tourism in their respective countries; they are learning that the average tourist is more interested in native dancing than in the new bus terminal, that he is more willing to spend money in the Casbah than to inspect new housing projects. For a while, after the demise of the violently unpopular Pasha of Marrakech, Thami el Glaoui, the great public square of Marrakech, the Djemaa el Fna, was used solely as a parking lot. Anyone will tell you that the biggest single attraction for tourists in all North Africa was the Djemaa el Fna in Marrakech. It was hard to find a moment of the day or night when tourists could not be found prowling around among its acrobats, singers, storytellers, snake charmers, dancers and medicine men. Without it Marrakech became just another Moroccan city. And so the Djemaa el Fna was reinstated, and now goes on more or less as before.

North Africa is inhabited, like Malaya and Pakistan, by Moslems who are not Arabs. The *Encyclopaedia Britannica's* estimate of the percentage of Arab stock in the population of Morocco dates from two decades ago, but there has been no influx of Arabs since, so we can accept its figure of ten percent as being still valid. The remaining ninety percent of the people are Berbers, who anthropologically have nothing to do with the Arabs. They are not of Semitic origin, and were right where they are now long before the Arab conquerors ever suspected their existence.

Even after thirteen hundred years, the Berbers' conception of how to observe the Moslem religion is by no means identical with that of the descendants of the men who brought it to them. And the city Moslems complain that they do not observe the fast of Ramadan properly, they neither veil nor segregate their women and, most objectionable of all, they have a passion for forming cults dedicated to the worship of local saints. In this their religious practices show a serious deviation from orthodoxy, inasmuch as during the *moussems,* the gigantic pilgrimages which are held periodically at the many shrines where these holy men are buried, men and women can be seen dancing *together,* working themselves into a prolonged frenzy. This is the height of immorality, the young puritans tell you. But it is not the extent, they add, of the Berbers' reprehensible behavior at these manifestations. Self-torture, the inducing of trances, ordeal by fire and the sword, and the eating of broken glass and scorpions are also not unusual on such occasions.

The traveler who has been present at one of these indescribable gatherings will never forget it, although if he dislikes the sight of blood and physical suffering he may try hard to put it out of his mind. To me these spectacles are filled with great beauty, because their obvious purpose is to prove the power of the spirit over the flesh. The sight of ten or twenty thousand people actively declaring their faith, demonstrating *en masse* the power of that faith, can scarcely be anything but inspiring. You lie in the fire, I gash my legs and arms with a knife, he pounds a sharpened bone into his thigh with a rock—then, together, covered with ashes and blood, we sing and dance in joyous praise of the saint and the god who make it possible for us to triumph over pain, and by extension, over death itself. For the participants exhaustion and ecstasy are inseparable.

This saint-worship, based on vestiges of an earlier religion, has long been frowned upon by the devout urban Moslems; as early as the mid-thirties restrictions were placed on its practice. For a time, public manifestations of it were effectively suppressed. There were several reasons why the educated Moslems objected to the brotherhoods. During the periods of the protectorates in Tunisia and Morocco, the colonial administrations did not hesitate to use them for their own political ends, to ensure more complete domination. Also, it has always been felt that visitors who happened to witness the members of a cult in action were given an unfortunate impression of cultural backwardness. Most important was the fact that the rituals were unorthodox and thus unacceptable to true Moslems. If you mentioned such cults as the Derqaoua, the Aissaoua, the Haddaoua, the Hamatcha, the Jilala or the Guennaoua to a city man, he cried, "They're all criminals! They should be put in jail!" without stopping to reflect that it would be difficult to incarcerate more than half the population of any country. I think one reason why the city folk are so violent in their denunciation of the cults is that most of them are only one generation removed from them themselves; knowing the official attitude toward such things, they feel a certain guilt at being even that much involved with them. Having been born into a family of adepts is not a circumstance which anyone can quickly forget. Each brotherhood has its own songs and drum rhythms, immediately recognizable as such by persons both within and outside the group. In early childhood rhythmical patterns and sequences of tones become a part of an adept's subconscious, and in later life it is not difficult to attain the trance state when one hears them again.

A variation on this phenomenon is the story of Farid. Not long ago he called by to see me. I made tea, and since there was a fire in the fireplace, I took some embers out and put them into a brazier. Over them I sprinkled some *mska*, a translucent yellow resin which makes a sweet, clean-smelling smoke. Moroccans appreciate pleasant odors; Farid is no exception. A little later, before the embers had cooled off, I added some *djaoui*, a compound resinous substance of uncertain ingredients.

Farid jumped up. "What have you put into the *mijmah?*" he cried.

As soon as I had pronounced the word djaoui, he ran into the next room and slammed the door. "Let air into the room!" he shouted. "I can't smell djaoui! It's very bad for me!"

When all trace of the scent released by the djaoui was gone from the room, I opened the door and Farid came back in, still looking fearful.

"What's the matter with you?" I asked him. "What makes you think a little djaoui could hurt you? I've smelled it a hundred times and it's never done me any harm."

He snorted. "You! Of course it couldn't hurt *you*. You're not a Jilali, but I am. I don't want to be, but I still am. Last year I hurt myself and had to go to the clinic, all because of djaoui."

He had been walking in a street of Emsallah and had stopped in front of a café to talk to a friend. Without warning he had collapsed on the sidewalk; when he came to, he was at home and a drum was being beaten over him. Then he recalled the smoke that had been issuing from the café, and knew what had happened.

Farid had passed his childhood in a mountain village where all the members of his family were practicing Jilala. His earliest memories were of being strapped to his mother's back while she, dancing with the others, attained a state of trance. The two indispensable exterior agents they always used to assure the desired alteration of consciousness were drums and djaoui. By the time the boy was four or five years old, he already had a built-in mechanism, an infallible guarantee of being able to reach the trance state very swiftly in the presence of the proper stimulus. When he moved to the city he ceased to be an adept and, in fact, abandoned all religious practice. The conditioned reflex remained, as might be expected, with the result that now as a man in his mid-twenties, although he is at liberty to accept or refuse the effect of the specific drum rhythms, he is entirely at the mercy of a pinch of burning djaoui.

His exposition of the therapeutic process by which he is "brought back" each time there is an accident involves a good many other details, such as the necessity for the presence of a member of the paternal side of his family who will agree to eat a piece of the offending djaoui, the pronouncing of certain key phrases, and the playing on the *bendir* the proper rhythms necessary to break the spell. But the indisputable fact remains that when Farid breathes in djaoui smoke, whether or not he is aware of doing so, straightway he loses consciousness.

One of my acquaintances, who has always been vociferous in his condemnation of the brotherhoods, eventually admitted to me that all the older members of his family were adherents to the Jilala cult, citing immediately afterward, as an example of their perniciousness, an experience of his grandmother some three years before. Like the rest of the family, she was brought up as a Jilalia but had grown too old to take part in the observances, which nowadays are held secretly. (Prohibition, as usual, does not mean abolition, but merely being driven underground.) One evening the old lady was alone in the house, her children and grandchildren having all gone to the cinema, and since she had nothing else to do she went to bed. Somewhere nearby, on the outskirts of town, there was a meeting of Jilala going on. In her sleep she rose and, dressed just as she was, began to make her way toward the sounds. She was found next morning unconscious in a vegetable garden near the house where the meeting had taken place, having fallen into an ant colony and been badly bitten. The reason she fell, the family assured me, was that at a certain moment the drumming had stopped; if it had gone on she would have arrived. The drummers always continue until everyone present has been brought out of his trance.

"But they did not know she was coming," they said, "and so the next morning, after we had carried her home, we had to send for the drummers to bring her to her senses." The younger generation of French-educated Moslems is infuriated when this sort of story is told to foreigners. And that the latter are interested in such things upsets them even more. "Are all the people in your country Holy Rollers?" they demand. "Why don't you write about the civilized people here instead of the most backward?"

I suppose it is natural for them to want to see themselves presented to the outside world in the most "advanced" light possible. They find it perverse of a Westerner to be interested only in the dissimilarities between their culture and his. However, that's the way some of us Westerners are.

Not long ago I wrote on the character of the North Africa Moslem. An illiterate Moroccan friend wanted to know what was in it, and so, in a running translation into Moghrebi, I read him certain passages. His comment was terse: "That's shameful."

"Why?" I demanded.

"Because you've written about people just as they are."

"For us that's not shameful."

"For us it is. You've made us like animals. You've said that only a few of us can read or write."

"Isn't that true?"

"Of course not! We can all read and write, just like you. And we would, if only we'd had lessons."

I thought this interesting and told it to a Moslem lawyer, assuming it would amuse him. It did not. "He's quite right," he announced. "Truth is not what you perceive with your senses, but what you feel in your heart."

"But there is such a thing as objective truth!" I cried. "Or don't you attach importance to that?"

He smiled tolerantly. "Not in the way you do, for its own sake. That is statistical truth. We are interested in that, yes, but only as a means of getting to the real truth underneath. For us there is very little visible truth in the world these days." However specious this kind of talk may seem, it is still clear to me that the lawyer was voicing a feeling common to the great mass of city dwellers here, educated or not.

With an estimated adult illiteracy rate of eighty to ninety percent, perhaps the greatest need of all for North Africa is universal education. So far there has been a very small amount, and as we ourselves say, a little learning is a dangerous thing. The Europeans always have been guilty of massive neglect with regard to schools for Moslems in their North African possessions. In time, their shortsighted policy is likely to prove the heaviest handicap of all in the desperate attempt of the present rulers to keep the region within the Western sphere of influence. The task of educating these people is not made easier by the fact that Moghrebi, the language of the majority, is purely a spoken tongue, and that for reading and writing they must resort to standard Arabic, which is as far from their idiom as Latin is from Italian. But slowly the transition is taking place. If you sit in a Moroccan café at the hour of a news broadcast, the boy fanning the fire will pause with the bellows in his hand, the card players lay down their cards, the talkers cease to argue as the announcer begins to speak, and an expression of ferocious intensity appears on every countenance. Certainly they are vitally interested in what is being said (even the women have taken up discussing politics lately), for they are aware of their own increasing importance in the world pattern, but the almost painful expressions are due to each man's effort to understand the words of standard Arabic as they come over the air. Afterward, there is often an argument as to exactly what the news contained.

"The British are at war with Yemen for being friendly to Gamal Abd el Nasser."

"You're crazy. He said Gamal Abd el Nasser is making war against Yemen because the British are there."

"No. He said Gamal Abd el Nasser *will* make war against Yemen if they let the British in."

"No, no! Against the *British* if they send guns to Yemen."

This state of affairs, if it does not keep all members of the populace accurately informed, at least has the advantage of increasing their familiarity with the language their children are learning at school.

There is a word which non-Moslems invariably use to describe Moslems in general: fanatical. As though the word could not be applied equally well to any group of people who care deeply about anything! Just now, the North African Moslems are passionately involved in proving to themselves that they are of the same stature as Europeans. The attainment of political independence is only one facet of their problem. The North African knows that when it comes to appreciating his culture, the average tourist cannot go much closer toward understanding it than a certain condescending curiosity. He realizes that, at best, to the European he is merely picturesque. Therefore, he reasons, to be taken seriously he must cease being picturesque. Traditional customs, clothing and behavior must be replaced by something unequivocally European. In this he is fanatical. It does not occur to him that what he is rejecting is authentic and valid, and that what he is taking on is meaningless imitation. And if it did occur to him, it would not matter in the least. This total indifference to cultural heritage appears to be a necessary adjunct to the early stages of nationalism.

Hospitality in North Africa knows no limits. You are taken in and treated as a member of the family. If you don't enjoy yourself, it is not your host's fault, but rather the result of your own inadaptability, for every attempt is made to see that you are happy and comfortable. Some time ago I was the guest of two brothers who had an enormous house in the *medina* of Fez. So that I should feel truly at home, I was given an entire wing of the establishment, a tiled patio with a room on either side and a fountain in the center. There were great numbers of servants to bring me food and drink, and also to inquire, before my hosts came to call, whether I was disposed to receive them. When they came they often brought singers and musicians to entertain me. The only hitch was that they went to such lengths to treat me as one of them that they also assumed I was not interested in going out into the city. During the entire fortnight I spent with them I never once found my way out of the house, or even out of my own section of it, since all doors were kept locked and bolted, and only the guard, an old Sudanese slave, had the keys. For long hours I sat in the patio listening to the sounds of the city outside, sometimes hearing faint strains of music that I would have given anything really to hear, watching the square of deep-blue sky above my head slowly become a softer and lighter blue as twilight approached, waiting for the swallows that wheeled above the patio when the day was finally over and the muezzins began their calls to evening prayer, and merely existing in the hope that someone would come, something would happen before too many more hours had gone past. But as I say, if I was bored, that was my own fault and not theirs. They were doing everything they could to please me.

Just as in that twelfth-century fortress in Fez I had been provided with a small hand-wound phonograph and one record (Josephine Baker singing *"J'ai deux amours,"* a song hit of that year), so all over North Africa you are confronted with a mélange of the very old and the most recent, with no hint of anything from the intervening centuries. It is one of the great charms of the place, the fact that your today carries with it no memories of yesterday or the day before; everything that is not medieval is completely new. The younger generation of French and Jews, born and raised in the cities of North Africa, for the most part have no contact with that which is ancient in their countries. A Moroccan girl whose family moved from Rabat to New York, upon being asked what she thought of her new home, replied: "Well, of course, coming from a new country as I do, it's very hard to get used to all these old houses here in New York. I had no idea New York was so *old.*" One is inclined to forget that the French began to settle in Morocco only at the time of World War I, and that the mushroom cities of Casablanca, Agadir and Tangier grew up in the 'thirties. Xauen, whose mountains are visible from the terrace of my apartment in Tangier, was entered by European troops for the first time in 1920. Even in southern Algeria, where one is likely to think of the French as having been stationed for a much longer time, there are war monuments bearing battle dates as recent as 1912. Throughout the whole first quarter of the century the North African frontier was continuously being pushed southward by means of warfare, and south of the Grand Atlas it was 1936 before "pacification" came to an end and European civilians were allowed, albeit on the strict terms laid down by the military, to look for the first time into the magic valleys of the Draa, the Dadés and the Todra.

Appearing unexpectedly in out-of-the-way regions of North Africa has never been without its difficulties. I remember making an impossible journey before the last world war in a produce truck over the Grand Atlas to Ouarzazat, full of excitement at the prospect of seeing the Casbah there with its strange painted towers, only to be forced to remain three days inside the shack that passed for a hotel, and then sent on another truck straight back to Marrakech, having seen nothing but Foreign Legionnaires, and having heard no music other than the bugle calls that issued every so often from the nearby camp. Another time I entered Tunisia on camelback from across the Great Eastern Erg. I had two camels and one hard-working camel driver, whose job it was to run all day long from one beast to the other and try, by whacking their hind legs, to keep them walking in something resembling a straight line. This was a much more difficult task than it sounds; although our course was generally due east, one of the animals had an inexplicable desire to walk southward, while the other was possessed by an equally mysterious urge to go north. The poor man passed his time screaming: "Hut! Aïda!" and trying to run both ways at once. His turban was continually coming unwound, and he had no time to attend to the scarf he was knitting, in spite of the fact that he kept the yarn and needles dangling around his neck, ready to work on at any moment.

We did finally cross the border and amble into Tunisia, where we were immediately apprehended by the police. The camel driver and his beasts were sent back to Algeria where they belonged, and I started on my painful way up through Tunisia, where the French authorities evidently had made a concerted decision to make my stay in the country as wretched as possible. In the oasis at Nefta, in the hotel at Tozeur, even in the mosque of Sidi Oqba at Kairouan, I was arrested and lugged off to the commissariat, carefully questioned and told that I need not imagine I could make a move of which they would not be fully aware.

The explanation was that in spite of my American passport they were convinced I was a German; in those days anybody wandering around *l'Afrique Mineure* (as one of the more erudite officers called this corner of the continent), if he did not satisfy the French idea of what a tourist should look like, was immediately suspect. Even the Moslems would look at me closely and say: *"Toi pas Français. Toi Allemand,"* to which I never replied, for fear of having to pay the prices that would have been demanded if my true status had been revealed to them.

Algeria is a country where it is better to keep moving around than to stay long in one place. Its towns are not very interesting, but its landscapes are impressive. In the winter, traveling by train across the western steppes, you can go all day and see nothing but flat stretches of snow on all sides, unrelieved by trees in the foreground or by mountains in the distance. In the summer these same desolate lands are cruelly hot, and the wind swirls the dust into tall yellow pillars that move deliberately from one side of the empty horizon to the other. When you come upon a town in such regions, lying like the remains of a picnic lunch in the middle of an endless parking lot, you know it was the French who put it there. The Algerians prefer to live along the wild and beautiful seacoast, in the palm gardens of the south, atop the cliffs bordering the dry rivers, or on the crests of the high mountains in the center of the country. Up there above the slopes dotted with almond trees, the Berber villages sit astride the long spines of the lesser ranges. The men and women file down the zigzagging paths to cultivate the rich valleys below, here and there in full view of the snowfields where the French formerly had their skiing resorts. Far to the south lie the parallel chains of red sawtooth mountains which run northeast to southwest across the entire country and divide the plains from the desert.

No part of North Africa will again be the same sort of paradise for Europeans that it has been for them these last fifty years. The place has been thrown open to the twentieth century. With Europeanization and national- ism have come a consciousness of identity and the awareness of that identity's commercial possibilities. From now on the North Africans, like the Mexicans, will control and exploit their own charms, rather than being placed on exhibit for us by their managers, and the result will be a very different thing from what it has been in the past. Tourist land it still is, and doubtless will continue to be for a while; and it is on that basis only that we as residents or intending visitors are now obliged to consider it. We now come here as paying guests of the inhabitants themselves rather than of their exploiters. Travel here is certain not to be so easy or so comfortable as before, and prices are many times higher than they were, but at least we meet the people on terms of equality, which is a healthier situation.

If you live long enough in a place where the question of colonialism versus self-government is constantly being discussed, you are bound to find yourself having a very definite opinion on the subject. The difficulty is that some of your co-residents feel one way and some the other, but all feel strongly. Those in favor of colonialism argue that you can't "give" (quotes mine) an almost totally illiterate people political power and expect them to create a democracy, and that is doubtless true; but the point is that since they are inevitably going to take the power sooner or later, it is only reasonable to help them take it while they still have at least some measure of good will toward their erstwhile masters. The die-hard French attitude is summed up in a remark made to me by a friendly immigration officer at the Algiers airport. "Our great mistake," he said sadly, "was ever to allow these savages to learn to read and write." I said I supposed that was a logical thing to say if one expected to rule forever, which I knew, given the intelligence of the French, that they did not intend to try, since it was impossible. The official ceased looking sad and became much less friendly.

At a dinner in Marrakech during the French occupation, the Frenchman sitting beside me became engaged in an amicable discussion with a Moroccan across the table. "But look at the facts, *mon cher ami*. Before our arrival, there was constant warfare between the tribes. Since we came the population has doubled. Is that true or not?"

The Moroccan leaned forward. "We can take care of our own births and deaths," he said, smiling. "If we must be killed, just let other Moroccans attend to it. We really prefer that."

Notes Mailed at Nagercoil

Cape Comorin, South India
March, 1952

I have been here in this hotel now for a week. At no time during the night
or day has the temperature been low enough for comfort; it fluctuates
between ninety-five and one hundred and five degrees, and most of the time
there is absolutely no breeze, which is astonishing for the seaside. Each
bedroom and public room has the regulation large electric fan in its ceiling,
but there is no electricity; we are obliged to use oil lamps for lighting.
Today at lunch time a large Cadillac of the latest model drove up to the
front door. In the back were three fat little men wearing nothing but the
flimsy *dhotis* they had draped around their loins. One of them handed a
bunch of keys to the chauffeur, who then got out and came into the hotel.
Near the front door is the switch box. He opened it, turned on the current
with one of the keys, and throughout the hotel the fans began to whir. Then
the three little men got out and went into the dining-room where they had
their lunch. I ate quickly, so as to get upstairs and lie naked on my bed
under the fan. It was an unforgettable fifteen minutes. Then the fan stopped,
and I heard the visitors driving away. The hotel manager told me later that
they were government employees of the State of Travancore, and that only
they had a key to the switch box.*

Last night I awoke and opened my eyes. There was no moon; it was still
dark, but the light of a star was shining into my face through the open
window, from a point high above the Arabian Sea. I sat up, and gazed at
it. The light it cast seemed as bright as that of the moon in northern
countries; coming through the window, it made its rectangle on the oppo-
site wall, broken by the shadow of my silhouetted head. I held up my hand
and moved the fingers, and their shadow too was definite. There were no

*Subsequently Travancore and Cochin have merged to make the province of Kerala.

other stars visible in that part of the sky; this one blinded them all. It was about an hour before daybreak, which comes shortly after six, and there was not a breath of air. On such still nights the waves breaking on the nearby shore sound like great, deep explosions going on at some distant place. There is the boom, which can be felt as well as heard and which ends with a sharp rattle and hiss, then a long period of complete silence, and finally, when it seems that there will be no more sound, another sudden boom. The crows begin to scream and chatter while the darkness is still complete.

The town, like the others here in the extreme south, gives the impression of being made of dust. Dust and cow dung lie in the streets, and the huge crows hop ahead of you as you walk along. When a gust of hot wind wanders in from the sandy wastes beyond the town, the brown fans of the palmyra trees swish and bang against each other; they sound like giant sheets of heavy wrapping paper. The small black men walk quickly, the diamonds in their earlobes flashing. Because of their jewels and the gold thread woven into their dhotis, they all look not merely prosperous, but fantastically wealthy. When the women have diamonds, they are likely to wear them in a hole pierced through the wall of one nostril.

The first time I ever saw India I entered it through Dhanushkodi. An analogous procedure in America would be for a foreigner to get his first glimpse of the United States by crossing the Mexican border illegally and coming out into a remote Arizona village. It was God-forsaken, uncomfortable and a little frightening. Since then I have landed as a bonafide visitor should, in the impressively large and unbeautiful metropolis of Bombay. But I'm glad that my first trip did not bring me in contact with any cities. It is better to go to the villages of a strange land before trying to understand its towns, above all in a complex place like India. Now, after traveling some eight thousand miles around the country, I know approximately as little as I did on my first arrival. However, I've seen a lot of people and places, and at least I have a somewhat more detailed and precise idea of my ignorance than I did in the beginning.

If you have not taken the precaution of reserving a room in advance, you risk having considerable difficulty in finding one when you land in Bombay. There are very few hotels, and the two or three comfortable ones are always full. I hate being committed to a reservation because the element of adventure is thereby destroyed. The only place I was able to get into when I first arrived, therefore, was something less than a first-class establishment. It was all right during the day and the early hours of the evening. At night, however, every square foot of floor space in the dark corridors was occupied by sleepers who had arrived late and brought their own mats with them; the hotel was able in this way to shelter several hundred extra guests each night. Having their hands and feet kicked and trodden on was apparently a familiar enough experience to them for them never to make any audible objection when the inevitable happened. Here in Cape Comorin, on the other hand, there are many rooms and they are vast, and at the moment I am the only one staying in the hotel.

It was raining. I was on a bus going from Alleppey to Trivandrum, on my way down here. There were two little Indian nuns on the seat in front of mine. I wondered how they stood the heat in their heavy robes. Sitting near the driver was a man with a thick, fierce mustache who distinguished himself from the other passengers by the fact that in addition to his dhoti he also wore a European shirt; its scalloped tail hung down nearly to his knees. With him he had a voluminous collection of magazines and newspapers in both Tamil and English, and even from where I sat I could not help noticing that all this reading matter had been printed in the Soviet Union. (After years of practice one gets to recognize it without difficulty.)

At a certain moment, near one of the myriad villages that lie smothered in the depths of the palm forests, the motor suddenly ceased to function and the bus came to a stop. The driver, not exchanging a single glance with his passengers, let his head fall forward and remain resting on the steering wheel in a posture of despair. Expectantly the people waited a little while, and then they began to get up. One of the first out of the bus was the man with the mustache. He said a hearty good-bye to the occupants in general, although he had not been conversing with any of them, and started up the road carrying his umbrella, but not his armful of printed matter. Then I realized that at some point during the past hour, not foreseeing the failure of the motor and the mass departure which it entailed, he had left a paper or magazine on each empty seat—exactly as our American comrades used to do on subway trains three decades ago.

Almost at the moment I made this discovery, the two nuns had risen and were hurriedly collecting the "literature." They climbed down and ran along the road after the man, calling out in English, "Sir, your papers!" He turned, and they handed them to him. Without saying a word, but with an expression of fury on his face, he took the bundle and continued. But it was impossible to tell from the faces of the two nuns when they returned to gather up their belongings whether or not they were conscious of what they had done.

A few minutes later everyone had left the bus and walked to the vil-

lage—everyone, that is, but the driver and me. I had too much luggage.
Then I spoke to him.

"What's the matter with the bus?"

He shrugged his shoulders.

"How am I going to get to Trivandrum?"

He did not know that, either.

"Couldn't you look into the motor?" I pursued. "It sounded like the fan
belt. Maybe you could repair it."

This roused him sufficiently from his apathy to make him turn and look
at me.

"We have People's Government here in Travancore," he said. "Not
allowed touching motor."

"But who *is* going to repair it, then?"

"Tonight making telephone call to Trivandrum. Making report. Tomor-
row or other day they sending inspector to examine."

"And then what?"

"Then inspector making report. Then sending repair crew."

"I see."

"People's Government," he said again, by way of helping me to under-
stand. "Not like other government."

"No," I said.

As if to make his meaning clearer, he indicated the seat where the man
with the large mustache had sat. "That gentleman Communist."

"Oh, really?" (At least it was all in the open and the driver was under
no misapprehension as to what the term "People's Government" meant.)

"Very powerful man. Member of Parliament from Travancore."

"Is he a good man, though? Do the people like him?"

"Oh, yes, sir. Powerful man."

"But is he *good?*" I insisted.

He laughed, doubtless at my ingenuousness. "Powerful man all rascals,"
he said.

Just before nightfall a local bus came along, and with the help of several
villagers I transferred my luggage to it and continued on my way.

Most of the impressively heavy Communist vote is cast by the Hindus.
The Moslems are generally in less dire economic straits, it is true, but in any
case, by virtue of their strict religious views, they do not take kindly to any
sort of ideological change. (A convert from Islam is unthinkable; apostasy
is virtually nonexistent.) If even Christianity has retained too much of its
pagan décor to be acceptable to the puritanical Moslem mind, one can

imagine the loathing inspired in them by the endless proliferations of Hindu religious art with its gods, demons, metamorphoses and avatars. The two religious systems are antipodal. Fortunately the constant association with the mild and tolerant Hindus has made the Moslems of India far more understanding and tractable than their brothers in Islamic countries further west; there is much less actual friction than one might be led to expect.

During breakfast one morning at the Connemara Hotel in Madras the Moslem head waiter told me a story. He was traveling in the Province of Orissa where, in a certain town, there was a Hindu temple which was famous for having five hundred cobras on its premises. He decided he would like to see these legendary reptiles. When he had got to the town he hired a carriage and went to the temple. At the door he was met by a priest who offered to show him around. And since the Moslem looked prosperous, the priest suggested a donation of five rupees, to be paid in advance.

"Why so much?" asked the visitor.

"To buy eggs for the cobras. You know, we have five hundred of them."

The Moslem gave him the money on condition that the priest let him see the snakes. For an hour his guide dallied in the many courtyards and galleries, pointing out bas-reliefs, idols, pillars and bells. Finally the Moslem reminded him of their understanding.

"Cobras? Ah, yes. But they are dangerous. Perhaps you would rather see them another day?"

This behavior on the priest's part had delighted him, he recalled, for it had reinforced his suspicions.

"Not at all," he said. "I want to see them now."

Reluctantly the priest led him into a small alcove behind a large stone Krishna, and pointed into a very dark corner.

"Is this the place?" the visitor asked.

"This is the place."

"But where are the snakes?"

In a tiny enclosure were two sad old cobras, "almost dead from hunger," he assured me. But when his eyes had grown used to the dimness he saw that there were hundreds of eggshells scattered around the floor outside the pen.

"You eat a lot of eggs," he told the priest.

The priest merely said, "Here. Take back your five rupees. But if you are asked about our cobras, please be so kind as to say that you saw five hundred of them here in our temple. Is that all right?"

The episode was meant to illustrate the head waiter's thesis, which was that the Hindus are abject in the practice of their religion; this is the opinion held by the Moslems. On the other hand, it must be remembered that the Hindu considers Islam an incomplete doctrine, far from satisfying. He finds its austerity singularly comfortless and deplores its lack of mystico-philosophical content, an element in which his own creed is so rich.

I was invited to lunch at one of the cinema studios in the suburbs north of Bombay. We ate our curry outdoors; our hostess was the star of the film then in production. She spoke only Marathi; her husband, who was direct-ing the picture, spoke excellent English. During the meal he told how, as a Hindu, he had been forced to leave his job, his home, his car and his bank account in Karachi at the time of partition—when Pakistan came into existence—and emigrate empty-handed to India, where he had managed to remake his life. Another visitor to the studio, an Egyptian, was intensely interested in his story. Presently he interrupted to say, "It is unjust, of course."

"Yes," smiled our host.

"What retaliatory measures does your government plan to take against the Moslems left here in India?"

"None whatever, as far as I know."

The Egyptian was genuinely indignant. "But why not?" he demanded. "It is only right that you apply the same principle. You have plenty of Moslems here still to take action against. And I say that even though I am a Moslem."

The film director looked at him closely. "You say that *because* you are a Moslem," he told him. "But we cannot put ourselves on that level."

The conversation ended on this not entirely friendly note. A moment later packets of betel were passed around. I promptly broke a tooth, withdrew from the company and went some distance away into the garden. While I, in the interests of science, was examining the mouthful of partially chewed betel leaves and areca nut, trying to find the pieces of bicuspid, the Egyptian came up to me, his face a study in scorn.

"They are afraid of the Moslems. That's the real reason," he whispered. Whether he was right or wrong I was neither qualified nor momentarily disposed to say, but it was a classical exposition of the two opposing moral viewpoints—two concepts of behavior which cannot quickly be reconciled.

Obviously it is a gigantic task to make a nation out of a place like India, what with Hindus, Moslems, Parsees, Jainists, Jews, Catholics and Protes-tants, some of whom may speak the arbitrarily imposed national idiom of

Hindi, but most of whom are more likely to know Gujarati, Marathi, Bengali, Urdu, Telugu, Tamil, Malayalam or some other tongue. One wonders whether any sort of unifying project can ever be undertaken, or, indeed, whether it is even desirable.

When you come to the border between two provinces you often find bars across the road, and you are obliged to undergo a thorough inspection of your luggage. As in the United States, there is a strict control of the passage of liquor between wet and dry districts, but that is not the extent of the examination.

Sample of conversation at the border on the Mercara-Cannanore highway:

Customs officer: "What is in there?"

Bowles: "Clothing."

"And in that?"

"Clothing."

"And in all those?"

"Clothing."

"Open all, please."

After eighteen suitcases have been gone through carefully: "My God, man! Close them all. I could charge duty for all of these goods, but you will never be able to do business with these things here anyway. The Moslem men are too clever."

"But I'm not intending to sell my clothes."

"Shut the luggage. It is duty-free, I tell you."

A professor from Raniket in North India arrived at the hotel here the other day, and we spent a good part of the night sitting on the window seat in my room that overlooks the sea, talking about what one always talks about here: India. Among the many questions I put to him was one concerning the reason why so many of the Hindu temples in South India prohibit entry to non-Hindus, and why they have military guards at the entrances. I imagined I knew the answer in advance: fear of Moslem disturbances. Not at all, he said. The principal purpose was to keep out certain Christian missionaries. I expressed disbelief.

"Of course," he insisted. "They come and jeer during our rituals, ridicule our sacred images."

"But even if they were stupid enough to want to do such things," I objected, "their sense of decorum would keep them from behaving like that."

He merely laughed. "Obviously you don't know them."

The post office here is a small stifling room over a shop, and it is full of boys seated on straw mats. The postmaster, a tiny old man who wears large diamond earrings and gold-rimmed spectacles, and is always naked to the waist, is also a professor; he interrupts his academic work to sell an occasional stamp. At first contact his English sounds fluent enough, but soon one discovers that it is not adapted to conversation, and that one can scarcely talk to him. Since the boys are listening, he must pretend to be omniscient, therefore he answers promptly with more or less whatever phrase comes into his head.

Yesterday I went to post a letter by airmail to Tangier. "Tanjore," he said, adjusting his spectacles. "That will be four annas." (Tanjore is in South India, near Trichinopoly.) I explained that I hoped my letter would be going to Tangier, Morocco.

"Yes, yes," he said impatiently. "There are many Tanjores." He opened the book of postal regulations and read aloud from it, quite at random, for (although it may be difficult to believe) exactly six minutes. I stood still, fascinated, and let him go on. Finally he looked up and said, "There is no mention of Tangier. No airplanes go to that place."

"Well, how much would it be to send it by sea mail?" (I thought we could then calculate the surcharge for air mail, but I had misjudged my man.)

"Yes," he replied evenly. "That is a good method, too."

I decided to keep the letter and post it in the nearby town of Nagercoil another day. In a little while I would have several to add to it, and I counted on being able to send them all together when I went. Before I left the post office I hazarded the remark that the weather was extremely hot. In that airless attic at noon it was a wild understatement. But it did not please the postmaster at all. Deliberately he removed his glasses and pointed the stems at me.

"Here we have the perfect climate," he told me. "Neither too cold nor too cool."

"That is true," I said. "Thank you."

In the past few years there have been visible quantitative changes in Indian life, all in the one direction of Europeanization. This is in the smaller towns; the cities of course have long since been westernized. The temples which before were lighted by bare electric bulbs and coconut-oil lamps now have fluorescent tubes glimmering in their ceilings. Crimson, green and amber floodlights are used to illumine bathing tanks, deities, the gateways of temples. The public-address system is the bane of the ear these days, even in the temples. And it is impossible to attend a concert or a dance recital without discovering several loudspeakers whose noise completely destroys the quality of the music. A mile before you arrive at the cinema of a small town you can hear the raucous blaring of the amplifier they have set up at its entrance.

This year in South India there are fewer men with bare torsos, dhotis and sandals; more shirts, trousers and shoes. There is at the same time a slow shutting-down of services which to the Western tourist make all the difference between pleasure and discomfort in traveling, such as the restaurants in the stations (there being no dining cars on the trains) and the showers in the first-class compartments. A few years ago they worked; now they have been sealed off. You can choke on the dust and soot of your compartment, or drown in your own sweat now, for all the railway cares.

At one point I was held for forty-eight hours in a concentration camp run by the Ceylon government on Indian soil. (The euphemism for this one was "screening camp.") I was told that I was under suspicion of being an international spy. My astonishment and indignation were regarded as almost convincing in their sincerity, thus proof of my guilt.

"But who am I supposed to be spying *for?*" I asked piteously.

The director shrugged. "Spying for international," he said.

More than the insects or the howling of pariah dogs outside the rolls of barbed wire, what bothered me was the fact that in the center of the camp, which at that time housed some twenty thousand people, there was a loudspeaker in a high tower which during every moment of the day roared forth Indian film music. Fortunately it was silenced at ten o'clock each evening. I got out of the hell-hole only by making such violent trouble that I was dragged before the camp doctor, who decided that I was dangerously unbalanced. The idea in letting me go was that I would be detained further along, and the responsibility would fall on other shoulders. "They will hold him at Talaimannar," I heard the doctor say. "The poor fellow is quite mad."

Here and there, in places like the bar of the Hotel Metropole at Mysore, or at the North Coorg Club of Mercara, one may still come across vestiges of the old colonial life: ghosts in the form of incredibly sunburned Englishmen in jodhpurs and boots discussing their hunting luck and prowess. But these visions are exceedingly rare in a land that wants to forget their existence.

The younger generation in India is intent on forgetting a good many things, including some that it might do better to remember. There would seem to be no good reason for getting rid of their country's most ancient heritage, the religion of Hinduism, or of its most recent acquisition, the tradition of independence. This latter, at least insofar as the illiterate masses are concerned, is inseparable not only from the religious state of mind which made political victory possible, but also from the legend which, growing up around the figure of Gandhi, has elevated him in their minds to the status of a god.

The young, politically-minded intellectuals find this not at all to their liking; in their articles and addresses they have returned again and again to the attack against Gandhi as a "betrayer" of the Indian people. That they are motivated by hatred is obvious. But what do they hate?

For one thing, subconsciously they cannot accept their own inability to go on having religious beliefs. Then, belonging to the group without faith, they are thereby forced to hate the past, particularly the atavisms which are made apparent by the workings of the human mind with its irrationality, its subjective involvement in exterior phenomena. The floods of poisonous words they pour forth are directed primarily at the adolescents; this is an age group which is often likely to find demagoguery more attractive than common sense.

There are at least a few of these enlightened adolescents in every town; the ones here in Cape Comorin were horrified when by a stratagem I led them to the home of a man of their own village who claims that his brother is under a spell. (They had not imagined, they told me later, that an American would believe such nonsense.) According to the man Subramaniam, his brother was a painter who had been made art director of a major film studio in Madras. To substantiate his story he brought out a sheaf of very professional sketches for film sets.

"Then my brother had angry words with a jealous man in the studio," said Subramaniam, "and the man put a charm on him. His mind is gone. But at the end of the year it will return." The brother presently appeared in the courtyard; he was a vacant-eyed man with a beard, and he had a voluminous turkish towel draped over his head and shoulders. He walked past us and disappeared through a doorway.

"A spirit doctor is treating him . . ." The modern young men shifted their feet miserably; it was unbearable that an American should be witnessing such shameful revelations, and that they should be coming from one in their midst.

But these youths who found it so necessary to ridicule poor Subramaniam failed to understand why I laughed when, the conversation changing to the subject of cows, I watched their collective expression swiftly change to one of respect bordering on beatitude. For cow worship is one facet of popular Hinduism which has not yet been totally superseded by twentieth-century faithlessness. True, it has taken on new forms of ritual. Mass cow worship is often practiced now in vast modern concrete stadiums, with prizes being distributed to the owners of the finest bovine specimens, but the religious aspect of the celebration is still evident. The cows are decorated with garlands of jewelry, fed bananas and sugar cane by people who have waited in line for hours to be granted that rare privilege; and when the satiated animals can eat no more they simply lie down or wander about, while hundreds of young girls perform sacred dances in their honor.

In India, where the cow wishes to go she goes. She may be lying in the temple, where she may decide to get up to go and lie instead in the middle of the street. If she is annoyed by the proximity of the traffic streaming past her, she may lumber to her feet again and continue down the street to the railway station, where, should she feel like reclining in front of the ticket window, no one will disturb her. On the highways she seems to know that the drivers of trucks and buses will spot her a mile away and slow down almost to a stop before they get to her, and that therefore she need not move out from under the shade of the particular banyan tree she has chosen for her rest. Her superior position in the world is agreed upon by common consent.

The most satisfying exposition I have seen of the average Hindu's feeling about this exalted beast is a little essay composed by a candidate for a post in one of the public services, entitled simply "The Cow." The fact that it was submitted in order to show the aspirant's mastery of the English language, while touching, is of secondary importance.

THE COW

The cow is one wonderful animal, also he is quadruped and because he is female he gives milk—but he will do so only when he has got child. He is same like God, sacred to Hindu and useful to man. But he has got four legs together. Two are foreward and two are afterwards.

His whole body can be utilized for use. More so the milk. What it cannot do? Various ghee, butter, cream, curds, whey, kova and the condensed milk and so forth. Also, he is useful to cobbler, watermans and mankind generally.

His motion is slow only. That is because he is of amplitudinous species, and also his other motion is much useful to trees, plants as well as making fires. This is done by making flat cakes in hand and drying in the sun.

He is the only animal that extricates his feedings after eating. Then afterwards he eats by his teeth which are situated in the inside of his mouth. He is incessantly grazing in the meadows.

His only attacking and defending weapons are his horns, especially when he has got child. This is done by bowing his head whereby he causes the weapons to be parallel to ground of earth and instantly proceeds with great velocity forwards.

He has got tail also, but not like other similar animals. It has hairs on the end of the other side. This is done to frighten away the flies which alight on his whole body and chastises him unceasingly, where-upon he gives hit with it.

The palms of his feet are so soft unto the touch so that the grasses he eats would not get crushed. At night he reposes by going down on the ground and then he shuts his eyes like his relative the horse which does not do so. This is the cow.

The moths and night insects flutter about my single oil lamp. Occasionally, at the top of its chimney, one of them goes up in a swift, bright flame. On the concrete floor in a fairly well-defined ring around the bottom of my chair are the drops of sweat that have rolled off my body during the past two hours. The doors into both the bedroom and the bathroom are shut; I work each night in the dressing room between them, because fewer insects are attracted here. But the air is nearly unbreathable with the stale smoke of cigarettes and *bathi* sticks burned to discourage the entry of winged creatures. Today's paper announced an outbreak of bubonic plague in Bellary. I keep thinking about it, and I wonder if the almost certain eventual victory over such diseases will prove to have been worth its price: the extinction of the beliefs and rituals which gave a satisfactory meaning to the period of consciousness that goes between birth and death. I doubt it. Security is a false god; begin making sacrifices to it and you are lost.

A Man Must Not Be
Very Moslem

Aboard m/s Tarsus,
Turkish Maritime Lines
September 25, 1953

When I announced my intention of bringing Abdeslam along to Istanbul, the general opinion of my friends was that there were a good many more intelligent things to do in the world than to carry a Moroccan Moslem along with one to Turkey. I don't know. He may end up as a dead weight, but my hope is that he will turn out instead to be a kind of passkey to the place. He knows how to deal with Moslems, and he has the Moslem sense of seemliness and protocol. He has also an intuitive gift for the immediate understanding of a situation and at the same time is completely lacking in reticence or inhibitions. He can lie so well that he convinces himself straightway, and he is a master at bargaining; it is a black day for him when he has to pay the asking price for anything. He never knows what is printed on a sign because he is totally illiterate; besides, even if he did know he would pay no attention, for he is wholly deficient in respect for law. If you mention that this or that thing is forbidden, he is contemptuous: "Agh! a decree for the wind!" Obviously he is far better equipped than I to squeeze the last drop of adventure out of any occasion. I, unfortunately, *can* read signs but can't lie or bargain effectively, and will forgo any joy rather than risk unpleasantness or reprimand from whatever quarter. At all events, the die is cast: Abdeslam is here on the ship.

My first intimation of Turkey came during tea this afternoon, as the ship was leaving the Bay of Naples. The orchestra was playing a tango which finally established its identity, after several reprises, as the "Indian Love Call," and the cliffs of Capri were getting in the way of the sunset. I glanced at a biscuit that I was about to put into my mouth, then stopped the operation to examine it more closely. It was an ordinary little arrowroot tea-biscuit, and on it were embossed the words HAYD PARK. Contemplating this edible tidbit, I recalled what friends had told me of the amusing havoc that results when the Turks phoneticize words borrowed from other languages. These metamorphosed words have a way of looking like gibberish until you say them aloud, and then more likely than not they resolve themselves into perfectly comprehensible English or French or, even occasionally, Arabic. SKOÇ TUID looks like nothing; suddenly it becomes Scotch Tweed. TUALET, TRENÇKOT, OTOTEKNIK and SEKSOLOJI likewise reveal their messages as one stares at them. Synthetic orthography is a constantly visible reminder of Turkey's determination to be "modern." The country has turned its back on the East and Eastern concepts, not with the simple yearning of other Islamic countries to be European or to acquire American techniques, but with a conscious will to transform itself from the core outward—even to destroy itself culturally, if need be.

Tarabya, Bosporus

This afternoon it was blustery and very cold. The water in the tiny Sea of Marmara was choppy and dark, laced with froth; the ship rolled more heavily than it had at any time during its three days out on the open Mediterranean. If the first sight of Istanbul was impressive, it was because the perfect hoop of a rainbow painted across the lead-colored sky ahead kept one from looking at the depressing array of factory smokestacks along the western shore. After an hour's moving backward and forward in the harbor, we were close enough to see the needles of the minarets (and how many of them!) in black against the final flare-up of the sunset. It was a poetic introduction, and like the introductions to most books, it had very little to do with what followed. "Poetic" is not among the adjectives you would use to describe the disembarkation. The pier was festive; it looked like an elegant waterside restaurant or one of the larger Latin-American airports—brilliantly illumined, awnings flapping, its decks mobbed with screaming people.

The customs house was the epitome of confusion for a half-hour or so; when eventually an inspector was assigned us, we were fortunate enough to be let through without having to open anything. The taxis were parked in the dark on the far side of a vast puddle of water, for it had been raining. I had determined on a hotel in Istanbul proper, rather than one of those in

Beyoğlu, across the Golden Horn, but the taxi driver and his front-seat companion were loath to take me there. "All hotels in Beyoğlu," they insisted. I knew better and did some insisting of my own. We shot into the stream of traffic, across the Galata Bridge, to the hotel of my choosing. Unhappily I had neglected, on the advice of various friends back in Italy, to reserve a room. There was none to be had. And so on, from hotel to hotel there in Istanbul, back across the bridge and up the hill to every establishment in Beyoğlu. Nothing, nothing. There are three international conventions in progress here, and besides, it is vacation time in Turkey; everything is full. Even the m/s *Tarsus,* from which we just emerged, as well as another ship in the harbor, has been called into service tonight to be used as a hotel. By half past ten I accepted the suggestion of being driven twenty-five kilometers up the Bosporus to a place, where they had assured me by telephone that they had space.

"Do you want a room with bath?" they asked.

I said I did.

"We haven't any," they told me.

"Then I want a room without bath."

"We have one." That was that.

Once we had left the city behind and were driving along the dark road, there was nothing for Abdeslam to do but catechize the two Turks in front. Obviously they did not impress him as being up-to-the-mark Moslems, and he started by testing their knowledge of the Koran. I thought they were replying fairly well, but he was contemptuous. "They don't know anything," he declared in Moghrebi. Going into English, he asked them: "How many times one day you pray?"

They laughed.

"People can sleep in mosque?" he pursued. The driver was busy navigating the curves in the narrow road, but his companion, who spoke a special brand of English all his own, spoke for him. "Not slep in mosque many people every got hoss," he explained.

"You make sins?" continued Abdeslam, intent on unearthing the hidden flaws in the behavior of these foreigners. "Pork, wine?"

The other shrugged his shoulders. "Muslim people every not eat pork not drink wine but maybe one hundred year ago like that. Now different."

"*Never* different!" shouted Abdeslam sternly. "You not good Moslems here. People not happy. You have bad government. Not like Egypt. Egypt have good government. Egypt one-hundred-percent Moslem."

The other was indignant. "Everybody happy," he protested. "Happy with Egypt too for religion. But the Egypts sometimes fight with Egypts. Arab fight Arabs. Why? I no like Egypt. I in Egypt. I ask my way. They put me say bakhshish. If you ask in Istanbul, you say I must go my way, he can bring you, but he no say give *bakhshish*. Before, few people up, plenty people down. Now, you make your business, I make my business. You take your money, I take my money. Before, *you* take *my* money. You rich with *my* money. Before, Turkey like Egypt with Farouk." He stopped to let all this sink in, but Abdeslam was not interested.

"Egypt very good country," he retorted, and there was no more conversation until we arrived. At the hotel the driver's comrade was describing a fascinating new ideology known as democracy. From the beginning of the colloquy I had my notebook out, scribbling his words in the dark as fast as he spoke them. They express the average uneducated Turk's reaction to the new concept. It was only in 1950 that the first completely democratic elections were held. (Have there been any since?) To Abdeslam, who is a traditionally-minded Moslem, the very idea of democracy is meaningless. It is impossible to explain it to him; he will not listen. If an idea is not explicitly formulated in the Koran, it is wrong; it came either directly from Satan or via the Jews, and there is no need to discuss it further.

This hotel, built at the edge of the lapping Bosporus, is like a huge wooden box. At the base of the balustrade of the grand staircase leading up from the lobby, one on each side, are two life-sized ladies made of lead and painted with white enamel in the hope of making them look like marble. The dining room's decorations are of a more recent period—the early 'twenties. There are high murals that look as though the artist had made a study of Boutet de Monvel's fashion drawings of the era; long-necked, low-waisted females in cloches and thigh-length skirts, presumably picnicking on the shores of the Bosporus.

At dinner we were the only people eating, since it was nearly midnight. Abdeslam took advantage of this excellent opportunity by delivering an impassioned harangue (partly in a mixture of Moghrebi and Standard Arabic and partly in English), with the result that by the end of the meal we had fourteen waiters and bus boys crowded around the table listening. Then someone thought of fetching the chef. He arrived glistening with sweat and beaming; he had been brought because he spoke more Arabic than the others, which was still not very much. "Old-fashioned Moslem," explained the headwaiter. Abdeslam immediately put him through the *chehade,* and he came off with flying colors, reciting it word for word along with Abdeslam: "*Achhaddouanlaillahainallah*. . . ." The faces of the younger men expressed unmistakable admiration, as well as pleasure at the approval of the esteemed foreigner, but none of them could perform the chef's feat. Presently the manager of the hotel came in, presumably to see what was going on in the dining room at this late hour. Abdeslam asked for the check, and objected when he saw that it was written with Roman characters. "Arabic!" he demanded. "You Moslem? Then bring check in Arabic." Apologetically the manager explained that writing in Arabic was "dangerous," and had been known on occasion to put the man who did it into jail. To this he added, just to make things quite clear, that any man who veiled his wife also went to jail. "A man must not be *very* Moslem," he said. But Abdeslam had had enough. "I *very very* Moslem," he announced. We left the room.

The big beds stand high off the floor and haven't enough covers on them. I have spread my topcoat over me; it is cold and I should like to leave the windows shut, but the mingled stenches coming from the combined shower-lavatory behind a low partition in the corner are so powerful that such a course is out of the question. The winds moving down from the Black Sea will blow over me all night. Sometime after we had gone to bed, following a long silence during which I thought he had fallen asleep, Abdeslam called over to me: "That Mustapha Kemal was carrion! He ruined his country. The son of a dog!" Because I was writing, and also because I am not sure exactly where I stand in this philosophical dispute, I said: "You're right. *Allah imsik bekhir.*"

Sirkeci, September 29

We are installed at Sirkeci on the Istanbul side, in the hotel I had first wanted. Outside the window is a taxi stand. From early morning onward there is the continuous racket of men shouting and horns being blown in a struggle to keep recently arrived taxis from edging in ahead of those that have been waiting in line. The general prohibition of horn-blowing, which is in effect everywhere in the city, doesn't seem to apply here. The altercations are bitter, and everyone gets involved in them. Taxi drivers in Istanbul are something of a race apart. They are the only social group who systematically try to take advantage of the foreign visitor. In the ships, restaurants, cafés, the prices asked of the newcomer are the same as those paid by the inhabitants. (In the bazaars buying is automatically a matter of wrangling; that is understood.) The cab drivers, however, are more actively acquisitive. For form's sake, their vehicles are equipped with meters, but their method of using them is such that they might better do without them. You get into a cab whose meter registers seventeen liras thirty kuruş, ask the man to turn it back to zero and start again, and he laughs and does nothing. When you get out it registers eighteen liras eighty kuruş. You give him the difference—one lira and a half. Never! He may want two and a half or three and a half or a good deal more, but he will not settle for what seems equitable according to the meter. Since most tourists pay what they are asked and go on their way, he is not prepared for an argument, and he is likely to let his temper run away with him if you are recalcitrant. There is also the pre-arranged-price system of taking a cab. Here the driver goes as slowly and by as circuitous a route as possible, calling out the general neighborhood of his destination for all in the streets to hear, so that he can pick up extra fares en route. He will, unless you assert yourself, allow several people to pile in on top of you until there is literally no room left for you to breathe.

The streets are narrow, crooked and often precipitous; traffic is very heavy, and there are many tramcars and buses. The result is that the taxis go like the wind whenever there is a space of a few yards ahead, rushing to the extreme left to get around obstacles before oncoming traffic reaches them. I am used to Paris and Mexico, both cities of evil repute where taxis are concerned, but I think Istanbul might possibly win first prize for thrill-giving.

One day our driver had picked up two extra men and mercifully put them in front with him, when he spied a girl standing on the curb and slowed down to take her in, too. A policeman saw his maneuver and did not approve: one girl with five men seemed too likely to cause a disturbance. He blew his whistle menacingly. The driver, rattled, swerved sharply to the left, to pretend he had never thought of such a thing as stopping to pick up a young lady. There was a crash and we were thrown forward off the seat. We got out; the last we saw of the driver, he was standing in the middle of the street by his battered car, screaming at the man he had hit, and holding up all traffic. Abdeslam took down his license number in the hope of persuading me to instigate a lawsuit.

Since the use of the horn is proscribed, taxi drivers can make their presence known only by reaching out the window and pounding violently on the outside of the door. The scraping of the tramcars and the din of the enormous horse-drawn carts thundering over the cobbled pavements make it difficult to judge just how much the horn interdiction reduces noise. The drivers also have a pretty custom of offering cigarettes at the beginning of the journey; this is to soften up the victim for the subsequent kill. On occasion they sing for you. One morning I was entertained all the way from Sulemaniye to Taksim with "Jezebel" and "Come On-a My House." In such cases the traffic warnings on the side of the car are done in strict rhythm.

Istanbul is a jolly place; it's hard to find any sinister element in it, notwithstanding all the spy novels for which it provides such a handsome setting. A few of the older buildings are of stone; but many more of them are built of wood which looks as though it had never been painted. The cupolas and minarets rise above the disorder of the city like huge gray fungi growing out of a vast pile of ashes. For disorder is the visual keynote of Istanbul. It is not slovenly—only untidy; not dirty—merely dingy and drab. And just as you cannot claim it to be a beautiful city, neither can you accuse it of being uninteresting. Its steep hills and harbor views remind you a little of San Francisco; its overcrowded streets recall Bombay; its transportation facilities evoke Venice, for you can go many places by boats which are continually making stops. (It costs threepence to get across to Üsküdar in Asia.) Yet the streets are strangely reminiscent of an America that has almost disappeared. Again and again I have been reminded of some New England mill town in the time of my childhood. Or a row of little houses will suggest a back street in Stapleton, on Staten Island. It is a city whose esthetic is that of the unlikely and incongruous, a photographer's paradise. There is no native quarter, or, if you like, it is all native quarter. Beyoğlu, the site of the so-called better establishments, concerns itself as little with appearances as do the humbler regions on the other side of the bridges.

You wander down the hill toward Karaköy. Above the harbor with its thousands of caïques, rowboats, tugs, freighters and ferries, lies a pall of smoke and haze through which you can see the vague outline of the domes and towers of Aya Sofia, Sultan Ahmet, Süleyimaniye; but to the left and far above all that there is a pure region next to the sky where the mountains in Asia glisten with snow. As you descend the alleys of steps that lead to the water's level, there are more and more people around you. In Karaköy itself just to make progress along the sidewalk requires the best part of your attention. You would think that all of the city's million and a quarter inhabitants were in the streets on their way to or from Galata Bridge. By Western European standards it is not a well-dressed crowd. The chaotic sartorial effect achieved by the populace in Istanbul is not necessarily due to poverty, but rather to a divergent conception of the uses to which European garments should be put. The mass is not an ethnically homogeneous one. The types of faces range from Levantine through Slavic to Mongoloid, the last belonging principally to the soldiers from eastern Anatolia. Apart from language there seems to be no one common element, not even shabbiness, since there are usually a few men and women who do understand how to wear their clothing.

Galata Bridge has two levels, the lower of which is a great dock whence the boats leave to go up the Golden Horn and the Bosporus, across to the Asiatic suburbs, and down to the islands in the Sea of Marmara. The ferries are there, of all sizes and shapes, clinging to the edge like water beetles to the side of a floating stick. When you get across to the other side of the bridge there are just as many people and just as much traffic, but the buildings are older and the streets narrower, and you begin to realize that you are, after all, in an oriental city. And if you expect to see anything more than the "points of interest," you are going to have to wander for miles on foot. The character of Istanbul derives from a thousand disparate, nonevident details; only by observing the variations and repetitions of such details can you begin to get an idea of the patterns they form. Thus the importance of wandering. The dust is bad. After a few hours of it I usually have a sore throat. I try to get off the main arteries, where the horses and drays clatter by, and stay in the alleyways, which are too narrow for anything but foot traffic. These lanes occasionally open up into little squares with rugs hanging on the walls and chairs placed in the shade of the grapevines overhead. A few Turks will be sitting about drinking coffee; the *narghilehs* bubble. Invariably, if I stop and gaze a moment, someone asks me to have some coffee, eat a few green walnuts and share his pipe. An irrational disinclination to become involved keeps me from accepting, but today Abdeslam did accept, only to find to his chagrin that the narghileh contained tobacco, and not kif or hashish as he had expected.

Cannabis sativa and its derivatives are strictly prohibited in Turkey, and the natural correlative of this proscription is that alcohol, far from being frowned upon as it is in other Moslem lands, is freely drunk; being a government monopoly it can be bought at any cigarette counter. This fact is no mere detail; it is of primary social importance, since the psychological effects of the two substances are diametrically opposed to each other. Alcohol blurs the personality by loosening inhibitions. The drinker feels, temporarily at least, a sense of participation. Kif abolishes no inhibitions; on the contrary it reinforces them, pushes the individual further back into the recesses of his own isolated personality, pledging him to contemplation and inaction. It is to be expected that there should be a close relationship between the culture of a given society and the means used by its members to achieve release and euphoria. For Judaism and Christianity the means has always been alcohol; for Islam it has been hashish. The first is dynamic in its effects, the other static. If a nation wishes, however mistakenly, to Westernize itself, first let it give up hashish. The rest will follow, more or less as a matter of course. Conversely, in a Western country, if a whole segment of the population desires, for reasons of protest (as has happened in the United States), to isolate itself in a radical fashion from the society around it, the quickest and surest way is for it to replace alcohol by cannabis.

October 2

Today in our wanderings we came upon the old fire tower at the top of the hill behind Süleymaniye, and since there was no sign at the door forbidding entry, we stepped in and began to climb the one hundred and eighty rickety wooden steps of the spiral staircase leading to the top. (Abdeslam counted them.) When we were almost at the top, we heard strains of Indian music; a radio up there was tuned in to New Delhi. At the same moment a good deal of water came pouring down upon us through the cracks above. We decided to beat a retreat, but then the boy washing the stairs saw us and insisted that we continue to the top and sit awhile. The view up there was magnificent; there is no better place from which to see the city. A charcoal fire was burning in a brazier, and we had tea and listened to some Anatolian songs which presently came over the air. Outside the many windows the wind blew, and the city below, made quiet by distance, spread itself across the rolling landscape on every side, its roof tiles pink in the autumn sun.

Later we sought out Pandeli's, a restaurant I had heard about but not yet found. This time we managed to discover it, a dilapidated little building squeezed in among harness shops and wholesale fruit stores, unprepossessing but cozy, and with the best food we have found in Istanbul. We had *pirinç çorba, beyendeli kebap, barbunya fasulya* and other good things. In the middle of the meal, probably while chewing on the *taʒe makarna,* I bit my lip. My annoyance with the pain was not mitigated by hearing Abdeslam remark unsympathetically, "If you'd keep your mouth open when you chew, like everybody else, you wouldn't have accidents like this." Pandeli's is the only native restaurant I have seen which doesn't sport a huge refrigerated showcase packed with food. You are usually led to this and told to choose what you want to eat. In the glare of the fluorescent lighting the food looks pallid and untempting, particularly the meat, which has been hacked into unfamiliar-looking cuts. During your meal there is usually a radio playing ancient jazz; occasionally a Turkish or Syrian number comes up. Although the tea is good, it is not good enough to warrant its being served as though it were nectar, in infinitesimal glasses that can be drained at one gulp. I often order several at once, and this makes for confusion. When you ask for water, you are brought a tiny bottle capped with tinfoil. Since it is free of charge, I suspect it of being simple tap water; perhaps I am unjust.

In the evening we went to the very drab red-light district in Beyoğlu, just behind the British Consulate General. The street was mobbed with men and boys. In the entrance door of each house was a small square opening, rather like those through which one used to be denied access to American speak-easies, and framed in each opening, against the dull yellow light within, was a girl's head.

The Turks are the only Moslems I have seen who seem to have got rid of that curious sentiment (apparently held by all followers of the True Faith), that there is an inevitable and hopeless difference between themselves and non-Moslems. Subjectively, at least, they have managed to bridge the gulf created by their religion, that abyss which isolates Islam from the rest of the world. As a result the visitor feels a specific connection with them which is not the mere one-sided sympathy the well-disposed traveler has for the more basic members of other cultures, but is something desired and felt by them as well. They are touchingly eager to understand and please—so eager, indeed, that they often neglect to listen carefully and consequently get things all wrong. Their good will, however, seldom flags, and in the long run this more than compensates for being given the breakfast you did not order, or being sent in the opposite direction from the one in which you wanted to go. Of course, there is the linguistic barrier. One really needs to know Turkish to live in Istanbul and because my ignorance of all Altaic languages is total, I suffer. The chances are nineteen in twenty that when I give an order things will go wrong, even when I get hold of the housekeeper who speaks French and who assures me calmly that all the other employees are idiots. The hotel is considered by my guidebook to be a "de luxe" establishment—the highest category. Directly after the "de luxe" listings come the "first class" places, which it describes in its own mysterious rhetoric: "These hotels have somewhat luxury, but are still comfortable with every convenience." Having seen the lobbies of several of the hostelries thus pigeonholed, complete with disemboweled divans and abandoned perambulators, I am very thankful to be here in my de-luxe suite, where the telephone is white so that I can see the cockroaches on the instrument before I lift it to my lips. At least the insects are discreet and die obligingly under a mild blast of DDT. It is fortunate I came here: my two insecticide bombs would never have lasted out a sojourn in a first-class hotel.

October 6

Santa Sophia? Aya Sofya now, not a living mosque but a dead one, like those of Kairouan which can no longer be used because they have been profaned by the feet of infidels. Greek newspapers have carried on propaganda campaigns designed to turn the clock back, reinstate Aya Sofya as a tabernacle of the Orthodox Church. The move was obviously foredoomed to failure; after having used it as a mosque for five centuries the Moslems would scarcely relish seeing it put back into the hands of the Christians. And so now it is a museum which contains nothing but its own architecture. Sultan Ahmet, the mosque just across the park, is more to my own taste; but then, a corpse does not bear comparison to a living organism. Sultan Ahmet is still a place of worship, the *imam* is allowed to wear the classical headgear, the heavy final syllable of Allah's name reverberates in the air under the high dome, boys *dahven* in distant corners as they memorize surat from the Koran. When the tourists stumble over the prostrate forms of men in prayer, or blatantly make use of their light meters and Rolleiflexes, no one pays any attention. To Abdeslam this incredible invasion of privacy was tantamount to lack of respect for Islam; it fanned the coals of his resentment into flame. (In his country no unbeliever can put even one foot into a mosque.) As he wandered about, his exclamations of indignation became increasingly audible. He started out with the boys by suggesting to them that it was their great misfortune to be living in a country of widespread sin. They looked at him blankly and went on with their litanies. Then in a louder voice he began to criticize the raiment of the worshipers, because they wore socks and slippers on their feet and on their heads berets or caps with the visors at the back. He knows that the wearing of the *tarboosh* is forbidden by law, but his hatred of Kemal Ataturk, which has been growing hourly ever since his arrival, had become too intense, I suppose, for him to be able to repress it any longer. His big moment came when the imam entered. He approached the venerable gentleman with elaborate salaams which were enthusiastically reciprocated. Then the two retired into a private room, where they remained for ten minutes or so. When Abdeslam came out there were tears in his eyes and he wore an expression of triumph. "Ah, you see?" he cried, as we emerged into the street. "That poor man is very, *very* unhappy. They have only one day of Ramadan in the year." Even I was a little shocked to hear that the traditional month had been whittled down to a day. "This is an accursed land," he went on. "When we get power we'll soak it in petrol and set it afire and burn everyone in it. May it forever be damned! And all these dogs living in it, I pray Allah they may be thrown into the fires of Gehennem. Ah, if we only had our power back for one day, we Moslems! May Allah speed that day when we shall ride into Turkey and smash their government and all their works of Satan!" The imam, it seems, had been delighted beyond measure to see a young man who still had the proper respect for religion; he had complained bitterly that the youth of Turkey was spiritually lost.

Today I had lunch with a woman who has lived here a good many years. As a Westerner, she felt that the important thing to notice about Turkey is the fact that from having been in the grip of a ruthless dictatorship it has slowly evolved into a modern democracy, rather than having followed the more usual reverse process. Even Ataturk was restrained by his associates from going all the way in his iconoclasm, for what he wanted was a Turkish adaptation of what he had seen happen in Russia. Religion was to him just as much of an opiate in one country as in another. He managed to deal it a critical blow here, one which may yet prove to have been fatal. Last year an American, a member of Jehovah's Witnesses, arrived, and as is the custom with members of that sect, stood on the street handing out brochures. But not for long. The police came, arrested him, put him in jail, and eventually effected his expulsion from the country. This action, insisted my lunch partner, was not taken because the American was distributing Christian propaganda; had he been distributing leaflets advocating the reading of the Koran, it's likely that his punishment would have been more severe.

October 10

At the beginning of the sixteenth century, Selim the Grim captured from the Shah of Persia one of the most fantastic pieces of furniture I have ever seen. The trophy was the poor Shah's throne, a simple but massive thing made of chiseled gold, decorated with hundreds of enormous emeralds. I went to see it today at the Topkapi Palace. There was a bed to match, also of emerald-studded gold. After a moment of looking, Abdeslam ran out of the room where these incredible objects stood into the courtyard, and could not be coaxed back in. "Too many riches are bad for the eyes," he explained. I could not agree; I thought them beautiful. I tried to make him tell me the exact reason for his sudden flight, but he found it difficult to give me a rational explanation of his behavior. "You know that gold and jewels are sinful," he began. To get him to go on, I said I knew. "And if you look at sinful things for very long you can go crazy; you know that. And I don't want to go crazy." I was willing to take the chance, I replied, and I went back in to see more.

October 16

These last few days I have spent entirely at the covered souks. I discovered the place purely by accident, since I follow no plan in my wanderings about the city. You climb an endless hill; whichever street you take swarms with buyers and sellers who take up all the room between the shops on either side. It isn't good form to step on the merchandise, but now and then one can't avoid it.

The souks are all in one vast ant hill of a building, a city within a city whose avenues and streets, some wide, some narrow, are like the twisting hallways of a dream. There are more than five thousand shops under its roof, so they assure me; I have not wondered whether it seems a likely number or not, nor have I passed through all its forty-two entrance portals or explored more than a small number of its tunneled galleries. Visually the individual shops lack the color and life of the *kissarias* of Fez and Marrakech, and there are no painted Carthaginian columns like those which decorate the souks in Tunis. The charm of the edifice lies in its vastness and, in part, precisely from its dimness and clutter. In the middle of one open space where two large corridors meet, there is an outlandish construction, in shape and size not unlike one of the old traffic towers on New York's Fifth Avenue in the 'twenties. On the ground floor is a minute kitchen. If you climb the crooked outside staircase, you find yourself in a tiny restaurant with four miniature tables. Here you sit and eat, looking out along the tunnels over the heads of the passers-by. It is a place out of Kafka's *Amerika*.

The antique shops here in the souks are famous. As one might expect, tourists are considered to be a feebleminded and nearly defenseless species of prey, and there are never enough of them to go around. Along the sides of the galleries stand whole tribes of merchants waiting for them to appear. These men have brothers, fathers, uncles and cousins, each of whom operates his own shop, and the tourist is passed along from one member of the family to the next with no visible regret on anyone's part. In one shop I heard the bearded proprietor solemnly assuring a credulous American woman that the amber perfume she had just bought was obtained by pressing beads of amber like those in the necklace she was examining. Not that it would have been much more truthful of him had he told her that it was made of ambergris; the amber I have smelled here never saw a whale, and consists almost entirely of benzoin.

If you stop to look into an antiquary's window you are lost. Suddenly you are aware that hands are clutching your clothing, pulling you gently toward the door, and honeyed voices are experimenting with greetings in all the more common European languages, one after the other. Unless you offer physical resistance you find yourself being propelled forcibly within. Then as you face your captors over arrays of old silver and silk, they begin to work on you in earnest, using all the classic clichés of Eastern sales-patter. "You have such a fine face that I want my merchandise to go with you." "We need money today; you are the first customer to come in all day long." A fat hand taps the ashes from a cigarette. "Unless I do business with you, I won't sleep tonight. I am an old man. Will you ruin my health?" "Just buy one thing, no matter what. Buy the cheapest thing in the store, if you like, but buy something. . . ." If you get out of the place without making a purchase, you are entitled to add ten to your score. A knowledge of Turkish is not necessary here in the bazaars. If you prefer not to speak English or French or German, you find that the Moslems love to be spoken to in Arabic, while the Jews speak a corrupt Andalucían version of Spanish.

Today I went out of the covered souks by a back street that I had not found before. It led downward toward the Rustempaşa Mosque. The shops gave the street a strange air: they all looked alike from the outside. On closer inspection I saw that they were all selling the same wildly varied assortment of unlikely objects. I wanted to examine the merchandise, and since Abdeslam had been talking about buying some rubber-soled shoes, we chose a place at random and went into it. While he tried on sneakers and sandals I made a partial inventory of the objects in the big, gloomy room. The shelves and counters exhibited footballs, Moslem rosaries, military belts, reed mouthpieces for native oboes, doorhooks, dice of many sizes and colors, narghilehs, watchstraps of false cobraskin, garden shears, slippers of untanned leather—hard as stone—brass taps for kitchen sinks, imitation ivory cigarette holders—ten inches long, suitcases made of pressed paper, tambourines, saddles, assorted medals for the military and plastic game counters. Hanging from the ceiling were revolver holsters, lutes, and zipper fasteners that looked like strips of flypaper. Ladders were stacked upright against the wall, and on the floor were striped canvas deck chairs, huge tin trunks with scenes of Mecca stamped on their sides, and a great pile of wood shavings among whose comfortable hills nestled six very bourgeois cats. Abdeslam bought no shoes, and the proprietor began to stare at me and my notebook with unconcealed suspicion, having decided, perhaps, that I was a member of the secret police looking for stolen goods.

October 19

Material benefits may be accrued in this worldwide game of refusing to be oneself. Are these benefits worth the inevitable void produced by such destruction? The question is apposite in every case where the traditional beliefs of a people have been systematically modified by its government. Rationalizing words like "progress," "modernization," or "democracy" mean nothing because, even if they are used sincerely, the imposition of such concepts by force from above cancels whatever value they might otherwise have. There is little doubt that by having been made indifferent Moslems the younger generation in Turkey has become more like our idea of what people living in the twentieth century should be. The old helplessness in the face of *mektoub* (it is written) is gone, and in its place is a passionate belief in man's ability to alter his destiny. That is the greatest step of all; once it has been made, anything, unfortunately, can happen.

Abdeslam is not a happy person. He sees his world, which he knows is a good world, being assailed from all sides, slowly crumbling before his eyes. He has no means of understanding me should I try to explain to him that in this age what he considers to be religion is called superstition, and that religion today has come to be a desperate attempt to integrate metaphysics with science. Something will have to be found to replace the basic wisdom which has been destroyed, but the discovery will not be soon; neither Abdeslam nor I will ever know of it.

Baptism of Solitude

Immediately when you arrive in the Sahara, for the first or the tenth time, you notice the stillness. An incredible, absolute silence prevails outside the towns; and within, even in busy places like the markets, there is a hushed quality in the air, as if the quiet were a conscious force which, resenting the intrusion of sound, minimizes and disperses sound straightway. Then there is the sky, compared to which all other skies seem faint-hearted efforts. Solid and luminous, it is always the focal point of the landscape. At sunset, the precise, curved shadow of the earth rises into it swiftly from the horizon, cutting it into light section and dark section. When all daylight is gone, and the space is thick with stars, it is still of an intense and burning blue, darkest directly overhead and paling toward the earth, so that the night never really grows dark.

You leave the gate of the fort or the town behind, pass the camels lying outside, go up into the dunes, or out onto the hard, stony plain and stand awhile, alone. Presently, you will either shiver and hurry back inside the walls, or you will go on standing there and let something very peculiar happen to you, something that everyone who lives there has undergone and which the French call *le baptême de la solitude*. It is a unique sensation, and it has nothing to do with loneliness, for loneliness presupposes memory. Here, in this wholly mineral landscape lighted by stars like flares, even memory disappears; nothing is left but your own breathing and the sound of your heart beating. A strange, and by no means pleasant, process of reintegration begins inside you, and have the choice of fighting against it, and insisting on remaining the person you have always been, or letting it take its course. For no one who has stayed in the Sahara for a while is quite the same as when he came.

Before the war for independence in Algeria, under the rule of the French military, there was a remarkable feeling of friendly sympathy among Europeans in the Sahara. It is unnecessary to stress the fact that the corollary of this pleasant state of affairs was the exercise of the strictest sort of colonial control over the Algerians themselves, a regime which amounted to a reign of terror. But from the European viewpoint the place was ideal. The whole vast region was like a small unspoiled rural community where everyone respected the rights of everyone else. Each time you lived there for a while, and left it, you were struck with the indifference and the impersonality of the world outside. If during your travels in the Sahara you forgot something, you could be sure of finding it later on your way back; the idea of appropriating it would not have occurred to anyone. You could wander where you liked, out in the wilderness or in the darkest alleys of the towns; no one would molest you.

At that time no members of the indigent, wandering, unwanted proletariat from northern Algeria had come down here, because there was nothing to attract them. Almost everyone owned a parcel of land in an oasis and lived by working it. In the shade of the date palms, wheat, barley and corn were grown, and those plants provided the staple items of diet. There were usually two or three Arab or Negro shopkeepers who sold things such as sugar, tea, candles, matches, carbide for fuel, and cheap European cotton goods. In the larger towns there was sometimes a shop kept by a European, but the merchandise was the same, because the customers were virtually all natives. Almost without exception, the only Europeans who lived in the Sahara were the military and the ecclesiastic.

As a rule, the military and their aides were friendly men, agreeable to be with, interested in showing visitors everything worth seeing in their districts. This was fortunate, as the traveler was often completely at their mercy. He might have to depend on them for his food and lodging, since in the smaller places there were no hotels. Generally he had to depend on them for contact with the outside world, because anything he wanted, like cigarettes or wine, had to be brought by truck from the military post, and his mail was sent in care of the post, too. Furthermore, the decision as to whether he was to have permission to move about freely in the region rested with the military. The power to grant those privileges was vested in, let us say, one lonely lieutenant who lived two hundred miles from his nearest countryman, ate badly (a condition anathema to any Frenchman), and wished that neither camels, date palms, nor inquisitive foreigners had ever been created. Still, it was rare to find an indifferent or unhelpful comandante. He was likely to invite you for drinks and dinner, show you the curiosities he had collected during his years in the *bled*, ask you to accompany him on his tours of inspection, or even to spend a fortnight with him and his *peloton* of several dozen native meharistes when they went out into the desert to make topographical surveys. Then you would be given your own camel—not an ambling pack camel that had to be driven with a stick by someone walking beside it, but a swift, trained animal that obeyed the slightest tug of the reins.

More extraordinary were the Pères Blancs, intelligent and well-educated. There was no element of resignation in their eagerness to spend the remainder of their lives in distant outposts, dressed as Moslems, speaking Arabic, living in the rigorous, comfortless manner of the desert inhabitants. They made no converts and expected to make none. "We are here only to show the Moslem that the Christian can be worthy of respect," they explained. One used to hear the Moslems say that although the Christians might be masters of the earth, the Moslems were the masters of heaven; for the military it was quite enough that the *indigène* recognize European supremacy here. Obviously the White Fathers could not be satisfied with that. They insisted upon proving to the inhabitants that the Nazarene was capable of leading as exemplary a life as the most ardent follower of Mohammed. It is true that the austerity of the Fathers' mode of life inspired many Moslems with respect for them if not for the civilization they represented. And as a result of the years spent in the desert among the inhabitants, the Fathers acquired a certain healthy and unorthodox fatalism, an excellent adjunct to their spiritual equipment, and a highly necessary one in dealing with the men among whom they had chosen to live.

With an area considerably larger than that of the United States, the Sahara is a continent within a continent—a skeleton, if you like, but still a separate entity from the rest of Africa which surrounds it. It has its own mountain ranges, rivers, lakes and forests, but they are largely vestigial. The mountain ranges have been reduced to gigantic bouldery bumps that rise above the neighboring countryside like the mountains on the moon. Some of the rivers appear as such for perhaps one day a year—others much less often. The lakes are of solid salt, and the forests have long since petrified. But the physical contours of the landscape vary as much as they do anywhere else. There are plains, hills, valleys, gorges, rolling lands, rocky peaks and volcanic craters, all without vegetation or even soil. Yet, probably the only parts that are monotonous to the eye are regions like the Tanezrouft, south of Reggane, a stretch of about five hundred miles of absolutely flat, gravel-strewn terrain, without the slightest sign of life, or the smallest undulation in the land, nothing to vary the implacable line of the horizon on all sides. After being here for a while, the sight of even a rock awakens an emotion in the traveler; he feels like crying, "Land!"

There is no known historical period when the Sahara has not been inhabited by man. Most of the other larger forms of animal life, whose abode it formerly was, have become extinct. If we believe the evidence of cave drawings, we can be sure that the giraffe, the hippopotamus and the rhinoceros were once dwellers in the region. The lion has disappeared from North Africa in our own time, likewise the ostrich. Now and then a crocodile is still discovered in some distant, hidden oasis pool, but the occurrence is so rare that when it happens it is a great event. The camel, of course, is not a native of Africa at all, but an importation from Asia, having arrived approximately at the time of the end of the Roman Empire—about when the last elephants were killed off. Large numbers of the herds of wild elephants that roamed the northern reaches of the desert were captured and trained for use in the Carthaginian army, but it was the Romans who finally annihilated the species to supply ivory for the European market.

Fortunately for man, who seems to insist on continuing to live in surroundings which become increasingly inhospitable to him, gazelles are still plentiful, and there are, paradoxically enough, various kinds of edible fish in the water holes—often more than a hundred feet deep—throughout the Sahara. Certain species which abound in artesian wells are blind, having always lived deep in the subterranean lakes.

An often-repeated statement, no matter how incorrect, takes a long time to disappear from circulation. Thus, there is a popular misconception of the Sahara as a vast region of sand across which Arabs travel in orderly caravans from one white-domed city to another. A generalization much nearer to the truth would be to say that it is an area of rugged mountains, bare valleys and flat, stony wasteland, sparsely dotted with Negro villages of mud. The sand in the Sahara, according to data supplied by the Geographical Service of the French Army, covers only about a tenth of its surface; and the Arabs, most of whom are nomads, form a small part of the population. The vast majority of the inhabitants are of Berber (native North African) and/or Negro (native West African) stock. But the Negroes of today are not those who originally peopled the desert. The latter never took kindly to the colonial designs of the Arabs and the Islamized Berbers who collaborated with them; over the centuries they beat a constant retreat toward the southeast until only a vestige of their society remains, in the region now known as the Tibesti. They were replaced by the more docile Sudanese, imported from the south as slaves to work the constantly expanding series of oases.

In the Sahara the oasis—which is to say, the forest of date palms—is primarily a man-made affair and can continue its existence only if the work of irrigating its terrain is kept up unrelentingly. When the Arabs arrived in Africa twelve centuries ago, they began a project of land reclamation which, if the Europeans continue it with the aid of modern machinery, will transform much of the Sahara into a great, fertile garden. Wherever there was a sign of vegetation, the water was there not far below; it merely needed to be brought to the surface. The Arabs set to work digging wells, constructing reservoirs, building networks of canals along the surface of the ground and systems of subterranean water-galleries deep in the earth.

For all these important projects, the recently arrived colonizers needed great numbers of workers who could bear the climate and the malaria that is still endemic in the oases. Sudanese slaves seemed to be the ideal solution of the problem, and these came to constitute the larger part of the permanent population of the desert. Each Arab tribe traveled about among the oases it controlled, collecting the produce. It was never the practice or the intention of the sons of Allah to live there. They have a saying which goes, "No one lives in the Sahara if he is able to live anywhere else." Slavery has, of course, been abolished officially by the French, but only recently, within our time. Probably the principal factor in the process by which Timbuktu was reduced from its status of capital of the Sahara to its present abject condition was the closing of the slave market there. But the Sahara, which started out as a Negro country, is still a Negro country, and will undoubtedly remain so for a long time.

The oases, those magnificent palm groves, are the blood and bone of the desert; life in the Sahara would be unthinkable without them. Wherever human beings are found, an oasis is sure to be nearby. Sometimes the town is surrounded by the trees, but usually it is built just outside, so that none of the fertile ground will be wasted on mere living quarters. The size of an oasis is reckoned by the number of trees it contains, not by the numbers of square miles it covers, just as the taxes are based on the number of date-bearing trees and not on the amount of land. The prosperity of a region is in direct proportion to the number and size of its oases. The one at Figuig, for instance, has more than two hundred thousand bearing palms, and the one at Timimoun is forty miles long, with irrigation systems that are of an astonishing complexity.

To stroll in a Saharan oasis is rather like taking a walk through a well-kept Eden. The alleys are clean, bordered on each side by hand-patted mud walls, not too high to prevent you from seeing the riot of verdure within. Under the high waving palms are the smaller trees—pomegranate, orange, fig, almond. Below these, in neat squares surrounded by narrow ditches of running water, are the vegetables and wheat. No matter how far from the town you stray, you have the same impression of order, cleanliness, and insistence on utilizing every square inch of ground. When you come to the edge of the oasis, you always find that it is in the process of being enlarged. Plots of young palms extend out into the glaring wasteland. Thus far they are useless, but in a few years they will begin to bear, and eventually this sun-blistered land will be a part of the green belt of gardens.

There are a good many birds living in the oases, but their songs and plumage are not appreciated by the inhabitants. The birds eat the young shoots and dig up the seeds as fast as they are planted, and practically every man and boy carries a slingshot. A few years ago I traveled through the Sahara with a parrot; everywhere the poor bird was glowered at by the natives, and in Timimoun a delegation of three elderly men came to the hotel one afternoon and suggested that I stop leaving its cage in the window; otherwise there was no telling what its fate might be. "Nobody likes birds here," they said meaningfully.

It is the custom to build little summerhouses out in the oases. There is often an element of play and fantasy in the architecture of these edifices which makes them captivating. They are small toy palaces of mud. Here, men have tea with their families at the close of day, or spend the night when it is unusually hot in the town, or invite their friends for a few hands of *ronda,* the favorite North African card game, and a little music. If a man asks you to visit him in his summerhouse, you find that the experience is invariably worth the long walk required to get there. You will have to drink at least the three traditional glasses of tea, and you may have to eat a good many almonds and smoke more kif than you really want, but it will be cool, there will be the gurgle of running water and the smell of mint in the air, and your host may bring out a flute. One winter I priced one of these houses that had particularly struck my fancy. With its garden and pool, the cost was the equivalent of twenty-five pounds. The catch was that the owner wanted to retain the right to work the land, because it was unthinkable to him that it should cease to be productive.

In the Sahara as elsewhere in North Africa, popular religious observances often include elements of pre-Islamic faiths in their ritual; the most salient example is the institution of religious dancing, which persists despite long-continued discouragement of the custom by educated Moslems. Even in the highly religious settlement of the M'Zab, where puritanism is carried to excessive lengths, the holding of dances is not unknown. At the time I lived there children were not allowed to laugh in public, yet I spent an entire night watching a dozen men dance themselves into unconsciousness beside a bonfire of palm branches. Two burly guards were necessary to prevent them from throwing themselves into the flames. After each man had been heaved back from the fire several times, he finally ceased making his fantastic skyward leaps, staggered, and sank to the ground. He was immediately carried outside the circle and covered with blankets, his place being taken by a fresh adept. There was no music or singing, but there were eight drummers, each one playing an instrument of a different size.

In other places, the dance is similar to the Berber *ahouache* of the Moroccan Atlas. The participants form a great circle holding hands, women alternating with men; their movements are measured, never frantic, and although the trance is constantly suggested, it seems never to be arrived at collectively. In the performances I have seen, there has been a woman in the center with her head and neck hidden by a cloth. She sings and dances, and the chorus around her responds antiphonally. It is all very sedate and low-pitched, but the irrational seems never very far away, perhaps because of the hypnotic effect produced by the slowly beaten, deep-toned drums.

The Touareg, an ancient offshoot of the Kabyle Berbers of Algeria, were unappreciative of the "civilizing mission" of the Roman legions and decided to put a thousand miles or more of desert between themselves and their would-be educators. They went straight south until they came to a land that seemed likely to provide them the privacy they desired, and there they have remained throughout the centuries, their own masters almost until today. Through all the ages during which the Arabs dominated the surrounding regions, the Touareg retained their rule of the Hoggar, that immense plateau in the very center of the Sahara. Their traditional hatred of the Arabs, however, does not appear to have been powerful enough to keep them from becoming partially Islamized, although they are by no means a completely Moslem people. Far from being a piece of property only somewhat more valuable than a sheep, the woman has an extremely important place in Targui society. The line of succession is purely maternal. Here, it is the men who must be veiled day and night. The veil is of fine black gauze and is worn, so they explain, to protect the soul. But since soul and breath to them are identical, it is not difficult to find a physical reason, if one is desired. The excessive dryness of the atmosphere often causes disturbances in the nasal passages. The veil conserves the breath's moisture, is a sort of little air-conditioning plant, and this helps keep out the evil spirits which otherwise would manifest their presence by making the nostrils bleed, a common occurrence in this part of the world.

It is scarcely fair to refer to these proud people as Touareg. The word is a term of opprobrium meaning "lost souls," given them by their traditional enemies the Arabs, but one which, in the outside world, has stuck. They call themselves *imochagh*, the free ones. Among all the Berber-speaking peoples, they are the only ones to have devised a system of writing their language. No one knows how long their alphabet has been in use, but it is a true phonetical alphabet, quite as well planned and logical as the Roman, with twenty-three simple and thirteen compound letters.

Unfortunately for them, the Touareg have never been able to get on among themselves; internecine warfare has gone on unceasingly among them for centuries. Until the French military put a stop to it, it had been a common practice for one tribe to set out on plundering expeditions against a neighboring tribe. During these voyages, the wives of the absent men remained faithful to their husbands, the strict Targui moral code recommending death as a punishment for infidelity. However, a married woman whose husband was away was free to go at night to the graveyard dressed in her finest apparel, lie on the tombstone of one of her ancestors, and invoke a certain spirit called Idebni, who always appeared in the guise of one of the young men of the community. If she could win Idebni's favor, he gave her news of her husband; if not, he strangled her. The Touareg women, being very clever, always managed to bring back news of their husbands from the cemetery.

The first motor crossing of the Sahara was accomplished in 1923. At that time it was still a matter of months to get from, let us say, Touggourt to Zinder, or from the Tafilelt to Gao. In 1934, I was in Erfoud asking about caravans to Timbuktu. Yes, they said, one was leaving in a few weeks, and it would take from sixteen to twenty weeks to make the voyage. How would I get back? The caravan would probably set out on its return trip at this time next year. They were surprised to see that this information lessened my interest. How could you expect to do it more quickly?

Of course, the proper way to travel in the Sahara is by camel, particularly if you're a good walker, since after about two hours of the camel's motion you are glad to get down and walk for four. Each succeeding day is likely to bring with it a greater percentage of time spent off the camel. Nowadays, if you like, you can leave Algiers in the morning by plane and be fairly well into the desert by evening, but the traveler who gives in to this temptation, like the reader of a mystery story who skips through the book to arrive at the solution quickly, deprives himself of most of the pleasure of the journey. For the person who wants to see something the practical means of locomotion is the trans-Saharan truck, a compromise between camel and airplane.

There are only two trails across the desert at present (the Piste Impériale through Mauretania not being open to the public) and I should not recommend either to drivers of private automobiles. The trucks, however, are especially built for the region. If there is any sort of misadventure, the wait is not likely to be more than twenty-four hours, since the truck is always expected at the next town, and there is always an ample supply of water aboard. But the lone car that gets stuck in the Sahara is in trouble.

Usually, you can go to the fort of any town and telephone ahead to the next post, asking them to notify the hotelkeeper there of your intended arrival. Should the lines be down—a not unusual circumstance—there is no way of assuring yourself a room in advance, save by mail, which is extremely slow. Unless you travel with your own blankets this can be a serious drawback, arriving unannounced, for the hotels are small, often having only five or six rooms, and the winter nights are cold. The temperature goes to several degrees below freezing, reaching its lowest point just before dawn. The same courtyard that may show 125° when it is flooded with sun at two in the afternoon will register only 28° the following morning. So it is good to know you are going to have a room and a bed in your next stopping place. Not that there is heating of any sort in the establishments, but by keeping the window shut you can help the thick mud walls conserve some of the daytime heat. Even so, I have awakened to find a sheet of ice over the water in the glass beside my bed.

These violent extremes of temperature are due, of course, to the dryness of the atmosphere, whose relative humidity is often less than five percent. When you reflect that the soil attains a temperature of one hundred and seventy-five degrees during the summer, you understand that the principal consideration in planning streets and houses should be that of keeping out as much light as possible. The streets are kept dark by being built underneath and inside the houses, and the houses have no windows in their massive walls. The French have introduced the window into much of their architecture, but the windows open onto wide, vaulted arcades, and thus, while they do give air, they let in little light. The result is that once you are out of the sun you live in a Stygian gloom.

Even in the Sahara there is no spot where rain has not been known to fall, and its arrival is an event that calls for celebration—drumming, dancing, firing of guns. The storms are violent and unpredictable. Considering their disastrous effects, one wonders that the people can welcome them with such unmixed emotions. Enormous walls of water rush down the dry river beds, pushing everything before them, often isolating the towns. The roofs of the houses cave in, and often the walls themselves. A prolonged rain would destroy every town in the Sahara, since the *tob*, of which everything is built, is softer than our adobe. And, in fact, it is not unusual to see a whole section of a village forsaken by its occupants, who have rebuilt their houses nearby, leaving the walls and foundations of their former dwellings to dissolve and drop back into the earth of which they were made.

In 1932 I decided to spend the winter in the M'Zab of southern Algeria. The rattletrap bus started out from Laghouat at night in a heavy rain. Not far to the south, the trail crossed a flat stretch about a mile wide, slightly lower than the surrounding country. Even as we were in it, the water began to rise around us, and in a moment the motor died. The passengers jumped out and waded about in water that soon was up to their waists; in all directions there were dim white figures in burnouses moving slowly through the flood, like storks. They were looking for a shallow route back to dry land, but they did not find it. In the end they carried me, the only European in the party, all the way to Laghouat on their backs, leaving the bus and its luggage to drown out there in the rain. When I got to Ghardaia two days later, the rain (which was the first in seven years) had made a deep pond beside an embankment the French had built for the trail. Such an enormous quantity of water all in one place was a source of great excitement to the inhabitants. For days there was a constant procession of women coming to carry it away in jugs. The children tried to walk on its surface, and two small ones were drowned. Ten days later the water had almost disappeared. A thick, brilliant green froth covered what was left, but the women continued to come with their jugs, pushing aside the scum and taking whatever fell in. For once they were able to collect as much water as they could store in their houses. Ordinarily, it was an expensive commodity that they had to buy each morning from the town water-sellers, who brought it in from the oasis.

There are probably few accessible places on the face of the globe where one can get less comfort for his money than the Sahara. It is still possible to find something flat to lie down on, several turnips and sand, noodles and jam, and a few tendons of something euphemistically called chicken to eat, and the stub of a candle to undress by at night. Inasmuch as it is necessary to carry one's own food and stove, it sometimes seems scarcely worth while to bother with the "meals" provided by the hotels. But if one depends entirely on tinned goods, they give out too quickly. Everything disappears eventually—coffee, tea, sugar, cigarettes—and the traveler settles down to a life devoid of these superfluities, using a pile of soiled clothing as a pillow for his head at night and a burnous as blanket.

Perhaps the logical question to ask at this point is: Why go? The answer is that when a man has been there and undergone the baptism of solitude he can't help himself. Once he has been under the spell of the vast, luminous, silent country, no other place is quite strong enough for him, no other surroundings can provide the supremely satisfying sensation of existing in the midst of something that is absolute. He will go back, whatever the cost in comfort and money, for the absolute has no price.

(Since this piece was written, the Algerian war has changed the Saharan picture. Now the hypothetical voyager would probably not go back, because without special documents it is very unlikely that he would be allowed in. The Sahara is not on display at the present time.)

AUTOBIOGRAPHY

Without Stopping

———————

I

In the early years of the century a certain Dr. Fletcher announced that it was absolutely necessary to chew each mouthful of food forty times, regardless of its consistency. This action, he claimed, made it possible to form a bolus. The practice was known as Fletcherization. My father explained it to me in detail many times, beginning when I was five, and I was obliged to use the method at table. I chewed diligently, but sometimes swallowed without meaning to, before I had counted to forty.

"Fletcherize, young man!" he shouted, and at the same instant I felt the sting of a large linen table napkin as he flicked it across my face. Often it caught me in the eye, which, being painful, was even more humiliating. "Keep chewing. Keep chewing. You haven't made your bolus yet." By this time I was so confused that I no longer knew whether I was chewing or swallowing.

"What'd I tell you? I told you *not* to swallow!"

"I couldn't help it." Sometimes I still had the bolus in my mouth, for I learned to hold it under my tongue while the involuntary spasm of swallowing took place, and then I would open my mouth to prove that I hadn't really disobeyed. This was always considered an "impertinence" and was followed by fresh recriminations.

I would beg Mother to let me eat in the kitchen early, so as not to have to undergo the ordeal of sitting at table. This she never allowed unless I was sick. To fall ill was thus a great temptation; half my early maladies were pretexts for lying in bed and eating alone. One night when I did have a high fever, Daddy stood at the foot of my bed with his hands in his pockets. He said to Mother: "You know, I think he likes to be sick."

"Yes," I thought, "I do. And the best part is, I *am* sick, and you can't forbid it." I regularly settled into protracted illnesses with a shiver of voluptuousness at the prospect of the stretches of privacy that lay ahead.

In the summer of 1916, when I was five, my parents moved into the house on De Grauw Avenue. After the Glenora season was over, they took me back to the Happy Hollow Farm and left me there. When they were all installed, Grampa went down to New York to spend a week with them in the new house. He returned and described it to me, making his eyes round with admiration. "Wait till you see it. It's a very fine house," he said. I believed him, but I did not look forward to living in it, because Mother and Daddy would be there.

Nevertheless, the house impressed me. Everything glistened with newness. The floors were so shiny and slippery that after a few falls I pretended the open areas were deep water; my task was to get from rug to rug without stepping into the water.

The house was on "the Hill," which was then a forested ridge above the town of Jamaica, Long Island. Here the newly laid streets came to sudden ends in the woods. At the beginning the land around the house was all unspoiled, so that we heard many birds singing in the early mornings. Then Judge Twombley built a house on the east. Two or three years later men came and cut down the trees across the street. Mother decided that she no longer enjoyed living there. The destruction of the trees was her bitterest complaint. There were further disadvantages, such as the fact that the house was one of those two-family structures that look like one-family houses, the other part being occupied by the young architect who had designed it. The young architect had a wife with whom Mother seldom agreed. Another drawback to the place was the elevation on which it had been built; thirty-five steps had to be climbed in order to get up to it from the street below. However, at the beginning there were robins and dogwood all around—even thrushes and violets—and it was certainly pleasanter for me than the dark apartment with its empty yard below.

We had a housekeeper named Hannah, a wonderfully calm Finnish woman who wore her eyeglasses on a chain that wound into a little reel pinned beside her collar. Hannah's husband was an official of the Socialist Party, and she became increasingly involved with his work and eventually left us, although for several years she occasionally came and stayed with me at night when my parents went out. Helping Hannah was Anna, also a Finn, but one who had just arrived in the United States. I did not particularly like her, but that was because I heard only adverse criticism of her. She was young and brash, she sang as she worked, and she made unnecessary noises with pails and mops.

"Aunt Adelaide's" was a magic phrase; it meant not only the person but the place. She was Daddy's sister, a librarian working with Annie Carroll Moore, who was the head of the Children's Section at the Fifth Avenue Public Library. Seeing Aunt Adelaide meant being recognized as a person who really existed, rather than being treated as a captured animal of uncertain reactions. That was pleasant and relaxing; besides, she lived in a Japanese apartment in Greenwich Village, full of strange objects and wonderful smells. Sometimes Miss Moore was in the apartment among the screens and lanterns and flickering candlelight; her presence gave the occasion an unmistakable air of celebration, low-keyed and mysterious, the very essence of festivity in its conscious exclusion of the outside world. During those early years the visits to Aunt Adelaide's provided the high points of life in the city.

"Your father's a devil," Gramma used to tell me. "He's impossible," Mother's sisters assured her again and again. At mealtimes his irascibility reached its peak. He insisted on knowing the ingredients and the preparation of each dish, and whenever he had time, he stood in the kitchen and supervised the cooking. If the food turned out to be not exactly as he wanted it, he had a temper fit, slammed down his napkin, and rushed to the bathroom to take one of his digestive remedies. A temper fit made him ill until at least the next day; it usually gave whoever else was at the table indigestion as well. His rages came like a bolt of lightning, even as the food went down his throat, and were the more inexplicable since Mother had studied cooking at Simmons in Boston and was an expert. Throughout my childhood she herself baked all the bread we ate. Any other bread was "synthetic," and Daddy would not touch it.

The new house made it possible for me to be alone much of the time, since I had the third floor all to myself. I could go upstairs and shut my door, leaving the sounds of wrangling behind. Quickly I began to invent more timetables. I established the routes by walking along and naming the rocks and bushes as I went, without, however, tagging them as I had done at Glenora. For there were other children around, and my intuitions warned me that everything must be hidden from them; they were potential enemies. I printed the lists of place-names in notebooks when I got home: Shirkingsville, 645th Street, Clifton Junction, Snakespiderville, Hiss, El Apepal, Norpath Kay.

Soon I invented a planet with landmasses and seas. The continents were Ferncawland, Lanton, Zaganokworld, and Araplaina. I drew maps of each and gave them mountain ranges, rivers, cities, and railways. All this was interrupted by my entry into school. In the autumn of 1917 they cut off my hair and took me to see the principal of the Model School. He made me read aloud to him for what seemed a long time. Then he had me assigned to the second grade, for, as he said, although I could print very fast, I didn't yet know how to write in script, and my arithmetic was nonexistent. It was fortunate that Dr. McLaughlin did not start me higher, since I was already the youngest in the class, a situation which could only make things more difficult for me.

School was no good. It took me one day to discover that the world of children was a world of unremitting warfare. But since I had suspected this all along, it did not come as a shock. I accepted the group beatings as part of the pattern and stealthily launched punitive attacks on loners who had got separated from the pack. This usually resulted in a permanent personal hatred for me on the part of the victim, inasmuch as I sharpened stones beforehand in order to draw blood. For a boy to participate in a mass attack against me was legitimate, but for me to ambush him later from behind was apparently unforgivable.

"Now he knows what it's like," Daddy once said to Mother, a satisfied grin on his face, when I had come in dirty and bruised. "This is what he needs to bring him down to earth."

In such instances I could only look at him, but since I firmly believed that I *had* to win in the struggle between us or I should be hopelessly lost, it seemed to me that it was merely a question of holding out.

One evening from up in my room I heard music downstairs. They had bought a phonograph and were playing Tchaikowsky's Fourth. This is the first time that I recall hearing music of any sort. At the beginning I was not allowed to touch either machine or records, but after a few months had gone by, I was playing it much more than they were. Soon I began buying my own records. The first one was "At the Jazz Band Ball," played by the Original Dixieland Jazz Band. When Daddy heard it, he berated Mother. "Why do you let him buy trash like that?"

"He plays the other music, too," she said.

"I don't want any more of that stuff brought into this house. Do you hear me, young man?"

As always, I let my face rather than my words express my emotion. "Of course," I said curtly. After that I bought military bands playing Latin-American pieces.

Daddy continued to buy records. He had Dr. Karl Muck directing the Boston Symphony. ("A Hun. I don't know why they leave him there.") He had Galli-Curci singing Rossini and Bellini. ("Homely as a hedge fence," said Mother.) He had Josef Hofmann playing "Venezia e Napoli." ("So conceited he doesn't even suspect there's anyone else in the world." Daddy had been to a Hofmann recital.)

My teacher Miss Crane and I did not like each other. I began by refusing to sing. No threats could make me open my mouth. I was marked "Deficient in Class Singing" regularly on my monthly report card, not to mention being given the lowest possible mark for Effort. In Proficiency and Deportment I always got top grades; fortunately my stubbornness was put down to a lack of effort rather than to purposeful sabotage. To avenge myself I hit on an idea which would prove to Miss Crane that I was capable of doing my work correctly, yet which at the same time would anger her. I wrote everything perfectly, only backwards. My papers were consistently marked with a zero. Finally Miss Crane made me stay after school. "What does this mean?" she demanded; her voice was trembling with rage. "What do you mean by this?"

"By what?"

She shook the papers in the air.

"There are no mistakes," I told her smugly.

"I'm going to call your mother," she said. "In my day they'd have known what to do with a little boy like you, I can tell you that." She shoved the sheaf of papers into a manila envelope and locked them away in a drawer.

The feud ended when Mother spoke with me seriously about it, simulating anxiety as to what Daddy would say if he were to hear about my behavior. "I don't know what's got into you," she complained. I did not know, either, but I felt a vague menace on all sides.

Later things went more smoothly. Once I had left Miss Crane behind I had a clean slate or imagined I did. In fact, Miss Crane went all over the school, warning my future teachers about me.

The day the war ended, no classes were held. They told us to go home and get combs. Back in school we were coached in the melody of "Marching Through Georgia." When we knew it fairly well, we were given toilet paper to put over the combs and instructed to sing the syllable "ta." There was a great amount of confusion, which every child did his utmost to augment and prolong, but finally we found ourselves marching down the street, always to "Georgia," with people smiling and waving flags at us. None of it made any sense, but I enjoyed it because no one noticed whether I was singing or not.

I was seven, and my second teeth were growing in crooked. "Your father's going to take you to the city tomorrow to see Dr. Waugh," Mother told me. So began the semiweekly visits to the corner of Fifth Avenue and Forty-seventh Street, where the orthodontist had his offices. Since my case involved broadening of both the upper and lower jaw, the visits continued until exactly ten years later, when the last bands were removed, and the enamel on certain of the teeth was found to have been pitted, possibly as a result of the treatment.

"Orthodontia's made great strides," Daddy told me. "If your mother or I'd had crooked teeth, they'd have yanked them out."

"It was like the Dark Ages," Mother said, shuddering.

"I just want you to know how lucky you are, that's all," he warned me.

Lucky had nothing to do with the way it felt to have a wide platinum band cemented around every tooth, each one with an interior and exterior screw attached to it, and four gold arches being held in place by the screws. Tuesdays and Fridays I went and had the screws tightened a little. The pain this caused lasted two or three days, generally until just before the next tightening, so that there were very few days in the year when I could eat without wincing. All this metal in my mouth made it necessary for me to take precautions not to let blows catch me in the face. When they did, it was disastrous. The only bright spot in the tooth straightening was the fact of missing school two afternoons a week in order to go to Dr. Waugh's. The next year, when I was eight, I began going alone to the appointments. This delighted me, because everyone was scandalized by the idea of allowing so small a child absolute freedom to go around New York City by himself.

"But don't you just worry yourself sick?" insisted Aunt Ulla. "I'd be a nervous wreck every time, until he got back."

"Oh, I get a little uneasy sometimes, of course," said Mother.

Aunt Ulla turned to me. "Your mother's got bats in the belfry."

"But what could happen to me?" I demanded. "Why should anything happen to me?"

Mother was quite right; nothing ever did. And I saw more and learned more going by myself than I ever would have if a grown-up had been along.

About once a month I stopped by the Public Library to see Miss Moore. She always had time to talk for a few minutes, and she generally gave me a book to add to my growing collection. Often she had the authors dedicate them to me beforehand. Hugh Lofting wrote a whole page in the front of *The Story of Doctor Dolittle* and embellished it with drawings, as did Henrik Willem van Loon in *A Short History of Discovery,* who drew me a portrait of himself smoking a pipe. She had Carl Sandburg inscribe his *Rootabaga Stories* for me, too.

The winter when I was in the third grade there occurred an epidemic of Spanish influenza. We all caught it, including Aunt Adelaide, but whereas Daddy, Mother, and I got well, Aunt Adelaide's case was complicated by pneumonia and pleurisy, so that she died. The news was given me by Mother in such a way that the very memory of Aunt Adelaide became an obscenity, and I could not mention her name for a good seven years. Mother said: "Your Aunt Adelaide has gone away. You'll never see her again." To my involuntary: "Where? Why not?" she gave no answer but turned and walked out of the room. I understood that Aunt Adelaide was dead and felt a blind rage which, needing an object, fastened itself upon Mother for being the bearer of the news and, above all, for giving it to me in such a dishonest fashion.

Aunt Emma came to visit, all pale and trembly. About her the others said: "Emma's the temperamental one in the family." This was because she spent her time painting landscapes in oil and playing the piano; anyone "artistic" was always temperamental by definition. She took to bed, where she remained for a month with every sort of ailment. When she was better, we used to eat breakfast in her room. One Sunday morning early I heard loud laughter coming from what was called "the yellow bedroom." I ran in and saw Daddy in his pajamas, in bed with Aunt Emma, who was squealing and shrieking, while Mother leaned over the footboard, holding her side from having laughed too much. As I came in, he sprang up, crying: "Let's get to those buckwheat cakes." Then he went out of the room.

In a few minutes Mother called to me. "I want to speak to you. You mustn't tell anyone you saw Daddy in bed with Aunt Emma."

"I won't, but why?"

"They might think it was terrible."

"What do they care? It's none of their business, is it?"

"That's right. Of course it's none of their business. So don't tell anyone."

I wrote a rhyme and made a little book of it for Aunt Emma. Each page had half a stanza printed in its own color of wax crayon. The rhyme, which for some reason I could not fathom, made her laugh, ran:

> Poor Aunt Emma, sick in bed
> With an ice-cap on her head.
> Poor Aunt Emma, sick in bed!
> She's very sick, but she's not dead.

"Why'd you laugh?" I asked her.

"Because I liked the poem. You love your old aunt, don't you?"

"Of course." This embarrassed me, and I went out of the room.

I was brought up to consider burglars an ever-present menace. The house was always completely locked. Even Hannah and Anna did not have keys but had to be let in when they came to work in the morning. Strangely enough, I was allowed to have my own key to the front door, and I kept it in an ostrich-skin Keytainer. One afternoon I got home from school, shut the front door behind me, and immediately suspected that I was alone in the house. The silence was overpowering. I went to the kitchen; it was all shining and empty. Reluctantly I crept from one room to another, not even daring to call out anyone's name and finding no one, anywhere. I went into the living room and sat on the couch, my mind boiling with awful possibilities. Perhaps already a burglar had got in and was hiding in some corner. I decided I must look into every closet, under every bed, even, unfortunately, in the garret behind the trunks, because if I went on sitting and worrying about it, I should become much too afraid. I went through my parents' bedroom thoroughly, beating my hands against their clothes hanging in the closet to be certain no one was hiding there in the dark. Then I went into the guest room. There was an enormous old four-poster bed in there. I bent down to look under it and felt my heart explode. Someone lay under there, all bunched up. I was unable to stand up and run; I could only stare.

Suddenly the thing under there snorted and began to wriggle. Mother's head came toward me, and she crawled forth, flushed and laughing. "Hannah and Anna had to go out, so I thought I'd see what would happen if I disappeared, too," she said. "You wouldn't like it much, would you?"

She tried to joke with me about it; I could see that she found the episode amusing. I walked out of the room, clenching my fists, climbed upstairs to my own quarters, and shut the door. Fear naturally turns to anger; the anger did not go away for several days.

On the whole Mother and I got on well, principally, I suppose, because she would listen to whatever I read her and give me a considered opinion, even of a list of invented place-names on a timetable. From the time when I had been two she had always read to me at bedtime for a half hour; this continued until I was seven. Then we alternated reading to each other. I remember wanting to stay in Hawthorne's *Tanglewood Tales* and the combination of repugnance and fascination I felt at hearing the stories of Poe. I could not read them aloud; I had to undergo them. Mother's pleasant, low voice and thus, by extension, her personality took on the most sinister overtones as she read the terrible phrases. If I looked at her, I did not wholly recognize her, and that frightened me even more. It was in this period that I began to call out in my sleep and to enact lengthy meaningless rituals, eyes open but unconscious, while Mother and Daddy stood watching, afraid to speak or touch me. The following day I would have no recall of the nocturnal drama. On one occasion I went to bed in my own room and woke up a minute later to find myself lying in the big bed of the guest room, Daddy bending over me shaking his forefinger in front of my nose, repeating: "You stay in bed, young man."

The winter I reached the age of eight, it was decided that I should start taking music lessons. This involved buying a piano, and since Mother would have only a grand, it also meant rearranging furniture. After prolonged and embittered discussion the piano was purchased, and I was taken to Miss Chase. Tuesdays I had theory, solfeggio, and ear training, Fridays piano technique.

The piano lessons were conducted in private, and so I did not mind them. I enjoyed practicing: it guaranteed privacy for the time that I sat there. No one thought of disturbing me when I was working at the piano, as long as I was either playing the pieces I had learned or running up and down my scales. I discovered, however, that if I improvised even for a minute, Mother would appear in the doorway and say: "Is that your work? It doesn't sound like it to me." So I learned to finish my practicing first, before I allowed myself the luxury of being free to experiment. Fortunately the theory, solfeggio, and ear-training lessons were obligatory, for it was thanks to them that I learned musical notation and thus was able to write down my own musical ideas. Had they been optional, I should carefully have avoided them, since there were other pupils present, and for me it could only be boring to listen to their attempts and errors, just as it could only be embarrassing to have them hear my own.

In the same way as I learned to complete my practicing before I amused myself at the piano, I always finished my homework immediately and only then turned to the various daily chores I had set myself: I issued a daily newspaper of which I made one copy of four pages in pencil and crayon, I made daily entries in the diaries of several imaginary characters, I continued to add to the books of information on my fictitious world, and I obsessively drew houses (front elevation, no perspective), complete with lists of their prices and purchasers, for a gigantic real estate development. The newspaper featured a daily report on an improbable sea trip being made by correspondents; "Today we landed at Cape Catoche. Guess where we will be tomorrow?" I had a huge loose-leaf atlas, so heavy that I could barely lift it. I would carry it to the center of the room and open it out on the floor to sit, lost, looking down at its maps. New loose sheets arrived every little while; the book had to be unscrewed and the maps inserted in their proper place.

I filled in the diaries each day, the entries being in the third-person present tense, like newspaper headlines. "Viper comes to house begging chickens. Adele turns him out." Many of the characters had diseases and lost weight at an alarming rate. At some point in each diary I would get too intensely involved in the developments and begin to fill in several pages at a time. Once that started, it was impossible to go back to day-by-day entries. The speed of events grew, and soon the book would be full. There were two volumes about a woman named Bluey Laber Dozlen, who sails from an unidentified European country to Wen Kroy, where she immediately finds a huge sum of money and buys herself a self-steering automobile. During her first year she has many illnesses and recoveries, several marriages and divorces, and becomes a spy. During the second year she learns how to play bridge and smoke opium. Everyone else catches influenza and pneumonia and dies, but Bluey, blessed with excellent health, manages to survive and is last seen hiding out in Hong Kong from a vengeful housemaid she was once foolish enough to dismiss.

I also made (and sold to visiting members of the family when I could) monthly calendars which I embellished with designs in crayon. The calendars were accurate and legible enough, but the vertical and horizontal lines which formed the squares for the days were always curved instead of being straight. Naturally, everyone called my attention to this defect. I explained that I had tried again and again to draw straight lines, but they always came out crooked. Daddypapa suggested I use a ruler. I did not consider that a solution to the problem at all; it would be almost like getting another person to help me. Besides, I had practiced a good deal making curved lines that were parallel, and I rather liked them that way. My calendars continued to look as though they had been designed for the side of a globe.

At this time I began to write a protracted work called *Le Carré, An Opera in Nine Chapters*. It was, of course, not an opera at all, but a story with a few lyrics inserted. For these I composed melodies; I assumed the songs gave me the right to call it opera. The plot concerned two men who agree to exchange wives. To accomplish this, each man must so lower himself in his wife's esteem that she divorces him. When the exchange has been effected, however, the women are discontented with the new arrangement and sabotage it in order to get their original husbands back. In the second chapter there was a soprano aria whose text went:

> Oh, lala,
> Oh daba,
> Oh honeymoon!
> Say, oh say when . . .
> But she got no further
> For there was her ex-husband
> Glaring at her like a starving pussycat.

I read *Le Carré* again and again to people who came to the house and discovered to my chagrin that the enthusiasm they showed for it came solely from the fact that they found it hilarious. When I was absolutely certain of this, I put the notebook away, and if anyone asked to hear it, I said it was lost.

Late one night there was a loud explosive cracking sound in the living room. In the morning it was discovered that the sounding board of the piano had buckled and split. Daddy flew into a rage against Wanamaker's and returned the instrument, insisting that no piano manufactured since the war could possibly be worth owning, because the wood was all unseasoned. Thus my music lessons came to a sudden stop. I did not mind too much, but Mother was unhappy about it for many months.

For relaxation Daddy had always played tennis. He looked very dapper in his white flannels. Much as Mother disliked having to play, she usually ended by giving in to his wishes, even though she knew a wrangle was inevitable. "I'm nearsighted!" she protested. "If my life depended on it, I couldn't see that ball."

"Nearsighted! You're blind as a bat."

Daddy had keen eyesight, but one morning he woke up blind in his left eye. A hemorrhage, his ophthalmologist told him. Although the damage was irreversible, he had several tests made. At breakfast one day he and Mother discussed them. I was busy pretending to look preoccupied, while following every word. Soon my curiosity overwhelmed me. "Why do they stick a needle into you?" I asked Mother.

"They have to take a sample of the blood . . ." she began, as Daddy gulped his coffee and slammed down his cup, roaring: "No!" And in answer to Mother's uncomprehending look he began in a singsong falsetto: *"My father blablablabla blablabla . . ."*

"I see," she said.

I felt slighted that he should imagine me capable of such abject behavior and could only conclude that he must have been like that when he himself was eight. This incident lowered my opinion of him considerably.

The doctors decided that Daddy had been working too hard. They ordered him to cut down on his schedule and to play golf three times a week. The suddenness of his partial blindness weighed upon him, and he brooded about his health, so that his hypochondria became more pronounced. The Hillcrest Golf Club was a few blocks from the house. A new routine began, in which all three of us marched off regularly to the club. Mother and I usually waited under the trees near the fifth hole. Sometimes, if he played alone, he insisted that we go along with him and help the caddy look for lost balls. One day he decided that I was going to caddy for him. It must have been obvious that I could not carry the bag properly, since when it was set down the top of it came level with my shoulder. Its regular bumping along the ground made Daddy so irritable that he could play only nine holes. "You make a fine caddy, I don't think," he said disgustedly when we got back to the locker room.

After they joined the club, Mother and Daddy made many new friends, and they began to go out nights to play cards. But now they did not think it necessary to have Hannah come and stay with me, so I had to be alone. Sometimes the card games were held in our house, and then there was a great racket throughout the house until two or three in the morning. Prohibition was brand-new, and people got drunk self-consciously; to show that one had been drinking was an elegant form of bravado.

Daddypapa came occasionally to visit us. He had a pleasant but embarrassing habit of going into the dining room before dinner and hiding money under my napkin. I could not understand why he never gave it to me in private so that Mother and Daddy would not know about it. I assumed that he liked me better than he liked them, because he constantly found fault with the way they lived. Each time he picked up a copy of *Vanity Fair* in the living room he snorted, riffled the pages noisily, and then slapped it down very hard on the table, remarking that it was not good to leave the magazine where I could get hold of it. But since I took its wrapper off when the postman brought it each month, I had already looked through it for as long as I wanted. While Daddypapa was staying with us, Mother often reminded me that he belonged to another generation and thus could be expected to disapprove of what went on in our house. He had never been a drinking man, so that when the Eighteenth Amendment became law, he made a point of expressing his condemnation of those who disobeyed it, and he did not invariably hold his tongue when cocktails were served by Daddy before dinner.

"It's a great mistake," he said testily.

"Father, be reasonable," Daddy would remonstrate. "The law's unenforceable in the first place. Can't you see that?"

"Only because people like you choose to disregard it. It's the law of the nation. That should be enough."

Gramma spent time with us nearly every winter. We seemed always to be going out together in the snow; on her feet she wore what she called arctics. During the long cold walks I took with Gramma, I discovered in her an inexhaustible lode of spleen against Daddy. I had only to listen and say: "Why?" from time to time, and out it came, including details which I could not believe, young though I was, until they had been either confirmed or explained to me by Mother.

"Your mother's afraid of him, so she always stands up for him. But I know what he had in his mind. Your father wanted to kill you."

I was startled. "Kill me?" I repeated. The thing seemed only too possible. You could never be certain of what anyone really had in his mind. Children were treacherous and grown-ups inscrutable.

"When you were only six weeks old, he did it. He came home one terrible night when the wind was roaring and the snow was coming down—a real blizzard—and marched straight into your room, opened the window up wide, walked over to your crib and yanked you out from under your warm blankets, stripped you naked, and carried you over to the window where the snow was sailing in. And that devil just left you there in a wicker basket on the windowsill for the snow to fall on. And if I hadn't heard you crying a little later, you'd have been dead inside the hour. 'I know what you want,' I told him. 'You shan't do it. You'll harm this baby over my dead body.' "

The idea of this dramatic confrontation excited me. "What'd he say?" I wanted to know.

"He was just jealous of the attention your mother was giving you. *He* was the baby. He felt she wasn't paying enough mind to him, that's all. So he thought: 'I'll let him catch his death of cold, and then I'll have her all to myself.' I know how his mind works. He's a devil, a devil! Like the old tomcat that comes back and eats his own kittens. He's got your poor mother where he wants her, right under his thumb."

Gramma enjoyed telling how just after I was born, she had gone to a clairvoyant, in order to make general inquiries about what my life was going to be like. The woman had claimed she saw piles of papers every-where, and that was all. "She certainly got *that* one right," Gramma told me. "I've never seen so many papers as you've collected. I don't wonder your mother gets nervous. The mere sight of so many would drive me crazy. Couldn't you get rid of some of them? The old ones?"

I had to put that suggestion down immediately. "No, no! I have to have them all. I don't want to throw any away."

"Your poor mother!"

"She doesn't ever see them. They're all piled together in the closet. I like to look at them."

"But they're just your own scribbles. Why do you want to look at them?"

I realized that she did not share my interest in my own literary achieve-ments; there was nothing to say.

In January, 1921, Daddy fell ill with pneumonia. The house was transformed into a hospital, with nurses coming and going, and Dr. Brush calling by several times each day. Mother decided to get me out of the way by sending me to Springfield to stay with the Winnewissers. I went to Grand Central Station by myself and took the New York, New Haven and Hartford, still stunned by my unbelievably good fortune. The idea of an indeterminate stretch of freedom ahead was intoxicating. I saw that life is potentially pleasant, and gained great respect for the unforeseen.

I had scarcely been at Springfield for two weeks when both Grampa and Gramma were stricken with pneumonia. Aunt Emma came down from Northampton to help, and once again I was sent away from the sickbed scene, this time to Northampton to stay with Uncle Guy. He and Aunt Emma had separate apartments in the same building. Uncle Guy was a novelty: he wore Japanese kimonos and spent a good deal of time keeping incense burning in a variety of bronze dragons and Buddhas. I was delighted with the apartment and imagined it as the setting for a murder mystery. As if to reinforce this impression there were a few Sax Rohmer novels on the table beside my bed. Nights I made the acquaintance of Dr. Fu Manchu.

So far I had been only three times in my life to see a moving picture. Uncle Guy in all innocence took me every afternoon to a barnlike building called the Academy of Music, where they showed two different films each day. I saw Mary Miles Minter and Charlie Chaplin and Viola Dana and William S. Hart, all with a sharp and delightful awareness of the degree of disapproval Mother and Daddy would feel if only they knew what was going on. Uncle Guy promised me he'd never tell them; he treated me in a very special way which made me feel he was "on my side," and he did not try to control my activities. I had never before known such freedom; it was inevitable that I should consider Uncle Guy a friend. But then he decided to give a big party. It would be in Aunt Emma's apartment; he had been planning it for several days. When Saturday evening came, he told me I was to eat early and go to bed. This was unwelcome news indeed. During the evening I found some pretext for donning my bathrobe and wandering through the corridors to the other apartment. I could hear the dance music being played on the piano, and a great racket of voices and laughter, before I got to the door. When I opened it, I had a brief glimpse of the studio. It was crowded with pretty young men dancing together. At that second a rough hand clutched at my shoulder, spun me around, and propelled me through the doorway. I glanced up and saw Uncle Guy's face transfigured by rage. With his other hand he seized the back of my neck and squeezed it painfully as he pushed me down the corridor toward his own apartment. "I told you not to come, and you disobeyed," he said between his teeth. "Now I'm going to lock you in."

Once I was back in my room I sat on the bed consumed by fury and frustration. Uncle Guy had proved the same as all the others. Above me on the wall hung a large framed photograph of a pretty girl with an inviting smile. I stood up on the bed and rammed my fist into the picture as hard as I could, smashing the glass and cutting my knuckles. That was for Uncle Guy. Then I went to sleep with a sore hand. The next morning when I worked up the courage to admit to Uncle Guy that I had broken his picture, instead of being angry about it, he smiled, which was upsetting. I said I would pay him for whatever it cost, and he agreed. No part of the episode was mentioned again by either of us, including the roomful of young men, which did not strike me as having anything unusual about it until at least ten years later when I recalled it. And until this moment of writing it, I have never mentioned it to anyone.

Uncle Guy had a mysterious, fat friend whom we used to visit. His name was Mr. Bistany, and he was even busier with his incense than Uncle Guy, so much so that the air in his apartment was almost unbreathable. The floors and couches and walls were covered with soft Turkish rugs, which he kept changing. He was a Syrian who kept an "Oriental" shop specializing in imported goods. Each time we went to see him he insisted on presenting me with a gift, but since Uncle Guy objected vociferously, I was placed in an embarrassing position. Uncle Guy would snatch the object away from me and put it down, whereupon Mr. Bistany would immediately hand it to me again. Toward the end of my stay in Northampton we no longer went to see Mr. Bistany.

When a letter came from Mother telling me I must return to New York in a fortnight, I sat down and wrote her a pleading missive, begging to be allowed to stay a little longer. Naturally, this had no effect. The fateful day came, and I was put on a train and sent home, feeling very sorry for myself.

I had not been back very long before Miss Naul called on Mother to suggest that I be sent ahead into Miss Miller's class. In other words, I was going from the fifth grade into the sixth. The process was called skipping. Because being sent ahead was a sign of official approval, any boy who received the honor risked ostracism by his classmates.

At the end of that term Miss Miller recommended that the sixth-grade class rise and applaud my achievement. I had got the highest marks of anyone in spite of my tardy entrance. It was a moment of nightmare, and I wondered then if Miss Miller realized what she was subjecting me to by calling attention to my defects. (For the qualities adults think of as virtues in a child are generally considered by other children to be sheer sycophancy.) The question surely would come: Why was he skipped? And the answer, illogical and brutal, but not without its element of truth, was bound to be: Because he thinks he's smart.

"Tell me about when I was born."

"You've heard about it a thousand times," Mother would say.

This was true, but somehow I felt there was more to the momentous event than I had so far extracted. I hoped that by constantly eliciting more details I would eventually get the whole picture.

The delivery took place in the Mary Immaculate Hospital. (For many years I remained under the impression that the word "immaculate" modified "hospital" and was a kind of cheap advertising, like the word "painless" which bad dentists of that era used on their signs.) "It was the most convenient and the best equipped," Mother explained. "But if I'd had any idea of what was going to happen I'd have given it a wide berth."

This was always thrilling, since I knew what was to follow. It had been a forceps delivery; my head refused to emerge. "When I came out from under the ether, there you were, with a big cut on the side of your head." But the best was yet to come. At dusk on that same afternoon it seems that two nuns wandered into the room and announced that I must be taken out and baptized. Mother refused, and they tried to lift me up by force, assuring her that I might not survive the night. That had nothing to do with them, she said; she would take the responsibility for my soul. They continued to clutch at me. "If you take that child out of the room, I'll follow you on my hands and knees screaming," she told them, and they went away.

When this tale was recounted, I always had the impression that Mother had scored an important moral victory, at the same time protecting me from what would have entailed a mysterious and obscene operation. She would hunch her shoulders and shudder. "Agh! Dirty creatures, with their old crosses dangling! They give me the shivers. Of course, some of them *are* very fine women, I make no doubt. But those black capes!"

"Nothing's so much fun as games you play with your own mind," Mother said one day. "You think you're running your mind, but then you find out that unless you're careful, your mind is running you. For instance, I'll bet you can't tell me exactly what motions you make to take off your topcoat. What do you move first? I've thought about it over and over, and I can't for the life of me tell you. Or this. Did you ever try to make your mind a blank and hold it that way? You mustn't imagine anything or remember anything or think of anything, not even think: 'I'm not thinking.' Just a total blank. You try it. It's hard. You may get it for a second, and then something flashes across your mind, and you lose it. I do it sometimes when I'm just resting in the afternoon, and I've got so I can hold on to it for quite a while. I just go into the blank place and shut the door."

None of this was lost on me. I said nothing, but I too began to practice secretly, and eventually managed to attain a blank state, although I was inclined to hold my breath along with it, which automatically limited its duration. Whatever powers of self-discipline I have now were given their original impetus at that time.

Early mornings in spring and summer had a particular magic. I could not go out, of course, nor could I get dressed and go downstairs before I was called, but I could go to the windows and look out and smell the air and hear the birds singing. That also was forbidden, but I was never caught at it. What did bring me to grief was my habit of sitting up in bed these early mornings, drawing houses to add to my collection of real estate. One cool July day I had got out of bed, tiptoed over to the door, locked it, and gone back to bed to work. Suddenly I heard Daddy bounding up the stairs. Long before I could get to the door he had tried it and immediately had begun to pound on it. I went and turned the key. His eyes were very narrow.

"What do you mean by locking that door, young man? What were you doing?"

"Nothing."

"Answer my question. Why was that door locked?"

"Because I was doing something I didn't want you to see."

"Oh, you were, were you? And what were you doing?"

"Drawing houses."

"And so you locked the door?" He did not seem to believe me.

"I didn't think you'd like me to be drawing houses before breakfast."

"I see. Well, just for that, I'm going to give you the whaling of your young life."

He seized me, threw me over his knees, facedown on the bedspread in my pajamas, and began to pummel my bottom. I lay there waiting for him to stop. When the tempo and volume of the blows had lessened, he said: "Have you had enough?" I did not answer, and so he continued in a desultory fashion for a moment, before he asked me again: "Had enough?"

I could never say yes.

I kept silent. "Speak up!" he told me.

I twisted my head to one side and managed to get out the words: "Whatever you say." Then he really pounded me.

When he was tired, he stopped and let me roll over on the bed. "Now I want all the notebooks you write in. Come on, hurry up." I got them out and laid them on the bed, and he went downstairs with them. Mother told me later in the day that I was to be deprived of them for two months, the shortest sentence she had been able to wangle for me. I was considerably relieved, having expected them to be destroyed once and for all. I also felt stronger, because I knew that no matter what physical violence was done to me, I would not have to cry; it was something I had not realized until that day. Decades later, looking through Mother's diaries, I found a reference to the incident. The entry for the day began: "Claude spanked Paul. Result: spent a miserable day with a sick headache."

This was the only time my father beat me. It began a new stage in the development of hostilities between us. I vowed to devote my life to his destruction, even though it meant my own—an infantile conceit, but one which continued to preoccupy me for many years.

II

. . . I took passage on an old American freighter called the *McKeesport*. There was only one another passenger aboard, a French count just divorced by his American wife in California, with a big album of photographs of her which he brought each time he came to the dining room. Most of the time he stayed in his cabin. This was understandable, since we ran into a violent storm the second day out of New York, and for days the ship heaved like a water buffalo in a mudhole. Both the dining room and my cabin, adjacent to it, remained awash, with the water sloshing from one side to the other and splashing against the walls. I piled my valises on the empty bunk and had the steward put my steamer trunk on blocks and wedge it between the wall and the chest of drawers. I might better have let myself be seasick, but I made it a point of honor not to, and walked the deck for hours in the wind and rain, breathing deeply. The ploy worked; I did not throw up at any point. After a week of storm and motion, I spied a gull one morning behind the ship and hopefully asked the captain if we were approaching the Scilly Islands. "Naw, we're off the Grand Banks," he said. It took us another eight days to get to Le Havre.

And there was Paris, with the trees in the Tuileries beginning to bud and the sweet smell of the Métro disinfectant wafting up from under the ground just as I had remembered it a thousand times during the past twenty months. I had only three weeks to spend there before Aaron would come from New York to pick me up and take me on to Berlin. One of the first things I did was to go around to 27 rue de Fleurus and find Gertrude Stein's door. When I rang the bell, a maid answered and said Mademoiselle was busy. I could hear the sound of women's voices coming down from the stairwell, and I said I had just arrived from America and must see her, if only for a moment. The girl made me wait outside. Soon Gertrude Stein appeared, looking just as she did in her photographs, except that the expression of her face was rather more pleasant. "What is it? Who are you?" she said. I told her and heard for the first time her wonderfully hearty laugh. She opened the door so that I could go in. Then Alice Toklas came downstairs, and we sat in the big studio hung with Picassos. "I was sure from your letters that you were an elderly gentleman, at least seventy-five," Gertrude Stein told me. "A highly eccentric elderly gentleman," added Alice Toklas. "We were certain of it." They asked me to dinner for the following night to meet Bernard Faÿ.

At the dinner there were only four. I was plied with questions; my answers seemed to please and amuse them. I liked Bernard Faÿ. He had the patience and charm that sometimes come as a result of prolonged physical suffering. Earlier in his life he had contracted polio and now had great difficulty in moving. Gertrude Stein insisted that I was really a Freddy and not a Paul. Accordingly, all three of them from that moment on refrained from using my name and addressed me only as Freddy. (Eventually Alice Toklas shortened it to Fred for her own use.)

"This is the season for *lancer*-ing Freddy," announced Gertrude Stein, who was in a jovial mood after dinner when we sat around the studio. "We're going to *lancer* Freddy." They discussed various people to whom I should be presented, laughed a good deal, and that was the end of it. The subject never came up again. A few nights later we all ate at the house of Bernard Faÿ's brother. A magazine called *The New Review* had recently been launched in Paris; its editors were Samuel Putnam, Ezra Pound, and Richard Thoma. At Thoma's that morning I had met Pound, a tall man with a reddish beard, and later had lunch with him, after which we had gone out to Fontenay-aux-Roses together to see Putnam. I had liked Pound and brought his name up during dinner. "Oh, I won't see Ez anymore," said

Gertrude Stein. "All he has to do is to come in and sit down for a half hour. When he leaves, the chair's broken, the lamp's broken." "And the teapot," Alice Toklas added. "Ez is fine," Gertrude Stein went on, "but I can't afford to have him in the house, that's all." This struck me as very strange until one afternoon during tea at Bernard Faÿ's I learned that Gertrude Stein had recently sent many of her acquaintances a standard note stating that henceforth Miss Stein would do without his friendship. The arbitrariness of such behavior defied belief, but two who had received such notices, Virgil Thomson and Pavel Tchelitchew, were present to attest to it. This was the first time I had met Thomson; I was rather put off by the casualness with which he pronounced his judgments. Being naïf, I imagined that the willingness to be amusing reflected inevitably a lack of serious purpose.

One day when I was at Gertrude Stein's, Maria Jolas came by. "I believe you've published some of Freddy's things in *transition*," Gertrude Stein said to her when she introduced me. Mrs. Jolas looked very vague. After she had left, we discussed her strange lapse of memory, which my hostesses insisted was feigned. Alice Toklas suddenly said: "You didn't by any chance ever write and ask to be paid, did you?" They joined in a great burst of laughter when I answered defensively: "They'd been owing me for a year." "That's the end of *transition* for Freddy!" Gertrude Stein announced with satisfaction. I realized then that she did not like the magazine or the people who ran it.

Another day Thoma took me around to the rue Vignon to visit Jean Cocteau. A maid let us into an antechamber one of whose walls was a huge blackboard with scrawls and doodles on it. This was where friends left messages when Cocteau was not in. On another wall was a very large sheet of brown wrapping paper where Picasso had inked some hieroglyphs and figures. We waited a moment, and then Cocteau appeared and led us into a much bigger room. He was extremely thin and intensely nervous, and the constant, expressive agitation of his hands was like a choreography perfectly devised to fit the course of his speech. For two hours he carried on a conversation without remaining seated for more than a minute at a stretch. The rest of the time he was a man playing charades, illustrating his remarks by the use of mime and caricature and changing his position and voice to give verisimilitude to his accounts. Once he crawled across the floor in imitation of a bear, and for a while he was a succession of disdainful ushers at the new Paris Paramount Theatre, which he loathed. Naturally I was fascinated by this performance; on another occasion I went back to see him, but was met at the door by Jean Desbordes, who before shutting it said firmly: *"Monsieur Cocteau est au fond de son lit."* When I told Thoma, he said: "Oh, he was smoking opium." I had just finished reading *Opium, Journal d'une Désintoxication;* ingenuously, I imagined that once disintoxicated, a smoker smoked no more.

Aaron Copland was about to arrive in Paris. I knew he would be much impressed when I told him that since seeing him I had met Pound, Stein, and Cocteau; accordingly when an American painter asked me to his *vernissage,* saying that André Gide would be there, I made a point of being present. I did meet Gide; we stood in a corner talking for perhaps two minutes, and I was so elated by the idea of being face to face with the master that I had no precise idea of what we were talking about. That was that, but at least I would have one more name to add when I came to give Aaron the list. One might expect a young man of twenty to have progressed beyond this sort of thinking and behavior or at least to be aware of its absurdity, but not at all. I went to the Gare St.-Lazare to meet Aaron, and we had scarcely settled ourselves in the taxi before I began. I had a plum for him, too: Gertrude Stein wanted me to bring him to dinner the following evening. The dinner went off very well. When we had left and were walking in the street, Aaron said: "When I opened the door and saw her sitting there, the only thing that went through my mind was: 'My God, the woman's Jewish!' "

So we went on to Berlin. Aaron had arranged his living quarters in an apartment on the Steinplatz, in the northern part of the city. I had to look for mine, but I found them the first day through an agency. My room was in the house of a Baronin von Massenbach, who turned out to be English by birth and more violently pro-German than the Germans themselves. I had a big balcony overlooking the Güntzelstrasse, near the Kaiserallee, and I could walk to the Kurfürstendamm in fifteen minutes. Architecturally Berlin was hideous, but as a compensation its streets were spotless and bordered by miles of carefully tended geranium beds. Each morning I had my breakfast on the balcony; it included an enormous bowl of *Schlagsahne* to put in my chocolate or over the strawberries. Very likely I was laying the foundations then for the liver complaints which plagued me many years later, but the breakfasts of the *Baronin* in the spring sunlight were one of the high points of the Berlin sojourn.

Berlin teemed with trolley cars in 1931, and there was little motor traffic. The sunlight was not the tentative, diffuse glow that hangs in the sky above today's cities; its unfiltered rays reached the ground. You could sit in a sidewalk café on the Kurfürstendamm and get a real sunburn. It was a new experience to be in a metropolis where one felt in constant touch with nature. The German obsession with nature had its comic side, of course, exemplified by such places as the Wellenbad at Halensee, where a monstrous contraption had been installed at one end of the pool; its mechanical heavings created huge waves which broke in surf at the opposite end. The important thing was to have a tan and to show as much area of bronzed skin as decency allowed. Pallor meant poverty, the East End, that vast slum beyond the Alexanderplatz, and no one wanted even to be reminded of the existence of such a region. The frantic insistence on enjoyment was in part a result of the suppressed knowledge that a few miles away great numbers of people were hungry.

Edouard Roditi was one of the poets to whom I had written the year before in order to get material for *The Messenger;* he had not only sent poems, but had also written several letters subsequently, in which he had given me a list of people to see in Berlin. Among them were Renée Sintenis, the sculptress; Wilfred Israel, who owned Wertheim's, Germany's largest department store; and two English writers, Christopher Isherwood and Stephen Spender. I presented the letters written to Germans first. When I came to Isherwood, he said he would take me himself to meet Spender. We walked one afternoon from the Nollendorfplatz to the Motzstrasse, where Spender had a room at the top of a house. Its windows faced west, and the sun was about to set as we walked into the room. Spender, who had reddish hair and was very sunburned, stood in the red light, looking as if he were on fire. I noted with disapproval the Byronesque manner in which he wore his shirt, open down to his chest. It struck me as unheard of that he should want to announce his status as a poet rather than dissimulate it; to my way of thinking he thus sacrificed his anonymity. To me name was all-important, the actuality represented by it less so. In a grammar-school reader I had once found a sentence: "Reputation is what people think about you; character is what God knows about you." References to God confused me. How was one to interpret them, since it was agreed that God was a figment of man's imagination? I ventured the opinion to Mother that this particular statement meant nothing at all. "Oh, yes, it does," she said. "It really means that character is what you know about yourself." In my fantasy the part of me about which there was anything to know did not exist; thus the knowing or recording part of me could scarcely learn anything about it. My deduction was that reputation was conclusive. Whether Spender wrote poetry or not seemed relatively unimportant; that at all costs the fact should not be evident was what should have mattered to him.

I soon found that Isherwood with Spender was a very different person from Isherwood by himself. Together they were overwhelmingly British, two members of a secret society constantly making references to esoteric data not available to outsiders. I reported all this to Aaron, who was amused, and who suggested that we all eat lunch one day. In this way we began meeting at half past one each afternoon on the terrace of the Café des Westens. Christopher often brought along Jean Ross, a pretty, dark-eyed girl who lived in the same rooming house on the Nollendorfplatz. She too was British, but from Cairo. (When Christopher wrote about her later, he called her Sally Bowles.) At all our meetings I felt that I was being treated with good-humored condescension. They accepted Aaron, but they did not accept me because they considered me too young and inexperienced or perhaps merely uninteresting; I never learned the reason, if there was one, for this exclusion by common consent.

I found German hard to acquire without regular lessons. After a month of riding on the tops of Berlin buses, I remarked to Aaron that usually I rode free of charge, since the man who came around to sell tickets seldom asked me to buy one. "But he always says: *'Noch jemand ohne Fahrschein,'* doesn't he?" asked Aaron. I had no idea of what the man had been saying, and I thought of the many times when I had looked straight at the ticket seller and not reacted to his words. It seemed a haphazard system they used, but now, knowing about it, I could no longer ride without paying. I ceased making an effort to learn the language. At least I knew the meaning of *"Fenster ʒu!"* the unceremonious phrase which my neighbors across the Güntzelstrasse shouted each time I began to work on the Baronin's big Bechstein. (Inspired by Aaron, I was writing a loud, dissonant piece for piano.) And I knew the word *Ausländer*, which the intolerant Berliners regularly applied to me; I had never been in a place where I felt so decidedly unwanted. In my fantasy I augmented this disagreement between us into a continuous feud and sought out details of behavior which I had learned would goad them into angry expostulation. I could get a reaction by tapping a fast rhythm with a coin on a café table, or by resting one foot on a chair opposite me, or even by ordering two *Schwedenfrüchte* in succession. Anything they were not used to seeing infuriated them because it was not in their manual; naturally this was too inviting a game for me not to be drawn into it.

Stravinsky's *Oedipus Rex* was about to be given in Munich. Since I had never heard it, I set out for Bavaria a week beforehand in order to be certain of not missing it. The city was bursting with vegetation, and the Isar churned through it, full of mountain water white as milk. I went on to Salzburg and the Salzkammergut for three days; in a village called Würgl I climbed through a glen and slipped into ice water up to my waist.

While I was in Munich, I received three letters of invitation: one from Gertrude Stein asking me to visit her in the country, another from the Comtesse de Lavillatte suggesting a stay at the château, and one which I had to decide and act on immediately. This letter was from another friend of Edouard Roditi's, an Egyptian named Carlo Suarès, who wanted me to go the following week to Holland and meet Krishnamurti. I wired Aaron that I should not be getting back to Berlin when I had planned to, and as soon as *Oedipus Rex* was presented, I left for Heidelberg. I wanted to explore the *Schloss*, but by myself. The only way of doing this was to get in at night. I had a small flashlight; with the aid of that and the moon, which was much brighter, I went over the building at my leisure. It was in an advanced state of disrepair then, with holes in the floors and bats overhead. I tried to feel that I was living in a poem by Novalis. The next day I continued to Deventer in Holland. Suarès met me at the station and we drove to Kastel Eerde, outside Ommen. The property had been given to Krishnamurti by a Dutchman, who a few years later changed his mind and asked that it be returned to him. Suarès was an Alexandrian banker who lived in Paris, where he edited *Carnets*, a monthly magazine devoted largely to studies of Krishnamurti's writings. Most of the texts he published in the review were his own, but now and then he printed a piece by Joe Bousquet or René Daumal on the same subject or a ramification of it. From time to time he spent a fortnight at Kastel Eerde with Krishnamurti. Madame Suarès was also a Krishnamurti follower; she sometimes accompanied him to Ojai in California and spent the winter there. I knew Krishnamurti's face very well, having seen it over a period of many years in the photograph of him which Aunt Mary had on her desk at Holden Hall, and when I met him, I was astonished to see that he still looked like a youth, although he must have been nearly forty by then. The first morning of my visit he came out of the castle and stood on the bridge that spanned the moat, tossing bread to the one swan that lived there. His shirt was open at the neck, at least as low as Stephen Spender wore his, and he had on white flannels and a scarlet blazer. Every morning after breakfast he appeared in the same costume and scattered the pieces of bread over the dark surface of the moat. The swan came sailing around the corner, white and fierce. It was an unfailing ritual.

In actuality I did not stay in the castle. I only ate there. The non-Indians lived in a dozen or so comfortable apartments that had been built on one side of the entrance driveway. In the castle itself was a man named Rajago-pal who was constantly with Krishnamurti; they were often in the company of two or three other very serious-looking Indians, possibly secretaries or simple followers. In the apartments there were several Americans, a French-woman with a small girl named Rolande, and Madame Pushkin, a very old Russian lady who had direct family ties of some sort with the poet. I went on walks in the lush Dutch countryside with Krishnamurti and Suarès. And I took an unforgettable stroll one sultry afternoon under the dramatic Dutch sky with Madame Pushkin and Rolande. A thunderstorm was rap-idly approaching. The flat terrain made it clear that the rain would soon reach us. Rolande was all for running in order to get back to the castle before we were struck by lightning. There was something to be said for her suggestion, but Madame Pushkin went on ambling unconcernedly, assuring Rolande that if one were not afraid of lightning it would not hit one. Even eight-year-old Rolande was not going to swallow that. *"Ce n'est pas vrai!"* she cried. *"C'est une décharge électrique. Papa m'a expliqué."* But Madame Pushkin actually believed what she had said; she went on to tell Rolande that the power of the mind enabled one to go along with natural forces rather than combatting them. Rolande, skipping nervously, kept interrupt-ing her, saying that it was impossible, and how could the lightning know whether somebody was afraid of it or not? As if in answer, a bolt struck a huge oak tree that stood alone a quarter of a mile out in the meadow. After the crash, Madame Pushkin sighed, turned to the child, and said: *"Ah, ma pauvre fille, comme tu es déplaisante!"* We continued in silence, albeit somewhat faster, until we got to Kastel Eerde.

I made plans to see Suarès the coming winter in Paris and returned to Berlin to work. Aaron was critical of my lack of seriousness in having spent so much time on holiday but I could not make myself feel guilty.

One weekend we went to Rheinsberg, where the hotel proprietor behaved in a typically German fashion. He allowed Aaron to sign the register as *Komponist*, but when he saw that I too claimed to be a composer, he objected, saying that I might sign myself in as a student if I wished, but certainly not as a composer. Aaron tried to argue with him, but to no avail. He crossed out what I had written and finally, as a special favor, he was careful to tell us, he rewrote my civil status as *Jazz-Komponist.* That was the best he could do for me. Back in Berlin Aaron told this as a joke; by that time I too could think it amusing.

Sometimes when I went around to see Christopher Isherwood, he would not be in, and I would ask for Fräulein Ross. Invariably I would find her stretched out in bed, smoking Murattis and eating chocolates; almost as invariably a German friend or two would appear, and she would involve herself in long conversations with them, only a small part of which I understood, punctuating her remarks here and there with her inevitable *"Du Schwein!"* Aaron told me I was not working hard enough. This was not surprising, since I wasted so much time moving around Berlin trying to see people. I decided, for instance, that I had to know Naum Gabo, the constructivist sculptor, and spent a whole day in his studio out at Potsdam, when I should have stayed at home doing figured basses. Another day I followed up a series of introductions which finally led me to the office of Walter Gropius, the architect, who looked like any businessman sitting at his desk, and who must have been mystified by my desire to talk with him, particularly since I had nothing at all to say. When Aaron announced that there was to be a Musikfest at Bad Pyrmont and that he thought we should go, I leaped at the opportunity because Bad Pyrmont was not far from Hannover, and in Hannover lived Kurt Schwitters, whom among all Germans I wanted most to meet. However, I said nothing about that until we were in Bad Pyrmont. The only concert of the festival I remember was the one at which Béla Bartók and his wife, both with cameo profiles, played at two huge black pianos facing each other across the stage. I have no idea of how I worded the wire I sent to Schwitters, but I recall my feeling of triumph when I went to the post office and read his answering telegram inviting me to Hannover. I set out the next morning, Aaron having gone back to Berlin.

Schwitters lived in a stolid bourgeois apartment house. The flat was relatively small and somberly furnished. I slept on a small glassed-in porch off the dining room. There was a huge chest near my couch; the first night I was astonished to hear distinct stirrings inside it. At breakfast I felt impelled to mention the phenomenon. The twelve-year-old Schwitters boy had filled it with guinea pigs. We went that day to the city dump and walked for two hours among the garbage, ashes and pieces of junk, collecting material for the Merz-Bau in the apartment below. On the trolley car returning from our outing people eyed us with curiosity. Schwitters, his son, and I each carried a basketful of refuse: we had bits of paper and rags, broken metal objects, even an ancient, stiff hospital bandage. It was all to be transformed into parts of the Merz-Bau. The Merz-Bau was a house within an apartment, a personal museum in which both the objects displayed and the exhibit rooms were inseparable parts of the same patiently constructed work of art.

Merz-Kunst was Schwitters' own brand of Dada, its lineage most evident in his poems and stories. That evening Frau Schwitters placed a big pan of strawberries on the dining-room table. Somehow we got the idea of making *Maibowle*. I went out to a nearby shop and bought a bottle of gin, which the Schwitterses claimed never to have tasted. Frau Schwitters made the *Maibowle*, and we all drank it, including the boy. It had a foul flavor, but the strawberries improved after they had soaked up the gin. When Schwitters was feeling happy, I begged him to recite some of his syllable poetry, which he did with great gusto. One which I liked particularly began:

> Lanke trr gll.
> Pe pe pe pe pe
> Ooka. Ooka. Ooka. Ooka.
> Lanke trr gll.
> Pi pi pi pi pi
> Tzuuka. Tzuuka. Tzuuka. Tzuuka.

I notated the words, the rhythm, and the vocal inflections and later used it without changes as the frame for the theme of the rondo movement of a sonata for oboe and clarinet. At my host's insistence I played two or three of my own pieces to them. Schwitters asked his son: "How do you like that?" and he replied: *"Schrecklich!"* without bothering to explain his reaction.

I went back to Berlin. The nights got shorter and shorter, until there were only two hours when the sky was uniformly dark. The sparrows began to chirp soon after two o'clock in the morning. The feeling came to me that I had had enough of this strange, ugly, vaguely sinister city, and I began to look forward to returning to France. The uneasiness Berlin induced had nothing to do with the little swastikas that were constantly being glued up everywhere by unseen hands. Hitler was unimportant, a feeble-minded Austrian fanatic with a gang of young hoodlums. Everyone said that. Everyone, that is, except a few people I met one day in the Baronin von Massenbach's salon, who believed he was going to save Germany, and an extraordinary young aristocrat named Von Braun, who invited me to his house for lunch with several of his friends, only to pause before sitting down to eat and point dramatically to his family tree on the wall, saying: "This is what Americans can never have. An American is worth only the number of dollars he has in his pocket." Then he sat down, and we ate, while he explained that Hitler was the only hope for cleaning out the rot that had attacked the German people's spirit. Had I met these people only a year later I should have recognized them as Nazis, but in 1931 they were only crazy Germans. It was not they, but a ride I took one day on the Ringbahn, that made Berlin seem sinister. With the exception of the quarters I already knew, the city was a gigantic slum, a monstrous agglomeration of uninhabitable buildings. Merely to see its geographic extent and the degree of unrelieved poverty it represented made me uneasy. The aura of desperation that I had found stimulating suddenly seemed ominous.

Just before I left for Paris, I met Julien Levy. At that time he was about to open a gallery in New York where he would show nothing but photographs. A week later in Paris it was Bastille Day, Aaron had gone to London, and I sat on the *terrasse* of the Dôme. Some friends walked up, bringing with them a fantastic girl in a very small bathing suit. Apart from being beautiful, she looked as though she had just come off the beach at Juan-les-Pins. Which, she explained charmingly, was exactly what she had done. In a fit of pique she had got onto the *Train Bleu* just like that, with no clothes and no luggage. And there was no way of buying anything for another three days because it was the *Quatorze Juillet*. What was she going to do? She shrugged, and we laughed. It soon became necessary to do something, however, inasmuch as the waiter arrived before long to say that the *patron* could not permit nudity on the *terrasse* of the Dôme. We were ordering plenty of drinks, the *soucoupes* were piling up, and we felt moved to protest. The *patron* sensibly suggested that we sit downstairs in the *sous-sol*. Jacqueline thought it a perfect solution; she had had enough of being stared at. We continued to drink in a corner of the basement near the *W. C. pour Dames*.

At some point Julien Levy came by and sat down to join us in our drinking, his beady eyes already on Jacqueline. When he heard of her plight, he grew very serious and began to rack his brain to think of some woman Jacqueline's size who might be in Paris during the holidays. "Don't you know anyone?" he said suddenly to me. I said no, I didn't, and then I took out my wallet and went through the cards and slips of paper until I came across one that read "Eva Goldbeck," with an address on the Boulevard Raspail. She was Marc Blitzstein's wife, whom he had suggested I go to see. "I've got someone here who might have something. I don't know her, though."

Julien thought I should call her immediately. I did. She was in, and I asked her if I might come over right away. She finally agreed, and I went back to the table triumphantly. One drink later I got up and set off for Eva Goldbeck's. She let me in, but she seemed disconcerted by the fact that I had been drinking and mystified by the course our conversation took. "Marc said you might look me up," she told me.

"You haven't got a dress you could lend me, have you?" I tried to paint her a picture of the serious emergency that existed back at the Dôme, but she looked confused and disapproving. "Came to Paris in a bathing suit?" she repeated.

"She's afraid she's going to be arrested," I went on. "That's why if you had any old thing, anything, it would save the day."

Eva Goldbeck looked doubtful, but she said: "Wait." She came out of her bedroom a moment later with three dresses on her arm. I took them, thanked her, and ran off, promising to bring them back as soon as Jacqueline could get to a shop.

Jacqueline was a tall girl, and Eva Goldbeck was short. Still, the discrepancy was not enough to explain what happened to the dresses when I carried them back to the Dôme. Jacqueline bore them off to the *W.C. pour Dames*. Fifteen minutes later she came back to the table looking glamorous in all three of the dresses. They had been partially ripped open and recombined with great skill. *"Dis donc,"* she said to me. "Your *petite amie* is not going to like it much when you take her clothes back to her." I assured her it would be all right, but of course I never took them back. (Two or three years later I learned from Marc Blitzstein that it had not been all right, at all.) The rest of the day has been lost in the mists of alcohol; I hope Julien remembers it, since it was he who finally carried Jacqueline off to his hotel, where she spent the remainder of the holidays.

A few days later I left for the Château de Lavillatte. This time there were several small children in residence. They had a toy phonograph which they played all day, and their favorite record was a popular song called "Constantinople." I was busy sending messages to Gertrude Stein, trying to arrange things so that I could go directly from the château to her. The

Comtesse de Lavillatte, who was still occupied with her petit point, became curious. "Who is this woman?" she demanded. When I said she was a famous poet whose works few people understood, she asked me to quote a line. I translated one I remembered from "Tender Buttons": "A little lace makes boils." She nodded her head in agreement and said without looking up: *"Ah oui, et la broderie anglaise fait des pustules."*

Gertrude Stein met me at the station in Culoz, along with Alice Toklas and Basket, the white poodle, and on the way to Bilignin I repeated Madame de Lavillatte's remark. She was overjoyed. "You see? You see how wonderful the French are?" she cried. Then Alice Toklas asked me what I thought of Germans. When I started to tell her, Gertrude Stein interrupted, saying: "We think they're *awful.*" There was no need to say any more on the subject.

The house looked very old; it was like a miniature château, with floors that slanted in various directions. It stood directly on the only street in the hamlet of Bilignin; there were often cows in front of the door. The walls were very thick, and inside the house it was beautifully quiet, a bit like the Happy Hollow Farm, I thought, with distant sounds of lowing cattle and crowing cocks. If you went straight through the house, you came out into a garden whose farther edge was a parapet. A valley lay below, its green lushness made sedate by rows of tall poplars that rose above the surrounding vegetation. (From the opposite side of the valley on a clear day, they said, you could see Mont Blanc.)

It did not take me long to understand that while I undoubtedly had her personal sympathy, I existed primarily for Gertrude Stein as a sociological exhibit; for her I was the first example of my kind. I provided her initial encounter with a species then rare, now the commonest of contemporary phenomena, the American suburban child with its unrelenting spleen. She wanted to hear every detail of life at home. Mother's activities particularly fascinated her, so much so that she wrote to her after I left. (Later, when I discussed it with Mother, she said: "Oh, yes, I answered old Sophie and poor Alice B. Luckless. I sent them some recipes of Grandmother Barkers'.") After a week or so, Gertrude Stein pronounced her verdict: I was the most spoiled, insensitive, and self-indulgent young man she had ever seen, and my colossal complacency in rejecting all values appalled her. But she said it beaming with pleasure, so that I did not take it as adverse criticism. "If you were typical, it would be the end of our civilization," she told me. "You're a manufactured savage."

Each morning Thérèse brought my breakfast tray to my room. After that she lugged up a two-foot-high pitcher of cold water so that I could wash. I was supposed to stand in the middle of a small circular metal tub and pour the water over myself. A little later she would bring a canister of hot water for shaving. Not of the opinion that cold water is useful for bathing, I would wash as well as I could with a washcloth, using the small amount of hot water and leaving the cold untouched. After a few days had gone by, Gertrude Stein began to question me. "Thérèse says you don't bathe in the morning." When I protested, she closed in on me, saying that I must use cold water. I had been through the cold water bit as a boy, when Daddy had obliged me to take a cold shower every morning, and I had made up my mind I was not going to use the cold water.

I told Gertrude Stein this; she shook her head impatiently. "It's of no interest whether you like it or not. We're not talking about that. All I'm saying is, you've got to use the water Thérèse brings you. It's simple." Then she delivered a short lecture on Americans. They were the dirtiest people on earth, really, she said, because unless they had access to a bathroom, they refrained from bathing. From then on she took to standing outside my bedroom door in the morning, calling out in a low melodious voice: "Freddy. Are you taking your bath?" I would make the appropriate noises and say that I was, indeed. "I don't hear anything," she would pursue, after a short silence. "Well, I am."

She would wait again, perhaps thirty seconds, before saying: "All right. Basket's waiting for you."

The huge poodle, Basket, being all white, also had to have a thorough bath in a tubful of sulfur water every morning. This was performed faithfully by Alice Toklas, who spent an hour at the task. The dog was bathed quite as if it had been a baby, and it squealed and whimpered during the entire hour. When for some reason the bathtime was postponed until later, it began to cry at the usual time and continued until the bath had been given. When the washing was finished, and the tub, brushes, and swabs had been put away, it was my job to give Basket his drying-off exercise. This consisted in running back and forth through the garden with the dog after me. For this work I had to wear a pair of lederhosen which reached just above my knees. These were what Gertrude Stein called my "Faunties." (She referred, of course, to the trousers little Lord Fauntleroy wore.)

"Ah, you've got your Faunties. That's right. Get out there and run Basket." If he could manage it, Basket liked to reach up as he ran and scratch the backs of my legs with his toenails. Gertrude Stein would lean out a second-story window watching us, occasionally crying: "Faster, Freddy, faster!" This advice was scarcely necessary, considering the sharpness of his nails. There would come a moment when I would call out: "Isn't that enough?" Invariably she answered: "No! Keep going!" There was no way of doubting that she enjoyed my discomfort. But since such behavior seemed to me a sign of the most personal kind of relationship, I was flattered by the degree of her interest.

A telegram arrived one day, asking if the sender might come to Bilignin the following Sunday. It added: AM IN EUROPE SPECIFICALLY INTERVIEWS YOU AND GB SHAW, and it was signed FATTY BUTCHER. Gertrude Stein was delighted with the name; nevertheless, she murmured: "What does he want with Shaw?" Instead of the heavy man we were all expecting, Sunday brought two expensively dressed American ladies, one of whom introduced herself as Fanny Butcher of the Chicago *Tribune*. A maid took their wraps upstairs, where Basket promptly went and shit on them. The fact was not discovered until much later, as they were leaving. Gertrude Stein apologized, shrugged, and said: "He doesn't like to have people come." A maid did some rapid cleaning, and Miss Butcher went away happy with her interview.

Mealtimes were fun, because then each of my hostesses expressed herself. This gave rise to a certain amount of contradiction; indeed, the words sometimes went across in front of me from one end of the table to the other like a ping-pong ball. "But, Lovit, I didn't say that." "Ohh, yes, you did, Pussy." Neither ever lost a shred of her equanimity, although it was always quite clear when Gertrude Stein was annoyed, because her face colored perceptibly. When there was an argument over a detail, Alice Toklas usually proved herself right, but then, having lost her point, Gertrude Stein would smile crookedly and with a certain mock commiseration, as if to imply the absurdity of caring whether one had been right or wrong in such a trivial matter. They were both fervent gourmets, but Alice Toklas liked her food hot, whereas for Gertrude Stein its temperature had no importance. She enjoyed dallying in the garden after lunch had been put on the table, in order to watch what she considered Alice Toklas' obsessive anxiety about getting inside and sitting down before the meal cooled off.

Gertrude Stein asked me one afternoon to get some of my poems and let her see them. After she had looked carefully at them for a while, she sat back and thought a moment. Then she said: "Well, the only trouble with all this is that it isn't poetry."

"What is it?" I demanded.

"How should I know what it is? You wrote it. You tell *me* what it is. It's not poetry. Look at this." She pointed to a line on the top page. "What do you mean, *the heated beetle pants?* Beetles don't pant. Basket pants, don't you, Basket? But beetles don't. And here you've got purple clouds. It's all false."

"It was written without conscious intervention," I told her sententiously. "It's not my fault. I didn't know what I was writing."

"Yes, yes, but you knew *afterwards* what you'd written, and you should have known it was false. It was false, and you sent it off to *transition.* Yes, I know; they published it. Unfortunately. Because it's not poetry."

Gertrude Stein had just inaugurated what she called the Plain Edition; this was to comprise a series of volumes published at her own expense. The first title was *Lucy Church Amiably.* It was a descriptive novel whose principal character was a small church in the nearby village of Lucey. We drove twice to look at it; she was fascinated by the juxtaposition of the building's somewhat Slavic-looking steeple and the very French landscape in which it stood.

There was an afternoon when I read to her for a long time from her own *Operas and Plays,* the Plain Edition proofs of which she was then correcting. Occasionally she would laugh appreciatively, and once she stopped me, saying: "That's wonderful! Read that paragraph again, will you, Freddy?"

One day she announced that we were all going to Aix-les-Bains to market. Alice Toklas shuddered and murmured: "Oh, Lovit, not by the tunnel!"

"Of course we'll take the tunnel. We're not going all the way around the Dent du Chat."

"It drips," Alice Toklas explained to me. "I don't like tunnels. Of course Gertrude loves them. She'll always take a tunnel if she can."

We took the tunnel; Alice Toklas showed her misery, and even Basket seemed disturbed by it. At Aix-les-Bains I sent a wire to Aaron in Oxford, where he was attending a music festival of the ISCM, telling him that he was invited to Bilignin and to let us know when he would arrive. In the market Gertrude Stein's eye lit on an enormous gray eel, which, in spite of Alice Toklas' protestations, she insisted upon buying. Along with the other provisions she bore it off to the car, and we went back through the tunnel to Belley and thence to Bilignin.

While it was being cooked, the eel gave off a revolting stench, and when the lid was lifted from its terrine in front of Gertrude Stein's radiant face, its appearance was totally unappetizing. I decided to subsist on a vegetarian meal that day, but it seemed there was to be no question of that. "You eat what you're served," she told me sternly. "It's all good food." She gave me a large helping, and I managed to get it down.

When Aaron came, they had talks about me, both privately and in front of me. "Why does he have so many clothes?" Gertrude Stein wanted to know. "He's got enough for six young men." Then she would ask Aaron if I really had talent as a composer and if I really worked at my music. Aaron said he could imagine someone who spent more time at it than I. "That's what I thought," she said. "He's started his life of crime too young." Aaron snickered and told her never to pay any attention to what I said—only to what I did.

"I know," she agreed, looking narrowly at me. "He *says* he bathes every morning."

At lunch one day we discussed where Aaron and I ought to go for the summer. I was holding out for Villefranche, and Aaron kept mentioning St.-Jean-de-Luz over on the Atlantic. Gertrude Stein thought both very bad ideas. "You don't want to go to Villefranche," she said. "Everybody's there. And St.-Jean-de-Luz is empty, and with an awful climate. The place you should go is Tangier. Alice and I've spent three summers there, and it's fine. Freddy'd like it because the sun shines every day. At least, in the summer."

At each succeeding meal we got more information about Tangier. Finally we came to a decision: Aaron and I were leaving for Tangier. The last afternoon as we sat in the garden, Gertrude Stein suddenly said to me: "What about those poems you showed me last week? Have you done any work on them?" I said no, because once a poem had been published there seemed to be no reason to rewrite it. She was triumphant. "You see?" she cried. "I told you you were no poet. A real poet, after one conversation, would have gone upstairs and at least tried to recast them, but you haven't even looked at them."

I agreed, chastened. The next morning we hugged, kissed on both cheeks, and that was the end of the visit. "Quite a woman, quite a woman," Aaron murmured as we drove off in the taxi. Thinking how mysterious it was that she should be lovable, I said she reminded me of my grandmother.

The trip to Morocco would be a rest, a lark, a one-summer stand. The idea suited my overall desire, that of getting as far away as possible from

New York. Being wholly ignorant of what I should find there, I did not care. I had been told there would be a house somewhere, a piano somehow, and sun every day. That seemed to me enough.

III

As we went aboard the *Iméréthie II*, they told us of a change in itinerary. The ship was not going to touch at Tangier, after all, but at Ceuta, in Spanish Morocco. On the second day at dawn I went on deck and saw the rugged line of the mountains of Algeria ahead. Straightway I felt a great excitement; much excited; it was as if some interior mechanism had been set in motion by the sight of the approaching land. Always without formulating the concept, I had based my sense of being in the world partly on an unreasoned conviction that certain areas of the earth's surface contained more magic than others. Had anyone asked me what I meant by magic, I should probably have defined the word by calling it a secret connection between the world of nature and the consciousness of man, a hidden but direct passage which bypassed the mind. (The operative word here is "direct," because in this case it was equivalent to "visceral.") Like any Romantic, I had always been vaguely certain that sometime during my life I should come into a magic place which in disclosing its secrets would give me wisdom and ecstasy—perhaps even death. And now, as I stood in the wind looking at the mountains ahead, I felt the stirring of the engine within, and it was as if I were drawing close to the solution of an as-yet-unposed problem. I was incredibly happy as I watched the wall of mountains slowly take on substance, but I let the happiness wash over me and asked no questions.

We landed at Oran that afternoon. It was hot and dusty, and to me, beautiful and terrible. Because I remembered the absurd name of a suburb from having studied a Baedecker obsessively when I was working at Dutton's, I wanted to climb aboard a tramcar and ride out to a place called Eckmühl-Noiseux.

We swayed through the city that reeked of light on an open trolley car to the outskirts. Cicadas screamed in the trees overhead and in the cane-brakes that covered the slopes of the ravines. At Eckmühl-Noiseux we got down, but only because it was the end of the line. The sun was incandescent; people must have been asleep, for there was no one around. Returning on the same car to the center of town, we changed to another one that was going to Mers-el-Kebir. The cicadas screamed here too, the savage cliffs increased the sun's searing heat, and when the wind hit, it was like having a hot scarf thrown over one's face. At the fortress we were suddenly challenged by an Algerian soldier, who pointed his gun at us and bellowed: "*Halte!*" Then he told us to turn around and start walking, and he kept us covered until we were back on the road. "Well, I'm glad we're not going to live in *this* country!" Aaron said. "Morocco's much wilder," I told him; I had been listening to conversations among the French aboard the *Imeréthie II.*

The next afternoon we put in at Ceuta. We disembarked with so much luggage that we needed a small detachment of porters to carry it. As we sat in a sidewalk café in the central plaza, we looked around at the extraordinary animation of the people in the street. I had the impression of something great and exciting happening somewhere offstage. Neither of us had ever before seen the Spanish. Soon Aaron shook his head and said: "They're like a lot of Italians who've gone raving mad." Alfonso XIII had abdicated only four months earlier; their agitation may have been part of the general euphoria that was so apparent all over Spain during the years of the republic.

We got aboard a narrow-gauge train which yanked us along the coast southward. In Tetuán the impression of confusion and insanity was redoubled. The Moroccans were even more excited and noisy; furthermore, they engaged in passionate arguments which continually seemed about to degenerate into physical violence. We sat and watched while buses came and went, unloading chickens and sheep along with the sacks and chests they brought down from the roofs of the absurd old vehicles. Each Moroccan gave the impression of playing a part in a huge drama; he was involved not only with the others in the dispute, but also with the audience out front (a nonexistent audience, since no one was paying any attention but Aaron and me). He would face his invisible public and subject it to formalized grimaces denoting exasperation, incredulity, indignation, and a whole gamut of subtler states of mind. "It's a madhouse, a madhouse!" declared Aaron. "It's a continuous performance, anyway," I said with satisfaction. Even before getting to Tangier, I knew I should never tire of watching Moroccans play their parts.

Gertrude Stein's habitual hotel, the Villa de France, was filled with vacationists; our cabdriver took us to the Minzah, a new hotel built at the end of the twenties and which now, in 1971, is still Tangier's best. We spent ten days or so looking for a house in town big enough so that we would not be in each other's way. One afternoon I took a tiny bus in the Grand Socco and stayed on it to the end of its run at the foot of a forested mountain, then began to climb the dirt road that led upward, until suddenly I came upon the house. When I got back to the hotel, I was able to talk of little else. The next day we hired a carriage in the Grand Socco and explored the property. Aaron hesitated because the house was big, run-down, unfurnished, and isolated. However, we decided to take it and immediately began buying the necessary beds, tables, chairs, and cooking equipment.

This was easy, if not economical. The complicated part was getting the piano. In the Calle de Italia we found an old black upright marked "Bembaron et Hazan," hopelessly out of tune, but which we were obliged to take if we expected to work at all. The salesman who rented it to us assured us that he could get a tuner to set it straight, so we arranged for the men and the donkey to deliver it. When they arrived and the donkey saw the gate, it decided not to go through it. In the struggle the piano crashed to the ground with an attractive but unreproducible sound, and Aaron and I saw our working possibilities growing dimmer as the two Moroccans pushed, heaved, and banged the instrument about some more. When it was finally left in a corner of the empty salon, however, it seemed to be no more out of tune than it had been in the shop.

Each day we went back to the piano store to find out when the tuner was going to appear. One morning they said to us: "You're in luck. The tuner came by a while ago, and we're sending him to you this afternoon." The man arrived at the house wheezing from the climb and got to work. Aaron and I sat in the garden listening; it soon became apparent that the man had no idea of how to tune a piano and no sense of pitch. However, we did not bother him. Presently there was silence in the salon, and the silence continued. I went inside. He was sitting with his head resting on his arms, and his arms folded on the keyboard. I coughed, but he did not react. Then I saw a pint bottle of cognac on top of the piano and realized that he had drunk himself to sleep. We awoke him; he seemed embarrassed, but jauntily ripped off some ragged arpeggios and barged into the "Pilgrims' Chorus" from *Tannhaüser*. The piano sounded, if possible, even more sour than before. Drastic action was essential. "The piano is tuned," said the man. "No," said Aaron. "You sit there, and we're going to tune it." And so for another two hours he loosened and tightened the strings while we cried *"Más alto!"* or *"Más bajo!"* until eventually the instrument sounded like any other piano in need of tuning—that is to say, one at least could tell what each note was supposed to be. By that time the tuner had finished his bottle and was in a mood not to mind the long walk back into town. The next morning Aaron got to work on his Short Symphony, and I on my little Sonata for Oboe and Clarinet.

If I said that Tangier struck me as a dream city, I should mean it in the strict sense. Its topography was rich in prototypal dream scenes: covered streets like corridors with doors opening into rooms on each side, hidden terraces high above the sea, streets consisting only of steps, dark impasses, small squares built on sloping terrain so that they looked like ballet sets designed in false perspective, with alleys leading off in several directions; as well as the classical dream equipment of tunnels, ramparts, ruins, dungeons, and cliffs. The climate was both violent and languorous. The August wind hissed in the palms and rocked the eucalyptus trees and rattled the canebrakes that bordered the streets. Tangier had not yet entered the dirty era of automotive traffic. There were, however, several taxis stationed along with the carriages in the Grand Socco, one of which Aaron and I took each evening to get home after dinner. Just as the absence of traffic made it possible to sit in a café on the Place de France and hear only the cicadas in the trees, so the fact that the radio had not yet arrived in Morocco meant that one could also sit in a café in the center of the Medina and hear only the sound of many hundreds of human voices. The city was self-sufficient and clean, a doll's metropolis whose social and economic life long ago had been frozen in an enforced perpetual status quo by the international administration and its efficient police. There was no crime; no one yet thought of not respecting the European, whose presence was considered an asset to the community. (This was not entirely true with regard to the Spaniards, of whom there were so many thousands that they scarcely counted as Europeans.)

Immediately after breakfast each morning Aaron gave me my harmony lesson; it included correcting the figured basses I had prepared the day before. I was still in the process of analyzing the Mozart piano sonatas. I worked lying in a deck chair in the lower garden, where I would not hear Aaron's chordal laboratory. Afternoons Aaron, who drank wine at lunch, took a nap upstairs, while I worked at the piano. We had a cross-eyed servant named Mohammed, who prepared breakfast and lunch and took care of the garden. In the late afternoon we walked down into town and had dinner on the beach.

Gertrude Stein had told us that a Dutch Surrealist painter named Kristians Tonny was in Tangier. He was living, she added, laughing sourly, with a girl named Anita, who it was clear did not have her approval. Since it was a foregone conclusion that we were going to see these two at some point, there seemed no reason to hasten the meeting. I foresaw a static evening with a square-headed Dutchman who would show us his canvases one by one, and I did not think it would be fun. Aaron, more interested in people than I, wanted someone to talk to, so we soon made arrangements to call on Tonny and Anita. I remember being pleasantly surprised by them: Tonny seemed more French than Dutch; he had been educated in France. His drawings were quite wonderful: Moroccan landscapes out of Bosch, alive with hundreds of tiny figures wearing djellabas and haiks. The second time we met, Tonny remarked to Aaron: "The young man with you is slightly off his head, isn't he? I noticed it the other night right away. I heard shutters banging in the wind in there somewhere." I found this a sympathetic observation and liked him better for having made it. They had a friend who was a soccer star on the Moghreb team. We went to a game and on the way back to town afterward saw members of the Hillal team ambush their rivals. Fists, rocks, and knives were used, and it was all because the Moghreb had won the game. Tonny and Anita smiled at our astonishment and said this always happened.

When I wrote Gertrude Stein, describing our difficulties with the piano, she replied that Chopin had had even worse ones when he went to Mallorca with George Sand. "So cheer up. It's the common lot," she told me. And she added: "This time you seem to have left nothing behind but an aluminum penny German piece and a very pleasant memory."

Aaron and I gave up the Tangier house in the autumn after selling all the furnishings we had so recently bought, and set out for Fez. Tonny had visited the city, staying at the house of a Swiss named Brown, to whom he gave me a note. Although Aaron was not delighted with Morocco (claiming that all the things that struck me as so exotic were nothing new to him because he had seen and heard their counterparts as a child on President Street in Brooklyn), he agreed to spend a few days in Fez before returning to Germany.

We arrived in Fez at sunset and took a carriage through the Mellah to Fez-Djedid. Tangier had by no means prepared me for the experience of

Fez, where everything was ten times stranger and bigger and brighter. I felt that at last I had left the world behind, and the resulting excitement was well-nigh unbearable. Still, I was not too agitated to be able to notice a hotel sign some distance down a side alley as we drove along. I stopped the carriage and ran to examine the place. It was called the Hotel Ariana. As soon as I saw the three outside rooms upstairs, I knew it was the right place, because they gave directly onto the ramparts of Fez-Djedid. You could step out the windows onto the top of the rampart wall. Below was the garden of Djenane es Sebir with its willows overhanging the Oued Fez, and to the right an ancient waterwheel turned slowly, dripping and creaking. The hotel was a primitive little establishment, but Madame did serve breakfast. In the morning Aaron and I would step out the windows of our respective rooms and have our coffee and croissants on the ramparts. We ate other meals at a Jewish restaurant in the Mellah.

A wire came from Harry Dunham saying that he was en route from Dresden to Fez and would arrive within a week. I suspected that Aaron was finding Fez even less agreeable than Tangier. In any case, he had to return to Berlin. I was very sorry to see him go, and probably if Harry had not already been on his way, I should have gone back to Paris. But Harry did come. He had decided to take a year off from Princeton in order to study the dance in Germany; in the meantime, however, he had discovered the delights of photography. As a result, he arrived in Fez in a febrile state and spent most of his time climbing into all kinds of places where he was not supposed to be, being screamed at by Moroccans and French alike, but snapping his pictures, several hundred of them each day.

Harry was from Cincinnati and often mentioned the old slave quarters behind his parents' house there. If we took a municipal bus to get back to the Hotel Ariana from the Ville Nouvelle, he would refuse to sit next to a Moroccan, for fear of catching vermin. Yet he thought nothing of being crowded in among French workmen who were infinitely less clean than the Moroccans. He did not like it when I pointed this out to him; his face would darken and he would say: "You don't understand. I was brought up differently."

Even with my past practice of pretending not to exist, I could not do it in Morocco. A stranger as blond as I was all too evident. I wanted to see whatever was happening continue exactly as if I were not there. Harry could not grasp this; he expected his presence to change everything and in the direction which interested him. I told him that was not an intelligent way to travel. Obviously he could not change; he continued to make his presence felt in situations where I believed we should both strive for invisibility. Harry thought in terms of confrontation rather than conspiracy. I, however, was so used to hiding my intentions from everyone that I sometimes hid them from myself as well.

We made a trip to Sefrou and walked for some distance out of the town, following a river which little by little became recessed in a gorge. A peasant passing by told me in bad French that farther up there was a cave behind a waterfall. He then added that people went there to sacrifice chickens and occasionally goats. Immediately Harry wanted to find the place in order to photograph the cave. I refused to continue translating at that point and sent the man on his way. Harry was annoyed, but so was I. I asked him if it wasn't enough to know the cave was there, and that for centuries the stones at our feet had been washed by sacrificial blood. "Why do you have to have a picture?" Harry shrugged and went on taking photographs.

One morning, taking along my introduction from Tonny, I went with Harry to see Brown. He had an old Moroccan house in an orchard outside Bab Sidi bou Jida; it was one of the very few places in Fez with a swimming pool. Richard Halliburton, the Baron Munchausen of the twenties, had been staying there and had left that morning for West Africa. There were several guests for lunch, but Brown added us to their number, and we all sat at a long table on the terrace. Thus we met a young Fassi named Abdallah Drissi, who insisted that we visit him for tea later in the afternoon.

Abdallah's manner of living was extraordinary. He and his married older brother (who, as he immediately explained to us, were the only two remaining direct descendants of Moulay Idriss, the founder of Morocco) had inherited a vast palace in the Nejjarine quarter. Most of the aristocracy had been ruined financially by the French presence, but not this family. The brothers owed their continued prosperity to the fact that they regularly collected money and large quantities of salable goods from the zaouias roundabout. When Abdallah wanted something, he clapped his hands, and the slave on duty in his courtyard appeared. (He consistently used the word "slave" rather than "servant.") The order was relayed to responsible people in another part of the house, who saw that it was carried out to the letter. Thus a few days later when he wanted to take us on an evening excursion to Sidi Harazem, one brief command dispatched two slaves ahead of time to Bab Fteuh. When we got there, the carriage was waiting, packed with food, braziers, charcoal, lanterns, rugs, and cushions. The slaves came along to prepare the food and tea at the oasis. Wherever Abdallah went, men insisted on bowing low to kiss the sleeve of his djellaba. This annoyed Harry, although he did not explain why.

I learned that Harry's parents had no idea that he was not in Dresden studying. His twenty-first birthday would be in another three weeks; he had to go back there in time for that, in order to send them a cable on the day (it was that kind of family) and also to arrange for his sister Amelia to visit him. Before returning he wanted to see Marrakech. We spent a night in Casablanca, to which I vowed I would never return if I could help it, and we left the following day for *la ville rouge*.

In Marrakech we stayed at a tiny hotel near the *quartier réservé*. It was run by a typical colonial couple who thought it their duty to warn us continually of the dishonesty and savagery in Morocco. When we came in at night from the street, we stepped over (and sometimes on) a boy whose job it was to lie across the doorway until dawn. Harry was indignant to see this and asked the woman why she did not give him a mat to lie on. "Ha!" she cried. "That's all he needs. He's already so spoiled he's no good. I'd fire him except that he owes me two months' work for one of my husband's shirts he ruined trying to iron it. He's an animal, that one!"

This information scandalized Harry. The next day I found him sitting on the roof talking to the boy. "It's perfectly true," he told me. "Two months for scorching a shirt. And the man's wearing it, what's more."

"They'll have their revenge some day," I said. "Don't worry."

"But that's not the point," he objected.

A quarter of an hour later when I went back to the roof, I saw that something had happened. The boy was looking at Harry as if he were the incarnation of God, and Harry was looking resolute and pleased. "I asked Abdelkader if he'd like to go to Paris and he said yes."

"But why?"

"I want a valet. I've never had one, and this is a good chance."

Harry went downstairs and calmly told Madame he was taking Abdelkader with him to Paris. I stood on the balcony above the courtyard and listened to the Frenchwoman's shrieks. *"Il me doit deux mois de travail!"* she kept crying. In spite of having no French, Harry had got his idea across.

When I saw Madame that evening, she was still very much excited. She rushed up to me, saying: "You know, if your friend attacks him, he'll defend himself." It was clear that she believed Harry's intentions regarding Abdelkader were sexual. "If he tries to take him away, I shall call the police!'' she shouted. At that moment Harry came into the courtyard and, passing behind us into the kitchen, suddenly stood in the doorway pointing a revolver at Madame. She swayed, nearly losing her balance, and screamed: "Lucien!"

The husband appeared from a back room and, seeing Harry, stood perfectly still. Harry swung around and aimed at him. Then he laughed and laid the weapon down on the table. The man immediately rushed over and seized it. By this time Abdelkader and a maid had come onto the scene and were watching with round eyes. Monsieur, Madame, and Harry now began to shout all at once. Harry's invective was in German, although I doubt that any one of them was aware of that. They were all red in the face, and they went on bellowing at one another for five minutes. We changed hotels that night, but the next day we had to confront Monsieur and Madame once again at the police station, for Harry had gone early in the morning to announce his intention of removing Abdelkader to France and to fill out the necessary papers. Since Abdelkader was working at the hotel, he had to be cleared by his employers, who steadfastly refused to give him up until they were paid a sum which suddenly included dishes and windows the boy had broken, as well as the scorched shirt.

The police warned Harry that the proceedings could take a long time, because Abdelkader's entire family had to be legally in accord with the project. Harry would go back to Dresden and I would stay on in Marrakech until I had straightened out official matters with both the French government and the Moroccan *adoul*. Then I would go straight to Paris with Abdelkader, where Harry would join me before Christmas. (He had just decided he wanted to spend the winter in Paris, rather than in Germany, because Man Ray was there, and he hoped to work with him.)

The proprietor of our new hotel was also a truck driver who regularly, twice a month, carried wine and food across the High Atlas to the Foreign Legion post at Ouarzazate. I questioned him at length about the place: he said no one could visit it without a pass from the governor. We checked on that bit of information and found it correct. Later he casually remarked that he himself would take us if we made it worth his while. He had done it once before, he said, arranging the matter at each checkpoint along the way by making generous gifts of extra bottles of wine and liqueurs.

A few days later we started out with him at three in the morning, a second truck following behind, as was the custom in those unsafe days. The trail over the Atlas was so hair-raising that the most sensible place to sit seemed the top of the truck, where at least we could see down over each precipice as we swayed along its edge. The road was in the process of construction, not a mile of it yet paved. Above the cloud line it was a mud track. We bogged down several times and once skidded to within inches of the abyss, when we got out and collected shrubs and stones to push under the wheels. And at each *poste de controle* the wine went out to the soldiers. Ouarzazate came into view just before sunset; we saw the painted towers of the Casbah above the palms, and when the truck came to a stop, the silence was broken by the faint sound of a bugle. A Greek had put up a hotel with eight tiny rooms at the edge of the camp. Each room had two army cots enveloped in one mosquito net that hung from the ceiling. There were no toilet facilities—not even a shed or a hole in the ground—nothing but the open desert. That night a sandstorm began to blow, so that the next day we could not leave the hotel. The following day was calmer, but unfortunately a French commandant burst in for drinks at the bar and, seeing Harry and me sitting there studying our maps, lost no time in demanding our papers. Harry jumped up, clicked his heels together, and saluted in best Junker fashion, saying *"Ja, ja! Natürlich, natürlich. . . ."* This so aroused the officer's suspicions that even though Harry quickly went into English, he questioned the validity of the American passport and placed us under house arrest, saying that we would be put on the first vehicle that went out of Ouarzazate. "And I know who brought you here," he went on. "And every guard along the trail is going to get fifteen days in prison." When he had gone, the Greek explained that often when legionnaires deserted, they acquired false or stolen American passports.

The next day the officer came back, accompanied by a civilian. "You had better have some money on you," he told us. "You paid to get here, and you're going to pay to get out. This man can take you to Marrakech tomorrow morning, and I hope he makes you pay through the nose." The man, however, wanted less than the other one had charged for bringing us, doubtless because there was no wine to be distributed, and so everyone was content.

Harry went back to Germany, leaving me with enough money to see that Abdelkader got to Paris. I waited in Marrakech, going each day with him to the notaries. His mother and grandmother had to go along as well; they rode always in a separate carriage and heavily veiled. It seems to me now that those days consisted largely of endless carriage rides along the dusty alleys, through flickering sunlight and shadow, the other carriage with the two covered figures in it, going on ahead.

Time passed, and nothing happened. The police themselves now were hindering progress by being slow to get certain documents stamped and signed. There was nothing I could do about that. I left my address with Abdelkader and went back to Tangier, where I stayed with Tonny and Anita. They had just moved to a small Moroccan house on the hill above Dradeb, reachable only by using a steep path bordered by cactus and boulders. The house always had Moroccans in it. During the day the maids, one of them noseless, worked in the courtyard, and at night friends came in to play cards and listen to the phonograph. The games were Moroccan, played with *naipe* cards, some of which looked as if they were part of the tarot pack.

Anita had come down to Tangier ostensibly to join an old friend, Dean, who was barman at the Minzah Hotel. But little by little I understood that it was Gertrude Stein who had engineered her departure from Paris, in order to make Tonny work more at his painting. With this in mind, she also had persuaded him to sign a long-term lease on a studio in Montparnasse, offering to pay the first two months herself. After he had lived there for a while, he began to hear rumors about the true reason for Anita's disappearance from the Paris scene. He promptly broke the lease and, leaving everything behind, came as fast as he could to Tangier to be with Anita.

At this point it was natural that my hosts had only the most disagreeable things to say about the Misses Stein and Toklas. Tonny was so totally infatuated with Anita that he seemed not to be aware of her continuous flirtation with the younger male population of Tangier. Or perhaps he blamed it totally on the Moroccan youths, who swarmed around her like bees over a honeysuckle vine.

Abdelkader arrived from Marrakech one morning by bus and straightaway began to find grievous fault with the way Anita managed the little house. "*C'est dégueulasse, mon ʒami!*" He would run his finger along the floor beside the wall and bring it up to hold it two inches from my eyes so that I could judge the truth of his statement. One evening Anita, having invited several Moroccans for dinner, prepared a couscous into whose sauce she decided to pour a quart of gin. Very likely it was a unique occurrence in Moroccan culinary history; with the exception of Abdelkader (who sensibly refused to taste the dish) everyone was violently sick afterward. From then on Abdelkader would not eat any food which Anita had, being persuaded that she had mixed poison with the couscous.

Since it was clear that Anita and Abdelkader were never going to get along together, I made a strenuous effort to leave quickly for Paris. The morning we set out, Tonny presented me with a fine drawing that I had admired, but he handed it to me as I was getting into the little motorboat that was to carry us out to the Algeciras ferry, so that it was damaged by salt water even before I left Tangier.

In Marrakech Abdelkader had gone several times to the cinema; that was the extent of his familiarity with the gadgets of the twentieth century. Of course, he had seen trains and automobiles, but as we boarded the ferry, a look of suspicion and terror came into his face, and he said: "Is this a bridge that moves?" I told him it was a boat, but the word meant nothing to him. "My grandmother told me that in Europe they have bridges that move, and she said never to go onto one of them, or I'd be very sick." We had scarcely got out into the strait before he was lying flat on the deck in an excess of nausea. Occasionally he moaned: "My grandmother told me," but that was all. In Algeciras he had to go immediately to the market to buy oranges, and he flew into a rage when he discovered that Spanish oranges were not identical to those in Marrakech. "This country is no good, *mon ẓami*, and the people are all crazy." This was still his opinion when we got to Seville. There in the dining room of the Hotel Madrid on Calle Sierpes he somehow met a middle-aged couple from Chicago who were traveling with their daughter and accepted an invitation for us both to accompany them on a carriage drive through the city. First the American went to Thomas Cook's and bought $5 worth of small coins, which he instructed them to put into several small cloth bags. Then he hired a carriage with two extra folding seats, on which Abdelkader and I sat facing the three members of the family, and we set out on the tour of Seville. The idea was for us all to stand up and scatter coins whenever we went through a densely populated quarter. Obviously it did not take long to collect a very noisy mob, which followed the carriage and was kept from trying to climb aboard by the driver's whip. All this delighted the American gentleman so much that when we got back to the hotel he sighed and remarked: "Well, I had fifty dollars' worth of fun for five. I call that pretty good!" That night we all went to a cabaret where the girls danced *sevillanas* up on a stage. At one point, however, they filed down into the other part of the room and danced among the tables. As one of them swirled by us, Abdelkader reached out and touched her. Then he pulled his hand back as if he had been burned and with consternation turned to me crying: "But it's not a cinema? They're real?" And a little later: *"Elles son vraies, alors? Ah, mon ẓami, c'est bien, ça!"*

In Madrid too, at the Prado, he stood looking at the Goyas, waiting for them to move. When they failed to change, he was disappointed, and we continued to explore the museum. We came to the Bosches; he was immobilized. Finally he said: "Come on! They're beginning to move. Let's go outdoors." In the street, after he had examined the world and satisfied himself that everything was still the same, he sighed and said: "Do you know who made all the cinemas in that house? I can tell you. It was Satan."

Abdelkader's ingenuousness was often staggering. The first morning in Paris we had breakfast on the Coupole's terrace. There were brioches topped with currant jelly in the dish bearing breakfast breads. He erupted in a series of anti-French remarks because he took it for granted that the jelly was coagulated blood. *"Ah, non, mon ʒami! Je ne mange pas le sang. C'est honteux!"* (In spite of this, a few weeks later, when I was thinking of having my tonsils out, he implored me to tell the surgeon to save all the blood that would come out of me when he operated, so that he could drink it.) That afternoon he said he was going to take a walk. He was gone several hours and returned to the hotel after dark, full of a story of having met a very nice old gentleman, quite like his brother, he stressed, who had invited him to his house and given him tea, *"comme elle le fait ma mère, la pauvre, jet te jure,"* by which I understood that he meant mint tea. It was not surprising, considering that he had gone wandering off fully dressed in Moroccan regalia. The old gentleman, who spoke Arabic, Abdelkader said, had pressed 50 francs into his hand when he left and insisted that he accept a djellaba which was hanging on a coatrack. He explained in an aside to me that he had not wanted to accept the garment because it would be shameful, but to be polite he took it and left it outside the door in the street. "It was very old," he added.

During the day I had telephoned Gertrude Stein. It was Sunday, her at-home evening. I told her about Abdelkader, and she said to bring him along. We were let in by a maid, who opened the salon door for us. The room was full of people; Gertrude Stein stood in the middle of it, talking. Suddenly she gave one of her hearty, infectious laughs and slapped her thigh, as she was wont to do in such moments. *"C'est elle?"* said Abdelkader in a stage whisper, wide-eyed. *"Mais c'est un homme, ça!"* I hushed him, and we went in. Soon I was in conversation with an engaging little Catalan whose paintings I knew and admired, but whom I had never met: Joan Miró. I told him about Abdelkader's behavior at the Prado two days earlier. He agreed with Abdelkader about the Bosches: they did indeed move. In case I ever passed through Barcelona he gave me his address there. But he also had a *mas* in Mallorca, which, like a true Spaniard, he said was my house whenever I wished. Then he asked me for a piece of paper and a pencil and drew me a map of Spain that looked just like one of his drawings. Now and then I glanced about to see what Abdelkader was doing. At one end of the room Alice Toklas presided over the tea and food, and here he had settled himself, beside her. They seemed to be deep in conversation. When the guests had thinned out a bit, she called Gertrude Stein and me over to the table. "Let him tell you about the Tonny ménage," she told Gertrude Stein, and to Abdelkader she said: "Tell Mademoiselle, was the house clean?" "*Oh, non, madame, pas beaucoup. Elle était dégueulasse.*"

Gertrude Stein grinned. They continued to ply him with questions; his replies all delighted them. Gertrude Stein turned to me. "Did you leave two and six on the dirty toilet cover?" I did not understand. "That's what Mr. Salteena did in *The Young Visitors,* and that's what Tonny and Anita were expecting you to do." "But they invited me," I objected. The two ladies joined in derisive laughter.

Harry arrived from Dresden to say that he had got a girl pregnant and was trying to persuade her to go to London for an abortion. My reaction was one of indignation at his carelessness, but he seemed rather pleased with the situation. Wires kept arriving, first from Germany and finally from London, but there was still a question whether she would go through with the abortion. Harry took a furnished studio at the top of 17 Quai Voltaire, the same building in which Virgil Thomson lived. The first thing he did after signing the lease was to go down the street to the Galerie Pierre, where Miró was having an exhibit of his works in a new medium, three-dimensional assemblages, and buy three of them to liven up the walls of the twenty-foot-high salon.

I went to see Nadia Boulanger, who was very pleasant, but who seemed not to have been expecting me. Or perhaps she had expected me several months earlier and had ceased to do so. At all events, she was not willing to accept me immediately as a composition pupil; she advised me to enroll in her counterpoint class at the École Normale, which I did with the intention of starting classes at the beginning of the year.

Aaron had arranged a London concert of new American music to be given at Aeolian Hall in Wigmore Street. He was to play his Piano Variations, and Virgil Thomson was to accompany the singers in his *Capital Capitals,* a cantata on a Stein text. Since my Sonata for Oboe and

Clarinet was on the program, I had to be there beforehand in order to rehearse the players. Harry and I left Paris a week before the concert. At that time Mary Oliver and Jock were living at Pembroke Lodge in Richmond Park, and she very generously offered to let me stay there. It was the sort of house that had Titians in the dining room and Gauguins and Picassos in the bathrooms. Its only disadvantage for me was its distance from central London, where I had my rehearsals each day. But Mary had just designed two extraordinarily smart-looking cars for herself, and she put one of them at my disposal, complete with chauffeur and footman. Harry made the mistake of mentioning the abortion to Mary, and she immediately began trying to persuade him to visit a witch she knew in Hampstead. The mere sound of the word infuriated Harry; his father was a doctor, he said, and he was having no truck with witches. The abortion took place a few days later, and there was no more mention of it.

In London I finally met Edouard Roditi, who had sent me so many letters of introduction to his friends. He was tall, suave, and polyglot. We went to his father's large export-import office in Golden Square. It was an international firm; Edouard had spent a time working for his father in the Hamburg branch.

Harry's older sister Amelia appeared at Aeolian Hall the night of the concert. She disliked the program intensely; for some reason my piece, even more than the others, incurred her wrath, perhaps because it had been described in the morning newspaper as "pagan." We went back to Paris together. On the ferry she told me: "If I had a little boy and he wrote a piece like that, I'd know what to do with him."

I was vaguely curious. "What would you do?"

"I'd see that he got hospital treatment," she said fiercely.

Amelia moved into the studio with Harry. From the moment she saw Abdelkader she loathed him, and it became her favorite occupation to persecute him by following him around, issuing impossible orders in a language no one could understand. *"Faites ceça or no spaʒieren, you hear?"* Abdelkader would stare at her uncomprehending; sometimes he would cry: *"Ah, je t'en prie, madame, laisse-moi tranquille!"* I could see that the pattern of life at the studio would be ephemeral.

JOURNALS

Days

Three years ago Daniel Halpern wrote me asking if I kept a diary. I replied that I did not and never had, not seeing any reason for engaging in such an activity. He wrote again, suggesting that I start one immediately, since he would like to include whatever resulted in an issue of Antaeus *to be devoted only to diaries, journals, and notebooks. I told him that I thought the result would be devoid of interest, since I would have nothing to report. All he wanted, he responded, was a record of daily life in today's Tangier. I agreed to try and did what I could with the project, although I was not very faithful, often allowing two weeks or more to elapse without writing anything. What went on during the periods of silence I have no idea, but doubtless the unrecorded days were even more humdrum than the others.*

I suppose the point of publishing such a document is to demonstrate the way in which the hours of a day can as satisfactorily be filled with trivia as with important events.

—PAUL BOWLES

August 19, 1987

Clear. Walked to Merkala. The *cherqi* was violent, and raised mountains of dust along the way. On the beach hundreds of small children, hardly any adults. The boys were beating each other with long strips of seaweed. Constant smell of the sewage coming out of the conduit at the east end of the beach. Lalla Fatima Zohra was right to forbid the public to use the place a few years ago. But that was during the cholera epidemic. A letter from Paris saying that Quai Voltaire will not agree to letting me inspect the galleys of any book they may publish. I never asked to see galleys. I wanted to see typescript before it was set up in type. They called my request *"légalisme excessif."* Buffie found her two thousand dollars and passport, hidden somewhere in the flat.

September 14

I looked through *Libération*'s questionnaire of two years ago: *Pourquoi écrivez-vous?*—this time to see what was the most usual answer. Very few writers claimed financial necessity as a reason for exercising their profession. Many admitted that they had no idea why they wrote. But the majority responded by implying that they were impelled to write by some inner force which could not be denied. The more scrupulous of these did not hesitate to admit that their principal satisfaction was in feeling that they were leaving a part of themselves behind—in other words, writing was felt to confer a certain minimal immortality. This would have been understandable earlier in the century when it was assumed that life on the planet would continue indefinitely. Now that the prognosis is doubtful, the desire to leave a trace behind seems absurd. Even if the human species manages to survive for another hundred years, it's unlikely that a book written in 1990 will mean much to anyone happening to open it in 2090, if indeed he is capable of reading at all.

October 3

Yesterday two men from the Wafa Bank called on me, handing me a letter from Casa, asking that I lend them two small drawings by Yacoubi for an exhibit they intend to hold there later this month. I said I had no Yacoubi drawings—only paintings—and they answered that drawings had been specified. Instead of shrugging and saying: *"Je regrette beaucoup,"* I added that I had had drawings, but that they had fallen behind the bookcases in one room or another, and I didn't know which room or which bookcases, and that I had no intention of moving those heavily laden objects in order to search. A bad idea, since they both volunteered to empty the shelves. Several thousand books. They're coming back this afternoon to do that work. In the meantime I've spoken with Abdelouahaid and Mrabet, both of whom advised me not to let them start. It would take several hours in any case. But A. and M. were in agreement that if the drawings were found and borrowed, I'd never see them again. So now I must face the two Wafa men and say the thing is impossible.

An even more unpleasant prospect is having the British TV crew and *animateurs* arrive week after next to do that interview. This I dread more than anything because of my disappearing voice. (Buffie insists I have

cancer of the larynx, and has no patience with me because I won't go for
X rays.)

October 13

"When a Jew is dead, he's dead," said Gertrude Stein. Yet both she and Alice
Toklas were bad Jews. Stein was a secret Christian Scientist; Toklas openly
embraced the Roman Catholic faith in her later years. Is this regression?

November 15

Rodrigo and I were in the Fez Market yesterday. He drew my attention to
a tray of mushrooms at a vegetable stall. "These look exactly like what we
call San Isidros," he said. San Isidros are psilocybin mushrooms, he went
on, in case I didn't know, which I didn't. He was excited to think they grew
in Morocco. I thought that if such a drug existed here, people would know
about it, and they very clearly don't. But he bought a dirham's worth and
went home, saying he was going to brew them in a tea. Today he came in
triumphant. "They're the same hongos. The same thing as in Guatemala."
The brew, which he said had a disgusting flavor, kept him awake all night,
writing rather than hallucinating. It's hard to believe that psilocybin is sold
here in the market and that no one is aware of it. This is probably because
mushrooms are not a part of the diet of Moroccans. Still, the Europeans who
buy them must have had some strange and unexplained experiences.

December 26

The most ridiculous gadget of the year, in the show window of an Indian
shop on the Boulevard Pasteur: a deodorant stick with a built-in compass.

January 20, 1988

Every morning, weather permitting, I set out on a long walk. It's supposed
to help my leg. It makes no difference whether it does or not; I go anyway.
Each day I walk to the inaudible accompaniment of a different popular song.
It's not necessary to look for them; they pop up from my unconscious. It
was some time last summer when I realized that all these old songs from
the 1920s were there. I can never remember what song it was that preoc-

cupied me on the preceding day, so now I write them down. Today it was "Red Hot Mama."

February 6

Rodrigo has bought a falcon. When Mrabet heard this, he decided that he was going to get it away from him, and began to announce his plans for teaching it to hunt.

February 7

The weather is so bitterly cold that I've abandoned my walks. Mrabet arrives early and makes a big fire in the fireplace. I get up to find it roaring. Wonderful these mornings when the temperature in my bedroom is 38° F. Rodrigo has the bird in a cage. He says it's gentle and seems to have no fear of him. It eats fresh raw beef.

February 12

Brazilian journalist with intriguing first name of Leda. Rodrigo brought the falcon here. A beautiful bird. R. wants to take it to the top of the mountain and set it free. "So it can eat people's chickens," says Mrabet.

February 13

Abdelouahaid and I drove with Rodrigo and the cage to the high point above Mediouna. There was a hard climb over sharp rocks to get up there. Abdelouahaid helped me. When the cage had been opened and the falcon had been persuaded to come out, Rodrigo threw it upward into the air, and we stood watching it as it flew. There was a strong *cherqi* blowing which seemed to keep it from rising very far. It flew straight toward the northwest over the pine forest, as though it knew where it was going. Little by little it went up. By that time the cold had got to my bones. I came home and got into bed.

February 20

Incapacitated with a cold since the day we took the falcon up to the mountain. L., my persevering biographer, has arranged a concert of my music as part of the Manca Music Festival in Nice for the third of April. Hard to be properly annoyed with him when he goes to such lengths to be agreeable. He even offered to come from Boston to Tangier and fetch me, if I'd go. I shan't go. I'm too old to put up with being stared at.

April 19

No one was certain whether today or tomorrow would be the first day of Ramadan. We knew only last night when the sirens sounded that today would begin the fast. (This is the second Ramadan with sirens instead of cannon. *Allez demander pourquoi.*) One shot, and you were over the boundary in the land where all is forbidden. They tell you that with today's traffic the cannon would not be heard. This may be true at sunset, but at half past four in the morning the city is silent. Strange that no Muslim has spoken of the ludicrousness of using an air-raid siren to herald a holy day of fasting.

Every year I have to remember to warn people who come for tea that they must leave well before sunset. The hour directly after that is the time to be inside, out of the street. It's the favorite hour for attacking foreigners. The streets are absolutely empty. Not a car, not a pedestrian, not a policeman in view, everywhere in the city. One of my guests, an elderly American woman, was knocked down, kicked, and robbed in the street in front of the apartment house. I felt vaguely guilty of living in a place where such things are taken more or less for granted. But the real guilt is that which I feel in the presence of Muslims. They are suffering and I am not. Here at home I'm obliged to eat and drink in front of them. They always claim that it doesn't affect them to see someone eating. If I want to eat, I can eat, they say. There's no one telling me I can't eat. This is true, but the social pressure is such that anyone seen to be eating in public is arrested and jailed.

Thirst is more painful than hunger, they say. Smokers are irascible for the first few days. As the month wears on, skirmishes between individuals increase in number. But no one will admit that he is short-tempered because of Ramadan. Says Abdelouahaid: "If you're going to be in a bad humor because it's Ramadan, your Ramadan has no value, and it would be better not to fast at all." Nevertheless they *are* likely to be fractious, and I take care not to contradict or criticize them.

April 24

I have a spider whose behavior mystifies me. It's the kind of spider with tiny body and very long legs, and it spins no web. It spends its days hanging by one filament from the bottom of a marble shelf behind the door. For the past three weeks it has been going every night to hang four feet away, near the washbasin. When morning comes it returns to its corner. There are no insects for it to catch at either location, but it never misses a night. If I let anyone know of its existence it's sure to be killed. Spiders are not encouraged to live in the house. Rahma is such a poor housekeeper that the spider probably can count on months of privacy. If Mrabet or Abdelouahaid should catch sight of it, they would unthinkingly crush it. I don't know why I assume that it's entirely harmless, except that it looks nothing like the spiders that attack. These have heavier bodies and thicker legs, and are intensely, militantly black.

May 3

Typical tale of Ramadan violence at the market of Casabarata. A man who prepared *chibaqia* was sitting on the ground, hoping to attract buyers. (*Chibaqia* used to be made with honey; now, there being no more honey, it's made with sugar syrup, and isn't very good.) Another man carrying a little portable counter of combs, pocket mirrors, toothpaste, and similar objects, sat down near the first, who immediately ordered him to go somewhere else. The second man said he was going to sit there only for a minute, because he was tired. Then he would go on. The *chibaqia* seller roared: "Safi!," whipped out a long knife, and slashed the other with a downward motion, severing his jugular. The wounded man rose, took a few steps, and collapsed. His four-year-old son stood watching while he bled to death. This was the second killing at Casabarata since Ramadan began two weeks ago. There have been others, in other parts of the town, but I didn't get eyewitness reports of them as I did of this one.

May 4

Jerez off to New York today. Unfortunately she came yesterday, bringing a big bunch of roses and lilies. Friday Mrabet had bought an armful of white roses from Kif Kunti, and had arranged them in a large vase. It was Jerez's fatal idea to put Mrabet's roses into a smaller receptacle in order to make room for her own more spectacular array. I didn't think Mrabet would be pleased to see this, but I wasn't prepared for his exaggerated reaction. The insults came fast and thick. Each time she tried to speak, he shouted louder. Anyone used to living here during Ramadan would have backed down and given up trying to reason with the adversary, but Jerez seemed to think conditions were normal, and continued to ask if she had ever done anything to harm him. His shouting grew louder; the insults came in Arabic, Spanish, and English. Then he began to hurl cushions at her, and finally hauled off and gave her a resounding crack in the face. Jerez was bending over him, so she did not fall. But Mrabet jumped up, seized a log from the fireplace, and swung at her, to hit her on top of the head. My shouting at him to sit down and shut up had no effect, but Abdelwahab, who was here as well as Abdelouahaid, came between them and calmed Mrabet for a moment. (Abdelwahab is a Riffian, so that Mrabet was more inclined to listen.) But then Mrabet must have felt that he had been bought too easily, and began to bellow that he was in a room full of Jews who should be killed and not allowed to pollute the air breathed by a Muslim. With this he left the room, and we heard him continuing his insults and obscenities as he banged around the kitchen. Jerez by this time was sobbing, and Abdelwahab decided to leave, which he did so quickly that he left his umbrella behind. Abdelouahaid merely sat, shaking his head. He whispered to me: "A horrible man. Heart of tar." I think he was shocked by Mrabet's behavior. I was not shocked, having seen other instances of his insensate fury, but I was ashamed that all this should have happened in my flat, and to a guest of mine. When Jerez went out, still weeping, he shouted: "If you come back from New York, I'm going to kill you!" Five minutes earlier she had whispered to me: "Do you think he'll kill me?" and I had smiled and said: "Of course not." So his parting shot was not calculated to comfort her. It's some consolation to know that when she returns it will no longer be Ramadan.

Before Mrabet went home he excused himself to me for his outburst, saying: "She wants to drive me crazy. She kept saying I was a thief. Can she prove it? Does she have a witness?" It's pretty absurd to consider that all this was ostensibly about a bunch of roses that got put into the wrong receptacle, or so it would have seemed to an onlooker. In reality Mrabet had a bad conscience, and when a Moroccan feels guilty, he attacks.

May 5

The spider, after having been absent for the better part of a week, has suddenly decided to return to its regular nocturnal haunt, where it stays the whole time, day and night. It seems to me there's something suspect about this. The identical spot where it used to spend its nights, yet I'm not convinced that it's the same insect. It looks smaller and feebler than before. If it's a different individual, what has happened to the original, and why does this one hang exactly in the place where that one hung? An entomologist could probably give a completely unexpected and satisfying explanation.

May 7

From time to time when we're driving in the country, Abdelouahaid recounts something that happened or is said to have happened in a village we're passing through. Some of the stories are of the sort that it would never occur to me to invent. Others are banal, like this one. A couple facing increasingly hard times in their *tchar*. Last few chickens die of an epidemic. If we want to go on living, we'd better leave now while we can still walk. With the girl enceinte, they start walking along the trails, and come to Bab Taza at night. A man sees them and realizes they are from the country, asks them if he can help them. The girl says: "We're looking for a place." "A house?" "Yes." "Come. I'll show you a good house." Takes them to a house he has just bought with the intention of selling it. Before they go in the husband asks the price. (He is entirely without a guirch.) The house is completely empty. After they have been shown around, they ask if they may spend the night in it, and give the owner the reply in the morning. He agrees. They bid one another good night, and the owner leaves them there. The husband goes to the well to draw water for washing and taking supper. Sees a small wooden box floating in the shadows down there. When he brings it up, it is locked. He and his wife decide that the owner knows nothing about it. They open it. Full of banknotes. In the morning when the owner comes, they agree to buy the house, which they do with half the amount in the box. Abdelouahaid loves stories about hidden treasure, which are invariably without interest.

May 16

The one enjoyable attribute of Ramadan was the *rhaïta* solo played in the minaret of each mosque at the times of the call to prayer. This year they have done away with music. I suppose someone came up with the idea that it was anachronistic or unorthodox. "People don't want to listen to somebody blowing a *rhaïta*, anyway," says Abdelouahaid. "They have music on the television." In 1977 I recorded the oboe concerts nightly for the entire month of Ramadan. Unconsciously I must have suspected that sooner or later they would dispense with them. Good things do not continue.

July 23

I think of how nowadays I never go near the beach. Fifty years ago it was where I spent my summer days. The days when for one reason or another I did not go, I felt were nonexistent, wasted. The Moroccans said I was crazy. Not even the men sunbathed in those days. They believed the sun was poisonous. After the war the younger men played football on the beach, and now and then you saw a female walking into the waves, heavily dressed, of course. The Moroccan girl who lived next door to us in Calle Maimouni got into the habit of taking the women of the neighborhood down to the beach in the afternoon. They would return before sunset in great spirits. Of the girl, Jane said: "She's a revolutionary. She's got the only pair of water wings in Tangier."

August 11

Yesterday an unfortunate day. Gavin Lambert and Phillip hatched a plan whereby we would go in two cars to Xauen, the two of them, Rodrigo, Krazy Kat, Abdelouahaid, and I. Before we started out, Gavin remarked facetiously: "Happy August the Tenth" (the title of the first story Tennessee published in *Antaeus* back in 1971). It was the wrong thing to say; in the story the tenth of August was not a happy one for the protagonists. This August tenth was hellishly hot. We in the Mustang were trying to keep up with Gavin, who hurried ahead of us at an unnecessarily high speed. At one point we saw his car slow down and stop. We all got out and stood uncomfortably in the strong sun. "It needs water," said Gavin. Abdelouahaid ran down to a river below and brought up some water. This did no good. Everyone got into the Mustang, sat one on top of the other, and went to Tetuan, where we drove from street to street in search of a garage which might still be open. Since it was midday everything was in the act of shutting. Gavin had to stay behind and find a *remorqueur* to tow him back to Tangier. The rest of us continued to Xauen. When we arrived it was just a little too late to get lunch at the Parador. We had to satisfy ourselves with omelettes and beer. It was even hotter up there than in Tangier, for the lack of any wind. After lunch we climbed up to Ras el-Ma and ordered tea. The bees were plentiful and insistent, and insisted on covering the rims of the glasses and sliding into the tea. Honey bees don't ordinarily sting, but there were so many here that there was nowhere one could touch one's lips to the glass in order to drink. Phillip took countless pictures and Krazy Kat made friends with everyone in sight. I wanted to get back to Tangier before dark, so we set out early. But with the extra people in the backseat, the car began to make agonized groans at each curve and pothole, so loud that it was hard to talk. The heat continued, because we were driving directly against the sun. Made Tangier just at dusk. End of Happy August the Tenth.

November 20

Got back last night. Acute euphoria going through the customs at the airport. Abdelouahaid had the Mustang outside, and Abdelwahab was inside to meet me. Getting to Paris was nerve-racking. Had to sit for five hours waiting for the plane to come in from Casablanca. Each time I asked for information, I was told that it still hadn't left the Casa airport. Never found out why. The flight was easy. It was nearly dusk when we hit Orly. Rondeau and Claude Thomas were waiting, and had been waiting all afternoon. There were great complications in the Paris streets. Strikers had built bonfires in the middle of the avenues, there were police swarming like ants everywhere, and traffic barely moved. Finally we got out and walked, leaving my luggage in the car for the chauffeur to deposit at the hotel when he got there. John Hopkins had come over from Oxfordshire to see me, and Claude, John, and I had dinner in my room. A fine dinner—the first good steak I've had in twenty years.

Next day very busy. Bibka (Madame Merle d'Aubigné) gave a huge complex lunch for publishers and critics. I was treated like a star, and enjoyed it. The afternoon was crowded with people who came to the hotel and asked questions and took photos. Rondeau and I dined alone, and were driven to the studio. Program [*Apostrophes*] longer than I'd expected, but it went off easily. Pivot obviously clever; how seriously devoted to literature I don't know. He was a bit hard on Miss Siegel, although if you bill yourself as Sartre's secret mistress, you can't object to a little rough treatment.

Saturday I went shopping with Claude, hoping to find a good bathrobe. The first shop we hit had one, but it cost nearly five thousand francs, which I had no intention of spending. Finally got one of cashmere for something over three hundred dollars, which still seems rather high for a garment no one but me will ever see. But I was glad to have a trophy to bring back to Tangier. It was already night when Claude, Rondeau, and Sylvaine Pasquier said good-bye at Orly. Paris more splendid than in 1938, but I wanted to escape from it before I began to remember it.

February 25

Books arrive practically every day from one place or another, and Abdelouahaid is indispensable in getting them through the censors and the customs, and to the postal authorities. But yesterday he came out to the car where I was waiting and in great excitement began to upbraid me. "A book that is killing people all over the world, and you want it. It's very bad. They're angry in the post office." I had no idea what was the matter. "What book? Where is it?" I got out of the car and went into the building, where I saw them all fixing me with baleful stares. One of the employees came to me and explained. "You have a book here that's forbidden." I asked him if I could see it, but he said it had already been repacked, and no one could see it. "Can't you show me the parcel so I'll know where it came from?" He went behind a counter and held up a package in the dark by its string, not wanting to touch it with his hands. By this time I'd guessed that the book was the one that was making all the trouble, thanks to the dictator of Iran. Still I had no idea who had sent it. Another official came up frowning. "This is contraband goods. You cannot have it." "I don't want it," I told him.

March 18

French TV crew came here today. Interviewer, intelligent and pleasant, seemed shocked by the humble aspect of the flat, saying he'd expected me to be living on the Mountain in a big house with a fine garden. Very earnestly he said: "Do you *like* living this way?" Then he decided that the interview should be conducted in the wine bar at the Minzah, a decor more in keeping with the expectations of his public.

April 25

Two disreputable-looking Moroccans rang my bell at about two-thirty in the afternoon. They didn't seem to know how to begin talking. Then the lift arrived and Abdelouahaid got out of it, standing behind them. "Your daughter wants to see you," said one. When I objected that I had no daughter, he only laughed. The other said: "Yes, you have, and she's here. The one named Catherine, from Germany. She's never seen you, and she wants to come and meet you." "I don't want to meet her," I told him. Abdelouahaid spoke up, assuring them that there was a mistake, but they carefully paid him no attention. "Shall we bring her here at five?" "No, no, no! I have no daughter. Thank you, but I don't want to see her."

They left. Abdelouahaid came in, warning me that they were criminals, and not to let them in if they came back. I felt fairly sure they wouldn't return. But after I got back from the market and post office and Abdelouahaid had gone home, the bell rang again. The two were there, looking as though they were supporting a woman between them. She wore a wide hat and kept her head down, so I could not see her face. "This is your daughter," they told me. "She comes from Essen." By this time it was all so unlikely and ridiculous that I yielded to temptation and decided to let her in, but I made the Moroccans stay outside. As if to introduce herself she pulled from her pocket a paperback copy of *So Mag Er Fallen*. Then she said in heavily accented English: "I have shame, but I go tomorrow to Germany." Apparently she could think of no way to meet me during her one afternoon in Tangier, save by going to the Zoco Chico and begging everyone who would listen to take her to her father, named Paul Bowles. The two outside the door, after arranging a price in the Zoco, had taken pity on her and claimed to know me, although surely they had never seen me.

Her conversation went in various directions and was hard to follow. I began to wonder how I could get rid of her. During the rambling she declared that she wanted to die. This made me even more eager to get her out. I gave her a cup of tea. As she drank it she explained that she had hoped to die in Merzouka on top of a big sand dune, but hadn't managed it. I said it was a pity, and she agreed. Finally she corrected herself. "I don't want to die. I want to change." Her glance was coy as she painted her lips.

I gave her a copy of *Gesang der Insekten* and signed it. She seemed disappointed to see that the locale was Latin America. It was clear that she had an obsession: she wanted to read only about North Africa. By the time I eased her out, her two friends were gone. I hope they hadn't already been paid, and were waiting downstairs, for she'd told me she had no idea of how to get back to her *pension*.

April 26

A house down the street has a large stork's nest on top of its chimney. Each spring a family of birds arrives, stays two months or so, and then goes on. Last year there were two young ones. They moved around the nest constantly and practiced flying by jumping up and down and flapping their wings. The male, apparently annoyed by all the hubbub, built himself another nest on the top of an electrical pylon about a hundred feet from the first. During the winter workmen came and pulled down the nest. Yesterday I noticed that the storks were in residence. Once again a big nest has been built atop the tower. Is it the same couple each year, and do the young birds return with their parents?

I haven't seen storks migrating for many years—thirty at least. I used to go down to Merkala and see hundreds of them moving past in perfect V-formations, so low that I could hear the regular beat of their wings. In the spring they flew out across the strait toward Spain, and in the autumn they came back. Storks strike me as particularly beautiful in flight, in spite of the two sticklike legs that dangle beneath. The long neck and the great wings slowly beating are what one notices.

June 7

Some advance crewmen from the BBC arrived with a view to shooting Jagger when he comes. *If* he comes, I thought. Their chief seemed pretty sure he would.

June 8

Today everyone is much less certain. Customs refuses to let any of the BBC equipment into the country. Great *Geschrei,* and much telephoning to London. Ultimatum from Stones' manager: If equipment is not through customs by nine o'clock tomorrow morning he will cancel the engagement. Jerez arrived this evening, panting with anxiety. "You've got to call the king," she told me, although she knows I've never met him and wouldn't call him even if I had. Then she mentioned that she'd been to see Lalla Fatima Zohra during the day and had been told to call her by telephone later. Her eyes lighted on me. "*You* know Lalla Fatima Zohra. You call her. Tell her how important it is for Morocco to have BBC make this film." I was in my bathrobe, downstairs with the others, in Buffie's bedroom. Everyone seemed to be of the opinion that the least I could do was to call Lalla Fatima Zohra and explain the situation, which I think Jerez had found it difficult to do because of language obstacles. (I had forgotten that Lalla Fatima Zohra speaks perfect English.) "But I can't speak Arabic well enough to talk to her," I objected. Abdelwahab made a suggestion that I call her and give my name, then pass the telephone to him. This we did, and she asked Abdelwahab to call back in a half hour. When he made the connection later, she seemed to be speaking into two telephones at once. There were very long waits, while everyone looked at Abdelwahab to see by his facial reactions what words were coming through from the palace of Moulay Abdelaziz. He merely said, "*Naam, lalla,*" from time to time. The conversation, if that's what it was, went on for ten minutes. At the end Abdelwahab hung up, saying that she had promised to call customs and ask that the television equipment be let in. By that time it looked as if The Rolling Stones would not be coming to Tangier. I said that I doubted Lalla Fatima Zohra had the power to force the airport officials to do anything, one way or the other. Both Bachir and Abdelwahab hotly disputed this. "Her word is law in Tangier," Abdelwahab cried. I said I certainly hoped so, and came upstairs to sleep.

June 8

Abdelwahab, who is almost as interested as Bachir in seeing that the film gets shot, came by at noon to tell me that Jagger and Keith Richards had gone to the Intercontinental and refused the suites reserved for them by Jerez.

So permission was given and the Stones came from London. All day yesterday and today Jerez, never once doubting that all would be well, has been rushing from one place to another, trying to find a likely place where the film could be shot. She has no time to eat, can't sleep at all, and will be ill in another day or two. She got a go-ahead from Malcolm Forbes for equipment to be set up in his garden, but the TV people turned it down in favor of the courtyard of the Akaboun house, which I suggested because it provides a more authentic background. About five o'clock Jagger arrived, accompanied by so many others that the room was *archicomplete*. Keith Richards was among them. He paid his respects to me and left, saying he was going to bed. Jagger sat down beside me, and we started to talk. It was a while before I noticed that our conversation was being filmed. After a quarter of an hour the filming stopped. "I'm tired," he said. "My kids woke me up at daybreak today. You see, Sunday's Father's Day, and they had to give me their presents today before I left. See you tomorrow at the show."

June 24

Last night Bertolucci sent a car for me, to take me to the Minzah for dinner. At the beginning of the meal he said: "At last, it's happening." "Yes. For two years I've been wondering whether it would," I told him. Everyone connected with the making of the film was there, including the producer, whom I'd met a few years ago when Bill Burroughs was here with him from London. Conversation was difficult. A very noisy floor show was going on for the benefit of a huge group of shrieking tourists. Bertolucci brought up the subject of music. He was still thinking of using David Byrne, although he mentioned Richard Horowitz as well and at one point said he'd like me to provide some of it. We didn't discuss it. I suspect he'd like electronic material rather than symphonic. Much easier, much cheaper. No parts or rehearsals needed. Scarfiotti had mentioned that he'd like to use Agadèz as the setting for the final city in the south. I hope this can be managed, and that they don't try to shoot everything in Morocco. I can appreciate their not wanting to get involved with the Algerians, but Morocco is no substitute for Algeria or Niger.

July 27

Abdelwahab tells me that the family of his bride came and demanded of his parents that they give them the nuptial sheet stained with blood. The bridal couple, after forty-eight hours of celebration with no sleep, had merely collapsed on the bed and lain inert for a two-hour respite before being called to continue the festivities. Thus there was no blood. Abdelwahab's parents were outraged. "Such backward people!" they commented, but they did agree to let the bride's family have the sheet once it was marked with blood, which presumably will be tomorrow.

August 15

Last night I heard drums—not the *darboukas* of Aachor, but in a variety of timbres. I had the impression that an *ahouache* was in progress. Never having witnessed an *ahouache* save in the High or Anti-Atlas, I decided that my hearing was deficient. When I opened my bedroom window and heard the chanting above the drums, I was no longer in any doubt. An *ahouache* was going on, up the street in the vicinity of the school. I ran out and found thirty men in traditional white robes, each with his dagger, dancing in a long line. Eight drummers crouched in front of them. I might have been in Tafraout. I stood motionless for about an hour, mystified and delighted, until they filed out of the courtyard. Then I asked a policeman sitting at the gate how it happened that such a group found itself here in Tangier. "They were brought by the American chief," he told me. "You mean the government?" "You know, the chief with the palace on the Marshan." That could mean only Malcolm Forbes. I have an invitation to a dinner he is giving on the nineteenth. A great idea, I thought, to bring performers from the deep south all the way here. There were nine very large buses parked outside the entrance to the school, which means that several hundred dancers and singers have come.

August 17

Jerez and Bachir came last night with the idea of going to the school with me. This time there was a crowd of two or three hundred men dancing, and perhaps fifty women. A great performance, including an astounding group of Haouara and even Bechara with her girls, dancing to the *guedra*. Bachir, who used to work in Goulimine and knew Bechara from that time, spoke with her after the rehearsal. She asked us to have tea with her upstairs in a room devoted to the *guedra* dancers. When she saw me she claimed to remember me, although I don't quite see how she could. The last time I saw her was in 1962 backstage in New York. (Katherine Dunham had imported her and three dozen other Moroccans to appear in her ill-fated musical; it lasted two nights.) I'd recorded her in Goulimine in 1959, but she wouldn't have been likely to have recalled that one evening. In any case, we were received with the traditional Moroccan hospitality. Some of the dancers reached into their bosoms and pulled out bundles of silver trinkets, which Jerez and Bachir bought. When we left, Bachir told me she had said to him: "If that American lives in Tangier, he must have a lot of money. Is he married?" We agreed to go back tonight and see her.

August 19

Last night we did go back, but everyone was out at the airport to welcome the planes arriving with Forbes's guests from New York. It must have been an impressive scene, with all those members of the Royal Guard on their black horses, and the long lines of dancers in white robes and turbans. On the airstrip there would have been ample space for everything, whereas later in the street it would necessarily be crowded. I'd like to have seen it, but security was so tight that no one could have gotten into the airport to see anything.

August 20

The party must be over by now. I'm told that it went on all night. By midnight I'd had enough. There remained only the birthday cake and the fireworks to look forward to, and I saw the pyrotechnical display from my bedroom window after I got home. A tiring evening. First, the police refused to let us anywhere within a quarter of a mile of the entrance, so that we had to park in the *plaçuela* behind the Café Hafa. The crowd in the street was so dense that Abdelouahaid had to push people aside roughly to make it possible for me to make any headway. When we got within sight of the Palais Mendoub, he wished me good luck and went back. There was a long queue of guests waiting outside in the street. As we moved slowly forward we were pelted with rose petals by girls standing on each side of the queue.

Beyond were the ranks of the dancers and drummers, and in the background, along the wall of the garden of the Palais du Marshan, stood the horses with their uniformed mounts, still as statues. I could think only of how fortunate it was that the weather was fine. Even a few drops of rain would have ruined a hundred evening dresses. It didn't seem an ideal manner of welcoming guests, to force them to stand in the street for a half-hour waiting to get to the bottleneck just outside the gate. There we exhibited our invitations, had our names checked on lists, and were admitted one at a time. The line continued through the courtyard, until we were given maps of the terrain and assigned to our tents. I counted nine of these objects, once I had passed through the receiving area, where our host stood grinning, flanked by his sons, and with Elizabeth Taylor seated by his side. "Wait till you see how fat she's grown!" people had warned me. To me she didn't look fat; she looked solid and luscious. She must have been tired; it's not easy to be introduced to nine hundred people one after the other. I refused the champagne and set out in search of the tent I'd been assigned to, pushing my way through the crowd until I'd found it. There were no place-cards. I sat down at an empty table until a waiter asked me to choose another, also empty. No one seemed to be in a hurry to eat. My table did eventually fill up—with, among others, the governor, the chief of police, and a military man decked with medals. At the next table sat Malcolm Forbes and his family. Miss Taylor was on his left, her back to me. The crown prince sat on his right. For three hours as I ate I watched their table. The French woman next to me made repeated comments in a whisper about Elizabeth Taylor's shoulders and the crown prince's face, which she characterized as "frightening" and "almost Japanese." All I could reply was that he never altered his poker-face expression and spoke very little. I myself thought he was unutterably bored; if that is so, it was understandable.

LETTERS

Selected Letters: 1947–1980

To Peggy Glanville-Hicks

Hotel Belvedere,
Bab el Hadid,
Fes-Batha,
Maroc.
Sat. [1947?]

Dear Peggy:

At last the weather has come off crystalline, and naturally the sky and the air grow hotter each day. Everything is thereby changed. One seeks the shade and the cooler currents of air, one's thoughts turn to drinks colored green: Menthe Verte à l'Oulmès. The young storks can fly fairly well by now, the fig trees smell strong all the time. And I can sit up here on the terrace of the hotel leaning against the loud scratchy sound of the cafe phonograph that plays Abd el Wahab, Louisa Tounsia, Om Khalsoum, and Salim Hillali. These would be ideal days to explore the regions round about, but it's impossible because Jane has a horror of buses, horses and trains, so that there's really no way of getting out of Fez save on foot. We are thinking in spite of everything of going to Marrakech before it grows too hot for her to be comfortable there. This summer if Oliver comes we shall doubtless go there, but it may well be that then Jane will stay in Tangier where she feels more at home and where the climate will permit her to work; she finds it impossible to work in the heat. Of course I have sent my novel off to New York and for the moment have nothing to do but lie about and read and revel in the magnificent weather. That proves to be highly disturbing to her, as she needs to have me in the next room working in order to be able to work. She has just completed a long story and wants to get back to the novel she started years ago and never got well into.

Thank you for the magazines; they arrived at the right moment, just when I needed something to read. And it had been so long since I'd read English, save for a clipping now and then. We have a great variety of books here in Fez;—the table in Jane's room is piled with scores of them, of every sort, but they're all in French, and sometimes that's not of much help. There are times when one definitely wants to read English. I'm enjoying the Palinurus book. I find myself agreeing with so much that he says, and yet the tone of the book is somehow alien. Perhaps it's his sentimentality and querulousness; he gives the impression of a very old, peevish and whining gentleman. And I know he isn't. Perhaps if one is an intellectual one automatically becomes that way . . . (I mean a 100% British one . . . or a 100% one and British to boot.) His difficulty in living in the present seems strange in one so young as he. But perhaps it's because he's condemned to live in London. Condemned by his own tastes. When I'm in New York my misery is boundless, and if I stayed there forever I should very shortly grow to be like him,—without his cleverness, it goes without saying.

I'm casting about for something to write about, but obviously I'm not ready so soon after finishing the other. What I ought to be doing is writing music, but I left the Concerto in Tangier, not thinking *The Sheltering Sky* would be done so soon. They are playing a fascinating record at the moment . . . the first I've ever heard of the sort. True Flamenco: a typical guitar background, but the singing, which is *almost* indistinguishable from Spanish style, happens to be in Arabic. A Fandango in Moghrebi. I've been waiting for modern inter-reaction. That was yesterday. Last night we made a fantastic walk by full moon, through the Guerniz quarter and along the river in the heart of the city, from El Qantara Ben Guezzam to El Zantara en Recif. Exactly like photos of Lhasa, the way the huge buildings are piled one atop the other, up the hills and down, in vast terraces. Also tried a very peculiar drug called Oisiset, Copravasanda, from the Senegal. I still feel strange from it, but I can't recall the exact effect it had, save that it seems to me I was wrapped in boiling rags and blankets and put away in an oven for the whole night, and it was pleasant, but nothing like hashish. Especially there was a feeling of being completely protected from all possible harm or trouble.

Forgive the amorphous letter.

Love,
Paul

P.S. I enclose one of a series of drawings by Ahmed ben Driss el Yacoubi. There are some incredible ones, but Jane has fallen in love with them and insists on keeping them. One of the parrot is the most extraordinary thing

I've seen in a long time. Hilarious and very sad, all at once. He names each one. I have one called "Three Men Running Past a Mosque in Aït Baza, Three Hundred and Eighty Kilometers from Fez!"

To David McDowell

British Post Office,
Tangier, Morocco.
15/XII/50

Dear Dave:

I returned last night from a twelve-day soujourn in the French Zone, to find, among the items of my mail, the first reviews of *Prey*. Shocked, scandalized and disapproving. And all wrong. I think some of the critics didn't bother to read all the stories about which they spoke so glibly. How could Charles Jackson make such a boner as to say that "How Many Midnights" was "a story about a suicide" if he had read it? There's not the suggestion of a suicide anywhere in the book, for the very good reason that the idea of suicide doesn't enter into my personal conception of the patterns of life and destiny. However, one would scarcely expect him to guess that. But neither would one expect him to guess at the outcome of the story instead of reading it, if he intends to single it out and make remarks about it. Another lovely error he made was the one in which he mentioned "the small town where" I "was brought up". Born, raised and educated in New York City, and never lived anywhere else until I went to Virginia for a bit of college. Of course, all these things are unimportant; I am just letting myself go in correspondence to you because I have no one to talk to about my reactions to the reviews. What does interest me is the fact that a while ago you mentioned to me the possibility of there being a second edition to the book, for which I might fashion some jacket notes. I certainly don't want to write the actual text, but I should like to furnish a clue as what I consider the stories to be and as to how they can be read in order to be understood,—if that is necessary, and it would seem that it is. No one seems to have realized that practically all the tales are a variety of detective story. Not the usual variety, I admit, but still, detective stories in which the reader is the detective; the mystery is the motivation for the characters' behavior, and the clues are given in the form of reactions on the part of the characters to details of situation and surroundings. If Chalia moves her bed out from the wall each night before she goes to bed, there is a reason for it. If Van says: "Gee, I was burned up last Friday," if Bouchta's eyes in Mohjtar's dream remind him of the eyes in the head of a roasted sheep at Aid el Kebir, if the employee on the river boat has a "somewhat simian" face and the husband walks toward him offering to pay the supplementary fare to him and then "remembers" that his wife has his wallet, there is a reason, and it is usually the reason for the entire story. Often the action of a story is predicated on a bit of unmentioned, subconscious knowledge on the part of a protagonist, but the suggestion is always made and placed in an emotional frame which serves as a clue to anyone who really read the story. If you could form a sentence or two for the jacket of that hypothetical second edition, which would embody these ideas, I should be delighted.

It is interesting to see the enormous disparity between the English reviews and the American ones. There is no indication of the English critics' having been morally outraged, no use of words as "decay," "putrescent," "revolting," "loathesome," "sensationalism," "horror," "disintegration," "evil." On the contrary, they speak of strength, directness, clean writing, being left breathless. Which I must say is a damned sight more pleasant to my eyes.

But what can one do? Hope to see more reviews.

Best,
Paul B.

To John Lehmann

British Post Office
Tangier, Morocco
October first [1953?]
Rosh Hashanah

Dear John:

I was glad to get your letter, because I had begun to wonder if it would ever come. I had wondered, too, if you wouldn't have reservations about the book [*Let It Come Down*]. I'm unable, of course, to offer a defence regarding the writing. I'm not an old enough hand at construction to be able to see where the interest lags in the first part. (I could, I suppose, find innumerable passages which could be deleted, but then what would be left? Not very much!) I'm sure you're quite correct about the jerkiness and random quality of the first chapters. If you would like them pared down I can do it. The Americans, I'm sure, are not aware that there *is* a "metaphysical theme," and so the story seems all of a piece,—a straight adventure story with particularly sordid trimmings, which is perfectly all right with me.

I was pleased,—perversely so, possibly—with your pointing out that you could find no "sense of moral choice" in the book, because that is a lack I meant it to have, (as you well know.) Of course it's extremely difficult to convince anyone that moral choice is nonexistent save as a social attitude, because everyone "knows" it just isn't so. However, it's a private fallacy of mine, and I think it strikes a sympathetic chord in the younger generation of Americans. Perhaps only because they're young, but perhaps also because they're Americans. I'm not suggesting that the young people emulate Dyar; I'm only suggesting that it would make no difference if they did, since all that keeps them from such behavior is the lack of opportunity and fear of the possible consequences. There are tens of thousands who would ask nothing better than the chance to live the part of Dyar's life described in the book, particularly as he is left at the end unpunished and with a considerable sum of money in his possession. In that sense it's definitely slanted toward an American public, and not an English one.

Personally I must admit that my sympathy remains with Dyar throughout the book, despite the murder, since nothing he does makes any particular difference to the texture of his life. He could have committed it before he ever left New York, save that it hadn't occurred to him. (Perhaps I ought to use the word "pity" instead of sympathy, but the two are confused in my mind. There are two types of people in the world: pitiful and hateful, and I don't know which I dislike more. So perhaps "sympathy" is not really a word for me to bandy about so glibly!)

In any case, while I defend the argument of the book, I am quite ready to make an effort to improve the technique, if you think it would make my point clearer. Only I should need concrete suggestions, I'm afraid, which would be putting rather a burden on you, since they won't be forthcoming from anyone else. There would be no particular objection to certain disparities between the texts of the American and the English editions, would there?

I did receive your telegram, and thank you for it. I hadn't replied earlier because the wire said: "writing very soon", and I thought our letters might cross.

Your prognostic for London's winter is dire; it makes me think twice before going ahead with any project of settling there. I suppose there are a good many pleasanter places to spend those weeks. I shall have to reflect and discuss and weigh, all those things I dislike so much.

The germ is gone. Now Mrs. Bowles, the maid and the Siamese kitten all have them. They (not the kitten) are having daily shots of Penicillin and Streptomycin. The kitten is given soporifics; it has become gaga.

Do you prefer *Fresh Meat and Roses* to *Let It Come Down* as a title? Brion Gysin has been insisting for so many months that a change should be made that I no longer have so strong a faith in my judgment. I have also asked Random House, but only recently, so that there has not been time for an answer.

I am working on the translation of a very bad novel in French, and I regret ever having taken on the work. However, now that the thing is begun, it must be finished. My plans depend somewhat on *Holiday* magazine. I have sent them several suggestions for articles, to write some of which would involve displacing myself, and I am waiting to hear their decision. Also I shall be waiting for yours, regarding the book. McDowell of Random House wrote me the other day that he will send you galleys if you want them. I should think it would be a good idea to ask for them even if you want me to make changes, just to have a more exact and compact copy of the original text than the one you have at present. They ought to be ready soon. He said that McKnight Kauffer had done a fine jacket. I hope he's right.

David Herbert is back here, living out at Vasco da Gama. He makes Tangier seem just like Wilton. Everyone exists in order to be entertaining.

best,
Paul B.

To James Leo Herlihy

2137 Tanger Socco
Tangier, Morocco
1/xii/64

Dear Jamie:
When I was living on my island off Ceylon a friend named Hugh Gibb came to spend a fortnight with me; he had just returned from a sojourn in

the Maldives, and was the only European to have gone and stayed with the people there. According to him they were all Moslems, and lived a fine windswept sort of life, eating fish and fruit, and plying among the hundreds of islands. The same year my ship, the *Issipingo,* took a course en route to Mombasa that brought it within a mile or two of certain of the outer Maldives, and I must say it looked incredibly pristine. I sat all morning on deck watching the strips of sand and palms slip by. I remember it moved me to start a novel at the moment, so that while I looked at the islands I invented the opening pages of the book. Perhaps if the Maldives had been more numerous, or more widely scattered, I should have got far enough into it to be able to hang on to it. As it was, once the stimulus had become invisible, (after lunch, that is,) I purposely forgot about it. By the time I got to Kenya I wondered why I'd thought of starting that particular story, and threw the pages out. But it always happens that way. *Sky* I started in order to make the hotel room at the Belvedere in Fez more real than it was. It began with the hotel room and extended itself beyond, fortunately. *Let It Come Down* I started while sailing past Tangier on the M.S. *Gen. Walter* one foggy winter night; I was going from Antwerp to Colombo, but Tangier was outside in the dark, so I had to be there, too. *The Spider's House* began on the *Andrea Doria* on the way to New York. Unthinkable situation; I had to be back somehow in Fez from where I'd come. I don't expect further difficulties when LWAFH [*Love With a Few Hairs*] appears in French, since it's already unequivocally banned now—in any form. I told you, I think, how one police chief said to me: "There are truths which are too bitter to be told," à propos of the book? (I translate literally, of course.) On another day, still regarding the same subject, another police-sergeant remarked: "A good writer doesn't just write about life as it is. He writes about it the way it *should* be, and then he does good to humanity." Every book-seller in Morocco was sent a form letter announcing that possession of the book was an offence. The proprietor of my neighborhood stationery store showed it to me, being a Russian (Soviet) citizen and interested in such matters. (Up until three years ago he sold mags and papers published in Peking; then he stopped.) Braziller will issue LWAFH in N.Y. The resistance is important, but one can't consider it anything less than a second front. Thus the danger of premature action. (probably inevitable)

best,
Paul

To Webster Schott

2137 Tanger Socco
Tangier, Morocco
2/ii/66

Dear Mr. Schott:

Forgive my tardy reply: I have been in the hinterlands.

Naturally enough, I was taken aback by your letter, never before having received a request for elucidation (save for the rhetorical questions put by disgruntled or suspicious readers, and those fall into a different category.) The wording of your key phrase inevitably suggests that I am to take a defensive attitude with regard to *Up Above the World*, and it goes without saying that I can't do that. (In case you haven't a copy of your own missive at hand, I'll quote from it: ". . . would appreciate very much hearing from you what you were trying to do in the novel.") The meaning here is that whatever I was attempting to do, or imagined I was doing, I did not do, and as a result, one reader,—but a pivotal reader—is left in doubt as to my intentions. I am the first to agree that these intentions ought to be crystal-clear, but I can't very well argue that they are, since you have already stated that they are not.

I was telling a story whose line is necessarily presented as a puzzle because the course of the plot is determined by the material. The "meaning" of the book is certainly not this convoluted and improbable tale of brain-washing as applied by the hero to his victims, however; nor is the book a *roman à thèse* any more than was *The Sheltering Sky*. (On the other hand, it has very little in common with that book save in the (probably obsessive) use of certain external situations.) But writing all this to you is farcical, because you are already aware of it. A sentence from Borges should have been included in the front of the book: "Each moment as it is being lived exists, but not the imaginary total." I've said nothing, but I have answered your letter.

Sincerely,
Paul Bowles

To James Leo Herlihy

2137 Tanger Socco,
Tangier, Morocco.
25/iii/67

Dear Jamie:

Yes, here I am, back under bright skies. (Thailand never had such a sky as we have here.) A little more than three weeks . . . long enough to have meshed again with the cogs of Tangier habits. Only Jane is very ill, having been for the past six months or so in a really bad depression. (They claim she's better now, though to me she seems fairly far gone, not being able to dress or wash, and resisting all helpful suggestions, naturally.) I am going to have to take her to Spain and leave her in a hospital, I'm afraid. But she should be having medication in any case. A clinical depression is not generally something one can climb out of by oneself. They say a month or so ought to do. Anyway, that's my present difficulty.

Their Heads Are Green. About half of each piece, I think, was written in the place with which it deals; the rest was out of memory later. As I'm doing (or shall be doing) with the Bangkok book that looms ahead of me menacingly. . . . deadline October first, God forbid. . . . About journeying, which you don't seem to enjoy too much, it would be good to do it in peace if it were possible, but the act itself militates against it. The only peace is that of being cut off from the outside world, and perhaps that is very important, although always one yearns to reestablish the connection, panting to get at mail, going miles to find a copy of *Time,* and dreaming of what it will be like when the test is over. If it ever is. (Since I often believe I won't return, what with microbes and other local hazards. I was convinced I wouldn't get back here from Southeast Asia. No anguish, just the dry conviction that this time would be the time.) Years ago in *Rien Que La Terre,* that unpleasant man Paul Morand wrote that it isn't important to be going somewhere, but that one simply feels better being en route, being, that is, nowhere for the moment.

I'll ask Holt, Rinehart to send you a copy of *The Time of Friendship* when it's ready, which ought to be out in June. I imagine next month I'll get galleys. At the instant I'm taping a novel in Arabic, for lack of something better to do. Imagine you haven't seen *Love With a Few Hairs,* which came out in London in January. Would you be interested in having it? I have three copies, and can send you one if you like.

I hear Alfred Chester is back here after having gone wild for a while and ended up in a London loony-bin. I haven't seen him in a year and a half. The Moslem grapevine has him living in a fisherman's house right on the beach, and fighting with the natives continually. But you probably don't know him, so my remarks mean nothing. As Susan Sontag insisted: You have to remember at all times that Alfred is crazy, but really crazy. I know he's adept at making you forget it, but remember it.

Malaysia, where I spent ten days after leaving Siam, is a better tourist land. Penang Island hasn't changed: one of the most propitious places for living. Singapore has far more traffic than the last time I was there, but is still pleasant. Kuala Lumpur, which I'd never before seen is overcrowded but very fine. Even Port Swettenham was a relief after Bangkok.

Let me hear.

Best.

Paul

To Don Gold

2137 Tanger Socco,
Tangier, Morocco.
23/II/69

Dear Don:

On the ship I put my memory to work and came up with a list,—nothing more—of events and people which would serve as nuclei from which to work in recapturing the material for each year.

The book [*Without Stopping*] would start off with a section dealing with the things that happened before memory begins, and go on through the recall of early childhood into late childhood, stressing the opposing pressures of the paternal and maternal family groups, and the resulting need for developing secrecy.

The anguish of adolescence is somewhat alleviated by my discovery of automatic writing (1927) and by subsequent publication in *transition* in

1928. From high school to art school; from there to University of Virginia, chosen because Edgar Allen Poe had gone there.

The tossing of a coin decides that I shall run away from college. Paris. (Tristan Tzara) the Paris Herald where I work, hikes to Switzerland and the Riviera. In Paris Prokofiev agrees to take me as a pupil in composition, but I go to Germany instead. Return to New York. (1929) Henry Cowell sends me to Aaron Copland, who teaches me music. Return to the University of Virginia, completing first year, then more study with Copland. (1930)

In March 1931 I go to Paris, meet Gertrude Stein, Cocteau, Tchelitchew, Pound, Gide. To Berlin. First meetings with Spender and Isherwood. To Hannover to see Kurt Schwitters and his Merzbau. To Holland, to stay in Kastel Eerde with Krishnamurti. During the summer Gertrude Stein suggests I go to Tangier. Copland and I go. The following winter I return to Paris to study with Nadia Boulanger. After a few lessons I have enough and go to Italy. Later to Granada to see Manuel de Falla, and back to Morocco (Spring 1932) where I catch typhoid. Convalescence in Monte Carlo with my mother.

In December 1932 to Algiers and down to the Sahara. By camel across the Great Eastern Erg into South Tunisia, arriving in Tunis in the Spring of 1933. Thence to Tangier. I take a house there and rent it to Djuna Barnes, who is writing *Nightwood*. Then from Cadiz to Puerto Rico. (Barranquitas) Next to New York, where I study harmony with Roger Sessions.

In the Spring of 1934 I return to Morocco and settle in Fez. In Autumn of the same year I sail to Barranquilla, Colombia. Amoebic dysentery in the Andes. To Los Angeles, then to San Francisco, arriving in the Spring of 1935 in New York to stay and write music. Meet Balanchine and Kirstein. Eugene Berman devises a ballet for him and me to do, and I begin work on it.

In 1936 Kirstein, not wanting the Berman subject, commissions me to write the score of the ballet *Yankee Clipper*. I compose my first theatre score for Orson Welles. Later in the year I write a second, also for Welles. Meet E.E. Cummings for first time.

1937. Miguel Coverrubias suggest I go to Tehauntepec, which I do. Visit Guatemala. First performance *Yankee Clipper* by Philadelphia Orchestra. In February 1938 I marry Jane Auer. Panama, Costa Rica, Guatemala, then France, where we settle at Eze-Village. In Autumn Orson Welles asks me to return to write a theatre score. We go back to New York. Meet Dalí for first time. In December we join Communist Party. Saroyan arrives in New York and asks me to write score for *My Heart's in the Highlands*. Clifford Odets gives me his apartment in which to work at it. Jane and I take a house on Staten Island. Leonard Bernstein spends week-ends there with us. (Summer and Autumn of 1939.) Meet Auden for first time.

Early 1940 I provide score for another Saroyan play: *(Love's Old Sweet Song)* (Theatre Guild) Am given commission to write score for film for the U.S. Department of Agriculture, in Albuquerque. After completing this work I leave for Mexico. In Acapulco Tennessee Williams comes to the house and introduces himself. I return to New York to write the score for the Maurice Evans–Helen Hayes *Twelfth Night,* then for Philip Barry's *Liberty Jones* and Lillian Hellman's *Watch on the Rhine*. Jane and I go to live at a rooming-house in Brooklyn Heights run by Auden. Benjamin Britten has his piano in the living room, and I put mine into the cellar where I work at a ballet commissioned by Kirstein. *(Pastoralas.)* I meet Carson McCullers for the first time. Receive Guggenheim Fellowship. We return to Mexico (Spring 1941) and spend remainder of the year there. I complete *Pastoralas* and begin work on *The Wind Remains,* (opera.) In the summer of 1942 we return to New York to live at Holden Hall, my aunt's house in the country, where we are visited by the F.B.I. I complete the opera. It is performed in the Spring of 1943 at the Museum of Modern Art, Leonard Bernstein conducting, with staging by Merce Cunningham. Jane's novel, *Two Serious Ladies,* is published by Knopf.

Virgil Thomson suggests I join staff of the *Herald-Tribune* to write musical criticism, which I do. I am asked by the Belgian Government-in-Exile to do the score for a documentary film called *Congo.* (Paul Robeson is narrator.) The Marquis de Cuevas commissions me to do the ballet *Colloque Sentimentale* with Dalí. I spend the Summer of 1944 in Mexico. Peggy Guggenheim issues records of my Sonata for Flute to sell in her gallery. Tennessee Williams comes to see me with the script of a play which needs music. *(The Glass Menagerie.)* I hear that Jean-Paul Sartre is in the U. S. and suggest to Oliver Smith that we obtain the rights to *Huis Clos,* which we do, meeting him in Washington. I begin to translate the play. I meet Elia Kazan and provide him with a score for *Jacobowsky and the Colonel*. Meet José Ferrer and furnish the score for *Cyrano de Bergerac.* Spend the Summer of 1945 in Cuba and Salvador. I am writing a series of short stories, most of which are being published in *Harper's Bazaar* and

Mademoiselle. I resign from the *Herald-Tribune,* but continue to write Sunday articles for the paper. I spend 1946 writing stories and doing more theatre scores, also a *Concerto for Two Pianos, Winds and Percussion.* In December I am asked to translate Giraudoux's *La Folle de Chaillot,* and go to the West Indies to do it.

On the strength of the short stories, Doubleday gives me (Spring 1947) an advance on a novel, and I go back to Morocco and write it. *(The Sheltering Sky.)* When I send it to the publishers, they tell me it is not a novel, and reject it. Libby Holman comes to Morocco and asks me to make an opera out of García Lorca's *Yerma.* I begin to translate it. New Directions accepts *The Sheltering Sky.* I return to New York to write the score for Tennessee Williams' *Summer and Smoke.* When the show is open, he and I go back to Morocco to stay at El Farhar. Afterward he goes to Rome, and Jane and I to the Algerian Sahara, and then to Paris, returning to El Farhar in the Spring. Truman Capote spends the summer at El Farhar with us. Gore Vidal arrives.

In the Autumn Jane and I go to London. *The Sheltering Sky* is published there. Meetings with Maugham, Angus Wilson, Cyril Connelly, etc. I leave for Ceylon to spend the winter, returning to London and Paris in the late Spring. Libby Holman returns to Morocco in the summer, and we spend a month in Andalusia. Back to the Sahara in the winter, Spain in the Spring (1951), where I pick up Jane, and to Tangier. I complete *Let It Come Down* and set out for Bombay. I stay in India and Ceylon until June, then go to the Italian Alps. Peggy Guggenheim invites me to stay with her in Venice. In the Autumn I go to Tangier and Madrid. While in Madrid I buy the island of Taprobane off the south coast of Ceylon. In January 1953 I go to New York to spend the Winter at Libby Holman's. Spring I spend in Tangier writing *A Picnic Cantata.* Tennessee Williams suggests my name to Luchino Visconti, to work on the scenario of a film *(Senso),* and I spend the summer in Rome, working on it. Then I go to Istanbul, returning to Tangier with Williams in the late Autumn. I go back to New York in December to write the score for Jane's play *In The Summer House.* When that is done I return to Tangier. I meet William Burroughs for the first time. In the Autumn Jane and I set out for Ceylon. I begin *The Spider's House.* We spend the Winter on Taprobane. Peggy Guggenheim comes to visit us there. I complete *The Spider's House.* Jane returns to Tangier and I go to Japan. By mid-summer I am back in Tangier. In the Autumn Christopher Isherwood visits. The following Spring my parents come to Tangier.

(1956) Later in the year I go to London, thence to Cape Town, and Ceylon, spending the winter there. In the Spring to East Africa (Kenya, Zanzibar) and back to Tangier. Allen Ginsberg arrives in Tangier for the first time. Jane being ill, I take her to England twice during the Summer, the second time remaining there until the winter, when we return to Tangier. In February 1958 we leave for Madeira, where Jane's passport expires. In Lisbon the American Embassy refuses to issue another (on orders from the F.B.I.) and Jane is obliged to go immediately to New York. I remain in Portugal until after the elections in June, and then go to Denver to try out *Yerma*. From there we take the opera to Ithaca, New York. Jane enters New York Hospital for three months. I go to Hollywood to work with José Ferrer. At the end of the year Jane and I go back to Tangier. I receive a wire asking me to return to New York to do the score of *Sweet Bird of Youth*. I go. Afterward I go to Madeira for *Holiday* magazine, then to Tangier. Tennessee Williams is there. I receive a Rockefeller Grant to record Moroccan music for the archives of the Library of Congress. The last six months of 1959 I spend making field trips in the interior of Morocco. In 1960 I continue recording, in various regions not previously covered.

In 1961 I rent a house in Marrakech. Tennessee Williams comes. Allen Ginsberg returns to Morocco and I take him to Marrakech. I pass a quiet year, writing short stories. In 1962 I begin the translation from the Arabic of *A Life Full of Holes*. Jane and I go to New York, where I write the score for *The Milk Train Doesn't Stop Here Any More* (Williams.) We return to Tangier at Christmas time. I continue translating. Random House publishes *Their Heads Are Green and Their Hands Are Blue*. I take a house in Arcila for six months, afterward going to the Sahara.

The following year (1964) Tennessee Williams again comes to Tangier. I am writing *Up Above the World*. I go to Spain. In March 1965 Jane and I go to New York. I continue to Santa Fe. In the summer we return to Tangier. I translate *Love With a Few Hairs*. In June 1966 Jane and I go again to New York, she to see Farrar, Straus about her collected works, and I take a ship to Bangkok. In December I hear from Jane's doctor in Tangier that she is ill, and return to Tangier, abandoning the book I am writing for Little, Brown. (In Tangier I suggest to Alec Waugh that he take over the project, which he does.) I begin the translation of *The Lemon*. *The Time of Friendship* is published. I translate ten short stories from the Arabic under the title of *M'Hashish*, and leave for Los Angeles. This brings us up to the present.

If this sequential listing serves no other purpose, at least it is useful to me as a basic memorandum; I have no notes with which to document the account. It is a chronological skeleton, nothing more, as you can see. I'll hope to hear your reaction soon.

all best,
Paul Bowles

To William Targ

2117 Tanger Socco,
Tangier, Morocco.
23/ii/71

Dear Mr. Targ:

Thank you for your three simultaneous communications. I'm not overly preoccupied about the title. I'm sure I can find something apposite sooner or later. But I am a bit worried about my ability to "flesh out" the people and make characters of them, as you suggested. Naturally I shall do what I can, but the truth is that I don't remember people very well—either what they wear or look like. For years critics have objected to the facelessness of my fictional people, although that is deliberate on my part. And at the time I was writing about in the section you mean, I did not have reactions to people as people, but only as forces to propel me, as a glider uses air-currents. For that reason any attempt now to describe them or my reactions to them risks being false; what one doesn't remember one ends by inventing, and I have been very careful to keep hazy recall and invention out of the chronicle. But as I say, I'll do what I can to suggest reactions on my part. I have a feeling that this can become a cause of friction between us at one point or another; if it does do so, I want you to know beforehand that I shall make every effort to provide the qualities you would like to find in the manuscript. If in spite of that I am unable to, I hope you will know that such is the case, and that I am not being difficult! I am sending you more of the manuscript in a few days, as soon as I have finished correcting it.

Sincerely,
Paul Bowles

To Hans Bertens

2117 Tanger Socco
Tangier, Morocco
25/i/80

Dear Mr. Bertens:

I was pleased to have your letter of January twenty-second. Re: *Up Above the World,* yes, I think your assumption of assessment and condemnation by the author was unjustified, and probably got in the way of your understanding what the book was about. It's interesting, too, that you mention the same assumption regarding Port Moresby. (Yes, I knew it was in New Guinea.) But clearly you're taking for granted a prejudice on the part of the author against one of his characters where absolutely none was either felt or shown in the text. The voice of the narrator in dealing with Amar is necessarily different from the voice of the narrator telling about Soto, but they are both noncommittal, neutral, content to describe and not judge. I'd say if the writer shows any feeling with regard to Norton, Moresby and Soto, it's one of sympathy—at least, sufficient sympathy to observe them in a tolerant fashion.

"The Hours After Noon" is a tale about how a woman's subconscious fastens together bits of information about a man in such a way that in ridding herself of his presence she also has him murdered; she becomes aware of what the hidden part of her mind has done only after the death of her victim. I didn't think it presented any problems. (With regard to Mr. van Siclen; the surname is what we think of in the States as an "old American name". There is a Van Siclen Avenue in Brooklyn. Also a De Kalb Avenue! It didn't occur to me that the name was specifically Dutch when I used it, I assure you. It's as American as Roosevelt or Vanderbilt. Very likely the spelling was altered three centuries ago. Perhaps I should have said Mr. Van Siclen was American; I suppose I thought it would be apparent from his dialogue. I certainly never meant him to be mistaken for Dutch.)

There was a point you brought up in your previous letter, when you said you had a Calvinist upbringing, and that you suspected I had as well. I don't know; to me a Calvinist background sounds vaguely religious, as though behavior were based on some fixed set of religious principles. This was not at all the case with me. None of my grandparents and neither of my parents was affiliated with any church; they did not believe in attending church. Being New Englanders, they were Puritans by tradition, but they were also agnostics. (I admit that the agnosticism would not necessarily cancel out the puritanism, but it might make it a little less codified in its application to behavior.)

To get back to Dutch names: it's not surprising that Kristians Tonny's name doesn't sound Dutch. His father's name was Antonius Johannes Kristians, and Tonny was Tony Kristians.

"Doña Faustina": the important consideration here is not the number of babies killed, but the number of their hearts devoured by Doña Faustina. She believed she could transmit the power of thirty-seven to her offspring. And although he knew nothing about the hearts, he suddenly was given the power of life and death over thirty-seven men. He exercised it and was thereby made happy, thus bringing good out of evil. I think it's made clear that the writer is sympathetic to the idea of freeing the bandits.

It was very conscientious of you to reread *Up Above the World;* I'm glad you came around somewhat to my viewpoint about it. Day Slade is not presented as any more admirable than Soto—just more ordinary. It would be confusing to let her views on Soto influence one. She is a completely uninteresting woman whose stock reactions to what the reader suspects are extreme situations help to set off Vero's eccentric personality. I think this is enough for one letter!

All best,
Paul Bowles

INTERVIEW

An Interview with Paul Bowles

DANIEL HALPERN: Why did you first come to Morocco?

PAUL BOWLES: Gertrude Stein suggested it. She had been here three separate summers, staying at the old Villa de France, and she thought I'd like it. She was right. I loved it. And I still love it. Less, naturally. One loves everything less at my age; also it's a little less lovable than it was forty years ago.

HALPERN: What is it that keeps you in Tangier?

BOWLES: It's changed less than the rest of the world, and continues to seem less a part of this particular era than most cities. It's a pocket outside the mainstream. You feel that, very definitely, when you come in. After you've been over to Europe, for instance, for a few days or a few weeks, and you come back here, you immediately feel you've left the stream, that nothing is going to happen here.

HALPERN: You were eighteen when you first left America. What lured you to Europe?

BOWLES: Everyone wanted to come to Europe in those days. It was the intellectual and artistic center. Paris specifically seemed to be the center, not just Europe. After all, it was the end of the twenties and just about everybody *was* in Paris.

HALPERN: Did you know many writers and composers in Paris?

BOWLES: Practically no writers. I met a lot but I didn't know them. Composers? Naturally, Virgil Thomson, and Henri Sauguet and Francis Poulenc. . . . Not very many, no.

HALPERN: Did you see much of Gertrude Stein while you were there?

BOWLES: I did see a lot of her in 1931. She had read some of the poems I had published, and she didn't like them. I went around in 1931, and I remember she mentioned Bravig Imbs, a poet at that time who wrote for various magazines, and she said, "Yes, Bravig Imbs is a very bad poet,

but you're not a poet *at all.*" She also had things to say about my music.
I played her my music in 1931 and she said, "It's interesting." And then
I went back in 1932 to her country house in Bilignin and played some
newer music for her, and she said, "Ah, last year your music wasn't
attenuated enough, and this year it's too attenuated." That's all she had
to say. Except that she told me to go to Tangier. She was liking me at
the time, which meant that I could trust her recommendation. The next
year, when she was not liking me at all, she suggested I go to Mexico,
adding after a pause, "You'd last about two days."

HALPERN: Was she in favor of your giving up writing and devoting
more time to your music?

BOWLES: I suspect she thought I had no ability to write. I remember we
were sitting in the garden at Bilignin and she said, "I told you last week
what was the matter with your poetry. What have you done with it since
then, with those particular poems? Have you rewritten them?" And I
said, "No, of course not; they've already been published that way. How
could I rewrite them?" And she said, "You see! I told you you were not
a poet. A real poet would have gone up and worked on them and then
brought them down and showed them to me a week later, and you've
done nothing whatever."

HALPERN: What was it about writing that made you put composing
aside?

BOWLES: I'm not sure. I think it had a lot to do with the fact that I
couldn't make a living as a composer without remaining all the time in
New York. I was very much fed up with being in New York.

HALPERN: When did you begin to write?

BOWLES: At four. I have a whole collection of stories about animals that
I wrote then.

HALPERN: But it was as a poet that you first published, in *transition?*

BOWLES: I had written a lot of poetry (I was in high school) and had been
buying *transition* regularly since it started publishing. It seemed to me
that I could write for them as well as anyone else, so I sent them things
and they accepted them. I was sixteen when I wrote the poem they first
accepted, seventeen when they published it. I went on for several years
as a so-called poet.

HALPERN: What ended your short career as a poet?

BOWLES: I think Gertrude Stein had a lot to do with it. She convinced
me that I ought not to be writing poetry, since I wasn't a poet at all, as

I just said. And I believed her thoroughly, and I still believe her. She was quite right. I would have stopped anyway, probably.

HALPERN: Were there any important early literary influences?

BOWLES: Well, I suppose everything influences you. I remember my mother used to read me Edgar Allan Poe's short stories before I went to sleep at night. After I got into bed she would read me *Tales of Mystery and Imagination*. It wasn't very good for sleeping—they gave me nightmares. Maybe that's what she wanted, who knows? Certainly what you read during your teens influences you enormously. During my early teens I was very fond of Arthur Machen and Walter de la Mare. The school of mystical whimsy. And then I found Thomas Mann, and fell into *The Magic Mountain* when I was sixteen, and that was certainly a big influence. Probably that was the book that influenced me more than any other before I went to Europe.

HALPERN: Before you actually begin writing a novel or story, what takes place in your mind? Do you outline the plot, say, in visual terms?

BOWLES: Every work suggests its own method. Each novel's been done differently, under different circumstances and using different methods. I got the idea for *The Sheltering Sky* riding on a Fifth Avenue bus one day going uptown from Tenth Street. I decided just which point of view I would take. It would be a work in which the narrator was omniscient. I would write it consciously up to a certain point, and after that let it take its own course. You remember there's a little Kafka quote at the beginning of the third section: "From a certain point onward there is no longer any turning back; that is the point that must be reached." This seemed important to me, and when I got to that point, beyond which there was no turning back, I decided to use a surrealist technique—simply writing without any thought of what I had already written, or awareness of what I was writing, or intention as to what I was going to write next, or how it was going to finish. And I did that.

HALPERN: What about your second novel, *Let It Come Down?*

BOWLES: That was altogether different. I began to write that on a freighter as I went past Tangier one night. I was on my way from Antwerp to Colombo, in Ceylon, and we went past Tangier and I felt very nostalgic—I could see faint lights in the fog and I knew that was Tangier. I wanted very much to stop in and see it, but not being able to, since the boat went right on past, I created my own Tangier. I started by imagining that I was standing on the cliff looking out at the place where I was on the ship. I transported myself from the ship straight over to the cliffs and began there. That was the first part I wrote. I worked backward and forward, as it were, from that original scene.

HALPERN: Where Dyar and Hadija stand on the top of a cliff and see freighters going by.

BOWLES: That's right. Then on the ship, before I got to Colombo, I worked it out—the sequence of events, the patterns of motivations, the juxtapositions. Again I decided to use exactly the same writing technique I had used with *The Sheltering Sky*. To get it up to a place from which it could roll of its own momentum to a stationary point, and then let go and use the automatic process. It's quite clear where it happens. It's on the boat trip.

HALPERN: When you wrote the scene in which Dyar was high on majoun, the evening he had dinner with Daisy, were you yourself under the influence of kif?

BOWLES: No. The whole book was written in cold blood, up to that point. But for the last section of the book I went up to Xauen and stayed in the hotel there for about six weeks, writing only at night after dinner. After I had worked for half or three quarters of an hour, and it was going along, I would smoke. That made it possible for me to write four or five hours rather than only two, which is all I can usually do. The kif gave me a much longer breath.

HALPERN: Are you in the habit of using kif in order to write?

BOWLES: No, I don't think that would be possible. When I was writing *Up Above the World* I smoked when I felt like it, and worked all day wandering around in the forest with a pen and notebook in my hand.

HALPERN: To what extent does the ingestion of kif play a role in your writing?

BOWLES: I shouldn't think it has an effect on anyone's writing. Kif can provide flashes of insight, but it acts as an obstacle to thinking. On the other hand, it enables one to write concentratedly for hours at a stretch without fatigue. You can see how it could be useful if you were writing something which relied for its strength on the free elaboration of fantasy. I used it only once that way, as I say—for the fourth section of *Let It Come Down*. But I think most writers would agree that kif is for relaxation, not for work.

HALPERN: Does your work require a great deal of revision?

BOWLES: No, the first draft is the final draft. I can't revise. Maybe I should qualify that by saying I first write in longhand, and then the same day, or the next day, I type the longhand. There are always many changes between the longhand and the typed version, but that first typed sheet is part of the final sheet. There's no revision.

HALPERN: Many critics like to attribute a central theme to your writing: that of the alienation of civilized man when he comes in contact with a primitive society and its natural man.

BOWLES: Yes, I've heard about that. It's a theory that makes the body of writing seem more coherent, perhaps, when you put it all together. And possibly they're right, but I'm not conscious of having such a theme, no. I'm not aware of writing about alienation. If my mind worked that way, I couldn't write. I don't have any explicit message; certainly I'm not suggesting changes. I'm merely trying to call people's attention to something they don't seem to be sufficiently aware of.

HALPERN: Do you feel trapped or at a disadvantage by being a member of Western civilization?

BOWLES: Trapped? No. That's like being trapped by having blond hair or blue eyes, light or dark skin. . . . No, I don't feel trapped. It would be a very different life to be part of another social group, perhaps, but I don't see any difference between the natural man and the civilized man, and I'm not juxtaposing the two. The natural man always tries to be a civilized man, as you can see all over the world. I've never yearned to be a member of another ethnic group. That's carrying one's romanticism a little too far. God knows I carry mine far enough as it is.

HALPERN: Why is it that you have traveled so much? And to such remote places?

BOWLES: I suppose the first reason is that I've always wanted to get as far as possible from the place where I was born. Far both geographically and spiritually. To leave it behind. I'm always happy leaving the United States, and the farther away I go the happier I am, generally. Then there's another thing: I feel that life is very short and the world is there to see and one should know as much about it as possible. One belongs to the whole world, not to just one part of it.

HALPERN: What is the motivation that prompts your characters to leave the safety of a predictable environment, a Western environment, for an unknown world that first places them in a state of aloneness and often ends by destroying them, as in the case of Port and Kit in *The Sheltering Sky* and Dyar in *Let It Come Down?*

BOWLES: I've never thought about it. For one thing there is no "predictable environment." Security is a false concept. As for the motivation? In the case of Port and Kit they *wanted* to travel, a simple, innocent motivation. In the case of Nelson Dyar, he was fed up with his work in America. Fed up with standing in a teller's cage. Desire for freedom. I suppose; desire for adventure. Why *do* people leave their native habitat and go wandering off over the face of the earth?

HALPERN: Many of your characters seem to pursue a course of action that often leads them into rather precarious positions, pushed forward by an almost self-destructive curiosity, and a kind of fatalism—for example, the night walks of Port, or the professor in *A Distant Episode*.

BOWLES: I'm very aware of my own capacity for compulsive behavior. Besides, it's generally more rewarding to imagine the results of compulsive than of reflective action. It has always seemed to me that my characters act naturally, given the circumstances; their behavior is foreseeable. Characters set in motion a mechanism of which they become a victim. But generally the mechanism turns out to have been operative at the very beginning. One realizes that Kit's and Port's having left America at all was a compulsive act. Their urge to travel was compulsive.

HALPERN: Do you think that these characters have an "unconscious drive for self-destruction"?

BOWLES: An unconscious drive for self-destruction? . . . Death and destruction are stock ingredients of life. But it seems to me that the motivation of characters in fiction like mine should be a secondary consideration. I think of characters as if they were props in the general scene of any given work. The characters, the landscape, the climatic conditions, the human situation, the formal structure of the story or the novel, all these elements are one—the characters are made of the same material as the rest of the work. Since they are activated by the other elements of the synthetic cosmos, their own motivations are relatively unimportant.

HALPERN: You have been accused of favoring neurotic characters in your fiction.

BOWLES: Most of the Occidentals I know *are* neurotic. But that's to be expected; that's what we're producing now. They're the norm. I don't think I could write about a character who struck me as eccentric, whose behavior was too far from standard.

HALPERN: Many people would consider the behavior of your characters far from standard.

BOWLES: I realize that if you consider them objectively, they're neurotic and compulsive; but they're generally presented as integral parts of situations, along with the landscape, and so it's not very fruitful to try to consider them in another light. My feeling is that what is called a truly normal person (if I understand your meaning) is not likely to be written about, save as a symbol. The typical man of my fiction reacts to inner pressures the way the normal man *ought* to be reacting to the age we live in. Whatever is intolerable must produce violence.

HALPERN: And these characters are your way of protesting.

BOWLES: If you call it protest. If even a handful of people can believe in the cosmos a writer describes, accept the workings of its natural laws (and this includes finding that the characters behave in a credible manner), the cosmos is a valid one.

HALPERN: Critics often label you an existential writer. Do you consider yourself an existentialist?

BOWLES: No! Existentialism was never a literary doctrine in any case, even though it did trigger three good novels—one by Sartre *(La Nausée)* and two by Camus *(L'Etranger* and *La Peste).* But if one's going to subscribe to the tenets of a formulated belief, I suppose atheistic existentialism is the most logical one to adopt. That is, it's likely to provide more insight than another into what attitudes to take vis-à-vis today's world.

HALPERN: But you do share some of the basic tenets of existentialism, as defined by Sartre.

BOWLES: He's interested in the welfare of humanity. As Port said, "What is humanity? Humanity is everybody but yourself."

HALPERN: That sounds rather solipsistic.

BOWLES: What else can you possibly know? *Of course* I'm interested in myself, basically. In getting through my life. You've got to get through it all. You never know how many years you've got left. You keep going until it's over. And I'm the one who's got to suffer the consequences of having lived my life.

HALPERN: Is this why so many of your characters seem to be asocial?

BOWLES: Are they? Or are they merely outside and perhaps wishing they were inside?

HALPERN: Do you think of yourself as being asocial?

BOWLES: I don't know. Probably very, yes. I'm sorry to be so stubborn and impossible with all this, but the point is I just don't know any of the answers, and I have no way of finding them out. I'm not equipped to dig them up, nor do I want to. The day I find out what I'm all about I'll stop writing—I'll stop doing everything. Once you know what makes you tick, you don't tick any more. The whole thing stops.

HALPERN: You are against Sartre's taking aspects of this life so seriously. Yet when you say about your life that you are just trying to get through it the best you can, it sounds to me as if *you* take living very seriously.

BOWLES: Oh, everyone takes his own existence seriously, but that's as far as he should go. If you claim that life itself is serious, you're talking out of turn. You're encroaching on other people's lives. Each man's life has the quality he gives it, but you can't say that life itself has any qualities. If we suffer, it's because we haven't learned how not to. I have to remind myself of that.

HALPERN: Then life is a painful experience for you?

BOWLES: You have to keep going, and try at least to keep a pleasant face.

HALPERN: Life seems to be inaccessible to many of your characters. By their going beyond a certain point, past which they are pulled by an unconscious force, they place themselves in a position where return to the world of man is impossible. Why are they pushed beyond that point?

BOWLES: It's a subject that interests me very much; but you've got to remember that these are all rationalizations devised after the fact, and therefore purely suppositious. I don't know the answers to the questions; all I can do is say, "Maybe," "It could be," or "It could be something else." Offhand I'd suggest that the answer has to do with the Romantic fantasy of reaching a region of self-negation and thereby regaining a state of innocence.

HALPERN: Is it a kind of testing to find out what it's like beyond that point?

BOWLES: It could be. One writes to find out certain things for oneself. Much of my writing is therapeutic. Otherwise I never would have started, because I knew from the beginning that I had no specific desire to reform. Many of my short stories are simple emotional outbursts. They came out all at once, like eggs, and I felt better afterward. In that sense much of my writing is an exhortation to destroy. "Why don't you all burn the world, smash it, get rid of everything in it that plagues you?" It is a desire above all to bring about destruction, that's certain.

HALPERN: So you don't want to change the world. You simply want to end it.

BOWLES: Destroy and end are not the same word. You don't end a process by destroying its products. What I wanted was to see everyone aware of being in the same kind of metaphysical impasse I was in. I wanted to know whether they suffered in the same way.

HALPERN: And you don't think they do?

BOWLES: I don't think many do. Perhaps the number is increasing. I hope so, if only for selfish reasons! Nobody likes to feel alone. I know because I always think of myself as completely alone, and I imagine other people as a part of something else.

HALPERN: And you want to join the crowd.

BOWLES: It's a universal urge. I've always wanted to. From earliest childhood. Or to be more exact, from the first time I was presented to another child, which was when I was five.

HALPERN: And you were rejected?

BOWLES: It was already too late. I wanted to join on my own terms. And now it doesn't matter.

HALPERN: And so now you alienate your characters, the way you were alienated?

BOWLES: I don't think the judge would allow that question. Life is much harder if one is alone. Shared suffering is easier to bear.

HALPERN: Sartre says somewhere that a man's essential freedom is the capacity to say "No." This is something your characters are often incapable of. Do they achieve any kind of freedom?

BOWLES: My characters don't attain any kind of freedom, as far as I'm aware.

HALPERN: Is death any kind of freedom?

BOWLES: Death? Another nonexistent, something to use as a threat to those who are afraid of it. There's nothing to say about death. The cage door's always open. Nobody *has* to stay in here. But people want freedom *inside* the cage. So what is freedom? You're bound by physical laws, bound by your body, bound by your mind.

HALPERN: What does freedom mean to you?

BOWLES: I'd say it was not having to experience what you don't like.

HALPERN: By the alienation that your characters go through in their various exotic settings, are they forced into considering the meaning of *their* lives, if there is meaning to life?

BOWLES: I shouldn't think there is meaning to life. In any case, there's not *one* meaning. There should be as many meanings as there are individuals—you assign meaning to life. If you don't assign it, then clearly it has none whatever.

HALPERN: In *L'Etranger,* Meursault is put in jail, a form of alienation, and at that point he considers "the meaning of life."

BOWLES: Camus was a great moralist, which means, nowadays, to be preoccupied with social considerations. I'm not preoccupied in that way. I'm not a moralist. After all, he was a serious communist; I was a very unserious one, a completely negative one.

HALPERN: What was it about communism that appealed to you?

BOWLES: Oh, I imagined it could destroy the establishment. When I realized it couldn't, I got out fast and decided to work on my own hook.

HALPERN: Back to destroying the world. . . .

BOWLES: Well, who doesn't want to? I mean, look at it!

HALPERN: It's one thing to dislike something you see and another to want to destroy it.

BOWLES: Is it? I think the natural urge of every human being is to destroy what he dislikes. That doesn't mean he does it. You don't by any means get to do what you want to do, but you've got to recognize the desire when you feel it.

HALPERN: So you use your writing as a weapon.

BOWLES: Right. Absolutely.

HALPERN: And your music?

BOWLES: Music is abstract. Besides, I was writing theater music. It was fun but it's a static occupation. I always have to feel I'm going somewhere.

HALPERN: Has your desire to destroy the world always been a conscious one?

BOWLES: Yes. I was aware that I had a grudge, and that the only way I could satisfy my grudge was by writing words, attacking in words. The way to attack, of course, is to seem not to be attacking. Get people's confidence and then, surprise! Yank the rug out from under their feet. If they come back for more, then I've succeeded.

HALPERN: If they enjoy your work you have succeeded—in the sense that their minds have been infected.

BOWLES: Infected is a loaded word, but all right. They have been infected by the germ of doubt. Their basic assumptions may have been slightly shaken for a second, and that's important.

HALPERN: But you don't regard your goals as being negative.

BOWLES: To destroy often means to purify. I don't think of destruction as necessarily undesirable. You said "infecting." All right. Perhaps those infected will have more technique than I for doing some definite destroying. In that sense I'm just a propagandist, but then all writers are propagandists for one thing or another. It's a perfectly honorable function to serve as a corrosive agent. And there certainly is nothing unusual about it; it's been part of the Romantic tradition for the past century and a half. If a writer can incite anyone to question and ultimately to reject the present structure of any facet of society, he's performed a function.

HALPERN: And after that?

BOWLES: It's not for him to say. *Après lui de déluge.* That's all he can do. If he's a propagandist for nihilism, that's his function too.

HALPERN: To start the ball rolling?

BOWLES: I want to *help* society go to pieces, make it easy.

HALPERN: And writing about horror is part of your method.

BOWLES: I don't write "about horror." But there's a sort of metaphysical malaise in the world today, as if people sense that things are going to be bad. They could be expected to respond to any fictional situation which evoked the same amalgam of repulsion and terror that they already vaguely feel.

HALPERN: Are you, as Leslie Fiedler suggests, a secret lover of the horror you create?

BOWLES: Is there such a creature as a secret or even an avowed lover of horror? I can't believe it. If you're talking about the *evocation* of horror on the printed page, then that's something else. In certain sensitive people the awakening of the sensation of horror through reading can result in a temporary smearing of the lens of consciousness, as one might put it. Then all perception is distorted by it. It's a dislocation, and if it's of short duration it provides the reader with a partially pleasurable shiver. In that respect I confess to being jaded, and I regret it. A good jolt of vicarious horror can cause a certain amount of questioning of values afterward.

HALPERN: Is that what you hope to accomplish through the horror you evoke?

BOWLES: I don't use horror. If reading a passage of mine triggers the suspension of belief in so-called objective reality for a moment, then I suppose it has the same effect on the reader as if I had consciously used horror as a device.

HALPERN: I'd like to talk a little about your translating. Some critics are convinced that the stories from the Moghrebi are really yours.

BOWLES: I know, but they're not. That's critical blindness. If they were mine, they'd be very different. They're translations. Each Moroccan writer has a different style in English because the cadence of each one's speech is different in Moghrebi. I keep the tapes. Anyone who listens to them and understands the language can hear the differences.

HALPERN: Has your writing been affected by the translations you've done?

BOWLES: A little. I noticed that it had been when I wrote *A Hundred Camels in the Courtyard*. I was trying to get to another way of thinking, noncausal. . . . Those were experiments. Arbitrary use of disparate elements.

HALPERN: You did some translating of Borges' work, didn't you?

BOWLES: I did one short story, which I particularly liked, called *Las Ruinas Circulares*—back in 1944, I think it was. He was completely unknown in the United States. His cousin, Victoria Ocampo, was in New York. She was the editor of *Sur*, in Buenos Aires, and was the woman who eventually bought *La Prensa* and went to jail under Perón. She was a very spectacular woman. One afternoon she tossed me a book, which she said was a new work by her cousin (it was one that she herself had published). It was called *El Jardín de los Senderos Que se Bifurcan*. A marvelous book. Since then it has been translated as *Ficciones*. I had read some Borges four years before that, and already admired him. I think that was the first translation into English of a short story by Borges.

HALPERN: Did you have much difficulty in translating that story?

BOWLES: Well, Borges writes in classical Castellano, and the ideas are simply put; he's an easy man to translate. I should think the important thing would be to retain the particular poetic flavor of the prose in each story.

HALPERN: What do you feel is the importance of the Moroccan translations you've done?

BOWLES: I think they provide a certain amount of insight into the Moroccan mentality and Moroccan customs, things that haven't been gone into very deeply in fiction. I haven't noticed many good novels about Morocco, so in that sense they're of use to anyone interested in the country. Literary importance? I have no idea.

HALPERN: As an admirer of Paul Bowles, I can't help but wonder why you spent so much time on these translations instead of on your own writing?

BOWLES: Because Jane, my wife, was ill, and to write a novel I need solitude and great long stretches of empty time; I haven't really had that since 1957. The summer of 1964, of course, I did go up on the mountain, Monte Viejo, you know, and write *Up Above the World*.

HALPERN: Are you a great fan of Jane Bowles's work?

BOWLES: I am indeed. I've read *Two Serious Ladies* ten times—I think I can quote most of it. Also, it was going over the manuscript of *Two Serious Ladies* that gave me the original impetus to consider the possibility of writing a novel.

HALPERN: You met Jane before she started writing *Two Serious Ladies*, didn't you?

BOWLES: Oh, yes. She began writing *Two Serious Ladies* in 1938, in Paris, the year we were married. She wrote a few scenes that were later much modified, but still they were the nucleus. And then she went on writing it in New York and finally in Mexico.

HALPERN: Was it difficult living with another writer?

BOWLES: That's hard to say, since I've lived only with Janie. She was the only writer I've ever lived with, and also the only woman I've ever lived with, so I don't know which difficulties come from her being a woman and which come from her being a writer. Naturally, you always have some difficulties with your wife, but whether these had anything to do with the fact that she was a writer, I can't tell you.

HALPERN: Was there ever any question of competition?

BOWLES: Competition between us? Competition's a game. It takes more than one to play. We never played it.

HALPERN: Among your own books do you have a favorite?

BOWLES: Of published volumes I like *The Delicate Prey* the most. Naturally that doesn't mean I'd write the stories the same way now.

HALPERN: Do you have much contact with other writers?

BOWLES: When other writers come through Tangier and look me up, I see them, yes. And I knew a few before I settled here. One of the first was Bill Saroyan, who came to New York with the script of a play for which he wanted me to write music. It was *My Heart's in the Highlands*, and the old Group Theatre produced it. About that time I met Auden. I always held him in great respect: he was erudite, and he had an unparalleled ability to use the English language. An infallible, like Stravinsky. And of course I knew Isherwood and Spender. There was one spring when I used to have lunch with them every day at the Café des Westens in Berlin. Although I never felt that I knew them, because they were English, and enough older than I to be intimidating. It was only much later, long after he had gone to America, that I knew Isherwood better. And Tennessee Williams. Certainly I've seen a lot of him and in many different places: Acapulco, New York, Rome, Tangier, Paris, Hollywood. . . . It used to be I who was the traveler, but nowadays Tennessee moves around a good deal more than I do. This is probably because he doesn't refuse to take planes. Truman Capote was here for a whole summer, staying at the Farhar, and we ate our meals together every day during those months. Gore Vidal came, and Allen Ginsberg, and Angus Wilson, and Cyril Connolly. And of course Bill Burroughs lived here for years. Even Susan Sontag came, although she didn't stay very long.

HALPERN: What about Djuna Barnes?

BOWLES: Yes, Djuna came here to Tangier and took my house on the Marshan one year. She was writing a book she called *Bow Down*. Later she called it *Nightwood*. I used to see a lot of Carson McCullers when we lived in Middagh Street, and then we used to go and visit her up in Nyack—spend weekends up there. And of course Sartre, who came to America for a while. We'd have lunch together and then wander around the poorer sections of New York, which he wanted very much to see. That was the year I got the rights to translate *No Exit*. Later he was annoyed with me in Paris, so I don't know him any more.

HALPERN: Annoyed about what, if I may ask?

BOWLES: He was annoyed because I was unable to keep the director of *No Exit* from changing the script. He considered that my province, which it should have been, but the point was that I didn't have a percentage in the show and he didn't know how Broadway works. I was simply the translator, so I had no rights whatever. He sent telegrams of protest from Paris before we opened, and I was obliged to send back replies that were dictated by John Huston. His anger should have been directed against John, not me.

HALPERN: What about contemporary writers? Are there any you enjoy reading?

BOWLES: Let's see, who's alive? Sartre is alive, but he did only one good novel. Graham Greene is alive. Who's alive in America? Whom do I follow with interest? Christopher Isherwood's a good novelist. They're mostly dead. I used to read everything of Gide's and Camus'.

HALPERN: Do you have an opinion on the writing being done in America today?

BOWLES: There are various kinds of writing being done, of course. But I suspect you mean the "popular school," as exemplified by Joseph Heller, Kurt Vonnegut, John Barth, Thomas Pynchon—that sort of thing? I don't enjoy it.

HALPERN: Why not?

BOWLES: It's simply that I find it very difficult to get into. The means it uses to awaken interest is of a sort that would be valid only for the length of a short piece. It's too much to have to swim around in that purely literary magma for the time it takes to read a whole book. It fails to hold my attention, that's all. It creates practically no momentum. My mind wanders, I become impatient, and therefore intolerant.

HALPERN: Is it the content that bothers you or the style of the writing? Or both?

BOWLES: Both. But it's the point of view more than anything. The cynicism and wisecracking ultimately function as endorsements of the present civilization. The content is hard to make out because it's generally symbolic or allegorical, and the style is generally hermetic. It's not a novelistic style at all; it's really a style that would be more useful in writing essays, I should think.

HALPERN: Let me go back to the critics for a moment. Do you think they have missed the point of your writing?

BOWLES: They have, certainly, on many occasions. I've often had the impression they were more interested in my motive for writing a given work than they were in the work itself. In general, the British critics have been more perceptive; language is more important to them than it is to us. But I don't think that matters.

HALPERN: One thing that particularly interests many who meet you is the great discrepancy between what you are like as a person and the kind of books you write.

BOWLES: Why is it that Americans expect an artist's work to be a clear reflection of his life? They never seem to want to believe that the two can be independent of each other and go their separate ways. Even when there's a definite connection between the work and the life, the pattern they form may be in either parallel or contrary motion. If you want to call my state schizophrenic, that's all right with me. Say my personality has two facets. One is always turned in one direction, toward my own Mecca; that's my work. The other looks in a different direction and sees a different landscape. I think that's a common state of affairs.

HALPERN: In retrospect, would you say there has been something that has remained important to you over the years? Something that you have maintained in your writing?

BOWLES: Continuing consciousness, infinite adaptability of human consciousness to outside circumstances, the absurdity of it all, the hopelessness of this whole business of living. I've written very little the past few years. Probably because emotionally everything grows less intense as one grows older. The motivation is at a much lower degree, that's all.

HALPERN: When you were first starting to write you were, emotionally, full of things to say. Now that that has faded somewhat, what springboard do you have?

BOWLES: I can only find out after I've written, since I empty my mind each time before I start. I only know what I intended to do once it's finished. Do you remember, in *A Life Full of Holes,* the farmer comes and scolds the boy for falling asleep, and the boy says: "I didn't know I was going to sleep until I woke up."

—Tangier, 1970

BIBLIOGRAPHY

Works by Paul Bowles

NOVELS

The Sheltering Sky. 1949. Reprint. New York: Vintage, 1990.
Let It Come Down. 1952. Reprint. Santa Barbara, California: Black Sparrow
 Press, 1980.
The Spider's House. 1955. Reprint. Santa Barbara: Black Sparrow Press,
 1982.
Up Above the World. 1966. Reprint. New York: The Ecco Press, 1982.

STORIES

A Little Stone. London: John Lehman, 1950.
The Delicate Prey. 1950. Reprint. New York: The Ecco Press, 1972.
The Hours After Noon. London: Heinemann, 1959.
A Hundred Camels in the Courtyard. San Francisco: City Lights Books,
 1962.
The Time of Friendship. New York: Holt, Rinehart & Winston, 1967.
Pages From Cold Point and Other Stories. London: Peter Owen, 1968.
Three Tales. New York: Frank Hallman, 1975.
Things Gone & Things Still Here. Santa Barbara: Black Sparrow Press, 1977.
Collected Stories 1939–1976. Santa Barbara: Black Sparrow Press, 1979.
Midnight Mass. 1981. Reprint. Santa Barbara: Black Sparrow Press, 1983.
Unwelcome Words. Bolinas, California: Tombouctou Books, 1988.
Call at Corazón and Other Stories. London: Peter Owen, 1988.
A Distant Episode: The Selected Stories. New York: The Ecco Press, 1988.

HISTORICAL TALES

Points in Time. 1982. Reprint. New York: The Ecco Press, 1984.

NONFICTION

Yallah. New York: McDowell, Obolensky, 1957.

Their Heads Are Green and Their Hands Are Blue. 1963. Reprint. New York: The Ecco Press, 1984.

Without Stopping. 1972. Reprint. New York: The Ecco Press, 1985.

Days, Tangier Journal: 1987–1989. New York: The Ecco Press, 1991. Paperback edition: The Ecco Press, 1992.

POETRY

Scenes. Los Angeles: Black Sparrow Press, 1968.

The Thicket of Spring: Poems 1926–1969. Los Angeles: Black Sparrow Press, 1972.

Next to Nothing. Kathmandu, Nepal: Starstreams 5, 1976.

Next to Nothing: Collected Poems 1926–1977. Santa Barbara: Black Sparrow Press, 1981.

TRANSLATIONS

R. Frison–Roche, *The Lost Trail of the Sahara*. New York: Prentice Hall, 1951.

Jean–Paul Sartre, *No Exit*. New York: Samuel French, Inc., 1958.

Driss ben Hamed Charhadi (Larbi Layachi), *A Life Full of Holes*. 1964. Reprint. New York: Grove Press, 1982.

Mohammed Mrabet, *Love with a Few Hairs*. 1967. Reprint. San Francisco: City Lights Books, 1986.

Mohammed Mrabet, *The Lemon*. 1969. Reprint. San Francisco: City Lights Books, 1986.

Mohammed Mrabet, *M'Hashish*. San Francisco: City Lights Books, 1969.

Mohamed Choukri, *For Bread Alone*. 1974. Reprint. San Francisco: City Lights Books, 1987.

Mohammed Mrabet, *The Boy Who Set the Fire*. 1974. Reprint. San Francisco: City Lights Books, 1988.

Mohamed Choukri, *Jean Genet in Tangier*. New York: The Ecco Press, 1974. Paperback edition: The Ecco Press, 1975.

Mohammed Mrabet, *Hadidan Aharam*. Santa Barbara: Black Sparrow Press, 1975.

Isabelle Eberhardt, *The Oblivion Seekers*. San Francisco: City Lights Books, 1975.

Mohammed Mrabet, *Look and Move On*. Santa Barbara: Black Sparrow Press, 1976.

Mohammed Mrabet, *Harmless Poisons, Blameless Sins*. Santa Barbara: Black Sparrow Press, 1976.

Mohammed Mrabet, *The Big Mirror*. Santa Barbara: Black Sparrow Press, 1977.

Mohamed Choukri, *Tennessee Williams in Tangier*. Santa Barbara: Cadmus Editions, 1979.

Abdeslam Boulaich, et al., *Five Eyes*. Santa Barbara: Black Sparrow Press, 1979.

Mohammed Mrabet, *The Beach Cafe & the Voice*. Santa Barbara: Black Sparrow Press, 1980.

Rodrigo Rey Rosa, *The Path Doubles Back*. New York: Red Ozier Press, 1982.

Mohammed Mrabet, *The Chest*. Bolinas, California: Tombouctou Books, 1983.

Rodrigo Rey Rosa, *The Beggar's Knife*. San Francisco: City Lights Books, 1985.

Jean Ferry, et. al., *She Woke Me Up So I Killed Her*. San Francisco: Cadmus Editions, 1985.

Mohammed Mrabet. *Marriage with Papers*. Bolinas: Tombouctou Books, 1986.

BOOKS BY
PAUL BOWLES

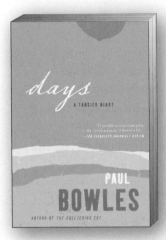

DAYS
A Tangier Diary
ISBN 0-06-113736-7
(paperback)

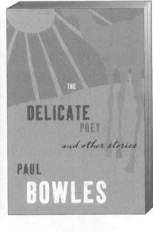

THE DELICATE PREY
And Other Stories
ISBN 0-06-113734-0
(paperback)

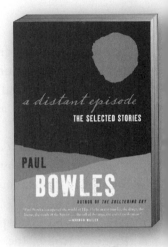

A DISTANT EPISODE
The Selected Stories
ISBN 0-06-113738-3
(paperback)

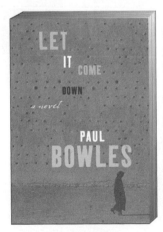

LET IT COME DOWN
A Novel
ISBN 0-06-113739-1
(paperback)

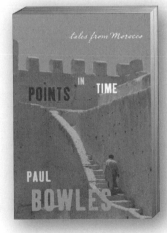

POINTS IN TIME
Tales From Morocco
ISBN 0-06-113963-7
(paperback)

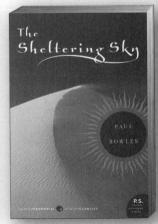

THE SHELTERING SKY
A Novel
ISBN 0-06-083482-X
(paperback)

THE SPIDER'S HOUSE
A Novel
ISBN 0-06-113703-0
(paperback)

THE STORIES OF PAUL BOWLES
ISBN 0-06-113704-9
(paperback)

THEIR HEADS ARE GREEN AND THEIR HANDS ARE BLUE
Scenes From the Non-Christian World
ISBN 0-06-113737-5
(paperback)

TOO FAR FROM HOME
The Selected Writings of Paul Bowles
ISBN 0-06-113740-5
(paperback)

UP ABOVE THE WORLD
A Novel
ISBN 0-06-113735-9
(paperback)

WITHOUT STOPPING
An Autobiography
ISBN 0-06-113741-3
(paperback)

For more information about upcoming titles, visit www.harperperennial.com.

Visit www.AuthorTracker.com
for exclusive information on your favorite HarperCollins authors.

Available wherever books are sold, or call 1-800-331-3761 to order.